Mysterious exes, a nosy neighbour...
and Interpol at her door.
Anjali's life is one hot mess.

A Goan Holiday

by

Anitha Perinchery

Copyright © 2019 by Anitha Perinchery

Publisher's Cataloging-In-Publication Data
(Prepared by The Donohue Group, Inc.)
Names: Perinchery, Anitha, author.
Title: A Goan holiday / by Anitha Perinchery.
Description: [Anitha Perinchery], [2019] | Series: [Indian summer series] ; [2]
Identifiers: ISBN 9781733798648 (paperback) | ISBN 9781733798631 (ebook)
Subjects: LCSH: Women physicians--India--Goa (State)--Fiction. | Clinics--India--Goa (State)--Fiction. | Criminal investigation--India--Goa (State)--Fiction. | Man-woman relationships--India--Goa (State)--Fiction. | LCGFT: Romance fiction.
Classification: LCC PS3616.I546 G63 2019 (print) | LCC PS3616.I546 (ebook) | DDC 813/.6--dc23

Editors:

Chase Nottingham https://chaseediting.com/

Elizabeth Roderick http://talesfrompurgatory.com/

Cover: http://EBookOrPrint.com

www.AnithaPerinchery.com

Dedicated to Friends:

Real and Fictional,

Online and Offline,

Friends Past, Friends Present, Friends yet to Come.

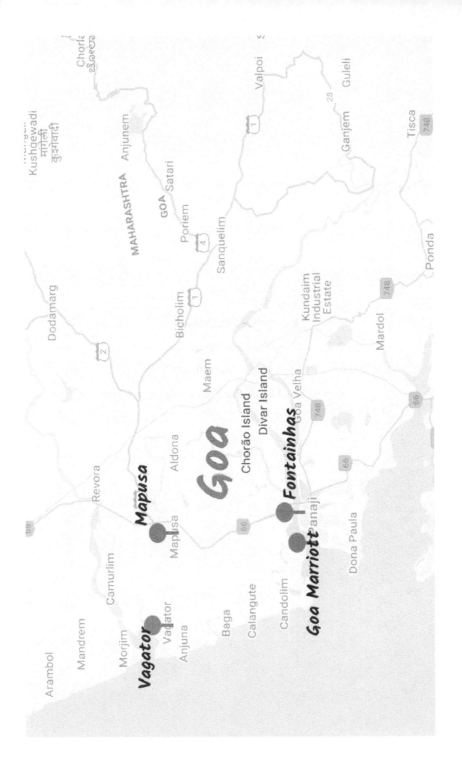

Table of Contents

Part I

Chapter I

Back in the 'sixties, Vagator was merely one more sleepy beach in the Indian state of Goa until a forty-year-old American tourist with only eight fingers trudged down the mud track to the nearby village, bringing with him a stampede of hippies.

Most of the locals scratched their heads in puzzlement as Eight Finger Eddie and his friends adopted the matted hair, rancid clothes, and broken sandals of the homeless, seeking enlightenment in LSD and heroin, but there was one enterprising fellow who saw a chance to make an easy buck. Gossip had it his ramshackle shed at the far end of the beach was the designated cop-free zone where hippies rented cots to crash at night.

To the surprise of no one who knew him, the owner of the establishment disappeared one day, only to resurface next week as the corpse in a fishing boat found adrift a few kilometres from the shore. Just three people showed up to grieve at his graveside—a couple of boyhood friends and his toddler son.

I

By the time Eight Finger Eddie went on to meet his maker half a century later, the shed's owner—part white, part Indian, and all hustler—had long been forgotten. Wealthy young locals and backpackers from around the world still partied to trance music amidst the dramatic red cliffs and green palm trees dotting the shore of the former Portuguese colony. Pungent smoke from industrial-sized rolls of *charas,* the homegrown weed, swirled all around, and white surf frothed over rocks, tickling the feet of stoned couples as they groped their companions and made promises which wouldn't last past daybreak.

The shed itself was converted by its current owners into a hip café which served delicious seafood and fine wines at exorbitant prices. It was where the rich and famous were frequently caught in carefully choreographed candid pictures. That's what the *kaamwaali bai*—the maid—employed at the Joshi holiday home a few kilometres away claimed. The woman showed up at her leisure and barely did any work if she could help it but always carried news of the movie stars spotted in the seaside village where her cousin lived.

None of the celebs seemed to have ventured outside this lousy night in April 2020. *Lucky for them,* thought Anjali Joshi, skirting the group of tourists dancing to ear-splitting music on the beach despite the ominous dark clouds rolling across the half-moon. Each screech from the synthesiser thrummed across her skull. Even her eyeballs were vibrating.

The ocean roared in displeasure, swatting the revellers with a storm wave. As the group screamed and dashed backwards, a white lightning bolt splintered the sky.

"No," exclaimed Anjali, her stiletto heels sinking into the wet sand as she plodded towards the electric torches marking the entrance to the café. Crashing thunder heralded the sudden descent of water from the heavens. "This is *not* happening." Rain fell in sheets, soaking through her hair, sluicing down her torso, plastering the red floral maxi to her skin. "Argh," she shouted, shaking a fist at the universe in general.

First, she'd lost her phone. Unable to find another way to cancel the stupid blind date her stupid cousin set up, she'd marched out to her car to tell the stupid man in person she *wasn't* meeting him for dinner, but the stupid car stalled half a kilometre from the café, and she was forced to walk across the beach in the insanely stupid shoes instead of just sashaying in from the parking lot. Now, this—a thunderstorm in sunny Goa in April, weeks before monsoon was supposed to hit. Couldn't it have waited five more minutes until she was safely inside the café?

The tourists from the beach were also making for the restaurant. With raucous laughter, a couple of young men sprinted closer to Anjali. One of them leered at her. "Hey, cutie," he bellowed over the sounds of the downpour. With a high-pitched giggle, he lurched sideways, the piercing odour of fermented coconut peculiar to Goan hooch wafting around him.

She blinked away the water spraying into her eyes and walked faster, keeping a firm grip on the strap of the purse hanging on her shoulder. On top of everything else, she didn't need to deal with a drunk lover boy or be robbed.

She was going to arrive soaking wet at the restaurant, but surely they'd let her make a call to whatever cab service could get there fastest. Or better yet, to the same stupid cousin who was responsible for Anjali being here in the first place. Said cousin came up with the bright idea of creating a fake Tinder profile with a picture of Audrey Hepburn. Only, she created it first and then informed Anjali. It wasn't the first time someone thought she looked like an Indian version of the yesteryear actress, but the photograph was actually that of the movie star, for God's sake.

Anjali would've dismissed the man who swiped right as a fool. Except, his DP was Gregory Peck. It tickled her enough that she'd agreed... and regretted it in the space of the afternoon. She wasn't in any sort of shape to get back into the dating pool, not after the year she'd gone through. But following the mysterious disappearance of her phone, her laptop apparently contracted some kind of virus and refused to let her log in. Then, Anjali's cousin vanished, taking *her* phone with her, leaving a note saying she'd be back at the family holiday home before midnight. Anjali had no way of contacting the fake Mr Peck to cancel.

Well, he'd have the pleasure of being turned down in person. Before she made the call to her cousin to pick her up, Anjali would tell Mr Peck: "Sorry, but not sorry." Anjali Joshi wasn't even about to wait at his table to be picked up. She wasn't giving the universe any chances to wreak further havoc in her life. If she sat quietly in a corner until her ride arrived, what else could possibly go wrong?

The electric torches on top of the gateposts flickered as she walked through. Except for the row of lit windows, not much was visible of the café, but she'd seen enough of the beach restaurants in Goa to know it most likely looked like a giant thatched hut. Behind the building, shadowed coconut palms gyrated in the wind. To the right of the glass double doors was a single bulb, casting a golden glow on the wooden board beneath it. Written on the plank in crimson lettering was the restaurant's name: Café Ishq. Anjali couldn't help a reluctant giggle. *Ishq*—the Urdu word for passionate love. The owner was surely a sucker for romance. She fervently hoped it didn't mean her supposed date for the evening chose the place because he was expecting action. He wasn't getting any.

Wiping away the water trickling down the back of her neck, she pulled the door open and walked in. A few others in the foyer were already following one of the employees inside, leaving small puddles on the floor. There were wet umbrellas in a couple of plastic buckets. Mandolin music was coming from the restaurant proper, the peppy cadence very European.

"Come in, come in," enthused a plump girl in a yellow tee and black slacks, her hair in pigtails. Only in Goa. Any other place, and the restaurant wouldn't have been so warmly welcoming to those running in from the rain, dripping all over their polished floors. Here, the local economy depended on keeping visitors happy.

With a grateful smile for the helpful hostess, Anjali peered into the interior. The band was on the left. Black pants, suspenders, billowy, white shirts, bowties—the overweight musicians with handlebar moustaches were swaying in place to the song they created. So were the diners and the wait staff moving around the tables. Lanterns hung from the high thatched ceiling, cane chairs were set around square tables, and yellow lighting created a cheery glow. There was a bar at the far end, built to resemble a shanty.

"Beautiful," Anjali breathed, tapping a foot in time with the song. Bits of mud fell off the toe of the red suede stilettos. Her ankles itched from the gritty sand coating them, but she couldn't very well lift her skirts here to scratch in peace. "How long have you been open?"

Anjali might have been from Mumbai, but she'd travelled enough times to Goa as a child and didn't recall... that *was* many, many moons ago, and she didn't remember venturing this way on her childhood visits. Once her grandparents made the family holiday home their retirement residence, she hadn't returned, not even after their passing.

No, not entirely true. Anjali *had* made one trip as a twenty-year-old, not informing any of her family about it. Eleven years, to be exact. That's how long it took her to work up the nerve to return. Except, she hadn't exactly worked up the nerve as much as been pushed by her family into making the trip to check on some problems which cropped up in the Joshi Charity Clinic. Anjali's brain added its own two *paise*—pennies—telling her she wouldn't be able to move on until she closed the door on painful memories, and she ended up acquiescing to her family's request.

The hostess murmured an answer to Anjali's question, but the words barely penetrated her mind. Eleven years since she'd last seen *him*. Eleven long years, during which she'd pretended everything was just peachy. Spectacular, in fact.

With a mental shrug, she shook off the memories. She'd wallowed in pain and regret long enough. Anjali was a new woman now. For New Anjali, a trip to Goa would be easy-peasy... until her cousin decided to tag along and pronounced a blind date was just what Anjali needed.

Nuh-huh. No way. Romance would have to wait until New Anjali got the rest of her life in order. Mr Peck was about to find himself dateless. "I have someone waiting for me," she said. "I'm Dr Anj—Audrey. My name is Audrey."

The hostess's eyes widened. "*You're* Audrey?"

"Umm... yes." Okay, so Anjali's dark brown hair might be hanging limply all around her head, her very wet floral maxi might reveal the slight belly flab on her short and skinny figure, and she likely had mascara smudged all around her brown eyes, but the hostess didn't have to sound so shocked. Anjali just came in from a thunderstorm. By God, she was allowed to look a little imperfect.

"All right," said the hostess, shaking her head as though she couldn't believe someone like Anjali could have a man waiting inside. A man presumably clad in dry clothes and not quite so dishevelled as the date he expected for the evening.

New Anjali squared her shoulders and tightened her fingers around her purse strap. Even if she weren't soaking wet, she didn't *need* to be perfect. She might not be a ravishing beauty, but for a thirty-one-year-old woman, she looked pretty good. Most people called her "classy."

The skirts of her sodden maxi flapping noisily against her legs, Anjali followed the judgemental twit into the restaurant. They headed towards a table on the right next to a row of windows overlooking the sea.

The cacophony created by the lousy weather was nearly drowned out by the music, but the view through the glass panes was still gorgeo—no, that wasn't the right word. Dramatic. Nature was putting on quite a show. Lightning bolts crackled across the black velvet sky, revealing coconut palms whipping into graceful dips, almost like the trees were dancing to the song from the café.

The suit-clad man waiting in one of the chairs must have agreed. He was looking out at the magnificent thunderstorm, leaving only a sliver of his profile visible. His fingertips were tapping out the rhythm on the rim of his brandy snifter. There were black-rimmed glasses on his nose. No grey in his hair that she could see, but something about the way he held himself said he'd left his twenties behind. That kind of confidence in posture came only with life experience.

Small mercies, Anjali muttered in her mind. At least her stupid cousin hadn't set her up with teenaged beefcake who could've gotten her arrested for paedophilia.

However old he was, the fake Mr Peck did seem trim. The way he was leaning back against the chair, long legs stretched below the table, ending in brown dress shoes... the set of his shoulders under the dark blue blazer and the streaks of light brown in the wavy hair brushing the top of his yellow shirt collar sent a tremor through Anjali.

No. It couldn't be *him.* She was imagining things. The mess her life had become was causing her mind to blast to the past, that's all. *New woman,* she admonished her wayward brain.

"Dr Joe," called the hostess. "Your guest is here."

"Hi," Anjali said, automatically. *Joe?* Her heart thudded. *No.* This was Goa, former Portuguese colony, stomping ground of ageing hippies. Men named "Joe" had to be a dime a dozen. Some of them were surely doctors. *Her* Joe left Goa eleven years ago.

Chair scraping the floor, the man stood and turned to face her. The light brown eyes behind the glasses crinkled in welcome. Bushy brows were combed into place like always. There was the same hint of a cleft in his chin and the crooked grin she remembered, now tinged with a strange uncertainty. If Anjali sniffed hard, she might smell the same cologne he always used, the one which reminded her of sun-warmed trees.

No. Anjali shook her head. Either she'd just lost the last of her marbles, or the gods were playing a prank on her, having a belly laugh at her expense.

The smile on the man's face morphed into shock. "Anju?" he asked, incredulously.

Anjali opened her mouth to speak, but sounds refused to come out. *This can't be happening,* her mind screamed, wildly. In her dreams, they'd met again a thousand times. Each time, she'd been a diva, unleashing royal fury on him for ripping her heart apart and trampling on the pieces. Each time, the agony of loss overwhelmed her pride and anger, and she cried loud, ugly sobs which left her humiliated even in her imagination.

She was finally—*finally*—trying to put the painful chapter behind her, and she ran into him exactly when she bore a close resemblance to a drowned rat. Anjali struggled to get her scrambled neurons in working order and remember the hurtful words she'd once longed to throw at him. "Joe," she croaked.

Dr Joseph D'Acosta, her onetime tutor. The man she'd loved and lost.

Chapter 2

2006

Long, narrow dissection tables stretched end to end in the physiology lab at the All India Institute of Medical Science in New Delhi. The recently hired tutor was walking up and down in front, methodically instructing first-year students on the experiment in progress. His deep, smooth flow of words was occasionally interrupted by the clatter of specimen dishes and steel instruments and a question or two from his audience. Unlike the anatomy lab where the smell of formaldehyde overpowered everything else, this place stank of mud and slime and frogs.

"I can't," Anjali whispered, her voice full from the puke she was trying to hold back. "I just can't." She was at one end of the table, and the rest of her classmates clad in white lab coats and protective gloves were already well into the lesson. In front of each student was a rotating drum covered by thick paper coated with black soot. With every twitch of a frog's thigh muscle, the contraction would be recorded on soot paper.

She had no idea how the rest of her classmates did it. They were all seventeen or eighteen like her, straight out of secondary school as was usual in India. Not a single one seemed to have a problem cutting open a live frog.

"You most certainly can," said the second new tutor, standing next to her. The lab attendant spent all of two minutes waiting for Anjali to pick a frog of her own from the specimen bucket before summoning *this* tutor—Tutor Two as opposed to Tutor One who was in front—for assistance. Unlike the rest of the people around, Tutor Two wore a surgical mask and safety glasses as though he'd been getting ready for the operating theatre when he was dragged into the lab. She'd been sure she'd be told off, but his kind smile was evident even under the protective garb. He was also careful to keep his voice low so none of the other students could overhear. Or it could've been the mask which muffled his voice. "Haven't you done frog dissections in school?"

"On *dead* ones." Not squirming, croaking creatures with great big eyes, blinking accusingly at her.

"Vivisection is the only way to learn how a live muscle works," Tutor Two insisted, puffing up. "Or a nerve or a heart. It's important. Galen, the ancient

Greek surgeon, wrote most of his treatises based on animal experiments. Galen, Sushruta, Hippocrates... you're following in the footsteps of the greats."

Was she supposed to clap and yell, "Bravo"? The pomposity of the man!

Kindness notwithstanding, he *and* his colleague were strutting about as though they'd been running the college for years when today was their first day on the job. Well, according to the whispers in the lab prior to the session, they *had* been big men on campus until they completed their undergraduate internships not long before Anjali arrived, making them twenty-two-ish to her eighteen. They were spending a year as tutors in basic sciences—the lowest possible position on the academic medicine totem pole—before starting the postgraduate course in surgery the next year. They could then do more cutting and sewing, blissfully imagining themselves on that list of greats someday.

"*I'm* not following in anyone's footsteps," she mumbled. "I can't even *catch* a frog." Anjali took a quick glance at the lab attendant, still holding the metal bucket towards her. In it were the last three of the captured animals, waiting to see which of them would be the final victim of this lab session. "How am I supposed to—" She couldn't complete the sentence: catch a frog, insert a needle into the soft spot at the base of its skull to immobilise it, strip the skin, isolate the thigh muscle, and attach it to the electrodes.

"Pithing makes sure it doesn't feel any pain," Tutor Two explained. "You have to do it to pass the course. No way around it."

"I don't have to," Anjali said, covering her mouth with a gloved hand. Tears blurred her vision. She furiously batted her lashes, willing the waterworks away. She didn't need to make a total fool of herself by blubbering in front of the whole class. "I could quit." She could tear off the lab coat and gloves. Before anyone objected, she'd run home to Mumbai in the same electric yellow salwar suit she was wearing underneath—the long tunic and leggings along with the brown flats she'd selected for her first day in the lab. She'd never imagined she'd freeze at the sight of the frogs.

"Quit—" With a muttered curse, Tutor Two straightened. "Don't be silly."

Anjali took a step back, her hand dropping to the table. Her knuckles collided with metal. The empty specimen dish slid sideways. It hovered on the edge of the table for a second. Both Anjali and Tutor Two dived for it, but—

A clatter. Then, there was a second loud noise, followed by a curse in guttural Hindi from the lab attendant. All chatter in the large, airy lab paused. Every head swivelled in their direction. Anjali didn't wait to check on the second noise. Hoping to God she hadn't knocked over one of the soot drums, she crouched to pick up the specimen dish, keeping her eyes pinned on the floor.

"Eek," squealed a girl a couple of places down. Something else clanged.

"What's going on, Dr Rastogi?" called a deep voice. Tutor One—the man who'd been instructing the rest of the students.

"Ahh..." grunted Tutor Two—Dr Rastogi. "Just a second... almost..."

Anjali frowned. For God's sake, it was just a specimen dish—an *empty* specimen dish—and maybe one of the soot drums or instruments. She *was* mildly embarrassed, but really, there was no need for so much drama. When she clambered back up, the other students were scampering away from the table. Dr Rastogi stretched his arm to the middle, lunging after... *an errant frog?*

The frog croaked as if taunting its pursuer and leapt a couple of feet, sending more specimen dishes crashing to the floor.

Anjali shook her head in confusion. "What happened—"

"Dammit, get back here," swore Dr Rastogi.

Titters rose. One of the students ran to take a stance on the other side of the table as though *that* would trap the frog. "*Idhar aa jaa,* baby," he crooned, asking the creature to go to him.

"What the hell—" said Tutor One from the front of the hall, taking two steps towards them.

"My fault," said Tutor Two, Dr Rastogi, positioning himself for another pounce across the table. "I caught my elbow on the specimen bucket."

The second clatter she heard... "Oh, my God," Anjali mumbled, both hands curled into tight fists against her mouth. Her *first* day in the lab, and she... maybe she could faint or something, and when she woke up, she'd just pretend today never happened.

"Get back here, or I'm gonna—" Dr Rastogi dived, again. So did the student on the other side. Two pairs of gloved hands met around the slimy amphibian. With a furious croak, the frog leapt almost straight into the air and atop the student's head.

Ignoring the shouts and the hoots and the guffaws from the audience, Dr Rastogi swiped at the student's head.

"Hey," screamed the student. "Let go of my hair!"

A giggle erupted from Anjali. Behind the hands held to her mouth, she laughed, helplessly. At least she'd have a story to tell her dad—

One more croak, and the frog flew through the air. Every eye in the lab followed its course as it made for Tutor One's chest. He took a startled step back, but the creature landed on his pristine white lab coat and slid a couple of inches straight into the front pocket. With a victorious grunt, the tutor clapped a hand over the lump. "Got ya." He looked around at the rest of the lab. "Show's over. Return to your specimens, please."

"Thanks, Joe," said Dr Rastogi, holding out a hand. "And sorry. Like I said, I caught my elbow on the specimen bucket." It happened only because Anjali sent her specimen dish flying to the floor, but he didn't mention it.

Tutor One—Dr Joe Something—was still holding his hand to his left chest, keeping the squirming frog prisoner. "Uh-huh." He glanced between his colleague and Anjali.

At the start of the session, he'd introduced himself. Busy as Anjali was, gaping in horror at the frogs in the bucket, she'd heard only a garbled echo, not his name. Nor had she paid any attention to the man.

Like his colleague and everyone else in the hall, Dr Joe wore a lab coat over his shirt, leaving only his frayed khakis and scuffed brown loafers visible. Unlike his colleague, Joe wasn't wearing glasses or a mask, and his face wasn't particularly kind. There was an edgy sort of attractiveness to him even with the bushy brows. The dark, wavy hair was a little too long for a doctor, and the chiselled jaw showed a slight cleft in the chin. A hint of stubble shadowed the sun-bronzed skin. His light brown eyes were narrowed and fixed on her. Oh, yes. He'd somehow guessed Anjali had something to do with the ruckus. The stiffness of his tall and trim form telegraphed his annoyance at disruptive students.

Anjali tried a cool smile, only then realising her hands were still curled into fists in front of her mouth. She dropped them in haste and straightened her shoulders, tilting her chin up ever so slightly. From her height of five feet and almost one inch, it wasn't easy to look down her nose at tall men.

"Lemme have the frog," said Dr Rastogi, "and I can help Miss... ahh..."

"Anjali," she supplied, thankful to have an excuse to drop her stare before her neck muscles froze into place. She tried a regal nod, something she'd seen her mother use on impertinent junior doctors at her maternity clinic. "Anjali Joshi."

13

"Right," said Dr Rastogi. "Miss Joshi asked a few questions about the procedure, so why don't you go ahead with the class while I show her how to do it?"

Joe's gaze was still on Anjali, and he opened his mouth as though to say something.

"Joe?" called Dr Rastogi, holding out a hand for the frog.

Turning his weirdly intent stare onto Dr Rastogi, Joe waited a couple of seconds. A strange expression flitted across his face before he shook it off with a jerky shrug and brought the hapless frog out of his pocket only to drop it back into the bucket. "Use one of the others. After the racket he caused, he deserves to live." Dr Joe turned away and sauntered to the next table.

The lab attendant snickered. Anjali hadn't even noticed he was still there. It was *his* job to set up the lab for experiments and clean up after, and the horrible man had made no attempt to help.

With a muttered exclamation and a blur of movement, Dr Rastogi dipped his hand into the bucket and came out with a writhing frog. Was it a different one? Anjali squinted. How could she tell?

"Here," said Dr Rastogi, tone brisk. Grabbing one of her hands, he placed the animal in it, keeping his fingers over hers to make sure the frog didn't get a chance to leap away.

God. Even through the latex glove, she could feel the slimy body squirming. A warmth spurted into her palm as the creature peed. Anjali whimpered. The pithing needle was tucked into her other hand.

"Hurry up," said Dr Rastogi. "Let's get this done before anyone notices." Three seconds. Even in their awkward side-by-side position with his fingers guiding hers, three seconds was all it took for the frog to become motionless. "Can you take it from here?" asked Dr Rastogi, his hands still holding hers.

Anjali was hot and sweaty, and her vision was slightly hazy, yet she craned her neck up, managing a watery smile. Darn it, he was as tall as the other one. But then, most males over the age of thirteen towered above Anjali. "I'll try. And thanks."

"That's better," he said, softly. He let go and stepped away but waited a bit to make sure she could, indeed, do the rest.

A snort intruded, followed by a snigger. When Anjali looked up from the frog in the dish, the lab attendant was covering his mouth with one gloved hand, the other still holding the bucket.

"*Kya hai?*" snapped Dr Rastogi, asking the attendant what the matter was.

The attendant—a lanky man, dressed in his uniform of white, half-sleeved shirt and white pants—moved his hand and shook his head. "Nothing," he responded, speaking in thickly accented Hindi. He immediately contradicted the denial by humming, "*Kuch Kuch Hota Hai.*" Only one of *the* most romantic Hindi songs ever from the eponymous movie, talking about the effect a small smile from the girl had on the hero.

Anjali frowned. Heavy glare evident behind the safety glasses, Dr Rastogi said, "*Abey, chup.*"

The attendant shut up as ordered, but he continued to titter as he walked away, the two remaining frogs tumbling about in the bucket.

Turning back to Anjali, Dr Rastogi said, "Get on with your work." His tone was once again kind.

There were only fifteen minutes left, and she just about managed to finish the experiment before the students dispersed, and a voice came booming from the other end of the hall. "Anju," called Meenakshi, Anjali's roommate, waving frantically. "What happened with the frog?" Meenakshi asked as soon as she got within three feet, pushing the designer eyeglasses further up the bridge of her nose.

"Nothing," Anjali mumbled. "I... umm... asked for help, and like Dr Rastogi said, the frog got out." She'd explain the rest in the privacy of their hostel room. Thick, heavy textbooks cradled in their arms, both of them joined the line of students heading to the biochemistry lecture.

The two tutors were still in the lab not far from the door, talking to a short man with a grey combover, heavy jowls, and the brightest, most intelligent eyes Anjali ever saw on anyone. The head of the physiology department was enthusiastically brandishing a sheet of paper, not paying any mind to the students, but Joe looked up as though aware of being watched. His gaze snagged on Anjali. The corner of his mouth curling, he glanced between her and his colleague.

She looked away, pretending not to have noticed his snarky amusement. No. Unlike Dr Rastogi, Dr Joe was not kind. The smirk totally ruined the broody sex appeal of his face. He knew very well she was responsible for the stupid incident, and he was mocking her for it.

"Lucky you," muttered Meenakshi. "Rishi was with you a long time."

"Who?" Anjali asked, resisting a sudden, insane impulse to stick her tongue out at Joe. Mentally, she urged the line to move faster so she wouldn't have to see the knowing grin, but the students in front were so busy gawking at the head of the department—a man who'd recently been shortlisted for the Nobel Prize in medicine—they were merely inching along.

Meenakshi clucked. "Rishabh Rastogi. Rishi."

Ah. "A bit pompous but very nice."

"Rishi *is* nice. He and Joe came to our house for my sister's engagement party." Meenakshi's older sister was in her final year in the same college. "But Rishi... he's so handsome."

"I never saw his face." Anjali craned her neck to peer past the exit, wishing she could snap out an order, asking her classmates to *move,* for God's sake.

Meenakshi nodded. "I know. The surgical mask. My sister says he wears it because he gets asthma from the chemicals, but believe me, he looks like a movie star. Gorgeous hair and bedroom eyes and a body to kill for. And that sexy voice!" She shivered. "Plus, all the professors agree he's going to be a fantastic surgeon."

"Down, girl," Anjali teased, squeezing past the door. *Finally.* Dr Joe could now keep his stupid smirks to himself.

"An observation, *yaar,*" Meenakshi said, calling Anjali her friend. "That's it. It's not like I have a crush on him or anything. Actually, I'm planning to have *no* crushes for the next five years. Nuclear medicine is not easy to get into."

Nuclear medicine—Meenakshi already knew what she wanted to be, unlike Anjali who in spite of being born into a family of doctors, had yet to consider any specialities. She was simply excited to finally be a medical student. At least until this morning. Well, the frog experience told her one thing. Surgery might not be her forte.

"I'm still allowed to appreciate male beauty, right?" Meenakshi asked. "You know, like a da Vinci painting or classical music."

Anjali giggled. "Right."

"Plus, there's the tragic backstory. My sister says there's some gossip about some girl Rishi was in love with who threw him over. Before medical college, I mean."

Taken aback, Anjali asked, "In high school? And he's still holding on to it? How weird."

"Romantic, not weird," Meenakshi said, firmly. "Hey, I forgot to bring my *Harper's* today. Can I share yours?"

"Of course." Arguing over the merits of various textbooks, they got to the lecture hall. As they settled into seats somewhere in the middle of the stadium-style hall, Anjali asked, "What about Rishi's friend? Dr Joe Something?"

"Joseph Francis D'Acosta," Meenakshi said, flipping through the pages of *Harper's Illustrated Biochemistry*. "According to my sister, they're not friends, just part of the same group. Joe's really driven—competitive. He and Rishi were always competing for the top rank in their class. My sister says Rishi was mellow about it, but Joe could never stand losing. He once asked to do the supplementary exam when he came in second."

"Really?" Retake the exam for coming in second in a class of almost a hundred medical students? "Crazy."

"Still, he's great fun. Such a dry sense of humour. When Rishi and Joe visited our home, Joe kept my *father* laughing. He never likes any of *my* friends."

"Fun?" That certainly wasn't how Anjali would've described Joe D'Acosta. "'What's going on, *Dr* Rastogi?'" Anjali quoted the man, her tone snide. Okay, maybe it was a silly thing to object to, but she couldn't help it. He annoyed her. "Didn't he just graduate six months ago? I mean, Rishi was also a bit pompous, but he didn't act so *totally* full of himself. I didn't hear *him* say '*Dr* D'Acosta.'" The name... Joseph D'Acosta... it sounded familiar. Had she heard it somewhere before?

Meenakshi laughed. "You know how it is when you first graduate."

"No, I don't," Anjali retorted. "You don't, either. We're still in our first year."

"My sister has one more year to go, and she told me if we run into each other on campus, I have to call her 'doctor.'"

"Rishi called Joe by his first name."

"True," Meenakshi acknowledged. "Rishi's more mature. I guess tragedy does that to a man."

Anjali rolled her eyes. The tragedy of a failed high school romance?

"Anyway, both of them are cool, but my sister's already warned me not to fall for either. Not that I was planning to."

"What? Dr D'Acosta also has a tragic past?" Anjali *had* heard his name before. She merely couldn't place it.

"Nope. Everyone says he has a one-year rule. No girlfriend has ever lasted longer."

"Maybe that's how long any woman has been able to tolerate him," Anjali suggested, snippily.

"Don't think so." Meenakshi snickered. "Or he wouldn't have gotten any more dates after the first couple. Word gets around, you know. They're called 'Joe's girls.'"

"*Yuck,*" Anjali said. "Why would any self-respecting woman want such a ridiculous label?"

Meenakshi waggled her eyebrows. "Don't dis it. Talk on campus is they all had a good time. If you know what I mean."

With a groan, Anjali said, "Double yuck. So anyone who goes out with him becomes the butt of every crass joke in college. No wonder your sister warned you away."

"Just as a romantic prospect. He's great to hang out with."

"Whatever," Anjali said. "Listen, next time in physio lab, stay with me. I need someone to catch the frog." She couldn't keep asking for help from the movie star doctor, and she wasn't about to give Joe D'Acosta another chance to mock her. "I can help you in the dissection hall." She had no problem with human cadavers, but Meenakshi's eyes watered from the formaldehyde the moment she started cutting.

The professor, a sari-clad woman with a bush of salt-and-pepper hair on her head, strode to the podium. "Amino acid metabolism," she started.

The sound of flipping pages went around the lecture hall.

Pushing Joe D'Acosta out of her mind, Anjali focused on the intricacies of deamination. Wherever she'd heard of him, whatever she'd heard, it hadn't been significant enough to remember.

Chapter 3

Present day

Outside Café Ishq, nature unleashed its rage on Vagator Beach, pelting it with violent rain. Thunder crashed, setting the glass windows vibrating. Inside the building, it should've been a safe, cosy cocoon beyond which nothing existed. Instead, another storm raged in Joe's heart.

Anjali was here in Goa, standing by his table. He couldn't take his eyes off her. The band switched from the playful song of a minute ago to a romantic ballad, but he couldn't hear much beyond the soft whisper of her breaths. She stammered, "I... I didn't know it was you..."

That much was evident from the stark horror on her face. Gritting his teeth, Joe reminded himself exactly how their romance ended. She was reacting as expected to a nasty memory from the past. "I got it. I didn't know, either. Not that I'm not happy to see you. I *am* happy... thrilled, to be honest."

At his unusual stuttering, her eyes widened. Joe mumbled a curse under his breath. He was no clumsy dork, but when his two brothers decided he needed to get laid and teamed up with his godfather—the crackpot parish priest—to set him up on a blind date from Tinder, he hadn't been expecting to run into the same woman who'd haunted his dreams for years. No reasonable person could hope to remain Mr Suave under the circumstances.

Or maybe he'd finally gone batshit crazy from the nightly fantasies and started hallucinating. *Lack of regular sex*, brother number two would say. Joe clenched his fist to stop himself from stretching out his arm and touching Anjali to make sure she was real.

A wet lock of hair clung to her cheek, its tip ending at the corner of her mouth. If she moved the hair even by a micron, the tiny black dot would become visible. That is if he peered closely at her face. He'd done it often enough. The little mark simply begged to be kissed, and he'd obliged every chance he got since he first gave into the impossible attraction he had for her.

Red colour washed across her skin as though she were aware of his thoughts. Her knuckles came up, but instead of brushing the lock of hair away as he wanted, her hand dropped back down.

The wet clothes were plastered to her petite frame, showing off every delicately sexy curve. Her figure was slightly fuller than Joe remembered, and—

"Excuse me," called a voice. The hostess. "Miss... er... Audrey, would you like a towel?"

Anjali's slim arms were wrapped across her torso, and the soft pink lips were quivering. The air conditioner in the café was set to a pleasant 23°C, but she'd just come in from a thunderstorm. With a muttered exclamation, Joe said, "Towels and something hot to drink, please. In fact, why don't you show her to the office so she can dry off?"

A light flared in Anjali's doe-shaped eyes. "Office?"

"Er... yeah." He gestured with his hand. "This is my brother's café." It used to be a teashop-turned-bar in his grandfather's day, selling bootlegged hooch and fried fish to tourists. By the time Joe met Anjali, the place was mortgaged to the hilt to a private bank. The rickety shed was one more symbol of the huge gulf between them, something neither had a prayer of crossing. She wouldn't have known it was now a Michelin star restaurant.

"Office?" Anjali repeated, as though she hadn't heard his explanation.

The band was loud but not *that* loud. The current song was a dreamy melody with the lead singer crooning about the mysterious connection between two people who'd met by chance. "It's my broth—"

"Office?" she asked a third time, her voice dangerously low. Her nostrils flared. Her chest heaved. "Is that all you have to say to me?"

Joe snapped his mouth shut. No, it wasn't all. He longed to ask her how she'd been. Had she thought of him once or twice without hating him? Did her mind ever wander back to the heady days of new love like his did night after night?

"After *eleven* years?" Anjali bared her teeth in a hiss. She stumbled around as though looking for something.

"Anju, I—" tried Joe.

"Miss?" called the worried hostess, her eyes darting to the rest of the diners. A few were looking interestedly in their direction. "Why don't you go with me?"

Not even glancing at the hostess, Anjali grabbed a fork off the table and raised her arm, as though to sink the prongs into his chest.

"What are you—" Joe took a rearward step, the back of his knees striking a chair. It fell with a clatter, but he didn't turn. He didn't dare. "Anju, let's talk inside."

"Argh." Tossing the fork onto the table with a clatter, she reached for the vase with the single yellow rose in it.

"Anju, no," he said, retreating further. A sudden, electric pain shot down his calf. The fallen chair. "*Oww.*"

There were more of the restaurant's staff around the table now, all of them dressed in yellow shirts and black pants. "Miss," called someone. Hands reached for her, trying to calm her. Every face carried the same expression: alarm and the urgency to get the crazy woman out of sight of the rest of the diners. Of course, they didn't have a clue what Joe did eleven years ago. He'd expected to live with guilt... never imagined he'd get a chance to tell her how sorry he was.

Without looking towards anyone, Anjali swatted away the hands and lifted the vase. Her face was now worryingly flushed. A splash—lukewarm water landed on his face, in his eyes, in his nostrils. The rose flew to his head and tumbled to the floor. Joe screwed his eyelids shut, spitting out slimy water.

There were a couple of shocked exclamations, followed by a smattering of claps. "You show him, sister," hollered a woman, the accent distinctly American. "The lying, cheating bastard."

Opening his eyes, he looked for the culprit. There—a black woman with curls all the way to her mid-back was sitting across a table from an Indian dude in khaki shorts barely hanging on to his twiggy legs. Through the droplets of funky-smelling slime dripping from his hair, Joe scowled in their direction. "Madam, could you please mind your own business? You have no idea what's going on."

White cloth suddenly blocked his vision. Fabric covered his eyes and face, mopping up the water and slime.

"What the—" Swatting aside the napkin and the hand of the waiter holding it, he said, "Stop. I need to talk to—Anju?"

Face still flushed, she was staring up at him. Her chest was heaving, and the empty vase was now rolling around on its side on the table. "How could you do it to me, Joe? How could you just walk out and never come back? Eleven years and not a word. Not one phone call, no emails, no texts."

There was a sudden gasp from the hostess. As one, all the employees turned accusing glares towards Joe. Even the music died down with the group craning their necks towards the tableau at the other end of the room.

Anjali's brown eyes filled with sudden tears. "Damn you," she whispered, and wiping away the added moisture on her cheeks with trembling fingers, she pivoted to glide regally towards the exit.

"Anju, wait." He pushed through the staff surrounding him and jogged after her.

She did stop before she got to the foyer but only to talk to the waiter manning the hostess station. "I don't have my phone on me," she said, her voice shaky. "May I use yours? I need to call a taxi."

Joe caught up. "It's not going to be easy to get a taxi in this weather. Anju, wait in the office, please. Or let me take you home." *Don't walk away,* he begged with his eyes.

Ignoring him, she asked the waiter, "I'll call my cousin, then."

"Er..." The waiter tugged at his collar and glanced between Joe and Anjali. "I'm sorry, Dr Joe. She's a customer." Pulling out a cordless phone from the podium, the waiter handed it to Anjali.

Watching her dial, Joe mumbled a curse. "Don't go, Anju. Please, please—"

She slapped a hand to her forehead and said into the phone, "Mohini, where *are* you? I need—as soon as you get this message—oh, God. What's the point? I'll have to wait here for a taxi."

"No, you don't," said the hostess, marching towards them with her mouth set in a straight, thin line. "I can have the delivery van take you home."

"Do you mind?" Joe snarled. "I'm trying to talk to her."

"Yeah?" asked the hostess, hostility radiating from every pore. "You had eleven years like she said."

"You work for me," Joe howled. Brother number one ran the place, but Joe and brother number two and their baby sister also owned shares.

"I work for Mr Dev," insisted the hostess. "He's not gonna fire me for it."

"Thank you," Anjali said, putting the cordless phone back on the podium and taking the hostess's hands in hers. Sudden chagrin appeared on Anjali's face as though she were just remembering something. "I do need to get back soon. My... umm... there's someone waiting for me."

Huh? Someone was waiting for her to return from her date in less than half hour after it was supposed to begin? Why? And who?

"The van will be here in two minutes." The hostess treated Joe to a particularly malevolent side-eye. "You go home and forget all this, Miss Audrey. Some men are not worth your tears."

Joe suppressed a groan. Was he going to have to battle the entire sisterhood of womankind for one measly minute with—

"Anjali," she corrected. "Anjali Joshi."

Joe frowned. The shock of meeting her had driven one important question from his mind. She'd been here on a blind date from Tinder, and now, she was introducing herself as Anjali Joshi. Last he heard, she'd been Mrs Rishabh Rastogi.

Part II

Chapter 4

The monitor on the wall beeped at regular intervals, showing steady heartbeats. Blood pressure, stable. Oxygenation, acceptable. On the ICU bed, the patient moaned in her unconscious state, restlessly moving her bandaged head on the pillow. Her eyebrows drew together in a grimace. A couple of hours had passed since she was wheeled out of the OR, but the faint smell of antiseptic still clung to her. Or it could be Rishi's nose, ultrasensitive to every damned odour.

Dr Rishabh Rastogi—Rishi—was still in his green surgical scrubs but ripped off the mask before walking into the patient's room. *Mistake.* Holding his breath, he quickly completed checking the neural reflexes on the soles of the patient's feet and stepped back.

"Stupid kids," muttered the nurse, the grey in her hair and the wrinkles on her face no detriment to the briskness with which she moved around her charge, adjusting pillows. "Always think they're indestructible." This particular one and her best friend thought it was a fine idea to race mopeds on Delhi's roads to celebrate the end of high school. "Her parents and brother are in the waiting room. They're lucky you were here, Dr Rastogi."

"If not, one of the others would've taken care of it," said Rishi, automatically. Evacuating hematomas—draining pooled blood from the brain—was something every neurosurgeon knew how to do. "But..." Curling the corner of his mouth into a smug smile, he grabbed the COW—computer on wheels—which was basically a laptop placed on a wheeled hospital cart. "...none of them would've been Rishabh Rastogi."

The nurse chortled. "Surgeons! Always so modest." She'd been a theatre nurse at AIIMS when he was training, and he'd lured her to this exclusive hospital in India's capital as soon as he was given charge of staffing the neurosurgery department. Not only was she excellent at her job, she had no qualms about telling him off when she felt he needed it. Talking to her and the rest of his staff, sharing *chai* and snacks during breaks—he felt like a human being with them. If he could, he would've spent twenty-four/seven in the operating theatre, scalpel in his gloved hand. It was the only place which offered him peace.

Rishi glanced quickly at the patient's electronic chart and signed off. "Hey, we both know who's the best." Tugging off his surgical cap, he tucked it into the back of his scrub pants. "I won't have any further updates for the parents until she wakes. I don't believe there's been any permanent damage, but no way to be certain until we see her responses."

On cue, the patient mumbled, "Water."

"Meds are wearing off," the nurse remarked. She leaned towards the patient and gently touched a shoulder. "Hey, girl. Can you hear me?"

Slowly, the girl's eyes fluttered open. Pain and confusion on her face, she peered at the nurse. "I... what..." Her gaze snagged on Rishi. For a second or two, she stared. Then, she gave a weak giggle. "You look like my husband."

The nurse laughed. "Husband? How old are you, child? Sixteen? Seventeen?"

"Seventeen, and I'm not married," the girl said, eyes drifting back shut.

"Heh? *Oh.*" The nurse turned to Rishi, her eyes brimming with mirth. "Looks like you got yourself another marriage proposal, Dr Rastogi."

Rishi could *feel* his face burn. He'd been on the receiving end of proposals before—decent and indecent. Many surgeons had when patients came out of anaesthesia. Rishi, being blessed with the even features, the sun-kissed complexion, and the lean, muscular build of his maternal ancestors, collected more than his fair share of lurid offers. He winced, remembering the ninety-year-old great-grandmother who pinched his bottom once. He'd laughed with the rest of the theatre staff over pervy granny, but this time, he couldn't meet the gaze of the nurse. He didn't want to see the sympathy sure to be in her eyes at the talk of romance. Not a soul asked directly, but they'd all heard about the divorce proceedings. How could they have failed to when Anjali was employed by the same place as an anaesthesiologist?

Yes, they'd all heard about Rishi's personal misery, but none of them had a clue of the extent of the trouble he was in. Earlier in the evening, a text popped up on his phone from an unknown number, asking him to check the hospital mailbox where something special waited for him. His heart thudded. Of all the people who'd come and gone through his life, there were only two left who'd care enough to send him surprise gifts. Anjali *did* care—of that Rishi was sure. Still, she wouldn't be in the mood to buy him gifts any time soon, and she certainly wasn't as callous as to send anything related to the divorce quite this way. The other one... the reason behind Anjali wanting a divorce... perhaps the anger at Rishi's desertion had subsided. Perhaps his pleas for understanding on his obligation towards his wife and family got through. Rishi was in no position to toss aside his responsibilities and travel the world with a lover.

The unstamped envelope delivered by Rishis' secretary contained only a single sheet of paper—a letter in Hindi typed with English alphabet. Each word in it dripped venom, telling Rishi news of the impending divorce reached the one person in the world he'd prayed would never hear of it—the blackmailing bastard Rishi thought he'd left in his past.

Daktar saab. Bohot din huve.

Rishi didn't bother looking for the signature—there wouldn't be one. The mangled greeting calling him "Doctor sir" and the statement it had been a long time since they talked was enough to remind him of the crime he'd committed so many years ago. The mistake no one knew about except him and the blackmailer. Rishi whimpered in panic and shivered in his chair for an hour until the call came through about this teenager who needed emergency surgery.

As soon as he slipped his hands into latex gloves, all thoughts of the disaster awaiting him fled. It was always the same. Being with his team drained the tension from him. Under the bright theatre lights focused on the delicate structure of the human brain, there was no Rishi—only Dr Rastogi, neurosurgeon.

The bastard who wrote the letter was threatening to rip it all away. He was threatening to slice off Rishi's identity, reducing him to a mere skeleton.

Fear tightened into a hot ball in his upper abdomen. *Stop*, he ordered himself. He was still in the patient's room. He couldn't afford to break down. The nurse was already looking at him with concern. She didn't know anything about the letter, did she? No, it was the patient's silly comment. Rishi tried a dismissive chuckle and turned, but the mirth seemed false to even his own ears. Marriage had dulled his reflexes against unwanted advances. He and Anjali had been together for eleven years, more if he counted from the year they met. But at the time, there was someone between them—Joe, Rishi's flatmate, the love of Anjali's life.

Chapter 5

December 2006

"Are you insane?" Rishi shouted over the sounds of cricket commentary drifting into the tiny bedroom from the living room TV. As he sat up higher on the twin bed, the yeasty froth of beer came up his nostrils. Coughing, he tossed the nearly empty bottle into the wastebasket in the corner and glared at the curly-haired woman in jeans and fuzzy pink sweater by the door—Gauri, final-year medical student and overall pain in the butt. He'd been chilling at home with a bottle of Kingfisher and a decent paperback when she barged in. "Darling," Rishi explained through clenched teeth, "I'm your sister's *tutor.* I can't have her as a guest for New Year's Eve."

This would be one of the handful of things Joe and Rishi ever agreed on. Gauri's fiancé, who was right now in the U.S. doing medicine internship, was best friend to both men, but there were limits to friendship, dammit—like risking their employability to keep the S.O.B.'s bratty betrothed entertained.

Stomping a foot, Gauri said, "The little snot complained to my parents I don't take her anywhere. If she can't be here, I can't, either. I can't even go any other place. You *know* how my family is."

Yup, Rishi did know and like a lot of young people in India, could painfully identify. Her parents—a retired history professor and his wife—were the conservative sort and kept strict control over all aspects of their children's lives. Rebellion would lead to withdrawal of social support and perhaps financial, as well. Their older daughter's romance with Rishi and Joe's best friend was initially met with intense hostility until the credentials and family background of the man in question were confirmed. Now, the intended son-in-law was treated royally, and *he'd* certified Rishi and Joe safe—including for the younger daughter. The flat was the only place the girls were allowed to visit without explicit parental permission.

"And *she* won't go anywhere without her pals," Gauri continued whining. "C'mon, Rishi. Help me out."

"Whoa, whoa, whoa. Back up a second. Did you say your sister wants to bring her *pals?*"

"Sorry, yaar. The girl she's always hanging with... the frog girl, Anjali? She and a boy from their batch. You know who I'm talking about?"

Rishi mumbled a curse. How could he possibly forget Anjali Joshi? The damned lab attendant from physiology spun a tale of love at first sight all around campus, and no matter where Rishi went, someone was humming the same silly movie song. After five years of successfully evading every attempt at pushing him into romances he didn't want, he was now starring in an imaginary love story. He'd hardly muttered two words to her since the incident in the lab, and she darted away anytime they came within ten feet of each other, but even the head of the department carried on about the girl's parents being practically royalty in medical circles, glancing meaningfully at Rishi as he made the remark. Apparently, Anjali was from Mumbai and came from a line of doctors extending back to the 1600s, all famed for their contribution to the development of modern medicine in India. Not only that, the Joshis were *über* wealthy, having made their money in land and gold and lately in stocks. It was more than Rishi ever wished to know about the girl. They were in Delhi—a major metro with almost fifteen million people—but in the medical college campus, he couldn't escape mentions of one Anjali Joshi.

Plus, Gauri's sister—Meenakshi—always hung out with the girl. Then, there was the third one in their little pack. The punk who'd tried to help Rishi capture the frog—wavy hair, dark poetic eyes, and a talent for making up dirty limericks about his teachers if the rumours were correct.

"I'm so bored," Gauri complained. "The only social life I have is with you and Joe. *Please,* Rishi? It will be just the three of them."

"Hell, no," Rishi said, gesturing her away. "I'm not losing my job just so you can keep yourself entertained." Nor was he going to give fodder to the gossip about him and Anjali. "Out you go."

"*Rishi,*" whined Gauri. "Why are you being so difficult, yaar? I need you to convince Joe."

"Ain't happening." Even if Rishi weakened, Joe wouldn't agree. Where career was concerned, there was no one more mindful of proprieties.

A hand to her heart, Gauri said, "I swear nobody's gonna know they were here. Except for a few of us, most everyone has gone home for Christmas break."

Gauri's parents were at some religious retreat their daughters recoiled from joining. Joe couldn't afford to travel to Goa, and Rishi... well... home was New Delhi for him, but he wasn't welcome in the family residence at the moment. If Gauri didn't show up, it would be only him and Joe staying home as neither had the money to go clubbing. Also, the nurse from Goa who was a friend of Joe's. When sozzled, they both tended to lapse into a weird mix of Konkani, Goa's official language, and Portuguese, neither of which Rishi knew. If not for Gauri, his Christmas would've been spent listening to the two Goans talking gibberish and drunkenly belting out carols.

Rishi growled. "Dammit, Gauri. You need to be here, or I won't have anyone to talk to on New Year's Eve! Give your sister some money to go watch a movie or something."

Gritting her teeth, Gauri asked, "Don't you think I would've... you got a couple of hundred on you? I'm broke."

"*Me?*" Rishi swung his bare feet to the floor and stood, turning the pockets of his flannel pants inside out. "Darling, I'm a tutor, not one of the professors. I barely make enough to pay rent and eat three times a day." Hence the flat-sharing arrangement with Joseph D'Acosta in this affordable neighbourhood as close as they could get to the AIIMS campus. People thought them friends, but people were thoroughly mistaken. Rishi and Joe *did* have a best friend in common, but they otherwise merely tolerated each other. "What if..." Rishi shook his head. He couldn't think of any alternatives.

"Exactly," said Gauri. "There's no other option. C'mon, Rishi."

With a huff, Rishi said, "Joe's not gonna agree."

"What are you guys talking about?" asked a deep voice.

Gauri squeaked and whirled to face the man walking by clad in flannel pants and cotton tee like Rishi. "Joe! I... umm... *we* thought..."

Rishi sighed. "She wants to bring her sister and two other first-years to dinner tomorrow. Anjali Joshi and the boy they hang out with."

"Heh?" Joe goggled. "No way. You're crazy."

For a second, Gauri didn't say anything. From where Rishi stood, only her profile was visible, but he could clearly see her eyes widening. Her lower lip trembled. Her shoulders shuddered.

"Oh, for God's sake," groaned Joe.

Rishi growled. "Gauri," he warned.

Before he could finish the sentence, the wailing started, loud enough to drown out the TV. Another sound joined her howling—the neighbour's dog, a Pomeranian with the lung power of an elephant. It took a couple of minutes for Rishi and Joe to cajole Gauri to the worn floral sofa in the living room. "I miss him *so* much," she blubbered, rubbing her tearful face on Joe's shoulder—"him" being her absent fiancé.

"We do, too," Joe soothed, exchanging a long-suffering glance with Rishi sitting on her other side. Even the dog's continued yips seemed to hold exasperation. They all knew how this would end.

33

Five minutes later, they were negotiating terms. "No alcohol for them," Rishi said, firmly. "Or for you." Hell, even he and Joe were below Delhi's drinking age of twenty-five and needed Joe's friend—the Goan nurse—to buy beer. "If anyone hears about them being here, they were walking by and something happened... an accident... someone sprained an ankle..."

"Done," Gauri agreed, her face now tear-free. "I just need to tell my mom I did my bit to get my sister settled into life on campus."

Face heating, Rishi added, "Also, you can't leave me alone with... ahh... you know..."

"Anjali?" Gauri asked, chortling.

Eyebrows drawn, Joe snapped, "She asked you for help exactly once. Stop acting as if she's throwing herself at you."

"Poor thing's sooooo embarrassed about the whole thing," Gauri agreed, eyes brimming again but with mirth. "She agreed to the party only because of my sister."

"He thinks he's irresistible," Joe muttered. "He doesn't even want her. *She* hasn't done anything for him to think..."

"I simply want to avoid any misunderstanding," Rishi insisted, choosing to ignore Joe's annoyance. An argument about some girl who'd somehow stumbled into their social sphere was not worth the discomfort it would cause them over the next few months as flatmates until the postgraduate course in surgery started, and God willing, each got a room in the hostel.

"All right, all right," said Gauri.

Joe looked around, cursing at the plastic Christmas tree on the coffee table. "Dammit. We have to clean. This place stinks."

The flat *was* cluttered but not really unclean. Still, the stink part was true. The smell of weed wasn't easy to get rid of. Rishi didn't give a damn what the pulmonologists said—the herb was the one thing guaranteed to stop his asthma attacks. That was his story, and he was sticking to it. Joe admitted to plain liking it.

"Open the windows for a couple of hours," said Gauri, rolling her eyes. "Then, burn some *agarbattis*." The incense sticks would beat the shit out of any weed odour strong enough to withstand the wintry winds of New Delhi. "As far as the snots are concerned, you two will be Gandhiji's avatars, okay? And don't worry about people finding out they were here. My sister and her friends are not gonna blab."

Moments after their arrival the next evening, they didn't even seem capable of opening their mouths. Oh, Gauri's sister was doing plenty of talking, mostly to the Goan nurse, but her batchmates were sitting stiffly on the sofa, wide eyes darting around the shabby living room.

Even with only seven people, it was a tight squeeze. Other than the threadbare sofa, there were the two wobbly wooden chairs which came with the flat and a couple of folding contraptions Joe managed to beg from their neighbour, the owner of the howling dog. The two windows which looked out to the narrow gap between apartment buildings were shut, and the space heater was on. Anjali, clad in jeans and a soft red sweater, was still shivering mildly, her sleeves pulled over her hands.

Mumbaikars. They constantly complained about the heat but dove for cover at the first hint of a chill. Except for Rishi and Joe, the rest were also dressed warm in jeans and sweaters and sneakers. Rishi was a Delhiite, used to cooler winters, and his thin fleece was absolutely fine for the occasion. After sunny Goa, Joe should've found the weather in the nation's capital uncomfortable, but he stuck to his usual khaki pants and Polo shirt—navy blue this time—along with the brown loafers which had seen better days. He'd at least bothered to shave to greet the new year. The bathroom reeked of his cologne. It did cover the weed stink.

Since Rishi and Joe usually ate in front of the TV, they'd never troubled themselves to get a dining set up, so they had to use the small coffee table.

"Wow," said Gauri, sniffing. "You guys went all out tonight."

Rishi recognised shrimp sautéed with coconut bits and the pork vindaloo—they were both Joe's specialities. Roti and fried rice were unmistakable. The red chunks Rishi wasn't quite sure about, but it looked like meat of some sort. Dessert—plum cake filled with nuts and bits of dried fruit—was still in the oven.

"This is not from a restaurant?" asked the boy in the group, speaking for the first time since his arrival.

"Did you copy your dirty songs from a book?" asked Joe, an affronted glare on his face.

Rishi tut-tutted and shook his head in mock awe before distributing paper plates to the group. "Poetry, my friend. Poetry. I heard he recited something at the freshers' party." The young punk's ditties were getting attention from even senior faculty. Academicians rarely appreciated mockery—salty mockery at that.

"It *is* poetry," said the punk, his dreamy black eyes snapping. "And I don't plagiarise. My lines are my own."

"*I* don't do restaurant food," Joe snapped back.

"Don't insult the chef," advised Meenakshi, plonking herself on the sofa, flanking the punk between her and Anjali. If Gauri were all about pinks and sparkles, her younger sister's giant polka-dotty butterfly glasses and high ponytail screamed Nerds-R-Us.

"Look how proud he is of his silly writing," marvelled Gauri.

Nose in air, the punk said, "It's not silly, and it's not dirty. It's erotic satire in rhyming verse."

"*Porn* poetry?" asked the Goan nurse, dragging a folding chair close to Meenakshi's end of the sofa.

As everyone else laughed, Anjali asked, her voice at once sweet and strong, "*You* made all this?" Joe and Gauri took the two chairs next to the nurse, leaving Rishi the one close to Anjali, but her eyes were on Joe, her pink lips parted slightly as though in surprise.

"Yeah," mumbled Joe. "I do the cooking around here, and whatshisname does the cleaning."

Gauri giggled. "Aren't they domesticated?"

Anjali leaned towards the coffee table with paper plate in one hand, sending the soft, lemon scent of her perfume drifting to Rishi. She pointed at the red chunks of meat. "What is this?"

For a second or two, Joe said nothing. Then, an unholy glee crossed his face. "It's a Goan dish. Jumping chicken."

His friend—the nurse—snorted, hiding her mouth with the back of her hand.

The faint suspicion in Rishi's mind was reflected on the other faces in the room. "What exactly is jumping chicken?"

Glinting eyes boring into Anjali, Joe admitted, "Frog legs."

***

Rage churning, Anjali stared unblinkingly at Joe, at his mocking smirk as he bit into... the thing. Around them, the rest were convulsing with laughter, stopping every few seconds to apologise to her. Pressure built inside her head. The muscles in her arms tightened almost involuntarily. She wanted—oh, she so badly wanted—to toss the paper plate in her hands onto his face. Too bad it was empty.

37

"Joe, you terrible man," squealed her traitorous friend. Meenakshi removed her butterfly eyeglasses to wipe the tears of mirth off her cheeks.

Wetness spurted at the corners of Anjali's eyes. Horror. Absolute horror. She was going to make a fool of herself any moment. Clumsily, she placed the paper plate on the table and stood, looking frantically around. "I... umm... I need to use the bathroom." No, she wanted to return to the hostel. She so badly wanted to stalk out and run to the security of her bed to have herself an angry cry.

Laughter sputtering to a stop, the second traitor complained, "C'mon, Anju. It was just a joke." Siddharth—Sid—attached himself to her and Meenakshi after his failed attempt to capture the frog in the physiology lab but switched sides exactly when Anjali was in dire need of support. Yeah, it was a joke like he said—the kind which was funny only if you were not the butt of it.

Anjali blinked hard, trying to keep her dignity intact. Staring at a spot somewhere above Joe's head, she said, "It's not that. I really need to use the bathroom."

"Sorry, yaar," mumbled Meenakshi. "It was not a joke. It was a horrible thing to do to you, and I shouldn't have laughed." Everyone else stopped guffawing, shifting uncomfortably in their seats.

"The bathroom?" Anjali repeated, keeping her voice even. She lowered her gaze to meet Joe's eyes.

"I didn't mean to..." He huffed out a breath and stood, pointing to his left. "Bathroom's over there."

As soon as she shut the door behind her, Anjali turned on the faucet and stood in front of washbasin, the hissing water camouflaging her furious sobs. She *wished* she hadn't decided to stay in the hostel when her parents offered to fly her to Mumbai for Christmas break.

Meenakshi stayed only because she refused to attend the religious retreat her parents were at, and Siddharth recoiled from spending time with his father and his new family in Boston. When Anjali heard her friends were planning to have Gauri take them to Joe and Rishi's flat for New Year's Eve, she didn't want to miss out on the fun and immediately made up a story about her parents going to a medical conference. Oh, Rishabh Rastogi would be at the party, and she really didn't need to feed the gossip, but who was going to find out? He would only be one among the group with Anjali, her friends, Gauri, and Joe D'Acosta. It would be Anjali's first time out as a semi-independent adult, and she would have fun. Instead, she ended up being the joke.

If she left now, she'd give the awful man the satisfaction of having driven her away. Splashing cold water on her face, she checked the mirror above the washbasin to make sure there were no tear tracks on her cheeks. She wiped the wetness from her hands on her jeans and took a deep breath before opening the door. Two steps, and she nearly collided with the tall form slouched against the opposite wall of the narrow passage. "Eek," Anjali said, heart pounding. "*You...*" She gritted her teeth. Didn't Dr Joseph D'Acosta already have enough fun for the evening, kicking around a poor first-year student?

"They're not frog legs," he said, abruptly.

"*What?*"

"I said they were because... I have no idea why I said it, but I'm sorry."

Utterly confused, Anjali shook her head. "But... what... come again?"

Enunciating each word in his buttery smooth voice, Joe explained, "I just said they were frog legs. They are not. I shouldn't have done it, and I'm sorry."

Anjali searched the light brown eyes under the bushy brows for some sign of mockery, but she saw none. There was no stench of deceit about him, only the scent of his cologne, something which reminded her of trees baking under the sizzling sun. Returning her silent regard, he scratched the slight cleft in his clean-shaven jaw with a single finger. An angry red line ran across the cleft, a shallow cut which was now healing.

The rest of the group was also silent, watching them from the living room merely ten feet away. There was a snort from Rishi, almost a laugh, but he immediately went into a coughing fit and turned his back until it subsided.

"So what *are* those things?" Anjali finally asked, crossing her arms over her chest to rub her shoulders.

"Soya chunks."

"Soya?" Siddharth exclaimed from the living room, his voice full from the food in his mouth. "Gimme a napkin. Hurry!" Rishi leapt from his chair as though to look for one, but there weren't any. Without waiting for anyone to locate one, Siddharth spat the half-masticated food onto his paper plate.

"*Eww,* Sid," said Meenakshi, leaning away from him.

"Are you all right?" asked Rishi. "You're not having an allergic reaction, are you?"

Joe straightened. "Get your EpiPen, Rishi." With his susceptibility to allergies, Rishi would need to keep pre-filled syringes of the lifesaving medicine with him.

"No," said Siddharth, holding a hand up. "It's just that I'm a strict non-vegetarian. It's against my religious code to eat anything without meat. You should've warned me."

It took a moment for the claim to sink in. Then, Anjali giggled. Everyone else erupted into shouts of mock-annoyance, pummelling Siddharth with pillows.

"He's asking to get his ass kicked," said Rishi, glaring and laughing at the same time.

"I agree." Joe stepped back into the living room, fists raised, but he was also laughing.

"Hey," Siddharth said, holding his hands up. "No violence, please. I'm delicate."

"You're certainly something," Rishi agreed. He leaned towards Siddharth as though to say more.

"I know what to do," said Meenakshi, holding her index finger up. Before Siddharth could object, she poked him in the tummy.

He bent double with a high-pitched tee-hee, setting Anjali and Meenakshi off while the rest guffawed. "Pillsbury doughboy," squealed Anjali.

Rishi glanced at the sofa where Siddharth was making faces at Meenakshi. Shaking his head slightly, Rishi scooted back into his chair.

When they settled down around the food a second time, Siddharth said, "Sorry, Anju. I shouldn't have said it's just a joke. You're so goody-goody all the time it's almost irresistible temptation to see what will make you crack." Ignoring Anjali's heavy frown, he nodded at Joe. "I get it, bro. Still, why health food junk on New Year's Eve?"

Joe was in the process of loading his plate with fried shrimp and stilled for a moment. Voice casual, he said, "I wasn't sure if any of you were vegetarian. There's some *khatkhate*, too, in the kitchen." His gaze swept over the group, skipping Anjali. "It's a sort of vegetable stew, very popular with Konkani brahmins."

Anjali fixed her eyes on the fragrant fried rice on her plate. Joe had been to Gauri and Meenakshi's home; he would've been aware they ate all kinds of meat, including beef. Of all the people in the flat, the only two whose dietary preferences he wouldn't have known were Anjali and Siddharth. She wasn't terribly keen on meat, preferring seafood, but lots of brahmins were strict vegetarians. A tremor went through her heart. Then, she frowned. *Konkani* brahmin? It was such a minute detail of their caste, how could Joe possibly have—

"I knew your grandfather," said Joe, as though he'd heard her unspoken question. "Dr Ram Manohar Joshi."

"Heh?" asked the nurse, Kokila. "Dr Ram was her grandfather?"

"*Really?*" Meenakshi tore off a piece of roti and dipped into the thick, tangy gravy of the pork vindaloo. "You never told us your family knew Joe, Anju."

"I didn't realise," Anjali said, trying to take in the information. Joe was talking about *Daadaji*—her paternal grandfather. He and *Daadima*—Anju's paternal grandmother—moved to Goa after Daadaji's retirement. Well, *semi-*retirement, since he ran a charity clinic there. They'd been a quiet couple, awkward with all their grandchildren, and Anjali hadn't known them all that well. She'd never visited Goa while they were living there. Not on purpose; it never occurred to her. Both passed very recently with Daadaji following Daadima mere weeks after her—Anjali sat up and waved her fork in Joe's direction. "*That's* where I heard your name. You found him."

The rest were glancing back and forth between her and Joe. He nodded. "Yeah. I'd gone home after the final-year exam. Your grandmother had just passed. Someone from the neighbourhood went by daily to make sure Dr Ram was doing okay. It was my turn that day. Plus, I needed some advice. He wasn't at the clinic, so I went to visit him at the house. He'd told all his employees to take the day off and was just resting in the living room, no TV, no nothing. He asked if I could buy him a pack of cigarettes."

Anjali smiled. The one thing she did know about Dr Ram Manohar Joshi, general practitioner, was that he'd smoked like a chimney. Where his health was concerned, Daadaji never practised what he preached, much to the frustration of his four sons, all doctors.

"When I returned," Joe continued, meditatively, "he was still in his chair. First, I thought he'd fallen asleep. But... it was too late for CPR, and he'd said many times he wouldn't want to be resuscitated. I called my godfather, the parish priest. He contacted the family." Setting his plate on the coffee table, Joe shrugged.

He'd left out a couple of details. Standing by her mother's side, Anjali had heard the conversation between her parents about Daadaji's protégé. The aforementioned parish priest and Joe hadn't been mere neighbours to Dr Ram Joshi. The priest and Joe's grandfather, a part Portuguese and part Indian man who'd died in a boat accident many years ago, were cousins and childhood friends of Daadaji.

Anjali's father asked Joe to return to Delhi to start his internship on time instead of travelling to Mumbai for the cremation. Daadaji would've wanted it that way. From among his circle in Goa, only the white-haired priest attended the funeral, the grief of loss clear in his red-rimmed eyes.

"Wow," muttered Kokila, Joe's nurse friend from Goa. She glanced at Anjali. "I worked a year at the charity clinic with Dr Ram. I never realised you're his granddaughter." No surprise with such a common enough last name. "How did *you* know, Joe?"

With a bemused look, Joe said, "He used to show me family photos and talk about his grandkids. He told me one of his granddaughters was dead set on going to AIIMS."

Daadaji had known it? Anjali supposed he and Daadima loved their grandkids, but the old couple were never more than distant figures in her life. *Joe* seemed to have enjoyed a closer relationship with them than her.

"Even on the last day..." He brooded.

After a couple of seconds, Anjali asked, "What happened on the last day?"

Joe shook his head. "Nothing. He just said I'd get to meet you soon."

"Of course," said Kokila. "You were already here in Delhi. Still, small world."

"Yeah," said Siddharth, fidgeting. "Hey, can we discuss something else? All this talk about death is going to give me nightmares."

Rishi raised a brow. "And you want to be a doctor?"

"Don't forget the poetry," Gauri said, chortling. "*Porn* poetry."

With a grin, Rishi said, "Erotic satire in rhyming verse. He does look the part."

Kokila gawked. "He looks like a porn star?"

"Like a poet," corrected Rishi, leaning back in his chair with a lazy warmth in his black irises. "The eyes and the long hair."

Anjali peered at her Siddharth's face and back at Rishi. *Hmm.* "I guess," she muttered.

"Stop," Siddharth said, swatting her away. "I feel like I'm one of the frogs."

The laughter resumed. Chatter continued. Anjali didn't talk to Joe one-on-one for the rest of the night except for when she caught his gaze on her face once. They'd somehow ended up sitting next to each other on the sofa, and he was peering intently at... *her mouth?*

With the tip of his finger, he gestured at the corner of his own lips. "You have something there." With a paper napkin, she rubbed it vigorously, but he shook his head. "Still there."

She touched her fingers to the spot in question. Nothing. "Is it a small, black dot? It's not food; it's a birthmark."

"Uh-huh... okay." Joe straightened.

"You have good eyesight." Anjali frowned. Or maybe the mark wasn't as tiny as she believed. "I should get it removed or something."

"Don't," he said, tone almost husky. Flushing, he added, "I mean, why do unnecessary surgery?"

Gauri's phone rang, and she squealed, announcing it was her fiancé. Both Joe and Rishi rushed to talk to him. So did Kokila and Meenakshi. They put him on speaker to introduce the new members of the group. He continued to stay on the phone until after the countdown to the new year. Even when he hung up, no one mentioned leaving.

Anjali bit into delicious plum cake and laughed helplessly at Rishi attempting to dance to the rowdyish movie songs picked by Joe. "You look like you're having seizures," she said, pointing a finger at a rueful Rishi. Whereas Joe... God, the man could move! He and Kokila put on quite a show for the rest, claiming the rhythm of the seas flowed in their blood.

The entire group stayed all night in the flat, chattering about this and that and everything. She didn't realise she fell asleep on the sofa until she woke the next morning, her head on Siddharth's chest, and Meenakshi's feet on his lap.

Chapter 6

Present day

Sitting in the leather chair in the wood-panelled office, Dr Rishabh Rastogi spun a pen on the desk and glanced at the clock. Eight AM? He'd been here all night? The wooden shutters were down, not letting him see the sun, and the air conditioner hummed, keeping the heat of the day away. No wonder he wasn't aware the night ended. Outside the closed doors, sounds of morning rounds started—shift change for the support staff, the clatter of carts, the ringing telephones, the heated discussions—but within his office, there was a forbidding quiet of impending disaster.

Rishi's mind fought to remain in the pokey flat near the AIIMS campus where he celebrated the birth of another year, unaware of the hidden enemy waiting to get him. In the flat where he was watching romance bloom between a couple, five more young people chatted that night, forming the first tentative bonds of friendship.

There were no plans made when the group scattered after breakfast, but somehow, they ended up spending most weekends in the flat. Cramming for exams, watching movies, arguing over cricket matches, while Anjali—not a fan of any sport, whatsoever—napped. Joe put the rest to work as his minions, cutting and chopping and cleaning while he cooked. The food bill was split seven ways. The young'uns managed to be deferential to Rishi and Joe in the lecture hall and call them by their title, but within the four walls of the apartment, they were equal—friends. Laughter, camaraderie, support, acceptance—they'd had it all until the day Rishi opened the letterbox and found an unstamped envelope addressed to him, threatening to reveal the crime he'd committed.

Rishi was still reeling from it when Joe—for reasons he never bothered to explain to his devastated girlfriend or anyone else—walked out of the flat for the last time. Anjali went to Goa, searching for Joe, only to be given the message he didn't want to be found. Rishi grabbed the lifeline Joe unintentionally left him—Anjali. Rishabh Rastogi deliberately used her and the political clout of her family to ensure his safety from the blackmailer. Whatever his reasons, he'd done his best to make her happy. Anjali had her own rationale for wedding him. No way could either ever claim they didn't get exactly what they wanted out of the marriage. It was an incredibly good life, too, with the mellow warmth of heart-whole friendship, deep affection, and shared interests. At least until Rishi was fool enough to seek romance with someone else.

Now, Anjali was gone, and it hadn't taken long for the news to reach his enemy. Rishi was no longer shielded by the political connections of the Joshi family. If he didn't do as he was told, his career could be destroyed. His identity as a doctor could be stripped away.

No. Rubbing his gritty eyes with a thumb and forefinger, Rishi stood and went to the window. He separated two of the slats and looked out into the sunlit street—the real world, the here and now. He'd invested too much of himself—in his past, present, and future—to let it be destroyed by the bastard who'd stayed in the shadows, waiting for the right time to strike. Rishi wouldn't let anyone wreck his career, and he certainly wasn't about shirk to his familial responsibilities towards Anjali to go chasing after a lover. Those who claimed to have feelings for him needed to understand it once and for all.

Rishi needed to talk to Anjali. He would get her to see how they could make it work. They needed to, dammit. Blackmailer aside, they got each other. Neither was ever going to find the peace they craved with anyone else no matter what emotional highs that particular someone might have promised. It took months of Anjali's absence to drive the point home to Rishi. He wouldn't stray ever again. She'd understand it. She'd forgive him. She *had* to.

Pressing the intercom button, Rishi said, "Farida, come to my office for a moment." When the secretary arrived, notepad in hand, he was back in his chair. "Don't say anything to anyone just yet but draft an email for me and send it as soon as I text you I'm out the door. I don't want to give anyone a chance to object... I'm resigning, effective immediately." At the startled squeak from her, he smiled, reassuringly. "No, you don't have to worry about your job. You'll continue to be my personal secretary."

"But... what... which hospital... are you going to teach?" It was no secret AIIMS would love to have him back.

"Maybe... I don't know yet. I'll keep you posted. Also... ahh... book me a ticket to Goa, will you please?"

"Oh..." Understanding dawning in her eyes, the secretary nodded. "Good idea, Dr Rastogi. There's no job more important than family."

Forget the job, forget the note still locked in his desk—there was *nothing* more important than family. When Rishi returned to Delhi, he and Anjali would be a family, again. There was nothing or no one he'd let stand in their way. "Also, a hotel room as close as you can get to Fontainhas."

The oldest Latin quarter in Goa's capital city was where the Joshi holiday home was. Anjali's grandparents once used the Portuguese mansion as their retirement place, but after their passing, the family only ever went there for holidays. Anjali asked her mom to inform Rishi of her location merely out of courtesy. He'd somehow managed to conceal his shock at the idea of her returning to the place which witnessed her devastation at Joe's hands. Family request or not, why the hell was Anjali going back to the scene of her heartbreak? She could've told the Joshis she was in no shape to handle the problems at the charity clinic. It wasn't as though the Joshi family suffered a shortage of doctors who could do the same job. Rishi got a single-word answer in response to his text. "Closure."

Closure, Rishi mumbled in his mind. She needed it before she returned to her life with Rishi. So did he. Together, they could bury the ghosts of their past in Goa.

His phone pinged. Taking a quick glance at the text message, he straightened in surprise. Anjali? After all the weeks of barely communicating? And precisely when he was thinking about her? Hope and anxiety battled for primacy in his heart as he dialled her number. "Anju, I'm so glad you—"

"Rishi," came her trembling voice. "He's back."

"Heh? *Who's* back?" The blackmailer? It couldn't be. Why would the bastard contact *her?* Rishis' heart thudded. Or was it someone else's last-ditch attempt to get Anjali out of his life?

"Joe," Anjali said with a soft sob.

Part III

Chapter 7

"How long is he going to hide from me?" Joe asked, cradling the phone on his left shoulder as he flipped through patient charts at the nurses' desk. The small building housing his clinic was set at the foot of a hill, and through the row of open windows, he could see the ocean and hear the surf crashing on the rocky shore. If he craned his neck, the Chapora Fort—an eighteenth-century structure occupied at various times by various conquerors—was visible at a distance. The air smelled like fresh-cut grass.

There was little evidence of last night's storm except in his heart. Mind thrown into utter chaos on seeing Anjali, he'd dumbly watched her leave instead of chasing after her. Memories of their days in Delhi sped through his mind like snaps on a carousel... the joy, the pleasure, the hurt, the anger... the mistakes he'd made. He stayed hours in the manager's office at the café, wishing he could go back in time and make different decisions.

When the rain finally slowed to a drizzle, he left his car in the parking lot and wandered down the dark, deserted street towards the family home. He barely saw the homeless under the awnings or felt the dying bursts of the monsoon storm trickling down his hair, dampening his clothes. All he could do was wonder at the miracle of her reappearance in his life. Except, Joe didn't believe in miracles.

He wished like hell he could believe she'd engineered it. But no. The Anjali he knew possessed too strong an awareness of social proprieties to chase after a man—especially one who'd discarded her without a backward glance. The only other person in Goa who even knew of her existence was the crackpot priest who considered it his second calling to interfere in his relatives' lives. Unfortunately for Joe, said priest was staying far away from his telephone today.

"I'm not just his godson... I'm a parishioner," Joe reminded the church caretaker at the other end of the line. "What if I need divine guidance?"

"Father is not hiding from you, Dr Joe," came the earnest voice of the caretaker. "He really has a wedding to officiate."

"With the new virus going around?" Joe asked. Goa wasn't impacted in a major way thus far, but the state government had ordered people to exercise caution and avoid crowds. He snapped the last chart shut and held a thumb up, signalling the two nurses who worked for him they could go on lunch break.

"The groom's dad is very active in the diocese *and* in politics," said the caretaker, primly. "They got special permission from the government. Plus, there are parish duties. Father doesn't have time to take non-essential calls. Tomorrow, it's Sunday, and he'll be busy all day."

Joe bit back a pithy retort. "Tell him I'll be at the morning service."

"That'll be a first," came the mutter from the other end. Joe hadn't darkened the church doorstep in years, limiting his involvement to dutifully sending weekly contributions to the collection box via his baby sister.

Ignoring the comment, Joe hung up and tucked the phone back into his pocket. When he got back to the family residence from the café, the pink rays of the sun were already brightening the sky. He dragged his brothers out of bed only to have both swear on the souls of their departed parents they didn't know Anjali's actual identity when they set up the blind date. They could be lying, but Joe had never mentioned her to either. Even now, he'd only said Anjali was an acquaintance from his college days. The idiots could've easily been in cahoots with the priest, but all *he* knew about her was that she was the granddaughter of his old friend.

Joe briefly considered beating the truth out of his brothers. His hands simply *itched* for a good old brawl like they used to have as kids when they'd beat each other to a bloody pulp. Joe was eight years older than the next in line, but the younger two teamed up to even the odds. Exhilarated by the fight, they'd all go to the beach to goggle at the bikini babes and make themselves sick on coloured ice masquerading as ice cream. Beer took over now they were all adults, but the babe part remained the same.

Regretfully, he discarded the idea. Two against one weren't great odds when brother number two outweighed him *and* possessed a black belt in karate. He didn't even bother asking his sister; she'd maintain her innocence to her last breath in spite of all evidence to the contrary. Father Franco, man of the cloth, wasn't supposed lie. He could pretend to be busy, but he'd have to be at the pulpit on Sunday—

Dammit, Joe couldn't wait until the morning. He really needed to go to Fontainhas tonight. It was all he could do not to race his old Ambassador car to the Joshi mansion and camp in front of the door until Anjali consented to talk to him. But he needed answers before they talked—her marriage to Rishi,

51

what she was doing back in Goa, and her weird statement about someone waiting for her while she was out on a date she clearly didn't plan to keep. The most important question of all was one Joe didn't dare ask: was there a chance she knew the real reason why he left Delhi, the terrible truth of what he'd done?

Chapter 8

2007

Did he even *want* a chance? Joe shifted in the padded chair, flipping through an old issue of the *Journal of the Royal Society of Medicine*. He'd come to the library to get the preliminary work done on his paper on xenotransplantation—species-to-species organ transplant. The department chief was very enthusiastic about Joe's hypothesis on nonhuman primate kidneys. If things went as planned, Joe would be a transplant surgeon before he turned thirty, and he needed cellular-level knowledge for the research he wanted to do. Every spare moment was spent in the operating theatre or the immunology lab or the library.

Unfortunately, further down the row of tables was Anjali, peering into a thick textbook—*Gray's Anatomy* from the looks of it—and making notes. Even in denim shorts and a pink, frilly blouse, she sat straight-backed, looking every inch a modern-day princess. Her dark brown hair was held back in a short ponytail. Between her and Joe, a dozen students were all poring over books, the only sounds being the rustling of pages and an occasional cough or sneeze. He still couldn't concentrate. She'd destroyed his focus the day they met. Her grandfather's last words to Joe before the old man passed less than two years ago never left his protégé's mind.

At nearly twenty-one, Joe was adamant he didn't have the luxury of going into academic medicine. Research was for people who didn't need to worry about cash, dammit, like the Joshis with their family trust supplying income to every member. As the eldest son in a long line of eldest sons, Dr Ram was the current head of the Joshi Trust.

Dr Ram had nodded his grey head in understanding and leaned back into the cane armchair, his bare feet on the matching ottoman. Dressed as he was for his day of solitude in a white undershirt and off-white cotton pyjamas, no one would take him for the wealthy man he was. Ostentatious displays were not really a Joshi trait, but everything around them spoke of money and privilege—the handcrafted furniture, the expensive art on the walls, even the silence of the air conditioner which kept the interior of the mansion cool and comfortable. The only sounds in the sun-drenched living room were of the birds chirping outside the large windows.

"I get what you're saying, JoJo." The old doctor was the only one left in Joe's life who still used the childhood name. "Private practice will bring you more money, but—"

Joe interrupted, "It's not just about money." Waving a hand, he gestured at the room around them. "When you walk out of here, everyone in the neighbourhood knows who you are. You're always Dr Ram Joshi. I want that."

"You'll be Dr D'Acosta after your internship." In only twelve more months. "Won't matter whether you're in clinical practice or working in a lab."

"Yeah, but..." Joe grimaced. "No one will know it."

With a sigh, Dr Ram said, "I was afraid of this. You went into medicine wanting the validation from society which comes with the title of doctor. JoJo, it's not something handed out so graduates can feel good about themselves. There's a responsibility which comes with the title. If your calling is in research, you'll regret every minute you spend in private practice. You won't be doing your patients any good. Even for those motivated purely by self-interest, there *is* something called job satisfaction, and it will impact the rest of your life. You've come this far; don't mess things up."

"But—" Joe huffed, slumping further into the plush cushions on the settee. "Follow your dream," he muttered. "Every loser who comes to Goa says the same."

Dr Ram guffawed. "I agree some people use it as an excuse for laziness, but in your case, you'll still be working your butt off and collecting a paycheck." A mischievous twinkle in his eye, the old man turned his head towards Joe. "Besides, Franco tells me one of his parishioners is trying to set you up with his daughter. Big money from what I hear. The girl is the only heir to her daddy's department store chain in Goa. Marry her, and you *will* have the luxury—as you put it—of going into academic medicine. I'm sure she'll tell all her employees to call you 'doctor.'"

"No," Joe snapped, instantly. "I'm not for sale." The D'Acostas might be known for their shameless willingness to bend any rule for cash, but not Joe. "I'm a man. I can take care of myself."

The mirth on his face intensifying, Dr Ram said, "A joke, my boy. I didn't mean to cast any aspersions on your manhood. I only said it because I knew damned well you'd never agree."

After glaring at the old doctor for a couple of seconds, Joe chuckled, reluctantly. "You know it, but the people around here... dammit, they either think I'm a loser who got lucky in life because of you, or they assume I'll trade my degree for a hefty dowry. No one expects me to be a success on my own terms."

"There you go again," said Dr Ram, softly. "You say you want to find success on your own terms, but what you're looking for is approval from society. JoJo, the society we live in *is* important but not to the extent you structure your life around its prejudices. Don't let other people's attitudes decide your future for you. Once again, clinical medicine requires an emotional investment you won't have if you're in it only for the money and to enjoy being the big fish in a small pond. Your patients will suffer for your lack of real interest. *Primum non nocere*, remember? Above all, to do no harm. The first thing any new physician must do is take an oath to that effect. You already recognise all this, which is why you're here, talking to me. Take a few weeks to think about it before you make your final decision. Whatever you decide, give it your all, and validation will come in one form or the other—if not from the rest of society, from your own self. Now, be a good boy and go buy me a pack of cigarettes, please."

Shaking his head in reproof at the doctor's blatant disregard for his own health, Joe stood. He was almost at the door when he heard his name called and turned.

"Anju will be in AIIMS in a year," Dr Ram mused.

Joe knew who she was. Dr Ram often bragged about his eldest grandchild, waving her pictures around and talking about her every accomplishment. Joe usually indulged the old man, silently marvelling at his confidence in her ability to get into India's most in-demand medical college.

Dr Ram stretched back in his cane chair and closed his eyes. "I wish I could be there... don't mess it up."

It was the old doctor's frequent admonishment to his protégé. Why he'd repeat the instruction where his granddaughter was concerned, Joe didn't get, and when he returned with the cigarettes, there was no chance to ask. Something about the old man's posture... there was no response to calls, to Joe's hand shaking his shoulder. Shock, disorientation, the grief of loss... Joe was numb from the gamut of emotions when Dr Ram's son—Anjali's father—told him to start his internship on time as the old man would've wanted instead of staying back for the funeral.

At the end of the flight back to Delhi, Joe decided to take his mentor's final advice. He didn't need to be the big fish in a small pond. It would take him a lot longer to become the king of the ocean, but he'd do it. He'd go into research medicine and rule it. He wasn't going to mess things up. Dr Ram's last disjointed order... the words played over and over in Joe's mind all through his internship. They surged back into his conscious thoughts when he laid his eyes on Anjali the first day in the physiology lab. It had to be the reason behind the instant connection he felt, an attraction so bizarre he was now in the medical college library, dreaming about her instead of focusing on his work.

Of all the dumb things... Joe snorted louder than intended, causing annoyed looks to be directed his way from the students on either side.

With an apologetic tilt of his head, he returned his attention to the journal in front of him, but his thoughts kept drifting to Anjali. Dammit, he was a practical man. He'd teased his departed mother often enough about her fantasies but now...

Anjali certainly didn't seem to feel any such connection. She hadn't even known who he was until he told her. Even afterwards, Joe's flatmate held her attention. She always went to Rishi when she needed help in the physiology lab. In the apartment, they were always chatting about art and music, Rishi throwing smirking glances at Joe while he was at it. Joe couldn't butt in. Beyond vaguely recognising some of the names, he knew nothing about oil paintings or Hindustani music. His jackass flatmate on the other hand... Rishi once brought out his old harmonica and played a piece simply to impress Anjali.

Joe flexed the fingers of his right hand, tightening his muscles against the urge to put his fist through the library desk. He took a deep breath and uncurled his fingers, setting the hand on the tabletop and studying the external markings of the extensor tendons. They were crucial to his future success as a surgeon. No way was he going to risk them over a girl.

Why, by God, did he feel the need? She wasn't even his type! He usually stayed away from the stiff princess kind, far preferring women who knew what they wanted from life—both in bed and out of it. Anjali lacked neither IQ nor ambition—no one wanting to get into AIIMS could—but everything about her screamed touch-me-not elegance. Plus, all his girlfriends to date were tall and stacked, and Anjali was... the top of her head barely reached his chest, and her boobs could easily fit into his palms. He would torment her with kisses on the tiny birthmark next to her mouth and nip his way down the course of her jugular vein, leaving love bites on that clear skin. The way she sometimes fiddled with the top button on her shirt... he'd imagined popping it open and giving her a hickey on her breast... caressing her until she lost all her polish and screamed in pleasure in his arms.

Bloody hell. The front of his jeans was now painfully tight, the sharp zipper digging into his plumbing. Of all the places to fantasise about sex... especially sex with *Anjali.* He, Joseph D'Acosta, was dreaming of planting a hickey on the Joshi princess. Even if his interest were real and not a delusion fuelled by Dr Ram's words, Anjali was out of bounds for Joe.

Narrowing his eyes, he forced his attention back to the journal in front and managed to jot down some notes. He didn't get far before the phone rang in his pocket, drawing more glares and throat-clearing from one of the library staff. Mumbling an apology, he turned off the phone without looking at the number.

Anjali's chair was empty and neatly tucked back under the table. When did she leave? Joe gathered his papers. It was no use. His brain was not in the mood today to cooperate with his career plans.

As soon as he walked through the door of the flat, he heard the sweet voice, raised in animation. Joe groaned. There was no escape. Anjali was on the sofa, talking to Rishi. She'd changed from the shorts and blouse she'd worn in the library, but it didn't matter. She remained a princess in the plain bluish-greenish salwar suit and three-inch platform sandals which didn't appear to have a single scuff mark on them. Joe's brown loafers were currently gasping out their last breaths with each step he took, and his jeans and grey tee were almost faded colourless.

Tossing the folder with his notes onto one of the chairs, Joe listened to Rishi's quick explanation for her presence. Apparently, she and Gauri and Meenakshi arrived, requesting Rishi or Joe's company on their trip to Chandni Chowk, the jewellery market. With all the stories floating around about attacks on women, they wanted someone of the male persuasion along on their night out on the town. Siddharth annoyed Gauri the week before by writing a limerick speculating on the reason behind her preoccupation with her boyfriend's absence, so Rishi or Joe it would have to be.

Before they could leave, some elderly relative called Gauri, stating he'd flown to Delhi specifically to visit her and Meenakshi. Promising Anjali they'd pick her up on the way back, the sisters left.

Joe made a noncommittal gesture with his hands and went to the kitchen to make himself some tea. Out in the living room, the conversation turned to some art exhibit Anjali attended. "...Nageshkar..." she said.

"Too European..." said Rishi. "Ravi Varma, on the other hand..."

Joe had barely returned to the living room and settled his butt into a chair with a glass tumbler of milky tea and a piece of *chikki*—peanut brittle—when Anjali twisted around. "What do you think, Joe? Nageshkar's paintings or Ravi Varma's? Nageshkar was from Goa."

Munching on the sweet, gooey chikki, Joe said, bluntly, "I have no clue what you're talking about. If it looks good, I'll like it."

"Oh, c'mon," said Rishi, smirking. "Surely—"

Joe drained the last dregs of the lukewarm tea, washing down the bits of syrup-coated peanuts in his mouth. "Yeah, well... some of us spent our childhoods either studying or working to make sure we didn't starve. We didn't have the cash for art classes and music lessons."

Rishi straightened. "I didn't mean—"

Anjali made a tiny sound of distress.

"How do you think I knew your grandfather?" Joe asked, his tone casual in spite of the sudden spurt of anger in his heart. All these years of hard work, all the single-minded focus on success so he could drag himself and his family out of poverty—everything was useless. He'd never be anything more than the boy standing outside the car showroom, dreaming of the day he'd own one of those shiny toys. "*He* knew my grandfather and Father Franco—my godfather—from when they were boys. When Dr Ram realised my father's army pay wasn't enough, he offered my mother a job in the charity clinic as a nurse's aide. He saw me trying to do my homework in the staffroom one day and took me under his wing."

"Man, I'm so sorry," Rishi said. Damned if the S.O.B. didn't look like he meant it. He already knew about Joe's financial situation, but knowing it in the abstract was very different from having the details shoved in your face.

"It's cool." The anger in him subsiding as quickly as it erupted, Joe uncurled himself from the chair and padded back to the kitchen, calling over his shoulder, "I have to leave. If you're still planning to go to Chandni Chowk, Rishi will have to go with you."

"It will be too late to go by the time Gauri and Meenakshi get back," Anjali's voice came floating behind. "Plus, I already called Sid; he's on his way here to hang out with us. We can go to Chandni Chowk tomorrow."

"I ain't going anywhere tomorrow," said Rishi, immediately. "It's world cup cricket final. Australia versus Sri Lanka. I'm not missing it."

"Joe?" Anjali asked.

"No can do," Joe bellowed towards the living room.

Tone worried, she called out, "Are you still mad at us? We didn't mean—"

"I'm not mad at you," Joe left the empty tumbler in the kitchen sink. Rishi could wash it as penance for the taunting. "I want to see if the Aussies win tomorrow. It will be three in a row for them. Today, I already had plans to go to the temple."

"Temple?" Anjali asked. "I thought you were Christian?"

"I am, but my mother was Hindu," Joe explained, walking back to the living room. "It's her birthday today, and I try to make it to the temple every year." God, religion, church, temple... he wasn't sure of any of it... hadn't been for a long time. Still, on his mother's birthday, he needed to believe in something beyond the mortal body.

Anjali was still on the sofa, her hands on her knees. "Did you send her a gift?"

"Ahh... Anju..." started Rishi.

"She died when I was ten," said Joe, keeping his voice gentle. Her grandfather had many charity projects he took on, and there was no reason for the Joshis to have discussed Joe D'Acosta in particular. Nor was Joe prone to discussing his family background with the people he encountered in Delhi, even the group hanging out at his flat every weekend. Except for the two friends he'd met as a first-year student, Anjali was the only one to hear even this much detail.

Anjali appeared to mull the information. "Which temple?" she finally asked. When Joe named a place a couple of kilometres from the flat, she stood. "If you don't mind, may I go with you? It's been months since I've gone."

Ignoring the slight upward tilt of Rishi's eyebrows, Joe huffed out a breath and tried to think up a reason—just one small reason—she couldn't go with him. "Sid's on his way here, right?"

"So?" she asked. "Rishi will be here." At the sudden cough from Rishi, she turned and asked, "Are you okay?"

"I'm good," said Rishi, both palms up, but his voice was husky, and there was a mild flush on his cheeks. "Scratchy throat."

She eyed him in silence for a second or two before standing. "Let's go," she said to Joe.

Half an hour later, he and Anjali were headed to the temple in an autorickshaw, having their bones rattled by every pothole along the way. While Joe slouched to avoid having the top of his head collide with the roof of the rickshaw with each jump, she was sitting as primly as she did on the ragged sofa in the flat, her spine straight, knees together, and her crossed ankles tucked a little behind. Her hands rested on her thigh, one on top of the other. If it hadn't been for the slight sheen of sweat on her skin and her rounded eyes peering through the open sides of the vehicle into the dusty street with its loud traffic, she could've been in a studio, posing for a portrait—or on a golden throne, dismissing queued-up suitors with a raised brow.

Trying not to burst into laughter, Joe advised over the phut-phut-phut of the engine, "Hold on to something before you get thrown out."

Anjali glanced at him and his grip on one of the steel bars to the side. "Oh, right—" Honking loudly, a red bus careened past. The rickshaw driver cursed, insulting the mother and sisters of the bus driver, and swerved the vehicle to avoid a crash. Anjali slid towards the open side. With an alarmed squeak, she clutched at Joe's elbow the same moment he shot out his right arm and dragged her back by the shoulders.

Heart pounding in terror at the near miss, he shouted at the driver, "Are you trying to kill us, you dumb—"

"*Arrey,*" said the rickshaw driver, the meaningless exclamation full of annoyance. "I didn't ask you to get into my auto. What kind of idiot doesn't know how to hold on?"

Anjali mumbled, "My kind of idiot." No way would she have known what to do in a rickshaw. She would've been sent to school and picked up by trusted employees of her family, riding each way in the cool comfort of a luxury car.

Joe glanced at the top of her head, somehow only then realising she was tucked against his side, his faded grey tee wrinkled in her grip. *Dear God.* The softness of her did something to his insides. The cool, fresh smell of her skin... he clenched his teeth, trying not to inhale deeply and scare the shit out of her that she might currently be in the company of a perv. "Is this your first time?" he asked, keeping his voice low enough so only she would hear. *Idiot.* Could he *make* it sound any more sexual?

"No," she said, her tone equally as soft. "I've done it a couple of times before, but the friend I went with kept trying to scare me, so I refused to go any more."

"He's a damned fool," Joe said, gruffly.

"Who?" she asked, peeking up at his face. She hadn't yet moved away.

"Er... the friend who..." Joe said, trying wildly to remember they were talking about rickshaw rides. Nothing else. Or were they?

Anjali stared unblinkingly at him for a moment. Then, red colour washed into her face, and she shifted away, this time taking care to hold on to one of the steel bars. Eyes on her shoes, she said, "I guess the company you're with matters in such cases."

What the— no, they couldn't still be talking about the rickshaw ride.

"I could've gone alone." She shrugged. "But there didn't seem to be any point. It wouldn't be much fun."

"Not true," Joe disagreed, devoutly. "It *is* great fun even alone. Better with... er... company, of course. Still, in a pinch, going solo can be just fine. You simply need to know what you're doing."

She looked up at him, her brows drawn together. "What special knowledge do I need to ride around in a rickshaw by myself?"

Dammit. She *was* talking about the vehicle. "I mean, how to call one, agreeing on the fare, etcetera." His throat was somehow dry. He coughed mildly, keeping an eye on Anjali's face.

"You still need someplace to go, right?" she asked, gaze solemn. "With my... umm... friend, we agreed it would be a short ride to the beach... to the park... wherever... you know, to celebrate the end of the school year... no real destination. Stupid idea. Now, I'm getting in only if I know where I'm headed."

Jesus. Joe was going to die before the end of *this* journey. "Pleasure rides are no longer an option?" he asked, hoarsely.

Soft pink lips slightly parted, she asked, "Heh?" Then, her eyes widened. The rose hue washed out of her nearly translucent skin.

Shiiit. She hadn't meant what he thought she meant at all.

With a loud squeak of the horn, the rickshaw came to a halt, throwing Joe and Anjali forwards and backwards. "We're here," announced the driver. As soon as she stepped out, Anjali scooted a few feet away to stand in the middle of the crowd thronging the place, peering fixedly into the temple compound. Cursing silently at his own stupidity, Joe dug out his wallet and handed the driver a couple of notes. The driver glanced meaningfully in Anjali's direction. "*Betay, mann mein laddu phoota kya?*" he muttered to Joe, asking if an explosion of anticipation went off in his brain. "Get your mind out of the gutter. She ain't talking about the same kind of ride as you."

***

God, God, God... stupid... oh, God, how stupid. Anjali scurried through the groups of devotees at the temple for evening prayers, wondering wildly if they could somehow divine how stupid she'd been. How could she have possibly not realised... she'd even talked about... he thought she meant... *eww...* she was never going to be able to face Joe in the lecture hall ever again.

He was practically sprinting his way around the main shrine, not even checking to see if Anjali was following. All around, there were chants to the celibate god, the rumble of traditional drums, swirls of fragrant incense. If Anjali were in a better frame of mind, she'd have enjoyed the coolly elegant architecture—the typically South Indian red-tiled roof, the brass and copper embellishments, and the thousands of glowing clay lamps.

Maybe she could just seek sanctuary here. She wouldn't get out until the day she died or Joe left Delhi, whichever came first. She'd never be a doctor, and her parents and brother would have to visit her here, but it was small price to pay for having propositioned her tutor, albeit inadvertently. *Get me out of this,* she begged the deity, *and I'll... I'll...* she'd follow in the god's footsteps and remain celibate for all eternity.

"Watch where you're going, young lady," snapped a voice. A sweaty man in glasses, carrying a sack full of whatever, skirted Anjali and continued on his way.

Yikes. She peered in Joe's direction. He'd halted his race around the shrine and was watching her. Great. Now, she wouldn't be simply a slut in his eyes, she'd be a klutzy slut. At least it rhymed. Maybe Siddharth could make up a new dirty poem about her. Joe took one step towards her. *God... is he coming here? Why's he coming here?* Why couldn't he simply pretend she didn't exist?

"Let's go," he said.

"Heh? Go where?"

"Home..." He flushed, and his eyes skittered away. "I mean, *I'll* go to the flat; *you* go to the hostel."

"Don't you have to pray?" She glanced at the queue of people waiting to visit the sanctum sanctorum.

"It's too hot tonight," Joe said. Delhi had swung from the chill of winter to scorching hot summer in a matter of days. He glanced at the cloudless sky which was fast turning the pretty pink-orange of twilight. "Plus, it's late. Gauri and Meenu might already be at the flat, waiting for you. Even if they're not, Rishi will be there." Hastily, he added, "What I mean is you could get Gauri and Meenu, and all three of you can go straight back to the hostel."

Did Joe think Anjali was waiting to get him alone or something? "Okay," she mumbled. After tonight, she'd *never* return to the flat.

He left a good ten feet between them on the crowded footpath while they waited to hail another rickshaw. Men, women, and children continued to stream in both directions. Cars and bikes sped by, horns blaring, but no rickshaw. One minute... two minutes... five minutes... the bright colours of the evening sky turned to velvety black, and the temperature dipped ever so slightly. Joe still wasn't looking at her. How was he going to avoid her in the physiology lab? What if she needed his help?

Muttering a quick prayer for courage, she took a few steps closer to Joe and immediately, something solid slammed into her back. "*Aaargh...*" she screamed as she fell against his side.

A couple of hands gripped her arms and straightened her. "Hey," Joe shouted at someone.

"Sorry, sorry, sorry," said a childish voice. A young boy, his printed tee stained with the juice dripping from the ice lolly in his hand, grimaced apprehensively at Anjali. His shock of black hair was thoroughly unkempt.

"It's all right," Anjali wheezed, trying to get her breath back. Were ten-year-old boys made of lead or something? She nodded at a plump woman stomping her way towards them, a fierce frown on her face. "Your mother's looking for you."

With a mumble of alarm, the boy sped in the opposite direction. "Idiot," said Joe, glaring after the boy.

"He reminds me of..." Anjali shook her head. "My brother always gets dirty like that." Their nanny used to complain he brought half the neighbourhood park home with him after each play session—twigs in his hair, mud caked on his shoes—while Anjali somehow managed to remain clean. He'd recently turned sixteen and still managed to track in dirt. Sometimes Anjali would watch Meenakshi and Gauri squabble, and she'd get a little ache in her heart, remembering her brother. She wanted so badly for them to be like Gauri and Meenakshi... bickering, bantering, laughing, gossiping... best friends for a lifetime.

"*Your* brother?" Joe asked, his disbelieving tone pulling Anjali back to the here and now.

She laughed up at him. "What? I can't have a brother? *You* do." Joe once fleetingly mentioned two brothers and a sister, all much younger to him.

"No... I mean, yes. Of course, you can. You do. It's just hard to imagine someone related to you running around the streets, getting dirty."

"You can be related and be different. My brother and I are very diff—" Suddenly, she realised Joe was still holding her by the shoulders. The awareness seemed to dawn on him as well. He dropped his hands so fast she barely saw the blur of movement. Biting her lip against the renewed surge of embarrassment, she stepped away. "I didn't mean it—"

"I'm not a—"

They both stopped at the same time, and a moment later asked, "What?"

Anjali peered up and down the street, making sure none of the passers-by was close enough to overhear. "You know... I didn't mean to make it sound like... in the auto, I wasn't hitting on you or anything... I hope you don't think I'm... umm... a ho."

"Ho—I *never* thought it for a second," he snapped, his tall form almost quivering with sudden outrage. "Why would you even—"

Phew. "Just making sure."

Scratching the cleft in his chin with one finger, Joe said, "Why would anyone think you... it was *my* fault. I have no idea how I got things so wrong, and I'm sorry. I swear I'm not a perv."

"This is the second time you've said it," she muttered.

"Heh?"

"That you have no idea why you did something."

"Wha—oh, the frog legs. Yeah, I seem to forget what to do around you." His face turned bright red. "I didn't mean... I should shut up."

A sudden warmth gushed in Anjali's chest. "I... umm..." What exactly was she supposed to say? What did she *want* to say? A tremor went through her body, accompanied by the mad thought that she should fall against him one more time. Before she was tempted to test out the crazy impulse, an autorickshaw rolled to a stop in front.

Headlights and traffic lights blended into a stream. Engines rumbled. The myriad smells of the city assaulted her nostrils—the exhaust fumes, the dust, the aroma of roasting peanuts. Inside the rickshaw, the driver hummed a cheery tune. Not a word was exchanged between Joe and Anjali. Forget placing his arm around her shoulders, he didn't as much as hold her hand. There was still an awareness—a bone-melting knowledge of attraction.

When they were at the door to the flat, she mumbled an apology in her mind to the deity she'd just visited, firmly taking back her vow of eternal celibacy. "Joe?" she called.

Key in hand, he glanced at her. "Yeah?"

Gathering courage, she admitted, "I'm glad I went with you."

His eyes widened. Before he could respond, the shrill ring of a phone had him blinking. With a frustrated huff, he drew out a flip phone, its silvery casing scratched and peeling. "Hello?" A few seconds later, he said, "Thanks, but no. I'm not looking for any moonlighting positions."

"Moonlighting?" Anjali asked as he hung up.

"Yeah. I don't know if it's legal since I'm employed by AIIMS. Even if it were, I have no time." Tucking the phone back into his pocket, he said, "Anju, I—"

The door was flung open. "Anju," Meenakshi exclaimed. "Where were— never mind. Joe, we need to plan snacks for tomorrow. World cup, babyyy."

Anjali rolled her eyes. *Cricket, cricket, cricket.* The Brits left India long ago. Why couldn't they have taken their ball and wicket with them?

Chapter 9

Present day

Joe parked the scratched and dented Ambassador car on one side of the narrow, cobbled street and stayed inside, adjusting his glasses to study the red-roofed, two-storey mansion, painted bright yellow. This was the first he was returning here after Dr Ram's passing, but it didn't look like anything had changed. The glass windows circling the upper level still glinted in the evening sun, the wrought-iron balcony would continue to tempt little boys to shimmy up, and roses bloomed in the flowerpots lining the wraparound porch.

Other than Joe's car, the only vehicle on the street appeared to be a moped, but the sounds of distant traffic filtered through. A bunch of tourists were wandering down the lane, clicking selfies next to the jewel-toned mansions and exclaiming over the most random things they found on the street like the red concrete roosters on the roofs. The fowl was the national symbol of Portugal, and most old houses in Fontainhas sported one. The Joshis kept their bird—

a cement creature with a worm in its beak and an evil glint in its eye—in the backyard.

At the door, Joe scratched his chin and eyed the big, brass knocker. *Damn.* He was sweating like a pig and probably smelled like one. His cream shirt and grey pants and black dress shoes were what he wore all day in clinic. No helping it now. Anjali wasn't likely to let him inside in any case, so it didn't matter.

In the absence of a firm "stay away" from her, he expected to be trying daily for weeks—even months—until she consented to talk. He lifted his hand.

The door flung open, and a rounded figure in a hot pink sari waddled out, her face red with rage. Joe leapt back to avoid being trampled. "I'm contacting your father," she fumed.

"You do whatever pleases you, Mrs Braganza," came the sweet, strong voice of Anjali from inside the house. "But you should know *I* make the decisions around here."

Mrs Braganza? Dammit, she's still around? Of all the people he could run into, it had to be Dr Ram's neighbour with a penchant for calling the cops on anyone who even looked at her cross-eyed. Unfortunately, she enjoyed the ear of her politician brother who was a board member at the Joshi Charity Clinic, so Dr Ram put up with her. The jet-black hair... she couldn't be that much younger than Dr Ram. "Ma'am," Joe said, inclining his head.

She stopped short and squinted at him. "Joseph Francis D'Acosta. I should've known! You always liked the company of loose women."

Annoyed, Joe asked, "What loose women?"

Anjali appeared at the door in her bare feet, dressed in a knee-length frock with yellow fruits and green leaves printed all over. Her dark brown hair was tied in a loose bun, and the familiar, lemony smell of her perfume wafted around her. Her furious eyes skittered in confusion when she spotted him. "Joe... umm..."

"Entertaining men at all kinds of hours," continued Mrs Braganza. "This used to be a good neighbourhood."

Joe's mouth dropped open. "*What?*"

"First of all, that's not what happen..." Anjali heaved in a deep breath. "You know what? Even if I were throwing an *orgy*, it's none of your business."

"What's going—" Joe tried.

Mrs Braganza snorted. "We'll see about that soon."

"Oh, we'll see right now," said Anjali, looking no less like an enraged bull than the older woman. "C'mon in, Joe. The orgy's about to start."

"*Wha*—" Anjali's fingers closed around his wrist. One quick tug, and he stumbled through the door and into the house.

Part IV

Chapter 10

Mistake, Anjali's mind screamed in a weird combination of anger and joy as soon as her fingers tightened around Joe's wrist. The warmth of the skin under her touch suffused her whole hand, threatening to radiate through the rest of her body.

He lurched into the bright, airy living room of the Joshi mansion, coming to a stop barely a foot from her. A surprised breath whooshed out of him.

"I suggest you return home and take up a new hobby," Anjali said to the nosy neighbour, slamming the door in her face before swinging towards Joe. "Why..." The slight tremble in her voice... darn it, at the café, she had the excuse of being caught by surprise. She'd been shocked to the point she'd almost forgotten the mess her life was in—the failure of her marriage to Rishi, the difficulty of the last nine months. All she could think of the night before was Joe, but now with almost a whole day to pull herself together, she was still acting like a silly twit. Anjali coughed. "Why are you here?"

He grinned, the familiar, wicked glee lighting up his eyes behind the black-rimmed glasses. When did he get glasses? She remembered them from last night at the café, but he had 20/20 vision during their time together in Delhi. Joe would be thirty-five now, his next birthday coming up in months. Ageing did cause changes.

The decade that had passed since they knew each other didn't matter. Somehow, his smile turned every colour in the sun-warmed room more vivid... the cream walls, the brightly hued pillows on the cane furniture, even the blue birds squawking outside the grilled windows. "Someone told me there would be an orgy here," he said, his buttery smooth voice lowered to a murmur.

Within her chest, her heart did a flip-flop. Forcing the fingers still wrapped around his wrist to open, she raised an eyebrow. "Really, Joe?" She pointed at the door, cursing the wild impulse which made her drag him in merely to thumb her nose at the judgey woman next door. "Get out."

"Anju, please—" he started, tone urgent. "I need to... can we please..."

She held up a hand. "No. Don't even—" Her throat tightening, she said, "I don't want to hear you call my name. I don't want to hear you say a word."

"Is he Gregory Peck?" asked a curious voice, rolling her Rs American style.

Anjali swung around. Darn it, she'd forgotten... "Umm... Mohini..."

Joe's head snapped towards the cane chair where a girl was curled up, pillow clutched to her chest. "Who are *you*?"

Mohini—Anjali's cousin—uncurled herself and stood. To Joe's credit, he didn't bat even an eyelash. Oh, Mohini wasn't beautiful—that was too tame a word for her. From her midnight black hair and bright green eyes to the lush and long-limbed figure, everything about her screamed wild child. The nineteen-year-old also possessed the same streak of stubbornness that ran through the rest of the Joshis—times a zillion—and had donned the teeniest shorts and tightest tee she could find to guarantee outrage from Mrs Braganza.

"You don't *look* like Gregory Peck," Mohini commented, eyeing Joe up and down.

"I never said I—"

"Why'd'ya use him as your DP, then? Also, you're in *my* house, dude. You can't ask who I am."

"Mohini, stop talking to him," Anjali ordered.

"Mohini?" Joe asked. "You're the cousin."

How did he— of course, he remembered Anjali asking for the phone at the restaurant to call her cousin. Joe rarely forgot little details like that.

Mohini shot him a cheeky grin. "That's *moi.*"

"Stop—talking—to—him," said Anjali, hands balled into fists.

"I have a couple of questions for you," said Joe, focusing on Mohini. "How do you know what picture I used for my DP?"

Eyes widening in sudden wariness, the girl said, "Anju said I can't talk to you."

"Anju," Joe called. "Did *she* sign you up on Tinder?"

"Oh, my God," said Anjali, slapping a hand to her forehead. "Are you deaf? I don't want to talk to you. I don't want you talking to me. I don't want you talking to Mohini."

"Don't you see, Anju?" Joe asked. "We were set up."

Anjali inhaled. "Can you *please* stop—what do you mean 'set up'?"

Narrowing his eyes, Joe again fixed his gaze on Mohini. "How is it possible out of the two million people in the state of Goa, Anju and I connected on Tinder when Vagator is twenty kilometres from Fontainhas?"

Mohini sniffed. "Dude, what have you been smoking? So effin' *paranoid.*"

"Oh, yeah?" asked Joe. "What I want to know is how—" With an impatient huff, he turned to Anjali. "Please, Anju? Can we talk in private? I need to ask you about... about you and Rishi. Are you still..."

So Joe knew she'd married his flatmate. Did he keep tabs on what was happening in her life after he walked out of it for good? What for? "How does it matter to you?"

"It does," he said, urgently. "If you're not still..." Pausing, he mused, "No, you're not. I know you. You wouldn't have been in the café for a date if you weren't completely free of him."

Completely free? How could she be completely free of Rishi when they shared a... Joe should know... Anjali eyed him. No, Joe rarely forgot details. He *didn't* know. She glanced back at the door leading to the interior of the house. The only good thing to come out of the last nine months—make that out of her entire marriage to Rishi—was sleeping in his crib, safe under the watchful eye of his nanny. Anjali and Rishi would forever be connected through their—

"And I assume your cousin wouldn't have been signing you up for Tinder," said Joe.

"You said he's an ex you didn't want to see," Mohini said to Anjali, frowning at Joe all the while. "So why did you pull him in here?"

"Because I..." Dragging her mind back from what Joe did and didn't know about her life, Anjali bit her lip. "I was angry at that Braganza woman..."

"You could've just told her the truth," Mohini said.

"Why should I tell her anything?" asked Anjali. "How is any of it her business?" New Anjali wasn't going to fuss over what society thought.

"What's going on?" asked Joe, looking thoroughly lost now.

With an impatient huff, Mohini turned to him. "The Braganza woman has been complaining about me since the day we got here. She doesn't like my clothes, she doesn't like how loud I play my music, and she spotted me sunbathing topless in the backyard. Arrey, my backyard, my boobs. Plus, there's an eight-foot wall all around! If she didn't want to see, she should've kept her damned window shut."

"*Mohini,*" Anjali moaned. The nineteen-year-old had arrived in India a few months ago with the purported intention of studying dance at Mumbai University's dance research school. Most of the Joshis recognised the ploy for what it was—a way to be closer to her childhood crush. Sadly for poor Mohini, said crushee fell madly in love with someone else. Her indulgent parents then allowed her to abandon her plans for college and "find herself" in Goa, where she proceeded to scandalise everyone around. "You simply can't talk about your... umm... body... with everyone you meet." Not with Joe, certainly.

"Didn't you claim you were going to stop worrying about what other people think?" asked Mohini.

Turning both palms up, Anjali tried, "Yes, but there are limits... something called *common sense.*"

"Uh-huh, okay," Joe said. "So Mrs Braganza came over to talk about your morals."

Mohini snorted. "Not *my* morals."

Anjali covered her mouth with both hands and looked heavenwards. "What did I do to deserve this?" More than God, her father owed her an answer.

When the name of the Joshi Clinic popped up in a police investigation, Anjali's father—chairman of the family trust—knew immediately it had to be about their purchase of generic forms of expensive medicines which was a violation of intellectual property law. Then, INTERPOL called, asking to discuss the clinic's recent buys.

The ninety-year-old doctor who currently graced the CEO position grumpily told the Joshis to find someone else to deal with the problem. Easier said than done since the chief executive of the charity clinic drew only a nominal salary. The one Joshi twiddling her thumbs at home happened to be Anjali, and she was offered/forced into the job. She'd meet with INTERPOL and simply smile pleasantly at whatever they had to say. Later, the clinic would call the media and make a production of the fight between the big, bad pharmaceutical industry and the idealistic, young doctor caring for low-income patients. Somehow, they needed to publicly shame the companies into providing lifesaving drugs at affordable cost.

One day on the job, and Anjali was wondering how on earth the clinic escaped getting into trouble before. The idea of keeping accurate records was apparently new to the administrative staff. Trying to avoid panic among the employees, the Joshi trust had decided against informing them of the investigation, but Anjali found herself with no choice but to involve her secretary. There was no one else who could possibly track down all the paperwork related to the purchase of medications over the last few months.

The stiff behaviour of the staff was another problem Anjali never expected. She didn't get it. She'd never been a life-of-the-party type, but people needed to wait until they spoke more than two words before rejecting her, darn it. Plus, everyone knew there were no other candidates for the CEO spot—a position with all the responsibilities and no perks, not even a decent paycheck.

The Saturday brunch at the Joshi mansion with some of the doctors and nurses was supposed to be an icebreaker of sorts, but Anjali got absolutely no answers from any of them. She'd been racking her brain for a Plan B when Mrs Braganza came knocking, followed by Joe.

Tone gleeful, Mohini continued, "Anju Didi already told the Braganza bi... *wi*tch to keep her nose out of my life. Plus, everyone in the neighbourhood calls me the wild chick from California. They don't really care what *I* do. This morning, some of the staff from the clinic came over, and the stupid woman immediately decided it was for... I really don't know what she thought Anju Didi was doing with them."

"What *Anju* was doing?" Joe goggled. No surprise at his surprise. The Anju he knew would've done none of what she did in the last ten minutes. Make it the last two days.

Mohini snickered. "I know, right? The witch probably has a more active love life than Anju Didi ever did."

"Do you mind?" asked Anjali, aggrieved. Okay, so it was probably very close to the truth, but Joe didn't need to know it.

"Maybe," he said, "it's because her family is setting her up on *blind dates with random men?*"

"Hey," snapped Anjali. "Don't yell at her." Mohini might need regular quashing, but she had her cousins to do it.

"It was with *you,*" returned Mohini, triumphant smile on her face. "Not a random man." Her smile faded as quickly as it appeared. "I mean... we didn't... *I* didn't know before but..."

Joe smirked. "Right."

"Mohini?" called Anjali. The mild panic on Mohini's face... unease crept up Anjali's spine. Was Joe right? Were they set up? After all, when she returned from the "blind date," her allegedly lost phone was on the kitchen table, and her supposedly broken laptop was back to working condition. "What did you do?"

"Nothing," came the pat answer. Green eyes widened. "Like I said, I saw his DP and thought you'd get a kick out of it. I mean, how many men in Goa would keep some actor from old Hollywood movies as DP?"

"Game's over, kid," Joe said before turning to Anjali. With a finger, he scratched the slight cleft in his jaw. His five-o'clock shadow was even more pronounced in the shallow groove, but Anjali could clearly see the thin, red line of a healing cut. Incredibly, she wanted to laugh. Gifted surgeon, almost an artist with his scalpel, and he still hadn't learned how to shave himself without nicking his skin?

But then, he *wasn't* a surgeon. When he left Delhi that last time, it wasn't just Anjali that he discarded. *Why?* she whispered in her mind. *No, don't tell me. I don't want to hear it.* What exactly was so bad about her he'd left the career he dreamed of for years? Couldn't he even bear to be in the same city as her?

"C'mon, ask your cousin what she did," he demanded.

He could've been back in the physiology lab at AIIMS, putting a smart-aleck medical student in his place. Sadly for him, Mohini was not easily put in her place. With a mock-sympathetic smile, she, too, turned to Anjali. "Anju Didi, the crazy is strong with this one. I think we should call your psychiatrist friend for help."

No. They weren't calling anyone. Anjali was beginning to have the same suspicions, but it didn't matter even if Mohini somehow deduced the whole story and in a fit of mischief, decided to send her cousin on a date with the very man she was trying to weed out of her mind. Five minutes in his presence, and Anjali was noticing things she had no business noticing. She was remembering, *feeling.*

She needed to be thinking about her life and her responsibilities, like the tiny bundle currently napping in his crib. The five-month-old would soon wake up and demand his mother serve his evening meal on time. Then, there was the job Anjali had taken on at the Joshi Clinic... the whole business with INTERPOL. Folding her arms across her chest, she rubbed her shoulders and looked straight at Joe. "You need to go."

His eyelids fluttered as though he were caught by surprise. "Anju, I— please, can we—"

"No," she said, stonily. Sudden moisture stung her eyes. "You're eleven years too late," she whispered.

"I know," he said, his tone as low and harsh as hers. "I wish... oh, God, I wish I could..."

"No, you don't," she said, her throat hurting. "You don't wish *any*thing. You never once tried to call. You never bothered to check how I was." He hadn't even cared enough to let her know he was still alive. Hot tears rolled down her cheeks. "You wouldn't have cared if *I* died."

"Uhh, Anju Didi..." Mohini was instantly at Anjali's side, wrapping an arm around her shoulders.

"No, Anju." Joe took a step towards her. "How can you—"

"You should leave now," Mohini said, tone firm.

Slashing the air with his hand, Joe said, "I have to talk to—"

"You need to leave," snapped Mohini. "*Now.*"

Anjali smiled through her tears. "I'm all right, kiddo." After the wretched year she'd suffered, the entire family worried about her, including Mohini. "Show Dr D'Acosta out, will you? I'm not sure what he thinks he has to say to me after all this time."

"I want to say I'm sorry," he said, stumbling over his words. "For all the things I did... things I should've done... I'm so very sorry. I wish I could go back and—"

"Stop saying that," Anjali demanded, her hands back to tight fists at her side. "You don't mean any of it, or you wouldn't have... you would've never let Rishi and me... you *knew* about him."

"I did," admitted Joe, pain etched in every line on his face. "But so did you. How was I supposed to stop you from marrying him when you were already aware he's..." Joe threw a wary glance in Mohini's direction.

He didn't need to complete the sentence and blurt out the secret in front of Anjali's cousin. Anjali knew what he would've said. Exactly like she knew Rishi was gay when she married him.

Chapter 11

2007

The exams were done. The preclinical portions of the course were complete. Nothing had so far tickled Anjali's fancy enough to consider it an option for a long-term career, but she wasn't worried. She fully expected to go into one of the clinical specialities. She needed to figure out which one, and she could take all summer to mull it. There were only *two days* left for her to make a decision on the other important part of her life.

Two more days, and they'd all disperse for the weeks-long break. In her hostel room, Anjali pulled her chair as close as possible to the noisy air conditioner at the window. She needed to devise a strategy for this fact-finding mission, but strategising could be done equally as well in the comfort of cool air as in the sweltering heat of the midday sun.

"*Now* you're okay with the AC?" teased Meenakshi, flipping over in her bed to lie on her stomach. After the first couple of months, they'd been offered single rooms, but both were too settled into their routine to move. Too lazy was closer to the truth, but hey. This room was precisely large enough to accommodate twin beds on either side, separated by two desks. Anjali and Meenakshi worked out a deal for the cupboard: keeping it tidy was Anjali's job as long as Meenakshi took care of the rest of the cleaning.

Anjali made a face. "I hope we don't get caught. What if we get kicked out?" Hostel rules clearly stated no air conditioners since they drained too much power, but Meenakshi thumbed her nose at Anjali's objections to the contraband device.

Lounging at the foot of her sister's bed, Gauri chuckled. She was almost done with the entire course. When she returned after the break, it would be for the final leg—the last six months before the mandatory one-year internship. "*Everyone* puts up ACs."

"Yeah, but—" Anjali worried.

"Look at it this way," said Kokila, her eyes closed as she curled her body into itself on Anjali's bed. "Which is preferable—broiling to death in this heat or taking a chance they'd kick you out of the hostel?"

Anjali giggled. "Well..."

"Oh, c'mon, Anju," said Kokila, laughing. "Little Miss Perfect." The other two groaned and threw pillows.

"Kidding," said Anjali, blinking as a sudden pain shot across her eyes. Weird. She used to get them in Mumbai all the time, but this was the first reappearance of the sudden zigzaggy eye pain after moving into the hostel. She pinched the base of her nose for a few seconds until the discomfort faded. Perhaps another visit to the eye clinic was in order. They'd said there was nothing wrong with her as did the neurologist, but there *had* to be some explanation for the repeated attacks. With a sigh, she dropped her hand. "It's nice hanging out like this—just us girls. I mean... it's great to hang out at the flat, too. But..."

Gauri nodded. "I know. Sometimes, you just want the company of your gal pals."

Plus, Anjali had questions to ask she didn't want Joe—or any of the men in their little gang—to overhear. Kokila and Gauri were best positioned to answer the questions. Gauri was not just Joe's best buddy's fiancée, they'd all been friends for years before Anjali appeared on the scene. Kokila knew him even longer. They met in Goa when she was working at the Joshi Charity Clinic as a brand-new nurse, and he was a high school student who ran errands for the old Dr Joshi.

Both women were frequent visitors to Anjali and Meenakshi's hostel room, so it was easy for Anjali to schedule this particular step in her plan for Joe. Not that she could let the ladies suspect anything. Narrowing her eyes, she studied each of her friends through her lashes. How should she do this? There wasn't much time left before they all went home for the summer. "I'm going to miss you guys."

Meenakshi snorted. "You'll be in Mumbai with your parents. At least they're not crazy like ours. Can you believe my ma has cooking classes arranged for us?"

"It's not a bad thing to learn," Kokila offered. "You're going to get tired of eating out at some point. Plus, the cash you'll spend on outside food..." She'd lived with her widowed mother while she was in Goa but on moving to Delhi, had to learn from scratch how to take care of herself. Right now, the major concern in her life was saving enough money to buy out her uncle's share in the family home so her mother wouldn't face daily harassment to get her to sell to a developer.

Sitting up, Meenakshi huffed. "You don't get it. Ma doesn't want us to learn because *we* have to eat. She wants us to learn so our *husbands* can eat."

Kokila finally opened her eyes. "You're crazy. I'm sure your parents are not that bad."

"Oh, no." Gauri shook her head. "They're worse. I'm just counting down days until I get married and move to New York."

The opening Anjali was waiting for. "Don't you miss having your boyfriend around—"

"Hey," called Meenakshi. "What about your job interview, Kiki? Did they call back?"

Kokila sighed. "No, yaar. I'm giving it six more months. If I don't find something in the U.S. by then, it's off to one of the Gulf countries. They do pay well."

"I heard Ireland is looking for nurses." Gauri went on to say something about a job placement agency.

Anjali suppressed a groan. Normally, they almost needed to sit on Gauri to stop her from talking about her boyfriend. Today, when Anjali wanted to talk about men—one man in particular—Gauri was all about career plans. Cannily, Anjali said, "Kiki, you're going to be so bored if you take a job in the Middle East. You won't have a social life."

"What social life do I have here?" Kokila asked, one hand mussing her pixie-cut dark hair. "The doctors at that stupid place?" She worked in a pricey private hospital in one of the posh areas of the city. Sitting up in bed, she crossed her legs guru-style, pillow on her lap. "Last week when I was doing night shift, one of the old doctors thought it would be great fun to pinch my butt."

For a second, Anjali thought she heard wrong. Meenakshi's eyes were also rounded in surprise, but Gauri snarled. "The same creep from last year?"

Kokila nodded, her large, black eyes snapping with helpless fury. Her tall, athletic form practically vibrated with rage. "I need to get away from that place."

"Can't you complain?" asked Anjali, both horrified and angry. "Especially if he's done it before..."

"Yeah," agreed Meenakshi, voice high. "First, you should backhand him. The bloody cheek!"

Gauri and Kokila turned towards the younger girls. "Kids," they said, almost at the same time.

"No one cares," Kokila explained, frustration evident in her tone. "Nothing's gonna change, and I could lose my job for starting trouble."

"That's so unfair," said Anjali. "But I didn't mean for you to do it directly. You don't want the whole hospital to hear your business. Kiki, there are women doctors there, right? If you went to one of them—"

Gauri clucked. "It won't make a difference. Some are in pretty much the same position, and some don't give a shit."

"My mother would," Anjali said. "In fact, I'm going to call her about this. She could talk to someone at your hosp—"

"*No*," said Kokila. "I can't afford to get into trouble until I find another job."

"You won't," assured Anjali. "Mom will make sure your name is kept out of it."

Kokila's eyes flashed. "I don't *want* my name kept out of it. All I'm waiting for is a job he can't get me fired from. Then, I'm going to backhand him like Meenu said—in front of all the staff."

Anjali stood. "Kiki, this way, no one will even know what happened. Trust me, my mother—"

"Anju," said Kokila. "I love you for offering, and I'm sure your mother will do exactly what you ask. But I won't have any peace of mind unless I tell the jerk exactly what I think of him. I don't care if the whole world hears. Would *you?*"

"I would *want* to tell him off." Anjali bit her lip.

"But you'd stew about it in silence, instead?" asked Gauri.

"I'd rather make the whole thing disappear and forget about it," Anjali admitted.

Gauri rolled her eyes. "No way. Kiki would go crazy. The creep is going to get exactly what he deserves."

"Once I find another job," agreed Kokila. Suddenly, she grinned. "You see why I don't care if there are no men around where I work?"

Anjali smiled back. She'd forgotten her mission for a couple of minutes. Now, she was no longer in the mood to investigate Joe D'Acosta's failure to make a move more than a month after she gave him the green signal.

Kokila glanced towards the foot of the bed where a full human skeleton hung from a standing pole. "Maybe you can lend him to me."

Anjali laughed with the rest of her friends. "Nuh-huh." She sashayed to the grinning skeleton and took the bony hand in hers before gazing soulfully into the empty sockets. "Gregory is all mine."

Another round of laughter started. "I can't believe you gave him that name," said Gauri, her eyelashes sparkling with tears of mirth.

"People say I look like Hepburn," said Anjali, twirling a lock of her shoulder-length hair around a finger. "So why not?"

"You need a boyfriend with flesh and blood on top of the bones," said Meenakshi, giggling. "I do, too." She sighed. "Hanging out with the gang is great and all, but it's bringing me bad luck in the romance department. People think I'm dating one of our three guys."

"Aren't you supposed to be off men?" asked Anjali, laughing. "Nuclear medicine, remember?"

"Oh, no," said Meenakshi. "I said I don't plan to fall in love. There's a difference." She groaned. "What am I supposed to do? Take out an ad in the paper I'm *not* dating Joe or Sid?" Grinning at Anjali, Meenakshi added, "Rishi, of course, is supposed to be all yours."

"God," moaned Anjali, letting go of the skeletal hand. "I wish everyone would give it up, already. We're *not* an item."

"It ain't stopping anytime soon," said Meenakshi. "Rishi's been the target of many women since he started at AIIMS, so people are curious about you."

Kokila sighed. "I'd kill for those eyes." Bedroom eyes as someone called them.

"The whole package," said Gauri. "The face, the hair, the bod... *and* a surgeon." Or he'd soon be one. He spoke well, too, his sexy voice melting many first-year hearts in the physiology lab. "Anjali, he's never paid attention to any girls other than Kiki and me. Everyone knows *we're* just friends. You're the first he's been romantically linked with."

Yeah, and Anjali was beginning to have a good idea why. The heat in Rishi's eyes when they landed on the poet in their group was unmistakable. It was to *Anjali*. Her Skinwalla Uncle—the dermatologist brother of her father's—who lived in L.A. was her absolute favourite relative, and she'd seen the same look on him when he was around his partner. *Pity, really*. What Meenakshi said the first day in the physiology lab turned out to be one hundred per cent accurate for Anjali, too. She'd gotten to be friends with Rishi, but that didn't stop the art enthusiast in her from marvelling at his physical form. He *was* a piece of exquisite art—flawless, including the fragrance he favoured which hinted of sandalwood and ginger. Womankind didn't know what it lost.

How was it possible the rest of the group couldn't see it? How could they possibly buy the silly story about mourning for his lost love from high school? Okay, so Meenakshi and Siddharth were new to AIIMS as was Anjali, but Gauri and Kokila knew Rishi for years. How could *Joe* not know? They were flatmates! Or were they more than... Anjali shook off the thought. Joe's now hot and now cold behaviour was making her crazy.

"Poor Joe." Kokila chortled. "It's been the exact opposite for him. Five years... five girls. Now, none at all."

"He's a *tutor*," said Gauri. "He's not going to ask any of the students out. If he didn't have to return to Goa instead of starting surgery right after MBBS, there would've been girl number six."

Anjali knew the story. Along with Gauri's fiancé, Rishi also left for the U.S., but his family demanded he return. Joe's family emergency required his presence in his hometown for a few months. Both men thus ended up spending the rest of the academic year as tutors instead of starting post-graduation right after internship as did the rest of their batchmates. Was *that* why Joe made no moves on Anjali? The evening at the temple, she'd thought for sure he was interested, but maybe it was just the light playing tricks. It *had* been getting dark... all those shadows... if he were really interested, wouldn't he have said something after, tutor or not? At least a "wait a few months until I'm back to being a student?" But then, there were all those heated looks he gave her when he thought no one was watching.

"As soon as he's done being a tutor, there's going to be girlfriend number six," agreed Kokila.

"Then seven, then eight," marvelled Gauri. "They all know how it will end but still jump into bed with him. Moths to the flame."

"*Andha Arabi Kadalorum*," Kokila sang the introductory bars to the bedroom song from *Bombay,* the movie, setting off hoots and whistles from the group. "They like burning in that fire, *babyyy!*"

Anjali bit back a moan. Did she even *want* Joe to make a move? She wasn't about to jump in anywhere unless they were at least exploring the possibility of a future. The idea of being slut-shamed all over campus... "What happened to the other ones?" she asked.

Kokila frowned in puzzlement. "Huh?"

"His previous girlfriends," Anjali clarified. "Weren't you two friends with them, at all?"

"Not really," said Kokila. "Yeah, they did hang out with us, but... hard to explain... we used to plan things, and if they happened to be around, we included them. Afterwards..." She shrugged.

"Ouch," said Anjali.

"They didn't seem to mind," said Gauri, a hint of doubt creeping into her tone. "It's not like we completely stopped talking to them after the breakup or anything. I still go to the gym with the last one."

Anjali pounced. "Who?" When Gauri named the lady in question, Anjali winced on the inside. Mile-long legs, double Ds. Enough *bindaas* attitude—cool factor—for a dozen Anjalis.

"Hey, you remember..." Kokila took up, going back in time to name the prior four women, all of whom could be clones of Dr Cool Girl.

Shoulders slumping, Anjali returned to the chair by the air conditioner. Mission successful. She had her answer even if not the one she liked. Anjali Joshi simply wasn't Joe's type.

They talked a bit more about Kokila's job hunting, about summer plans, about a movie they all wanted to see. Anjali barely heard any of it. *Maybe a push-up bra?* She gritted her teeth. What in God's name was she thinking? If Joe D'Acosta didn't want her as she was, she didn't want him, either. Even if he did, she wasn't anxious to be merely number six in a list of women.

Biting back a huff, she wished like crazy there was someone she could talk to. The girls were out of the question; she'd get teased until the end of time.

Someone who could help her navigate the thinking process of men... if she had a closer relationship with her brother... nah, she wasn't likely to ask *him* how to convince Joe a five feet and almost one inch woman with fair to middling boobs was what he needed, not the glamour goddesses he'd thus far dated.

But in the rickshaw... why had Joe... more to the point, why *hadn't* he done anything since? Some other reason? The flat-sharing with Rishi... Joe... no way. He wasn't gay. God, the man was driving her bonkers. If there was no hope for any kind of future with him, she needed to know it with no trace of lingering doubts.

❊❊❊

Rishi stayed by the kitchen door, keeping a good ten feet between himself and Anjali. She was sitting on the sofa as composedly as she usually did, dressed in cotton shorts and matching off-white, peasant blouse, ankles crossed below, hands on her lap. She hadn't said a single unkind word... actually, she didn't say much in the ten minutes since she and Siddharth got to the flat an hour ahead of the rest for their final dinner before summer break. The air around her though... Rishi lived with his three sisters for enough years to know there was feminine silence, and then, there was *silence*. Which of the two men in the flat were at the receiving end of the muted ire was anyone's guess.

"Thanks for offering to pick up the food," Rishi blurted. Joe was still with the ethics committee, presenting his hypothesis on xenotransplantation to get permission for further research, and no one would want to eat Rishi's cooking, so takeout Chinese it would be tonight. With each clanky rotation of the ceiling fan, the smell of soya-soaked noodles permeated the room. "I could've, but..."

"You needed to pack," she completed, tone snippy.

Rishi directed a questioning glance at Siddharth who was perched on the edge of one of the chairs. With an infinitesimal shrug, he blinked his ignorance.

"Sid," she called, a determined smile now pasted on her face. "I need a favour."

"What?" he asked, clearing his throat.

"I left my phone in my room," she said. "You think you can run down to the hostel and get it for me? The girls are not there, or I'd have called Meenu and asked her to bring it." Expression turning imploring, she added, "Please?"

Rishi straightened. *What the hell—*

Siddharth glanced between her and Rishi. "Sure," he said, easily. Muttering something that sounded like "good luck," Siddharth brushed past Rishi on his way to the front door.

When it clicked shut, Rishi glanced wildly around for an escape route. *Shit, shit, shit, shiiit.* He should've made it clear to her... he hadn't dreamed for a moment she actually bought the silly gossip about him and her... he'd only been trying to have some fun by needling Joe, dammit... jump out the window, maybe? Did every damned opening to the outside world have to be barred except for the front door? He wasn't even wearing shoes!

Looking straight at him, Anjali said, "He's not gay."

Rishi heard the words, but they didn't... they somehow ricocheted around his brain, getting louder each time. "He... *what?*"

"Siddharth is not gay," Anjali said.

The noisy ceiling fan clanked to a halt. *Power outage?* Silence filled the room. There was no audible breathing, no shuffling of shoes, no rustling movement. There wasn't even a ticking clock to mark the passage of time. The Pomeranian next door howled long and loud once, the noise then dying down to yelps and whimpers. Through it all, Anjali sat on the sofa, not moving an inch, not taking her eyes off Rishi. His stomach knotted hard, sending acidic terror regurgitating to his mouth. Sweat drenched his tee and shorts, plastering them to his skin. "I... ahh..." Through stiff lips, he asked, "How did you know?"

"I know someone who's... it wasn't difficult to guess. I haven't said anything to anyone else." Her eyes... they were still the same soft brown... the same doe shape... the same warmth of friendship... *phoney* friendship.

She'd so casually thrown the charge at him—an accusation which could get him life imprisonment under India's laws. He'd lose his medical licence, his family, *everything* he held dear. Without warning, a red haze exploded around the periphery of his visual field. "Look at you," he snarled, taking a step towards her. "Sitting there, judging me. Who *are* you?"

"Rishi—"

"Who *are* you?" he shouted, not giving a damn any longer. "Pretending to be a friend, mocking me behind my back. Plotting against me."

She stood, her hands held to her mouth. "I swear I'm not mocking. Or plotting. I told you I haven't said anything to anyone else. Rishi, please—"

"Get out," he ordered. He wasn't sure how much longer he'd have self-control enough not to grab her by the scruff of her neck and toss her through a window. His head hurt. His throat hurt. His chest burned from the sting of betrayal.

"I only asked because I wanted to know about Joe," she cried, her eyes now wide and moist.

"*What?*" Thoughts screeched to a halt, only to be thrown into a bewildering muddle. "What about Joe?"

"What's the equation between you and him?" she asked, finally dropping her hands to tilt her chin up.

Now, Rishi was slightly dizzy. "Siddharth... Joe... you think I hump every man I meet?"

"No," she said, stomping a foot clad in red platform sneakers. "I've seen you checking out Siddharth, okay? I only mentioned him... I don't know... I wanted to tell you I knew. What I really want to know is about Joe and you."

"Joe and me?" Rishi frowned, trying to bring some order to the chaos in his mind.

"Yeah." Vaguely, she waved a hand. Almost as though she'd summoned some sort of electrical genie, the ceiling fan clanked back up, sending blessed breeze circulating through the room. "Are you two together?"

"No," said Rishi, automatically. "He's not gay or bi, and even if he were, he ain't my type. I prefer the laid-back artist kind."

"Like Sid."

"Like him," Rishi agreed. "I already know he's not gay, by the way."

She bit her lip. "How? Did you ask him?"

"No. Most times, I can tell. What are you—" Slashing a hand through the air, Rishi snarled. The red-hot anger was dissipating, but now, there was intense annoyance. His fingers itched with the urge to twist her ear hard. "You force me into confessing my sexuality... for *what?* Because you're curious about Joe? Of all the thoughtless, self-centred..."

Eyes wide, she heaved in an uneven breath. "I'm sorry. I didn't mean... I'm so sorry. One of my uncles is gay, and he always talks about how he met his partner. It didn't occur to me you wouldn't want to discuss it. So, so sorry."

"How does *that* make it any bett..." Rishi blinked. "You have a gay uncle?"

"My father's brother," she said, distractedly. "He's a dermatologist in California. I sometimes go there on vacations."

"You do?"

"Yeah. He has five kids, so it's great fun."

"He does?" Rishi was beginning to sound like a parrot, but Anjali was so blasé about it.

"Him and his partner. They trust me. You see? I simply wanted to know about you and Joe."

Rishi really wanted to learn more about this gay uncle, but Anjali's jump from topic to topic was making his head spin. "You thought Joe and I might be partners?" Rishi rubbed his temple hard. "Where does Sid come in? Side action?"

"No," she said, stomping her foot, again. "I mean, yes... maybe. *God*, I don't know what I mean. Didn't you hear me? I've seen you checking him out, but I didn't think you were the kind to cheat, and I didn't think you and Joe were... you know."

Unexpected mirth bubbled up through Rishi's confusion. "*I've* seen Sid checking out you *and* Meenu."

"Checking... *eww*... the jerk. We're supposed to be friends."

"Oh, yeah?" Rishi sauntered over to one of the chairs and collapsed into it. "So why were you asking me about Joe if you didn't think he and I were 'you know'?"

A pink flush working its way up her neck, she mumbled, "I was trying to figure out why he hasn't... does he know about you?"

"Yeah." Rishi thought back to the night after the results of the paraclinical courses were out.

It was two years ago, right after his twentieth birthday. He'd topped the class in most subjects, decimating Joe who until then had managed to stay more or less at the same level. On campus, Rishi was congratulated at every corner. He'd foolishly hoped it was the right time to bring up his sexual orientation with his family. And he did. At his usual Saturday lunch with his parents. In under ten seconds, a blow landed on his left cheek. Pain zinged up his temple, but Rishi managed to stay put in the dining room chair. He'd expected this. After all, his sisters got slapped for much less. As the youngest of four and the only boy, Rishi had never been at the receiving end of his father's disciplining hand, but his news was bound to elicit strong reaction. Still, it was a shock to see his beloved father towering over him, face contorted into an ugly snarl. "This is not the kind of joke you use on your elders, boy," said the grey-haired investment banker.

Rishi swallowed hard. "I'm not joking. I *am* gay." He saw the open palm swinging through the air, felt the second blow on the same cheek. Darkness hovered for a moment before disintegrating. Hands curled around the edges of the chair, he begged, "Papa, please." He'd explain how he felt... they'd understand... they had to.

"You're not my son," screamed his father. "No child of mine would have the gall to say such things to me."

"Hey, *bhagwan*," fretted Ma, asking God for help. "What will people say? Do you realise we're looking for alliances for your sisters? Their future is at stake. We can't let you ruin the whole family."

"Ma, I——" started Rishi, eagerly. This was precisely what he wanted to discuss. He'd go abroad after his MBBS course and away from the laws which would brand him a criminal and strip away his identity as a doctor. Far from the strictures of their social circle, he'd finally get breathing room to be himself. No one would know his secret except his beloved parents who'd protect it at all costs. As far as their friends were concerned, he'd be the son who dedicated his life to science, forgetting even to get married and start a family. Yeah, Ma and Papa would want grandchildren with the Rastogi last name, but there were ways... surrogacy, adoption...

"He will not say a word to anyone," stated his father, finality ringing in the edict. "He will either forget all this nonsense and understand his obligation towards us, or he won't be part of us. He will face the consequences of his actions on his own."

"What—" Rishi sat up. What were they... were they threatening to... no, he was their son... they wouldn't...

His mother nodded. "Thank God the girls weren't here to hear this. Rishi betay, I don't want you saying another word about this gay stuff."

"Not one word," warned his father. Turning to his wife, the investment banker said, "Jaya, call your friend in Singapore. The psychiatrist."

Ma nodded. "Good idea. She won't say anything to anyone, and the clinic is in Singapore. No one will find out."

They got up and left in search of the shrink's number, leaving Rishi alone and dazed. What was he supposed to do now? A chill ran through him. His teeth chattered. The air conditioner... it was set too low. Outside the windows of the bungalow in the upscale neighbourhood of Asiad Village, couples sauntered arm-in-arm, children played cricket. The faint noises of a distant car horn filtered in. What *was* he supposed to do? Go to the shrink? Wait and hope his parents would come around? What if they didn't?

He dragged out the cell phone from his pocket and dialled Nikhil's number. Nikhil was the only other person who knew. They'd been best friends since kindergarten and were batchmates in AIIMS. Brothers, really, going through pretty much every milestone together. They'd snuck out of school Rishi's one and only time to hang out at the mall, darting into shops each time they imagined their parents' reflections on a glass surface. When they were sixteen, Nikhil promised his older brother a month of slave labour if he'd buy them *bhang lassi*—weed-infused buttermilk—on Holi, the festival of colours.

At seventeen, frantic to disprove what his brain was telling him, Rishi accompanied Nikhil to G.B. Road, Delhi's redlight district. When Rishi heaved aside the half-naked woman on his lap and ran out the door, Nikhil wasn't too far behind. He waited silently while Rishi retched into the open gutter on the side of the road and in response to his mumbled admission, said only it explained a few things.

"Pick up," Rishi mumbled into the phone. "Pick up, dammit."

"Bro, where are you?" Nikhil screamed even before Rishi could utter a greeting. "Did you forget about the match?"

Match—right, the football match. AIIMS allotted hostel rooms to all their undergraduate students whether or not they planned to stay in it. Rishi went home most weekends, but this Saturday, he'd promised to return for a football match—soccer, as the Indian-born Yank whom Rishi's parents were considering as potential groom for his oldest sister called it. "Give me ten minutes," said Rishi, desperately needing relief from the sudden, silent chill permeating his childhood home.

Just before the match was about to begin, someone laughingly asked Rishi if he heard what happened. Joe had put in a request to take the supplementary exam in one of the papers where he came second to Rishi. Jogging to the edge of the field where Joe was watching their teammates kick the ball around, Rishi wiped the sweat from his upper lip with the back of his hand. "What makes you think you'll be able to beat me this time?"

Ignoring the taunt, Joe sprinted to the centre of the field. Grunting, kicking, chasing... they were on the same team, but somehow, they ended up colliding when they tried to be the one scoring the goal. The ball escaped their possession and was captured by the captain of the rival team.

"What the hell?" shouted Joe, shoving Rishi by the shoulders. "*I* had the ball."

Rishi remembered swinging his fist; he remembered Joe's angry roar before a punch landed on the same cheek battered by his father's slaps. More blows rained in both directions until they stumbled to the ground. Feet thundered towards them. Shouts and whistles rent the air. When Joe sat up, there was a trickle of blood coming out of one nostril—something Rishi could barely see through his rapidly swelling left eye.

"Enough," said Nikhil—not yet Gauri's boyfriend—walking back to the men's hostel with them. "Joe, you're an idiot to retake the exam. Rishi, what's your effing problem, bro? He's not taking anything away from you. Also, aren't you two planning to go into surgery? You can't afford to hurt your hands."

"I wasn't thinking," admitted Joe, spitting blood-stained saliva to the side. "I should've remembered jackasses like him are not worth it."

"Trust me," huffed Rishi. "There's no bigger jackass than you." Turning to Nikhil, Rishi added, "How the hell do you put up with him?" While Nikhil and Rishi's friendship started before either could read, they met Joe at the anatomy dissection table. Rishi didn't appreciate Nikhil including Joe in the best friends' circle, but Nikhil simply told the other two to get along—or else.

Nikhil stopped short. "I have an idea."

All were underage, but Joe knew someone in Goa who knew someone who worked as a guard at the club. Only after they got to the door did Joe tell them the burly guard with track marks on both arms was the ex-boyfriend of Joe's musician pal from Goa—a *male* musician.

Joe's expression was watchful, almost daring his classmates to say one wrong word. Rishi stayed silent, his pulse pounding as he tried to figure out how to respond. Joe couldn't know. It was impossible. Nikhil wouldn't have said anything. He could talk your ear off, but he'd never divulge things he'd been asked not to. If Joe harboured secrets, Nikhil would keep those, too.

"Oh, yeah?" Nikhil asked the guard, his friendly grin in place. "How come you don't mind doing favours for your ex? Mine tried to chop off my—"

Rishi managed a casual snort. "Next time, don't sleep with her cousin."

"Man," said the guard, tone awed. "She let you live?"

Joe's shoulders relaxed, and he nodded. "Let's get beer. I have just about enough money for two."

In the bar, Rishi kept glancing towards the entrance where the guard was. Granted the burly man was from liberal Goa, but he hadn't simply been gay. He had a boyfriend—an actual relationship, which was matter-of-factly accepted by the people in their social circle, like Joe. Rishi's introduction to intimacy was the clandestine coupling with one of his high school teachers soon after the incident with the prostitute on G.B. Road. Since then, nothing.

Two bottles of cheap beer each later, the three of them were sauntering back to the campus. Trying not to lose his nerve, Rishi blurted, "I told my parents at lunch today. You know... that I'm gay."

"Ah," said Nikhil, clapping a hand between Rishi's shoulder blades.

There was a split-second hesitation in Joe's next step, but he continued walking. "You're still a jackass."

From that night until this evening in the flat while having this bizarre conversation with Anjali, the topic never came up between Rishi and Joe. Why would it when they'd never talked about any of *Joe's* conquests? Anjali Joshi was the only one who'd been nosy enough to ask.

Dragging his mind back from the past, Rishi said to Anjali, "Joe has his moments, but he's not a bad sort. He's known about me for a couple of years. It was not one of the issues we discussed when we agreed to split rent on the flat. I don't think it ever occurred to him other people might misunderstand." Even Rishi's parents, well aware of Joe's reputation with the ladies from information Nikhil let slip, never suspected there was anything romantic between the flatmates.

Anjali shrugged and returned to her seat on the sofa, her back to the front door.

"What?" Rishi asked. "You're not impressed?"

"With what? He doesn't get bonus points for basic human decency." Relief. Rishi relaxed into the chair—as much as anyone could relax in the rickety contraption. "Once again, I didn't misunderstand your situation," Anjali added. "I didn't *think* he was gay or bi, but everything's so confusing. *He's* confusing." Glumly, she looked down at her shoes. "I guess he could simply be not into me."

"What do you mean?"

Something about an autorickshaw ride... disjointed mumblings about a mix-up in their conversation... "You see?" she ended.

"Lemme recap." Rishi leaned forwards. "You like Joe. You thought he doesn't like you back because he's gay." Laughing, Rishi taunted, "Talk about ego!"

Anjali glared. "It's not about ego, okay? What was I supposed to think when he says things like... and then... I thought maybe he's seeing someone else, but there are no girlfriends around, so..."

"So you thought it might be me." Guffawing hard, Rishi said, "You're wrong. Trust me, Joe is *not* into men."

Rishi didn't know what made him look towards the door, but when he did, he saw his astounded flatmate, folder in his hands, sweat patches decorating his khakis and cream-coloured tee. The brown loafers were brand-new, Joe having decided he couldn't risk the old ones falling apart in the middle of his presentation. He didn't seem to be thinking of his project, though. Horrified look on his face, Joe was staring at the back of Anjali's head.

"I needed to make sure," she explained to Rishi. "I have to move on, right?"

"Anju," called Rishi, casting a warning glance in the direction of the door.

She wasn't looking at him. "But how am I supposed to move on when... argh... sometimes, he looks at me like..." With her index finger, Anjali poked

99

at one corner of her mouth. "Why would he keep staring at me there if he didn't want to kiss me?"

Behind her, Joe nodded as though in agreement. Shoving the fingers of both hands into his hair, Rishi pleaded, "Anju, stop!"

"Sorry, sorry," she said, biting her lower lip. "I didn't mean to embarrass you, but he's driving me crazy. Tell me, does he have a neck fetish or something?"

Joe's eyes snapped wide open. Shaking his head, Rishi groaned, then laughed, helplessly.

"I'm not kidding," Anjali insisted. "You watch when we're all here. He starts eyeing my hair and moves down my face until he gets to the neck and the collarbone." She frowned. "Just when I think he might go lower, he goes back... it's really frustrating!"

"Stop!" Rishi exploded out of his chair and went down on a knee in front of her. "Anju, darling. For the love of God, *stop talking.*"

"I'm so sorry," she said. "I don't usually discuss such stuff with *any*one. I wish I could talk to the girls, but they know the gossip about you and me is fake, and they *still* tease me for it. Imagine if I told them I have the hots for Joe! I came here to talk to you because only you could tell me..." For the first time since starting her tirade about Joe's inaction, she looked directly at Rishi. "Are you all right? Why are you so..."

Rishi glanced over her shoulder to where Joe stood.

Anjali stilled. Then, she gulped. "Is there someone behind me?"

Rishi closed his eyes once and inclined his head.

She looked upwards as though desperately hoping for clemency from the heavens. "Sid or the girls?"

Silently, Rishi shook his head.

Colour leached out of her face. Tone strangled, she asked, "Rishi... could you... umm... could you ask him to go straight to his room? I'll leave, and we'll all forget this ever happened, okay?"

Joe didn't respond either by speech or action.

"I don't think he's going to agree," Rishi murmured.

For a second or two, she simply stared. "Can you knock him out or something? When he wakes up, we can tell him he imagined the whole thing."

"Do me a favour, will ya?" Joe finally spoke. "Hold off the others for a while."

"Will do," said Rishi.

When he tried to stand, Anjali darted out a hand and grabbed his arm. Her French tipped nails dug into his flesh. "Don't go," she begged, tone panicked.

"Sorry, darling." Rishi pried her fingers loose. "You're on your own here. Got to say this was the most fun I had in a long time." Which said much about *his* love life.

✹✹✹

This is not real, Anjali thought wildly, staring hard at the cracked mosaic tiles below her feet. It couldn't be. Any moment now, she'd wake up and laugh at the embarrassing dream. Maybe the floor could disintegrate, letting her fall through the hole. Perhaps a meteor could strike the exact spot she sat. She'd die in front of Joe's eyes, and he could spend the rest of his life sobbing over her memory. The front door clicked shut behind her. Rishi was gone. The clanking of the rusty ceiling fan accompanied Joe's treads. Her heart thumped against her ribcage. She grabbed a pillow and set it on her lap, clutching it tightly as though it would stop her bouncy soul from leaping with each of his footsteps. *Closer... closer...* brown loafers appeared in her field of vision. *New,* she noted, idiotically.

"Anju," called Joe, with a slight tremble in his voice.

This was it. He'd either tell her—gently, of course—it wasn't happening, or he'd hold his arms open for her to fly into. Anjali made a sound somewhere between a gurgle and a "yes?"

"What you said—you know I can't—"

"I lied," she blurted. Biting her lip hard, she forced herself to look up. Gaze uncertain, Joe was standing there with a folder in his hands—his research proposal. Some explanation the scientist in him would buy... what could she say... "There was a lot of teasing about Rishi and me, and I wanted to let him know it was all right. I wasn't romantically interested in him."

Joe's bushy brows drew together, forming one furry line above his light brown eyes. "Huh?"

"I thought it might be more believable if I said I was interested in someone else," she said, rushing her words together.

Joe stood in silence for a few seconds, his frowny regard fixed on her face. "You said you had the hots for me."

Cringing inwardly, Anjali tilted her chin up. "I got a little carried away."

Slowly, he nodded and dropped into the chair Rishi vacated, sweeping the bags of Chinese food to one end of the coffee table to make room for his folder. "All right," Joe said, his gaze sweeping from her eyes to the corner of her mouth before jerking back up in a hurry. "Hypothetically speaking," he started, "if you *weren't* lying—"

"I was," she interjected.

"Hypothetically," he repeated. "If I told you the hots are mutual, what would you say?"

She gawked at him. *What... how... he wasn't teasing her, was he?* No, he wouldn't. Not about this. It would be so, so hurtful. "Hypothetically speaking," she said, her tone high, "I'd want to know why."

The uncertainty on his face morphed into confusion. "Huh?"

"I mean..." Anjali gulped. "Is it only hots or something more?" Hastily, she added, "Hypothetically, of course."

"Of course," he agreed. "You're not my usual... I usually know what I want going in. With you, I'm not sure. What if it's because I'm—"

"Because you're... what?"

Visibly swallowing hard, he asked, "If I'm falling in... you know... what if I can't fall out?"

Her silly soul leapt straight from her chest to her throat. "Would it be—" The words came out tinny and thin. With a small cough, she continued, "Would it be a bad thing?"

"It would be if you didn't feel the same way." When she opened her mouth to speak, Joe held up a hand. "Don't say it, please. Anju, there are things about me you don't know. We come from very different worlds... my family background, my connection to your grandfather... you might not want to have anything to do with me after you hear. I couldn't ask you to wait until next year without explaining. I was working up the nerve to do it, but if you said no, it would be the end. So..."

"There are lots of things you don't know about me, either," Anjali said, her pounding pulse now making her dizzy. She laced her fingers together, trying to stop the trembling. "I already know the important stuff about you— that you sometimes do strange things but are still thoughtful of others, that you apologise right away when you hurt someone's feelings, that you don't use someone's weakness against him, that you're crazy ambitious, that you love your mother."

With a sudden grin, Joe leaned towards her. "That you don't like to kill frogs, that you try not to hurt people's feelings to begin with, that you don't mind if dirty, little boys bump into you, that you get embarrassed by silly things, that you pretend you're not in the least embarrassed, that you don't know yet what you want to do with your medical degree." His eyes crinkled. "That you're the crazy chick who named the skeleton you keep in your room."

Anjali giggled and scooted to the edge of the sofa where his chair was. They were so close their knees were almost brushing. "That you always cut yourself shaving, that you pretend you only cook because you have to, not because you like to."

"You forgot something," Joe said, the smooth tones now husky. He shifted slightly, bringing them a lot closer. They weren't touching, but she could feel the moisture in his breath on her cheek, smell the warm, woodsy scent of his cologne. "That I like to look at you." His gaze wandered leisurely over her face before dropping to her mouth.

Inside her sneakers, her toes curled. The breeze from the clanking ceiling fan was barely enough to dry the sweat on her skin, but her body trembled in anticipation. "You forgot something, too," she whispered.

"What?"

"That you never went below the collar bone."

Joe's eyes snapped back up to meet hers. "Anju?" he called, his breathing uneven.

"Hmm?" She couldn't look away from the longing in the light brown irises. How could she have thought—

"We still need to talk about... about..."

"About what?"

His brows furrowed for a moment. "I don't have the faintest idea."

One of them was breathing really loudly. Was it her? Anjali couldn't tell. Her chest was heaving as though she'd run a marathon. Running the tip of her tongue over her dry upper lip, she murmured, "Joe?

"Yeah?"

"Hypothetically speaking, shouldn't we kiss?"

"I'm *trying* to find the key," someone yelled outside the front door—Rishi.

Anjali jumped in place, knocking her knee on the coffee table. Her racing heart arrested for a second before hurtling into the unpleasant gallop of shock. Joe leapt back into his chair, cursing under his breath.

"You don't *need* the key," said Siddharth's impatient voice. "Anju's inside. Hey, *Anju*." A loud knock sounded on the door. "Open up. Everyone's here, except Joe."

Anjali bit back a hysterical giggle. With a muted groan of frustration, Joe stood and went to open the door. "I'm here, too," he announced.

"Oh, hey, Joe," said Rishi, an elbow on one doorjamb, his leg extended across the entrance. Behind him were the rest, clearly annoyed and confused at the human barricade. "I was right outside, getting some fresh air. Didn't see you come in."

Both hands held to her mouth, Anjali would've laughed like a mad woman if Joe's phone hadn't rung, startling her. As the rest of the group took their places around the coffee table, he barked into the phone, "Hello?" A few seconds later, he asked, "How many times do I have to say I'm not interested in any kind of moonlighting no matter what the pay? I'm not allowed to. Even if I were, I don't have time."

"Same people?" Rishi asked as Joe hung up.

"Yeah," he said, tucking the phone back into his pocket. "This has to be the ninth or tenth time. They just won't take no for an answer. I don't get it. It's not like there aren't hundreds of doctors in Delhi."

Chapter 12

Present day

Joseph D'Acosta had, indeed, been "crazy ambitious." He wanted everything in life—Anjali in his arms, his career in transplant research, a way to keep his family afloat. After his conversation with Anjali in the flat, they didn't get a chance to discuss anything else. Joe flew home for the summer and walked along these very streets in the Goan town of Mapusa, deciding he *was* going to get everything he wanted, and he'd do it all while feeling like a man.

Nothing much seemed to have changed in the small town since then. It was Sunday, and some of the spice stores and the shops selling *chorizo*—Goan pork sausage—were closed, but crowds still thronged the unpaved lanes. Joe shouldered his way through until he reached the fish vendors. Wrinkled women lined the narrow path on both sides, sitting on low stools with their colourful saris hitched all the way up to their knees. Fish of all kinds were piled in baskets in front. In a multitude of languages, the women called out to the shoppers, announcing the prices. There were very few tourists. Mapusa market was meant mostly for the locals.

"God, it's hot as hell, and it stinks," muttered Dev, Joe's brother, tugging at his collar. A bead of sweat ran down his temple. His fair skin was sure to burn by the end of the expedition.

The air *was* almost too thick with moisture and fishy aroma to breathe, but Joe laughed, peering at the faces of each seller, looking for the one he wanted. "There was a time when I had to threaten you with a stick to get you to return from the market and do your homework. You *and* Romeo." The younger of Joe's two brothers was currently in his room, cramming for exams.

Grinning, Dev said, "You remember the stall a couple of streets down which sold homemade sweets?"

"Oh, yeah," Joe mused. "They had the best chikki." He'd never found peanut brittle with quite the same stickiness and sweetness elsewhere. "I used to buy it in bulk to take to Delhi."

"*Bhai,*" called Dev, addressing Joe as "brother." He stepped over a puddle of greyish-green water, scattering the flies buzzing above it. "Is that why we're here? You could've just asked one of the restaurant staff to get you some."

"Nope. I'm looking for someone, a former patient."

Dev stopped short, causing the man behind to bump into him. Ignoring the curses of the annoyed fellow, Dev caught Joe by the elbow. "Former patient? Why did you ask me along, then? Bhai, it's the weekend. The restaurant is busy."

"How long did we live in this town?" Joe asked, gesturing at his brother to follow as he moved to the relatively secluded spot next to a dumpster overflowing with fish entrails. The black cow hanging out next to it let out an annoyed moo at the interlopers. "Haven't you ever had an attack of nostalgia?"

Tone puzzled and mildly irritated, Dev said, "*You* were the one who insisted on moving to Vagator. If you felt so nostalgic about this place..." When the D'Acostas left Goa eleven years ago, Joe had only been twenty-four and his siblings, sixteen, twelve, and eight. They'd returned three years later but chose Vagator instead of Mapusa.

Joe swatted away a couple of flies hovering by his face. "I thought a fresh start would be good for all of us." Plus, their family was originally from the Vagator area, and they finally got their father's property back from the bank.

"So what's the point of a trip down the memory lane?"

"*I* wasn't asking for it, either," said Joe, tone even. "You sent me on one anyway."

Dev drew out a packet of tissues from his pocket and wiped the sweat beads from his temple, chucking the wad into the middle of the pink, bleeding fish innards in the dumpster. "Is this about the Anjali woman? Look, I get it." He held up both hands and made air-quotes. "She's a former *acquaintance* you didn't want to meet. Then, don't. As simple as it gets."

"I didn't say I didn't want to meet her. It's just—Dev, I need answers. I wasn't *expecting* to meet her. Her cousin mentioned something about the Joshi Clinic, and I'm assuming it's what brought her to Goa. Even so, it's too much of a coincidence how we ran into each other. I want to see what's happening at the clinic, and the patient I mentioned has a daughter who works there. I also want to hear *your* explanation. You more than Romeo and Laila will remember how bad things were when we left Goa." At twelve, Romeo wouldn't have picked up on the details of the constant visits from the cops. For their baby sister, the then-eight-year-old Laila, the whole thing made for a big adventure. The two of them would consider Joe's worry over his blind date cause for a laugh, but not Dev as long as he were away from them. "I need to know if the person who arranged this with you is aware of the circumstances, what he or she might've said to Anjali."

"I didn't think of the possibility." Scratching his chin, Dev eyed Joe for a few moments. The habit was another thing they had in common. Apart from the startlingly fair skin they inherited from their Kashmiri mother, all three of Joe's half-siblings shared the D'Acosta looks with him, including the dents in their chins. Joe owed his bronzish tone to *his* mother, the first Mrs D'Acosta. Then, there was their culinary skill, though Dev was hands down the best chef of the four. "All Fr Franco and I heard was you were crazy about her, and after you left, she got together with someone else. They're now getting divorced."

Divorce. Joe had been sure she wouldn't have been at the café if she were still committed to Rishi, but her behaviour that night couldn't entirely be explained by the shock of meeting an ex she preferred to forget. There was a weird niggle in Joe's mind which started when he heard her mention someone waiting for her to return from the date. But it hadn't been Rishi. They were getting divorced. Joe nodded in relief. "*Where* did you hear about her and me?"

"We hired an investigator."

"*What?*"

Dev clucked. "Don't get mad. Like you keep telling *us,* it was for your own good."

Joe gritted his teeth. "I'm eight years older than you."

"Bhai," Dev said, reprovingly. "You've been both father and mother to us. We all know Dad was pretty much useless, and Ma... well... she didn't have the faintest idea how to cope. I was sixteen when you quit AIIMS. I watched you give up everything for us. Romeo and Laila might not know the details, but they also understand as much. Even after things settled down, you never showed any signs of wanting anything for yourself." Dev grinned. "I remember the ladies from before, but afterwards, you were like Fr Franco."

"Not as bad," Joe muttered. He definitely hadn't taken any vows of chastity.

"Almost. We thought we'd check if something happened in Delhi before setting you up with someone new."

It took them about ten minutes to locate Joe's former patient in a covered shed with a bunch of fisherwomen. Without looking up to see who it was, she spat to the side the blood-red remnants of *paan*—the psychoactive combination of betel leaf and areca nut. "Five mackerels for a hundred," she quoted, "and not a paisa less."

For five hundred, she informed them her daughter, the lab technician, wouldn't know anything about Anjali's presence at the Joshi Clinic, but the idiot son-in-law might. He was now Anjali's secretary.

After dropping Dev off at the restaurant in Vagator, Joe was driving home when a thought occurred. There weren't many people who could've told the investigator about Anjali and Joe. Who among those he knew—no, not true. One other person was aware of Anjali's importance to Joe.

The man who called on the phone so many years ago knew about their romance to the minutest detail, his disguised voice promising Joe everything he dreamed of could be his if he would consent to their request. Take the moonlighting job they offered, and he'd have it all—financial security for his family, introductions to the well-connected in the field of transplant research, and most of all, the social standing to walk into Anjali's home with his head held high. Anjali was the lure leading Joe into the trap from which it took him three years to escape, and now, she'd somehow been thrust back into his life.

Part V

Chapter 13

Rishi smiled his thanks at the employee of Goa Marriott and accepted both the seashell garland and the offering of beer. Drinking himself into a stupor was not an option, but by God, he needed *something*.

"...just a short walk to Casino Carnival..." said the young man in the crisp, cotton uniform, showing Rishi to the waterfront restaurant as requested instead of his room.

Tables were arranged on the narrow strip of solid ground between the swimming pool and the mouth of the river where it emptied into the bright blue sea. On the other side of the pool, palm trees swayed in the wind, and a group of teenagers in bathing suits were running past the palms into the hotel, their excited shouts reaching Rishi. He drew a deep breath, relishing the smell of sun and hot sand. Getting a permit to travel in the middle of a pandemic wasn't easy, but it *was* good to be outside without worrying about viruses.

111

Rishi shook his head. He wasn't here to take in Goa's scenery. On his phone were notifications for dozens of messages he didn't bother looking at—from the CEO of the hospital, his colleagues, his angry family, and random people apparently dying to know what went wrong between the perfect couple. *Why didn't you just tell them, Anju? You could've included it at least in the court filings. Tell everyone I'm gay.*

She knew he recoiled against revealing it to the world, but why would she bother about the emotional damage she inflicted on the husband she was divorcing? As far as Anjali was aware, there would be no physical repercussions for her to feel guilty over. All she knew was someone blackmailed Rishi for his sexuality, and he, desperate for a way out, asked if she'd consider marrying him. The law had since changed. Rishi was no longer at risk of being branded a criminal or losing his medical licence. She didn't know what else he'd done—his deepest shame, the secret which could still cost him his identity as a doctor, the blackmailer's real weapon.

Still, except for their immediate families, she'd told no one the reason behind the divorce. With the tips of his fingers, Rishi rubbed his temple hard. Even the parents who adored her didn't know the reason she'd agreed to the *marriage*—the man who was now back in their lives. Every ghost from Rishi's past seemed to be making a reappearance at the same time.

"I'll take a cashew feni," he said to the hovering waiter. One glass of Goan hooch for liquid courage.

Slouching in the chair, Rishi stared holes into his phone. Missed calls... messages... nothing from Anjali. She hadn't called back after their conversation about Joe's reappearance. Half-sobbing, half-ranting, she said she ran into him at a beach restaurant, but when Rishi asked questions, she hung up on him mid-sentence. Nor did she pick up *his* calls.

"Café Ishq," Rishi muttered.

"Their brunch is to die for," said the waiter, returning with the feni. "I hope you have a reservation, or you could end up waiting a long time."

"Ahh... no reservation." Rishi took a sip of the yellowish-orange drink and blinked as the fruity liquid pleasantly burned its way down his gullet.

"Good, no?" asked the waiter. "Forty-three per cent alcohol. Do you have other plans for lunch? If not, you should try one of *our* restaurants."

"I haven't decided yet," Rishi said, nodding dismissively. The only thing he knew with certainty was he was not going to Café Ishq.

Anjali said something about the place belonging to Joe's brother. Bringing up the restaurant on the web browser, Rishi huffed. The site hadn't changed in the last couple of days since he first typed in the address. There was nothing on it about the owner's identity. Googling Joe's name was useless. Who knew Joseph D'Acosta would turn out to be not-so-rare a name in India? But if Joe owned a medical practice in the Vagator area, Farida—Rishi's secretary—would locate it. She once claimed she belonged to an underground network of medical secretaries where information useful to their bosses was traded. Rishi still had no idea if she'd been joking, but once Farida said she'd do something, she always got it done. Rishi would soon know if the man Anjali ran into was actually Joe.

The idea... it was still so damned vague... like a disquieting, half-remembered dream. Or maybe it was simply the nice little buzz he already got from the feni. "Forty-three per cent alcohol," Rishi muttered. Raising a hand, he beckoned the waiter who was walking by. "I'll take one more."

Could Anjali have been imagining things, some kind of post-traumatic stress from the terrible few months she'd gone through? What better way to get your mind away from the turmoil of the present than to return to a happier past?

Rishi sipped his second drink—or was it the third? He couldn't remember. There was a time when he could've drunk three times this much and not batted an eye. He'd lost his taste for alcohol during the years of his marriage, imbibing mainly for show at social events. No wonder his head was already floaty. Any moment now, he'd start imagining things like running into an ex.

Anjali *had* to have imagined the whole thing. As soon as the waiter returned with the bill, Rishi would ask if he knew who owned the restaurant. It couldn't be Joe or any of his relatives. The world had changed in the decade past. It was almost impossible to hide someone's identity from the prying eyes of big tech. If any of the D'Acostas owned Café Ishq, Google would've known it. Anjali's mind—fragile from the trauma of the last few months—surely played tricks on her. No ex-boyfriend was waiting in the wings to foil Rishi's plans. When he left Goa, it would be with Anjali. They'd return to Delhi and tell everyone concerned—his family, hers, their colleagues—they'd decided to give their marriage another shot. His parents would again accept him into the family fold as the son they were so proud of. The blackmailer would slink back into the shadows, never again to show his face.

Feminine laughter pealed from the direction of the palm trees. A boy and a girl from the group of teenagers were returning to the pool arm-in-arm, talking. They stopped under a swaying palm to kiss, oblivious to the rest of the world the way only teenagers could be. More diners trickled in behind the couple. There was a *gora*—a white man—sauntering in with nothing more on than swimming trunks and a string of colourful beads around his neck, his friendly grin directed at Rishi. Muscles loosening, Rishi raised his glass.

The gora's eyes went to the glass, and with a half-frown, half-smile, he turned away.

Rishi mumbled a curse. His wedding ring. As though he weren't already juggling a wife and a lover, he *had* to respond to a random fellow with a flirtatious smile while advertising the fact he was married. He hadn't been able to take the ring off, this symbol of the one person in the world who'd stayed when everyone he thought of as family or friend abandoned him. Not even the lover who'd begged Rishi to break the chains holding him down could compete with his history with Anjali. She was friend *and* family. No exes—imagined or real—were going to tell him otherwise.

He needed to let her know—gently, of course—how the best option for them was to stick together. He'd shower her with affection until she knew he was the only man who could give her everything she wanted—happiness, family, peace of mind. Rishi picked his phone back up. He already knew where the Joshi mansion was, but chances were she wouldn't let him in. She'd be at the clinic now, anyway. Today was Monday.

An hour and one more feni later, Rishi was getting out of the cab, staring up at the two-storey concrete building which extended through the block— the Joshi Charity Clinic. He'd been to Goa exactly once. Eleven years ago, he and Anjali came to Mapusa in search of Joe and left with broken hearts. He never expected to return to the town.

A faint smell of antiseptic clung to the air. Sunlight glinted off the large arched windows lining both floors. The yellow paint was surely meant to be cheery but bore the dullness wrought by time. Otherwise, there were no piles of garbage or stray animals to indicate the clinic served a low-income population.

There was a guard booth by the glass-doored entrance, but it was empty. When Rishi entered the cramped but well-lit waiting room, there was a mild lull in the hum of chatter. Quite a few curious stares were directed his way from the rows of plastic chairs. His twill chinos, half-sleeved shirt, and expensive sneakers were just fine for a day at the Delhi Golf Club but didn't exactly allow him to blend in with the crowd at the Joshi Clinic.

"Sir?" called an employee clad in pink scrubs, a folder held to her chest. Wrinkling her nose, she took half a step back. Rishi cleared his throat and tried not to huff acidic, feni-scented breaths onto her face. "Can I help you?" she asked.

"Anjali... I mean, Dr Anjali Joshi? Is she here?"

With a professional smile, the employee said, "Dr Anjali is in her office, but she has meetings all day."

"Yes." Not missing a beat, Rishi lied, "One of those meetings is with me." Damn. He was good at this.

"Uh-huh." The employee eyed Rishi up and down. Clearly, she had no clue she was looking at the boss's husband. "I'll get her secretary."

"Excellent," agreed Rishi, waiting only until she'd stopped glancing behind to follow her into the interior.

There was plenty of traffic in the long, narrow corridor. Stretchers being pushed, patients in squeaky wheelchairs, a couple of doctors arguing over a case, nurses in their old-fashioned white dresses. Unlike the private hospital in Delhi which employed Rishi, there seemed to be no guards. But then, this place was hardly likely to be visited by VIP patients.

Twists and turns and turns and twists, Rishi hummed in his mind as he followed the employee in pink scrubs down the corridor. *Great stuff, this feni.* What more did a man need in his life? A friend, a family... a friend who was family... and feni. When he and Anjali got back home to Delhi, they could mark the occasion with a bottle. A couple of bottles. Why not? It would almost be like getting married a second time. They'd be starting over with a clean slate, no imaginary exes to mar their celebration.

A door swung open, nearly hitting Rishi on the nose. "Sorry, sir," said a lab-coated technician.

Rishi nodded and held his breath until his chest was ready to explode. *Damn the feni.* The smell was going to give him away as a drunk and an interloper.

The employee in pink scrubs stopped at the far end of the corridor where there was a wooden door, a moustachioed man sitting at the tiny desk outside. The secretary? There was someone else next to the desk, his back to Rishi, looming over the moustachioed secretary. Dress pants and the crisp cotton shirt and gleaming shoes suggested the man was a professional of some kind— a doctor, a medical sales rep, even a patient's well-to-do family member. From the frown on the secretary's face, the man was arguing. Strangely, there was a dog next to him, sitting on its haunches.

Rishi jogged the last few feet up to the desk. The nameplate on the door said, "Dr Anjali Joshi, CEO." He frowned. Had she formally taken over management of this place? She couldn't. Her life was in Delhi.

Holding a hand up to silence the employee in pink scrubs, the secretary said to the other man, "I'm sorry, Doc. I realise my mother-in-law was your patient, but I can't let you simply march in. Dr Anjali is busy today, and she told me to tell you if you want to see her, you have to make an appointment."

Rishi didn't care about any other business; Anjali was his *wife*. Surely, the fact entitled him to cut the line. Hell, if they could announce their reconciliation to the staff by the end of the day, the man might be making an appointment to see some other CEO altogether. They'd soothe everyone's disappointment with a party. Music, dancing, food. Feni all around!

"Excuse me," Rishi said to the secretary.

The third man at the desk turned, and Rishi looked into the face of Joseph D'Acosta.

Chapter 14

Summer 2007

"*Dhoom machaale*," the singer bellowed the tune from *Dhoom*, the hit action-musical, inviting the guests at the *sangeet*—the pre-wedding party—to have a blast.

And so they did. Shoes off, the ladies danced, kicking the gold glitter dust all around the floor, mimicking the mini-clad actress from the Bollywood hit. Rishi twirled the groom's sister into a deep dip, causing catcalls and claps all around. Flushed and sweaty, when they straightened to take a bow, the reception stage was empty except for the MC, Rishi's uncle, standing by one of the four white lattice pillars which formed the corners of the stage. Wrapped around each pillar were dozens of garlands of pink and red roses. The peach-pink drapes at the back of the stage glowed from hidden lighting. The throne-like love seat in plush, bronze-coloured fabric was unoccupied. The bride—the second of Rishi's sisters—was making her way towards him, her intended in tow.

"Whatta show, Rishi," said the soon-to-be brother-in-law, clapping.

Show was the right word. This was the second wedding in his household, and as before, Rishi had been told in no uncertain terms to "show up and act normal." Hating himself for the pathetic spurt of joy at the command to join the family, he agreed. He talked, cracked jokes, seated guests, ran errands. While dancing was not exactly his forte, looking glamorous in a black silk kurta-pyjama and maroon brocade vest was easily achieved, especially when his partner was content to sway sexily without actually moving her feet.

"Bhai saab," said Rishi, playfully. "Your turn to show us your magic." He turned to the crowd around and shouted, "What say, everyone? One last dance for them as boyfriend and girlfriend?"

Amidst the whoops of approval, Rishi escorted the groom's sister off the dance floor. "Boyfriend and girlfriend!" She laughed. "Everyone knows this is an arranged marriage."

With a wink, Rishi said, "Arranged love." He took a quick visual sweep of the hall for the rest of his family. *There.* Sister number one, heavily pregnant, was seated on a sofa a few feet away. Rishi's parents were with her. Her Yank hubby was nowhere to be seen. Sister number three was probably off dancing with *her* fiancé. In another six months, Rishi would be the only one in the household without a partner.

Long fingers tightened around his forearm. "Is that what you want?" asked the groom's sister. "Arranged love?" Somehow, she seemed closer, her cheek brushing against his shoulder.

Before Rishi could answer, sister number one called his name. *Phew.* "God. I hope she's not going into labour."

"Oh," said the sister of the groom, her mouth contorting into a dismayed moue. "You'd better check."

When Rishi got to his sister—alone—she frowned heavily at him. "What were you talking about with *her?*"

"Nothing," said Rishi, a sick feeling in his heart. Did she know? Did *all* his sisters know? He glanced at his father and mother. Thus far, they'd kept his announcement of his sexuality a secret, not sharing it even with their daughters, only telling them Rishi moved out as he needed to be closer to the hospital. Now, it looked like Papa and Ma couldn't be bothered to do even that much for him. Why? Was his entire family ganging up on him to make sure he didn't embarrass them? "We were dancing. There wasn't much chance to talk."

"Good," said his sister. "You could do a lot better."

For a second, it didn't sink in. "What?"

His sister ptchaaed. "Rishi, you're a doctor. Handsome, family background, money—you could have most anyone you wanted. Her family's all right, but she's already been through a few boyfriends. Her parents told her to settle down, or she'll have to find a job and support herself. Don't let her trap you into anything."

"Didi, I—" Rishi turned to his parents, his mind in turmoil. Did they tell his sisters or not? How was he supposed to respond? Or was this a trap of a different kind? They weren't planning to force him into an arranged marriage, were they?

"Get a chair, betay," ordered his mother. "We want to talk to you."

In a daze, Rishi complied and waited until the relatives who came by to say hello left. What the hell did Ma want to discuss? Some girl she had in mind? He couldn't. He'd have to... he needed to get out, run as far away as possible. Hide. His job... his plans... he'd be alone. *God.* What was he going to do?

"Tell us about this girl, Anjali," said Papa's firm voice.

"Anjali—" Startled, Rishi rubbed his temple and nodded at an old granny limping by on her way to the buffet table. "Anjali Joshi? At AIIMS? How do you know..."

"We heard some stories, betay," said Ma, leaning forwards. "One of your professors is close friends with my friend, Dr Bharti. You remember Bharti Auntie, right?"

How could he forget? Dr Bharti Sachdev, the shrink his parents took him to, tried her best to convince him being gay was only a figment of his imagination, borne out of a fear of sexual intimacy. On Nikhil's advice, Rishi nodded in agreement and zipped his lips long enough to finish his MBBS course. All he needed was to get to the U.S. with Nikhil. He'd finally be able to breathe.

He should've never returned from the States. His father found out about his visits to the gay bar and ordered him back. Rishi didn't dare disobey. Papa was... Papa. No one said no to him. Rishi returned but couldn't bring himself to deny his sexuality to his parents any longer. Thank God, the job at AIIMS and the flat came within a day of his parents telling him he was no longer welcome in the family home. All they said to their daughters was Rishi needed to be closer to the campus, but he was still afraid they'd call the college, accusing him and Joe of illegal sexual acts. Nothing of the sort happened. Somehow, Joe gave out very strong straight vibes. Still, there was no communication between Rishi and his parents since then. Damned fool he was, he'd hoped their demand he attend this wedding meant they missed him.

"The professor was saying you're 'really friendly' with the girl," said Ma.

Slowly, Rishi said, "I am. But..." Shooting a wary glance at his sister, he turned back to his mother. "Dr Bharti doesn't discuss... ahh... our family matters with her friends, does she?"

Ma shook her head ever so slightly, letting Rishi know his secret was safe. So far.

"How come you didn't tell us about this Anjali?" asked his sister, her tone prickly with hostility. "What's her background?"

Papa held a hand up. "Dr Bharti gave us a quick bio on her."

Bio? Rishi laughed, tiredly. "Are you planning to offer her a job?" As his father's face darkened with anger, Rishi lowered his eyes. "Sorry," he mumbled.

"*Kya kar rahe ho?*" admonished Ma, asking Rishi what he was trying to do with the smart-aleck comment. "Betay, we got the basic information on her already. Good family, reasonably pretty, parents are rich. That's not enough. She needs to fit into *our* family."

"Ma," Rishi said, "Anju is... we're friends."

"*Haan, haan,*" agreed his mother. "Whatever you want to call it is fine. She's always at your flat, but you feel compelled to protect her reputation in front of us. We understand. We were also young once."

Absurdly, Rishi wanted to laugh. The idea of Ma and Papa sneaking around... a giggle erupted from Rishi's pregnant sister. Within a couple of seconds, they were both laughing hard.

"Enough," said Papa, tone stern, but there was a twinkle in his eyes.

Elation. Rishi's heart suddenly felt unbearably light. This was the beloved papa of his childhood, the man who'd carried his only son into kindergarten every single day until the teachers pleaded, "Let the boy walk." This was the mother who'd wept buckets when he moved fifteen minutes away to the medical college hostel. His sisters were the same sisters who'd demanded he play the harmonica while they practised dance steps.

"Go," Ma muttered, poking her husband in the shoulder with a finger. "You said *you'll* talk to him."

A few minutes later, Rishi and his father were squeezing through the crowd of guests at the bar. "Scotch?" asked Papa.

Rishi shook his head, immediately. Alcohol flowed freely at Punjabi weddings, but he'd never imbibed in front of his father before and wasn't about to start now.

"Arrey, yaar," said someone from the crowd. "Who says no to free whiskey?"

Quelling the third party with a stern look, Papa said, "You're twenty-three now, Rishi betay. A man, not a boy. You can drink in your father's presence. Plus, I want to talk to you as an equal today."

Whiskey glasses in hand, they'd been standing for at least five minutes in the relative quiet next to a large urn with a profusion of roses, and Rishi still couldn't bring himself to take a sip. Damn, but he wanted to. It was Scotch, too. His budget didn't run to things like fine whiskey.

"I'm proud of you," said Papa, finally breaking the silence.

Was he, really? For what? Ignoring the sliver of cynicism, Rishi stammered, "Ahh... thanks."

"Everyone has weaknesses," continued Papa. "You fought yours and won."

Rishi closed his eyes in misery. "Papa, I—"

"You can't imagine how happy you've made me and your ma. It's hard when you see a child going wrong. You won't understand until you're a parent. It's our daughter's wedding, and we couldn't find any joy any it. Then, Dr Bharti called. Betay, it was the best gift we got."

Rishi stared at his father's grey head, the lines on his face. Papa was older than the fathers of most of his peers. The investment banker was already in his late thirties when he married Rishi's ma, and Rishi was their youngest. Like most Indian parents, Papa and Ma were strict with their children—the girls, especially—but they'd been such a happy family... until the day Rishi opened his big mouth. What was he supposed to say now? How was he supposed to break this old man's heart, yet again?

"It doesn't mean we're going to give our blessing so easily," said Papa, almost teasingly. "Like your ma said, we need to know if this girl will fit into our family."

Rishi looked around at the happy faces. The bride was still on the dance floor. The other two Rastogi girls joined her, the pregnant one barely able to move. Ma was clapping along to the music. *The wedding... God, let me have this day, at least.* Mumbling an apology in his mind to Anjali, to Joe, to his own wounded self, Rishi said, "Anju would fit in anywhere."

***

Guitar chords vibrated through the open door, across the hallway of the South Mumbai duplex, and into Anjali's room. She sat smack in the middle of her queen-sized bed in the pool of afternoon sunlight filtering through the large windows. She might've planned to stay in her room all day and make progress on the oil sketch she was attempting, but that didn't mean she couldn't dance. Raising her arms, she rocked in time with the music.

Vikram crooned, "SexyBack." Anjali's sixteen-year-old brother was a huge fan of the singer, Justin Timberlake.

Anjali clapped a hand over her mouth, muffling a giggle. Vikram could play the guitar like a dream, and he had a lovely baritone voice, but with his shaggy hair and torn jeans and one-word grunts, he wasn't gonna deliver anything even remotely resembling sexiness.

Sexy was... she flopped back onto the pile of fluffy pillows. Sexy was Joseph D'Acosta. Closing her eyes, she imagined herself back in the autorickshaw with him, on their way to the temple. The only time they'd touched. Darn it, did she *have* to move away right then? What would he have done if she'd stayed in his arms? Would he have lowered his head and brushed his lips against hers? Maybe not. They hadn't acknowledged anything at the time. Still... he could've been drawn in by the feel of her body against his... drowning in the passion promised by her melting gaze...

"Anju," shouted a voice.

Eyes snapping open, Anjali jerked up in the bed. Her heart was practically pounding its way out of the ribcage. A hand to her chest, she glanced towards the door. "Vikram, you scared me half to death."

His thick, slashing brows drew together into a frown over the broken nose. "Sorry. I called you a couple of times, but you didn't hear me. Mom said you need help with your laptop."

"Yes." Anjali leapt out of bed. "It's soooo slow. *Please* take a look, Vikram." Joe had asked if she'd instal something called Facebook so they could message each other, but her computer simply wouldn't cooperate. Calling daily on the phone cost money he didn't have, and Anjali didn't want dozens of calls to the same number in Goa popping up on her parents' bill.

Vikram took the laptop and settled into the armchair by the window. One click... two clicks. Pushing the sleeves of her cotton pyjama shirt to her elbows, Anjali hopped from foot to bare foot. "My God," Vikram breathed, eyes wide in horror.

"What's wrong?" Anjali asked, nearly tripping over the lace-trimmed, wide hem of her pants.

"So many viruses," Vikram muttered. "No wonder you're slow."

"Can you fix it?"

He looked up, the expression in his eyes saying *Duh.*

"Just asking," she mumbled. Without responding, he returned to the job at hand. Anjali bit her lip hard and stared at his bent head. *Say something to me, Vicky, you doofus.*

He used to be such a cute little boy, always asking to tag along when she went to school. All it took was one mistake on seven-year-old Anjali's part of ignoring him when he was being taunted over something stupid, and in time-honoured Joshi fashion, Vikram decided she no longer mattered. All of five years old, and Vikram could already hold on to a grudge harder and longer than the worst of the Joshis—eleven years and counting now. Anjali started medical college after high school as was the practice in India, and Vikram would be off to college in one more year, but age failed to bring about reconciliation.

"You didn't call me all semester," she ventured.

Eyes fixed on the computer, he said, "You didn't call me, either." Anjali winced. She'd dialled his number a few times—usually after hanging out with Gauri and Meenakshi or after overhearing Joe chat with *his* brothers on the phone—only to change her mind before hitting CALL. "'S all right," Vikram added, tone dismissive. "What would we have talked about, anyway?"

It was precisely her reasoning—her *fear* as well—that they'd stay on the line in awkward silence until one or the other mumbled an excuse. "You could've asked how I was doing in a new place."

"I'm sure you did all right. No matter what you do, it always comes out perfect."

A lightning-hot pain shot across her eyeballs. Anjali gritted her teeth and counted down from ten until it passed. Darn. She'd forgotten to make the eye clinic appointment. She really needed them to run some tests. Even if she didn't need glasses, there had to be *something* causing the acute flashes of blinding pain. The neurologist called them tension headaches, but Anjali suspected the label basically meant the doctor didn't want to hurt her feelings by saying she was imagining things.

"I'm running a clean-up," Vikram said, setting the laptop on the desk. "It will take a couple of hours. Don't use the computer until it's completed."

"*Hours?*" Anjali asked, dismayed. She'd told Joe she'd message him soon. His entire family would be at church, and he'd finally have enough privacy to use the desktop which was in their living room.

"Something wrong?" asked Mom's voice.

Anjali jumped. She hadn't even heard their mother approach. "Umm... no. I'd planned to chat with one of my friends is all."

"You can use the PC downstairs," offered Mom, rolling her hennaed hair into a neat little bun and sticking a bronze pin into it. For a Sunday, she was dressed quite spiffily in a silk maxi wrapped around her short and slightly plump figure, the collar of the matching shirt opened a touch to reveal the string of glittering stones around her neck. The bronze-coloured stilettos put her a couple of inches above Anjali's height. "Your dad and I have a leukaemia benefit to attend, and I think Vikram's visiting Nanaji, so you'll have the place to yourself." Nanaji—Mom's father—had to be Vikram's absolute favourite person in the world. Actually, the only human being he seemed to like.

"I'll be back by the time the clean-up is done," Vikram interjected, padding into the room across the hallway.

Anjali glanced at his disappearing back and for a moment contemplated marching in and demanding he talk to her. Shoulders slumping, she huffed. What was the point? He'd simply stare away and mumble once again they had nothing to say to each other.

"Everything all right?" asked Mom, glancing between Vikram's now closed door and Anjali.

"Nothing," said Anjali. "You know how he is." They all did. If there was anyone Vikram talked less to than Anjali, it was their parents. He seemed to prefer pretending to be an orphan with only a grandfather for family.

A shadow crossed Mom's face before it dissipated in a flash of hope. "He's been hitting the books pretty hard. I think he's planning to follow you to AIIMS."

"Really?" Anjali asked, doubtfully. Vikram was super smart and possessed the awards from school to prove it, but nothing in his demeanour shouted "doctor." Still, there *was* a certain expectation that all Joshi sons would be doctors. Mom and Dad met as classmates during their first year in medical college. "Mom, you have a minute? I need some advice."

"I thought you said no way you're going to be a gynaecologist?" Mom teased.

"I haven't changed my mind," Anjali said, waving a hand. She couldn't imagine... she had no idea how her mother dealt every single day with all the screaming and the slime and sometimes poop. *Gak, no way.* "This is about something else." She poked her head out into the hallway and glanced up and down, making sure the coast was clear.

127

"What are you doing?" asked Mom, laughing.

"Let's sit," said Anjali, pulling at her mother's arm.

"Do I *need* to sit for this? That doesn't sound good."

"*Mom.*" Anjali stomped a foot.

"Okay, okay," said Mom, both hands raised. "I'm sitting." She plunked herself down on the bed and fixed her gaze on Anjali as she climbed onto the mattress to cross her legs, guru-style.

"You can't tell Dad I asked this," Anjali warned.

"Uh... okay."

"I'm serious," Anjali insisted. Mom and Dad were the ideal couple, staying in love through thick and thin over the twenty-some years of their marriage. If there were secrets between them, Anjali didn't know. "Promise me."

"I can't until I know what you're going to tell me," Mom said, bluntly.

Anjali bit her lip. "It's nothing major. I only wanted to ask... when you met Dad, did you know right away he was the one? Also, how did you figure out how *he* felt?"

"Ahh," said Mom, a wealth of meaning in the long, drawn-out syllable.

Heat rushed into Anjali's cheeks. "It's not about me." At the raised eyebrow on Mom's face, Anjali added, "Okay, so it is... I don't know for sure. How do I decide? How did *you* decide?"

"Anju," called Mom, reaching out to cup Anjali's cheek before dropping her hand. "You can't model your life after mine or anyone else's. For what it's worth, your dad and I used scientific method."

Anjali's mouth dropped open. "How?"

"We weighed the risk versus benefits." Mom shrugged. "The risk was mostly about family and the circumstances we grew up in. We eventually decided the problems were something we could handle, but living without each other would make life meaningless."

What if Joe were to vanish from Anjali's life? Would she find further living meaningless? Would he?

"Now, I want to hear about this young man," said Mom, mock-sternly.

Anjali giggled. "He's... umm..." How much did she want to divulge? Joe had said something about his family and circumstances and how she might not want to get involved if she knew. He was being ridiculous. Nothing around him was going to change Anjali's mind about the man himself, but Mom and Dad... they knew he was Daadaji's protégé and that he grew up poor. Anjali didn't think *they'd* object, but Joe... she needed to talk to him first. "One of the tutors," Anjali said. "He's starting post-graduation this year."

"And?"

"He's cute and smart and does the weirdest things sometimes." Anjali sighed, dreamily remembering the soya chunks he'd claimed were frog legs. The dish he'd made only for her. "I don't want to say any more until I know for sure, but he's thoughtful and nice, and he loves his mother."

"Very important," said Mom, immediately, causing Anjali to chortle. "Tutor, huh?"

Narrowing her eyes, Anjali said, "Don't go asking any of your friends in AIIMS about him."

"Of course not," agreed Mom, her tone smooth. "I wouldn't embarrass you that way."

***

"Want me to knock some sense into the delinquent?" Joe asked into the phone, enjoying the feel of the ocean breeze riffling through his hair and the silvery light from the full moon on his face. Yeah, his back was coated with gritty sand, but it was a small price to pay for a couple of peaceful hours on the beach. He'd long considered this secluded space between the two large rocks his own except for the skinny puppy with the half-bitten left ear. The beast popped up this summer and sometimes napped in the same spot, forcing Joe to leave. It was now staring at Joe from the top of a rotting log. *Ha, I got here first tonight,* Joe telepathically told the animal. A few feet away, noisy tourists partied on, but Joe and the pup were well hidden in the shadows.

Besides his idiot brothers and his baby sister, this was what Joe missed in Delhi—chilling on the beach in nothing but his swimming trunks and a towel rolled up under his head. What he missed in Goa was at the other end of the line—Anjali, the euphoria of being near her, the excitement zinging along his nerve endings whenever she talked or laughed or hummed a little tune, the painful erections brought on by imagining the trim little figure under the cool and casual clothes she preferred.

"Vikram's not a delinquent, just a bit moody." Anjali snickered. "Plus, he's not little. He's actually bigger than you."

Joe snorted. "*Your* brother?"

"Believe it or not, he's six-foot-two and likes to work out. He takes after our great-grandfather."

"Okay, so beating him until he sees the light is out."

"Also, aren't you going to be a surgeon?" she asked, severely. "You can't risk your hands."

"Anything for my *sundari,*" he said, huskily.

After a surprised moment, she asked, "What did you call me?"

"Sundari," he repeated. "It means beautiful woman in Malayalam language. My mother was Malayali."

"I know what sundari means." It was the same in many Indian languages. "You think I'm beautiful?"

Joe guffawed. "All the way from the tips of your hair to your toes. And yes, I've looked below the neck. I've just been careful to do it from far away with no one near. Didn't want the gang spotting any problems downstairs." He waited for it to sink in. One... two...

A tickled giggle. Then, "You really have?"

"Hell, yeah." He growled. "I could write an essay on your—"

"Nuh-huh. No essays. Lovers are supposed to write poetry for each other."

"Says who?"

"Says me," she said, firmly. "And Shakespeare. Haven't you read *Romeo and Juliet?*"

"Is that the one where the dude kills himself when he thought the chick did?"

"Joooeee."

Laughing, he quoted, "'Did my heart love till now? Forswear it sight! For I ne'er saw true beauty till this night.'"

She hissed, triumphantly. "You *have* read it."

"Yeah," he admitted. "I used to sit in Dr Ram's library for hours. Jules Verne was my favourite, but I did spend one entire summer with the works of Shakespeare and Tagore."

"I *adore* Tagore," she said, immediately.

"I thought you might." Joe adjusted himself on the towel-pillow, keeping a careful eye on the dog. It was now close enough to telegraph the smell of wet fur. Rabid stray dogs were not unknown in Goa. Joe was vaccined to the max

131

given his work in xenotransplantation research, but he still didn't fancy getting bit.

"What does that mean?" Anjali asked. "How could you possibly know?"

"Because, Miss Joshi, you're a refined chick... art, literature, classical music. Naturally, you'd like Tagore."

"Oh, naturally," she said, her tone snippy. "Talk about assuming things."

Grinning, he said, "I'm not wrong, am I? My younger brother is called Romeo, by the way. Actually, my stepmother named all three of her kids after famous lovers—Devdas, Romeo, and Laila."

"So cute."

"You realise all those famous love stories end in tragedy?"

"You have no appreciation for romance," she accused, sniffing.

"I do, too. I'm very romantic." He leered. Unfortunately, there was only the mangy dog to see.

Anjali giggled. "Prove it. Write me a poem."

"I could borrow one from Sid's collection. I'll just tell him it's for a girl I want to impress. He wouldn't mind."

With a sound somewhere between a snort and a laugh, she said, "*I* would. I want you to write me a real poem, rhyme and rhythm and all. You said you'd do anything for me. Plus, isn't it your birthday next month?"

"Heh? Sundari, you're supposed to give *me* a gift on my birthday."

"I already have something planned."

"Oh, yeah? What?"

"I was going to ask you... you think you can return to Delhi one day early? I... umm... don't want the gang to see my gift. It's meant only for you to see. Kinda personal."

Only for his eyes? An image of her clad in a giant red bow and nothing else popped into his mind. One small tug at the end of the bow, and it would slither to the floor, leaving her body completely bare. *Jesus!* In less than a second, his groin was primed to explode. "*How* personal?" His voice came out sounding strangled.

"Not what you're thinking," she said, snickering.

"Damn." Her correction did nothing to deflate any of his body parts. Tone still thick, he charged, "You did that on purpose, you little tease."

"Refined enough for you?"

He should've known. He'd seen the rage in her eyes the night of the New Year's party. If it hadn't been for his remorse at having teased her, he would've recognised the wildness concealed by her grace and polish. "Evil woman," he said, wanting all of it—the elegance *and* the stormy abandon, waiting to be unleashed. "Me likey." When her delighted laughter subsided, he asked, "Since we've ruled out you in lingerie, what *am* I getting for my birthday?"

"Nuh-huh. You'll have to wait and see. And since you didn't give me any special gifts for *my* birthday, I want a poem from you before our celebration."

"Wasn't your birthday a week before we met?" Joe asked. Her eighteenth.

"Doesn't change the fact you didn't get me a gift."

"Heh... how would I... you're gonna drive me crazy, aren't you? Okay, I'll have your poem ready before we get back to Delhi." He yawned and took a quick glance at the time on the phone. *Oh, shit.* He'd spent two hours talking to her. If they continued this, he was going to go run out of minutes within a couple of weeks. "Got to go now," he said.

"Umm... okay. I'll be on Facebook tomorrow."

"'Goodnight, goodnight,'" he quoted. "'Parting is such sweet sorrow—'"

"Your own," she insisted, laughing. "Not Sid's, not Shakespeare's." With the smacking sound of a kiss, she hung up.

Joe stood and dusted the sand from his person, turning at the low whimper from the dog. It was also standing. Correction: it was tottering. Joe moved backwards, tilting his head to see the pup better in the dull light of the full moon. The white and brownish-orange patches of colour on the fur were evident enough, but the hind leg had a dark stain on it. Blood, of course. Anger swelled. "Bastards," he muttered. The world was full of them, the cruel kind who liked to throw stones at stray animals.

Towel slung over a shoulder, he was almost out of sight of the dog when he heard the same low whimper. With a muttered curse, Joe turned back and wrapped the sand-coated towel around the quivering animal. There was no resistance.

"Don't bite me," Joe warned.

Half an hour later, he was padding as quietly as he could through the dark living room of the tiny apartment in Mapusa the D'Acostas called home. It was way past midnight, and the rest of the family would've long gone to bed. Kneeling on the cracked tiles of the only bathroom, Joe washed the pup's wound with soap and water. The towel was now wrapped around the animal's neck, serving as buffer zone between its teeth and Joe's hand. The beast wasn't pretty, its ribs almost poking through the skin and its countenance mean, but the yips and whines sounded tired and scared rather than aggrieved. Finally, damp dog tucked under one arm and a bowl of milk in the other hand, Joe manoeuvred between the plastic furniture cluttering the living room to the room he shared with his brothers. The barred window was left wide open to let air in. The streetlamp outside was working for once, throwing Dev and

Romeo into silhouettes on their bed. Romeo was practically falling off one side. Joe's bed was set against the opposite wall. At twenty-two, he got his own.

Joe placed the pup and the bowl on the floor and waved away a buzzing fly. "This will have to do. Tomorrow, you'll have to go back to doing what you did before." Which was to say, it would again be begging from shopkeepers and scrounging through garbage piles.

There was a sudden flash of pink and the wet slide of a rough tongue across Joe's hand. The pup's eyes... they were so pathetically grateful, almost disbelieving that he was in this safe, dry place.

"I get ya," Joe muttered. Somehow, they both seemed to have wandered into a realm beyond the circumstances of their birth. The animal at least wasn't here under false pretences. Joe had yet to tell Anjali about his background— his family history. Each time they talked, he hesitated to bring it up. What if afterwards, there were no more phone calls? He couldn't put it off much longer. She deserved to make an informed decision about where she was going with him. She needed to consider how her parents would react if they heard about their daughter's romance with Joseph D'Acosta.

How would *his* family react? Dev and Romeo would be the dorky idiots they always were around girls, and Laila would be tickled as she usually was by the idea of romance. Their mother—Joe's stepmother—would squeal and clap and leap ahead to planning a wedding without understanding why Joe was worried. With his index finger, Joe scratched his chin. *Dammit, old man,* he muttered at the memory of Dr Ram. *Where are you when I need someone to talk to?* Yeah, right. As though Joe could've marched into the Joshi mansion in Fontainhas and announced his intention to pursue Anjali.

Dr Ram always said the Joshis as a clan didn't believe in ostentatious displays of wealth. Luxury needed to be understated. Very *déclassé* to show off your good fortune, and it inspired negative feelings in others. The one time he'd forgotten it... with a sigh of profound regret, Dr Ram would fall silent.

It didn't matter how modest the Joshis were about their money. One look around the living room, and Joe would see stark evidence of the differences between him and Anjali—in class, in wealth, in family background. He would have no reason left to pursue her; his libido would shrivel into nothingness.

He eyed the pup, now busy slurping milk. It would've been a heck of a lot easier if he and Anjali were born dogs. No dog ever worried about falling in love when he didn't mean to or about impressing the parents. Canine romance seemed very simple. Basically: *Let's hump.* Wherever they pleased, whenever they felt like it. Dogs never griped about poor timing.

If Anjali had come into Joe's life a few years down the line, he could've let himself follow her to where his mind was telling him this was going. He could've walked up to her parents and introduced himself as Dr D'Acosta, transplant surgeon, someone respected by society. Not Joe D'Acosta, former charity boy and current tutor who did things like counting the minutes left on his phone plan. By the time Anjali completed her MBBS course, he would be a senior resident at least, pursuing subspecialisation in urology with focus on kidney transplants. He'd already have his general surgery completed and the ability to earn a decent paycheck even if he'd instead chosen to study further. Perhaps that would be enough. If he could persuade her to keep things quiet until then...

Chapter 15

Present day

Shock reverberated through Rishi's mind. *Hide,* screamed his psyche as though Joe were a terrifying ghost from a nightmare. But Rishi's feet were rooted to the mosaic tiles lining the long, narrow corridor in the Joshi Charity Clinic. At the end of it was the CEO's office—Anjali's office. The door remained closed, but even if she suddenly popped out, Rishi didn't think he could look away from the man to his front. The square-rimmed glasses on Joe's nose were new, and the restlessness Rishi was used to seeing on his flatmate's face was no longer there, but otherwise, there was no real change. Joe was staring equally as intently, his eyes wide with every bit as much shock.

The moustachioed secretary sitting at the desk next to the closed door frowned. "Who are you?" he barked at Rishi.

"You were supposed to wait in the lobby," exclaimed the woman in pink scrubs, the one who'd said she'd check with Anjali's secretary if Rishi actually had an appointment with her as he claimed. The pink scrub girl sniffed. "He says he's here to meet Dr Anjali, but I think he's drunk."

"Yeah," agreed the secretary, coughing. "I can smell the fumes from here."

"I'm not drunk," Rishi enunciated, forcing his eyes away from his former flatmate. "Two or three drinks... four, maybe... I am *not* drunk." He glanced at the mutt next to Joe's feet. Its fur was white and brown, but there was plenty of grey around the muzzle. If the animal had been an elderly male of the human kind instead of canine, its face alone would've earned it the title of the meanest crank in the neighbourhood. "You can let that dog in here, but not me?"

"Emotional support animal," corrected the secretary, his dry tone broadcasting his scepticism at the owner's claim.

"Scher doesn't reek of feni," Joe snapped. "You do."

The pressure within Rishi's chest skyrocketed. "You," he snarled, "stay the hell away from her."

Lips twisting into an ugly sneer, Joe asked, "Like you stayed away from my girlfriend?"

"What?" asked the secretary, mouth open in confusion.

Neither Joe nor Rishi answered the secretary. "Girlfriend?" Rishi mocked. "After you showed her very clearly you didn't need her?" Not like Rishi needed her. His heart stumbled over a beat before pounding hard against his ribs. Joe couldn't be allowed to see her. Anjali was supposed to return home to Delhi... if she didn't... *everything* would be ruined. The bones of Rishi's thoracic cage seemed to stretch, sending agonising pain shooting all over his body. His vision took on a dark hue. His muscles bunched.

There was a soft growl from the dog. It was now on all fours, hackles up, lips drawn to show fangs.

The pink scrub girl screamed. The secretary stood in a hurry, the chair clattering to the floor. "Security," he bellowed.

Rishi was too angry to give a damn about the dog. All his hopes... his family, his career... he was about to get it all back, and then, this. Baring his own teeth, he hissed.

"Calm down," said Joe, and he bent to pat the dog. The half-bitten left ear twitching, it obeyed Joe's command and returned to its position on its haunches. "Scher is an old man now," Joe assured the rest. "He's not going to hurt anyone."

"I don't care how old he is," shouted the secretary. "Get him out of the building."

The door to the CEO's office opened. "What's going on here?" asked Anjali, her sweet, strong voice tinged with annoyance. Clad in a navy capri business suit and matching stiletto heels with her dark brown hair tied in a neat chignon, she looked more a business executive than a doctor. "Joe, stop bothering my staff. I already told them I can't see you today." Her eyes fell on Rishi. "Oh, for God's sake. You, too?" She slapped a hand to her forehead. "This is all I need right now."

"You *know* him?" asked the secretary.

"I'm her husband," announced Rishi, triumphantly.

"I'm her boyfriend," added Joe, mumbling "used to be" almost under his breath.

The secretary and the pink scrub girl—apparently struck dumb by the revelations—scrutinised the other three. There were a few more onlookers now, mostly employees from their attire.

"Ex," corrected Anjali, her teeth clenched. She pointed a finger at Rishi. "*Ex*-husband." Turning to Joe, she added, "*Ex*-boyfriend."

"Ex-dog?" asked someone, prompting a giggle from the small crowd.

Anjali quelled the mockery with a hard stare. "Get in here," she snapped at Rishi and Joe. "Him, too," she said, pointing at the dog.

The secretary followed the two men in. "Are you sure about this, madam?" he asked. "What if they..." He eyed Joe and Rishi. "Just yell if they start a fight. I'll be right outside."

"Trust me, Chandekarji," said Anjali, her tone dry. "Neither one is going to throw a punch. They're surgeons. Can't afford to hurt their hands."

"*He* isn't," Rishi mumbled. Joe never completed his course. No one in the suite paid any mind to Rishi's correction, not even Joe who was close enough to have heard.

"What about the dog?" asked the secretary.

"Scher won't hurt anyone," insisted Joe.

"I'll be all right," said Anjali, and hustling the secretary out, she closed the door to the suite.

"You don't look like an anaesthesiologist, anymore," Rishi remarked, eyeing her pantsuit. "Anaesthesiologists should be in scrubs."

"I didn't ask for your opinion," Anjali said, moving a bundle of papers from a chair and dumping it on the floor. "Anyway, I'm not here as an anaesthesiologist. I'm the administrator. The CEO. And this—" She waved a hand around. "—is my office."

For a CEO suite, it wasn't much. With the fluorescent lamps and the large windows on the far wall, the room was brightly lit, but besides that, it looked like a standard-issue government office. There was a desk with a computer and a couple of phones, and the wall on the right was lined by empty shelves. Crumbling folders and a few thick medical tomes were piled on the floor.

"What are you doing to this place?" Joe asked, sounding bemused. His dog made straight for the air-conditioning unit rumbling noisily below the windows, sticking its tail up to enjoy the cold draught on its hind end.

"Digitising administrative records," Anjali explained, dragging two chairs in front of the desk. Almost to herself, she muttered, "I'm no computer expert, but this is the new millennium. We don't *have* to keep losing paperwork."

Joe pointed at a spot on the wall above the air-conditioning unit. "Dr Ram used to have a brass plaque here." Sounding alarmed, he asked, "You didn't throw it away, did you?"

Anjali nodded. "Primum non nocere." The first duty of every physician— above all, to do no harm. "Beautiful engraving. No, I haven't thrown it away. It's at the restorer's."

"Ha... ha... haaatchoo." Rishi sneezed into his shoulder. "This place is dusty."

"You're free to leave," Anjali said, her tone extra sweet.

"You're mean," he complained.

Anjali frowned. "How much did you drink?"

"One glass," Rishi mumbled. "Feni."

Walking around the room, Joe said, "He said four before. Dr Ram liked to do things the old-fashioned way. He preferred paper records."

"Dr Ram isn't here," Anjali said. "*I* am the CEO now. I prefer electronic records and letting nurses wear comfortable clothes instead of those ridiculous outfits men like to look at. And no one's going to pinch anyone's bottom."

"Heh?" asked Rishi.

Shooting Anjali a puzzled look, Joe continued his tour of the room.

"Where are you going—" In two quick strides, she was at the wall on the left, barricading the two closed doors there. "That's my private space. You're not allowed in."

Joe held up both hands. "Just curious. Dr Ram used one of the side rooms to rest. The second one was supposed to be for lunch and such, but he let me study there."

Anjali inclined her head. "It's being used at this time, and I don't want you barging in. Besides, I didn't call you here to give you a nostalgia tour. I was simply trying to stop you and Rishi from embarrassing me in front of my staff. I already have problems with them on top of the issue with the pol—" Abruptly stopping, she bit her lip as though just remembering something. Then, she tilted her chin up. "Sit down, Joe. You, too, Rishi. Say what you came to say, then leave. This is my place of work. I'm sure neither of you would tolerate it if I showed up at your office and threw myself a tantrum. I expect you to extend me the same courtesy. After today, there will be an automatic order to call the cops if either of you is spotted on the premises without an express invitation from me. Is that clear?"

Like Rishi, Joe was staring at her, open-mouthed. "You *are* tough." He leered. "Me likey."

Anjali shot him an incredulous look. "Sit down," she repeated her command, waiting at the closed doors on the left until both Joe and Rishi were in chairs. Walking around to the other side of the desk, she settled into her own fabric-covered swivel chair. "You have five minutes each."

Rishi didn't need five minutes. "I came to take you home," he stated, baldly.

Anjali raised an eyebrow. "*Bas?*" she asked, querying if that was all Rishi wanted. There was a tinge of humour in her voice.

"Yes." He should've said something more, pretty words to melt her heart, but all of a sudden, Rishi was drained. He didn't know if he could muster the energy to get up from the chair, let alone fake emotions he didn't feel. "Anju, we're a family. Divorce won't change the fact."

Almost imperceptibly, her gaze went to the closed doors on the left wall. "We've been over this so many times," she said, glancing back. "Once again, my answer's no. And I don't want to discuss this further in front of a third person."

With a mocking laugh, Joe asked, "What's there I don't know already? He needed you for cover and somehow convinced you to agree. It took you this long to figure out it was a mistake."

"Shut the hell up," said Rishi, anger breaking through fatigue. "You're nobody in this discussion. You didn't even know we were getting divorced until last week."

Elbows on the table, Anjali rested her forehead on linked hands. "Rishi—"

"I didn't," Joe admitted. "After I heard you got married, I tried my best to keep away from any news of you and her. I stayed as far away as I could from this clinic. Now that I do know..." He stopped, looking uncertain. "Anju, I came here to talk to you. Only to you. Please? If not today, I'll come back anytime you want, anywhere you want."

"For what?" Rishi asked. One breath. Two breaths. *Don't let panic take over.* All Rishi needed to do was get rid of the interloper. Then, he could confess to Anjali what was going on in his life. He would *have* to confess.

Thanks to Joe, Anjali was not in a mental place where Rishi could tempt her back to Delhi with the pleasant life they used to have, and the reason he'd given before their marriage no longer existed. The law had changed, and Rishi could no longer be branded a criminal for his sexuality. No one could take his medical licence away merely for being gay. Anjali would want to know what else the blackmailer had on him. She'd be disgusted but wouldn't hang him out to dry. She couldn't. There was their family to consider. She'd return to Delhi and use her parents' clout to help him get rid of the blackmailer. Rishi's parents—Papa and Ma—were old now. They didn't know anything about the blackmailer, but the divorce was killing them. Surely, Anjali wouldn't break their hearts by refusing to return. Rishi would once again be the beloved son of the Rastogi family. Everything would go back to normal as soon as Joe vanished from their lives. "You think you can talk her into leaving me and our family so you can take up with her again?"

"She has *already* left you," snapped Joe. His dog whined as though in agreement. "If she chooses to 'take up' with me, it will be none of your bloody business."

"Shh," said Anjali, her eyes again going to the closed doors on the left wall. "Can you both please keep it down?"

Pushing his chair back, Rishi stood. "Hell, yeah, it's my business. I won't let you win this round, Joe. I won't allow Anju to let a callous bastard like you back into her life and ruin our family."

"You won't *allow* me?" asked Anjali, her tone dangerously low.

Rishi could feel his face heating. "I didn't mean it the way it sounded."

"Doesn't matter even if you did mean it," Joe taunted, hooking an ankle over a knee and leaning back in his chair. "It ain't up to you, jackass. You keep talking about family, but you're not her family. You're only an ex. An ex who wasn't even a real husband. I was actually her boyfriend. If she's willing to gimme a second chance, I'll take it."

143

Only an ex? Rishi stared. Then, he grinned. "You don't know. She hasn't told you." He turned to Anjali. Her face was pale and rigid, and her chair... it was swivelled to keep her back to the doors on the left, almost as though she were getting ready to physically prevent anyone from going into those rooms. "Is he in there?" Rishi asked.

"What are you talking about?" Joe asked in irritation. "Is who in there?"

Hands on the edge of the desk, Anjali heaved herself up. "Rishi, stop—"

He couldn't stop. Victory. Beautiful, beautiful victory was within reach. All he needed to do was grab the weapon and plunge it into his enemy's heart. "I might only be a fake husband, but you're still going to lose," Rishi snarled.

"Stop, Rishi," Anjali said. "I'm warning you. Let *me* tell him—"

"Oh, no, darling. The pleasure will be all mine." Relishing every bit of the confusion on Joe's face, every note of trepidation in Anjali's voice, Rishi said, "Real boyfriend or not, you won't win with a mother against her son. *My* son."

For a moment, Joe merely looked puzzled. Then, his colour changed, healthy flush draining out of the tanned skin. "Son?" he parroted. He glanced at Anjali. "You have a son?"

Eyes stiffly fixed on Joe, she said, "I... yes. I would've told you—"

In one quick move, he was out of his chair, staring hard at the doors on the left wall. "You have a son," Joe mumbled, voice shaky. "*That's* why you said at the café someone was waiting for you." Face still ashen, he snapped his fingers. "Scher." Joe wheeled around and strode out of the suite with the dog padding arthritically behind.

The door to the suite swung shut. Rishi blinked. He'd won? This easily? The sonuvabitch was out of his way. He could take Anjali and their child home. With her guarding his back, no damned blackmailer was going to get near him. No one could snatch his life away—his family, his identity as a surgeon, everything making him who he was. Laughing exultantly, he turned to Anjali.

Her eyes... they were so stark against the pale skin. Lips trembling, she was still looking at the door to the suite as though hopelessly yearning for Joe's return.

Rishi bit down on a pang of regret. "I'm sorry, Anju. Maybe I shouldn't have done that."

"Get out," she said, turning away.

"C'mon... he should've known... we were married."

Shoulders heaving on a shuddering breath, she said, "It wasn't the way to tell him, and you know it. In all the years we've been married, I've hated many things about our life together, but I've never hated you. Get out now before I start."

"We need to talk," Rishi said, urgently. He had to tell her about the blackmailer. The situation wasn't the same from all those years ago when she agreed to marry him. This time, she wouldn't be saving only Rishi from ruin. Their baby's future was at stake. As parents, he and Anjali couldn't let their personal desires get in the way of their responsibilities, be it her dreams of a lost love or his longing to stop pretending to be someone he wasn't. "There's something—"

"*I don't care!*"

Rishi took an involuntary step back. Anjali was shouting at him? The woman he knew all these years was too proper to shout at *anyone*, even the husband she was in the process of divorcing. It was Joe. Had to be. She'd never restrained herself in front of Joe, and the moment they met again, she'd stopped caring about the rest of the world. She'd stopped caring about Rishi, about their baby. Darkness rushed into the periphery of his vision. If she refused to help him... *no.* He couldn't lose everything over one stupid mistake from years ago. Only one mistake, born out of desperation.

Part VI

Chapter 16

"Thanks, Dev," said Anjali, struggling up from the chair in the manager's office at Café Ishq. It wasn't easy to do with a five-month-old strapped to her chest in a baby carrier. "I don't need anyone to go with me. Just point me towards Joe's hiding spot."

Dev D'Acosta, Joe's brother, scratched his chin. "Will do." For the hundredth time since walking into the café and asking to speak to him, Anjali thought how like Joe he looked except for the peachy complexion. Dev's mother had been a Kashmiri Muslim while Joe's skin tone was a mix from his Portuguese-Indian father and his Malayali mother. Dev studied her and the baby as intently. "You know about bhai's... I mean, Joe's hiding spot?"

Anjali smiled. "He's mentioned it a few times, and you said he was at the beach, so..."

Outside the door of the café, Dev straightened the board which proclaimed the name of the place. "You wanna come by later on?" he asked, tone carefully casual. "My other brother and our sister will be here."

Meet Joe's family? There was a time she'd begged him to let her. Even now, her heart leapt at the idea. "I... umm..."

"My brother's a paediatrics resident," Dev said, eyeing the baby. "You can't beat the company, and I can tell you the food's good. Michelin three-star."

The expression on his face... Joe used to brag about the surgeries he'd scrubbed in for with the same smug look. Fingertips to her mouth, Anjali smothered a laugh. "I'll keep that in mind. Lemme talk to Joe first." *If* he still wanted to talk to her. The way he'd simply walked out after learning about her child... it could've been from the shock, but she needed to know for sure.

She was halfway to the rocks Dev pointed her towards when the baby gurgled.

"Shh, sweetie," she crooned, dropping a kiss on the soft, fuzzy hair on his crown. He wasn't crying, simply startled by the sea breeze and probably puzzled by his mother's decision to go trudging along the sandy beach at sunset with him. They were dressed in matching white Mommy & Me tees over her denim cut-offs and his fresh diaper. She'd placed him in front-facing position, and his little head was bobbing this way and that way, taking in the crowd and the music and the smell of peanuts. "Look at the pretty colours," she said. The bright pink sun was sinking rapidly into the blue-grey sea, streaking the sky a wild palette of warm hues. Perhaps the heavens were the canvas of some artist who in a fit of mad genius splashed purples and reds and oranges all across.

"Guh," said the baby.

Tucking a flying strand of hair behind her ear, Anjali asked, "Can you say Mama? Ma-ma." Five months was a little too early, but it didn't hurt to try.

"Guh," the baby repeated, stubbornly.

She chuckled. "Man of few words, aren't you? Just like your Vikram Uncle." Flip-flops slapping against her feet with each step, she made her way to the cliffs at the far end. A couple of tourists were wandering around, but they seemed to be headed towards the crowd and the noise, not the relative seclusion offered by the rock formations.

There. The gap between the two large boulders came into view. Running the tip of her tongue over her suddenly dry upper lip, she stepped into the space.

With a soft woof, the dog alerted his master to the presence of intruders. The man clad in black swimming trunks sat up. Joe's eyes swept over Anjali, lingering on the infant strapped to her chest.

The baby kicked his legs and said, "Guh," once again, but to the dog, not the man.

"Is there room for two more?" Anjali asked. When Joe inclined his head, she padded over, and keeping a hand on his sun-warmed shoulder, she lowered herself to the ground. The dog settled on Joe's other side, his head on his paws but eyes wide open and darting from Anjali to the baby.

She didn't speak. Neither did Joe. They sat in silence until the sun sank into the sea, and the half-moon cast a silvery glow over the water. A warm breeze drifted around them, almost hypnotic in its effect. Resting his back against her chest, the baby grabbed his bare foot to suck on his big toe, a sure sign he was preparing to nap. Somewhere, a cricket chirped, causing the dog to whine in annoyance.

"What's his name?" Joe finally asked.

"We haven't gotten around to a naming ceremony yet." In the Maharashtrian tradition, there was a lot of family involvement in the naming of a child, and the Rastogis declined to cooperate until Anjali toed the line and withdrew the divorce petition. Had the baby's father been willing, she would've done the ceremony without the grandparents, but... she and Rishi needed to figure something out. Anjali made a vague gesture with her hand, reluctant to explain further at the moment. "Did you think I'd simply waste away over you? Are you really that egotistical?"

Joe shifted, restlessly. "No. I knew I had no right to expect anything. You moved on."

"With a gay man," she said, mocking herself. "You must have been happy."

"Believe it or not, there were a couple of moments here and there when I hoped *you* were happy with the jackass."

"Of course, you did," she taunted. Hot tears stung her eyes. "Why not? Easy to do when you didn't care what happened to me."

Joe turned to face her, but he was only a silhouette, his expression masked by the shadows. "Not true. Anju, you have no idea how much I cared. Some nights, I'd lay awake and pray you were hurting for me like I was for you. In the morning, I'd remember it was all my own doing, and I'd beg for the strength to move on. I'd tell myself I wanted *you* to move on. It took me years to accept I'd lost you for good. Then... you walked into the café."

Throat hurting from anger, Anjali taunted, "You walked *out* as soon as you learned Rishi and I have a baby. Why? You claim you wanted me to be happy, but you don't like the idea I actually might have been happy enough with another man to make a child with him? Or did you simply want *me* to chase after you?"

She'd leapt at the hint and raced in pursuit, going to the extent of cancelling her plan to work late. The upcoming meeting with INTERPOL about the clinic's purchases of cheap medicines from unlicensed vendors, the hostility of the staff towards their new CEO... she'd put everything aside this evening only for Joe.

"*No.*" Joe's hand came up to stroke the baby's head. "I never meant for you to... it simply didn't occur to me before... I didn't realise until today it wasn't only you I lost. He could've been mine."

Her heart squeezed hard. Grief, pain, fury... a short, guttural scream erupted from Anjali's chest. She slapped away his hand and scrambled up. "You *lost?*" she asked, voice trembling. "You *threw away* everything we had." The love, the passion, the friendship, the trust... he'd tossed it all aside. "For *what?*"

Chapter 17

Summer 2007

"Five thousand euros?" Anjali asked into the phone, shoving aside the clothes in her closet. She needed accessories to match her outfit for this last get-together at the Taj Hotel with her old friends from high school. The pink, ostrich leather purse lying on its side on the shelf at the back would do nicely. She'd bought the Hermes bag on her last trip to L.A. to visit her cousins and never had a chance to use it. "Is that the usual for a moonlighting job?"

"Are you kidding me?" Joe asked. "Haven't you checked how much AIIMS pays interns and postgraduate residents? Five thousand euros would be about four months' stipend for me. I don't get it. Why would someone offer a trainee surgeon so much cash for one weekend of moonlighting?"

Anjali eyed the purse in her hand. She didn't remember exactly how much she paid for it, only that it was way more than the dollar equivalent of five thousand euros. Downplaying their wealth was practically a religious edict for the Joshis, but understated indulgences cost even more money. She tossed the purse back onto the shelf, next to the oil sketch she'd worked on all summer. "Maybe the agent heard how good you are."

Laughing, Joe said, "I wish I could believe it. I know I'm good, and I go to the O.R. as much as I can, but I haven't officially started my training. Every surgeon in there is more experienced than me."

"Ask the agent next time he calls," she suggested.

"Nah," said Joe. "I'm not going to bother. The whole thing reeks of a scam. The only reason they're making such crazy promises is they know they're not going to keep it. I'll be lucky if I get five thousand in Indian currency."

"You're probably right. Let's talk about something more pleasant. Are you keeping the puppy?"

"Only until his leg heals," Joe said, firmly. "My sister named him Scheherazade."

Anjali smiled. After two weeks, Joe was still pretending the dog's leg hadn't healed. "The *Arabian Nights* princess? Didn't you tell her he's the wrong gender?"

"By the time we realised what she did, the dog was already answering to the name. We're trying to change it to Scher."

"Princess to tiger?" Anjali asked, laughing.

"He has the spirit of one," Joe defended. "We... I mean, my brothers are working on getting him to answer to it. I'll be leaving soon." Voice turning husky, he added, "Three more days, sundari, and we'll meet in the flat. Are you going to give me the surprise you promised?"

She bit back a giggle. That's what *he* thought. After they decided to get to Delhi a day ahead of the rest, she asked Rishi for help in getting her surprise ready. It would be waiting at the flat when Joe walked in. "When *I* make a promise, I try my best to keep it. Joe, I'm so glad you didn't take the hostel room."

"Damned difficult to sneak a girl in," Joe agreed, laughing. "Plus, Rishi didn't get a room." As a resident of Delhi, he would've been at the bottom of the list for post-graduate room allotment on campus. "He told his family he needed to stay closer to AIIMS. They're not very... anyway, it worked out." The two men were back to sharing a flat.

"Hey, did you forget *your* promise?" she asked. "Weren't you supposed to send me the poem before the end of summer?"

"I didn't forget. I still have a couple of days. Tell you what... it will be in your messages first thing in the morning."

She should've asked Joe for his definition of "morning." Her dinner with friends lasted past midnight, but she still woke at six to check Facebook. Nuh-huh, no poem. Not in her email, either. Refreshing the page every fifteen minutes didn't change anything. She even carried her laptop to the breakfast table, prompting curious looks from her parents. Usually, it was her brother, Vikram, the grump, who pulled stunts like that. She was just biting into buttery toast when the computer pinged.

"What in the world?" Anjali muttered, staring at the My Messages page. "It doesn't make any sense."

Joe: My sweetheart, you're like a buzzing honeybee.

You make my heart sing an interlude.

You're the yellow myna bird, showering your love on me.

None of the people in the dining room of the duplex responded. Vikram was already on his way out the front door, and only Mom and Dad were around to finish breakfast with her, but they were also in a hurry to get to work. The laptop would be company for Anjali until the evening when her family gathered for one last dinner together before she flew back to Delhi the next day. Still staring at the computer screen, she set the partly eaten toast on the plate and took a sip of the orange juice, barely noticing the cold sourness.

"Do I look yellow?" she asked. Honeybees, myna birds... what was Joe trying to say?

Dad, bald-headed and almost as short as Anjali and Mom, paused in the act of getting up from his seat to shrug on his doctor's coat. "Why? Are you feeling ill?"

Mom peered into Anjali's face. "I don't see any obvious jaundice. Any nausea or vomiting?" She extended her hands, thumbs upright. "Lemme check your eyes."

Anjali swatted away her mom's hands. "No! I don't mean I feel sick. Is my skin tone normally yellow?"

Mom tilted her head this way and that way, studying her. "You're brown as you've always been. Sharp Parsi features and nice, clear skin." Mom was mostly Parsi—Persians who'd migrated to India centuries ago to escape religious persecution following the Muslim conquest of the Middle East—and Anjali took after her. "A little pink in the cheeks. Why do you ask?"

"No reason." Anjali shrugged. "I thought I needed better makeup."

"You're my gorgeous daughter without any makeup," Dad said, warmly.

"Uh-huh," Mom said, still staring.

"C'mon, Rattan," said Dad. "We need to get to work. Don't you have surgery scheduled?"

He hustled Mom out, mumbling something about being supportive to young women so they wouldn't be insecure about their looks.

Anjali bit her lip. She might not be a ravishing beauty, but she'd been quite secure about herself until this morning and Joe's strange message. Apparently, he *liked* the fact she looked yellow. The computer pinged a second time. Oh, cool. There was a new message. Perhaps he wanted to tell her how her skinny hips and short form enthralled him.

> Joe: I cast my eyes on you, sitting on the bed, dreaming of us making love on a boat.
>
> My sweetheart, you're like a buzzing honeybee.
>
> You make my heart sing an interlude.

This at least made some sense. They hadn't even kissed yet, but she did—frequently—dream of them making love. She never imagined them on a boat, though.

> Joe: I'm not naïve. I know how to please a woman. I'm impatient for you.

Anjali growled. Seriously? This was Joe's idea of wooing her? Buzzing bees and yellow birds and bragging about his bedroom skills? Anjali blinked. Something about the imagery...

She set the glass of juice aside and pulled up the web browser. Fifteen minutes later, she was on the phone.

Two rings, and Joe's voice said, "Hello?"

"I'm gonna kill you."

"Why?" His buttery smooth voice was oh, so innocent. "You didn't like my poem?"

"*Your* poem? You just took a Tamil song and more or less translated it!" What sounded mischievous and romantic in Tamil was plain weird in English.

After a second or two, he said, "Damn. How did you figure it out?"

"I've only seen the movie like about a dozen times! I'm a huge Thalaiva fan." Rajni Kanth, a.k.a. Thalaiva, might be a mere mortal and an actor, but he was practically God to his fans.

"You are?" Joe asked, voice raised. "Me, too! Which one's your favourite?

"Some of the old—don't you change the subject, Joe D'Acosta. You sent me a plagiarised poem."

"I tried to write something new," he said, sounding disgruntled. "It wasn't as easy as I thought, and there was a deadline. I was going to confess after a day or two. Are you really angry?"

Anjali laughed. "No, it just confirmed for me you're a madman. I still think you're cute."

"I have another one if you'd like to see."

"Oh, yeah?" she asked, frowning at nothing in particular. "From which movie?"

"Not from a movie. This is an actual... er... poem."

Something in his voice... "I don't believe you."

"Check your messages." The high-pitched tone said he'd hung up.

> Joe: Shapely and graceful are your sandaled feet, and queenly your movement.
>
> Your limbs are lithe and elegant, the work of a master artist.
>
> Your body is a chalice, wine-filled.
>
> Your skin is silken and tawny like a field of wheat touched by breeze.
>
> Your breasts are like fawns, twins of a gazelle.

There was no one else in the duplex except the housekeeper, and she was in the kitchen, too far to see Joe's message. Anjali still snapped the laptop shut. God, she was sweaty. With trembling fingers, she reached for her glass and gulped more cold juice, crossing her legs for good measure. Then, she frowned. Her boobs were like fawns? And what the heck did Joe know about wheat? Like her, he was an urban creature.

Another Google search later, Anjali was again on the phone. "Seriously, Joe? Ripping off the Bible?"

He guffawed. "You know how many chicks King Solomon got with those lines?" Anjali rolled her eyes and started to ask something, but Joe interjected, "I know... it has to be my own. I'm going to email you something else. This one is all mine, I promise."

"Where did I hear that before?"

"I never said I actually created the first two. But this I did. Read it, please."

"Okaaay," said Anjali, still suspicious. "I'll call you back right away."

"No, don't. In fact, I'm gonna be off radar for a day so you have a chance to chew over things before we talk. Better yet, let's talk when we get to Delhi. I want you to be absolutely sure."

"What do you mean—"

"Bye, sundari. See you soon."

***

The pristine white façade of the church at the end of the tarred driveway shimmered under the blazing sun. The voices of the faithful inside the building reverberated out through the doors, singing *"Ave Maris Stella."* The green palms surrounding the church complex promised at least mild respite from the heat. Tossing the silent phone in his hand, Joe dropped to the ground under one of the trees.

Maybe he could turn it back on for a few minutes just to see... "Idiot," Joe mumbled. Why the hell did he ask Anjali not to call? Now, he wasn't gonna know if she weren't calling because of his request or because she was so disgusted by his story she didn't want anything more to do with him.

Brushing away the red ants crawling in the vicinity of his sandaled foot, Joe groaned. He'd told himself to back off and give her space to think about things, and that's what he was going to do. He had errands to run, anyway. Like this visit to Fr Franco, the man whose words he'd recounted in his email to Anjali—the tale of the three preteen boys who'd met on the beach when Ram Joshi, Anjali's grandfather, was a lonely kid holidaying in Goa with his parents.

Young Ram returned every summer to meet the two Portuguese-Indian lads. The three of them played, fought, fished, explored, even got drunk the first time together. Then, Franco—the oldest—heeded the divine voice in his head and went to Rome to take up priesthood. By the time he returned in 1961, Goa was liberated from Portuguese rule and joined India. Most of the D'Acostas emigrated to Europe except for Franco's cousin—Joe's grandfather—who'd somehow convinced a local lass to marry him. Franco also stayed, believing his calling was to serve the Lord's flock in India.

"Joe," called a voice, bringing him to the present.

When he looked up, the faithful were streaming out the doors of the church, some glancing curiously in his direction. Fr Franco, still clad in clerical vestments, was the one who called his name. The old priest was with one of the parishioners, the owner of a local department store chain who'd been trying to set Joe up with his daughter for years. The businessman wanted a doctor for a son-in-law, and he believed Joe could be bought. Suppressing a groan, Joe raised his index finger and put his silent phone to his ear.

Fr Franco raised a disbelieving eyebrow and glanced at the phone but soon dismissed the businessman with a friendly nod. The priest waited patiently while Joe stood and loped towards him. "You came this far," remarked Fr Franco, thankfully not saying anything about the proposed marriage/alliance. "Couldn't you just pop your head in and say a prayer?"

"Nah, I'm good," said Joe, hands raised. "If God exists, He already knows what I'm going to say. If He doesn't, what's the point?"

With a long-suffering sigh, Fr Franco said, "The last time I saw you in church was when you were in high school. For your confirmation, I believe."

Joe had already been leaning towards agnosticism and was disinclined to go through the ceremony meant to confirm his Catholic faith, but Fr Franco and Dr Ram insisted. "Thanks to your mother, you go once a year to the temple. I have my doubts about how much praying you actually do there, but maybe it will be enough to drag you across the finish line." Sudden chagrin passed over the priest's face. "Don't tell the bishop I said that." When Joe laughed, the priest chuckled, reluctantly. "Off to Delhi for another year, heh?"

"Yeah. Came to make sure you're still alive and kicking before I left."

Five minutes later, Joe was on his way out. He tugged at the collar of his tee to get *some* relief from the humid heat and glanced back at the church.

According to Fr Franco, Joe's grandfather married his grandmother in this very building. Franco hadn't yet returned from Rome, but he was the priest who baptised the baby boy born to his cousin's Goan wife. Franco was also the one who led the prayers at her funeral a week later. Thus, Joe the First—simply Joe at the time—became a single father at the age of twenty-one and the sole proprietor of the teashop he'd gotten as dowry. The near-mandatory wedding gift owed by the bride's parents had long been a curse on Indian women, but it sure came in handy for Joe the First.

Mrs Joe the First didn't have much family left, either, so the father was the only caregiver for the baby which didn't leave much time for anything else. Then, an eight-fingered American trudged down the path to the village, bringing with him a stampede of hippies. When Ram got to Goa in 1966 for one last holiday before submitting to the marriage arranged for him by his parents, there were new faces around. Gone were the staid and old Portuguese expats he was used to seeing. Most of the new arrivals were in their twenties—carefree, uninhibited, and looking for enlightenment in sex, drugs, and rock 'n' roll. There was one pretty, young thing—

Fr Franco had been red-faced and stumbling when he recited this part of the story to Joe the Third. Old Joe was apparently a good-looking guy. He wasn't expecting to lose to Dr Ram. What Ram Manohar Joshi lacked in looks, he more than made up for in wealth, and he wasn't above flashing enough of it around to entice said pretty, young thing away from the Joe the First's arms and into his bed. According to Fr Franco, Joe was enraged. He'd already turned the teashop he got as dowry into a place for the hippies to crash and had experience scamming people here and there. The one way he could see to making enough money in the little village they called home was supplying drugs to foreign visitors. The next time Ram returned, Joe would be flush with cash. Fr Franco worried constantly what Joe intended to do with the money, but the priest never found out. There was no next time.

Joe—the doctor, not the drug dealer—was thinking about second chances and how sometimes, there were none, when he landed in Delhi. Waiting for his taxi, he took a deep breath and turned on the phone. Before he could tuck it back into his pocket, it rang. He glanced at the number and murmured in relief, "Thank you."

Anjali had only one demand—that he provide details. "I thought your grandfather died in a boat accident?" she asked.

Joe the Third heaved his two battered boxes into the trunk of the taxi and slammed the lid. "Nope, not an accident. Old Joe was *found* dead in a boat... knifed or shot or something. Fr Franco didn't give me the details, only it was quite evidently not a natural death."

Ram Joshi was just a few months into his marriage, but when Fr Franco telegraphed him the news, he and his pregnant wife drove to Goa. Young Dr Ram was in shock. What had been a mere game of one-upmanship over women ended at the graveside of one of his best friends. A four-year-old boy was now an orphan.

Ram couldn't very well take the child back to Bombay without questions being raised, but he paid enough cash to the cops to cover up the details of the gruesome death so the kid wouldn't face life as the son of a murdered criminal.

Unfortunately, it didn't stop the news from spreading. "Fr Franco managed to get a local woman to foster my father," Joe the Third explained. Things were easier back then in some ways. No government to poke around and demand adoption paperwork. Dr Ram kept a close eye on the boy, ready to assist in whatever way he could to give the child a decent life. "Dad was an easy-going chap. Unfortunately, he got all the D'Acosta good looks but none of the brains."

Anjali snorted. "You had to squeeze that in there, didn't you?"

"Why not?" Joe asked, watching the streets of Delhi as the taxi sped in the direction of his flat near the AIIMS campus. Within a matter of moments, day gave way to twilight, and the streetlamps came on. "The D'Acosta genes usually include both." Only, there wasn't much of a moral compass. "Plus, didn't you say something about having the hots for me?"

"I fell for the beauty of your soul first," she claimed, grandly.

"Of course," Joe returned, grinning. "Me, too. I especially like seeing your 'soul' in the pink tee you wear all the time. Very perky."

When the laughter subsided, he talked about his mother—his Amma. "I used to call her a weirdo," he muttered.

At seventeen, she'd rebelled against her landowner father and joined a group of young people fighting for the rights of the *adivasis*—the indigenous peoples of India. She was working as a shop clerk in the state of Kerala when she met a handsome, young soldier and eloped with him, not giving two hoots for the family which disowned her. By the time she got to Goa with the smooth-talking infantryman, she was married and already pregnant. The soldier wasn't allowed to take her with him where he was stationed, so he rented her the cheapest flat he could find in Mapusa.

The infantryman returned to duty, and the girl he married found it difficult to make ends meet with the pittance he sent home. With her poor grasp of

English, no one would give her a decent job. Plus, there was the baby—Joe the Third—who didn't have anyone else to mind him while his mother was working. When she informed her disinterested husband about it, he took the easiest route available. The teashop once owned by Mrs Joe the First was mortgaged to a private bank at an exorbitant interest rate.

When Dr Ram and Fr Franco heard about it, they were exasperated but eventually decided the property would be safer with the bank than with Joe's father and made minimum payments—enough to avoid foreclosure. Once Joe the Third reached adulthood, they'd help him get it back. But the loan money soon ran out, leaving Amma and Baby Joe back in financial difficulties.

"So that's why Daadaji offered your mother a job," Anjali completed.

"Yeah." Joe chuckled. "She was highly suspicious of all rich people—including Dr Ram—but it was either the job or starvation." Amma—the quasi-Communist—was taken aback by liberal Goa. She was horrified by the free flow of alcohol, the uninhibited women on the beach, and yes, by the very concept of homosexuality. "She used to insist ghosts existed, but not gay men. That, apparently, was a *bourgeoisie* capitalist myth, invented by Westerners to deliberately degrade Indian culture. She chased me around the flat with a ruler when I called her crazy."

Tone warm, Anjali murmured, "You loved her."

Joe sighed. "Yeah... I wish you could've met her. She died when I was ten... ovarian cancer which went undiagnosed for a long time." He remembered the long days he spent at her bedside, terror quaking his insides as he watched her waste away. He remembered waking up every two hours to make sure she was still alive. He remembered weeping in one corner of the room as the Hindu priest brought in by Fr Franco gave her the last rites. "After her funeral, Dad brought my stepmother back from Kashmir. Dev was two." The salwar-clad woman with a toddler sleeping on her shoulder seemed as shocked as young Joe at the meeting.

Anjali hissed.

"No, Dad hadn't divorced Amma," Joe clarified. "That was the reason he never had enough money for Amma and me. Poor Ruksana... Dev's mom. I'm not sure if Dad told her he was already married. I think Dr Ram and Fr Franco knew what was going on... not that they ever told me so, specifically."

"Joe," Anjali sobbed.

"It was a long time ago," he assured her.

Even as it was happening, he wasn't sure what to think. Dad said the last bullet he'd taken fighting the enemy at the Indo-Pak border in Kashmir was in the hip. Since he'd put in enough years to retire, he was in Goa to stay, but to Joe, he was a near-stranger who'd appeared once or twice a year to play with him. Now, there was a woman with him, also a stranger. Was Joe supposed to care?

He remembered sitting in the backyard of the Joshi mansion in Fontainhas, silently following Mrs Ram's instructions to eat his samosa and drink the milk. Staring at the red concrete rooster, he listened obediently as Dr Ram and Fr Franco talked. Apparently, two-year-old Dev would forever be considered illegitimate if Dad didn't marry his live-in lover and adopt his own son. Dad hadn't actually talked about marrying her, but Fr Franco was adamant they do. He and Dr Ram merely wanted to make sure Joe was kept in the loop.

"I don't know how they could do it to you," Anjali whispered.

Joe shook his head. "I was all right. I mean... I was only ten, but even I could see Dad was kind of an idiot... irresponsible with other people. Which is funny because the army gave him a medal for distinguished service in the Kargil war. My stepmother was—is—a ditz, and that's putting it mildly. The kid already had a bad start in life while *I* had a decent mother until then." By the time Dev was ready to go to school with his twelve-year-old big brother, Romeo was born. Then, came Laila. "They knew how to pop out kids at regular intervals but not a clue how to take care of them. Fr Franco had to make sure all the paperwork was done. Vaccines, school, etc. Eventually, he started asking me to do everything, including the household budget."

The army pension wasn't nearly enough. Dr Ram got the charity division of the Joshi Trust to arrange a special scholarship for Joe so he could prep for the medical entrance exams as he wanted. Somewhere around then, Ram Joshi decided to retire from his private practice in Bombay and move to Goa to devote his days to the charity clinic he'd started a few years ago. Young Joe spent more and more time at the Joshi mansion, being tutored by Dr Ram on the proper use of cutlery, on high society mannerisms, on speaking English with an upper-crust accent. Dr Ram was delighted when his protégé developed an interest in literature—science fiction classics, especially. He ordered books for Joe in all the languages he could read—Goan schools taught at least three, including Portuguese. One day, the protégé caught the mentor by surprise by vowing to be a doctor like him, deferentially treated by society.

"I actually said I was going to build a bigger house." Joe chuckled at the memory. Dr Ram had stared for a while and warned Joe not to mess up his life. Ram Joshi said it frequently to Joe, even to the last day of his life. The Latin admonishment to do no harm as a physician—primum non nocere—was another of Dr Ram's favourites, but it was his advice to *every* doctor who crossed the threshold of his office with a question. "I think he was worried I'd turn out like my grandfather."

"You?" asked Anjali, tone warm. "Not a chance."

"Thanks." The old doctor *had* been worried, or he'd have helped Joe recover the old teashop from the private bank when he turned twenty-one. Even after the passing of Dr Ram, Joe wasn't particularly bothered the property was still mortgaged. Now that he was in charge of the family budget, they were managing to keep up with the minimum payments. Once he completed his training, he'd get the place back. With real estate prices in Goa having skyrocketed, the place would give the D'Acosta kids a nice cushion. Then, towards the end of his internship at AIIMS, Dad passed from a heart attack.

"Your family emergency," Anjali murmured.

It kept Joe from starting his post-graduation in surgery. After settling things in Goa, he took a job at AIIMS as the tutor in physiology. All the years he'd been Dr Ram's protégé, Joe never met his mentor's granddaughter. Not surprising since Dr Ram lived in Goa, returning to Mumbai when he felt like visiting his family. If Anjali ever visited the Joshi mansion in Fontainhas, Joe never heard of it, and *he'd* never been to Mumbai. The first time they laid eyes on each other was at the frog vivisection session. "There you have it," he said. "My story in a nutshell. Still wanna risk it with me?

After a tense second, she said, "Depends. Are you with me because I'm Daadaji's granddaughter?"

"*No.* God, no. I used to wish like hell you weren't his granddaughter. Or you were just an itch I could scratch. It would be so much easier. What he said to me the day he died... I don't know if he were warning me away from you or..." Joe stopped, feeling ludicrous. He wasn't a man prone to fantasies. Dr Ram wasn't clairvoyant to order Joe away from his granddaughter *or* to give them his blessing. "Anju, I... goddammit, I'm with you because I can't help myself. You somehow got hold of me—mind and body and soul—and won't let go."

"Good," she whispered. "Because I don't think I can get you out of my mind, either."

Joe huffed in relief. "Sundari," he called. "I can't wait to see you. What time tomorrow are you getting here?"

"How long will it take you to get to the flat?"

"Another ten minu—what do you mean 'the flat'? Anju, are you there?"

With a delicious giggle, she said, "Hurry."

***

Heart pounding, Anjali stayed in the rickety chair and listened to the bounding footsteps, the sound of the key being turned, the door squeaking open. She saw Joe—a mere shadow in the darkness—backing into the flat and lugging his two boxes. One click, and yellow light flooded the room. As was his habit outside the classroom, he was dressed in worn jeans and a faded tee with brown loafers on his feet. His hair was neatly trimmed but still a little longer than usual for doctors.

In turn, he stared at her, not even glancing at the cake on the coffee table or the thin package next to it. His gaze swept over her newly acquired bangs, her pink tank top, and the fringe denim mini, lingering leisurely on her bare legs. Inside her platform sneakers, her toes curled.

"Welcome home," Anjali whispered.

Joe took one step towards her. "Anju," he called, his smooth voice now thick.

She wasn't quite certain how it happened, but she did hear the chair clatter to the floor. Suddenly, she was trembling in his arms. His hands were wandering all over her back and hips almost as though he couldn't help himself. Clinging to his shoulders, she went on tiptoes, sobbing in frustration when she couldn't quite reach his lips.

His fingers dug into her hair, and he tilted her face up. "May I?" he asked, hoarsely.

Anjali only barely finished nodding, when his bristly jaw scraped the smooth skin of her cheek. The scent of his cologne filled her lungs, leading her mind to a sun-warmed forest where they were the only people. Soft lips touched hers—once, twice, three times, until she opened her mouth to invite him in. God, the dizzying heat. The taste of cinnamon. "Joe," she moaned into his kiss.

Suddenly, he lifted his head, leaving her quaking in unquenched thirst. Her arms went around his neck to drag him back down. She tugged at his shirt, wanting it off. Kissing her over and over, he slipped his hands under her tank top and fiddled with the strap of her bra. "You sure?" he asked.

"Yeah," she mumbled, running her lips down his jaw.

It was as if a cyclone suddenly struck the flat, stripping them of all control. Her bra snapped open. Buttons popped on his tee. The faded green fabric of his shirt ripped, her nails leaving marks on his chest. Somewhere, something crashed. Then, they were in his room, tumbling onto the twin bed.

The back of her hand struck something. There was another crash, the sound of shattering glass. She didn't care. Joe's mouth was on her neck, his hands tugging down her skirt. "Please, do something," she shrieked. There was an ache inside her only he could soothe.

With an animal snarl, he nipped the soft skin of her bare shoulder. She lifted off the mattress on an answering growl and shoved him onto his back. Laughing exultantly, he shoved her right back and loomed over her.

Then began a contest to tease and frustrate and make each other beg for mercy. His hands and mouth were everywhere, but so were hers. She tasted the salt on his skin, threw her head back and laughed when he bellowed in wild pleasure. She revelled in the musky scent of sex—on her body, on his, on the sheets, *everywhere.*

"Need you," he finally rasped, his glittering eyes boring into hers. There was the ripping sound of a condom packet. Sobbing his name over and over, she welcomed him in. They clung to each other for dear life and let the storm take them.

When Anjali woke in the darkness of the room, her heart did a little flip-flop as she realised where she was. Her back was tucked against Joe's chest, the heavy warmth of his arm holding her close. There was a thin cotton sheet pulled over both of them. In the street outside, a car honked.

Attempting to slide out of bed, she lifted his arm. "Careful," he said into her ear. "I think we broke the lampshade. There's probably glass on the floor."

"I need to—" God. Was she about to tell Joe after their wild, lampshade-breaking sex that she needed to pee? Talk about taking the magic away! "I... umm... need to use the restroom."

"You need to..." Laughter in his voice, Joe said, "All right, sundari. Get out on my side, and you should be okay. After you 'use the restroom,' it's my turn at the facilities."

Rewarding him with a light punch on his shoulder, she slid past, only to realise she didn't have a stitch on her. "My clothes," she mumbled.

"Why?" His leer was evident even in the darkness. "I think you look better this way."

"Joooeee!"

"All right, all right. Here, use this." He tugged something from underneath the pillow and tossed it to her. His torn tee.

She was still wearing it when he left the bathroom and came to the living room, clad only in his jeans. "We didn't cut the cake," she said, lighting the single candle on top.

Blowing out the candle, Joe pinched off a bit of cake between his thumb and forefinger and tasted it. "From Wenger's?" he asked, naming one of the oldest bakeries in Delhi. When she nodded, he bent to take her upper lip between his, giving her a taste of Swiss chocolate cake. "Delicious," he murmured.

"Your gift," she reminded him.

Taking the flat, twelve-by-sixteen package, Joe eyed the glossy cover. "Best sex ever certificate?"

She giggled. "Open it." He unwrapped packages as carefully as might be expected from a surgeon. Which was to say, he was driving her crazy. "C'mon," she complained, hopping from foot to foot at his side. Finally, he took out the cardboard pieces and separated them.

Joe gaped at the oil sketch of him—a nude she'd done from imagination. Now that Anjali had seen him up close and personal, she could honestly say her art closely matched the real thing. Except, in place of his equipment was a giant green frog. "Look at the size of the critter." Guffawing hard, he said, "Hope I lived up to expectations."

"More than," she said, waggling her eyebrows. "But there's always room for improvement, Dr D'Acosta."

"Oh, yeah?" Setting the sketch carefully back on the coffee table, he bent his head towards her as though to kiss. Anjali puckered her lips, only to have Joe swoop down and lift her off her feet.

"What—" The world tilted as he tossed her over his shoulder. "Don't drop me, you crazy caveman," she squealed. "Ahh..." She fell back onto the bed. "You could've at least carried me in romantically."

"I can do romance." He climbed onto the mattress on all fours and stared intently at the corner of her mouth. "Damn. Your birthmark... it's bloody tempting." Bending down, he proceeded to kiss the mark over and over. Soft, sweet kisses and whisper-light touches. The longing in his eyes and his murmurs of love.

It was as though they were on a cloud, thunder and lightning all around but still floating in the sky. Slowly, they drifted back to the planet... a shrieking sound penetrated her consciousness. "What's that?" she asked, drowsily.

"The alarm clock," said Joe, yawning. He turned on his side and groped around on the floor. The noise stopped. "I think I knocked it off the nightstand."

When Anjali woke again, it was to the aroma of coffee. The only view through the narrow window was of the wall of the next building and the graffiti on it, but the night was clearly done. Hair dishevelled and mouth twisted into a happy grin, Joe was still at her side. Still asleep. Anjali glanced at the closed door. The coffee... who...

She pulled on Joe's tee over her denim mini, but the tear she'd made on the shirt left most of her back exposed. It would have to do; half her clothes were still in the living room. Silently, she crept to the kitchen.

"'Morning," said Rishi, handing her a cup.

✳✳✳

"Sorry, darling," said Rishi. "I know I'm not supposed to be here." When she asked him to let her into the flat, she'd made him promise not to return until two nights after. "But I had no choice."

Yawning loudly, Joe appeared behind her. "Problems in the family?" he asked, tone matter of fact.

Jerkily, Rishi nodded. Yes, there were problems, but not the kind Joe imagined. Anjali's phone calls to Rishi hadn't gone unnoticed. He'd said something about her not being sure of a future together, but it didn't stop the Rastogis from making plans—his oldest sister, especially. She'd found out more about the prospective Rastogi *bahu*—daughter-in-law—and was apparently in awe. Ma and Papa, not so much. Arrey, wealthy and well-connected girl or not, Anjali would be getting their precious son for a life partner. She and her parents needed to be grateful.

When Ma said something about educated moms being important in ensuring the IQ of future Rastogis, Rishi knew he needed to get out. One more day, and he'd go crazy and scream the truth. He'd tell his parents he'd never been Anjali's boyfriend, how he was damned well not going to change his mind about being gay. He'd again be tossed out of the family.

"I got here late last night," he said aloud. Glancing between Anjali and Joe, he asked, "Is this going to be a regular deal? In that case, I need to order industrial-strength earplugs."

Anjali's face turned bright red.

Joe simply smirked. "You do that."

"Also, your brother told Kiki you're already back in Delhi," Rishi said to Joe. "She's on her way here. Apparently, there's been some news on the job front she wants to tell us about. Unless you don't mind the rest of the gang knowing, you'd better clean up the stuff in the living room before she gets here."

"No way," said Anjali, looking dismayed. "They'll all have their opinions, and Sid... I don't even want to imagine what kind of poem he'd write."

"I'll put the cake away," said Joe.

"I'll get my clothes—" Anjali started. "Oh, no," she wailed, clapping a hand to her mouth and eyeing Rishi with horror. "The sketch. You *saw* it?"

"Darling," Rishi said, laughing. "I'm doing my best to unsee it."

Chapter 18

Present day

Anjali turned one of the panels of the Venetian blinds in her office side-to-side, her eyes on the employee parking lot outside but not really seeing any of it. What happened to those three people in the flat? How did their lives end up careening in such wildly different directions from what they imagined that morning in Delhi?

"Dr D'Acosta's practice..." Behind Anjali, the secretary continued talking, reciting whatever information he'd gathered on Joe's personal and professional life.

After she stormed away from him at the beach, he'd stopped trying to contact her, sending only a handwritten note with his phone number on it. Maybe she should've called him. If only for her own peace of mind, she needed answers. She needed to know why he left her, why he left the career he wanted. Anjali might have deputised her secretary to find what he could about Joe D'Acosta, but the search only led to more puzzling questions.

Perhaps she hadn't mattered as much to him as she'd imagined. Perhaps he'd decided making money was more important than his dream of being a transplant surgeon. He'd landed on his feet according to Anjali's secretary—a beach restaurant in Goa, a thriving medical practice in a tourist town, and an eye-catching home set on a clifftop. While Joe might be driving a beat-up old Ambassador car, Anjali recognised the smartwatch on his wrist as one of the high-end brands. How did he manage it all? *When* did he do it? Eleven years ago, he and his family packed up and left Goa; when had they returned to rebuild their lives?

Joe once said something to her about a teashop owned by his family, but she assumed it was somewhere near Mapusa where he used to live, where the Joshi Charity Clinic was—not Vagator, where beach property the size of the café could fetch bids as high as a million American dollars. Still, he'd somehow made enough money to wrench it back from the private bank which held the mortgage, and his brother Dev created a wildly successful restaurant out of it. Then, the recently built family home. There were no outstanding loans. Joe did it all on a general practitioner's income?

Anjali moved a few steps rearwards and looked up at the brass engraving which was back on the wall and the Latin motto on it—primum non nocere.

Rishi and Anjali had the combined paycheck of two specialists working at a private hospital, but they certainly couldn't have managed to buy property in Goa without help from a bank or from her family. Unlike Joe, Rishi never expressed any discomfort with her spending the quarterly cheque she received from the Joshi Trust, or she wouldn't have been able to maintain the lifestyle she was used to in her parents' home.

"What about Dr Rastogi?" she asked the secretary. "Did you find where he's staying?"

The secretary cleared his throat. "Not yet."

Anjali nodded. She already knew Rishi was still in Goa. He'd left enough messages on her phone, pleading with her to be allowed to visit. She also knew what she was doing wasn't fair to him. Her baby wasn't hers alone. Rishi had a right to see his son. But if she called back, if she let him visit them at home, he'd start again about wanting to get back together. She could let him see the baby at whatever hotel he was staying in. Perhaps her cousin, Mohini, could take the baby to visit Rishi.

Yet another man Anjali didn't understand. Years ago, when they decided to get married, each had reasons they thought were compelling. Rishi had his family and the need to keep his identity secret from men who would harm him. But now... the world changed even if his family chose not to. The law changed, and the blackmailer was long gone. Anjali was prepared to tell his parents they couldn't see their grandson as long as they refused to treat Rishi with respect. For the sake of her child and the man she'd lived with all these years, she could and would pull every dirty trick she knew. She'd already said all this to Rishi.

Yeah, he was still adamantly opposed to the divorce, but she'd thought he'd eventually come around. There was the man, the immediate cause of this divorce, who was desperately in love with Rishi. The feeling was fully

173

reciprocated. Anjali knew Rishi well enough to recognise the yearning in his eyes.

Yet he was practically shaking with fear and desperation the day he came to the charity clinic to talk to her. The bond of friendship between them was unbreakable, but both knew it would never develop into anything else, and neither ever wanted anything more. Not with each other, anyway. Still, he'd thrown the existence of their child in Joe's face in an attempt to get him out. Rishi's voice was dripping malice when he told Joe about the baby. It wasn't enough to get an old rival out of the running; Rishi was intent on inflicting injury even at the risk of wounding her. No, Anjali had no idea what was going on with him. What was he so afraid of he didn't care how badly he hurt those around?

She'd agreed to take this job in Goa to exorcise her ghosts. Unfortunately, said ghosts followed her to Goa, insisting on squatting rights in her thoughts.

Anjali squared her shoulders. She'd already wasted enough of her workday on personal problems, going to the extent of setting her secretary to the task of investigating her exes. Enough was enough. She needed to get her act together and do her job. The mistakes she'd made in her private life would have to wait their turn.

"Chandekarji," she called, turning to face the secretary. "Do we have the papers ready for the meeting with the man from pharmaceutical crimes division?" There was slightly more than an hour until said meeting, and she planned to go over the documents once more while breastfeeding her baby. It would give the nanny time to get some fresh air.

"Yes, madam," said the secretary. "We have copies of all the purchase documents from the last six months."

When Dr Pratapchandra Joshi—cardiologist and chairman of the Joshi Trust—got a tip from an old friend that the name of the clinic popped up a couple of times during some kind of police investigation, he knew it had to be about the violation of intellectual property law and their purchase of generic forms of expensive medicines. Charity hospitals couldn't afford to be sticklers for IP law. The call from INTERPOL confirmed they wanted to discuss the clinic's recent purchases.

The latest in the succession of CEOs since Dr Ram Joshi's passing—a local doctor in his early nineties—did not want to deal with it or with the confusion created by the new viral pandemic. He was only too glad to step aside for anyone the Joshis appointed. As the only Joshi doctor currently at loose ends, Anjali was asked to take charge of the situation, and the lawyers from the family trust helped her draw up a plan for this first meeting with the INTERPOL man. She was to say nothing today. Later, the clinic would call a press conference and readily admit to buying medicines from patent-breakers. They would agree to pay whatever fine was imposed. Then, Anjali would present her side to the media. An idealistic young doctor fighting Big Pharma would make a good story and perhaps force those companies to strike a deal of some sort to provide lifesaving drugs.

It took only one day at the job for Anjali to learn the clinic would be in deep doo-doo with the cops. The men who'd graced the CEO position since her grandfather's demise could've been clones of Dr Ram Joshi in their aversion to computers. Paperwork was actually *paper*work—a large chunk of which was missing, misplaced, or plain undecipherable due to someone's bright idea of using the chamber next to the main water tank as the file room. The only bright spot was that it took weeks for the concerned clerks to send the documents to Records Department to be stored in the dank chamber which meant the newer papers were still scattered in the dry parts of the clinic.

"Thanks to you, Chandekarji," Anjali said to the secretary, "we found records at least from the last six months. This can't happen ever again. Once we're done digitising administrative records, we'll take care of patient charts."

Chandekar patted his thick moustache. "Madam, you might want to rethink the idea."

Anjali frowned. "Why?"

"This clinic was started by your grandfather. Most of our senior employees were hired by him. They're comfortable with the procedure he established."

Anjali fixed her eyes directly on the secretary's face, taking care to hold the stare for a few seconds. "My grandfather—God bless him—was a man of his times. The world has changed. Within reason, we at the clinic need to change with it or get left behind. The clinic is supported financially by the Joshi Trust, but that doesn't mean we can afford to ignore wastage caused by poor record-keeping. Nor can we provide substandard care to our patients, which we will if we don't ensure access to information. Plus, look at what happened with this INTERPOL thing. I hope to God they'll be happy with six months of documents. If they ask for more..." The ensuing legal trouble might even lead to the government shutting down the clinic, something that would severely impact the lower-income patient population in town.

Blinking rapidly, the secretary said, "Those are all good reasons, madam. I'm just saying the staff won't like it. Dr Ram Joshi preferred the traditional way of doing things, and they're happy with it."

The staff can just take a hike. No, she couldn't say that. *I'm CEO now?* No, not that, either. "We'll hire technicians to train the staff," Anjali soothed. "It won't be as difficult as they imagine. *I* learned, and all I knew about computers was how to browse the internet. Anyway, it will take us a few months to be completely digitised. Let's focus on this meeting with the police for now, shall we?"

"There's another thing," grumbled Chandekar. "I wish you'd said something to me before. I'd have arranged someone to sit with you on this. Cops cannot be trusted. They'll twist every word you say into whatever they want."

It wasn't the first time they had the discussion since the week before when Anjali asked the man to squeeze the meeting with the officer into her schedule. "INTERPOL asked for a private meeting with the CEO. As a matter of courtesy, we have to allow it. Moreover, if we insist on lawyering up at every encounter with the police, they're going to think we actually have something to hide."

"We don't need it to be a lawyer. You could pick any one of the staff who knows what he's doing. Since there's no time to bring a third person up to speed, it will have to be me."

Chandekar served as secretary to the CEO for a good number of years. He'd started in the position in the last months of Dr Ram Joshi's life and continued with the series of retired local physicians who'd held the title. Anjali had no doubt Chandekar did know more about the clinic's running than her. She needed his help. Trying not to snap at the man, Anjali inclined her head. "Thanks for the suggestion, but I should be able to handle one meeting on my own. If the cops ask questions I feel uncomfortable answering, I'll let them know I'll have to get back after consulting our lawyers."

"The board members of the clinic may feel more comfortable with two representatives from our side."

"The board members are here only in advisory capacity. Like I said, the Joshi Trust foots the bills for the clinic. *They* have faith in my ability to handle this."

"Yeah, but..." With one of his deferential coughs, Chandekar asked, "May I speak freely?" When Anjali nodded, he continued, "Madam, you're a doctor, but you're also a young woman. Thirty-one, correct? This is your first time running anything. When your father appointed you CEO, there was some talk among the employees about nepotism."

Anjali sighed. "I'm sure they understand the administrative setup in the clinic." The staff got paid market wages but not the CEO. Dr Ram Joshi had been adamant he didn't want his project turning into a business proposition run by doctor-managers with their eye mainly on profit. The chief executive of the clinic would be someone willing to give back to the community at least in terms of time and effort. All of which meant the very few applicants for the position were grey-haired physicians who'd already made their retirement money. Anjali was appointed only because there was no one else. "Besides, I have *you* to help me, and I can always call my father for advice." In fact, Dr Pratap Joshi made it quite clear while he knew she'd quickly figure things out, he also expected her to request assistance when she needed it.

"True," Chandekar said. "Precisely what I said to the staff—if you made a mistake or two in the beginning, we could always contact the Joshi Trust."

With a huff, Anjali said, "Chandekarji—"

"There's one more thing." Once again, the secretary patted his moustache. "There have been some rumours about you... that you're not quite stable."

Humiliation gushed, almost choking her. *Of course*, the rumours got to the clinic. Her parents paid cartloads of cash to everyone and anyone they could think of to keep her breakdown a secret, but there was no way to seal every mouth. The perfect Anjali Joshi had lost her marbles. She'd then not only divorced her perfect husband for reasons no one could fathom, she'd done so was while she was pregnant with their child. Poor thing, she hadn't even been able to handle her job as an anaesthesiologist.

Chandekar nodded. "I'm sure you understand how it changes things if word gets out we're being investigated for pharmaceutical crimes. The staff *and* the board members would want someone less delicate in charge. Someone with more experience. Nobody will say anything to your face because you're Dr Pratap Joshi's daughter, but I'm sure the employee association will call the Joshi Trust office to protest. You'll end up being removed or having to step aside. If the trust refuses to do either, staff morale will go down. Patients will suffer."

One... two... three... Keeping her breaths slow and even, Anjali said, "I decided to keep this issue with INTERPOL quiet precisely because of possible panic. And before you ask, my father agreed with the decision." Unfortunately, she couldn't track down the necessary documents and had needed to involve Chandekar. "Outside of the Joshi Trust, the only people who know about the problem at this time are you and me. Neither of us is likely to discuss it with the staff, are we?" She waited a beat and added, "Please get the copies I requested on my desk in ten minutes."

"Yes, madam," said the secretary, tone resigned.

As the man reached the door, Anjali called, "Chandekarji?" When he turned around, she tried a gracious smile. "Don't worry. I'll be careful not to say anything that could hurt the clinic or offend the staff." Nor would she allow the employees to dictate how she managed the clinic. Once the meeting with the cop was done, she needed to put a plan in place for her recalcitrant secretary.

An hour later, Anjali didn't know if the clinic would survive long enough for any of her plans. The INTERPOL man wasn't from the pharmaceutical crimes division. He introduced himself as SP Naidu—superintendent of police—an officer with the Central Bureau of Investigation, assigned to the INTERPOL division of the agency. His words made no sense to Anjali, whatsoever. A few young men—ones who'd been treated at the clinic at some point over the last year—went missing from the neighbourhood, and the cops were investigating for criminal activity. Did they think the clinic was involved in the disappearances?

The thin wail of the baby interrupted her stream of confused thoughts, followed by the nanny's soothing murmurs. From her chair, Anjali glanced at the closed door on the left wall of the suite. Two days ago, her boy slept through the whole drama with the men in her life. Today, he'd decided he wanted his mother. More like he wanted his afternoon snack. The nanny would give him infant cereal, but that didn't stop Anjali's breasts from suddenly and painfully engorging with milk.

"Doctor?" called the cop, his voice stern and impatient. With his neat beard and the side-parted, dark hair, SP Naidu could've been in front of a lecture hall of grad students, not interrogating hospital CEOs on behalf of INTERPOL.

Clearing her throat, Anjali said, "I heard every word of what you said, Officer. I'm simply trying to understand how the Joshi Clinic got mixed up in your case. We're a charity organisation. For God's sake, the Joshi Trust is set up to eat the losses from the clinic. As long as the trust is able to balance it out with gains from other ventures, the clinic will stay open. We don't *need* to run a criminal operation for money."

"Be that as it may," said Naidu, "we still have no explanation for the patient disappearances from your clinic."

Dad, Anjali muttered in her mind. *You didn't send me here to handle* this. Out loud, she said, "I have to consult with our lawyers before giving you access to records, but if there were any patients who disappeared from our clinic, someone would've talked. The people of this town would've been up in arms. There would've been some kind of noise, I'm sure. Plus, the patients didn't exactly disappear if you spotted them in the Philippines."

The INTERPOL officer inclined his head. "Let me word it correctly. There have been a few disappearances from in and around Mapusa. Migrant labourers from other states who work in construction. All of them young, and most of them male. No one reports them missing because they do tend to move in search of better pay. The only reason law enforcement noticed it was the foreman at a construction site was sure one of the young men absconded with his scooter. The cops weren't expecting to have him and a friend pop up on airport security cameras, flying to Manila."

"A migrant labourer, working for pennies, flying to Manila," Anjali murmured, disbelievingly.

"Precisely. The first thought was terrorism, so Goan police alerted INTERPOL. From our investigation, it appears as though Manila is now the favoured holiday spot for male migrant workers from Mapusa."

"Couldn't you ask them? Assuming the Filipino government cooperates, of course."

The officer's mouth twisted into a smile. "Thank you for telling me how to do my job."

Anjali winced. "I didn't mean to—"

SP Naidu continued as though she hadn't spoken, "Dr Joshi, all we know is they flew out of Goa and arrived in Manila. Except for two, we haven't been able to track the rest. Maybe they're still in the country. Maybe they returned to India. The two we found..." The officer leaned forwards, looking directly at Anjali. "They were dead."

"Oh, my God."

"No kidneys, no liver, no heart," said the officer, tone emotionless. "They were butchered."

"What—" A yelp escaped Anjali. Pushing her chair back, she stood and looked frantically around for a non-existent washbasin. All she could find was the half-empty bottle of water on the windowsill above the air conditioner. Her breaths harsh and raspy, she poured the lukewarm water down her throat, some of it spilling onto the front of her blouse.

"Dr Joshi," called Naidu. "I'd assumed you could handle it. You are an—"

"Anaesthesiologist," she agreed, returning to her chair. "I'm in the business of keeping people alive while they go under the knife. Murder is beyond my purview."

The cop nodded. "Murder is exactly right, but I should've been more specific. Those labourers were cut upon with great precision, and their internal organs were harvested with extreme care. The murderer... or at least one of the murderers... was a surgeon. No question about it."

Lips stiff, she said, "Organ smuggling."

"Yes."

"And the connection to the Joshi Clinic?"

"For one, most of the migrant labourers who disappeared seem to have been treated at this clinic at some point. And..." Naidu paused as though approaching a delicate subject, somehow more delicate than the butchery he'd described moments ago. "INTERPOL wouldn't have approached you if we didn't feel your family had nothing to do with it. All the Joshis even peripherally involved with the clinic were thoroughly investigated, and the belief among the team was you'd cooperate. We were actually expecting to interview your father about this and request his assistance, but at some point, we would've had to talk to you, as well."

"Me?" Anjali asked. Wildly, she laughed. "I never as much as park in the wrong spot."

A glimmer of a smile passed across the cop's face. "We're aware of the fact. You're not a suspect at this time, but we have some concerns about a couple of men closely associated with you—Doctors Rishabh Rastogi and Joseph D'Acosta."

Part VII

Chapter 19

"No," screamed Rishi, throwing the wadded sheet of paper at the wall. The blackmailer had tracked his quarry to Goa. Silently, the note fell to the carpeted floor of Rishi's room at the Goa Marriott.

An invisible clamp snapped itself around his chest, tightening its grip until his muscles hurt with each breath. Rishi stumbled to the side table and grabbed his inhaler. One puff, two. Fingers trembling, he slammed the inhaler back into the drawer and went to the window. Air. He needed air. Outside, tourists thronged the sandy beach and the bright blue water beyond, laughing and shouting in the sheer pleasure of their Goan holiday. Rishi took a deep gulp of the hot wind and tried to bring his thoughts into focus.

One mistake. The one mistake was all it took to leave him at the mercy of the blackmailer. Rishi wished like hell he could go back in time and fix it.

Heart quaking, he reviewed options. There was no Anjali around to rescue him. She wasn't returning any of his calls. He could go to her home and beg her help for the sake of their son, but he'd run out of time to convince her. He needed to do something *now*. But what?

Rishi rubbed his temples hard. Curling his fingers, he eyed the wall next to him and fought the urge to slam his fist into it. Fractured bones, ruptured tendons—the world's best hand surgeons could put it all back together, but none of them would be able to get him the same dexterity which made him the skilled neurosurgeon he was. But he'd be free from the blackmailer's threat to his medical licence because there would be nothing left to threaten.

"No," he said, gritting his teeth. "I will not..." He would not live out his life staring at his deformed hand, mourning the surgeon he used to be. He'd rather be dead.

Death was always the final solution to every problem. It could be his or the blackmailer's. Or both. Perhaps he should've considered it to begin with. Rishi nodded. He grabbed the scrunched paper from the floor and smoothed it. No phone number, and unless he chose to approach the cops, no way to track who sent it. It was only a demand to do as he was told. He'd have to wait until the inevitable call came. In the meantime, there were plans to make. He was a surgeon—good with the knife. If things went well, he'd be free of this nightmare. His son wouldn't grow up as the child of a disgraced doctor. If it didn't go well... Rishi needed to make sure no one else got affected by the fallout from his attempt to stop the blackmailer—not Anjali, not their son.

There was one person he owed a call to before doing anything. Unplugging his phone from the charger, Rishi brought up a number. *Ring, ring, ring.* "Pick up," he muttered. "Pick up, dammit." He glanced at the alarm clock on the nightstand. Thursday afternoon. The OR schedule would be packed. Maybe the phone was switched off. Maybe it wasn't even—

A click. "Rishi?" said a voice, tone at once hopeful and wary. "Did you decide you're gay after all, or are you calling to tell me you're back with your wife for good?"

The clamp around Rishi's chest loosened. A sound of relief escaping his lips, he sank into one of the plush chairs by the window. "There's nothing to decide. I've never denied my sexuality to myself, and you know it. There were circumstances... Farhan, can we talk? I need to tell you something."

Chapter 20

January 2008

Rishi glared at the closed door to his flatmate's room. He about had it up to his eyeballs with Joe and Anjali. The thin walls meant Rishi was privy to their long and barf-inducingly cheesy phone conversations—at least Joe's side of it. Rishi knew everything they discussed from a Thalaiva movie both wanted to watch to Anjali's unexpected liking for pharmacology to her annoyances with her little brother who wasn't talking to her. Joe, when he wasn't spouting weird sounding poetry on the sexiness of her body or talking classic novels, elaborated on his theories about pig kidneys in primates or told her all about *his* brothers and sister. Or he cooed into the phone how everything took on new purpose after she came into his life. The delighted laughter which followed had to mean the sentiment was returned.

As if their talks on the phone weren't enough to drive Rishi stark, raving mad with exasperation, there were the booty calls. Anjali couldn't stay overnight without Meenakshi, her roommate, finding out, so it was pretty much whenever they could, wherever they could. For the last few months, Joe and Anjali managed to keep their secret partly thanks to Rishi. She got to the flat way before the rest was supposed to arrive, giving them time for whatever. Both the men were there, so no one suspected anything. Rishi, idiot he was, even alerted the couple when their other friends were almost at the door. But there were limits, dammit. They needed to have some sympathy for him, surrounded by horniness but lacking a mate.

185

A piercing squeal erupted from Joe's room, followed by a thump and an "Oh, shit. My ankle."

Groaning, Rishi tossed the neuroanatomy textbook onto the coffee table and laughed as the Pomeranian next door howled in synchrony. He eyed the front door and glanced back at Joe's room. Raising his voice, he called, "Gimme a second, Sid. Something in the kitchen…"

There was a scuffling sound in Joe's room. In under thirty seconds, Anjali was racing to the sofa, slipping on her sneakers along the way. Crossing her legs, she put on her earphones and swayed along to whatever song was on her phone. *If* there was a song. Rishi held on to the back of a chair and guffawed.

It took her a moment to realise there was no Siddharth at the front door. "Jerk," she mumbled, tugging off the earphones.

"What the hell, man." Pulling on his tee, Joe padded gingerly to the sofa.

"I'll tell you what the hell," Rishi said. "We need to create some rules for this sort of thing. Divvy up the days of the week we can have personal guests over."

Anjali waggled her eyebrows. "You met someone?"

"He just likes being a pain in the ass," grumbled Joe. "Who'd put up with him?"

"I'll ignore that," Rishi continued. "My days will be mine to use as I wish. I might bring a guest, or I may just choose to enjoy the peace and quiet."

Joe smirked. "Ha, you're simply—"

Finger to her lips, Anjali shushed her boyfriend. "I shouldn't have called you a jerk, Rishi. You're right, of course. You deserve some time to yourself. And thank you for keeping our secret."

"No problem," Rishi mumbled, his pulse skipping a beat. He'd gladly continue doing it. If and when Anjali and Joe decided to go public, Rishi didn't know what the hell he'd do. The lies he'd told his family...

It didn't take long. Oh, neither Anjali nor Joe meant to out themselves. She hadn't even initiated the conversation. A week later, Meenakshi was at the window of the flat, griping about the view. "Don't you guys get sick of it? All you can see is the graffiti on the next building."

"I hope we get an apartment with a water view," murmured Gauri, slumping into the sofa with a dreamy look on her face. Nikhil was expected in India towards the end of November for a two-month vacation he'd somehow arranged with his residency program in the U.S. When he returned to New York, it would be with his new bride. "Kiki, yaar. I wish you could stay for the wedding."

"So do I," said Kokila, tone glum. She'd pushed aside the folding chairs Rishi added to the furniture and stretched out on the floor, a small pillow under her head. "But the hospital won't wait." Her visa was finally ready, and she'd fly to the U.S. in a week. "We'll meet in New York and *partyyy.*"

"Yay," said Gauri. "It's gonna be so much fun."

Clearing his throat, Siddharth said, "In honour of the occasion of your wedding, I've written a new poem."

"No," said Gauri, immediately.

"C'mon, yaar," Siddharth complained. "It's my gift to you and Nikhil *jeeju.*"

"Jeeju?" Meenakshi howled. "Sister's husband?"

"Aww," Kokila and Anjali went in unison.

Slouching against the wall, Rishi and Joe exchanged glances. The punk could play the ladies very easily when he put his mind to it. Womankind was fortunate he was too intent on provoking people with his poetry, instead.

"The answer's still no," Gauri said.

Siddharth opened his mouth to respond, but Anjali leaned left from her chair and poked him in the belly, causing him to double over, laughing. "Not fair," he complained. "You know I'm ticklish in my tummy."

"I hope you get your water view, Gauri," said Anjali. "I want one, too. Imagine waking in the morning and hearing the ocean waves."

"You can't hear the waves from your parents' flat?" asked Rishi. All he knew was she lived in Cuffe Parade, a wealthy neighbourhood with stunning views of the sea.

Anjali laughed. "No. The view is there, but I want a house closer to the beach." With a faraway sigh, she continued, "There will be a big master bedroom with French windows which open onto a garden. Roses, maybe. I wouldn't mind a pond, either. Lilies or something. Six bedrooms in total."

Meenakshi pulled one of the folding chairs to her side and sat. "Wow, Anju. You've been planning this."

"Only forever," Anjali admitted. "I used to do sketches of my dream home."

"Six-bedroom beach house with a garden," muttered Joe. "I'd love to live near the sea, too, but that's damned huge. It will take a lot of money."

Giggling, Anjali asked, "Why? You afraid I'm gonna bankrupt you?"

No one said anything for some time, all of them glancing between her and Joe in varying degrees of confusion. *Laugh it off, Anju,* Rishi muttered in his mind, frantically. If she and Joe went public with their romance... word would get to his parents. They'd know he lied. He'd again be thrown out of the family. *Please, Anju,* Rishi begged. *Say it was a slip of your tongue.*

Face frozen in comical dismay, she continued to stare at Joe. His gaze was fixed on her, as well. Eyes glittering, he smiled. "The income of two doctors should easily get us a loan."

Panic rose in an acidic surge to Rishi's mouth. He coughed, trying to bite down on it.

A murmur went around the room. Siddharth hissed. "Anything you wanna tell us?"

"Yes," Joe said, baldly. He walked to Anjali's chair and went down on his haunches next to her. "But I want to tell Anju first. Not—" he added, a firm eye on Siddharth, "—in front of you."

***

"You know they're all probably listening," Anjali whispered, glancing at the closed door to Joe's room.

With a low laugh, he dragged her into his arms. "I don't care." He bent down to brush his mouth against hers. They swayed to some unsung song, barely managing to avoid bumping into the bed and the other furniture crowded into the small room. "I just wish I had a chance to plan this out. Cook your favourite crab masala, couple of candles, nice music..." Grimacing, he looked at down at his customary tee—faded blue this time—and worn jeans and sandals. "Better clothes."

Her dusty red tunic and black leggings were chosen more for the warmth offered than fashion, and her black platform sneakers barely brought the top of her head up to Joe's chin. "Does it matter?" she asked.

"No." He cupped her cheek with a warm hand. "Anju?"

"Yeah?" She couldn't look away from his yearning gaze.

"I love you."

With a shuddering sigh, she went on tiptoes to kiss him. "I love you, too."

Trailing soft kisses along her cheek, he asked, "We're planning to make this a permanent thing, right? Marriage and that dream home of yours?"

"You haven't asked me."

Joe laughed. "Sundari, I think *you* already asked me out there. My answer was yes."

Smiling foolishly at him, she said, "Mine, too. Yes, I'll marry you."

A cheer went up outside the door. Joe groaned and called out, "See? This is why she didn't want to tell any of you idiots."

"Hey," yelled Meenakshi. "We're being supportive. What else are friends for?"

Apparently, friendship also meant sharing all the details of your romance with your girl gang. They did mean *all* the details. In their hostel room, Meenakshi paced up and down and grilled Anjali on how it started, complaining all the way she wasn't kept in the loop while Rishi was.

"Forgive me, yaar," Anjali begged from her usual spot in the chair by the window. "I had no choice with Rishi. He lives in the same flat! He knew every time we... umm... every time I visited."

Sitting in the centre of Anjali's bed, Kokila held up a hand. "Wait, Meenu. Argue later about that stuff. What I want to know is..." Leaning to her side, she smacked Gauri's hand away from her laptop. "Email Nikhil later. This is important business."

"I *am* telling him about this business," Gauri said, rubbing her hand.

Kokila clucked. "Wait. First, I want to hear about Anju's 'visits.'"

As one, they all turned towards her. "Well?" asked Meenakshi.

"Well what?" Anjali asked.

"C'mon, girl," said Gauri. "Don't act coy. What's he like in bed?"

Tilting her chin up, Anjali sniffed. "That's so private. How could you possibly ask?" She waited a beat until the curiosity on their faces was tinged by chagrin. "*Andha Arabi Kadalorum,*" she sang the raunchy song from *Bombay,* the movie.

With a collective whoop, the three women tossed pillows into the air. In a couple of minutes, Kokila said, "I hope this doesn't mean I'm going to miss two weddings."

"I don't think so," said Anjali. "We haven't actually talked about any of that, but I think he'd want to finish at least junior residency first." It would be a long three years as a junior surgical resident, followed by three years of specialisation in urology with focus on kidney transplantation.

"Makes sense," said Kokila. "He'd have a postgraduate degree to fall back on in case the subspecialisation doesn't work out. Some kind of income guarantee is important when there's a second person in the picture." She sighed. "God, I hope I'm able to save some money. Every day, there's a new developer asking to buy our house in Goa, and every day, my uncle comes by to harass my mother into agreeing to sell. I really need to buy his share."

"They pay good overtime in the U.S.," said Anjali. That's what she'd heard from her uncles who lived in L.A. It was likely the same in New York, where Kokila was headed.

"I'll do all the hours they offer," stated Kokila. "In whatever department they want." She was primarily a paediatric nurse but had some experience working in surgery and OB/GYN.

"Hey," said Gauri. "Maybe I'll get accepted to residency in your hospital. You can show me the ropes." As soon as Gauri arrived in the U.S. as Nikhil's wife, she'd start applying to residency spots in obstetrics and gynaecology.

Anjali groaned. "I can't imagine doing OB all my life."

Flopping onto her own bed, Meenakshi said, "Your mom's one."

"Still..." said Anjali. "I'm kind of jealous of you, Meenu. You already know what you want to do. Two years in, and I still don't have a clue." Siddharth hadn't known at the beginning, either, but even he'd since figured out he wanted to be a forensic psychiatrist. Apparently, the way to get over his fear of death was to confront it head-on, especially the gruesome kind. Choking down his resentment towards his journalist father who lived in Boston with wife version 3.0, Siddharth asked for help reinstating his American permanent residency so he could do his training there. "Any advice, Gauri? You're the senior medical student in this room."

"Me?" Gauri shrugged. "How can I advise you on what you might like? It's something *you* need to figure out."

"That's what Joe says," Anjali grumbled. The only comment he'd offered was whatever she decided to do with her life, to make sure she left some room in it for him. Her heart fluttered at his words, but her problem remained.

"Don't you still like pharmacology?" asked Kokila.

"Yeah, but..." Restlessly, Anjali plucked at a non-existent thread on her flannel pyjamas. "I like the rest of the courses I've done so far, too. Anatomy, pathology, etcetera, etcetera. In pharmacology, you get to hear all about how medicines work. Put it together with the research protocols... you get to see the whole process of how it gets to the patient. The overall view is what interests me."

"You want to work for a pharma company?" Gauri asked, doubtfully.

"Nah, you're not the type for a research lab," Meenakshi opined. "Or even a diagnostic lab like me. Oh, I didn't tell you. I talked to the nuclear medicine professor yesterday. He thinks my paper has a good chance of being accepted to one of the bigger journals."

Chattering excitedly with her friends about Meenakshi's prospects, Anjali thought about the gynaecology seminar scheduled the next month in AIIMS. Her mom was invited to speak and would expect to meet Anjali's friends; she'd expect to be introduced to the man her daughter mentioned. In fact, Anjali was sure Mom had already asked her friends in the college to check on her daughter's social circle, hoping to find more about said man. She would already know Daadaji's former protégé was part of the group, but she wouldn't know it was him Anjali talked about.

Anjali hadn't been sure how to handle the meeting, but now... she smiled to herself. *Mom, meet Dr Joe D'Acosta, surgery resident, future transplant surgeon. You've heard about him before. He's the man I plan to marry.* "Hey, girls," she called, waiting until their attention turned to her. "Don't say anything to anyone about Joe and me, please. I don't want it to get to my parents before I have a chance to tell them myself."

✶✶✶

Staring into the darkness, Rishi stayed silent on his bed. From the room to the right, Joe and Anjali's voices were raised in argument. Their first fight as a couple. At least the first Rishi witnessed. If he were a better man, he would've put a pillow to his ears and tried to sleep, but he needed to know the outcome. Whether or not Rishi copped to the lie he told his parents depended on Joe's decision.

"Why does this have to be so difficult?" asked Anjali, frustration evident in her tone. "Joe, I'm telling you my mother is not the sort to judge anyone by social class. *She* didn't come from money. My parents don't even belong to the same religion, caste, whatever. Dad's Hindu Brahmin, and Mom's Parsi."

"It's different in my case," Joe insisted. "I wasn't even thinking about religion. Anju, we're equal only on campus. The minute we step outside, there's a huge difference between you and me. Hell, between the rest of the group and me. None of you has ever had to worry about money... even Kiki... she's not

193

rich, but no one mocks her for her family. *I'm* not merely poor or your grandfather's protégé; he paid for my education from your family's trust. My father and I were both charity projects—*your* family's charity. My grandfather was a criminal. The D'Acosta history is a horror-comedy full of irresponsible and unreliable men. I can't simply walk up to your mother and introduce myself as your boyfriend."

Anjali groaned. "How many times are we... what difference does it make at this point? You're a doctor now. If that doesn't say reliable, what does?"

"A doctor with only a bachelor's degree. Your parents *might* take your word for it I'm not a leech, but the rest of the world won't. My God, I won't feel like a man. Anju, please. Let me complete my junior residency. I could at least claim I can afford to feed and clothe you."

"Feed and clothe me?" she asked. "For one, I asked you to meet my mother, not marry me right now. For another, did I *ask* you to feed and clothe me? I should check with my mother if she said the same thing to my father when they decided to get married."

"Oh, c'mon," scoffed Joe. "It's not the same thing. She wouldn't have been expected to..."

"Expected to... what, Joe? Say it. She wouldn't have been expected to be much more than a trophy, so it was okay for her not to be ready to pull her own weight when she got married?" Tears evident in her voice, Anjali asked, "Is that what you think of me? A rich, spoilt brat who expects everything to be simply handed to her? Forget the doctor title. My *real* job will be to warm my husband's bed?"

"What the hell? Why are you putting words in my mouth? Society has certain expectations of men is all I meant. Your family will, too, whatever you believe. But I've never seen you as anything less than the whole you."

"Oh, really?" Anjali asked. "What about the women you used to date? Did you pick them for their IQ or their bra size?"

Joe hissed. "Stop, Anju. You're going too far."

"*I* am? You ditch all your lovers after a year and go on your merry way while they get slut-shamed. I won't let people talk about *me* like they do about your other girlfriends. You *told* me it was different... so why are you refusing to meet my mother?"

Tone dangerously low, Joe said, "The women I dated were beautiful *and* intelligent, some way more than me. The only one who has ever slut-shamed them in my presence is *you*. Just now."

A shocked silence followed, broken by a sob. "I didn't mean to—"

The sharp sound of a slammed door reverberated through the wall into Rishi's room. He closed his eyes in relief. Joe wouldn't be meeting Anjali's mother as her boyfriend. She'd already instructed all her friends not to mention the romance around general public, thus risking her parents finding out before she had a chance to talk to them. Rishi's dirty little secret was safe for now. His lies wouldn't be exposed just yet.

A low keening reached him, punctuated by the subdued gasps of someone trying to keep her crying a secret. Rishi gritted his teeth. He needed to cover his ears right now. He hadn't caused them to fight. Anjali's tears were none of his business. An image of her crying in the bed her lover abandoned her in flickered in front of his closed eyelids. She wouldn't stay there for long. Anjali had too much pride for it.

With a growl, Rishi stood and padded to the door of the other room. The thin moonlight was enough to show Anjali, sitting on the mattress with her knees drawn up to her chest, her face turned away. "Anju?" he called. When she looked up, he said, "I'll go away if you'd rather stay here. If you're planning to return to the hostel, lemme take you there." This time of the night wasn't safe for women to be out and about in the city.

Walking to the women's hostel under the moonlit sky, she murmured, "You heard everything, didn't you?"

"Hmm." He nodded, tucking his hands into his pockets to keep them warm. A few cars were going up and down, honking at nothing in particular, and a drunk slumped under a lamppost, reeking of cheap alcohol, ignoring the orders of the cop next to him to get up and move before he froze to death in the chilly night.

"Was I wrong?" Anjali asked, tone subdued. She tugged the collar of her winter coat tighter around her neck.

To ask her boyfriend to meet her mother? No way. "You did take it too far," Rishi muttered, finally. The phone rang in his pocket. Grimacing at the number, he took the call. "Hello?"

"Rishi," came Joe's frantic voice. "Is she—"

"She's with me. We're walking back to the hostel."

"Oh, thank God," Joe huffed. "Her phone seems to be switched off, and I was afraid she barged out all alone... lemme talk to her, please."

"Here," said Rishi, holding his phone out to her. Walking a few feet away, he waited until they finished the conversation.

"I'm so sorry," Anjali said, sobbing. "I swear I didn't mean to say anything bad about... I was just so worried I wasn't any different to you." There were squawks from the phone. With a watery smile, she said, "I love you, too... you don't have to keep apologising... I understand. I mean, I don't really, but you feel what you feel. I'll tell my mom I'm not ready yet to introduce anyone to her." In a few moments, Anjali nodded. "Yeah, we'll work something out."

When Rishi and Anjali got to the hostel, there were curious looks directed their way from the few female students they ran into. Gaze faraway, Anjali didn't seem to notice their knowing smirks. Rishi nodded at one he recognised. There was a painful hardness within his chest. Grabbing his inhaler from the back pocket of his pants, he puffed in a couple of breaths.

"Your asthma," Anjali said, regretfully. "And you came out in the cold with me."

"Don't worry about it," Rishi said, coughing. His asthma was usually triggered by smells, dust, pollen, etcetera. It never before happened with cold air. "Get some sleep. Things will look better in the morning."

Half an hour later, he stood at the entrance to the apartment building and looked up. Joe was in there. Rishi took one step forward, preparing to go into the warmth of the flat and face his colleague's anxious questions about Anjali. His chest... he took another puff and waited for his lungs to relax. His pulse was already racing—effects of the adrenergic agonist which helped him fight the asthma.

Pivoting, he strode down the footpath. Where to... home? No, he couldn't face his family... Papa, Ma... these days, they always wanted to know about Anjali. Nikhil was in New York. Who... who... maybe Gauri. But she'd be asleep, and she certainly wouldn't condone what he was doing. The invisible fingers wrapped around Rishi's chest tightened.

"*Aey, theek hain kya?*" a passer-by asked, wanting to know if Rishi were all right.

For a second, Rishi didn't get why he was being asked the question. Then, he heard a harsh, raspy sound. Was it him? Trying to control the loud wheezing, he nodded. He grabbed the inhaler again and with trembling, sweaty fingers, puffed more medicine into his lungs. His heart was thumping so hard his vision was getting blurry. With a raised hand signalling his well-being, he sent the passer-by on his way.

Weaving his way down the footpath, Rishi continued walking. The buildings... had he been here before? He stood in the pool of light thrown by a streetlamp and looked around. The shops lining the road were dark. What time was it? Where *was* he? There were fuzzy lights in one building at the end of the block. Rishi squinted. The place did seem familiar, but he didn't remember going there.

Rishi staggered to the door and peered at the board above. Eclipse, it said. There was a vector image of two muscular men dancing together. *Ahh.* The nation might have laws against homosexuality, but some mustered enough courage to defy it and gather in public. Not Rishi, though. He remembered Googling gay clubs in Delhi but never finding the nerve to visit. With a short laugh, he admitted, *No cash, either.* Now, he did. Pleased with his apparent change of heart, his parents had transferred money to his bank account.

The smell of tobacco greeted him. The burly bouncer sitting inside the door didn't even look up, let alone ask for ID to check age. Dim, reddish light, low tables, a dance floor—nothing to set the place apart from any other club in the city except for the lack of women. The music was muted as though to keep the club's presence in the neighbourhood as unobtrusive as possible.

Swallowing hard, Rishi sauntered to the bar, trying to keep his gait casual and nonchalant. He eyed the drinks in front of the other men. What the hell did he order without looking like an ignorant idiot? He was used to drinking plenty of cheap beer but had no clue about cocktails. The few times he'd been to gay clubs in New York, he was too awed by the smell of freedom to enjoy it fully. The Americans he met laughed at him for saying so, but they didn't understand how good they had it. In Delhi, the lack of money and the obsessive need to control impulses held him back. "Bloody Mary," he finally said.

"Coming right up," said the bartender, cheerfully.

The sour, spicy drink warmed Rishi's insides. The muscles of his chest finally loosened. Inhaling a lungful of smoke-filled air, Rishi looked about, noting the couples at the counter, around tables, on the dance floor, and two elderly gentlemen in suits, sitting quietly together.

"Couples' night," explained the bartender, following Rishi's gaze. "We do it once or twice a month."

Rishi winced. He'd never been part of a couple. Something told him he would never be. After his initiation into the joy of intimacy by one of his high school teachers, there was a long dry spell for Rishi, broken only in New York. Since then, the only time he got lucky was in his imagination. Except, in his parents' minds, he was involved in a passionate romance with Anjali Joshi. "Gimme one more," he said to the bartender.

Ten minutes, thirty minutes, an hour... he had no idea how much time passed. Covering a burp with the back of his hand, he asked for the latrine. A few men were going in and out. It wasn't until Rishi was at the washbowl, scrubbing his hands clean, he heard a voice call, "Oh, *hellooo,* Doctor."

His heart leapt to his throat. Suds still dripping, he wheeled around. A fellow close to his own age stood there, waggling fingers. His hair was shaggy, and he could definitely use a shave, but the dark, snapping eyes were arresting. The graphic tee and skinny jeans were meant to show off the lean, muscular build. "Who?" Rishi croaked.

A look of incredulity passed over the fellow's features. "Parth. Parth Kumar. I'm an actor."

Rishi shook his head. "I'm sorry. I don't remember—"

Flushing, Parth said, "Theatre artist, so you might not have watched my work. I'm very close to getting a break in the movies, though. I just auditioned for one of the big production companies. Does that ring a bell?"

Actor... audition... "The indigestion case," Rishi muttered. "You were convinced your appendix had ruptured. You called me a quack and threatened to have your agent sue if you died before your audition."

Parth ptchaaed. "Not my fault. The website said it could be. I still thought you were cute. I didn't realise you were... you know."

"I... ahh..."

With a sympathetic cluck, Parth brushed his fingertips against Rishi's forearm. "I get it. You're not out. Me, neither. I mean, my agent knows, and some of the casting directors have asked me to put out, but I haven't gone public. I can't afford to. My audience won't like it."

"Many stage and screen artists are gay," Rishi said, encouragingly.

The sympathy dissipated from the actor's face, replaced by mischief. "Doc, you're a hypocrite." He snort-laughed. "Hypocritic doctor. Get it?" At Rishi's confused stare, Parth added, "Don't you guys take an oath or something?"

"Hippocratic Oath?" Rishi asked, feeling slightly dizzy. "It's not the same thing."

"Whatever. Anyway, your secret's safe with me, Doc. What's your name, by the way? I can't keep calling you 'doc' all night."

"Rishi. I'm not staying—"

"Aw, c'mon." Parth pouted. "Have you *seen* the peeps out there? You're the only good-looking man to come this way in months... did you come here with someone?"

"No, but—"

"Cool. So it's you and me tonight." Flinging an arm around Rishi's shoulders, Parth led him out. "You can tell me all about the Hypocritic Oath."

"Hippocratic."

Clapping a hand to his mouth, Parth marvelled, "You're so smart. I adore smart men. I hope you like slightly dumb actors."

Rishi laughed. For the first time in several months, the sound didn't seem false to his ears. "Let me buy you a drink."

It was only one more drink. There wasn't any more alcohol Rishi could use as an excuse for what happened later. Someone offered Parth cocaine, but he refused, stating simply his body was his temple. They were both perfectly sober when they danced in the far corner of the club, concealed by shadows. They both knew exactly what they were doing with the first, tentative kiss. Rishi was trembling with excitement when he accepted Parth's invitation to his flat.

Hours later, tepid sunlight struck Rishi's eyes, annoying him awake. In a matter of moments, he knew where he was. Grabbing his phone from the side table, he swore. "Oh, shit. I'm gonna be late."

Parth barely stirred when Rishi scrambled out of bed and dressed. It was only when Rishi was at the door that Parth called out, "Hey. You wanna hang out later on?"

"Ahh... I'm working through the weekend."

"I could come by the hospital," Parth offered.

"No," exploded Rishi. Softening his tone, he said, "I can't. I'm sorry, but I can't." When Parth frowned, Rishi explained, "I could get into trouble. Not only for this. You're a patient. I'm not allowed to. I could lose my..." God, he could lose his licence. What had he been *thinking?* "Listen, I can trust you, right? You said you won't say anything."

Raising both hands, Parth said, "We're cool. I get ya. Pity. You're a looker. Plus, a doctor. My ma would've been happy."

Taken aback, Rishi asked, "Really?"

"Yeah. She always wanted a rich son-in-law."

In the evening, Rishi surprised his friends by bringing out his old harmonica. He hadn't played in months, but now, he took requests while the rest stumbled around the room, trying to keep up with the peppy songs.

Chapter 21

Present day

Rishi felt bloody weird telling the man he considered the love of his life the story of the one-night stand which changed the course of his existence, but Farhan had a right to know.

"Playing the harmonica?" Farhan shouted over the phone. Farhan Zaidi, respected anaesthesiologist like Anjali, was easy-going most of the time but was a stickler for ethics. "Were you out of your effing mind? Sex with a patient after buying him a drink. My God. Do you realise they could've arrested you for custodial rape?"

In the plush chair by the hotel room window, Rishi winced. The Indian Penal Code considered hospital managers—which presumably included doctors—custodians of patients, and as such, the burden of proof was with the accused. "I never operated on Parth. He'd eaten the wrong thing, and I told him so. It wasn't his appendix. He was discharged from my care. The American Medical Association only says a sexual or romantic relationship should not be concurrent with the doctor-patient relationship. He'd already left my custody, and one beer was all he had. No way was he drunk. *I* had more drinks than him."

"Don't make excuses," said Farhan. "The *Indian* medical council considers even former patients off-limits. It wouldn't have mattered how many days ago he left your care or how many drinks you had. All anyone would've heard is *you* bought *him* a beer before having sex. You might not have gotten officially charged with rape, but everyone would've been thinking it just the same."

Rishi groaned. "It was twelve years ago, and I was young and stupid. I admit it."

"You think that will be enough justification?" Farhan asked, incredulously. "If you were straight, you might have gotten off with a reprimand, but..."

"My identity will be reduced to my homosexuality," Rishi finished, bitterly. "No matter what else I am, any judgement passed on me will eventually come down to my sexual preferences. My skill as a surgeon, how hard I've tried to be a dutiful son, a responsible husband, a loving father... none of it would've mattered then; none of it will matter now." At the time, gay sex was still criminal in India. When it involved a doctor and a former patient— with alcohol thrown into the mix—Rishi would've had no hope for leniency. His medical licence would've been stripped away, and he would've been sentenced to life imprisonment. "It won't matter that the supreme court has now decriminalised homosexuality. It won't matter it *wasn't* custodial rape. On paper, I will merely be the doctor who had sex with a patient, but in the minds of society, I'll be the *gay* doctor who had sex with a patient. The courts won't throw me in jail, but they'll order the medical council to act. The council's rules are meant to be equally applicable for all, but in my case, there will be no benefit of the doubt or chance for redemption. Public opinion will make sure of it. I *will* lose my licence."

Tone gentling, Farhan said, "I wish I could claim you're wrong, but it *is* the world we live in... so that's how you ended up with your wife. The note you mentioned had to be from the actor fellow. You married your wife for cover. Her family *is* pretty high up there in hierarchy."

"No. I mean, yes." Rishi shook his head. So much else happened in between. "Look, I wanted you to know... Farhan, since we met, there was never any doubt in my heart what I want to do or who I want to be with. What I *must* do is a different matter. It's not only about my medical licence. I have a responsibility towards my son. His needs come first."

Tiredly, Farhan stated, "You're planning to stay married."

"No. Anjali won't——" Rishi swallowed hard. He needed to be honest about this. No more half-truths. "Anjali won't consider it. I know she's right not to——right for her, right for everybody else but me. It would be so much easier for me if she would..."

"Easier only in the short run," murmured Farhan. "Would you advise one of your patients to do what you're doing?"

No way. "Be that as it may, I need an immediate solution to my problem." Rishi went over the happenings of the last couple of weeks, including the new notes from the blackmailer. Taking a deep breath, he said, "I don't have the time to try and change Anju's mind. I don't know that she ever will."

"Good for her. Rishi, you need to think about——"

"Coming out? Don't you think I have? Not just since I met you, and you started asking me to. For years... since I first realised..." His heart leapt at the idea of finally being free. "I could do it, but my parents and sisters..." The family he adored would forever forsake him. There would be colleagues and acquaintances who distanced themselves. In spite of it, there was a part of Rishi which fervently wished Anjali had announced his sexuality in the divorce papers. If she'd taken the decision out of his hands, he wouldn't have been living with this constant fear of discovery. But... "Even if I risk everything else in my life and come out, the blackmailer problem won't go away, and I can't do what the bastard wants."

"You can't," agreed Farhan. "Pay once, and the demands will never stop."

"Yes. I'm going to meet him."

"Eh... *what?*"

"I can't live like this anymore. What if it comes out one day? My child will be mocked as the son of a disgraced doctor wherever he goes. I can't risk his future like that. I need to put an end to things."

"Rishi, my love... *are you insane?*" Farhan huffed. "You're not going to meet any blackmailer, got it? You're going to sit right there and wait for me. I'm flying down tonight. We'll have to make the first payment while we figure something out. We'll pool cash. It will give us enough for a few payments. How much is the bastard asking for?"

"My soul," Rishi muttered.

"Heh?"

Rubbing his temple hard, Rishi said, "He's not asking for cash." The demand hadn't come yet, but it would, and it would be the same as the one made all those years ago—that Rishi take a weekend moonlighting gig, performing just one illegal kidney transplant for a client who really wanted a surgeon from a top institute.

Part VIII

Chapter 22

Sitting at the large teak desk in the library at the Joshi mansion, Anjali eyed the numbers scrolling down her laptop, not really seeing any of it. She hadn't even been able to talk the first few moments after the INTERPOL officer's revelation. The father of her child and the man she'd once loved with all her heart were both suspects in a criminal investigation. Not suspects, the officer explained. Rishi and Joe's names popped up in electronic communications intercepted by the cops. The police didn't know in what capacity the doctors were involved. "*Connections, connections, connections,*" the officer muttered. Rishi and Joe to Anjali, from her to the Joshi Charity Clinic, and from the clinic to the migrant workers who'd been lured to the Philippines to sell their organs for cash. Somehow, two of the donors ended up dead. The officer wanted Anjali to agree to an interview by the local investigator.

A shrill ring broke into her thoughts. Her phone... it was vibrating mere inches from her fingertips. Her heart leapt to her throat. She glanced at the screen and closed her eyes in disappointment. Not Joe—only the alarm she'd set to remind herself to prepare for the upcoming police interview. Of all the times for Joe to stop trying to contact her. After their encounter at the beach, there was a single message from him, a handwritten note delivered to her home, which had only his phone number.

Call me, Joe, she begged. She needed to hear that there was some other explanation behind his sudden wealth. Anjali didn't dare call him. The INTERPOL man had warned her not to divulge anything to Joe or Rishi, and she didn't want her phone records showing calls *she* made to either. She didn't need to come under scrutiny when she was trying to convince the cops neither man would've done what INTERPOL suspected. She would keep repeating it to the officer until her last breath.

Joe *had* to call and tell her how he'd made the money to do all that he did in the last eleven years. He simply couldn't be involved in organ smuggling. INTERPOL was wrong.

And Rishi... why did *he* stop calling? There were no more desperate messages since the week before. What caused him to be so terrified when he came to see her at the charity clinic? It *couldn't* have anything to do with what the cop said. Rishi was a doctor, for God's sake, bound by honour to save lives, not take them. So was Joe. But then, the killer had been a surgeon, too, bound by the same oath.

No, the cops were mistaken. Of all the people in the world, there was no one who could claim to know Rishi and Joe better than Anjali. Nothing short of a confession would convince her of either one's guilt.

In the meantime, she needed to set the stage for the interview. She'd done the best she could about finding herself a lawyer. Well... someone other than the divorce attorney and the Joshi Trust legal team's point man on the charity clinic. If the police didn't like it... she wasn't quite sure what she'd do, but the lawyer she called cheerfully told her to flip the bird at the cops. She was an adult, and she was *compos mentis*—in full possession of her mental faculties.

No one got a say in her choice for legal representation. Now, if he'd actually shown up on time, she could've breathed easier.

From a distance, she heard the doorbell ring. The cops, most likely, since the lawyer had missed his flight and was driving down. Her maid would bring the officers straight to the library as she'd been told. The quiet, temperature-controlled hall with no windows was the right place for a private conversation. The characters in the books lined up on shelves built into three of the four walls would not divulge what was said in the room.

Anjali waited until the footfalls reached the door. Pasting a gracious smile on her face, she stood. Two men—the INTERPOL officer she'd met before and a cop in the Goan police uniform of khaki shirt and pants—walked in. "Thank you for agreeing to talk to me here," she said, meaning it fully. If they wished, they could've ordered her to the police station.

Nodding briskly, SP Naidu—the INTERPOL man—looked around. "Your lawyer?"

"He... umm... is running late—"

Raised voices sounded outside. "Don't start without me," a man called, agitatedly. "Wait just one... goddammit, this is heavy... wait one second, please." The door was flung open. "Anju, could you ask your maid to..." The man in the Sherlock Holmes cap stopped short and grinned at the cops. "Oh, hello, officers."

Smiling in relief and pleasure, Anjali walked around her desk and greeted him with a hug. "Long time, friend."

Wrapping his arms around her waist, he practically lifted her off her feet. "Long time," he agreed, before setting her down. "Lots to catch up on after the meeting."

Anjali nodded. "Lots." Turning to the cops, she said, "My lawyer."

Tossing the cap on his head to one of the three armchairs arranged in front of the desk, the lawyer held out a hand. "Siddharth Menon, MD, LLB, ETW."

"ETW?" asked the Goan official, frowning even as he shook hands with the new arrival.

"Erotic thriller writer," said Siddharth, sounding quite pleased with himself.

"Heh?" The cop's mouth dropped open. "A writer?" Incredulously, he stared at Anjali. "You hired a writer to represent the clinic?"

"I'm legit," said Siddharth, putting on his best shyster smile. "I could show you my degree certificate if you want. I carry it with me, you know. People keep asking for proof I'm a real lawyer."

"He's not the Joshi lawyer," Anjali explained, awkwardly. The questions for her involved the men in her life, and she didn't really want the clinic's legal adviser around when she answered them. Siddharth could always coordinate with the clinic's lawyer if it came to that. "Dr Menon is representing only me."

"I've heard about you," interjected the INTERPOL officer, staring at Siddharth. "You've done some work for Bangalore police. That case with..." The officer named the apparent murder of a movie star by a stalker which eventually turned out to be the handiwork of her producer husband. "Professor at NIMHANS, right?" The mental health institute in Bangalore was the one place in India which offered a course in forensic psychiatry.

"I teach there off and on," said Siddharth, waving the cops to the chairs as though the library were *his* office.

Anjali shook her head and took her own place behind the desk. "Off and on" was the right description for what Siddharth did. Fresh from his forensic psychiatry fellowship in Massachusetts General Hospital, he'd joined NIMHANS but later decided it wasn't enough to interpret the criminal mind. He quit his job to join an LLB course and continued writing through his three years of law college, switching from poetry to thrillers. Last Anjali heard, he was a genuine bestseller. Not that it stopped him from sauntering by NIMHANS a couple of times a month to give lectures, usually to packed audiences. High-profile police cases, papers in psychiatry journals, sporadic articles in newspapers... Siddharth couldn't seem to stay put in one place. High-functioning attention deficit hyperactivity disorder as Meenakshi once commented. When Anjali called, frantic with worry, he told her to "chillax"; he'd be there as soon as he could.

"So your speciality is criminal law?" asked the Goan cop. Clearly annoyed, he glanced between Anjali and Siddharth. "You work with the police?"

"Yes to both," Siddharth stated, baldly. "Any problem?"

"None at all," cut in Naidu, the INTERPOL officer. "My colleague and I were expecting to meet the clinic's adviser, that's all. Would've made things a bit easier if we could get the permission to review records today."

"Life can be difficult," agreed Siddharth, mild mockery in the words. "Dr Joshi felt she'd be more comfortable with me. Rest assured we'll cooperate to the fullest so you can proceed with your investigation."

"Shall we start?" Anjali asked, eager to get the interview over with.

It took the Goan official a couple of moments to unslit his eyes and clear his throat. "First of all, I want to reiterate what my INTERPOL colleague said to you before, Dr Joshi. This is an extremely serious matter we're looking into. Goan police asked INTERPOL to take the lead in contacting the Joshis only to drive home the gravity of the situation."

Anjali nodded. "I understand. I've already agreed to hand over the information about the treatment received by the vanished workers. All I'm waiting for is clearance from the clinic's legal adviser."

"Good," said the Goan cop. "Secondly, need-to-know discussion only. Lawyers are unavoidable, I suppose. Thank you for agreeing not to share this discussion with the clinic's board or the rest of your family."

Siddharth sat up. "*What?* Why not?"

"Umm... Sid..." Anjali muttered, "they're talking about the part which involves Rishi and Joe. I've already informed my father of the rest of it." Dr Pratapchandra Joshi was the chairman of the trust which funded the clinic. She had a fiduciary duty to notify him of any developments concerning the clinic, but the problems in her personal life were no one else's business unless and until she chose to share the information. As far as the rest of the case was concerned, both Anjali and her father were ordered to use the violation of intellectual property law regarding medications as cover. Even her secretary, Chandekar, didn't know what was really going on.

Nodding, Siddharth said, "Well then, we'll need to make sure this interview stays strictly within the realm of her personal observations of Dr Rastogi and Dr D'Acosta."

"Of course," said the INTERPOL officer, smoothly.

Back and forth they went over any potential connections the men might have had with the clinic. With the exception of Joe's long-dead mother who'd worked as a nurses' aide, Anjali knew of no such connection. Still, the questions continued—about her life in AIIMS, her friends, the people she saw around Rishi and Joe. At one point, the Goan cop asked, "What was your equation with Dr D'Acosta? Just friends or..."

"I... umm..." Anjali mumbled, mildly panicking. What was she supposed to say? It was illegal to lie to the cops, wasn't it? But she didn't really want to go into the details with complete outsiders.

With an annoyed cluck, Siddharth said, "You don't have to answer if you don't want. They can't force you."

"Doctor," said the Goan cop, his eyes snapping with impatience. "You work with law enforcement. You know as well as I any detail could eventually turn out to be important."

With a genial smile which was all the more tough for its friendliness, Siddharth said, "That's your problem, sir. Not Anju's, and I'm here as her lawyer, not the police psychiatrist. I'm sure she wasn't expecting to be embarrassed in this manner."

Anjali raised a hand. Lips stiff, she said, "I'll answer. There was a time when Joe and I dated, but he left."

"Any idea why?" asked the Goan official.

She'd asked herself the same question for the last eleven years.

Chapter 23

Summer 2008

Arms wrapped around each other, Anjali and Joe waltzed to peppy Goan music in the cluttered living room of the flat, laughing helplessly whenever they bumped into the sofa or one of the chairs. There was no one else present, Rishi having made himself scarce. She'd returned from what had been a miserable vacation, and this time, Joe surprised her with dinner.

"Thank you for this," Anjali murmured. "Summer was horrible. People keep asking what I want to do, and I don't have an answer." Groaning, she added, "I need advice, Joe."

"Tell 'people' to mind their own business," he suggested.

She laughed. "On my *career*. And don't just say you want to be part of my life whatever I decide."

"I do," he said, immediately. "From boyfriend to girlfriend, it's the only thing I have to say. From surgery resident to third-year medical student... well... you have two more years. If you still don't know, try general practice while you decide." His hand rubbing soothing circles on the small of her back, he said, "Sundari, don't let the idiots get to you. A couple of nosy questions shouldn't mess up your vacation."

"Oh, it wasn't only that. I told you about my nanaji." Her mother's father passed away a mere month ago. "In a brothel! Can you believe it?"

Joe shook with laughter. "Why not?" he teased. "Best way to go."

Rolling her eyes, Anjali said, "Mom and Dad were so embarrassed. And Vikram... he's just..." Anjali's seventeen-year-old brother lost the only person he talked to. He packed his bags and moved to the men's hostel on the IIT campus—the elite engineering school he'd gotten into. Mom and Dad were super understanding about Vikram breaking the Joshi tradition of all sons going into medicine, but he still thumbed his nose at them and moved out. "He could've stayed at home. IIT's only thirty kilometres from our parents' flat."

"The commute?" Joe asked.

Grudgingly, she admitted, "An hour."

"C'mon, Anju. You can't expect the kid to do an hour each way every day."

"I'm not talking about doing that forever, but he could've stayed for a month or two until Mom got over it. *I* would've if I could."

Joe placed a soft kiss on the birthmark at the corner of her mouth—his favourite spot to kiss on her whole body. Tenderly, he said, "You would've because you're my sundari."

Kissing him back, Anjali smiled. "How was *your* summer? Did you talk to your brother about what the school said?" Sixteen-year-old Dev D'Acosta was apparently well-liked by both faculty and the student body, but unfortunately,

213

he wasn't in the least interested in academics. The principal had doubts about his chances of graduation.

"Yeah," said Joe, frustrated look on his face. "This is his final year in high school, and he doesn't care. All he talks about is getting Dad's teashop back from the bank and starting a restaurant. Worse part is Rosanna... Ruksana's all for it."

Anjali murmured, soothingly. The woman who was Joe's stepmom was a complete ditz according to him, but she was aware enough to hide her religion by using the Christian version of her name in public. Interfaith marriages weren't exactly uncommon. Except, the lady was a Kashmiri Muslim, and the man in question was a soldier at the time. The army wasn't bothered by it, but if the facts were openly known, two-bit politicians from every side of the debate would march to the D'Acosta residence to score cheap points by holding forth on terrorism in the troubled Indian state and the loyalty expected from the armed forces. It would be akin to an American military officer marrying an Iraqi. Then, there were the religious fanatics who would've unleashed violence on the poor woman and her family for the sin of marrying outside her faith.

Anjali was the only one in the gang who knew the whole truth about Ruksana/Rosanna, but they had all heard Joe scolding her over the phone about making the kids do their homework. "She's his mother for God's sake," Joe grumbled. "She should want a more stable life for him than running a teashop."

"You're so *desi*, yaar," Anjali teased, calling him a stereotypical Indian. The music had changed to a slow tune, and they were barely swaying in place now. "You think your brother should get a college degree and work nine to five."

"Ha, ha," said Joe, grumpily. "It's not as if I *want* him to be miserable, but starting your own business comes with some risk. A fall-back plan is essential.

For those of us who're not independently wealthy, education is the best security."

She leaned back against his embrace and stuck her tongue out at him. "You insulting me?" She was aware she'd basically won the ovarian lottery in being born a Joshi, but she worked hard, darn it. The entire clan did. There wasn't a single relative of hers she'd call a slacker.

"Heh?" Joe laughed. "No, I wasn't even thinking about your family. Dr Ram worked his butt off at the charity clinic when he was supposed to be semi-retired, and being a Joshi wouldn't have helped you get into AIIMS." There were no quotas for the privileged at India's premier medical college. Only the best and the brightest were allowed in. "But you gotta admit being rich gives you options. You have the freedom to fail. I can't afford to. Dev can't, either."

True enough. "You need to make a deal with him. Say you'll help him get financing for the restaurant but only if he finishes college."

Joe pursed his lips for a moment. "Might work." With a sudden grin, he added, "I can't wait to tell them about you." The younger D'Acostas never interacted much with Dr Ram Joshi, and they'd never heard of Anjali. Except for Fr Franco, no one in the family knew of her existence, but even he didn't know his old friend's granddaughter and the man who was more or less his grandson were wildly in love. "We'll tell everyone as soon as my junior residency is done," vowed Joe. Kissing her again, he asked, "Can you believe we've been together one whole year?"

"Our first anniversary," Anjali murmured, dreamily.

"Hope the year was as good for you as it was for me."

"Oh, yes," she whispered. The only fight they had was over his reluctance to meet her mother, and he managed to be off campus the day Rattan Joshi was in AIIMS, thus avoiding the possibility of Anjali's awkwardness with the situation giving them away. Otherwise, life was perfect. A sudden, sharp pain shot across her eyeballs, almost blinding her. She stumbled against Joe's shoulder.

"Hey," he said. "Are you all right?"

Anjali loosened herself from his embrace and took a couple of steps backward. "Yeah." With her thumb and index finger, she massaged her brow. "The stupid tension headache." She'd had them a couple of times this last year. It was always the same—excruciating pain for a few minutes which resolved so completely, she was left wondering if she'd imagined it.

"Here," said Joe, taking her by the shoulders and gently directing her to the sofa. "Sit."

She ended up lying down, her head on his lap while his thumbs rubbed circles at her temples. "I don't want to mess up our anniversary dinner."

"It was supposed to be dinner *and* the new Batman movie," Joe said, ruefully. "But we'd better stay home."

"Movie?" she asked. "I thought we weren't going to go public until you're done with your junior residency?"

"Yeah, but... Anju, lemme tell you something. If I were in a position to do so, I would've put an engagement ring on you right now."

"I understand."

His thigh shifting restlessly at the back of her neck, he said, "I wish we could go around together on campus. You know... make it clear we're a couple. Most of them think you're with whatshisname. I bet even your parents have heard the rumours."

"Rishi?" Anjali laughed. She really hoped Mom was keeping her promise not to poke her nose into her daughter's social life, but there was always the small chance one of her acquaintances on campus had volunteered the information. "Are you jealous?"

"Kind of."

"Aww," said Anjali, reaching up to pat Joe's cheek. "I'll talk to Mom and Dad as soon as you're ready."

"That's two years from now. I thought we could start small right away and make the big announcement later."

"The movie," she murmured, dropping her hand.

"Yeah. What do you think?"

"If I started going out with you, my parents *will* get to hear of it," she warned. With Rishi, there were merely rumours. With Joe, people would be convinced there was romance. Or at least sex. He had what they called a reputation. Someone was bound to inform her parents.

"I meant we could keep it friendly and casual in public for the moment. You go with Sid all the time without worrying about your parents. They know we're all in the same group."

Friendly and casual on a one-on-one basis with Joe? There was already talk on campus on why he'd been partnerless for two years in a row. The moment he appeared with Anjali on his arm, gossip would begin. She sat up and brushed back her hair. "What if people start saying stuff about me? Will we tell them?"

Joe frowned. "Why would anyone say... you're still worried about the slut-shaming thing, aren't you? Anju, all you have to say is we're friends. Which we are."

The claim wouldn't stop the malicious gossip. The engagement ring Joe mentioned would, but he wasn't ready for that step. "I don't think it's a good idea," she finally mumbled. "Let's wait until your junior residency is done." When he didn't respond, she added, "What you're suggesting will leave me in a difficult position, Joe. You kinda want everyone to start thinking we *might* be together, but you don't want to actually tell them for the next two years. People will start talking, and I won't have anything to say except—" Anjali made air-quotes with her fingers. "'—we're just friends.'"

After a second or two, Joe muttered, "I guess you're right."

Her headache didn't melt away like it usually did, so Joe got her in bed and cuddled her from behind. While he was still teasing her about already having wifely headaches, she drifted off to sleep.

They did get to see the Batman movie, but as a group. Classes, exams, the hospital, Joe's research work. Hanging out with the gang on the weekends, talking to a homesick Kokila on the phone, stealing moments alone with Joe. With some satisfaction, Anjali checked off three months on her desk calendar, humming the new Beyoncé song, "Single Ladies." Twenty-one more months to go. Anjali could hardly wait.

***

"The number you have dialled does not exist," said the pre-recorded message.

Standing at the bottom of the staircase of the crowded hospital building, Rishi hung up his phone and frowned at the list of missed calls from the same unknown person. Nope, the number was correct—one call every hour on the hour on the busiest night in the burn unit when Rishi didn't have time even to take a piss. Now, when he returned the call, the number was no longer in existence? Shrugging, he slipped the phone back into his pocket. Whoever it was could call again if they wanted to talk to Rishi badly enough.

He was exhausted beyond imagination. It happened every year with Diwali—the festival of lights. Idiots all across the city would decide to tempt fate with fireworks, leading to more business for burn management teams. The hospital seriously needed to consider giving extra pay to those on duty on Diwali night.

Pushing out through the noisy throng of patients at the main entrance, Rishi encountered Joe walking in, lab coat slung over one shoulder. When Rishi got home, there would be *poori* and *aloo*—deep-fried bread and sautéed potatoes—waiting.

Breakfast, shower, and straight to bed. Rishi was not willing to do anything else the rest of the day. He stopped at the mailbox in the lobby of the apartment building and looked through the papers. Flyers advertising sales, a donation request, and an unstamped envelope addressed to Rishi. Frowning, he stared at it. The landlord of the flat sent messages this way, but it was usually addressed to both his tenants. Yawning, Rishi gathered all the papers and jogged up the stairs to the fourth floor, his backpack bouncing against his spine with each step.

The smell of spiced potatoes greeted him as soon as he opened the door. Rishi tossed his backpack and the mail in his hands to the floor and made his way to the kitchen. He was tucking in even before he got to the living room sofa. In five minutes, he demolished all the food on his plate. Joe could be difficult, but sharing a flat with him had its perks. He'd even left tea in the kitchen to wash the food down.

Rishi eyed his backpack and the mail still lying on the floor by the front door. *The envelope...* he needed to check. "Later," he mumbled. At the moment, he was too full and lazy to get up.

Someone was shouting his name. Groaning, Rishi turned on his side, and the world dropped under him. A sudden pain shot up his elbow, waking him up. "What?" he mumbled in shock. He was on the floor, not on the sofa, any longer.

There was a loud banging on the front door. "Rishi," shouted Gauri.

Staggering to his feet, he went to the door. His backpack and the mail from the morning were still there. He kicked them to the side and opened the door. "Whatchu doing here, darling?" he asked, voice sleep-slurred. "I thought you were on duty in the paediatric ward today."

Gauri pushed in. "You weren't picking up the phone, and Anjali was in class, so Joe asked me to come here. There's been an accident in Goa. His stepmother. He needs to go right away."

"Oh, God," said Rishi, fully awake now. "Is she..."

"Alive as of now," said Gauri. "The priest—Joe's godfather—didn't really know the extent of injuries, but she's unconscious. Joe's planning to fly down tonight. He's trying to get someone to take today's duty instead of him. He asked if either you or I would pack some stuff for him and meet him at the airport."

"Of course," said Rishi. "What about the ticket?"

"He'll have to buy it at the airport." Gauri grimaced. "Gonna be expensive."

By the time Rishi got to the airport with a small box crammed with his flatmate's stuff, Anjali called and said she'd meet him at the Air India counter. She'd claimed a headache and missed the rest of the afternoon's classes. Purse on her shoulder, she was peering through the streaming crowd. "Oh, good," she said, spotting him. "Joe isn't with you." At Rishi's puzzled frown, she zipped open her purse and grabbed an envelope with the airline logo on it. "Give it to him," she shouted over the announcements going on. "Tell him you bought it. I got here after you if he asks. Say he can pay you back later."

"What—"

Anjali clucked. "Just do it, please?" She glanced over his shoulder and yelped. "He's here. There's no time to explain. For God's sake, take it."

Rishi tucked the ticket into his shirt pocket and turned.

Pale-faced, Joe was striding towards them. This was conservative Delhi, not Goa or Mumbai, but he still hugged Anjali tightly for a long minute. When Rishi said he'd already bought a ticket, Joe muttered a "Thanks, man" before scratching his chin. "God," he mumbled. "I hope Rosanna pulls through." He'd said plenty of times the woman his father married was a total ditz, but she *had* spent years in the same household with Joe and was mother to his half-siblings.

"You'd better check in," said Rishi. "Not much time left."

With one more hug for Anjali, Joe strode to the counter and soon, disappeared into the crowd.

Rishi escorted Anjali back to the hostel. She didn't offer any explanations for the ticket thing, and he didn't ask. He'd been caught by surprise when she shoved it into his hand. Otherwise, he would've realised what was going on. Joe and the giant chip on his shoulder.

The adrenaline rush which fuelled Rishi through the afternoon was wearing off when he got back to the flat, leaving him bone-tired. The damned backpack was still on the floor, the unstamped envelope and the rest of the mail next to it. If the envelope contained communication from the landlord, it was for both Joe and Rishi. Well, Rishi needed a shower first. The landlord could wait.

Twenty minutes later, he exited the steamy bathroom in a pair of boxers. It was good to feel clean and smell of lemony soap instead of sweat and grime. Rubbing the moisture off his head with a small towel, he picked up the backpack and the mail from the floor.

The bag went on one of the chairs, along with the damp towel. The flyer advertising some kind of car show went straight into the trash can. So did the donation request. Neither Rishi nor Joe was in a financial position to buy cars or donate to charity, but the doctor title meant they received more than usual such junk in the mail. Rishi turned the envelope over with his fingers. The

221

writing didn't seem familiar. It was almost... *childish?* Ripping it open, he drew out a single sheet of paper.

Daktar saab, it began, calling Rishi Doctor sir in Hinglish. *Phone uthao. Nahi tho sab ko patha chalega tu ne klab mein kya kiya. Raat mein call lagaunga.* Pick up the phone, or everyone's going to know what you did at the club. I'll call at night.

"What the——" Rishi's heart slammed against his chest wall. His head swam. The club? Eclipse? The phone... he needed to get to the phone. Dropping to his knees, he unzipped his backpack and dug through. Nothing. He flung the pillows on the sofa to the floor. Where was the damned phone? The last time he used it... Anjali... she'd called him, asking him to go to the Air India counter.

He ran to the bathroom. Soapy steam hit him in the face. Coughing, he grabbed the pants off the damp tiles and tugged out the device from one of the pockets. The missed calls from the night before... three from Joe while Rishi was napping on the sofa this morning... a couple from Gauri... the call from Anjali he'd picked up. Nothing else. He glanced outside the window. It was almost dark. The note said the call would come at night.

His chest... he couldn't breathe. Rishi dug into the other pocket and brought out his inhaler. Two puffs. Somehow, his chest got tighter. His vision greyed. He needed to get out of the steam, or he would soon be unconscious.

Wheezing loudly, Rishi staggered back to the living room. The note was on the floor, next to the chair. He went down on his haunches and reached for the sheet of paper, but he couldn't. Wildly glancing between the sheet and the phone in his hand, he scrambled rearwards until his spine hit the side of the sofa.

Everyone... everyone would know. His parents... they'd know he'd been lying to them. His professors, all his colleagues, the students... they'd all mock him. If it got to the medical council, they'd take away his medical licence.

"No," Rishi whimpered. He was a surgeon. No one could take it away from him. Except, they could. They could even send him to prison. Panting, he glanced around the room. He needed to leave the campus. Hide. His family... Papa and Ma would refuse to let him in. The doors of his home would forever be closed to him.

When the shrill ring of the phone ripped apart the silence in the flat, Rishi sobbed. With fear-blurred eyes, he glanced at the number.

"Hello?" he mumbled into the phone.

"Daktar saab," said a muffled voice. "*Darr gaye kya?*" Was he scared?

Acidic fluid surged to Rishi's throat. Swallowing hard, he asked, "What do you want? Money?"

"No." The voice at the other end continued in guttural Hindi, "I want you to take the money I give."

Voice trembling, Rishi said, "I don't have much, but... huh?"

The bastard on the phone said, "I have a job for you. You'll be paid well, too."

"A job?" Rishi parroted, stupidly.

"Yes. A moonlighting gig. Accept it, and you'll be all right."

Feeling dizzy, Rishi asked, "What kind of moonlighting?"

The bastard grunted, satisfaction evident in the sound. "I'll let you know the time and place."

"But what do you want me to *do?*" asked Rishi. Nothing made sense. Why would anyone...

"Not to worry," said the blackmailer. "It's right up your alley. A small surgery. I'll give you the details once I have the rest arranged." A click, then the dial tone. The bastard had hung up.

223

Rishi didn't know how long he sat on the floor, his mind foggy. It could've been minutes; it could've been hours. "Moonlighting?" he mumbled. *Joe* had been offered a moonlighting gig. Rishi glanced at his phone and brought up Joe's number. *No.* Rishi tossed the phone aside. He couldn't tell *anyone*. Not even those who knew he was gay would condone what he'd done, and if he were to ask about the moonlighting offer while Joe was in the middle of a family crisis, he'd immediately know something was wrong. Rishi would have to wait and see.

***

"How old is your stepmom?" Anjali questioned Joe, her stomach churning in helpless anxiety for him. "In her fifties? Otherwise healthy?"

After a week in Goa, Joe had just flown back to Delhi. There were shadows under his eyes and the beginnings of a beard on his cheeks. "Forty-nine," he said, slouching into the sofa next to Anjali. "I can't believe it still... some drunk idiot going ten kilometres an hour on a moped... she didn't even fall. The neurologist thinks the shock shot Rosanna's blood pressure so high she bled into the cerebellum. He says she's recovering... otherwise healthy as you said except for the BP... but..." Making a helpless gesture with his hands, Joe continued, "She's still off-balance. Our flat in Mapusa is on the second floor. Dev says he'll make sure she takes her meds, but how's he going to stop her from going in and out on her own? He'll be in school. He has to be. Missing these many days when you're in your final year of high school is not helpful."

"Tell her about the risk, man," Siddharth commented, chewing thoughtfully on a piece of Joe's stash of peanut brittle.

"How many times?" Joe groaned. "You guys haven't met her. I feel like I'm dealing with a fourteen-year-old most of the time. Rosanna is pleasant, but if she's told she shouldn't be doing something, she sulks and whines and sometimes does it anyway. Whenever I asked if she were taking the meds her doctor prescribed, she'd tell me everything was all right. Apparently, she fired her regular doctor and went to some kind of herbal healing quack who gave her some sugar tablets and assured her she was cured. In her mind, she *was* doing what the 'doctor' asked her to."

"She has three children," Anjali muttered. "How could she be so irresponsible?"

Joe snorted. "Fr Franco and I have three children... make that four. But Rosanna is an adult under the law and entitled to do as she pleases. Unfortunately, she's also the only adult in the house for now and the legal guardian of the actual children."

"Oh, God," Anjali said. "I hope she gets her balance back soon." She glanced towards the window where Rishi was standing, staring out at the next building. He hadn't talked much—actually, not at all. Meenakshi was busy with her research paper, so she wasn't around. Gauri's wedding was a mere six weeks away, and she was trying to get all her work done before, so she was absent as well. Kokila, of course, had been in New York City for a few months now. "What do you think, Rishi? This is your area of expertise."

There was no response.

"Yo, Rishi," yelled Siddharth.

Rishi started. Turning around, he asked, "I'm sorry... were you talking to me?"

"Trying to," said Siddharth.

"Are you all right, Rishi?" Anjali asked, noticing for the first time the shadows around *his* eyes. He'd also been taking extra duty to make sure he'd get enough time off for his best friend's wedding to Gauri.

"Yeah, I'm fine," he said. "I was thinking about... ahh... moonlighting."

Joe frowned. "You know we're not allowed to. Don't get yourself into trouble. I'll return the ticket fare as soon as I get a chance to go to the bank."

Gaze directed away from a cringing Anjali, Rishi said, "It's not about the fare. I was simply thinking about it. Have you gotten any more calls?"

"God, yes," said Joe. "They're up to seven thousand euros now. Crazy."

"What if they're serious?" Rishi asked, abruptly.

Laughing, Siddharth said, "C'mon. It's a scam. Next thing you know, they'll ask for your bank account number so they could deposit all the cash."

"You know," said Joe, leaning forwards. "That possibility never occurred to me. I thought they were going to simply refuse to pay after I did all the work."

"You've never asked what kind of work they want you to do?" Rishi asked.

Joe shrugged. "What for? I'm not allowed to do it, so I'm not going to."

"Not even if they paid you more?" Rishi asked, doggedly.

"What's up with you?" Joe asked, mild irritation in his tone. "I worked damned hard to get this far. Why would I consider ruining it all for any amount of money? Why would *you?*"

"We all have our price," muttered Rishi.

"Don't do anything stupid," warned Siddharth.

Shaking his head, Rishi said, "I won't. I was looking up something on medical ethics and thought I'd ask."

Before she left the flat, Anjali found a moment to talk to Rishi in private. "Hey, do you need any money?" She wasn't quite certain how things stood with his family, but the fact he rarely went home surely meant something. It wasn't easy to survive in a big city like Delhi on a resident's stipend.

Surprise lit his eyes, followed closely by gentle humour. "You're a good friend, Anju. No, I don't need any money. At least not at the moment. Like I said, I was only doing some reading on medical ethics."

She eyed him for a moment. "Okay. Get some rest, all right? Or you're not going to look your usual, glamorous self at Gauri and Nikhil's wedding."

He laughed. "Worry about your boyfriend. What if your parents want to meet him when he's in Mumbai?"

"Don't remind me," she said, groaning. Gauri and Meenakshi's mom was from Mumbai, and the wedding would be in the city. Anjali would be travelling to the venue from her parents' home. They had to know Joe was part of the same group of friends. What if they expected grandfather's protégé to pay them a visit while he was in the neighbourhood? *Awkwaaard.* "I'm just glad his stepmom's all right, and he can be at the wedding. Nikhil's one of *his* best friends, too."

Another week later, Anjali was exiting the exam hall with Meenakshi and Siddharth after the Microbiology paper when they spotted Gauri waiting for them. "Joe's stepmom had a second stroke," she said. "She didn't make it."

***

The world was falling apart around Rishi. He sat on the threadbare sofa, the strange buffer zone surrounding his mind causing the voices in the flat to sound far, far away. Joe was on the phone, talking to his sixteen-year-old brother, frantically asking him to hold on. A cup of tea in her hand, Anjali was in one of the chairs, but her eyes were fixed on her boyfriend, following him around. Gauri, Meenakshi, Siddharth... they were all talking at once, trying to find a way to travel to Goa with exams going on for the younger ones in the group and Gauri's wedding coming up in about a month. None of them could hear the screams in Rishi's head; they couldn't see his murderous rage.

The bastard, Rishi thought, savagely wanting to slit Parth Kumar's throat. He had to have been the caller. There was no other soul on earth who knew what Rishi did that night—no other soul who could be threatening to reveal all.

227

A moonlighting gig... it had to be the same person who'd kept calling Joe the last couple of years. Joe refused to take the bait, declining even to ask what was involved.

Stupid, Rishi muttered in his mind. He should've simply noted the time and place when the second phone call came an hour earlier. Instead, he simply *had* to ask what he'd be doing.

"It will be easy for you," the voice at the other end said, calmly. "There's a woman who needs a kidney. She's insisting on a surgeon from a top institute."

Joe wasn't in the flat, but Rishi hadn't wanted to take the slightest chance of anyone outside the front door overhearing. "I'm not the right person for a transplant," he whispered into the phone. Fool him, he didn't understand what they were asking.

There was an annoyed grunt from the line. "Who's asking you to do the transplant? We have experts for that part, but none of them wants to be involved in getting the kidney from the donor. Our lawyer called it plausible deniability. The transplant surgeons we have want to be able to claim ignorance of where the organ came from. There was a general surgeon who took care of it for us, but the last time this same patient got a transplant, the kidney got rejected. She's convinced it was because the surgeon didn't know what he was doing. She'll be happy to hear this time around it will be done by someone from AIIMS."

Rishi's heart stopped. "You want me to... *no.* No way, you damned bastard. I won't do it. I'd rather die than steal organs from my patients." How did they think Rishi would do it, anyway? He was a junior resident. It wasn't as though he could sneak a patient into the operating theatre and perform clandestine surgery.

"Calm down, Doctor," snapped the voice. "You don't have to steal anything. We have willing donors."

Understanding finally dawning, Rishi said, "The patient is *buying* the kidney." A wealthy patient, bribing a starving man or woman into selling body parts for survival. Except, trading organs for cash was illegal in most countries, including India.

"Don't act so superior, Doctor. You know what the life expectancy is for a dialysis patient? Five years. Worse than some cancers. What would *you* do in her place? If it makes you feel better, remember you'll be saving her life. Think about it that way, and your conscience will be clear. Better yet, think about what will happen to you if you decide not to cooperate. Plus, you'll be paid well."

A scream of fury erupted from Rishi's chest. "No," he sobbed. "I can't."

"Are you sure?" asked the bastard. "I'll give you two more weeks to make a decision. The patient won't be ready for surgery until then. Think hard, Doctor."

"Rishi," shouted a female voice from outside the flat. Gauri. "Open the door!"

Whimpering in fear, he glanced between the phone and the front door.

"Rishi," Gauri shouted a second time. "There's an emergency. Joe's stepmom had another stroke."

Chaos. Utter chaos. Gauri, Anjali, Meenakshi, Siddharth... Anjali calling the airlines for Joe... Siddharth throwing Joe's clothes into his suitcase... finally, Joe striding in.

None of them glanced a second time at Rishi. No one asked why he was sitting motionless on the sofa. Nobody saw the thick, iron chains wrapped around his soul. If he didn't want to lose his licence, if he didn't want to be thrown in prison for being who he was, he'd have to break the oath he'd sworn as a doctor. He'd have to do what was told, go where he was asked.

"I'm going with you," said Anjali, her strong, sweet voice penetrating Rishi's mind. With a small clatter, she set the teacup on the coffee table.

"What—" He followed Anjali's gaze to Joe who was now off the phone and looking vaguely around.

"You can't skip exams," muttered Joe. These were the second professional exams, held at the end of the fifth semester. If she missed them, it would be six more months before she could redo, and it would eat into the time allotted to the clinical part of the course.

"Exams will be over in one more week," argued Anjali. "I'll fly to Goa after."

"Anju," Joe sighed. "Things will be done by then."

Gauri broke off from her discussion with her sister and Siddharth. "You're still going to need help. Your brothers and sister... I guess your Fr Franco can help, but you still need someone."

Joe held both hands up as though at the end of his tether. "No. It won't work."

Clambering to her feet, Anjali said, "You can't handle it all on your own. Plus..." Her eyes filled with hurt. "I'm your girlfriend, Joe."

"Look, Anju," Joe said, his voice raised. Throwing his hands into the air, he lowered his tone. "Not now, okay? I can't deal with this right now. You don't need to come to Goa. I'll manage."

Rishi gritted his teeth. *Idiots,* he wanted to rage. Lovers, insecurities, arguments... all self-inflicted wounds. Which among them was staring at criminal charges for merely being them? Which among them was about to lose everything he'd ever worked for?

"Maybe we should leave," Siddharth muttered.

"Yeah," said Meenakshi, standing. "We can see about a ticket while Joe talks to the surgery chief." She took one step towards the door and hesitated. "Anju, you gonna be okay here, or do you want to go with us?"

"I'll be fine," said Anjali, nodding without taking her eyes off Joe. As soon as the front door closed, she said, "We need to talk. In private."

As though there was any privacy to be had in the flat. Eyes tightly shut, Rishi tried to tune out the argument in Joe's room. The noise... it needed to stop, but it didn't, not even when Rishi held pillows to his ears and rocked back and forth.

"My God, Anju," Joe shouted. "Can we not do this today of all days?"

Tears clogging her voice, she asked, "What exactly am I doing? Trying to help you?"

"You're *not* helping. Think about it. How are you going to help by coming to Goa? It won't be with the rest of the group. Gauri and Meenu won't be allowed to go anywhere near a home with a recent death because of... bad omen... whatever... for the wedding. Rishi can't miss Nikhil's wedding. Sid can't come now because of exams, and later, what's the point of asking him to skip the wedding to help me deal with paperwork? You'll be the only one there. Your parents—"

"Stop right there," said Anjali, her fury evident in her tone. "Don't make this about my family and your crazy ideas on how they will react to us. This is about you and me. You said you wanted to marry me. Know what that makes me? Your fiancée, not simply your girlfriend. Fi-an-cée. You hear me?"

"Yeah. And? We're not public yet. You're going to stay with me in the flat and claim we're only friends? You didn't even want to go to a movie with me."

"Movie—oh, God. You've been holding on to that all this time? And how can you possibly see the two things as the same?"

"No, it's precisely because they're not the same—" Joe groaned, loudly. "Okay, how about this, sundari? My brothers share the room with me. My sister used to sleep next to her mom, and I don't know what I'm going to do with all of *them* when I get home. Where will I put you?"

Voice slightly lower, Anjali said, "I get what you're saying. Joe, I only want to help. I'll stay at the Joshi house. Maybe the kids can stay with me while you take care of the paperwork—"

"No."

"Why not?"

"What do you mean 'why not?'" Joe asked, incredulity in his tone. "I'm not going to take any more charity from your family."

"Charity? Anytime you need my help is charity to you?"

"Anytime you use your family to help me *is* charity. You may not see it that way, but the rest of the world will. What are you going to do after? You don't think your parents will have questions once they know you—and only you—were in Goa with me? It isn't like watching a movie together. You won't be able to claim we're only friends. They won't believe you."

Anjali hissed. "Your problem is not that you don't want to take my family's help. You simply don't want to acknowledge me. You're afraid you'll have to if anyone finds out I was in Goa. You'll feel forced to acknowledge me because I'm Daadaji's granddaughter."

"What?" Joe shouted. "Don't put words in my mouth—shit, I don't have the time for this."

"Where are you—you're leaving?" The door to the room was flung open, and Joe stalked out, wheeling his box behind him. Anjali, her cheeks stained with tears, followed. "Joe, if you go now..." She ran to the front door and blocked his way.

"Anju, please," said Joe. "We'll talk when I get back."

"Oh, yeah?" she asked, eyes wild. "Unless you're prepared to acknowledge me, don't bother coming back."

Chapter 24

Present day

"He didn't," Anjali whispered, hot tears rolling down to her jaw. "He simply didn't come back." She was on the porch swing, looking out at the cobbled street in front of the Joshi mansion. The tourists walking around in the afternoon sun threw furtive glances at her, but she couldn't stop crying.

Even the baby on her lap twisted around to stare. "Guh?" he enquired. Anjali laughed and nuzzled his head.

Settling an arm around her shoulders, Siddharth said, "You finally have a chance to ask why."

"I thought about it," Anjali said, wiping the moisture from her face. "*Joe* tried to tell me, but I walked away each time. What's the point after all these years?"

"You tell me," said Siddharth, "why the man can make you cry even after eleven years, and I'll tell you what the point is."

Anjali laughed through her tears. "Don't play shrink with me, Sid. Or I'll start asking inconvenient questions."

"Like?"

"Like what's going on with you and your publisher lady."

Removing his arm from her shoulders, he mumbled, "Shut up." He brought a knee up to his chest and balanced himself with his heel on the edge of the cushioned seat. "How do you know something's going on? You've never met her. Hell, *she* doesn't know something's going on."

Anjali clucked. "One-way traffic?" At Siddharth's glare, she raised her left hand. "I won't make fun of your love life if you leave mine alone. Kiki told me there was something off in your behaviour when she and her hubster had dinner with you and Ms Publisher in New York."

"Damn," said Siddharth. "And I thought I was a good actor. Hey, did you know Kiki wants to move back to Goa?"

Nodding and laughing, Anjali said, "Mr Kiki luuurves the idea." The Russian-American Kokila married took one look at the beaches and the sun and fell head-over-heels for the state. She'd managed to buy her uncle's share in the family home, but her mother for whom Kokila did all the work passed before the paperwork was signed. Nevertheless, Kokila started renovations on the property, planning to return to India very soon.

The expression on his face changing, Siddharth asked, "Anju, does Kiki know Joe's back? What about Gauri and Meenu?"

"No, I called Kiki for something else. She's worked at the Joshi Clinic before, and I needed some advice... staff problems, etcetera." Anjali looked down at her baby. "I was planning to tell her about meeting Joe, but I kept thinking about what those policemen said. My mind was too messed up to say anything at the time."

"Do you believe Joe could've done it?" Siddharth asked. "Or Rishi?"

"No," Anjali said, instantly. "But there are so many things I don't understand. Joe... Rishi... they're both acting strangely."

"You're never going to understand unless you ask," Siddharth pointed out.

"Yeah, but..." Anjali dropped a kiss on the baby's head. "The officers said they don't want me talking to anyone about it. Sid, am I *legally* obliged to keep quiet?"

"No. And don't let them convince you otherwise."

"Hmm," she brooded. "But if the employees somehow hear about it, I'll end up with clinic-wide panic on my hands. If it gets to the general public—" Pressure from the media, from politicians... the clinic would very likely be forced to cease operations.

"You won't be talking to the staff," Siddharth argued. "Just Rishi and Joe."

"I can't," dismissed Anjali. "I know neither of them will blab, but I don't want to take any chances. If I were in Rishi's place, I'd talk to Farhan. And Joe..." Anjali shook her head, not wanting to imagine any romantic partner he might choose to confide in. "What if he goes to Fr Franco or his brothers or someone else? If there's a leak, I need to know it didn't start with them or me. For one, I'm *not* going to be the one to pull the trigger on the clinic's destruction. For another, any leak might point the cops in the direction of the actual culprits."

"True," Siddharth acknowledged. "But you don't need to tell either Joe or Rishi about the situation at the clinic. Just keep the lines of communication open."

Anjali mulled the idea. "Maybe it will help us figure out what the heck is going on." She glanced sideways at Siddharth. "What I said about Rishi... his boyfriend... you won't mention it to anyone, right? I had to tell you the reason for the divorce because the cops will probably ask, and you're my lawyer." Vaguely, she noted Siddharth hadn't appeared terribly surprised by the news. Writer, shrink, and friend of many years... he surely noticed something before. Thankfully, he'd never confronted her with it.

"It stays between us," Siddharth swore, a hand to his heart. Glancing thoughtfully upwards, he added, "And between Rishi and his boyfriend... you said Joe knows? Rishi's parents? Your family?" When Anjali poked him in the belly with a finger, he doubled over, laughing. "Not fair," he complained. "You know I'm ticklish there."

"Another one?" exclaimed a strident voice.

Anjali looked up and groaned. "Mrs Braganza." The nosy lady was dragging her rotund self up the steps of her own porch, huffing and puffing all the way. She glanced between Siddharth and the rental car parked in front of the Joshi residence.

"Who's that?" asked Siddharth.

"My neighbour. She's convinced I'm a harlot."

Siddharth stared for a second and then, guffawed. "Harlot? Not a slut or a ho?"

"That was the word she used. For Mohini *and* me." Mrs Braganza's brother, a local politician, was a board member at the Joshi Charity Clinic. According to Anjali's secretary, the old lady was the power behind her brother's throne and could inflict real damage to the clinic if she chose to. Anjali wished she'd known this before picking a fight, but there was no helping it now. In any case, Anjali was darned sure she wouldn't have reacted any differently to being called out for loose morals, and Mohini would've thumbed her nose at La Braganza's demands for decorum, the clinic be damned.

"Who's Mohini?"

"You probably met her at my wedding, but she was a child then. She's my cousin from California. She came to India to study dance." All the Joshis knew it was only an excuse; Mohini arrived in Mumbai to pursue her childhood crush. Sadly for her, the man in question had eyes only for the lovely lady *he* was pursuing. Anjali gave Siddharth a quick rundown of the one-sided romance. "Mohini's the first slacker Joshi... actually, no. She lacks purpose is all. Says she's going to 'find herself' before returning to L.A. So far, she's found one-oh-one ways to drive the neighbours crazy. Deliberately!"

"Ha!" said Siddharth. "*That's* purpose. It simply needs channelling in a different direction." Looking around, he commented, "Interesting circle of acquaintances you have, Dr Anjali Joshi. Gay husbands, mysterious exes, INTERPOL officers, crazy cousins, nosy, old broads for neighbours..."

"To be honest, I might've provoked Mrs Braganza a bit." Anjali mused, "I should give her something to *really* think about. I'm going to invite Meenu and Gauri to stay here with me a couple of days. Let La Braganza think we're having a group orgy." Cuddling her baby close, Anjali murmured, "Gauri needs to know... Joe owes *all* of us answers on why he didn't call her even after Nikhil died."

Part IX

Chapter 25

Joe plucked a card from the stash at the reception desk outside his exam room and offered it to the short, silver-haired woman. "I'm sorry, Mrs Mehra," he said, firmly. "My staff and I are happy our treatment plan worked for your lung cancer, but I cannot order chemotherapy for your dog." From the size of the animal, malignancy was not the cause of his trouble breathing. "Go to this veterinary clinic, and they'll take a look."

Sniffling, the woman cuddled the obese pug in her arms, tilting her head back to keep her nose out of its thick neck. "I thought you'd be more understanding," said Mrs Mehra. "You're a pet parent, too."

Behind the reception desk, Scher merely twitched an ear, not bothering to dignify the woman's remark with a response. The clerk was red-faced. Any moment, she was going to burst out laughing. The nurses—traitors, both—left Joe alone to deal with Mrs Mehra. The ladies were probably in the staff break room, rolling on the floor and hooting.

"Scher goes to the same clinic," Joe said, glancing down at the card in his hand. The veterinarian would *not* be happy with Joe for sending the duo his way. "They close in a couple of hours, so you'd better hurry." Watching through the glass windows as the receptionist hustled the old lady to the parking lot, Joe mumbled, "She's good for a laugh at the end of the day."

"That she is," agreed a female voice.

Joe swung around. "Anju?" Joy exploded in his chest. She was here in his clinic. Looking like a million bucks, too, in the printed blue harem pants and the tight black tee. The baby on her hip chortled and kicked his legs, almost as though he recognised Joe from their brief encounter at the beach. His presence was a good sign. It had to be. Anjali hadn't called as Joe hoped, but showing up at his clinic with her son—albeit a week after he sent her his phone number—was better. It showed the beginnings of trust. At least Joe hoped like hell it did.

"We were in the bathroom," Anjali said, her eyes glistening with mirth. "But I caught enough of it. You should be happy she trusts you with her baby."

Joe stared. "What—oh, Mrs Mehra. Yeah, I know it's a compliment. Especially, coming from her."

The receptionist, walking back to her seat, snorted. "The old woman doesn't like anyone, but she *adores* Dr Joe. And he loves her. Two crabby people. Match made in heaven."

"Hey," Joe objected. "I'm not crabby."

"Crabbypants," said the receptionist, firmly. "With us, not with patients. *And* you make us work on weekends."

Anjali eyed the lab coat Joe wore over his dress shirt and striped navy pants. "Tomorrow, too? That's terrible!"

"The temp agency covers staffing on Sundays," explained the receptionist. "The regular nurses and I are off tomorrow." She smiled widely at Anjali.

"We've all been dying to meet you, Dr Anjali. Let me get the other ladies here; they were just waiting for Mrs Mehra to leave."

Anjali threw a startled look at Joe.

Groaning, Joe explained, "My brothers." Had to be. Thanks to Dev, the employees at the café were fully aware of Anjali's importance in Joe's life. Romeo D'Acosta, paediatrics resident, recently started showing up at the clinic when he found time off. Thank God, Laila knew how to keep her mouth shut, or Joe would've been facing an audience comprised of the church congregation and the entire Goa University choir.

With muffled giggles from the younger one, his nurses rushed out. The senior of the two poked Joe in the ribs. "Introduce us."

He waved a hand between the women and recited everyone's names. "Don't you ladies have to go home?" he asked.

Ignoring him, the receptionist cooed, "And who is *this*?" She pinched the baby's cheek. "Hey, sweetie." The boy let out a loud, ripping sound and stared unblinkingly at the young woman. "Oh," she said, taking a step back. Her face turned a mild shade of green.

Anjali grimaced. "Sorry. He's been a little gassy since I started weaning him off breast milk."

A little? It was a full-blown stink bomb explosion. Death by the smell of rotten eggs. *Way to go, kid,* Joe cheered. On cue, the baby whimpered. "He probably needs his diaper changed," Joe said to his staff. "You guys head on home before it's too late."

"We're not leaving *now*," said the younger nurse.

"Yes, you are," said Joe, firmly. "It's Saturday night. I'm sure you and Romeo have plans."

The junior nurse's mouth formed a tiny "o." The bright pink of embarrassment washed over her face. As she practically ran out of the clinic with her purse, the other two followed, the senior woman casting reproving glances at Joe.

"What happened?" asked Anjali, confused.

Joe shook his head, laughing. "My little brother has been volunteering here. Believe me, he's not the sort to do extra work—*unpaid,* extra work." The receptionist had a fiancé, so nurse number two was the likely inspiration behind Romeo's newfound interest in volunteering, a fact verified by Dev's staff who'd delivered dinner for two to the young lady's flat. "They thought they were so clever, hiding it from me."

Jiggling the cranky baby on her hip, Anjali grabbed a black satchel from one of the chairs in the waiting area. "You don't approve of your brother dating your staff?"

"It can cause problems, but she's leaving in a couple of months to do her master's degree. Once she's no longer my employee, it's entirely up to them." Joe glanced at the baby. "There's a changing table in the exam room."

The thick drapes covering the windows looking out to the ocean were drawn, letting the late afternoon sun into the exam room. Then, there was the glimpse of the eighteenth-century fort at a distance. Otherwise, it was the same as any other GP's office, with a computer desk and a couple of chairs and a table to evaluate the patient. There were a few basic instruments neatly arranged on a stainless steel cart. The patient charts from the day were piled on a side table. Outside lab reports, etcetera, went into the folders until they were scanned in every Sunday.

Anjali stopped at the side table and eyed the two medical journals lying on top of the patient charts: *Xenotransplantation* and the *American Journal of Transplantation.* She threw a quick glance at Joe before moving on to the changing table. Scher followed them into the exam room and after one sniff at the infant in Anjali's arms, made for the opposite corner.

"Hold on, my love," Anjali cooed at the baby, struggling with the zipper on her satchel.

"Let me," said Joe, holding out his hands. "I keep a couple of extra diapers here for patient emergencies." On the changing table, the baby straightened his chubby legs and stiffened his quads, glaring at Joe with challenge in his eyes. *Your ma,* Joe acknowledged. *But c'mon, kid. We're both men. We gots to have each other's backs. Don't make me look like a loser in front of her.* The baby didn't as much as blink. *Okay. How 'bout this? If she lets me, I wanna try once more.* The "if" was a big "if." When she heard all he had to say, once she knew what he'd done, she might tell him to get the hell out of her sight. Also, he was quite certain he hadn't gotten the whole story on how she suddenly appeared at the café—his brothers could've hired the investigator, but how did they coordinate with her cousin? It didn't matter. If Anjali didn't order him away, if she gave him another chance, he'd get things right this time. He *would* make her happy. *Take my word for it, kid; happy ma, happy you.* The baby looked thoughtful for a moment. Then, a gummy grin appeared on his face, and he relaxed. *Phew.*

As Joe wiped poop off infant butt and applied a coating of protective cream, Anjali clapped. "You're an expert!"

There was an explosive chuckle from the changing table. *Wingman of the Year award,* Joe promised the baby. "It's my superpower. I was twelve when Romeo was born. We used cloth diapers, but Dev and I still managed a team record of under one minute." Joe lifted the baby and handed him to Anjali. "Here you go. Clean, fresh, and ready for chow." Face heating, he tried to explain. "I didn't mean..."

"I always carry a bottle when I take him outside," Anjali said, settling into one of the chairs with her son on her lap. Public breastfeeding was rare in urban India.

The baby quaffed milk with the expertise of a barfly. "Nice work, champ," said Joe, washing his hands at the sink. Bumping the tiny fist with his own, Joe dragged a chair close to Anjali's. "Kid lucked out. Got the jackass's face."

"Excuse me?" asked Anjali, tone outraged.

"What—" *Shit.* "I only meant... Dr Ram used to show me pictures of his family." The old man had not exactly been pretty. Nor were his sons. Anjali glared. "Sundari, you already know you're gorgeous top to toe. I meant the men in your family." Her glare got even more ferocious. Groaning, Joe said, "Can I just take it back? I have no idea why I always do the wrong thing around you."

Anjali bit her lip, but the giggle still came through. "Not always."

"Yeah?" He leered.

"Heh? Oh..." She laughed outright. "That's not what I was talking about."

"You gotta admit 'that' was pretty good."

"Hmm." The mirth on her face morphed into sweetness, then faded into bewildered sorrow as though remembering their breakup and the years since.

Joe waited a minute before saying, "Thank you. For coming here, I mean. I was beginning to get worried when I didn't hear from you."

"After only a week?" she snapped. "Try eleven years."

Damn. He'd walked into that one. Even the baby paused his milk binge to stare in disbelief—or it could've been to finally take a breath. There was a derisive honk from Scher. "Can we start over?"

Eyes widening in incredulity, Anjali asked, "From the time we met? That doesn't work even in the movies!"

"Not if you're Thalaiva," Joe said, immediately. "He can do anything."

"*What?*" When the baby mewled in irritation, she softened her tone and said, "Doesn't matter. I didn't come here to fight you." Unexpectedly, she chuckled. "Thalaiva can put out a forest fire with a single breath." Mundane things like physics and biology did not apply to his movies.

"Yeah, but how fast can he change a diaper?" Joe asked, craftily.

"I don't know. Maybe we can ask his wife."

"Maybe." Laughing, Joe said, "I only meant if we could redo the last minute. The time we had in AIIMS... I wouldn't give it up for anything."

Once again, her mirth changed to pain. "You did give it up. We had everything, and you threw it all away." Her eyelashes sparkled with sudden tears. "My insecurities were a problem, but so were yours. Did things get so bad you couldn't even stay in the same city as me to complete your surgery residency? One stupid fight, and you never returned. Do you know what I went through? Do you have *any* idea?"

Chapter 26

November 2008

"There's something wrong," Anjali muttered, walking up and down the lobby of the movie theatre she'd been dragged to by the members of the group still in Delhi. Around her, people swarmed, chattering about the comedy that was playing. The smell of *samosa*—fried potato pastry—permeated the area.

"C'mon, Anju," chided Meenakshi. "Joe messaged you when he got there, didn't he? He hasn't had time to call is all. There's been a death in his family!"

Sure, he'd sent the Facebook message. It was still on her laptop.

Joe: I'm sorry. We'll figure it out. I promise. Love you.

She didn't have a clue if he'd seen her response.

Anjali: I know. Love you, too.

"It's been more than a week since then," she fretted. The funeral was surely long over. He'd know she was worried sick, so why hadn't he called? Not only her. He hadn't called *anyone* in the group. Nor did he respond to her messages. "Gauri, would Nikhil do this to you?"

"Uhh..." Gauri grimaced. "No, he wouldn't. But they're different people, no?" She didn't say anything else, but Anjali saw the sympathy in her eyes all the same. Nikhil and Gauri would soon be married in the presence of family and friends. Joe hadn't even mentioned Anjali to his brothers and sister, not as anyone special.

"Still..." Anjali said. It wasn't like Joe to be uncaring. He'd once called Rishi only to make sure she had company when she returned to the hostel after dark.

Anjali hadn't thought of anything else since Joe left. Each day passing with no communication from him, the knot in her lower belly got tighter. Every night, she stared into the darkness, worrying about what was going on, wondering how he was coping. She'd managed to go through the rest of her exams, but God only knew how her scores were going to turn out.

Slurping the last of his soda, Siddharth tossed the cup into the trash can. "Look, Anju. Give the man some time to settle things. He'll call; I'm sure of it. Our exams are done, and we came here for one weekend out with Gauri before she gets married. So enjoy it." He nodded at Rishi who was slouching against a pillar. "Yo, friend. Are you worrying about Joe, too? You haven't said a word in the last couple of hours. Actually, make that the last few days. What's going on, man?"

Rishi straightened. "Ahh... nothing. Just tired."

"You have your time off all arranged, right?" Gauri asked, anxiously. "Joe won't be able to make it. *You'd* better be there."

With a strained smile, Rishi said, "Wouldn't dare miss it." He glanced at the entrance to their hall. "Intermission's over; we should go in."

Anjali barely saw any of the movie. Her friends guffawed at the ridiculous antics of the cast, but Anjali couldn't have said what the gag was. Joe... why hadn't he called? What was he doing? One seat down was Rishi, also silent. She'd hardly talked to him lately. With the exams going on, she hadn't even been to the flat since Joe left.

The next day, Gauri's classmates and other friends gave her a grand send-off. They rented a car and decorated it, embarrassing Gauri by taking her to her relative's house in the city in the vehicle. From there, she and Meenakshi would travel to Mumbai for the wedding. Nikhil was expected to get there in a couple of days. Rishi, Anjali, and Siddharth would join the wedding party once winter break started in three weeks.

Returning from the airport after dropping off Gauri and Meenakshi, Anjali stopped at the flat. When the door opened, she couldn't really see anything.

"Rishi?" she called, tentatively.

"Yeah," he said, from close vicinity of the open door.

Anjali jumped. "Why are you sitting in the dark?" Why *was* it dark? It was only early afternoon.

"No particular reason."

His voice... it was so shaky. "May I come in?"

With an exclamation, Rishi said, "Yeah, of course." The light clicked on.

Anjali took a step in and eyed the bedsheets draped over the windows, blocking the sun. Rishi had to have put them on sometime in the two weeks since Joe left—the last she was here. Strangely, there was a teacup exactly where she'd left it on that day, a half-eaten chocolate bar next to it. Rishi was still in the same jeans and tee he'd worn to the movies the night before. There was a funky smell about him as though... Anjali sniffed. "You've been smoking pot." She knew both he and Joe did. Well, Joe *used* to. When she complained about the stink in his bedroom, he quit cold turkey.

Rishi waved a clumsy hand, almost hitting the doorjamb with his knuckles. "I needed something. My asthma was acting up."

She peered at him. "Did it help? You don't sound so good."

For a second, it seemed he was going to say something. Then, he swallowed. "I'm okay. It's just the extra hours I've been working. Are *you* all right?"

"Not really." She covered her mouth with the tips of her fingers. "Umm... Rishi, do you happen to have any other phone numbers for Joe? Fr Franco's, maybe?" It had never occurred to her she might need it someday. She didn't even know where the priest worked. Googling the churches in Goa didn't help. No Franco D'Acosta popped up, and there were apparently many plain Francos in the state. Even Joe's middle name was Francis.

"I don't. Sorry."

She'd been pretty sure he wouldn't. "You think you can check with the dean's office or something? They probably won't give *me* the number, but you and Joe are flatmates."

"I... sure. Why not? Better than sitting here and waiting for whatever."

Huh? What a weird thing to say. Besides, she'd meant for him to call the office, not walk there with her in tow. "Rishi—" But he was already striding out, key to the flat in his hand.

Half an hour later, the clerk in the office called the security guard to escort Anjali and Rishi out. "Policy is policy," the clerk muttered, returning his attention to the computer on his desk. "We can't give out phone numbers."

Anjali shook off the guard's hand on her elbow and walked off. Tears blurred her eyes. *Joe, please be all right,* she begged. *What am I going to do? Oh, God, why aren't you calling me?*

Her foot tripped on the edge of something. The air shifted around her. Warm fingers closed around her arm, steadying her. "Careful," said Rishi. Wiping her tears away, she clambered down the steps and stood staring out into the street. "Kiki might know," he said. "Wait a few hours. We can call her when it's morning in New York."

"I already did," Anjali said, tiredly. "Her phone's switched off. She's at some kind of certification class. I left a message with her roommate. I even asked Gauri if she knew any other numbers."

"If Gauri doesn't know, Nikhil definitely won't," Rishi said. "Is there anyone in Goa you could ask to check in person? Your grandfather lived there."

"My dad might, but I—" Anjali blinked. Her grandfather, Dr Ram Joshi, paid for a good chunk of Joe's education from the family trust. Surely, there were records somewhere. "I'm going to call someone."

"Ahh... okay," said Rishi. She half-expected a reminder from him about Joe's wishes, but Rishi said nothing further.

"Thanks for trying to help." She tried to smile. "I know you're not feeling well. You should get some rest." She needed to get back to the privacy of her hostel room and make the phone call to Mumbai.

Before she got ten feet, Rishi called, "Anju, why don't you come with me to the flat? You don't need to be alone right now." Besides them, Siddharth was the only one of the group left on campus, but he'd sworn to sleep the next two days to recover from exam week.

"You sure?"

"Yeah. *I* need the company." Restlessly, Rishi glanced up and down the street. "I feel like... hang out with me for a while, please?"

An hour later, Anjali was on the worn sofa in the flat, one eye on Rishi tidying up the living room. *Ring... ring... ring...* Did she even have the right number?

"Anju?" a voice said into her ear.

"Vikram," she said. "Oh, thank God."

Five minutes, and her brother still hadn't given her the information she asked for. He kept asking "but why?"

"Look," Anjali said, impatiently. Of all the times for Vikram to show interest in her life! "I told you a hundred times I'm doing this as a favour for a friend of mine. He's really worried about his flatmate. *Please,* Vikram? Just get Sharma Uncle's phone number from Dad." The Joshi Trust lawyer would have all the contact info on the D'Acostas. "I can't ask directly because..." She racked her brain for an excuse. "It's a girl thing."

Rishi paused in the act of moving a pillow from the floor to the chair. A hint of a smile appeared on his face—something that had been all too rare lately.

Hoping Vikram wouldn't ask her to explain the "girl thing," Anjali continued, "Tell Dad you need Sharma Uncle because..." Why *would* her seventeen-year-old brother need a lawyer?

An insulted snort came over the phone line. "I don't need to tell Dad anything. Give me ten minutes. You'll have the number. Too bad the trust hasn't computerised their records."

If the trust's records were computerised, they wouldn't need to contact the lawyer. Vikram could've broken in and gotten any number he wanted. He'd won awards for hacking—security research as the companies which ran the contests called it. Anjali pushed the thought out of her mind. Her little brother wasn't really doing anything wrong. It was as simple as looking up a number in the directory. The fact the phone directory was their dad's computer was merely a minor detail.

Advocate Sharma, the Joshi lawyer, wasn't quite as trusting as Vikram. "Anju, dear. You know I can't. You need to go to your father."

"Sharma Uncle, please," Anjali begged, her voice cracking. She stared unseeingly through the window at the graffiti on the building across. "We... Rishi's just trying to make sure his friend's okay. Joe won't like it if we involve Dad and Mom."

The lawyer sighed. "All right. I can't give you the number, but I can make a few calls myself. I'll let the boy know he needs to call you back."

"Thank you," she whispered, closing her eyes against renewed tears. "Umm... don't tell my mom and dad. Joe won't—"

"—like it," finished the lawyer. "I got it."

Seconds turned to minutes, minutes to hours, and Anjali stayed on the sofa, waiting for the phone to ring. Rishi finished tidying up and went to take a sorely needed shower. The light outside the window faded into darkness, but the sounds of traffic continued unabated. Every now and then, the neighbour's dog would howl. The door to the bathroom squeaked open. A few minutes later, Rishi returned to the living room, bringing two plates of roti and grape jelly.

"I'm not feeling too good," Anjali said, waving the plates away. "My tummy." The queasiness was the aftereffect of not eating properly for days, but she really couldn't stand the thought of food right now.

"All right," he said, walking back to the kitchen. "I'm not hungry, either. Let me get you something to drink."

Accepting the mug of black coffee, she sat next to him in silence. *Please, be okay, Joe,* she murmured in her mind.

Any moment now, he'd call back, apologising for the agony he'd put her through. He'd explain why he hadn't been able to contact her. Maybe he lost his phone... her number was stored in it... he didn't want to embarrass her by calling the hostel... he hadn't called anyone else because... because... he'd better have a good reason, or she was going to beat him to death with her bare hands.

A shrill ring interrupted her thoughts, making her jump. She pounced at the phone on the table. *Blank screen?* "Rishi?" she called. He was staring straight ahead as though he couldn't hear the sound. "Rishi," she called, her voice louder. When he turned her way, she glanced at his pocket. "Your phone."

"I... ahh..."

"Pick it up," she said. "What if it's——" Reaching out, she plucked the phone from his pocket and peered at the caller I.D. She groaned in disappointment. "Not Joe."

Rishi took the phone from her. "My mother," he muttered, a peculiar expression crossing his face. "I'll call her back later."

"You sure? I could wait in Joe's room if you want privacy."

"Don't worry about——"

The peppy sounds of a flute heralded the opening of a Bollywood song. *Her* phone. In a few moments, she was biting her lip hard, trying not to sob in desperation.

"Sorry, Anju," said the lawyer. "I tried every number I had for the family. Their landline, the priest's phone number, even the mom's number... God rest her soul. I did contact an old associate of mine who lives around there. He'll send someone to the boy's flat to check what's going on. It won't be for a couple of days, though. My colleague's dealing with an important case."

Couple of days? Anything could happen in a couple of days. Joe could be injured... sick... worse. She'd go crazy. "Thanks, Uncle," Anjali murmured. Hanging up, she turned to Rishi. "I need another favour. Could you go with me to the airport?"

***

Through the small window of the plane, Anjali watched the sky turn the pink of dawn. It had only been a two-hour flight, but none of the passengers seemed to have the energy to do more than mumble their gratitude to the airline staff handing out breakfast trays.

Next to her, Rishi stirred. "Thanks," he said to the sari-clad flight attendant. "I'm not hungry, but I'll take some tea." Grazing the back of Anjali's hand with his fingers, he called, "Anju?"

"Thanks, but I don't want anything," she said. "My tummy." When the flight attendant moved on to serve the next row of passengers, Anjali said, "Gauri's going to kill me if you end up missing the wedding."

"I won't. Nikhil will get to Mumbai tomorrow, but I'm not going for any of the pre-wedding stuff." Rishi's work schedule didn't allow extended time off for things like best friends' weddings.

"Still..." Anjali murmured.

Tone reassuring, Rishi said, "We have three more weeks until D-day. It will take us *one* day to go to Joe's flat and kick his ass. Then, you and I are going to drag him and his family to your grandfather's house. I'll leave you two alone and go back to Delhi. Sid and I will fly to Mumbai. Try to make it even if Joe can't. You don't wanna face Gauri's wrath if you don't."

Anjali inclined her head. Joe could either go quietly to the Joshi mansion or put her up in his flat. She was beyond caring about gossip on campus, and if he fussed again about her parents knowing, she'd... she'd... she didn't know exactly what she'd do, but it wouldn't be good for Joe's health. He wasn't gonna say a cross word to his flatmate, either.

"Thanks for going with me," Anjali said to Rishi. All she asked for was his company on the nighttime cab ride to the airport to ensure safety amidst the worry in Delhi over crimes against women. He'd called the surgery chief for emergency leave of absence under the pretext of his long-dead grandmother falling deathly ill. The chief definitely hadn't been happy at having two of his residents out, but Rishi promised to do extra duty over New Year's Eve in return. "You're such a nice guy."

Rishi flushed. "I... ahh... didn't want to stay in the flat by myself. Plus, I'm worried about Joe, too."

"Yeah, you keep checking your phone."

"Who knows who's going to call?" Rishi muttered, looking away. "Joe... Gauri... Nikhil... the wedding's so close."

The mid-morning sun was beating down on the tarred road in front of the Joshi Charity Clinic when Rishi and Anjali exited the autorickshaw, their backpacks their only luggage. There were boys playing cricket on the footpath across the street, ignoring the annoyed shouts of the motorists trying to avoid the ball.

"I'll wait here," she mumbled, glancing vaguely at the scraggly beggar loitering by a lamppost. He reeked, the unwashed smell combined with the gasoline fumes making her slightly nauseous. Still, Anjali couldn't take the risk of going inside. She'd never been to the clinic before, but... "The staff might recognise me." *Joe* did from the photos her grandfather proudly showed off. She wasn't going to embarrass him in front of the clinic staff if she could possibly help it.

Anjali checked the clock on her phone a few dozen times, mopping the sweat off her upper lip even more frequently with a tissue. Rishi popped his head out once or twice to update her on his progress in finding someone who knew Joe's mother from way before and would know the address.

Backpacks on their shoulders, she and Rishi finally walked down the street and past the crowds in the local market to a five-storey building, its walls a dull green. A couple of cars and a motorbike sped by, but there were no pedestrians. The painfully thin cat on the stoop stopped washing itself and yowled in alarm before dashing away. Gingerly, Rishi pushed open the steel front door with his fingertips.

Anjali blinked a couple of times before her eyes adjusted to the relative lack of light. Rishi sneezed into his shoulder. "Sorry," he muttered. "Something in the air. Mould, I think."

The air *was* musty. There were a couple of narrow windows on one side, but facing a dumpster. No wonder they were kept shut. The stairs to the left were unsoiled, but there was a gaping hole in the second to last step, and the railing was clearly loose, kept tied to the bottom post by a plastic rope. A kitchen knife and a half-peeled onion rested on top of the post with no one around to claim ownership. Breaking the silence, a Hindi song blasted from somewhere above, and a masculine voice bellowed, asking whoever to turn off the damned television before he threw it in the trash.

Anjali swallowed hard. She'd been to the *chawl*—the working-class tenement building—where her mother's father rented rooms until his death. "*This* place..." It wasn't grim, exactly, and everything looked quite clean and reasonably safe, but it wasn't the Mumbai chawl where residents prettied up their homes with gaudy colours and bright lights and plastic flowers, celebrating life with music and chatter while hoping for better days.

Nodding, Rishi said, "I know. Let's get Joe and get the hell outta here."

"Second floor," Anjali said. Belly knotting in mild anxiety over Joe's possible reaction, she stood in front of the door, knuckles raised.

"Let me," said Rishi. Pounding hard, he bellowed, "Joe, it's us. Open up." Anjali listened intently for the sounds of surprise, of approaching footsteps. Nothing. Nada. Not even mild scuffling. Rishi tried again, the metal vibrating under his blows. "Joe! Open the door, man." The other three doors in the narrow passageway also remained shut. No one appeared to check on the ruckus. Eyeing Anjali, Rishi said, "They're probably out doing something. We could wait... ahh..." He looked around. "Let's go get some lunch and come back after."

Out doing something? *All* of them? This soon after their mother's death? "What's going on?" she whispered, a hand to her mouth. Everything see-sawed around her. Her vision blurred with tears. "Where is he?"

Rishi's arm settled around her shoulders. "We'll figure it out. Right now, you need to sit someplace. You need to eat. Look at you; you're going to fall any second." Leading her outside, he said, "We'll check again in a couple of hours. If they're still not back, we'll ask the neighbours... the kids' school... the post office... now that we have the address, we have options, darling." He peered into her face. "Anju? Are you crying? Oh, my God. You're crying."

A school bus careened past, horn blaring. He tugged her further away from the road. Suddenly, her face was buried in his shoulder, her weeping muffled by his shirt. "I'm so afraid," she said, sobbing. "I knew—I *knew*—something was wrong." Joe wouldn't have gone completely silent for almost two weeks. "Something's happened to him." If it hadn't been for the stupid exams, she'd have... "I should've come sooner." He could've gotten sick or injured or something. "What am I going to do?" She shoved away from Rishi's chest, almost stumbling to the ground. "What am I going to *do?*"

"What's going on here?" yelled someone.

"Sorry, sir," called out Rishi. "She didn't eat anything all day. I'm trying to find a restaurant."

Somehow, they found themselves in the back of a police jeep, being dropped in front of a crowded café at the local market. She pushed away the menu Rishi got for her. "I can't right now. Maybe a lemon soda or something."

"I'll get you lemon soda, but you need to eat." He flipped open the menu. "The cops said this place has great Goan food. Look... prawn fry, fish platter... you love seafood, right? Try one of these. Or maybe the beef patties. Oh, sorry. You don't eat beef. How about chicken? Chicken fry, chilli chicken, jumping chicken..."

He continued reciting, but Anjali didn't hear anything else. She grabbed the menu from his hands and stared at the words. *Jumping chicken? Frog legs?* Her belly cramped. Acidic fluid burned its way up her throat. Clapping a hand over her mouth, she clambered up and looked wildly around for the restroom.

"What's wrong?" asked Rishi.

Without answering, Anjali pushed through the group of teenagers in her way, racing to the entrance. Shouts, clatters... she ignored them all. Hanging on to the edge of the garbage can outside, she retched. Questions of concern and offers of help echoed all around. She heard the words, she knew what they meant, but she couldn't answer. Her mind was so fuzzy.

A comforting hand patted her back. "She hasn't eaten all day," Rishi explained to the onlookers.

Someone clucked. "My wife was the same way. Couldn't keep anything down with any of our kids. Saab, she needs something light."

"She... ahh... okay," Rishi stammered. "C'mon, Anju. Let's get you that lemon soda."

They returned to the dreary apartment building in under an hour. Once again, Anjali watched hopelessly as Rishi banged on the door and yelled Joe's name. "It's no use," she said. "He's not here. I'm going to check with the neighbours."

Through the crack left by the safety chain, the matronly woman from the second flat said, "The whole family left."

"Yes, but where did they go?" asked Rishi, impatiently. "And when did they leave?"

The woman shrugged. "Don't know."

It took three more tries to figure out where Joe's brothers and sister went to school. "The school office will be closed by now," Rishi said. "We're going to have to check tomorrow."

"Tomorrow?" Anjali whispered. One whole night without knowing what happened to Joe. One whole night when anything might happen to him.

"Yeah," Rishi said. "We don't have any other option. Do you want to go to your family's house for tonight?"

Anjali started. The Joshi mansion in Fontainhas? She'd been prepared to drag Joe and his siblings to her family's home, but without him... what was she going to say to her parents when they heard from the housekeeper she was there? "I took cash out before leaving Delhi. Let's find a hotel."

She didn't go to bed all night, somehow unable to get up from the couch in the suite's living room. The blinds were drawn, and the lights were dimmed, but she couldn't close her eyes. It didn't matter. All she could see was Joe... his face, his fingers gripping the pull-on bag. She should've grabbed his hand, forced him to stay. She should've chased after him and insisted he take her with him.

Doors opened and closed, and Rishi said something, but Anjali had no idea what. It was only when he draped a blanket over her shoulders she realised she'd been shivering under the draught from the air conditioner. "Thanks," she said, sniffling.

He tossed his phone to the coffee table in front and dropped to the couch next to her. "Can I ask you something personal?"

"Go ahead," she said, automatically.

"Is there a chance... ahh... Anju, are you pregnant?"

"*What?*" Anjali shook her head. "*No.*" It wasn't possible. She and Joe always used protection.

Red-faced, Rishi said, "Just thought I'd ask. You were saying something about your tummy, and at lunch..."

"I'm not," Anjali said. Mentally, she counted back to her last period. When *was* her last period? Before the exams for sure. Had it been before Diwali? She didn't go home to Mumbai for the festival. Was it more than four weeks ago? "I don't think so."

"I didn't mean to offend you by asking, but if there's a chance you could be, you shouldn't be stressing yourself out like this."

As if he could offend her after all he'd done so far. "If I'm pregnant, I have more to stress about than a missing boyfriend."

"We'll find him," Rishi vowed.

With a wobbly smile, she said, "You're such a good friend. There's a wedding going on, and you came with me all this way."

A peculiar look crossing his face, he glanced at the phone on the coffee table. "Don't give me too much credit. I didn't want to stay in Delhi by myself."

"Still... I don't know what I'd have done without you. I haven't been able to think the last few days."

The phone rang. Eyes widening in shock, Rishi jumped. Panting audibly, he stared at the device for a moment before mumbling an expletive and turning it off.

"Are *you* all right?" she asked. "You look... I don't know... weird."

"I'm okay. It was my mother. I'll have to call her after we get back."

Mother? Anjali had done things she didn't want her dad and mom finding out, but phone calls from them never induced the stark panic evident at the moment on Rishi's face. Then again, she was almost certain his relationship with his family wasn't great. Why else would he stay on campus every single weekend when his parents lived mere minutes away?

"Tomorrow..." Rishi said. "The school will know where the kids went. We'll find Joe and ask what the hell he's doing."

At nine sharp, Rishi and Anjali were in the principal's office of the all-boys school in Mapusa. The bearded priest settled into the chair behind his desk and after a quick sideways glance at Anjali, focused on Rishi. "You're Joe's flatmate?"

"Yes," said Rishi, respectfully. "He hasn't contacted any of us after he left Delhi. It's been almost two weeks."

The priest sighed. "I was hoping you were here with some news."

Anjali mewled. With a pat on her fingers, Rishi asked, "What do you mean?"

"Most of the teachers here know Joe. He was one of our star students. Dev..." With a frown, the priest continued, "This is his last year in school. He's barely scraping through. We all understand the situation... his mother passed... there's some money issue... but he can't afford to miss so many days. A week at the most. If he were going to miss more, Joe should've informed us so we could prepare homework. Romeo is a bright boy like Joe, but that doesn't mean he can skip school, either."

"What about Laila?" Anjali asked. "Their sister? I think she's eight."

"She goes to..." the priest named a convent school. "The principal there tells me she's been absent, too. A couple of the nuns went to their flat to check,

259

and I called Fr Franco." Shaking his head, the priest said, "The Archbishop House says he took emergency leave."

"So no one knows where they are?" Anjali asked, covering her mouth with her fingertips. "Oh, God," she moaned.

The priest glanced between her and Rishi. "The nuns said they ran into the homeowner. He's very angry because this month's rent hasn't been paid. He says he spoke to Joe after the funeral. Joe said he was going somewhere to make arrangements, but a couple of days later, the kids simply left. They didn't even take any of the furniture with them. There was a note from Dev they'd mail the rent money as soon as they had it."

Rishi growled. "Joe leaves; the kids vanish without taking any of their belongings. No one thought of filing a missing persons report?"

"That's why I contacted the archbishop's office," explained the priest. "They say Fr Franco has taken leave from the church to take care of the kids. What am I supposed to tell the police when their great uncle is supposedly in charge?"

"I don't understand any of this," Anjali said, despairingly. "If Fr Franco took the kids, he would've told the school, right? Even if they moved out of town, they'd need paperwork for the new school." Almost blindly, she turned to Rishi. "Something's really wrong. I know it."

Rishi nodded. "I agree. Father, if you don't mind telling us... where's the nearest police station?"

The note with the directions in her hand, Anjali stumbled along next to Rishi, not understanding any of his soothing words. She was so, so cold. Why was she so cold when the sun was bright and hot? The office the cops showed them to was quiet, but her last words to Joe echoed louder and louder in her mind. "*Don't bother coming back.*"

The half-door swung open with a squeak. The chunky officer introduced himself as the inspector and asked Rishi to the side office to fill some forms. There was a mumbled conversation. "*What?*" came Rishi's voice.

Anjali glanced towards him. His face... it was so pale. She sat up. "Rishi?" Inclining his head slightly, he returned to his conversation with the inspector. She strained to listen, but they were taking good care to make sure she didn't overhear.

Rishi finally came striding out. "We need to go to the medical college hospital."

"Back to AIIMS?" Anjali asked, confused. "We haven't found Joe."

Shaking his head, Rishi said, "Not AIIMS. Goa Medical College Hospital."

Her heart stilled for a moment. "How badly is he hurt?" she whispered. If there were any way Joe could've called, he would've. Or he'd have asked someone to notify her. "He's not conscious, is he?" she asked, sobbing.

"Anju..." Rishi swallowed hard. "Let's go and see."

She had her face buried in folded hands through the thirty-minute ride in the back of the police jeep, begging God to let Joe recover. *Please, let him live*, she prayed. She needed him. His family needed him. Where *was* his family? Had they moved somewhere near the hospital?

Neither Rishi nor the two cops riding with them said much. Rishi's lips were moving as though he were also praying. Once or twice, he hugged her to his side, murmuring, "Hold on, Anju. You've got to hold on, okay?" His words ended in a muffled sob.

"Rishi—" Before she could ask what he wasn't telling her, the vehicle screeched to a halt. Fingers trembling, she jiggled the lock on the back door. One of the policemen reached over her shoulder and snapped it open.

Anjali scrambled out, ready to run in and find Joe. There was an ambulance blocking her way, parked right in front of the large red pillar announcing the name of the building: Forensic Medicine & Toxicology Faculty, Mortuary Block.

"Mor... mortuary?" She swung to face Rishi. "Why are we *here?*"

"Anju, please." Tears rolling down his cheeks, he took her by the shoulders. "Darling, you need to hold on—"

She swatted his arms aside. "Why are we here, Rishi?" It must be a mistake. He'd tell her this was the easiest place to park, that all they needed to do was walk ten minutes to the patient wards.

He turned to the cops. "Does it have to be her? I can do it."

"*Why are we here?*" Anjali screamed. Grabbing Rishi's lapels, she shook him. "*I asked you to tell me why we're here.*"

"Madam," said the policeman, holding a hand up. "Identifying a body is traumatic, but you need to remain calm."

"Identifying?" Letting go of Rishi, she looked wildly around, not really seeing anything. "Is that why you brought me here?"

"Anju—" Rishi called, sobbing.

"*Answer me,*" she screeched, swinging back to him.

"Please," he begged the cops, trying to gather her into his arms at the same time. "Let *me* do it. We don't need to upset her."

"*Bastard,*" Anjali spat, struggling to free herself. He was wrong. They were all wrong. "Filthy, rotten bastard. You never liked him. You're trying to get rid of him, somehow."

"You said she's the fiancée," said one of the policemen. "We haven't been able to find any other family. She's the closest."

Restraining both her wrists with one hand, Rishi wrapped his other arm around her shoulders. "I lived with the man for the last two years."

"Procedure has to be followed," said the cop. "Or the body won't be released. He'll eventually be buried with the other unidentified corpses."

Buried? Her Joe buried? Shrieking savagely, she twisted around. She could hardly see the cops through the hair hanging in front of her eyes. "*Don't you dare touch him.*" Joe wasn't dead, and they were trying to bury him alive. "*I'll kill you. All of you.*"

"Bring her in," the cop snapped at Rishi. "Everything's ready."

"We have to do this, darling," said Rishi, sobbing while he dragged her stiff form towards the entrance.

"No," she said, trying to tug her wrists loose from his hold. She didn't want to see what they wanted her to. They were all wrong. Wrong, wrong, wrong. "I can't."

"There's no other way," Rishi mumbled, relentlessly moving her towards the building.

"*No,*" she screamed. "I won't do it. *Let me go.*" There were strange hands on her hair and body. Someone was putting something on her... cap, gown... she didn't want any of it. The air suddenly turned cold, and there was a metallic shriek as though... shivering violently, Anjali turned her face into Rishi's shoulder. "Please, don't make me."

"You have to," Rishi whispered into her ear, forcibly turning her towards the metal cabinet being pulled out by a technician.

"*No.*" One look at the pale, frozen face of the corpse, and her grip on Rishi's shirt loosened. There was no cleft in the dead man's chin. The build was similar to Joe's, but the features were all wrong. "No," she sobbed, her knees buckling. "It's not Joe."

"It's not," agreed Rishi, holding her up and weeping into her hair.

"Are you sure?" asked the cop. "There's been some decomposition, but the description you gave matches the dead body."

Anjali's stomach heaved. There was no time to free herself from Rishi's hold and run to the restroom. She retched, splattering sour liquid on his clothes, on hers, on the floor.

The hands on her shoulders immediately loosened, but he didn't completely let go. There were exclamations from the policeman and the technicians. A trash can was shoved under her nose, but she pushed it away. There wasn't any more in her belly to chuck up. "Towel?" she asked, voice hoarse.

While she was mopping off vomit with the thin rag provided, Rishi gave his explanation to the officers on why the corpse wasn't Joe.

The cop muttered, "If your friend has been gone these many days without contacting any of you, he's either dead, or he doesn't *want* to come back. I checked our prison management system; he ain't inside, and he's not rich or famous enough to get kidnapped."

The soiled rag in her hand, Anjali paused. She refused to believe Joe was dead. Someone would've notified his friends. He was still somewhere out in the world, hiding from her for reasons she couldn't fathom. *Where are you?* she asked, but the memory of the man in her heart gave no answer.

Rishi and Anjali returned to the police station to give details of Joe and his family. She didn't say much. It was as though all strength drained out, leaving her body a feeble shell. Neither she nor Rishi talked in the cab ride back to the hotel. Her phone rang as they were walking into the suite. She didn't even have the energy to dig through her backpack for the device.

"Aren't you going to check?" Rishi asked.

"You do it," she requested, curling on the couch with a pillow held to her chest.

"Hello?" Rishi said into the phone. "Yes, sir. I'm the flatmate she talked about." Rishi mouthed "lawyer" at Anjali.

She sat up but shrugged, declining to attend the call. Sharma Uncle would immediately sense something was wrong and inform her parents.

"Ahh... she's in the bathroom," said Rishi. "I'll let her know you called." There was a long pause during which he hmmed and nodded his head, his expression growing more and more puzzled. When Anjali stood in alarm, he held up a hand, asking her to wait. "The dean was certain about who called? It's easy to be confused over the phone." In tone filled with confusion and hurt, he mumbled, "I don't understand" before hanging up.

"What happened?" she asked, eagerly. "Joe called the dean?"

"Yeah."

Anjali huffed in relief. "Oh, thank God." She was wrong. They'd all been wrong. Joe wasn't hiding from her, and he certainly wasn't dead. He was *about* to die at her hands, but for the moment, he was still alive.

Rubbing his temple with a fingertip, Rishi said, "Your lawyer knows one of AIIMS's lawyers. Apparently, Joe called the dean's office and said he's quitting."

"Quitting?" Anjali blinked. "What do you mean quitting? He can't quit. He hasn't even finished general surgery." Joe and his ego. She was prepared to relent a little, but giving up on his cherished dream of being a transplant surgeon to go work as a GP rather than accepting her offer of financial help was beyond the limits of tolerance. Firmly, she nodded. "Just let me get to him. I'll put an end to this nonsense."

"Anju," Rishi called, worry on his face. "The dean says Joe left specific instructions not to give his contact information to anyone at AIIMS. He asked them to let me know he's changed his phone number. Anything I have to say to Joe will need to be conveyed via the dean's office."

"What do you mean?" She shook her head, not quite understanding. "Joe doesn't want to talk to you? Why?"

Voice at once angry and sympathetic, Rishi clarified, "Not just me. He doesn't want any contact with anyone from AIIMS."

Her whole body went painfully numb. "Me," she said, dully. "He doesn't want any contact with *me.*" The cop at the mortuary was right, after all. Joe was missing because he did not want to be found. He didn't want to talk to her ever again. He hated her so much he was even prepared to give up on his career to avoid her. Something tore inside her ribcage.

"You should sit." Rishi was next to her, his hand on her elbow, urging her to the couch.

Anjali shrugged off his touch. "It's all right, Rishi," she said, her tone calm. She was shocked by how calm she sounded when inside, her soul raged in pain and anger. "We should return to Delhi. There's a wedding to attend. I assume Joe won't be showing up, but you need to." Joe couldn't have anyway because of the death in the family, and now... at Rishi's silence, she added, "Your flatmate's made his thoughts quite clear. He doesn't want *any* of us around."

Rishi eyed her for a good minute before swearing, colourfully. "He's doing this only because he can't bring himself to ask you for help. Give him a month or two; he'll come to his senses."

"Maybe," Anjali said, tonelessly. "Or maybe he decided fifteen months with me is long enough." He didn't want her any longer but couldn't discard her like he discarded other girlfriends. She was his mentor's granddaughter.

"C'mon, darling. You honestly think Joe couldn't find any other way to break up with you? And I thought *he* had an ego."

"Call it whatever you want... ego, self-respect, pride..." She closed her eyes and heaved in a painful breath. Even if Joe's actions had nothing to do with him getting tired of her, the fact remained while she'd been prepared to meet him halfway, he wasn't. "If he can go this far, I don't want him back." Glancing down at her clothes, she said, "We've wasted two days over this when there's a wedding coming up in three weeks. Your friend, Nikhil, should be in Mumbai by now. *We* need to go back to Delhi and get our stuff together. Also, Sid must be worried." They'd tried calling him before leaving but had to leave a message. Since then, neither Rishi nor Anjali had been in any mood to call anyone else. "We need clean clothes, or the airline won't let us in." They'd brought exactly one extra set of clothes each in their backpacks, now soiled with Anjali's vomit.

Rishi huffed. "Fine. We're going to talk about this after we get to Delhi, but for now, we'll do what you want. Let's go get some new clothes."

"Could you take care of it?" she asked, not wanting to face the outside world yet.

When he left, she returned to the sofa and willed herself to rest, but her brain refused to cooperate. Every scene from her life since the moment she encountered Joe sped through her mind like a slideshow—the irresistible attraction, the sweet confession, the joy of banter, the wild lovemaking, the arguments, the anguish, and the heartbreak. Over and over, she relived everything, her soul bleeding anew at the end of each cycle.

Stop, she ordered herself. She'd known going in what his *m.o.* was with women. Somehow, she let him convince her she was different. Now, he'd told her bluntly they were over. He couldn't quite pretend she didn't exist like he did with his other girlfriends; their worlds were too intertwined for that. He preferred to sacrifice the future he'd toiled for, instead. Or he couldn't stand feeling beholden to the Joshis, and *she'd* convinced herself he cared enough to work through the issue with her.

It didn't matter *what* his reasons were. The agony of the last few days... he couldn't help but know what she'd go through. He'd still... why wouldn't he? She'd been the one who did all the chasing, all the compromising. The only thing she insisted on was protecting her reputation. No thanks to him, it was still stellar. She wouldn't have to pretend not to hear the vicious murmurs on campus. Anjali squared her shoulders. There would be no private tears, either. Joseph D'Acosta didn't deserve it; he didn't deserve her love.

The door to the suite opened silently, letting Rishi back in. He placed a couple of shopping bags on the coffee table and drew something from his pocket. "You need to make sure before deciding what to do about Joe," he said, handing the rectangular box to her.

Pregnancy test? Five minutes later, she returned from the bathroom, wiping her wet hands on the seat of her jeans. "I'm all right." Her upset stomach was the result of the stress of the last two days, not impending maternity. She really hadn't expected anything else, but she didn't want Rishi worrying about her for the next few weeks, especially when he was supposed to fly to Mumbai for his best friend's wedding.

He twisted around on the couch to face her. "Good."

She supposed it was. She wasn't ready for a baby yet. There were many things she wanted to do before taking up motherhood. Joe wouldn't be at her side as she once dreamed, but she would still do it all—her medical career, a happy life, even her dream house on the beach. And as far as the rest of the world knew, Anjali Joshi had suffered nothing—no heartbreak, no damaged reputation, no unexpected pregnancy to mess up her plans. No one—*no one*—would be able to call her a slut or a fool who'd lost her head over a man. Nodding, Anjali said, "Life *will* be good. Perfect, actually." A sharp pain shot across her eyeballs, making her stagger.

"Anju?" Rishi called.

She held up a hand. "Headache. I'll sleep it off in the plane."

***

11 PM, November 26, 2008

New Delhi

The phone in Rishi's hand glowed. It turned a bright orange, then flaming red, burning through his palm. "No," he screamed, but he couldn't let go.

"Rishi," called a sweet voice. "Are you all right?" A warm hand landed on his shoulder, shaking him.

Heart pounding hard against his ribs, he opened his eyes. The monstrous features of the blackmailer from Rishi's imagination morphed into Anjali's pale face. Yeah, right... the cab... they were on their way from the Indira Gandhi Airport back to the AIIMS campus. "Sorry. I fell asleep. Are we there—" Sirens blared. Lights flaring against the night sky, a police car raced past, followed by half a dozen more. Gritting his teeth against the ear-splitting noise, he peeked outside the window. They were smack in the middle of a sea of vehicles. "Accident?"

"I don't know," said Anjali, tiredly. "The driver said he needed to make a detour because the usual route was blocked."

Rishi glanced at the familiar ruins of the fourteenth-century fort. They weren't far from Asiad Village where his parents lived. "Bhai saab," he called the turbaned driver. "There's a side road you can take. Just follow my direction."

The driver grunted. "Side roads won't work, saab," he said, speaking in a mix of Hindi and Punjabi. "Everything's blocked. I think some kind of terrorist threat."

"God," Rishi muttered. India suffered enough such attacks to take even the smallest hint very, very seriously. They were bound to be stuck on the road for hours. "Wanna walk it?" he asked Anjali. It would only be thirty or so minutes, and all they had for luggage were their backpacks.

269

"Sure," she said, rubbing her eyes. "I can go straight to bed once I get to the hostel." Thus forestalling any thoughts of her missing boyfriend.

As usual, Anjali was overreacting to Joe's hot-headed behaviour. He was going to come crawling back. How he could do something insanely stupid like announcing he was quitting was what Rishi didn't get. AIIMS wouldn't be as forgiving as his girlfriend.

Rishi itched to plant his fist into the idiot's face. Joe blithely declared he was giving up what Rishi would've killed to have—a chance to be the doctor he wanted to be. If he did what the blackmailer demanded... the bastard called twice, and Rishi didn't pick up, claiming to Anjali it was his mother calling. There was probably another note waiting for him at the flat.

He couldn't do it. No way. Maybe he could string the bastard along while he tried to get another visa to the U.S. or any place that would take him. But if the authorities in India stripped away his medical licence because of the damned actor, Parth Kumar, no other nation would let Rishi practise medicine. The reason behind the disciplinary action wouldn't matter to authorities anywhere, not even in places which didn't consider homosexuality criminal. Dammit, he should never have returned from New York. *God, what am I going to do?*

Shaking his head, Rishi tried to dislodge the thought he should silence the blackmailer. Permanently. He desperately needed to talk to someone before he completely lost it. He'd have to confess to Nikhil, but with the wedding coming up soon... afterwards, perhaps.

"Let's go," said Anjali, opening the car door. His mind yanked back to the problem of getting back to the AIIMS campus, Rishi followed.

There was no moon in the sky, but the street was bright with headlights from the stalled vehicles. The crowds on the footpath went in all directions, talking on phones, puffing on cigarettes, yelling curses at police vehicles. Rishi turned to ask Anjali to stick close... where *was* she? Swearing under his breath,

270

he walked back to where she was standing, digging through her backpack for her ringing phone. "Stay close," he shouted into her ear. With a crowd this size, there was no telling what would happen.

She nodded and dropped the phone back into the bag. Gesturing with her head to the side of the footpath, she said, "Safer over there."

They managed to inch their way along the wall with her ignoring the nonstop ringing of the phone in her backpack. It wasn't long before they were stopped by the cops. "No entry," shouted the constable, waving his *lathi*—the police baton—at the crowd.

"Sir, please," Anjali said to the constable, tone frustrated. "I need to get back to the hostel. I have my ID." The man wasn't listening to her or any of the rest who were demanding to be allowed through. "Sir... *sir*... will you *please*... I need to... for God's sake, please—"

"Anju," Rishi called, tugging her back by the elbow. "No point arguing. They're not going to let us through."

"We can't stay here all night," she exclaimed. "God, this ringing..." She tugged the backpack off her shoulder and glared at it.

Rishi eyed the pallor of her skin, the shadows around her eyes, the messy, brown hair. "You look beat." The jeans and the pink tee he'd bought from the hotel's gift shop were expensive, but they hung loose on her short, skinny frame. The sports shoes on her feet were her old ones, now dirty and worn from their two days in Goa.

"I'll be all right once I get to the hostel."

Shaking his head, Rishi said, "Not gonna happen soon." He made up his mind. "My parents live around here. We could crash there for the night. I'll tell them we were out for a movie or something and got caught in the crowd."

"Umm... they won't mind?" Anjali asked, nervously.

Mind? They'd be thrilled to meet her—the girl who'd supposedly turned their gay son straight. Rishi didn't know how he was going to stop them from asking awkward questions, but he couldn't take the risk of having Anjali wait in the middle of this large and angry crowd of mostly men. "Let's go," he said.

Only a few minutes' walk into the upscale neighbourhood of Asiad Village, the crowds petered out. The noise receded. The phone in her backpack continued to ring. "Just a second," she muttered, unzipping the bag. Mild confusion on her face, she said, "Hello?" Her eyes widened. "Who—" A stream of unintelligible squawks came from the device. Every trace of blood remaining on her face drained out, leaving her paper white. "Oh, my God," she screamed. "Are they all right? Tell me they're all right—"

"What happened?" Rishi asked, urgently. At some distance, a dog barked, but there were no passers-by to witness the conversation.

"Bomb blasts," Anjali said, her voice shaking. "In South Mumbai." Where her parents lived. Where Gauri and Nikhil were supposed to have their wedding in three weeks.

✻✻✻

Phone glued to his ear, Rishi walked up and down the living room of his house, muttering frantic prayers with every step. *Nikhil, man. You'd better be safe.*

"All circuits are busy," the electronic voice intoned at Rishi. "Please, try again later."

With a desperate groan, he turned to the bronze-coloured leather sofa. Anjali was still flanked by Rishi's parents, all three listening intently to the silver-haired man who'd shown up the doorstep almost at the same time as Rishi and Anjali. "Minister Verma," the man introduced himself. His only son was apparently a good friend of Anjali's brother. The secure line used by father and son to communicate with each other worked even as the rest of the nation

272

descended into chaos. The boy asked the minister to reassure Anjali the Joshi parents were safe. The minister—on his way to an emergency cabinet meeting in his helicopter—asked Anjali for her location and decided to offer reassurances in person. Anjali's father, Dr Pratapchandra Joshi, was out in the city as part of the emergency medical team, but he was all right so far.

The minister's secretary was by the front door, talking into his phone.

Padding to him, Rishi asked, "Anything?"

The secretary shook his head. "None of the numbers you gave me are going through. I've already verified with the girls' family they and their mom went out shopping. They're not back home yet. Your friend, Nikhil..." Grimly, the secretary continued, "Apparently, he took a colleague from New York to see the Mumbai nightlife. Let's hope they're not at any of the places which got hit."

"Please, God," Rishi mumbled. They needed to be safe—Nikhil, Gauri, Meenakshi.

"Rishi?" Anjali called from the sofa, tone anxious. "Have you tried Sid? Maybe he heard something. Also, I have Meenu and Gauri's cousin's phone number."

"We can try," said the secretary. "I doubt it will work. Everyone's trying to call... no one knows what's happening in the hotels. There's gunfire at the railway station, bombs in taxis... the whole city is a war zone."

With a small sob, Anjali said, "My father's out there on the streets. I need to talk to him. Maybe I can rent a car and drive down."

"No," said the minister, firmly. "I understand your worry, but the best thing you can do for your parents at this time is stay here where it's safe."

"But—" She covered her mouth with both hands, trying to quieten her weeping.

"*Beti*," called the minister, addressing Anjali as daughter. "Your father is fine. My staff is in constant contact with him, and they'll keep you updated. If you need to return to your hostel, I can arrange it. Otherwise, stay right here where your parents know you're safe."

"She can stay with us as long as she needs to," said Rishi's father, immediately.

Rishi barely managed a polite "Thank you" as the minister and entourage announced their departure. "If you hear anything..." he muttered to the secretary.

"I'll let you know," the minister promised.

Rishi and Anjali spent the rest of the night on the sofa, sobbing as they watched on television the blood-stained streets of Mumbai. His parents walked in and out, offering tea and sympathy but asking no questions. Towards dawn, Siddharth called. He'd managed to connect with Gauri. They'd been stuck in one of the shops but were now allowed out.

"Thank you," Anjali muttered, looking heavenwards with folded hands and a tear-blotched face.

"Nikhil wasn't in his hotel room when the attack on the Taj started," continued Siddharth. "All Gauri knows is he was going to take his friend from New York to one of the clubs. He's not picking up his phone. Poor girl, she's going crazy."

Relief flooding him, Rishi said, "He wasn't at the hotel, so he's got to be all right." But why wasn't he picking up his damned phone?

Within an hour, they got their answer. The minister's secretary called. In the list of those who'd fallen victim to the gunmen at the Leopold Café was one familiar name: Dr Nikhil Arora.

The world spun crazily around Rishi. Someone was keening loudly. Shouts echoed. His mother, father, one of the maids... they were making soothing sounds, asking him to be calm. Their faces... he didn't know them... everything was so distorted, monstrous. Every colour turned to red.

A pair of arms slipped around Rishi's torso. He knew the touch. Anjali... he'd held her... was it only yesterday? "Anju," he said, frantically clinging to her. "They're wrong." They had to be. The cops at the mortuary had been.

She didn't utter a word and simply tightened her embrace, burying her face in his shoulder. Rishi wouldn't let go of her. If only he held on, the horrible news would turn out to be untrue. It would be someone else who died, not Nikhil. Rishi clung to her until three days later when he came face-to-face with Nikhil's lifeless body in his Delhi home, already prepared for cremation.

The thick smoke of incense swirled around the priests chanting hymns. Nikhil's distraught mother wept inconsolably as guests wearing white surrounded her. Sitting by her fiancé's side was Gauri, so pale. She wasn't crying, simply staring dully at the body in front of her as though she couldn't believe what she was seeing.

"Nikhil," Rishi sobbed. The friend he'd met in kindergarten, the brother of his heart. "Nikhil," Rishi wept, again. He freed himself from Anjali's arms and stumbled towards Gauri. Loud sobs racking his body, he dropped to his knees. Gauri turned to look and without making the slightest sound, slumped unconscious against his chest.

She was sleeping off the sedative the doctor gave her in Nikhil's old bedroom when his brother came to the door, whispering it was time to take the body to the cremation site. Anjali and Siddharth flanked a weeping Meenakshi on the small sofa someone previously dragged into the room.

Rishi stood from his chair. "Now? But..." Frantically glancing at Gauri, he asked, "How can you take him now? She needs to wake up and say goodbye."

Tears pouring down his cheeks, Nikhil's brother said something about the stars and timing.

"What timing?" shouted Rishi. "Get another time. Don't take him away just like that. The people who loved him... they need a chance to..." Weeping, Rishi said, "The people from school... from AIIMS... Joe's not here yet." Siddharth had called the dean's office and left an urgent message to be conveyed to Joe. "He was one of Nikhil's best friends, too. Joe needs to see him."

"Rishi," called his father, appearing behind Nikhil's brother.

"*Bas,*" said Rishi, holding up a hand and telling them firmly to stop. "Nikhil's not going anywhere until Joe gets here."

Rishi's screamed threats at the men attempting to take his friend away had no effect on Gauri's drug-induced sleep. His violent struggles couldn't break Siddharth's hold. Neither Meenakshi nor Anjali would relent when Rishi begged them to open the door and let him out. Through the barred window, he watched helplessly as Nikhil's body was loaded into the back of the long, black car and driven away. Rishi dialled Joe's old number a hundred times, leaving messages to come and help him get Nikhil back, but Joe didn't return the call—not even once.

Chapter 27

Present day

Joe kept his eyes fixed on the baby on the changing table. Frowning ferociously, the boy tried to reattach the head of the monkey-shaped rattle to the handle. With a low bark, Scher padded to the table and settled down below it, resting his jowls on his front paws. Outside the windows of the clinic, the sky turned orange, and the seagulls shrieked, heading to their nests. Inside the brightly lit exam room, neither Joe nor Anjali said a word. His fingers itched to take her hand in his, to hold her close and beg for forgiveness, but he couldn't find the courage.

"How could you, Joe?" Anjali finally asked, her eyes red-rimmed. "Even if you didn't want to talk to *me*, how could you possibly have ignored Gauri? She needed you. How could you not call her? And Rishi? The group started with you, him, and Nikhil. Rishi and I weren't together at the time. How could you not call *him?* Do you know how many days he kept insisting you would, how many times he contacted the dean's office to check if you bothered to respond? Do you? *Do you?* Have you any idea how much he hates you for it?" Tears dropped from her lashes. "He'd tell me you'd return when you got a chance to think things over. I'd tell him to stop hoping, but somewhere in the back of my mind, *I* was also hoping... I should've known better. We both learned our lesson."

Urgently, Joe said, "I'll explain everything."

"Oh, yes, you will." Anjali stood and went to the changing table to gather her baby into her arms. "I came here to tell you Sid is in Goa. He asked me to say hello. Meenu and Gauri will also be here in a few days." Pausing, she added, "Kiki is flying down, too. Her hubby's babysitting for the next three weeks." She grabbed her black satchel and slung it on her shoulder. "You're going to answer all our questions. Unless, of course, you again decide to vanish."

"I'm not going anywhere," he swore, jogging after her as she walked out. Scher followed at his heels. "Anju, wait. Gimme a chance."

But she was already outside the front door, stomping towards the yellow Volkswagen Beetle in the well-lit parking lot. His Ambassador was parked close to the entrance.

A motorbike roared in—a monstrous vehicle which looked like something James Bond would drive—startling all of them. The baby cuddled closer to Anjali. Scher growled in anticipation even though his days of chasing bikes were long gone.

A man got off and removed his helmet. "Excuse me?" he called, shaking out his shoulder-length mane. "Is this the D'Acosta clinic?"

"Yes," Joe said, impatiently. "We're closed. There's a hospital in town which is open twenty-four/seven." Anjali had walked on and was strapping the baby into the car seat in the back of the Beetle. "Anju, please. *We* need to talk first."

"Is that Anjali?" asked the biker. "Wait, please. *Anju.*"

What? Joe glared at the biker before turning back to Anjali. She was opening the driver's side door. "*Anju,*" shouted Joe, jogging towards her.

"*Anju,*" called the biker.

Joe stopped short. "Do you mind?" he snapped. "I don't have time for this. I need to talk to her."

"Oh, yeah?" the biker snapped back. "I need to talk to her, too."

"What the hell?" Joe glanced at Anjali. Forearm resting on the roof of the car, she was staring open-mouthed at the two of them. "Do you know this dude?"

"Yes, she does," said the biker. Hands turned up, she shrugged, telegraphing her ignorance. "Of course, you know me, Anju," he insisted. "I'm Farhan. Rishi's boyfriend."

"Heh?" said Joe, pivoting towards the biker. "Rishi's—"

"Oh, no," said Anjali. Before either of the men could say another word, she slid into her car and slammed the door.

Joe turned back. "Don't go—"

The biker raised a hand. "You need to talk to Rishi—"

"No, I don't," she shouted through the open window. "Whatever any of you wants to say, you can say it to *all* of us." The car engine revved. Tyres screeching, Anjali zoomed out of the parking lot.

Part X

Chapter 28

Going to tiptoes on the step stool, Anjali swept aside the pill bottles on the top shelf of the wall-length metal cabinet. Dust rose in small clouds, tickling her nose. "Ha... ha... hatchoo." Sneezing into the cotton sleeve of her blouse, Anjali glanced at her grimy fingers. "Next time, I'm wearing a mask and gloves," she mumbled. Inventorying the stock of medicines at the clinic was turning out to be a dirty job. Also, depressing in how poorly managed the place had been. "Look at all this, Chandekarji." The secretary was waiting at the door of the storeroom of the ambulatory surgery suite, notepad in his hand. "Some of these are two *years* past expiry date. Plus, this is the storeroom of the *operating* theatre. How was this place allowed to get so filthy?"

Chandekar clucked. "Thank God you found this before the cops. I'll get the pharmacists to go through everything, shelf by shelf. We'll clean the whole place."

It was way after six, and all the staff already went home, but Anjali took a quick glance around to make sure there was no one who could've overheard the secretary's remark about the police. Through the door, she could see the operating room proper. The lights were on, and the ceiling fan twirled noisily, circulating warm air, but there were no doctors, no nurses, no technicians. One of the clinic's many problems remained a secret for now.

She'd meant to carry out a section-by-section inspection and make a checklist of all the things which needed to be done, but Chandekar imagined it was only because of the INTERPOL investigation. As far as he knew, INTERPOL was concerned about the clinic buying generic drugs for cheap from companies which broke patent laws. While it wasn't nearly as bad as organ smuggling, Anjali didn't want the employees panicking over *any*thing. "Make sure you tell them it's routine," she instructed.

"Of course," said Chandekar, deferentially.

Huffing in mild irritation, she clambered down from the step stool. The secretary had done a one-eighty from doubting his new boss could even feed herself without making a mess to being unconditionally supportive. *Too* supportive. Maybe he regretted being as forthcoming as he'd been with his feelings about her appointment as CEO, but he didn't have to scramble to attention whenever she walked by. That, too, in front of other employees, leaving her cringing. "What's the latest talk among the staff?" she asked, keeping her tone casual.

"Nothing I can't manage," said Chandekar, patting his thick moustache.

Hmm. His management was what she was afraid of. Washing the dust off her hands at the sink, she strode over to the operating room proper and the number-locked steel cupboard at the far right corner. At least there were enough disposable instruments, and the medicines inside—anaesthetic agents, sedatives, analgesics—were all well within expiry date.

She tugged at the door of the noisy refrigerator next to the cupboard—locked as it should be. She nodded in relief and approval, then frowned. The nursing staff clearly did their job, making the dust and the expired medicines in the storeroom even more surprising. The charge nurse was conscientious enough, so why did she fail to notice such glaring problems on her own turf?

"Key?" Anjali asked, holding out a hand. "I want to see what's inside the fridge."

"You should delegate this sort of thing," said Chandekar, handing over the bunch he'd obtained from the charge nurse earlier that day. "The CEO should be more concerned with the big picture." He bounced once on the balls of his feet. "As I'm sure you know."

Anjali bit her tongue to keep herself from retorting all the CEOs since Dr Ram Joshi did precisely that, getting the clinic to the sad shape it was in today. For the umpteenth time, she reminded herself Chandekar was only trying to be helpful.

She opened the refrigerator and for just a few moments, let herself enjoy the cool blast of air on her face. Eyeing the sparse contents, she remarked, "We need to restock." Antibiotics, insulin... Anjali tilted her head to view the red-capped glass vials. Succinylcholine—a.k.a. sux—the neuromuscular relaxant used frequently in surgeries to induce paralysis. When used, the patient needed to be ventilated to keep him breathing. But the procedures done at the clinic were minor and would not routinely involve paralytic agents. Sux was also used to paralyse patients to aid rapid sequence intubation in emergencies, which would be the one reason for the ambulatory surgery suite at the clinic to carry it. Emergencies could happen even with a breast biopsy. "Where's the crash cart? And the mechanical ventilator?"

"In the side room."

"What do we do if someone needs intubation?" The clinic didn't offer inpatient services required to monitor intubated patients. "Where do we send them?"

"It's never happened in all the years I've been here," Chandekar proclaimed.

"No emergencies in the last what... fourteen, fifteen years?" she asked, dryly. "You realise how improbable that is?"

Chandekar insisted, "It hasn't happened, and we don't expect it to."

Anjali considered telling him how succinylcholine worked, why it wouldn't have a place in the outpatient clinic if it weren't for potential intubations. The two doctors and the nurses who covered ambulatory surgery knew what they were doing even if management didn't have a clue. So how was it possible there weren't any plans in place for the patients who *did* crash? Plus, the labour room had transfer arrangements in place with the government hospital.

Anjali needed to talk to the staff directly, and she needed to do it without worrying what they'd heard about her breakdown and what they thought about her ability to handle the pressures of her position. Plus, there was Chandekar. She simply couldn't shake the guy at work. He was always hovering over her, insisting that wasn't how things were done or bowing and scraping as though she were a loony dictator who needed to be humoured. Unfortunately, he was also the one person in the entire clinic who knew anything about how the administrative side of things functioned in the last decade or so. Without his help, it would take Anjali a *loooooong* time to bring some order to all the chaos.

Maybe if she sent him out on some errand... injecting a no-nonsense tone into her voice, she said, "Tomorrow, I'd like you to set up a preliminary meeting with the district hospital about emergency transfers. For you and the CEO's office there, I mean. Feel them out on it."

Scribbling on his notepad, he muttered, "Lots of things to do tomorrow."

Anjali glanced at the wall clock. Almost seven. They'd put in eleven hours of solid work. Mrs Chandekar—the fiftyish lady whose mother was a former patient of Joe's—worked as a lab technician at the charity clinic, and she would've clocked out exactly at five. "Why don't you go home before your wife reports you missing?" Plus, Anjali was expecting an important phone call she definitely didn't want Chandekar overhearing.

"There's no one else here for company except the night watchman," he warned.

The retired police officer pretty much napped the entire shift. Even if he carried a gun—which he didn't—Anjali doubted he could see well enough in the dark to use it. Another problem she needed to sort out. "I'll be out of here in a few minutes. You go ahead."

As soon as he left, she ran down the stairs instead of using the clanky lift meant for transporting patients to the upper floor for minor procedures and emergency deliveries. Back in her office, she did a quick visual sweep of the side rooms to make sure the nanny had indeed returned home with the baby as expected.

Kusum had been Anjali and Vikram's nanny, too, and she always demurred when told she was free for the evening if Anjali were still working. All Kusum needed to do was take the baby home and hand him to Mohini. Kusum, unfortunately, sniffed disdainfully at poor Mohini's babysitting capabilities. "That girl," Kusum frequently said, "needs her own babysitter."

A second nanny, perhaps? Anjali mused. *For the evening shift?* She had the money to do it. She glanced at the empty hallway outside the open door. The employees of the clinic were mostly female. None of them enjoyed the luxury of bringing their children to work or hiring sitters. Joe's mom, when she worked here as a nurse's aide, had brought him along, but that was with Dr Ram Joshi's blessing. What they needed was a daycare centre. One more thing to add to the long to-do list for the CEO of the charity clinic.

But first... Anjali settled into her chair and tugged open the drawer. The featherweight laptop was inside. Checking Facebook, she smiled. One message, as she'd received every evening for the last four days from the newly reactivated account of Joe D'Acosta.

She'd left Joe and Farhan in the parking lot, refusing to talk to *either* of them until the rest of the group got to Goa. Joe tried to call her but eventually acceded to her demand to do what *she* wanted for a change. He'd wait as long she gave him a chance to speak privately afterwards. That promise didn't cover the dozen roses which arrived daily at the house, causing Siddharth and Mohini to waggle their eyebrows meaningfully at Anjali. It certainly didn't preclude Facebook flirting.

Joe: Your eyes are round and shiny.

Your nose is small and straight

If I were a fish all briny,

I'd hope your lips were the bait.

Anjali groaned, then laughed. She typed the same response she'd given him the last four days.

Anjali: Terrible.

Joe: Not giving up. I'll send a new one tomorrow.

Anjali: Goodnight, Joe.

Joe: Goodnight, sundari.

Nope, Joe was no longer pressuring her into listening to what he had to say, but he certainly hadn't called a halt to his pursuit of her.

Swivelling her chair towards the window, Anjali grimaced. Farhan hadn't given up, either. He arrived at the clinic every afternoon since the week started, trying to cajole her into a discussion. What about, Anjali had no idea. He should've been working on getting Rishi to see the light.

The shrill ring of the phone interrupted her thoughts. Opening the drawer again, she dug into her purse. She really needed to develop the habit of keeping the phone with her. When she'd been working as an anaesthesiologist, it was easy to simply drop it into one of the pockets on her lab coat, but regular female work attire didn't lend itself to practicalities such as carrying the smartphone on her person. She didn't get it. If science could send human beings into space, why couldn't working women get decent clothes which let them... well... work?

Anjali glanced at the American number and smiled. Another working woman who'd heartily agree with her. "Hello, Kiki," she said, closing her eyes and leaning back into her chair.

Without preamble, Kokila asked, "So did you smack him across the face like I told you to?" She seemed to be talking over chatter in the background. A loud voice echoed, making an indecipherable announcement. Kokila was at the airport, waiting for her flight to India. Travel permits were difficult to obtain these days, but she managed it by stating she was an Indian citizen who wished to return home. "Walking out on you like that!"

Laughing, Anjali said, "No. And I'm not going to." She'd lost her composure for a few moments when she and Joe first ran into each other but no more.

"Anju, you can't let him get away with what he did."

"I won't," Anjali promised. "But I can't go around hitting people, Kiki." Nope, Anjali had never been the slapping kind. Nor was she going to avoid life's little glitches any longer. "I'll deal with problems my own way."

A beat later, Kokila muttered, "You have to do you, I guess."

Anjali sighed. "He keeps saying he wants to explain."

"*Let* him," said Kokila. "I want to hear what possible excuse he can have for what he did."

So did everyone else, and Siddharth asked Anjali to keep the lines of communication open. She'd still told Joe he'd be making his explanation to the entire group. There was really nothing stopping her from granting him the request for a private conversation. Except... she'd once forgiven his reluctance to meet her family, forgiven his demand to have her acknowledge him before he deigned to do the same, forgiven his refusal to have her around when his stepmom died.

The moment she met Joe, memories of their time together rushed back in. The bonds of their friendship, the utter joy of their love, the wild passion... all of it. The shattered look in his eyes when he'd learned about her baby... she couldn't stand it. She'd gone searching for him. She'd smiled in inward approval at the easy camaraderie between him and his staff, sweet warmth welling in her heart as she watched him change her baby's diaper. They'd bantered as they used to do. Heck, they still did.

"I need you and Meenu to keep my feet on the ground when I talk to him next," said Anjali. Between speaking with Siddharth and visiting Joe at his clinic, she'd updated the remaining members of the gang on Joe's reappearance. Meenakshi and Gauri were expected in Goa later in the week. Kokila's flight would also take a couple of days, stopovers and all. "Enough about him. What did you find?"

Many, many years passed since Kokila's time at the clinic, but she'd promised to sniff out the talk among the staff about the new CEO. Anjali wished she could tell Kokila about the missing migrant workers as well. The staff had to have heard something. It was impossible there hadn't been a single murmur about it, and Kokila could've collected useful gossip. INTERPOL demanded Anjali keep her mouth shut, but she wasn't legally obliged to do so.

Still, it was never a good idea to annoy the cops, and she didn't want to risk any leaks.

Kokila's huff was audible over the phone. "I spoke to all the nurses I knew. They're aware you and I are friends, so it wasn't easy to get them to open up, but—" Tone hesitant, she warned, "It's not good. Anju, most of them don't care much about nepotism. They know how Dr Ram set things up. But there's some nasty gossip going around about you."

Tiredly, Anjali asked, "That I lost it?" It wasn't merely gossip, but the news about her breakdown hadn't gotten to New York.

Kokila clucked. "All kinds of stories start when a woman files for divorce. Some say you have mental health issues... er... there's a rumour you're keeping kind of a male harem."

"*What?*" Anjali groaned. "Mrs Braganza."

"Yeah, her," said Kokila, grimly. "Girl, you're always so careful not to piss people off. How did you manage to piss *her* off? Do you know who she is—"

"I didn't at the time," Anjali admitted. La Braganza was in a position to do a lot of damage to the clinic through her board-member brother who was big in the hierarchy of local politicians. "Let me tell you something. Even if I knew, it wouldn't have made a difference. The nerve of the woman! She practically accused Mohini and me of turning the house into a brothel!"

"Heh? She's always been a bitch, but why did you have to pick a fight with her? *I* would've done something crazy like that, but you?"

Anjali gritted her teeth. "Arrey, how could I not? She said it to my face!" Plus, her nerves were shot from meeting Joe the night before.

Kokila sighed. "Regardless, we now have a problem on our hands."

"*One* problem?" Anjali detailed the results of her inspection of the outpatient surgery suite. "I mean, if they're incompetent, it should be a complete mess, right? But it's not." The clinical part, the one the doctors and nurses could handle on their own, looked decent. The expired medicines on the other hand... and the dust... where the staff required cooperation from the management, it was clearly lacking. Anjali needed to talk to the employees directly, but it wasn't going to get her anywhere in the current situation—not when the staff thought she was a loon and a ho. Chandekar's attitude wasn't helping any.

"First thing to do is get rid of the Chandekar fellow," stated Kokila, firmly.

"I wish it were that easy," Anjali muttered. "He's been handling all the paperwork all these years. I still need him for things."

"Tell you what," said Kokila. "When I get there, I'll invite the nurses I know to dinner and talk about all the stuff. You need inside support."

Anjali nodded. "I've been thinking along similar lines. After you meet your friends, I want to call a townhall-style meeting for the entire staff and explain some things. They need explanations. They also need to hear we're all on the same side. Once they understand it, I'll take care of Chandekar."

Something metallic clattered outside. Kokila responded enthusiastically to the suggestion of a townhall meeting, but Anjali missed her exact words. Pulse skittering, she jerked up and glanced at the hallway beyond the open door. The fluorescent lamps reflected bright, white light on the mosaic tiles. Plastic chairs were lined up outside the haematology lab, and there were a couple of empty stretchers as well as a lonely wheelchair, paint peeling off its handles. The lemony smell of the disinfectant used by the evening cleaning crew still clung to the air. Except for the watchman outside the glass-doored entrance, no one was *supposed* to be here this time of the evening. Even Chandekar left as ordered. The watchman, perhaps? Making his night rounds? Or perhaps a misplaced piece of equipment, tumbling to the floor?

"Anju?" called Kokila. "Are you there?"

"Do me a favour," Anjali muttered, keeping her tone low. "Stay on the phone. If you hear anything strange, hang up and get Sid to call the cops."

"Huh? What's going on—"

"Play along." Raising her voice, Anjali continued, "I'm switching to video call. You want to see what the clinic looks like now, don't you?"

Kokila's anxious face came on the screen. In the years since leaving India, she'd dyed her jet-black hair a reddish-brown, but the pixie cut remained the same. The hum of chatter and the booming announcements continued in the background. "Anju? What—"

Putting a finger to her lips, Anjali tugged the drawer open and grabbed her purse with trembling fingers. The featherweight laptop went in. Her slingback stilettos... if she needed to run... she slipped the shoes off and stuffed them into the purse. Thank God, the baby and the nanny already left. They were safe.

Purse slung over her shoulder, Anjali padded out hurriedly and continued with the video chat. "So this is the hallway outside the CEO suite... the haematology lab..." The mosaic tiles were cool under her bare feet. As her nervous voice echoed down the passage, she glanced sideways at the rooms on both sides. Most featured two doors—one leading to the hallway and one to the lobby/waiting room of the clinic. She could cut through, but the noise... if it hadn't been the watchman or something accidentally falling to the floor... no, she couldn't risk running into an intruder. She'd have to get to the door at the end of the passage. *One... two...* still talking to Kokila, Anjali counted her heartbeats until she got to the lobby.

The lights remained on with the expectation Anjali would turn off the master switch locked inside the electric box by the front entrance. Rows of plastic chairs stood in empty glory. The reception desk on the left was dark, the sole computer shut down. On the right were the pharmacy, the cashier's counter, and the lift with its grille gate left open.

"This is the lobby," Anjali exclaimed, turning a three-sixty with the phone. "You're seeing everything, aren't you?"

"Yes," said Kokila, her eyes confused and worried. She glanced away for a second. "They're calling the flight."

"Almost there." Ten more feet, and Anjali was by the glass-doored entrance. Not bothering to turn out the lights, she rushed outside. Night had already fallen on the town of Mapusa. Horns blaring, cars and buses careened past on the dark street. The watchman, a turbaned man with a greying beard, was sitting in his glass-walled booth by the front door.

"Sardarji," Anjali called the man. Her racing heart settled into a less painful speed. "Walk with me to the parking lot, please?" When the watchman stepped out of the booth, she glanced between him and the phone in her hands. "I was showing my friend the place. She used to work here."

The watchman touched his turban with the tips of his fingers—an expression of respect. "Hello, madam," he said to Kokila.

As Kokila smiled, Anjali said, "You can hang up now, Kiki."

"Wait," said Kokila. As another announcement boomed in the background, she huffed in annoyance. "I need to get to the gate, but I'm going to WhatsApp you from the plane. You'd better explain."

"I will." Dropping the phone into her purse, Anjali asked the watchman, "Were you inside the building a few minutes ago?"

The watchman had been staring at Anjali's bare feet. Head jerking up, he said, "No, madam. I do my night rounds after dinner."

"Did anyone else go inside?" she asked, tugging the shoes from her purse and hopping about as she shoved her feet into the slingbacks. "Or come out?"

"The last one to come out was Chandekar saab," said the watchman.

Anjali hadn't imagined the noise. Maybe it was only something hovering at the edge of a table or a shelf, clattering to the floor while she'd been on her phone call. "Don't do your rounds tonight," she instructed the watchman. "Lock the door and stay in your booth, okay?"

A frown on his face, the watchman asked, "Why?"

"I heard something... just stay in the booth for tonight, please? It makes no sense for a single person to do the rounds on his own. What will you do if there *is* an intruder?"

"Uhh... okay," said the watchman. His frown morphed into pity. "Are you feeling all right, Doctor? I could get someone to drive you home."

Poor, unstable Anjali Joshi, walking around barefoot in the clinic and hallucinating noises. If she hadn't been the CEO, her precarious mental state would surely have been reported to the CEO. "We don't exactly live in a paradise with no crime, sardarji," she said, trying to keep her tone even. "All of us—working women, especially—have to be careful. It's best not to take chances. There was a sound inside, and I thought I'd better get out fast."

"Oh." Face clearing, the watchman said, "That's why I told my daughter she can't go into nursing. All those late hours! It's not safe."

Outraged, Anjali said, "That's not the solution—" She flung her hands into the air. "Let's get to the parking lot. And stay in the booth as I said. No rounds tonight."

The chirping of crickets got louder as they got to the brightly lit parking lot. Empty this time of the night except for her yellow Beetle and one monstrous motorcycle with a long-haired man leaning against it. "Hello, Anju," said Farhan.

She groaned. "Don't you have to eat and sleep?" The reception desk called her about his presence sometime before four, and it was now past seven.

"I'll stay here all night if that's what it takes," he said, grimly.

Huffing, Anjali turned to the watchman. "You can return to the booth, sardarji. Thank you." As soon as the man disappeared from the lot, she asked, "Didn't I tell you we'll talk after this weekend? I'm just for waiting for the rest—you were here the entire time? You didn't go anywhere?"

"The entire time." Farhan smoothed back his hair with a hand, revealing the tiny gold hoop in his right ear. There were shadows under his eyes.

She glanced towards the main entrance. It wasn't visible from her position, but if she were five feet down and leaning against the bike as Farhan was... "Did you see anyone come out of the front door just now? Just before I did, I mean."

"That man with the moustache who's always with you?"

"Chandekar's my secretary," Anjali said, shaking her head. "*He* left about fifteen minutes ago. After him and before me... did you see anyone?"

"No, he didn't leave fifteen minutes ago. He ran out right before you did."

Anjali stared. "Are you sure?"

"Yeah, I'm sure." Eyes darting between her and the direction of the main entrance, Farhan asked, "Problem?"

Anjali bit her lip. "Maybe... I don't know." If Chandekar made the clattering sound, why didn't he simply call out? Actually, why was he still there? Even if he'd forgotten something, why hadn't he simply walked to the desk right outside the CEO suite where he usually sat? Did he hear what she'd been discussing with Kokila? Why had the watchman said... the watchman only said Chandekar came out the door. There was no time frame given. "I heard something inside. I thought everyone already left."

"Ahh. Carry a gun when you're working late. I always do."

Taken aback, Anjali asked, "Really?" The bike, the weapon... when Rishi first mentioned the anaesthesiologist who played the drums, she hadn't exactly pictured a badass type.

"If you don't like the idea of packing heat, you could always have someone with you." After a pause, he added, "Like Rishi. You know he quit his job, right? He'd be happy to help you with the clinic for a few months, *and* you'd have the benefit of muscle."

Heh? Exasperated, Anjali asked, "Arrey, what's your problem, yaar? What's *Rishi's* problem? Why aren't you with him, making plans?" Stopping short, she asked, "Is this some kind of guilt trip? Look, I told Rishi a thousand times I don't have any ill will towards either of you. I knew what I was getting into when I married him. I'd just come off a difficult relationship, and he was looking for a way to survive."

"*That's* what he wants to talk to you about. You never got to hear the whole story."

Chapter 29

December 2008

The words of the chief of surgery echoed around his office, making no sense whatsoever to Rishi. Nothing was real anymore. His childhood home, the streets of the city he'd grown up in, the medical college campus... all reduced to indistinct apparitions of the world he used to live in. The world of one week before, the world before Nikhil's death, before Joe's disappearance.

Rishi was summoned to this room—the office of the department chief—his first day back on campus. He'd been here several times. Somehow, he couldn't remember the framed certificates on the cream-coloured walls or the oil painting of Sushruta, the ancient Indian surgeon, operating on a patient while his students looked on in fascination.

From across the desk, the chief—a burly man with a greying moustache—was looking at Rishi expectantly, so he murmured, "Yes, sir."

"What do you—you weren't listening, were you?" The chief drummed the tabletop with his fingertips.

Staring at a glass paperweight, Rishi stayed silent.

"Look, betay," said the chief. The leather chair squeaked as he stood and came around the desk. Settling a hip on the edge of the table, the chief continued, "My own son is your age; I don't know if I've ever told you that." The chief grimaced. "He didn't want anything to do with medicine. Or working, for that matter. I only hope..." Shaking his head, the chief said, "Back to the topic. You, Nikhil, Joe... I've known all of you since the day you showed up on campus as seventeen-year-old know-it-alls. Granted, my grief at Nikhil's passing cannot come remotely close to yours, and if I could get the dean to tell me where to find Joe, I would personally kick his ass... what a waste of potential. Can you believe he got someone to pack his stuff and mail everything? He couldn't even be bothered to... anyway, that's a problem I can do nothing about. Right now, my concern is *you.*"

"I'm sorry," Rishi said, automatically.

"You haven't done anything to be sorry about. We're all simply concerned about you—the professors, your parents, everyone."

The words pierced through the fog surrounding Rishi. He sat up. "My parents?"

"Yeah, I called them," said the chief. "I wanted to know how you were doing. They said you stayed in your room all day, every day. The girl... Anjali... your father was hoping she might be able to pull you out of your funk. She got back to classes a couple of days ago, but the hostel warden tells me she doesn't even get out of her room after-hours. I guess the problems in your group affected all of you, but *she's* making an effort to get on with her life. You... if I hadn't told you to get your butt back here today... when were you planning to return?"

"I don't know," muttered Rishi. Anjali had made no attempt to contact him since leaving Nikhil's home with Siddharth. Rishi didn't want to call her. They would only remind each other of the losses they'd suffered back to back. Rishi never even checked his phone; the call from the chief ordering his return to work came on the landline. Heart thundering in sudden panic, Rishi sat up. The blackmailer... did the bastard call?

The chief continued, "You don't seem to be doing well at your parent's home, and returning to your flat right now is probably not a good idea. If you agree, I'll talk to the hostel superintendent and arrange a room for you. It will be a break from all the problems. What do you think?"

The flat... Rishi needed to get to the flat and check for notes from the blackmailer. Or was it too late? His chest was so bloody tight. With trembling fingers, he grabbed the inhaler from his pocket and puffed twice. "My asthma," Rishi wheezed, glancing at the chief. No, they wouldn't be having this conversation if the blackmailing bastard already carried out his threat. As his breathing slowly steadied, Rishi added, "Thank you for the offer, sir. It's very kind of you."

Huffing, the chief asked, "Are you going to take it or not?"

Move from the flat? Rishi wished that would solve all his problems, but in the hostel, he wouldn't be running into memories at every corner. "I'll take the room as soon as it's ready."

Late in the evening, he stood at the bottom of the apartment building, not daring to go in. Pivoting on his heel, he strode down the main road and took a cab to his parents' home. He wasn't allowed to go straight to his room. His oldest sister had arrived, her baby in tow. The child was asleep by the time the adults gathered around the dining table.

Casually, Rishi's sister asked, "Did you see Anjali today?"

"No," he said, his eyes on the *sabzi*—curried vegetables—on his plate.

"Why not?" His sister clucked. "Rishi, Papa and Ma really liked Anjali. They said she didn't leave your side the entire time, and her background seems perfect. The *minister* came here personally to talk to her. Imagine that! *I* want to meet her, too. Invite her here for the weekend, please."

He stared incredulously for a few seconds. "You realise the 'entire time' you're talking about was Nikhil's funeral? You remember him, don't you? You've only seen him come here with me since I was in kindergarten."

Face paling, his sister said, "I—"

"There is no need to take that tone," said Papa, reprovingly. "All of us grieve for Nikhil. We can't imagine what his family is going through."

"He wasn't even *inside* the café," mumbled Ma, her gaze troubled. One of the terrorists who'd targeted the Leopold Café casually fired a couple of shots before entering the restaurant. "His poor mother. I'm just so relieved you weren't in Mumbai at the time."

Suddenly, violently, Rishi *wished* he'd been in Mumbai, that he were the one whose ashes were now floating in the Ganga, the holy river. There would've been nothing left to worry about. No blackmailer, no more threats to the career he'd dreamed of for years, no bleak, lonely future to fear. No pretence to keep up about a girlfriend who wasn't actually his. Nikhil—the man with plenty to live for—would still have been around. Gauri would now be his wife instead of being cooped up in her ancestral home, all her chatter and laughter gone, replaced by silent grief.

"Betay," called Papa. "It's precisely because of Nikhil's passing... we were prepared to wait until you were ready for marriage, but I don't think we should

297

wait any longer. Life can be cut short any time, and I'm going to be seventy in a few months. For another, the minister's son and Anjali's brother are such good friends the man came here and talked to her just because the boys asked him. If someone of his standing can come to our house on the Joshis' behalf, the next step has to be from our side, or they're going to think we're not interested."

"Let the families take care of it," said Rishi's sister. "All this boyfriend-girlfriend stuff in college doesn't fit in the Indian culture."

Rishi snarled, "If you're so interested in sticking to Indian culture, why are you living in Boston?" She hadn't waited a day longer than necessary to join her husband in the U.S., and now that she was there, she was all about India.

"Enough," snapped Papa. "I'm prepared to give you some leeway because of Nikhil's passing, but don't forget you have parents who're still alive. It would be nice if you treated us with a modicum of respect for as long as we're with you."

Tears brimming in her eyes, Ma asked, "Or would you rather we were *not* with you? I thought you continued staying at the flat because you needed to be as close as possible to the hospital, but you were home all last week, and you've been acting as though we don't exist." Voice catching, she continued, "You slept next to me until you were seven... my beautiful baby. I went away for three days to visit my family, and you refused to eat anything even at school. *I* had to fix your lunchbox, not the maid, not your sisters. Papa had to finally lie and say I'd left lunchboxes in the freezer. When I returned, you clung to me and told me I could not go anywhere anymore without taking you." Sobbing in earnest, she said, " *That* child doesn't want anything to do with me now."

Each of her words pierced Rishi's heart; her tears fell on the wounds, searing them. This was the woman whose entire life was spent taking care of her husband and children. She'd enveloped all four of her brood in her loving warmth, but Rishi forever remained her favourite. Both Ma and Papa were so proud of him, bragging about his accomplishments to all and sundry. He'd already broken their hearts once by announcing his sexuality, and the lies he said about Anjali went a long way towards healing their wounds.

His oldest sister—she'd mother-henned him at the school they all attended, saving for him the candy she bought with her pocket money. She didn't know why Rishi was reluctant to bring Anjali home to meet the family as his girlfriend. None of them knew about the lies he'd told.

"Ma," Rishi called. Shoving his chair back, he stood and walked around to her side of the table. "Ma," he called again and dropped to his knees next to her. Taking one of her hands in both of his, he said, "I'm sorry about the way I've been acting with you and Papa." Glancing across the table, he nodded at his sister. "With you, too."

Tone gruff, Papa said, "We understand. Nikhil was your best friend, and your chief said Joe unexpectedly left the course. The three of you were together for how many years now?"

"Eight," Rishi said, shoving every memory of Joe from his mind. The bastard never considered Rishi or Nikhil his friends. Anjali was nothing more than time-pass for Joe. He'd simply vanished from their lives, letting them know through the dean's office not to bother looking for him. He hadn't wanted to return even to pick up his things; according to the surgery chief, someone else did it for him. He never made a single phone call to the grieving fiancée of his supposed best friend.

Papa nodded. "It's not easy to adjust to huge changes, and you lashed out at the first people you saw. *We're* just trying to make sure you get through this okay. That's why we asked you to invite Anjali—"

"Papa, please," said Rishi. "This is not the right time. I'm not in the mental space to think about such things." God, how was he supposed to get out of this? Eventually, he'd have to admit what he did. All his lies would be exposed. And then...

Inclining his head, Rishi's father said, "All right. We can back off for now, but you need to talk to the girl and tell her it's only a matter of time. Your phone's been in the living room for the last one week, so I know you haven't called her. Don't leave her and her family thinking you've changed your mind."

"The minister," fretted Ma.

"Exactly," said Papa. "He controls the *finance* ministry. After the president and the prime minister, he's the most powerful man in the country. He could snap his fingers and make wars happen. *He* came to our house on Anjali's brother's request. Do you realise the kind of clout that is? We need to let the Joshis know we *will* respond as soon as you feel able."

Rishi's head swam. Was there a possibility the Joshis thought there was something romantic between their daughter and him? After all, Anjali never talked about Joe to her parents, and the gossip circulating on campus could've gotten to them the same way it got to the Rastogis. When Rishi's lies were finally laid bare, he was going to add the third most powerful man in the nation to his list of enemies. The blackmailer, the minister, the Joshis, even Anjali... how many people were going to call for Rishi's blood? If the blackmailer revealed Rishi's one-night stand to the world, none of the rest would matter. He'd be in prison, his medical licence gone, his future as a surgeon ripped away.

Trying to clamp down on panic, he said, "I'll call Anju. I swear. Just lemme have some space for now."

In ten minutes, he was jogging down the dark footpath, phone tucked into his fleece jacket. Mildly chilly air slapped at his face, but the cold meant there weren't many on the street to overhear him, thank God.

Standing in the circle of yellow light thrown by a lamppost, he dialled Anjali's number. He needed to tell her, somehow get her to help him. "Hello, it's—"

"What's going on, Rishi?" asked Anjali, tone puzzled and angry. "I've been trying to reach you for two days. My mother called me. Apparently, your ma contacted her to discuss wedding plans."

***

Accha. Tho tumhaare dost ko wo Pakistan waale off kiya. So your friend was offed by those Pakistanis, said the note. Apparently, the blackmailer and his cronies decided to give Rishi time to grieve. Something about their surgeon needing to be in top form. They'd be on the lookout for his return to work before trying to call. The blackmailing bastard actually said he was sorry for Rishi's loss before ending the message with a patriotic *Jai Hind*—victory to India.

"*Saala,*" Rishi cursed the blackmailer. He scrunched up the sheet and shoved it into his pocket. Since he'd returned to work the day before, the call wouldn't be long coming.

He glanced towards the stairs. No, he couldn't go up to the flat for the same reason Anjali refused to meet him there. Each step he took into the flat, happy memories would attack, leaving him bleeding. At some point, he'd have to return to pick up his stuff but not this evening.

Plus, Anjali agreed to give him one day and no more to come up with an explanation, and she'd be waiting. After hanging up last night, it had been all Rishi could do not to sprint back home and demand to know why his mother did something so insanely stupid without checking with him. Except, it wasn't stupid as far as the Rastogis knew. Hell, even as far as the Joshis knew.

He got through his shift in the operating theatre somehow, discarding one lie after another he could try on Anjali. No matter what excuse he came up with, she'd tell her parents there never was any romance with Rishi. His family would come to know his truth. He'd once again be the pariah. If he could talk her into keeping his secret a little longer... maybe he could persuade the blackmailer too to wait until he finished his junior residency. He could say he'd actually be a legit general surgeon then even if there were three more years left to the neurosurgery part of course. The delay would help him devise a route out of being forced into illegally harvesting organs. Maybe he could get out of the country during the time. What the hell was he going to say to *Anjali* to get her to cooperate?

He so badly needed to talk to... Rishi had been planning to confess everything to his best friend after the wedding was done, but Nikhil was gone. Blinking back the tears welling in his eyes, Rishi walked into the shopping mall close to the medical college campus and made for the food court where Anjali would be waiting.

At the McDonald's, Rishi and Anjali ordered Chicken Maharaja Macs neither wanted. They pushed through a crowd of chattering teenagers towards the table in the farthest, most secluded corner of the store.

"You look... different," he said, chewing on a greasy French fry. She'd lost weight in the last week, and there were purplish shadows under her eyes as though she hadn't been sleeping.

A ghost of a smile appeared on her face. "I look terrible." Staring down at her burger, she muttered, "I'm trying to move on, but it's not easy. Whenever I close my eyes... I don't *need* to close my eyes... I actually thought I heard Joe call me a couple of times. If Meenu were there, I could've coped better." Meenakshi was still with her grieving sister and not expected back for at least a couple of weeks. "Sid keeps suggesting things for us to do, but I don't feel up to it."

"Not yet."

"Not yet," Anjali agreed. "But I *will* get through this." She looked up. "Did someone tell your parents the gossip from campus or something? Is that why she called—"

"I did," Rishi blurted.

"Heh?"

"*I* told them about the gossip." Then, it came out—the reaction in the Rastogi household when he revealed his sexuality, his short stay in New York, the forced return to India, finally his re-entry into the family on the basis of lies. "I'm sorry," he finished, miserably.

"Oh, my God," Anjali groaned, her hands covering her mouth. "My parents... I'd said something to my mom about Joe without mentioning his name, now she believes it was you. What am I going to do?"

"I'm really, really sorry," Rishi said. "I'll talk to your mother and confess everything, I swear. I just need a little bit of time—"

"You don't understand," said Anjali, eyes wide in near panic. "She knows there was someone. I was simply going to say we drifted apart, but now, I have to say it wasn't *you* before anyone starts planning a wedding. She's gonna guess it was Joe. There's no one else who fits the profile."

"You can tell them about Joe. He's not around to stop you, and it's not like *you* did anything wrong." Indian families tended to be stricter with their daughters' love lives, and broken relationships could lead to social ostracism, but Anjali's family accepted a gay couple, for God's sake. Her uncle in California and his partner. Surely, the Joshis would be supportive of their own daughter. "Only, gimme a little time before talking to your parents, please."

"I can't tell them. I can't tell *any*one. God, I was such a fool. I trusted Joe. Everyone on campus is going to know I was with him for the last fifteen months. They're all going to talk. Oh, God. Fool, fool, fool." Burying her face in her hands, she moaned.

"Anju, stop," said Rishi. "No one will know except your parents, and they're not going to blab, are they?"

Dropping her hands from her face, Anjali hissed, "I don't want them to know. They can't find out I was so *stupid*. God, I practically ran to the flat every time Joe called. Every. Single. Time. You know what that makes me? The whole world will call me a slut, and I don't want my family to hear it. They'll be crushed."

Rishi glanced both ways and said, "Shh." The low tables around them were empty, but there were customers walking towards the counter. "Your dad and mom are not going to look at it that way." The way she always talked about her family, it seemed they enjoyed a great relationship. Even the brother she always complained about. The boy was the one who asked the minister to make sure his sister was safe. "And how is 'the whole world' going to hear about you and Joe?"

"Rishi," snarled Anjali. "When your mother called, my mom didn't deny it because she thought it was true. All the gossip... plus, what I said to her before... she was just waiting for me to confirm the man I talked about was you. It's been three days since then. If I confess to my parents and my mom takes back what she said to yours, your family's going to know something's wrong. If they say a word about it, people are going to start putting things together. How are you going to get *your* ma and papa to stop talking? You don't even dare tell them you haven't changed your mind about being gay." Abruptly, she asked, "You said you wanted a little time. How much time?"

Rishi blinked. "Dunno. A few months, maybe."

"After that we can say we drifted apart?" Anjali shook her head. "What am I saying? This is so stupid."

"No, it's not," Rishi said, urgently. For once, things seemed to be falling in place for him. "I need time to make some arrangements to go abroad."

"Abroad? What for? Even if you don't want to tell your parents you're still gay, all you have to do is say you don't want to marry *me*. String them along. Don't quit your course like—"

Like Joe. "*I* have no choice," Rishi said, bitterness welling up. One mistake, and he was going to pay for it with the sacrifice of his career. "I'll go someplace... Canada, probably." The country accepted asylum applications based on sexuality. He hoped like hell it meant he stood a better chance of retaining his medical licence there even if the Indian government stripped it away. Plus, the visa process was easier than the U.S. It would still take some time, and he'd have to delay the blackmailer somehow. Maybe by claiming his customers would be better served by someone who'd actually completed at least general surgery which wouldn't be for another year in Rishi's case. Nor could the bastard find out Rishi was trying to leave India. He could apply for a visa from some other city... Mumbai... travelling there under the pretext of being Anjali's fiancé. "Once I get to Canada, I'll try to get into a surgical residency. You'll be free."

"But why?" Anjali asked, tone confused. "I get that you want to live free, but if you wait until you finish your course here—"

"I can't." Rishi swallowed. This was Anjali Joshi, the girl who didn't want anyone to hear of the failure of her perfectly legal, one hundred per cent ethical association with a single man. Yeah, she was supportive of gay rights, but what would she say about Rishi's one-night stand with a patient? Forget Anjali— there would be no doctor in India with any ethics who'd condone what he'd done. He'd be labelled a predator. His licence, his freedom... "Someone's blackmailing me."

"*What?*"

Squinting sideways towards the other diners, Rishi again said, "Shh."

Elbows on the table, Anjali leaned forwards. "What do you mean by black—for being gay?"

"Yeah. They want me to... ahh..." Rishi looked Anjali right in the eye and lied, "They want money."

Puffing out short, sharp breaths, she glanced wildly around the restaurant before returning her gaze to Rishi. "Who's 'they'? And how much?"

"I'm not sure, but I think it's a former... former boyfriend. I get these phone calls, but the voice is kind of muffled. They haven't said how much."

Anjali frowned. "If it's a former boyfriend, won't *he* get into trouble, too?"

Not with Rishi accused of sex with a former patient and not when alcohol was involved. Even if custodial rape weren't part of the charges, Parth Kumar would be considered a victim. "It was only a guess. Could be anyone else. The point is I need to leave India before I get arrested."

Eyes softening with concern, Anjali said, "I know there's a law about it, but I've never heard of anyone actually getting arrested for being gay."

"Anju, you... you come from a different world, all right? My parents are reasonably well-to-do, but they're not exactly free thinking. Nor is the rest of India. Yeah, I could get arrested." Life imprisonment, simply for the way he was born. Even if *that* didn't happen, Rishi could still lose his licence for having sex with a patient. He shook his head. "Can't take a chance. Please, Anju? It will work out for both of us. Play along for a few months and once I leave for Canada, tell everyone you changed your mind. I swear, we'll behave so carefully no one will be able to slut-shame you."

"Once you leave, everyone will know *you* changed your mind. There *will* be talk about me."

"It can't happen," Rishi said. "*You* have to break the engagement. Say something like... I don't know... that you don't want to move out of India."

"But Rishi—"

"I don't want your family angry with mine," he said. When her eyes widened in confusion, he explained, "Look, Anju. Your family is powerful. I can't risk—"

"Stop," Anjali said, a hand raised. "Joe always used that excuse. I'm not putting up with it any longer."

"I'm sorry, but they are," Rishi insisted. "My God, the finance minister of India came looking for you. In the middle of a national emergency! If that doesn't say powerful, what does?"

"The minister came to talk to me because *his* son asked him to. That boy happens to be my brother's best friend."

"Do you seriously imagine the minister would've shown up in person if you'd been the daughter of a regular middle-class couple? He came because of your family. There's no question about it." Rishi folded his hands. "Anju, we both need this time. Please, just this one favour. Nothing will happen to your reputation. Our behaviour will be so circumspect no one will be able to shame you in any way. In fact, you'll be the girl who preferred to break an engagement to stay in your own country, near your family. *I'll* be the ambitious S.O.B. who put career over love."

With a small huff, Anjali quipped, "If my family's so darned powerful, maybe we should threaten him back. You know, the horrible man who's blackmailing you?"

***

"Listen, you son of a bitch," Rishi snarled into the phone, walking up and down the small living room of the flat. Thanks to Anjali's casual suggestion, he'd finally found the courage to return to the privacy of his former home and pick up the phone when it finally rang. *She'd* returned with him and was now on the sofa, listening to his side of the conversation. "Call me again, and I'll have your ass thrown in jail for blackmail."

307

"Really?" mocked the bastard. "You'll be right there with me, doctor saab. Did you somehow forget what you did?"

Rishi glanced at Anjali. "I haven't. *You* have forgotten something. You're clearly having me followed, so you should know by now who my fiancée is."

"Huh?" The bastard laughed. "Fiancée? You?"

"Yeah. Me. A friend of her family was at our house the other night," Rishi said, an almost violent satisfaction surging through his limbs. His muscles bunched. "The finance minister of India. He's a friend of the Joshis. You think it's going to be difficult for them to make my little problem go away?"

"Oh, c'mon, doctor saab. *Kya bakwaas.* You're claiming that the little girl, Anjali, is *your* fiancée?"

"It's not nonsense," Rishi insisted. "She's here with me. Anju?" He turned on the speaker.

"I'm here," said Anjali, her strong, sweet voice carrying exactly the right decibel level. "Rishi and I are engaged to be married. And yes, he has told me everything."

He turned off the speaker function before the blackmailer got a chance to reveal anything incriminating. "You heard what she said. Now, go back to whatever hole you came from and stop bothering me."

"*Dhat teri ki,*" muttered the blackmailer, the exclamation announcing his shock. "That was... unexpected."

Relishing every bit of his victory, Rishi said, "Your game stops right here, right now. If you call me again, if you *breathe* a word about me to anyone, we'll give the phone numbers you called from to the minister. I might not be able to trace it, but I'm betting *he* could. If I go down, I'll take you and your pals with me. What's more, the minister could probably get me out in no time. *You* will die in jail."

***

Six months flew by. Six months of peace from the blackmailer. Six months of family visits, of phone conversations with far-flung relatives, of celebratory dinners with friends and faculty. Six months of occasional trips to the temple with his ma where Rishi prayed for forgiveness for what he was doing.

He was fêted once again as the beloved son of the Rastogi clan. Ma waited up for him on Friday evenings when he got the weekend off to spend at home, cooking all the dishes he liked. Rishi was forced to beg his sisters to stop inviting Anjali on their shopping expeditions. She was in her third year of medical college with plenty of studying to do and no time for shopping.

Papa even started taking Rishi to the Delhi Golf Club to introduce him to the city's elite. The CEO of a pricey private hospital network was quite interested in signing Rishi and Anjali as future employees. It didn't matter that she had yet to decide what she wanted to do though the gentleman did have a suggestion. "Anaesthesiology is a very good speciality for lady doctors, especially surgeons' wives," the CEO said to Rishi's father. "The hours are flexible. Working women have to think about things like children, right?"

Rishi barely refrained from rolling his eyes. Mentally, he counted the days remaining to the tentative timeframe the Canadian consulate gave him for visa approval. No matter when his application was approved, the farce of an engagement would have to last at least until he completed his general surgery course—which would be in one more year. Then, he'd leave the country in the middle of the night. Only then would Anjali break the engagement, telling everyone Rishi left clandestinely to force her hand because she'd refused to consider the possibility of moving abroad. Their entire social circle would despise him for what he'd done, but he'd be safely out of the blackmailer's reach.

Rishi would be away from his beloved family, from the professors he'd revered since he walked into AIIMS at the age of seventeen. He'd be leaving behind the city and the streets which witnessed his every joy, his every sorrow and fear. When he was in New York for the first few months after his undergraduate degree, Nikhil was with him. Now, Rishi would be alone in a new city—Vancouver, perhaps—where every face would be unfamiliar.

While he and Anjali were making plans, the families made theirs. Apparently, their horoscopes were a perfect match, delighting all the old aunties and uncles in the two clans. The *official* engagement ceremony— religious rites and ring exchange—would be in Lonavala, the hill station near Mumbai where the Joshis owned a bungalow.

The week before they were supposed to fly to Mumbai for the engagement, Rishi sat silently on the sofa in his apartment at the AIIMS postgraduate hostel. Next to him was Anjali, talking to what was left of the gang.

"Seriously, Sid?" she asked, tone angry. "An intervention?"

Kokila was on the speakerphone while Siddharth and Meenakshi occupied the chairs on the other side of the coffee table. "Look, Anju," said Sid, patiently. "Both you and Rishi suffered major losses back to back. Within one month, you announced your engagement. As your friends, we have a responsibility to tell you this is crazy! I asked you a zillion times what the hell you're doing. So did Meenu and Kiki. Neither you nor Rishi has given us a rational explanation."

"This is the right thing for us," Anjali insisted.

"So you keep saying," grumbled Meenakshi. "I have a hard time buying it."

"You're the only ones," snapped Rishi. "The rest of the campus has no problem with us."

Behind Meenakshi's butterfly glasses, her eyes flashed. "The rest of campus thinks you've been together for the last three years. Sid and I and Kiki know better. If Gauri were here..." Meenakshi swallowed hard. "If she were here, she'd tell you the same."

Gauri hadn't returned to AIIMS to complete the remaining six weeks of internship. She was still in her ancestral home in Nasik. According to Meenakshi, her sister did nothing except stare silently into the distance, mechanically eating the food placed in front of her. She didn't even seem to hear what anyone might say. The prescription antidepressants had little effect. Her desperate parents took her to at least three different psychiatrists, but all the advice the shrinks offered boiled down to one word: time.

If she were there, she'd do much worse than merely tell Rishi and Anjali they were crazy. Nikhil never revealed his friends' secrets—except to his fiancée. Gauri, for all her glitzy attitude, was equally as close-mouthed and never said a word about Rishi's sexuality to anyone else. But if she knew what he was currently up to, she would've pulled every trick in the book to get him to see the light.

Anjali said, "Guys, I appreciate what you're trying to do, but look at it this way. We're only engaged. The wedding's not going to happen for another year. If ours is a rebound thing as you think, it's not going to last that long, right?"

Meenakshi and Siddharth exchanged glances. Huffing, she called, "Kiki?"

Over the speakerphone, Kokila agreed, "I guess one year is good enough time for you to figure things out."

"Thank you," Rishi said, rolling his eyes and flopping back onto the sofa.

"Does that mean you're coming to Mumbai next week for the engagement party?" Anjali asked.

"I can't," said Meenakshi. "The last time we were there... Sid will have to represent all of us."

"It's all right, Meenu," Anjali said. "We'll have our little party when I return."

Rishi bit back a sigh of relief. If Meenakshi showed up, Gauri might have, too. If her grief somehow lifted enough for her to understand what was going on... he needed this pretence of a romance to continue for another year. At the end of it, he'd be off to Canada, and Anjali could call the whole thing off.

He might be alone, but he'd be safe. Anjali would have the delay she needed to keep her pristine reputation.

✳✳✳

Anjali leaned her forehead against the iron fence surrounding the hilltop property and took in the impossible green of the grass-covered cliffs around her. At some distance was a thin silvery waterfall, wispy mist floating all around. Her brother, Vikram, and his best buddy went off hiking. They said they'd be going to see the waterfall, but it was too far from the Joshi bungalow to spot the two boys.

"It's hot," complained Rishi, tugging at the collar of his silk navy blue and beige *sherwani*—the Indian version of a frock coat.

She laughed. "It's May in Maharashtra." Her jewel-encrusted, burgundy velvet *lehnga* and golden *choli*—ankle-length skirt and cropped blouse—were also completely unsuitable for the muggy weather. Thank God, the matching silk stole didn't weigh three kilogrammes like the rest of the attire. The wedding planners chose the outfits for both bride and groom with photography in mind, not comfort. "Do you wanna go back inside?"

The Joshi bungalow was set a few feet away from the edge of the cliff. With the exception of the finance minister and Siddharth, both of whom would fly in only the next morning, all the guests invited to the engagement ceremony the next day were currently in the building. Their chatter and laughter echoed across the grassy yard to where she and Rishi stood.

"Nah," he mumbled. "They start talking and teasing... I feel like a bloody fraud. I *am* a fraud."

"We don't have another option," she pointed out.

"Yeah, but..." Frustrated look on his face, Rishi huffed. "Didn't you ever have dreams of what your wedding was gonna be like? Don't you feel this is all a bit... I don't know... unreal?"

Anjali turned her gaze back to the cliffs. "These things are always only as real as we want them to be." In her heart, she'd been engaged to Joe the moment they promised each other forever. There were no prayers, no lavish house party, no diamond rings. But the pledge they'd made was as real as it could get for *her*. For Joe, the words meant absolutely nothing. "Besides, I'd always imagined getting married on a beach, not here." A Hindu wedding, followed by an exchange of rings blessed by Joe's uncle, Fr Franco. Afterwards, the bride and the groom and all the guests would've danced barefoot on the sand. Holding hands, she and Joe would've snuck away sometime during the night to the honeymoon suite.

"You could still do it," Rishi said. "Someday, you'll find a man you'll really want to marry."

Would she? Silently, Anjali continued to stare at the cliffs, tracing the path of the distant waterfall with her eyes. There were a few houses at the bottom. Maybe a newlywed couple lived in one of those houses. Maybe it was a home she'd dreamt of living in since she was a little girl. Maybe the man was so wildly in love he'd built it for her as he'd once promised.

A small sob escaped her mouth. Suddenly, hot tears gushed, scalding her cheeks. She gritted her teeth to hold back the sounds, but it only made her head hurt.

Rishi's arm was around her shoulders in an instant. "Careful," he murmured into her ear. "Someone might see."

Nodding jerkily, she brushed the moisture off her cheeks with the edge of her silk stole. "I'm all right," she muttered.

"No, you're not."

"I... God, how long is it gonna take?" she asked, despairingly. "It's been six months." There wasn't a day she hadn't thought about Joe. She recalled every word of their sweet banter. The touch of his hands on her body. His fascination with the teeny, tiny birthmark at the corner of her mouth. The dreams they'd woven. "How am I going to find someone else when I feel like this? If he'd actually told me we were over—" If Joe had looked her in the eye and told her she no longer mattered to him, she could've moved on.

Perhaps.

"I keep thinking... what if he returned?" If she weren't careful, her mind slipped into daydreaming she was back in his warm arms, that the scent of his cologne was in her breath. There was a constant ache in her left chest. "I need to, *need to,* forget."

"I can't tell how long it will take to forget," said Rishi. "I can only hope you get every good thing life has to offer. You deserve it."

With a tremulous smile, she turned to face him and patted his chest. "Thank you. You're a lovely man, you know. Inside and out." He did look handsome in his Indian finery. "Why couldn't I have fallen in love with you?"

He laughed. "Anju darling, don't forget I'm gay."

"Why did you have to be gay?" she asked, quite seriously. "Everything matches in our case... background, interests, even our horoscopes. You wouldn't have left me. We'd have married and lived happily ever after."

"My *family* would've been happy," he murmured. "They are now."

"They're very important to you," Anjali stated. "Most of the things you do are to keep them happy."

"Are you telling me you don't do the same?"

"I do, but..." She shrugged. How did she say it was different with the Joshis without insulting Rishi and his parents? Anjali simply didn't want to hurt her

314

dad and mom's feelings or fail to meet their expectations. She had no doubt they'd continue to love her even if she didn't. Whereas the Rastogis...

"My family's a bit old-fashioned." Rishi grimaced. "I saw Papa talking to your uncle from California."

"Skinwalla Uncle?" Anjali asked. The dermatologist was the second of the four Joshi brothers and lived in L.A. with his partner and their five children. "Your father was quite pleasant, actually." If Rishi hadn't told her of the investment banker's reaction to his own son's announcement, she'd have never suspected him of such virulent homophobia.

"Papa used to work for a multinational bank. Of course, he knows how to behave." Rishi's arm slipped from her shoulders. "Man, *your* parents... I wish..." He glanced back at the house.

"What?"

"Nothing." He shook his head. The yearning in his eyes... at some level, he had to know the difference between the two families. "I wanted to talk to your uncle and see how he managed. It couldn't have been easy back in the day. It's not easy now. He went to the U.S. all by himself, met someone, made a life. But then, he still had the support of all his brothers. *I'm* going to be all alone." With a small smile, Rishi asked, "Why couldn't you have been a man?"

"Heh?" Anjali laughed. Then, she couldn't stop laughing. "First time in my life..." she wheezed between guffaws. "...ever... someone said that to me."

He laughed with her for a few moments before saying, "I meant it. I would've married you just for your family."

"Really?" Anjali crossed her arms and tapped a foot. "What about love?"

"Meh." Rishi waved an airy hand. "You can live without love. It's difficult to live without acceptance. We all want that one place where we fit in. You know... what we call home."

315

When he fell silent, Anjali murmured, "Nikhil. He was your home." More than the Rastogi parents.

"Yeah. Joe, too, to some extent. The bastard." With a quick glance at her face, Rishi mumbled, "Sorry. Didn't mean to—"

"It's all right," she said, quickly. "I have to learn to stop going to pieces every time his name is mentioned."

"Sonuvabitch doesn't know what he lost," Rishi brooded. "Your parents care only that you're happy. They accepted your uncle and his partner. They would've welcomed Joe with wide-open arms. They accept me, too, but as your fiancé. That acceptance will be gone the moment I leave for Canada." Melancholy look on his face, he repeated, "I will be alone."

"I'll still be there," swore Anjali.

"For how long?" Rishi asked. "At some point, you *will* meet a man you want to marry. What story are you going to tell him for keeping in touch with a fake fiancé who left you?"

"What story am I going to tell this man now?" Anjali asked, heart once again heavy. "That I practically lived with a very real boyfriend? That *he* left me without a word?" Her vision blurred with tears. "That I don't think I'll ever be able to forget him?"

"Hey," Rishi murmured. "Hey, hey, hey." He reached out and gathered her into his arms. "Maybe we should get married for real," he said, tone teasing. "It would solve both our problems."

Anjali was about to respond when she heard a squeaking sound. Vikram and his friend—the minister's son—pushed open the gate at the far end of the fenced property and sauntered towards the bungalow.

"The perfect couple," Vikram said, tone low but his mockery quite evident. Catching his sister looking at him over her fiancé's shoulder, he stumbled.

Vikram scrambled up and shot her an awkward half-grimace, half-smile. "Shit," he muttered. "She heard me."

Rishi let go of her but didn't turn around to check who threw the taunt. "Your brother?"

With the tips of her thumb and forefinger, Anjali massaged the base of her nose, hoping to ward away the headache threatening to attack. "Yeah. I don't think he realised we could hear." Still, it hurt.

"What's his problem?" asked Rishi. "He was glaring at me all last evening and today whenever I talked to your parents."

Anjali huffed. How could she possibly explain her little brother's stubbornness, his lack of forgiveness towards the sister who'd made the thoughtless mistake of ignoring him when he was being bullied? How did she explain his hostility towards their parents when she didn't understand it herself? "We all have our demons, I guess." Anjali wished like crazy Vikram and she could share theirs, but when she needed a brother, *he'd* found one— his best friend, Adhith Verma. Minister Verma's son.

With a snort, Rishi asked, "Demons? Your brother? He's rich, straight, clearly smart, and has the most supportive family imaginable. To top it off, he's friends with the finance minister's son. Now, *that* kid actually seems like a decent fellow. He knows how to be polite at least. Your brother, on the other hand, is an entitled ass. Mocking us like that! You're his sister. What he needs is a good thrashing."

A sharp pang went through her heart. "Joe once said something similar."

"What—" Rishi dissolved into sympathetic laughter. "Darling, you're hopeless. So am I."

✳✳✳

Six months later, Anjali was on the sofa in Rishi's apartment at the postgraduate hostel when he received the visa approval letter from the Canadian consulate.

"This is it," he said, collapsing next to her on the sofa. "By the end of this academic year, I'll be done with general surgery. The day after, I'll be able to leave India."

"This is it," she agreed, feeling somewhat cold. She crossed her arms to rub warmth into her shoulders. "Good luck, my friend."

Rishi tossed the letter onto the coffee table. "Anju?" he called. "Remember the engagement party?" When she nodded, he continued, "I've been thinking... we talked about... will you seriously consider making things real between us?"

"Real?" Anjali dropped her arms to her sides. "As in really marry you? C'mon, Rishi—"

"Hear me out before you decide. I know you're not over Joe, and you've already ruled out getting into another relationship because of it. *I* don't really want to go to Canada."

She sighed. "Getting over Joe is not the issue." With the rest of her life settling into an even keel, Anjali learned to function around the core of dull ache in her chest. "I don't want to explain Joe to anyone else, and I can't marry someone without explaining Joe. But you... there's nothing stopping you from meeting someone. I mean, Delhi High Court just decriminalised gay sex." Even if Anjali weren't paying attention to the issue, the recent headlines would've been unmissable.

"The rest of India hasn't caught up. What am I supposed to do? Stay in Delhi all my life? Plus, there are idiots moving the supreme court to overturn the judgement, and who knows how that will end. If I leave the country to scratch my itches, there will be no coming back. The blackmailer will get me if I do. I will lose everything I ever knew. The only way I can stay here is if you really marry me. Anju, I've thought about this for a long time. The one difficulty I see is children. I assume you'd want one or two brats at some point. But even that is not really a difficulty. You and I... ahh..." He flushed. "I'm sure we can somehow manage."

Anjali laughed. "Do you think 'somehow managing' will be enough?"

"Yes," said Rishi, firmly. "Marriage and family involve a lot more than sex. You said it yourself: we're a match in all other ways. Which is actually a lot more than most other couples start with if you consider all the arranged marriages in this country." When she didn't respond, he leaned over and pressed his lips to her mouth.

Anjali made a surprised mewl but didn't say anything. Rishi smelled of sandalwood and spice as he usually did. He didn't attempt to go further in, limiting himself to a soft—almost virginal—kiss. It wasn't unpleasant, but there was none of the crazy hunger she'd experienced at the first brush of Joe's lips against hers—no racing heart, no pooling blood.

"See?" Rishi asked, withdrawing. A sheen coated his face as though his sweat glands just leapt into overdrive. "It's not impossible," he insisted, voice trembling.

"I might have believed you..." she said, dryly. "...if you didn't look like a dying duck."

He glared for a moment before sighing. "Point one: you're prepared to be alone and miserable rather than risk explaining Joe to another man who might be interested in you. Point two: you wouldn't have to explain Joe to *me*. Point three: if I leave India, it will be forever. Everything... every*one* who made me what I am will be on the other side of the world." Rishi looked down at the floor. "*I* don't want to be alone."

"That's the thing," she pointed out. "You won't be alone for long. You'll meet new people in Canada... maybe someone to love."

"Maybe," he muttered. "But I'll lose my *family* forever. My parents are going to know why I left no matter what story we feed them. They won't accept me back. The only one left for me in this world will be you, Anju. You'll eventually drift away, too."

"Rishi, yaar." Anjali leaned close to pat his knee. "What are you suggesting? That we can be together and miserable instead of alone and miserable?"

"Only in the worst-case scenario. Chances are we'll get along just fine. We do *now*. As for the rest of it... this is a country of one billion people. I'm sure all those baby daddies weren't straight. If they can do it, so can I."

"Insert Tab A into Slot B?" she teased. "Your passion for me is overwhelming."

"Just don't say no right away, okay? Take time to think about it." He twisted around to face her fully. "You know what you should do? Weigh the risks and benefits before deciding."

Anjali blinked. Her mom had once said something similar—to consider life without the other. Life without Rishi, the one person who'd seen her at her lowest, the one man she'd trusted with all her secret fears.

For two weeks, she thought about little else. She walked by the physiology lab where she'd first met both Rishi and Joe. There was a look of concern on Meenakshi's face when Anjali asked the cabbie taking them to the movie theatre to stop by the flat where the two men used to live. She didn't go in... merely stared up at the fourth floor, struggling to close a mental door on the bittersweet memories. But then, the memories included Rishi, too. Kind-hearted Rishi in whose presence she'd found tranquillity. If he left, there would be nothing stopping the pain from crushing her.

"What's going on?" asked Meenakshi.

Anjali shrugged. "It's been a year." Exactly twelve months since Joe walked out of the flat for the last time. "I wanted to make sure I'm over him. Now, I'm sure."

Meenakshi didn't look completely convinced by the lie, but thankfully, she didn't ask further questions.

Later that night in their hostel room, Anjali waited until Meenakshi fell asleep before dialling Rishi's number.

"What's up?" he asked. The clatter and chatter in the background suggested he was in the patient wards.

Before she lost her nerve, Anjali blurted, "Okay."

"Huh? Okay what?"

"Okay, I'll marry you."

Two weeks after Anjali's final exams in 2010, she and Rishi were back in Lonavala. Endless strings of lights, bouquets of roses, colourful fabrics... the bungalow and the family temple nearby were decorated to the max for the wedding of the Joshi princess to her handsome prince. Cousins and aunties helped Anjali don the traditional nine-yard sari in green and gold. Rishi opted for the simplicity of a cream silk kurta and matching *dhoti*—woven cloth wrapped around the hips and legs and knotted at the waist.

The sweet smoke of incense swirled around as the priests chanted prayers to the accompaniment of music. Friends and family showered the couple with rice to bless them with abundant happiness. As Rishi put *sindoor*—vermillion—on Anjali's forehead, signifying her new status as his wife, she saw in his eyes the same doubts lurking in the shadowed corners of her own mind. Holding his hand, she took the *saat phere*—seven rounds around the sacred fire—and recited the vows of lifelong love and commitment she'd once dreamed of making with Joe.

Every guest who came up to the reception stage to greet the couple said how perfect Rishi and Anjali were for each other, how perfect their love story was, how perfect their life was going to be. Anjali thanked all of them, smiling through the blinding pain pulsing across her skull.

Much later in the night, Rishi was shoved with a great deal of laughter and hilarity into the wedding chamber where Anjali was waiting. They stared at each other in uncomfortable silence as the crowd in the hallway left, and their chatter receded. For the first time since they started their pretend engagement, Anjali didn't know what to say to Rishi.

His eyes went to the king-sized bed before jerking hastily away. At least there were no rose petals as the wedding planner originally intended. The groom's allergies needed to be taken into account. "Shall I turn off the light?" he finally asked.

In the darkness, a clumsy kiss landed somewhere in the vicinity of her ear. His fingers—trembling and sweaty—closed around her wrist.

It was at the tip of her tongue to tell him they didn't have to do this. Not tonight, anyway. At her side, Rishi took a long, deep breath before kissing her earlobe a second time. The trembling in his fingers stopped. He seemed determined to prove something at least to himself.

Anjali swatted back the objections crowding her mind, clamouring to be vocalised. Praying desperately not to cringe at his touch, she brushed her lips against his smooth jaw.

There were no words said, no frantic whispers of love, no screams of passion. Most of their clothes remained on. He was quite gentle throughout, but she held on to his shoulders and gritted her teeth, wanting for it to be over, struggling not to remember her wild lovemaking with another man.

When Rishi left the bed in twenty minutes, Anjali turned on her side, letting silent tears fall on the pillow. She listened to the sound of running water as her new husband stayed in the shower for an hour, scrubbing the scent of her from his body.

In the morning, she would learn he'd merely been trying to fulfil expectations. It took him twice the usual dose of Viagra. They agreed not to torture each other like that ever again until sperm needed to meet egg someday.

Chapter 30

Present day

"You lied to me, Rishi?" Anjali asked, fiercely. When she pushed herself up from the chair, the straps of her purse slid down her arm. Her laptop slipped out, falling to the plush carpet of the brightly lit room at the Goa Marriott, but she didn't pause to pick it up. Her former husband was in the armchair by the window, his features almost unfamiliar under the beard he now sported. At least the wedding ring was no longer in evidence. Anjali didn't know what she'd have done if he were still wearing it, but it wouldn't have been pretty. The two-faced man pretended to be her friend, gave her his shoulder to cry on, when all he wanted was the support of her family to slither out of trouble. "You *used* me. For what? To cover up the fact you had *sex with a patient?*" Her words ended in a near shout.

"Shh," said Farhan. He was leaning against the wall on the other side of the room. "Anju, please—"

"Don't," she said, raising a hand. "Don't say a word." She didn't take her eyes off the culprit, now cowering in his chair. "You made me complicit in your *crime,* never even considering how it might affect me."

"There was no crime," Rishi said, doggedly. "Except for the gay sex part which you already knew about. Parth Kumar was not my patient at the time. I was young, bloody frustrated, and I'd been drinking. I know none of it excuses what I did, but it was *not* a crime."

"You think it's only about that?" Anjali asked, tone wild. "My God. I was with you for *eleven* years. We were married for nine of those years. We have a child together. You were the one person in the whole world I thought I could trust with everything, but you... you were only *using* me."

"*No.*" Rishi nervously patted the new beard on his face before meeting her angry gaze. "I mean, yes. I did lie to you about the reason for needing help, but I never denied needing it to begin with. I told you it was about... ahh... a former boyfriend. It was... sort of."

"But you..." Heaving in an angry breath, she paused. No, he'd never denied using her name to get back into his family's good books or lied about being blackmailed for his sexuality. He simply neglected to explain that the "sort of former boyfriend" was also a former patient. All Rishi begged her for was time to get out of the country. *She* was the one who brought up the minister, urging Rishi to use the connection to get rid of the blackmailer.

Rishi clambered out of the armchair and held out a beseeching hand. "I lied only because I didn't think you'd help me, otherwise. It was a lousy thing to do to a friend, but I was being blackmailed into organ smuggling. It's banned in every country in the world except Iran. If you didn't agree to help, I would've been forced to kill that bloody actor."

Anjali stared. "Kill? Oh, my God, *Rishi...*"

"I didn't know what else to do, okay?" he snapped, shoving his fingers into his hair. "Actually, I *wish* I'd done exactly that. We wouldn't be in this situation today."

"Are you *crazy?*" Anjali shouted.

"No, but I was getting there," said Rishi. "What were my other options? Go to jail for a one-night stand or do what the bastard ordered and illegally harvest organs?"

"What would *you* have done, Anju?" asked Farhan.

Pivoting to face him, she said, "I wouldn't have slept with a patient."

"But if you did—" At her glare, Farhan held up both hands in surrender. "You wouldn't have, I know. But do you think Rishi deserved jail time for it?"

"Jail time?" Anjali asked. "The actor was not a current patient... I know there were laws at the time against gay sex, but..."

"No buts," said Farhan. "A gay doctor who slept with a patient? Even a former patient? They would've thrown his ass in jail. There would've been no leniency."

"They would've at least taken my licence away," Rishi finished, miserably. "You know they would've. They still could." He wouldn't go to prison since the laws changed, but his medical licence could still be taken away for the ethical violation. Then and now, it would be no less than a life sentence for Rishi—the end of his identity as a doctor.

"That's why you decided on Canada," she said. The country had liberal asylum laws which covered homosexuality. "You thought they might let you keep your licence even if the Indian government took it away."

Rishi nodded. "Yes. Anju, I never *meant* to use you or lie to you or anything. It just sort of happened... out of my own stupidity... and then, I kept getting deeper and deeper into it."

She hadn't known how to get out of the *truths* she'd told her parents about the man she was involved with. She'd used Rishi to protect her reputation and her pride. "Why did you ask me to marry you?"

"I told you I didn't want to be alone," said Rishi. "It was one hundred per cent true. Also, because you were, in a weird way, already my family. You still are. That part is never going to change whatever you decide tonight."

"You never actually did any harvesting," she said, her words partly a question, partly a statement.

"God, no," said Rishi, taking half a step towards her. His shoe was perilously close to the laptop she'd dropped on the floor.

"So that's why you were so anxious about getting back together," she murmured, glancing between Rishi and Farhan. Going down on her haunches, she stuffed the laptop back into her purse. "I couldn't figure out... I thought you'd be happy."

"I was half-hoping you'd say something in the divorce papers about me being gay," Rishi admitted. "All the pressure would've ended."

Frowning, Anjali said, " *You* have to make that decision, not me."

"Doesn't matter now," said Rishi, his tone fatigued. "The blackmailer problem won't go away whether I come out or not. If the bastard says something... I don't want our son growing with that kind of stain on him. His needs must come first. For me *and* you."

"You don't need to tell me about prioritising my own child." Hands on her knees, she heaved herself up and turned to Farhan. "I don't know why Rishi imagined I wouldn't help him unless we were married. I honestly don't know what I'd have done eleven years ago, but today... as he said, we were and will always be family. The question is... will the blackmailer buy the threat without us actually being married? There is another problem. The minister quit politics last year." It was quite a scandal. Rumours were the gentleman reported the corruption of his colleagues to the Intelligence Bureau before turning in his resignation.

"I was thinking along a different line," said Farhan. "Your father has connections on the medical council, right? Will you talk to him? Rishi won't go to prison, but they *can* take his licence away for what he did."

"A pre-emptive strike?" asked Anjali. "It might work if we can control the narrative."

"What if it doesn't?" Rishi asked.

"Then," said Farhan, "you're going to reapply for that Canadian visa. This time, you won't be alone. I'll be with you."

"I can't go anywhere," muttered Rishi. "My son is here. I need to meet the goddamned blackmailer and—"

"Don't start," warned Farhan. "You're a doctor, not some idiot actor playing superhero. The blackmailer is actually a real-life criminal. You won't stand a chance."

Covering her mouth with her hands, Anjali muttered, "Of all the stupid, insane... stupid... argh... are you *crazy?*"

"I—" started Rishi.

"So what if you're in Canada?" Anjali asked. "Don't you think I'd take the baby to visit? Don't you think he'd rather have you alive in a different country than dead before he could even talk?" She stopped to take a calming breath. "I'll call my dad tonight. Let's see what he can do."

There was one other way Anjali could help her former husband. If she gave INTERPOL this information, they could clear Rishi of any wrongdoing in the organ-smuggling case. The blackmailer's phone calls might even give the cops an opening. As reward, INTERPOL could easily make arrangements with the medical council to let Rishi off with a rap on the knuckles. But then, there would only be one surgeon left on the list of suspects: Joe.

Part XI

Chapter 31

"What's wrong with you, old man?" Joe bellowed, hanging on for dear life to the pillion seat of the scooter as the crackpot priest driving the vehicle took a hard right. They careened into the crowd thronging the nighttime street. "Are you *trying* to get us killed?"

"Oh, calm down," shouted back Fr Franco. "We're both wearing helmets." The priest added something else, his words lost in the sudden roar of voices.

"*Har, har, Mahadev,*" chanted devotees of the residing deity of the village. The sleepy settlement near Mapusa where the Joshi Charity Clinic was located came alive one week a year for the festival. Strings of bright lights turned night into day, with flowers and incense setting up a storm of fragrances.

The priest took the scooter through an unpaved lane, the crowds dwindling to nothing as they went farther. The sounds of the festival were only a distant roar when they came to a stop in a clearing lit by a single lamppost. A couple of cars and motorbikes were already there, as well as an autorickshaw, but no people. They seemed to be at the back of the new office building of the temple. Fr Franco explained, "The festival committee told me I could park here if we planned to visit."

As a gesture of goodwill, Fr Franco made it a point to show up at the festival whenever he was in town, and Joe went with him. The temple priest here had consented to give Joe's mother—a Hindu woman who'd eloped with a Catholic—her last rites. They usually used Joe's car, though, and parked some distance away to walk through the noisy, colourful fair. Fr Franco's eyes glowed like neon bulbs whenever they landed on the plastic toys lined up in the stalls. This was the first time in years Joe rode pillion on the priest's scooter.

Joe leapt off the vehicle and unstrapped his helmet, mussing his hair to get some relief from the sweltering heat. "Leave the damned thing parked here. I'll get Romeo to drive it back later. Better yet, just donate it to the temple committee. I don't want to find you dead in a ditch someday."

"Language," reproved the priest. Clambering off, he smoothed the white cassock over his lean frame before doffing his helmet.

"The way you drive..."

"You chicken?" The eighty-year-old fellow flapped his elbows and clucked.

"Oh, for—" Still holding on to his helmet, Joe guffawed. "What would the bishop say if he saw you?"

"The bishop is a frail, old coot," said Fr Franco, nodding his grey head with great spirit.

The bishop was fifty-five and did an hour of cardio exercises daily. He expected strict discipline of himself and his flock, especially his priests. As his doctor, Joe knew all of it. "'Old coot?'" Joe snickered. "Language."

"I'll do an extra Hail Mary as penance," retorted Fr Franco. "So are you, by the way... an old coot. How many days has it been since I got you and Ram's granddaughter together?"

"Heh?" Though Joe knew from his siblings how they and Fr Franco had been investigating Joe's love life, this was the first time the priest copped to it. "What does it have to do with—"

"Three weeks," said Fr Franco, holding up the same number of fingers and nearly hopping about in agitation. "That's *twenty-one* days. Plus, all the time you knew her from Delhi. Dev says she's come looking for you at least twice he knows about, but you haven't invited her home even once." Face suddenly turning red, the priest glanced both ways as though to make sure there was no one to overhear. "I'm not recommending sex outside marriage, mind you, but I never thought I'd have to ask this question to a D'Acosta. Everything all right down there?"

"Down—*what?*"

"I'd been thinking for years it was because something happened in Delhi... some girl... I thought it was Anjali. But now..." The priest shook his head. "Men—even doctors—would rather die than admit there's a problem in a certain department, but Joe, if you need help, you must ask for it."

"I don't *have* any problem," Joe said. Unfortunately, his voice came out sounding high. Clearing his throat, he swore, "I don't."

"So what's the delay?" asked the priest. "Why is *she* the one making all the moves? I'd like to see a great-grandchild before I die, and I want to know if I should focus on Dev instead of you. Tell the truth, Joe."

"I *am* telling the truth," said Joe, vehemently. He could not possibly be having this conversation, explaining to his octogenarian relative—a *cleric*—why he hadn't gotten laid. "Anju needs space, and I'm giving it to her. No other reason." Plus, he *had* made moves. The roses, the ridiculous poetry... did he need to put on an effing public display?

Fr Franco snorted.

"There ain't nothing wrong with me," Joe insisted, snarling. "Old man, don't cast aspersions on my manhood, or I'm gonna—"

"Joe," snapped a female voice. "Don't use that tone with him. He's like a grandfather to you. Plus, a priest."

Wheeling around, Joe adjusted his glasses further up the bridge of his nose. Anjali was at the narrow back door of the temple office, yellow light spilling out from behind her. The baby was on her shoulder, asleep from the looks of him. "Anju?" Joe asked, incredulously. "What are you doing here?"

Voice loud enough for only Joe to hear, the priest said, "Third time she's come looking for you."

Joe didn't respond. He was busy taking in the sight of her in a rose silk sari, holding the infant. The boy's tiny form hid part of her torso, but the draped portion of the sari had shifted, giving Joe a tantalising glimpse of her curvy midriff. A thick braid lay over one shoulder, its end curling against her shapely breast. She'd come to the temple for him? Dressed like *that*? His hands simply itched to tug mother and son into his embrace. While they cuddled the baby between them, his fingers would slide over her bare belly. He'd tease the birthmark next to her mouth with kisses.

Bloody hell. Any moment now, the world was going to get visible evidence Joe was quite capable of propagating the D'Acosta genes. Casually, he moved the helmet in his hand in front of his crotch. Too bad he couldn't do anything about the holes in his old jeans or the missing button on his cream tee.

Marching towards them, Anjali patted her son's back and eyed Joe up and down. "You should apologise."

"Huh?" he asked, glancing at the crackpot priest. "For *what?*" Fr Franco was standing there with a pitiful expression on his face, somehow managing to look every day of his eighty years when he'd been prancing about like a grasshopper on drugs only a minute ago. Encountering Anjali's glare, Joe groaned. "Fine, I'm sorry."

With one more stern look for Joe, she turned to Fr Franco. "Thank you for arranging this."

"The least this old man could do for my friend's granddaughter," said the priest, a slight quaver in his voice.

Rolling his eyes, Joe mumbled, "Faker."

Fr Franco ignored the remark and smiled benevolently. "Anjali sent her nanny to the church and requested a meeting with you—a *secret* meeting. This was the best place. You always come here with me, Joe. And no one would've wondered why the CEO of the Joshi Clinic was showing up at one of the local temples. Plus, I have connections here."

"Secret meeting?" Joe asked, shaking his head in confusion. "Anju, you could've just called—"

"I couldn't," she said.

"Her personal situation," reminded the priest.

Personal situation? As in the divorce proceedings? This was the twenty-first century. Plus, it hadn't stopped her from going on a Tinder date.

Anjali glanced towards the door at the back of the temple office building. A man was standing there, clad only in a white dhoti—the *pujari,* a.k.a. the temple priest. "Let's talk inside. Pujariji was kind enough to offer his office."

"I'll take him while you talk," Fr Franco offered while holding his hands out towards the baby. Glancing pointedly at Joe, the priest added, "After all, Ram's great-grandchild is just like mine."

Subtle, old man, Joe mumbled in his mind. *Real subtle.*

Five minutes later, he was in the chair next to Anjali in a small, windowless room crammed with folders, wondering what the hell was going on. Fr Franco and the temple priest left with the baby some time ago, but Anjali had yet to say a word. She was staring holes into the floor.

"You know," started Joe. "I wasn't intentionally rude to Fr Franco. He was... er..." Nope, Joe wasn't about to tell Anjali there were any doubts whatsoever about his plumbing. It worked fine, dammit.

A hint of a smile appeared on her face. "I heard what you were talking about."

"You did?" *Shit.*

Anjali glanced up at him, finally. "I was rescuing you, doofus."

Joe grinned. "Er... thank you. Anju, I assure you I don't have a problem there." She should know. They'd gone at it every chance they got when they'd been together.

A giggle erupted from her. "I remember. But I couldn't tell your Fr Franco that." Her smile faded.

"What's wrong?" he asked, gently.

Visibly swallowing hard, she started, "Joe, my family sent me to Goa to... there's been some trouble at the clinic."

"Yes," he said, instantly.

"Huh? Yes what?"

"Yes to whatever you want me to do."

"Oh, it's not about... yeah, there's been some mismanagement. Kiki and I are arranging a townhall meeting with the staff to hash stuff out. I need to get them to trust me."

Joe nodded. "Great idea. You're new... you're young... you're a Joshi. The employees are probably worried about what you might be planning. Kiki's a known entity. Once the two of you talk to the staff as a team, they'll start trusting you."

"I'm going to ask them to at least withhold judgement for a reasonable period," said Anjali, tone firm. "But Joe... there's something else. I wasn't sure if I should tell you, but circumstances are such that you might need to start putting together a defence." Her teeth peeked out, pressing down on her lower lip until it turned blood red. Words running together, she said, "The police came to see me about a couple of patients from the clinic who'd turned up dead. Their organs were harvested."

"Organs?" Joe asked, not quite understanding at first. "*Organs?*" A vicious storm roared to life in his mind. Memories swirled like pieces of shattered glass, piercing every atom of his being. The pungent odour of fear, the anger, the crippling panic when he realised he wasn't going to escape the trap so neatly laid for him... all the images from his dark past returned *en force*.

"The cops think you might have something to do with it." Anjali's brows drew together in a mutinous expression. "I told them you wouldn't. You would never, ever do something like that."

Joe looked down at his hands, vaguely surprised not to see blood dripping from his fingers. "Wouldn't I?" he murmured.

Chapter 32

November 2008

"No," said Joe, turning off the gas stove before adding milk to the tea in the glass tumblers. He'd walked in the door to the Mapusa flat a mere ten minutes ago and got no time to do anything more than reassure the kids their big brother had arrived. Fr Franco immediately called Joe into the kitchen to make some tea. Neither man was in the mood for the hot drink, but it was as good a thing to do as any while they carried on this discussion on where to bury poor Ruksana who was right now in the morgue. "She wouldn't want her kids to be put at risk simply to get a religious funeral."

The Kashmiri Muslim woman married outside Islam, but she never missed *namaz*—the obligatory five prayers a day—and faithfully kept all the fasts. Everything was done at home, though. In secret. Ruksana might've been ditzy, but even the totally clueless couldn't miss the explosive effect the combination of the words Kashmir and Muslim had in India. More so when she was the widow of a former infantryman. Joe's dad was a piss-poor husband and a useless parent, but he was also a loyal soldier who won a medal for distinguished wartime service. Still, every damned thug with an interest in politics would've acted as though the *havildar*—junior non-commissioned officer—who took bullets for his country committed treason. If the D'Acostas were wealthy and well-connected, they could've warded off the attacks, but not while they were barely keeping their noses above water.

There would also be the religious crazies who took Ruksana's choice of a husband as personal affront. Violence over such interfaith marriages was not unknown in India.

Ruksana constantly worried about her children being targeted by both sides, and they were all taught not to mention their mother's religion to anyone. The army knew the truth, but as far as the general public was concerned, she was Rosanna D'Acosta. She wouldn't want Joe contacting the local mosque to arrange her funeral.

From the wooden stool next to the utensils cupboard, Fr Franco threw a wary glance towards the living room outside where the three younger D'Acostas were huddled together on the sofa, Scher at their feet. The last of the visitors—the couple of women Ruksana knew from the apartment building—left right after Joe walked in. "But Joe, we can't give her Catholic prayers at the cemetery. It's not allowed."

"Is it allowed to bury her with her husband?" Joe asked, teeth clenched.

"I already told you it is," said Fr Franco, patiently. "The point is I can't give her a Catholic *mass* before the funeral, and she wouldn't have wanted one, anyway. We need to bring in someone who can—"

"*Xapai*, please," said Joe, calling the priest "grandfather" in colloquial Konkani. "No matter who we bring in, there's risk involved. What if they notify the mosque? What if some religious loon decides we're the perfect family to be made examples out of? Even if no one does anything violent—" Lowering his voice, Joe continued, "I'm not the kids' legal guardian. Neither are you." Ruksana had only been forty-nine, but after her first stroke, Fr Franco planned to have her do the paperwork giving Joe custody of her children in case of her death or incapacitation. She passed before it could happen. "If it gets to the courts, all three could go to someone from Ruksana's side."

Joe was a half-brother, but he was not a Kashmiri. The Indian government maintained special rules for everything in the Himalayan state as part of the deal made back in the 'forties when it first joined the nation. He didn't know if a non-Kashmiri would be allowed custody without documentation from the deceased Kashmiri parent. Plus, Joe was a student with only a stipend, and the legal system surely considered income in deciding such matters. Who knew what kind of financial situation Ruksana's relatives were in? The woman never kept in touch with them which told Joe all he needed to know about the equation. He'd seen his own mother in a similar situation. Amma never needed to hide her religion, but the bastards in her family refused to show up even after Fr Franco notified them about her impending death.

"I'm trying to tell you there's a way," whispered the priest. "Lazar Noronha somehow found out about Ruksana being Muslim. He's willing to help."

It took Joe a second to remember who the priest was talking about. Lazar Noronha—the owner of a local department store chain—had zeroed in on Joe as the doctor son-in-law he wanted. "No," said Joe, instantly. The price for Noronha's help was too high. Even if Anjali weren't in the picture, Joe was not for sale, dammit. "*How* did he find out?"

Fr Franco ptchaaed. "Could've been anywhere... army records... the kids' birth certificates..." The priest never let Ruksana lie where she could get into legal trouble. "Lazar is not fool enough to think you'll agree to marry his child in return for one small favour. He simply wants to get into your good books. He has a friend who can do a quick, private service for Ruksana. No one's going to say a word because trust me, no one wants to rub Noronha wrong."

"Exactly what I'm worried about. What happens after the funeral when I tell him there's no way I'm going to marry his precious daughter?"

"Nothing will happen because we'll tell him *before*." Fr Franco pleaded, "C'mon, Joe. Let the woman go to God in peace."

Joe snorted. "What kind of God plays games with the dead?"

With a sigh, the priest asked, "How about giving your brothers and sister a measure of comfort? You willing to do so?" When Joe didn't respond right away, Fr Franco added, "Think about it this way. Noronha already knows. If you *don't* accept his offer of help, he'll realise you're never going to agree to the marriage. He'll have no reason to stay mum."

The next few hours were a blur. Fr Franco dealt with Lazar Noronha, and Joe informed everyone in Ruksana's small social circle the service would be limited to immediate family. There would be a gathering sometime after... as soon as he came up with the cash to pay for it. The two unexpected trips between Delhi and Goa dented his bank account in a big way, but there was still the payment on the mortgage to make if they wanted to keep the old teashop from foreclosure. Yeah, there was the pension from Dad's military service, but with his widow's passing, there would be paperwork delay before it started going to his children. The government was not exactly the most agile of beasts.

Close to midnight, Joe slid down the chair in front of the living room computer to lean his head against the backrest. Staring at the bank's webpage wasn't going to add any more cash into his account. Forget paying for the funeral services. What would happen afterwards? The kids couldn't stay home by themselves. Fr Franco said he'd take a few years off active church duties, but how well would a man in his late sixties deal with two teenage boys and a girl? Joe didn't have the cash to hire help. Plus, the kids needed him around now that their mother was gone.

Moving the family to Delhi was next to impossible. A flat close to the AIIMS campus with a minimum of two bedrooms, school, someone to stay home with them when Joe was on night duty... cost of living in Delhi was a lot higher than in Mapusa. Even if Fr Franco moved with them, the money Joe made wouldn't cover all expenses. The other option was to quit his surgery training and stay in Goa as a general practitioner which he couldn't imagine doing. Transplant research was a bloody calling for him. Not to mention Anjali was in Delhi.

"What am I going to do?" he murmured.

At his feet, Scher whined. For all the care the younger D'Acostas lavished on the dog, the second Joe entered the flat, Scher made it clear whom he considered best friend.

With a pat on Scher's head, Joe picked up the phone lying next to the keyboard and eyed the list of the calls he'd missed *en route* to Goa. There were a couple from the moonlighting agent; the idiot simply wouldn't take no for an answer. No Anjali. After the way Joe walked out, he needed to be the one to call, but she'd be asleep now. Grabbing the scratched mouse, he clicked his way to the other page on the browser: Facebook. Anjali's profile was already open. Dragging the keyboard to him, he typed.

> Joe: I'm sorry. We'll figure it out. I promise. Love you.

He'd started missing her five minutes after he left the flat, but what the hell else could he have done? Yank her into the chaos? God, he badly needed to talk to her about things. Simply to hear her voice would be enough, but he was beginning to realise she liked to manage the world around her to her satisfaction. Even the money Rishi loaned for the airfare... the expression on his face when it was returned... somehow, Joe *knew* it was Anjali's doing. If she'd been around during the conversation, they would've probably brought the roof down with the commotion they made—first fighting, then loving. Yeah, yeah, she was only trying to help, but no, he wasn't gonna collect the kids and walk hand-in-hand with her to the Joshi mansion like she demanded. She loved him too much to see why not, but her parents would. By God, the whole world would call Joseph D'Acosta a leech.

A notification popped up on the computer.

> Anjali: I know. Love you, too.

Something loosened within Joe's ribcage. She was awake. He needed to call—

"Bhai," called a tiny voice.

Joe closed the browser and turned in his chair. "Laila? Couldn't sleep?" He'd told her to use his cot in the boys' room instead of sleeping in the same bed she'd shared with her mother, but it clearly hadn't worked.

Standing at the door in a faded sleeveless frock, the eight-year-old girl shrugged. "Too cold."

Cold? Sweat was rolling down Joe's back, sticking his tee to his skin. He stood from the chair and gestured at the sofa with his thumb. "Wanna sit for a while with Scher and me?"

The moment they settled with her tucked against big brother's side, there was a shuffling sound from the bedroom. The boys trudged in. Without saying a word, they, too, crowded the sofa, causing Scher to yelp and slither to the floor.

Five minutes... ten minutes... half an hour... none of them slept. The silence in the flat weighed a ton.

"Will we go back with you, bhai?" Dev eventually asked from one end of the sofa. "To Delhi?"

"Of course," mumbled Romeo. "We can't live on our own."

"But I heard Fr Franco say..." Eyes troubled, Dev continued, "Is he going to stay here with us?"

Cuddling closer, Laila said, "Fr Franco is almost seventy. Ma was forty-nine." With a small sob, she buried her face in Joe's shoulder. Her tears dampened his shirt.

"Shh," he said, stroking her hair. "I'm here. We're all here." Romeo's skinny arms wrapped around Joe's chest. Dev practically draped himself over his siblings. Even Scher placed a paw on Joe's knee. "Everything will be all right," he murmured.

How the hell, though? The last time the world fell apart around him was when his own mother passed. He'd only been ten at the time with a number of adults to help. Dr Ram, Fr Franco... even Joe's dad and stepmom were presences which helped stabilise his life. *Joe* was the one in charge now, and he didn't have a clue how to handle this.

He needed money fast, and the only thing of value he owned was the bloody teashop, but the shed and the land it sat on were mortgaged to the bank. If he could find a buyer for it... but they'd never imagined selling it before the loans were paid off; it wouldn't fetch a decent price. In the last couple of years, Dev had actually been talking about keeping it and converting it to a restaurant. If they could get even half the market value for property of its size, the cash would buy Joe breathing room. He'd be able to complete at least his junior residency and keep his siblings with him in Delhi. He'd be with Anjali. Perhaps he could work a few years as a general surgeon until Dev finished college and found a job. Then, Joe could return to complete his training in transplant surgery.

He threw a glance at Dev. Joseph D'Acosta would be a transplant surgeon and would eventually marry the girl of his dreams, but there would be no D'Acosta restaurant. No, wasn't gonna happen.

He needed to talk to Anjali so damned bad. But if he did, she'd immediately bring up approaching her family for help. If Dr Ram were around, Joe could request a small loan, promising it would be repaid before he put a ring on Anjali's finger.

Joe shifted, causing his sister who was resting against his side to mumble a protest. "Try to sleep," he soothed. "Fr Franco will be back in a couple of hours for the service."

The priest knew Dr Ram's son—Anjali's father. If Fr Franco were to talk to Dr Pratap Joshi, perhaps he'd be willing to loan Joe some money with the teashop as collateral. The Joshis already knew about the existing mortgage. If Joe failed to repay the loan, they'd easily be able to pay off the bank and take the property. Not an arrangement any other private lender would entertain without charging backbreaking interest rates.

Somehow, Joe needed to manage things without bringing up Anjali's name. If he did... no, he couldn't. There was no way he could present himself to the family as her fiancé and ask for a loan. The Joshis would eventually know he'd been romancing their daughter while accepting cash from them, but he could hold his head high and point out he'd repaid every paisa.

After the funeral, he'd talk to Fr Franco. Joe huffed. He needed to talk to *Anjali* before anyone else. She'd heartily approve except for the secrecy part and the inevitable delay it would cause in getting married.

Lazar Noronha, the department store magnate who was angling to get Joe as son-in-law, sprang into action before daybreak, sparing the D'Acostas the job of finding women to ritually clean and dress Ruksana's body in the morgue. It was still dark when the kids left for the cemetery church with Fr Franco. Joe waited outside the morgue's doors, leaning back in the passenger seat of the Noronha department store delivery van, hoping like hell the businessman's driver/flunky wouldn't start a conversation.

An ambulance drove in and parked in the large pool of light thrown by the fluorescent lamps at the doorway. Two uniformed technicians plodded out of the building, one of them yawning loudly. Without much fuss, the ambulance doors were opened, and a body—covered with a green hospital sheet—was unloaded onto a metal stretcher. The sheet slid to the ground, revealing the corpse of a man around Joe's own age. The build was similar... maybe the colouring, too. There was the bloating of decomposition, but no obvious marks to suggest trauma. God only knew how he died... drug overdose... suicide...

"Everything's done," said the impatient voice of Lazar Noronha, startling Joe. The businessman was standing by the window on the driver's side. Average height, pot belly, ample grey in his hair and moustache... he was close to Fr Franco's age. A late marriage to a trophy wife produced only one daughter. Even at this early hour, Noronha was in dress pants and shirt. But then, he was here for a funeral.

The van carrying the casket followed the businessman's Mercedes to the cemetery. In a small prayer room at the back of the chapel, a bearded *imam*— Muslim cleric—led the service. Behind him was Dev, the oldest male related to the deceased by blood. After quick prayers, Joe and Fr Franco helped

Ruksana's sons carry her to her husband's grave. Laila—her little head wrapped in a black scarf—stumbled along next to Joe. Copious tears ran down her cheeks, but the only time the eight-year-old made a sound was when she tossed the three fistfuls of dirt into the grave. Before the town woke to a new day, Ruksana D'Acosta was buried.

Joe waited until the taxi carrying his siblings and Fr Franco disappeared down the street. The first bus of the day was rumbling to a stop a few feet away, thick, black fumes spilling from the exhaust. Standing next to his Mercedes, Lazar Noronha sneezed before making a production of patting his pockets for keys. Joe took a deep breath and approached the businessman. "Thank you," he said, stiffly. "It was very kind of you to help us."

Tone gruff, Noronha said, "No problem. I was happy to." He gestured towards the road down which the taxi went. "How are you getting home?"

"I'll take the bus." He wanted to visit his own mother's resting place before returning to the flat. Amma was cremated per Hindu customs with the open help of the temple priest from the village near Mapusa. Her ashes were scattered around Chapora Fort. She'd once visited Vagator to see the teashop on which hinged her hopes for financial stability for her son. The dilapidated shed didn't tickle her fancy, but she fell in love with the fort at some distance from the property. The greenery around reminded her of the hometown she'd abandoned to marry Joe's father. If there were such a thing as a soul, hers would be happy there.

God, spirits, afterlife... not really things Joe believed in, but if she could somehow hear him, he wanted her blessing for what he planned to do with the teashop. Someday after he paid off the loans, he'd take Anjali there.

"You don't need to wait for the bus," said Noronha. "I have to get to work, but if you don't mind stopping by my house for a few minutes, I'll have my daughter drive you home."

Here it was. No matter what conditions Fr Franco placed on accepting help, Lazar Noronha was going to push his own agenda. "It's not necessary," said Joe, keeping his tone even.

"It is," insisted Noronha. "How else are you going to get to know her?" At Joe's silence, the businessman added, "I'm sure Fr Franco has talked to you about it."

"He has," Joe admitted. How the hell did he do this without pissing off Noronha? Naïve Fr Franco imagined his parishioner would keep his word and stay mum about Ruksana, but Joe harboured no such misplaced faith. If it weren't for the fact Noronha already knew about Ruksana's religion and the growing certainty she'd end up in her grave with no prayers whatsoever to give some peace to her hurting children, Joe wouldn't have agreed to the idiotic plan. Now, he was gonna have to deal with Noronha. "Sir, I'm not in a position to think about anything other than my family right now. I can't—"

"This is precisely the time to think of it," said Noronha, tugging his pants further up his ample belly. "You need me. How are you planning to take care of everything and continue in Delhi?"

"I'll manage," said Joe, doggedly.

"How?" Noronha asked a second time. "I talked to your landlord yesterday. He was planning to let your stepmother know..." Crossing himself, the businessman continued, "The rent is going up. Even if Fr Franco gets time off from active church duties, he can't take care of the little girl. You'll still need to hire a woman. Face facts, boy. You need my help. Just meet my daughter this morning, and we'll discuss the rest in the next couple of days, including the wedding."

Wedding? Suddenly feeling an invisible hand strangling him, Joe coughed. "Thanks for the offer, but I'll figure something out about the situation at home. As for... er... the rest... gimme a month or two. I need time to think. I'm sure your daughter won't want a husband who was pushed into it, doctor or not." Long before the two months ended, Joe and his siblings would be in Delhi. He hoped like hell the Goan businessman's reach did not extend to the nation's capital.

"Huh?" Noronha snorted. "I don't have to push anyone. You think there's a shortage of young doctors willing to marry for money? I chose you for other reasons, not your medical degree." His snort turned into laughter at Joe's confusion. "I've been watching you, boy. You have your grandfather's drive." With a firm nod, Noronha patted Joe on his shoulder. "Yeah, I was in my teens when Old Joe ended up dead. Pity. Not that I'm sympathetic towards criminal activities, mind you. But with the right kind of support, your grandfather could've learned how to get what he wanted while staying out of trouble with the law. He could've reached great heights. Your father was useless most of the time, but the army did give him a medal. You, my boy, have the same energy, or you wouldn't have gotten this far. Smart and ambitious young men are not rare, either. But I want a smart, ambitious fellow who needs *my* help which you certainly do."

"In other words, you want to control this smart and ambitious chap," Joe muttered.

Noronha inclined his head. "It will be a mutually beneficial relationship. Like I said, your grandfather could've benefitted from—"

"I am *not* my grandfather," Joe said, his teeth clenched.

"No, he was shrewder," agreed Noronha. "He would've jumped at this chance. But you can be trained."

"I don't want to be trained," snapped Joe.

"Why not? Ram Joshi did it."

Joe battled himself not to swat the businessman to the floor and squash him like the bug he was. "Dr Ram was my *guru*—my teacher."

"I will be, too," said Noronha.

"What you're offering is a transaction," Joe snarled. "Not teacher-student relationship. I'm not for sale, and neither is my degree."

"Not for sale?" Laughing again, Noronha asked, "Are you trying to tell me you're going to work for free? Or when you do get married, it won't be to the woman with the most to offer? In money... in looks... connections... or something else which will benefit you? Trust me, boy. You *are* for sale. Everyone is. Only the price varies. People like to tell themselves they're above actual cash. I didn't expect it from you. Your grandfather was an honest man."

"My grand—" Incredulously, Joe stared. "He was a criminal. You just said so."

Noronha nodded. "Yeah, but he never lied to himself or anyone else about what he wanted. You, on the other hand, are pretending you're different."

"I *am* different," Joe said, seething. "I am *not* my grandfather. I will never be him."

"If it hadn't been for Ram Joshi and his financial support, you would've turned out exactly like Old Joe," retorted Noronha. "Ask anyone who knew him. Joshi is gone now. When you realise ambition alone won't get you anywhere, you'll name your price and will go to whoever's willing to pay. Might as well admit it now and not waste time."

Everything around Joe blurred for a second before sharpening into a clarity which hurt his every sense. He could see every pore on the businessman's florid face, hear the shift of his large, metallic watch against the cuff of his shirt. His every breath stank of power and the arrogant certainty Joe would eventually be brought to heel. Taking a deep breath, he struggled to remind himself not to antagonise Noronha further. "I'm not my grandfather," Joe said for the third time in the conversation.

Noronha asked, "Who're you trying to convince? Actually, *why* are you bothering to convince anyone? You're lucky people don't pile false expectations on you. You don't need to explain your career choices. Haven't you ever wondered why no one from the parish other than me has ever tried to set you up with a relative—good-looking doctor and all? You have a reputation, boy. Most of them know you mess around with girls. They think you're waiting for the highest bidder. If the girl's family refuses to cough up cash, you're out the door."

Joe took half a step back. Anjali... Dr Ram's granddaughter... he was about to ask the Joshis for money. If they refused... he never thought about the possibility they might. What would happen between him and Anjali? If the Joshis agreed, would they eventually see him as a hustler like his grandfather? Would the rest of the world? Voices clamoured in his brain, demanding to be heard... Anjali, Fr Franco, the kids, Noronha. "I need to go," Joe said, abruptly. "Fr Franco will let you know of my decision."

Without waiting for Noronha's permission, Joe pivoted on his heel and strode away. At the bus station, he eyed the vehicle bound for Vagator. What was he going to say to his mother? That all her efforts at bringing him up as a decent human being were wasted? That all his struggles to make something of himself would never matter to society? That regardless of his desperation, if he took a paisa from Anjali's family, he'd be considered a conman?

"Are you getting in or what?" shouted the driver, poking his head out of the window.

Joe looked up at the impatient fellow. "I changed my mind," he said. "Sorry." He started jogging, shoving his way through the morning crowd.

Down the streets of Mapusa he went... his heart speeding up, keeping time with his treads... blood pulsing through his arteries, thundering in his ears, until his entire body burned from within. The faces along his path blurred, voices and honks and rumbles raised in discord. He bumped into someone—many someones—continuing to sprint without offering apologies. He didn't stop until he got to the Joshi Charity Clinic, staring up at the row of large, arched windows along the upper floor.

What should I do? Joe asked the ghost of his mentor. Accept the label society already slapped on him and beg the Joshis for cash? Forget about being a transplant surgeon and move to Goa, away from Anjali? Or sell the teashop and destroy his little brother's dreams? *Answer me, dammit,* his mind screamed, but except for the incessant buzz within his skull, there was no response.

"Pick up the phone," said an irate voice.

Someone jostled Joe's elbow. Startled, he swung to face the person intruding on his thoughts. A painfully skinny and deeply tanned beggar with scraggly hair stood there, dented aluminium bowl in his hand. The pungent odour in the air around suggested the strong need for an immediate shower. Almost out of habit, Joe's hand went to his pocket to bring out coins.

"Your phone," snapped the beggar. "It's annoying. Pick it up or turn it off. Or go someplace else. This is *my* spot, and I ain't moving."

The recurring buzz in his head... Joe became aware of the shrill ring of the phone in his shirt pocket. He looked at the number and swore hard. The moonlighting agent. Picking up, he barked, "Listen, you damned—"

"Having trouble with the girlfriend, eh?" the amused voice of the agent asked over the phone.

"*What?*"

"*Koi baat nahin,*" said the agent, telling Joe it didn't matter. "There's a solution to everything. In your case, it's money—something I've been offering you."

"How do you—" Joe took in an angry breath and moved a few feet away from the curious beggar. Pedestrians streamed around him; cars and buses continued to rumble down the road. "What's your problem, dude? I told you a thousand times I don't want your bloody job."

"Not even if it gets you Anjali?"

"What the hell do you mean?" asked Joe.

The agent clucked. "You like the pretty girl, but you don't want her family to know because you don't have any money. She's angry with you because of it. Also, you probably need cash now for your stepmother's funeral. Do I have it right?"

So the agent somehow knew what was going on in Delhi but not the fact Ruksana's funeral was already done. "Are you having me followed?"

"I keep an eye out for opportunities," said the agent. "What I don't understand is why you're not taking my offer. Seven thousand euros would go a long way, Doctor. Plus, you'll get to meet a number of the movers and shakers in your field."

Seven thousand euros would let the D'Acosta family move immediately to Delhi. So would winning the lottery. With an angry growl, Joe said, "Call me again, and I'll break your neck, you—go find someone dumb enough to believe this crap."

"C'mon, Doctor. What do you have to lose? How are you going to take care of your family without money? You'll have to quit your training and—"

Joe hung up. "Seven thousand euros," he muttered, desperate tears sprouting in his eyes. If only... raising his arm, he used his shirt sleeve to wipe the moisture off his cheeks. The phone rang, again. "*Saala*," he swore, calling the persistent agent a foul name. Not bothering to look at the number, he answered the call with a stream of filthy curses.

"Bhai?" came the uncertain voice of Romeo, tone lowered to a high-pitched whisper.

"—shit," finished Joe. Gritting his teeth, he said, "Sorry, didn't realise—everything all right? Why are you whispering?"

"Can you get home fast?" asked Romeo. "The landlord's here, talking to Fr Franco and Dev. Something about the rent."

As Joe opened the door to the flat ten minutes later, the first thing he heard was Fr Franco's promise. "You will have the money," said the priest. "Give me a day or two." Dev—his face thunderous—was next to Fr Franco. The younger two were nowhere to be seen. Hiding in the bedroom, most likely.

"You're a man of God," said the landlord, his thin back to the flat's front door. "So I'd like to believe you. But how are you going to come up with the money? You don't have any income."

"What the hell?" Joe asked, incredulously. "Do you realise we just returned from the cemetery?"

The landlord swung around. "Doctor! Good. You're here. I'm sorry about your loss, but this can't wait. We got into a bit of trouble with the government about the water supply. They've given us only a short time to fix it. Frankly, I don't have the money. I'm raising the rent and asking all the residents to pay a little early this time."

"How's all this the residents' problem, sir?" Joe asked, his teeth clenched. "Why do we need to pay early?"

Frowning, the landlord said, "Maybe if one of you idiots in the building hadn't reported me, we wouldn't have gotten into trouble. If I don't fix it, the government will ask all of you to get out. So yeah, it *is* the residents' problem. Pay up or vacate the flat at the end of the month."

"This is illegal," objected Dev.

"Be grateful I'm only raising the rent," retorted the landlord. "I mean, I know you just suffered a loss. I can show some leniency. With the rest of the residents, I'm asking for three months' rent right now."

350

"Three—" Dev goggled.

"You—" started Joe.

Fr Franco folded his hands. "Thank you. It's considerate of you." Raising a firm eyebrow at his great-nephews, he asked, "Right, boys?"

Counting to five, Joe unclenched his fists. "Very considerate," he ground out.

The landlord nodded. "So when can I expect my cash?"

"In a couple of days," said Fr Franco.

"I'd like to hear it from the doctor," the landlord insisted.

"What Fr Franco says goes for me as well," snapped Joe. "There's no need to insult him."

Shrugging, the landlord said, "I would take *his* word any day. But he doesn't have any money, and I don't have his faith in his family. Don't forget I knew your father. I can't trust you not to go back to Delhi and simply forget the three children here."

"Forget the—" hissed Joe. "Sonuva—"

"Enough," shouted the priest. He glanced meaningfully at Dev. The hot, angry eyes of the sixteen-year-old were fixed unblinkingly on the landlord.

As though Dev weren't thinking the exact same thing as his older brother. As though they weren't both battling the same overwhelming need to thrash the landlord until he begged for mercy. "I'm not my father," Joe finally said, voice hoarse. "You *will* have your money in a couple of days."

As soon as the door shut behind the fellow, Fr Franco turned to Joe. "I can sell my scooter."

Raising a hand in acknowledgement, Joe said to Dev, "I'm not Dad. I won't ever abandon any of you."

"I know, bhai," said Dev, some of the tension leaving his shoulders.

Nodding, Joe strode towards the room which belonged to his stepmother and eyed the furniture. The twin beds side-by-side, a small desk, the steel cupboard... he marched to the cupboard and tugged the door open.

"What are you doing?" asked Fr Franco, Dev following at his heels.

"Dad's medal," muttered Joe, shoving piles of colourful clothes to one corner.

"The medal?" asked the priest. "You're going to *sell* it?"

There... a built-in locker at the back of the cupboard with the little door ajar. Thanks to Ruksana's carelessness, Joe didn't need to spend hours looking for the key. "You can't do without your scooter. How will you get around? The medal it will have to be." Pausing, Joe threw a glance at his brother.

"Dad's gone," Dev said, immediately. "*We're* still here, and we need to survive."

"But—" With a rueful huff, Fr Franco said, "I realise he wasn't a good parent to any of you, but his military service was pretty much the only thing he was successful at."

Dad was so bloody proud of the medal. The two perfectly decent women he'd somehow convinced to take a chance on him were equally proud of the thing. Now, his oldest son was going to trade the one shining moment of his life for cash.

"Either this or live on the street." Joe's fingers shook when he reached for the silver disc. With a muttered curse, he grabbed the medal and stuffed into his pocket. The pawnshop would pay more than the value of the metal for a genuine service decoration. "It should keep us until the pension gets sorted out."

"And then?" asked Fr Franco.

Joe didn't answer. How could he when he didn't know what to say? He still had no idea when he was walking back from the illegal pawnshop in Mapusa market with Dev. The damned shop owner had taken one look at the D'Acosta boys and smelled their desperation. The money they got wasn't anywhere near what Joe hoped for.

Darkness invaded Joe's mind, shrouding the sights and sounds of the crowded street. Dev was reduced to a shadowy figure, walking next to Joe. Monsters loomed, threatening to destroy his family... the landlord, Noronha, the world around them.

"You're no better than your grandfather," said Noronha.

Joe shook his head. "I'm not him."

"I knew your father," said the landlord, smirking. "You're the same."

"I'm not," shouted Joe.

"Bhai?" asked Dev.

Joe started. "Uhh... nothing. Just thinking about stuff." They were at the door of the apartment building. His foot was on the bottom step of the stoop when his phone rang yet another time. Glancing at the number, he groaned. "Give up, man," he said to the caller, tiredly. "I've had my share of vultures today."

"I'm not a vulture," objected the agent.

"Yeah, you are." Waving Dev into the building, Joe continued, "You're trying to take advantage of the situation. Like I told you before... I might be desperate, but I'm not dumb enough to buy what you're selling."

"You'll get your money," swore the agent. His voice brightening, he added, "What if we advanced you half of it?"

"Heh?"

"My man will meet you in front of your bank with a draft for three thousand five hundred. Tomorrow."

"Three thous—*euros?*" Joe asked, nearly stumbling before steadying himself on the door jamb, his hand slippery with sweat. The thin cat which had made the stoop its hangout yelped and scampered away. There were a few pedestrians on the street, but none close enough to overhear. "Tomorrow?"

"You heard the offer," said the agent.

"What would I have to do?" asked Joe, feeling disoriented. If this turned out to be a genuine offer... he couldn't miss the chance.

"A surgery. And don't worry about not getting time from college. One weekend. You'll be back home before the mourning period is done."

"What kind of surgery?"

"Nothing too complicated for a man of your talents. It's a lifesaving procedure which hasn't been approved."

"But what—" A lifesaving procedure... not approved... something worth a mindboggling fee to a mere junior resident... something not too complicated for Dr Joseph D'Acosta, future transplant surgeon. The offer of cash was real. Slamming a mental door on further thought, Joe said, "Meet me at the bank tomorrow morning and bring a draft for five thousand euros."

"*Five* thousand?" asked the agent.

"For now," said Joe. "Five after the surgery. It will be a one-time deal. After it's done, there will be no more calls."

***

"Someone I know promised me a loan," Joe said to Fr Franco. The priest and the kids were gathered at the bedroom door as Joe stuffed an old book bag with a change of clothes. "I have to do a small job for him, so it may be a couple of days before I return. I'll put a cheque in the mail as soon as I get the money." The agent had been firm Joe wouldn't have time to return to the flat with the cash.

"What kind of job?" asked Fr Franco, tone troubled.

With a reassuring smile, Joe said, "A weekend gig at his private clinic."

"Won't you get into trouble with AIIMS?" asked the priest.

Joe clucked, noncommittally. "It's not a big deal. I'll explain what was going on here. At the most, I'll get reprimanded." Unwelcome thoughts jostled each other at the periphery of his mind. Fear and guilt clamoured to be heard. *No,* he snapped. The time for thinking was over. There was no room left in his psyche for doubt, not when the survival of his family was at stake.

Fifteen minutes later when he stepped into the bank, an employee approached. "This way, Doctor."

Startled, Joe stared at the pleated pants and buttoned-up shirt and metal frame glasses. He hadn't been expecting an accountant type. Without much fuss, five thousand euros were deposited into Joe's account via a draft from a supposed uncle who'd migrated to Portugal decades ago. As the accountant fellow explained in a low tone, foreign remittances by family members were neither questioned nor taxed by the government of India. Within another five minutes, a cheque for the rupee equivalent of a thousand euros was in the mail, addressed to Fr Franco.

When Joe turned from the mailbox in front of the bank, the accountant held out another envelope. "The flight's in a couple of hours."

Pulling out the ticket, Joe glanced at the destination. "Kochi?" he asked, suddenly feeling numb. The seaside city was in Kerala, his mother's home state.

Somehow, he imagined the smell of coconut oil in his lungs—the scent Amma always carried about her. Her face haunted his thoughts on the cab ride to the airport and during the ninety-minute flight. Her long, dark hair was always worn in a thick braid. The large, black eyes used to widen in hero-worship when she went to the movie theatre with him to watch Thalaiva in action. She sulked like a child the day she heard her ten-year-old son carry on a conversation with his mentor in a language she barely understood. Joe caught her going through his old textbooks, trying to teach herself English. She might've succeeded, too. Amma was always a determined woman. Except, the cancer attacked.

Dr Ram swore to Amma he'd be there for her little boy. So did Fr Franco. She still told Joe she wouldn't be able to die in peace until *he* promised he'd grow up to be a son she'd be proud of. It was her dream he'd join the army like his father, but she knew his heart was set on being a doctor. She advised him not to chase money and never to trust rich people, pointedly ignoring Dr Ram and his wife's presence in the hospital room.

Joe was sitting by her sickbed one of the nights when she started humming a lullaby in her native tongue. He thought she was delirious until she said it was something *her* mother—Joe's grandmother—used to sing. Silent tears ran down Amma's cheeks. The next day, he begged Fr Franco to call her family and learned the priest did so as soon as the cancer was diagnosed. The bastards stated she was already dead to them. Nor did they want anything to do with her half-breed son.

Joe never imagined he'd be visiting the place one day. He exited the Arrivals terminal in Kochi and glanced at the crowds, vaguely disappointed not to feel the pull of familiarity. He snorted. What in God's name did he expect? Some sort of umbilical cord connection?

"Doctor Joseph?" someone called. When Joe whirled around, there was a skinny man with a deep tan and a thick moustache, jangling car keys. "This way," said the man, gesturing towards the parking lot.

Sweat rolled down the back of Joe's neck as he peered from the backseat of his cab at the thick groves lining the tarred roads. Amma used to say every wall, every small rock, in Kerala was draped in velvety moss, and it was no hyperbole. The green was so impossibly bright under the evening sun, it almost hurt the eyes.

When they made it to the city proper, the driver ignored the cacophony of horns and rumbles and loud chatter, weaving in and out of traffic. Joe glimpsed water, but the driver swerved right and went into an equally crowded side road. Tyres screeching, the taxi jerked to a stop in front of a red and yellow building. "High Court of Kerala," said the sign. Startled, Joe glanced at the driver.

"Our office is near here," said the driver.

Joe swallowed hard as he saw the small whitewashed church next to the one-storey building which served as the office. Fr Franco took time off to deal with the crisis in the family, but the old priest was a genuine believer, and he'd sorely miss celebrating the daily mass with his parishioners. Not knowing what the boy he thought of as his grandson was up to, Fr Franco would be praying Joe returned successful from his weekend gig. The blood on Joe's hands would spatter onto the pristine white robes of the priest.

Inside the tiny office with the single window looking out into the churchyard, Joe came face-to-face with the agent—the owner of the Pomeranian from the flat next door in Delhi. The man had claimed to be a lecturer in one of the local colleges. With his side-parted dark hair and neat beard, he looked the role.

Noting Joe's silent shock, the man guffawed. "Didn't you wonder how I knew so much about you?" The coarseness in his tone was gone, but it *was* the same voice which talked to Joe several times over the phone. Somehow, he never recognised it. "If you could hear my dog, don't you think *I* could hear every word of what you said?"

A second man walked in, followed by a third fellow. "He knows more about your girlfriend's preferences in bed than his own wife's."

"You—" Joe growled. The dog owner/moonlighting agent always seemed a reticent fellow, declining to meet any of Rishi and Joe's friends, but the bastard had listened every time Joe and Anjali...

The agent frowned and held up a hand. "There's no need to be crass," he said to his colleague. "We're done with all the playacting." The agent nodded at the last man to walk into the room and spoke in Hindi. "Mustafa, this is the doctor. He will need to examine you."

There was no further explanation given on what Joe was expected to do. The gang clearly assumed he was intelligent enough—and criminal enough— to have guessed. He eyed the donor—a fellow with a weather-beaten face. In his thirties, perhaps. Joe took the chart handed to him and glanced back up in surprise. Twenty-four? Same age as him? A quick physical examination later, Joe took his seat behind the desk and studied the chart—blood type, immunology report, urine tests, scans of the donor's organs. "I need to see the reports from the recipient... crossmatching and tissue typing."

"Why?" asked the agent. "You have nothing to do with the actual transplant. Your only job will be to safely extract the donor kidney."

Joe nodded partly in relief. He'd assisted in enough transplant surgeries to believe he could do it, but leading a procedure was way different. Removing a kidney was much, much easier. It was illegal all over the world except Iran to sell kidneys, but not a difficult surgery to perform for someone like Joe. "I still need to know the kidney is a match," he stated. "Or the risk of rejection will be high."

"You think our transplant surgeons aren't aware of this?" asked the agent, dryly. "Trust me. They've gone over every detail. They simply don't want to be involved in the harvesting... plausible deniability."

"What do you mean?" asked Joe.

Tone impatient, the agent explained, "It means they don't want to take any legal risks. If the cops get involved, the only doctor going down will be you. The other surgeons will claim they didn't know where you were getting the organs from." At Joe's sudden stillness, the agent added, "C'mon. You're earning enough money to make it worthwhile. Plus, the girlfriend. I thought you wanted to walk into her parents' home with your balls intact. Oh, I did tell you we could introduce you to the surgeons. These connections will be important for you in your career. Consider it a bonus."

Joe stared unblinkingly at the agent, not vocalising his thought the surgeons who'd cooperate with any part of this criminal operation were not worth trusting, including Joe D'Acosta. "I take pride in my work," he said. "And I don't work without complete access to records."

Ten minutes later, Joe was glancing in surprise between the papers in front of him and the donor sitting silently on the exam table to the left. A manual labourer from Bengal was a near-perfect match for the fifty-year-old wife of a wealthy Arab?

"Satisfied?" asked the agent. "Now, get some sleep or something. We have a few hours before ten. Then, we'll go to the ship." At Joe's puzzled look, the agent clucked. "We have a vessel anchored at twenty-five nautical miles from the coast which means we'll be outside India's control. The surgery is going to be done in the sickbay, but we can't use the boat jetty to go there until after the last service at tennish."

Ships, the boat jetty, plans to evade the coastguard, Arab patients, transplant surgeons... this was no small operation. The phone rang, startling Joe. He glanced at the number—Anjali. Powering off the device, he tucked it back into his pocket.

"We'll be outside, making some calls," said the agent, walking out with his colleague.

On the exam table to the left, the donor stretched out, preparing to nap as instructed. Joe sank deeper into the chair and tried to relax, but Anjali's face kept crowding his mind. It was the third day since he left Delhi. She'd know the funeral would be over. She'd want to hear what else was going on. She'd be worrying herself sick over why he didn't answer her call, but Anjali was too smart, loved him too much not to pick up on his tension.

I'm doing this for us, sundari, Joe murmured in his mind.

For us? taunted the image of her in his heart. *Is that why you don't dare take my call?*

There's no other way, he insisted. Time and again, she said she'd proudly present him to her parents as her fiancé, refusing to acknowledge his lowly status in society. She simply didn't get it. *I won't ever give you up, but I can't sacrifice my brother's dreams for mine, either.*

You could ask my parents for help, she reminded him.

No, he snapped. *It's impossible. What will they think of—*

Stop it, she screamed. *Don't make it about them. If you wanted to, you could explain things to my father and mother. They've heard enough about you from my grandfather to give you the benefit of the doubt. I could talk to them for you. You could ask Fr Franco to call my father. You're choosing not to because you're afraid of what the rest of the world might say.*

I'm not gonna have anyone think I'm with you for money, he argued. He wasn't his grandfather, willing to do anything for cash. Nor was Joe his father, irresponsible with his family. *I'm the one who's going to be the object of ridicule. This is important to me, Anju. Why won't you understand?*

Tone full of hurt, she asked, *More important than me? More important than everything you've learned from the people around you? From your mother, from Fr Franco, from my grandfather? More important than the oath you took as a doctor?*

"Primum non nocere," Joe murmured. Above all, do no harm.

"Doctor?" called an uncertain voice.

"Hmm?" Joe turned to the patient. The man was now sitting up on the exam table. "I was just—" What language did Joe use with the chap? He didn't know any Bengali, and he doubted the manual labourer spoke English or Portuguese or Konkani. The agent had introduced them in Hindi. "I was only thinking of something someone told me... er..." Mustafa. The donor's name was Mustafa.

The man squinted as though computing the words. "Ahh... I understand... maybe."

"Sorry," Joe continued in Hindi. "I don't speak any Bengali."

Mustafa chuckled, the worn look on his face dissipating for the moment. "Me... Bengali, little bit Hindi, Malayalam."

"Malayalam?" Joe sat up. It was the local language. Joe spent the first ten years of his life conversing with his mother in her native tongue. *"Athengane?"* he asked, wanting to know how a man from the other side of the subcontinent picked up the language. Joe explained to the surprised donor his mother had been Malayali.

Apparently, Mustafa joined a wave of labourers migrating to the west coast in search of jobs. Some went to Mumbai and Goa, and some reached Kochi. Mustafa found love in a fellow labourer and married her. Life went swimmingly until a year or so ago when their firstborn got sick. Mr and Mrs Mustafa were told their child's acute myeloid leukaemia could be cured, but chemotherapy cost money they didn't have. One of the other migrant labourers told Mustafa about an organisation recruiting able-bodied men for kidney donation. While the moonlighting fellow was apparently in charge of finding surgeons, the second criminal Joe met in the office was the donor recruiter for a couple of cities in southern India, including Kochi. Mustafa smugly reported having struck a hard bargain—one thousand euros.

Joe blinked. Only a thousand euros for a kidney which was a near-perfect match for the wife of an oil sheikh? The woman would live a long time on the borrowed organ while Mustafa's child... it wasn't nearly enough to cover the treatment.

Finishing the story, Mustafa peered warily through the door as though watching for the agent and his colleague.

"Do they understand the language?" Joe asked, making sure there was no one outside the window, either. The sky was fast turning the orange of dusk, throwing the room into gloom. There was surely a light switch somewhere, but he didn't feel like getting up to search for it.

"I don't think so," said Mustafa, shaking his head.

"Listen," Joe said, leaning forwards. If he told Mustafa he was making a mistake... the agent was not working for some small-timer... Joe would pay for his slip of the tongue. "I'll... uhh... send you some cash when I get back to Goa."

Mustafa's broad smile was visible even in the deepening darkness. "Thank you, Doctor. You realise I might not be able to pay you back?"

"Doesn't matter," Joe said. The plaintive cry of *adhaan*—the Islamic call to prayer—sounded from a distance, startling him.

"Time to thank God for blessings," said Mustafa, leaping off the exam table. He turned on the power switch, flooding the room with dull yellow light. Joe watched in silence as the man went through his prayers. When it was over, Mustafa returned to the exam table. "There's a church next door. You're Christian, right?"

Responding with a shrug, Joe asked, "How do you manage to pray at a time like this? Don't you feel... I don't know... angry?"

"Angry with *God?*" Mustafa asked, his eyes rounding with near-comical horror. "Don't say that!"

"Why not?" Joe argued. "You're talking about *thanking* God. For what? Putting you in this position?"

"For giving me a way to earn my living, for my lovely wife, our child, and allowing me to save her life." Mustafa grinned. "Plus, He sent me someone like you. You offered to give *me* money. How many doctors do that?"

Yeah, the Almighty sent Joe D'Acosta to someone like Mustafa. In all the frantic desperation of the days after Ruksana's death, it never occurred to Joe to sacrifice his ego for his family, let alone his physical self. Here was Mustafa, literally putting himself under the blade. Joe couldn't even bring himself to tell the poor labourer his kidney was probably worth fifty times as much. Gritting his teeth in abject misery, Joe asked, "What if I make a mistake? Aren't you worried?"

"The agent said you're from a big institute. I trust you."

The pressure around his chest was so damned intense, Joe couldn't answer. He glanced through the window at the church next door where the cross on the roof gleamed under the silver light of the nearly full moon. *If You exist, You bloody well better not let me make a mistake. Not for my sake. For his.* "I'm gonna take a nap," he said, hoarsely. "I want to be fresh for the procedure."

When he closed his eyes, there was Anjali, asking him what in the world he was doing. His mother, Fr Franco, even Ruksana... the only one who didn't make an appearance was Dr Ram. If Joe opened his eyes, there would be Mustafa's trusting face. Fidgeting in the chair, walking to the window to stare at the church, venturing to the front door where the agent and his colleague stood... Joe refused the roti and fried beef offered for dinner, gulping down ice-cold water, instead. He counted minutes until it was ten, but it was after eleven by the time they left the office.

Traffic had quietened when they stepped out. There weren't any streetlamps to speak of, but the moon lit their path as they walked to the boat jetty less than five minutes away. "Marine Drive," said the agent, gesturing at the two-lane road. The buildings on one side were shrouded in darkness, and there were no bobbing pinpricks on the waters lapping softly on the other side to suggest boats. A few pedestrians—mostly men—were walking up and down. With a metallic clang, the chap minding the food stall at the entrance of the jetty brought down the shutters, but the smell of spice and grease still clung to the air. "The water you see is actually the canal, and we won't reach the sea until we're past the islands," continued the agent. "Then, we have to go twenty-five nautical miles to the ship. We'll make it there in under an hour."

With each step Joe took down the shadowed ramp towards the deserted jetty, his calves got heavier and heavier. The mild breeze billowing his shirt should've brought comfort, but the stench of motor oil made the air thick the closer they got to the end of the narrow ramp. Once they were in the boat, there would be no turning back for Joe or Mustafa.

"Hurry up," said the agent, striding in front. His colleague brought up the rear, sandwiching Joe and Mustafa in between. The railings on two sides didn't leave room for more than single file walking. "We don't have all night."

What would happen to Mustafa after the procedure? Would they let him recover in the ship? Joe hoped like hell there would be no complications during surgery, but what about after? What if there was an infection? Joe wouldn't be around to make sure the patient received proper care. He'd be on his way back to Goa with the rest of his fee.

"Did they give you the whole amount?" he asked Mustafa, speaking in Malayalam. If they hadn't... there was no trusting these criminals.

"Yes," Mustafa mumbled from behind.

"Hey," snapped the agent's colleague. "What's going on? Speak in Hindi, you—"

The agent raised a hand. "Shut the hell up and get in." One agile leap, and he was inside the boat.

Fingers clutching the wooden post at the end of the ramp, Joe paused for a second. The light cast by the single bulb hanging from the roof of the ramp was weak at best, but it showed a motorised skiff with a seating capacity of four. The silvery glow of the moon reflected off the red and white colours of the craft. Written on one side in royal blue letters was the name: *Sundari*— beautiful woman.

Joe wheeled around and pushed Mustafa aside before shoving the agent's colleague to the ground. "Run, Mustafa," Joe shouted.

The man on the ground bellowed for help and kicked hard, getting Joe in the shin. He fell on his knees.

"What—Doctor?" asked Mustafa, fumbling around.

"Run," Joe ordered in Malayalam, struggling to keep the enemy from scrambling back up. "These people are cheating you," he gasped out as he grappled with the criminal. "Your kidney is worth at least fifty grand." Straining against the hold on his hair, he twisted his head towards the boat. The agent was clambering out. "Run!" shouted Joe. "You said you trust me."

Mustafa turned and ran.

The agent was back on the ramp now. Joe brought his knee up, slamming it on the groin of the criminal on the ground. The man grunted in pain. The painful hold on Joe's hair slackened. Joe crawled over the criminal and swiped at the agent's leg as soon as it was near. All it got him was a hard wallop to his shoulder.

Time... Joe wasn't gonna win the fight, but he didn't need to. He only needed to buy enough time for Mustafa to escape. Summoning every ounce of strength in him, Joe threw his arms around the agent's leg. There was a thud, a stream of colourful curses.

A blow landed on Joe's cheek, snapping his neck back. The light from the bulb dimmed, then brightened. He glanced down the ramp and snarled in satisfaction. The access to the jetty was empty except for the three of them. If Mustafa's God were with him, there would be a bus or autorickshaw waiting to carry him to safety. Joe had done his part.

More blows... more kicks... he rolled, twisted, did everything he could to keep his hands out of harm's way. There were fingers gripping his collar, jerking his head up. He shoved his elbow back, hitting bone. There was a roar of anger before Joe's head was slammed into the iron railing. Pain, terrifying pain... a steely warmth in mouth... the world around greying, whirling.

"Stop," the agent ordered. His voice sounded so far away. "We need him alive."

"What the hell for?" asked the other criminal, continuing to pound Joe. "Do you realise how much he cost us?"

"Yeah, and if we don't get him to admit what he did openly, the bosses are going to blame *us*. The sheikh is not going to be happy about this development. Plus, we still need a surgeon."

Joe was dragged by his wrists, his shoulders stretched to the point of popping out of their sockets. When he was tossed into the skiff, he must've fainted for some time, because the next thing he was aware of was lukewarm water spraying into his face. The motor was rumbling, and there was a light on in the skiff.

Legs clad in faded jeans appeared in Joe's field of vision. Every muscle in his arms burned in pain, but he managed to slide his hands under his hips, keeping them out of danger. A punishing kick landed on his ribs, sending sharp pain shooting up to his neck. He curled into himself and retched. Blood gushed out.

The criminal colleague of the agent crouched next to Joe's head. "Listen well, you little—you're going to tell the bosses what you did, and once we hunt down the other bastard, you're going to do the surgery. What's more, you're gonna do it for free."

Barely able to even shake his head, Joe mumbled, "No."

"*What did you say?*" Fingers gripped Joe's throat. Everything went dark. There was distant shouting, arguing. "You will do it," screamed the criminal.

Blearily opening his eyes, Joe laughed in the criminal's face. "No, I will not." Once again, he was dragged by his arms. "What—" Before he could complete the sentence, his head was slammed into the frothing sea. Water rushed up his nostrils, choking him, stinging his eyes. "Stop," he gasped, but there was more water in his mouth, draining into his lungs until they weighed a ton. He twisted his head this way and that way, trying to get air, but the hand holding him down wouldn't let him. Arms and legs flailing, he struggled to break the hold, but there was no escape.

The world blinked out. This time, there were no sounds to tell him he was still in the boat. The pain—the beautiful, life-affirming agony—was gone.

"Kinda nice if you think about it," said a voice sounding strangely like that of John Lennon, the Beatles singer. "Yesterday..." the voice hummed.

Joe pivoted on his heel, only then realising he was standing. He was in a large room, the walls whitewashed but empty of adornment. There was a round table with chairs set around it, one of them occupied by an insolent-looking chap with a cigarette dangling between his teeth. He was dressed in deep blue bellbottom pants and a tight-fitting shirt. "Who are you?" Joe barked.

The insolent fellow stopped humming and spat out the cigarette, not seeming to care about the fire hazard. "You don't recognise me?"

The same build, the same features, the same cleft in the chin Joe saw in the mirror. "Are you... er... my soul?" Was he dead? Why was his inner self dressed like a leftover hippie?

Laughing heartily, the insolent chap asked, "When did you start believing in the magical crap? Franco and his—I told him once not to teach my son such nonsense. Should've included grandsons, too."

Joe goggled. "Grandpa Joe?"

Shoving the chair back, Grandpa Joe stood. "Finally, some sign of intelligence! Of course, I'm your grandfather. Who else would be here to welcome you into the afterlife? We share the same blood. We *are* the same."

"No." Shaking his head, Joe said, "We might share the same blood, but we're *not* the same. You're a criminal. I'm nothing like you."

"Oh, yeah?" asked Grandpa Joe, devilment in his eyes. "They say you're smart. Where do you think you get it from? Plus, you were so intent on proving to the Joshis you were not a criminal like me, you decided to do a bit of organ smuggling. Do you not see the absurdity of it?"

"I... uh..."

"You should've let things be, son," said a second voice, sounding only vaguely interested.

When Joe whirled, there was a young man dressed in military formals. "Dad?" Joe asked. "You look..." It was strange to have both his grandfather and father appear the same age as him.

"Yup," said the soldier. "This was how I looked the day I met your mother." His eyebrows crinkled in sudden confusion. "Or was it when I met Ruksana?"

Irritated, Joe started, "You will never change—" A sharp pain shot across his chest. Water came gurgling through his lips. He staggered to the table and supported himself with a hand on the backrest of a chair. "What's going on?" he asked, groaning.

"They're trying to bring you back," explained Dad. "Happened to me, too. The hospital did CPR, you know. I decided not to return. I mean, all the worries and responsibilities... I was feeling beat." He looked around. "This is nice."

"Responsibility?" Joe asked, trying to breathe through the pain. "Like towards the children you left behind? When did you ever show any?"

"So?" Dad shrugged. "It's not like *you* showed any."

"No," insisted Joe. "I'm your son, but I've never been irresponsible."

Dad chuckled vaguely. "This is getting tedious, but I was told I *must* talk to you. Lemme leave you with this... I was a terrible parent, but my duty as a soldier was something I took very, very seriously. I thought we had at least as much in common. Unfortunately, you proved me wrong. What do you think will happen to your brothers and sister with you gone? Who's the irresponsible one now?"

"Leave my baby alone," demanded a female voice. Draped in a cream and gold sari, Amma came scurrying to the table, followed closely by Ruksana in her Kashmiri costume. The two women glared at the man they'd been married to, sending Grandpa Joe into belly laughter.

"Gimme a break," muttered Joe, gasping as another spasm of pain rippled across his chest wall. Was this his version of hell? To be trapped for all eternity amidst this family farce?

"You're not trapped," said the deep tones of Dr Ram Joshi. Perhaps for reasons of maintaining sanity, he was in a lounge chair at some distance from the D'Acosta table. Thank God, *he* looked his age and was dressed in pyjamas exactly the way he'd been his last day on earth.

"What took you so long?" complained Joe. "I would've thought Amma and you would be the first to welcome me to this place."

"Say what?" Dr Ram joined in the laughter of the rest of the room. "You think we're real?"

"Aren't you?" countered Joe, refusing to feel foolish. He was dead... dying... something. Who knew what happened afterwards?

"We're whatever you imagine us to be," stated Dr Ram, no trace of laughter left on his face. "The ghosts from your past who haunt you still... your conscience... spirits sent to torment you... whatever. I wasn't here before because of your behaviour with Anju. Because of your breach of the trust placed in you by your patients. You did not remember what I taught you: above all, do no harm. The guilt in your heart prevented me from coming to you."

"I made a mistake," Joe said, miserably. "I tried to fix it." He hoped like hell Mustafa managed to get away. "As for Anju... I fell in love with her. Not because she's your granddaughter... I just love her, okay? I didn't mean to hurt her, but I did. If I get a second chance..."

"Sometimes, there are no second chances," intoned Grandpa Joe. "I didn't get one. I died in a fishing boat. So will you."

"Second chances are meant for those who regret things," said Amma, somehow speaking fluent English. "When did you ever regret anything, Grandpa Joe? Neither did my husband, but he was merely irresponsible. He never deliberately hurt people for his own benefit. JoJo is nothing like either of you. He made a couple of foolish mistakes he badly wants to set right. He is *my* son. Fr Franco is his grandfather."

"And *I* am his teacher," stated Dr Ram. "JoJo, it's now up to you to decide what you want to be, where you belong."

Joe snorted. "What's the point of deciding now? I'm dying." Or already dead. "In any case, I'm my own man. I can't blame my family for my mistakes. I'm grateful for the help I got, but *I* worked damned hard for my successes, too. I belong to all of you, and I belong to none of you. I'm Joseph D'Acosta. *Doctor* Joseph D'Acosta. 'I am that I am.'"

"Popeye, the Sailor Man," crooned Ruksana, speaking for the first time. She used to love watching cartoons with her kids, especially the one with the eponymous theme song she just sang.

"What JoJo said is from the Bible, not the show," corrected Dr Ram. After an exasperated glance at her, the old doctor turned back to Joe. "If you're comfortable enough with yourself to accept credit *and* culpability for your deeds, why are you so bothered by the labels society tries to stick on you? The criminal's grandson... the loser's child... the rich man's project?"

"Because I..." Joe D'Acosta always knew who he was. His identity was a problem only for the world beyond him and those he cared about. Wanting the same world to admit its mistake and acknowledge him as a brilliant doctor... a successful man... a worthy boyfriend... cost Joe his life. "I don't have to be bothered," he allowed. Yeah, he was obligated to pay his dues to society just like everybody else, but he didn't have to contort himself to fit into the slot the people around picked for him. Nor did he have to prove he didn't belong there. If he hadn't set out to do so, he would've still been alive.

A fist slammed into his belly, sending every last drop of fluid regurgitating to his mouth. A disgusting mixture of blood and seawater seeped through his teeth. Every cell in his body was on fire.

"What's happening?" he tried to ask, but the occupants of the room were reduced to mere shadows. Whitewashed walls morphed rapidly into moonlit sky. Below him, the boat's floor vibrated from the motor. He was wet—soaked through—and there was the stench of evacuated body waste about him.

"He's back," snapped the agent. "No thanks to you."

"Arrogant sonuvabitch needed to learn to obey orders." The agent's colleague kicked out casually with a foot, sending pain radiating down Joe's hip. "You're gonna do the surgery now, aren't you?"

The muscles in his face screaming in agony with each word, Joe mumbled, "No, I will not."

He saw the boot coming down towards his right hand and closed his eyes, prepared to hear the crunch of his bones as they were smashed beyond repair.

There was a thud, followed by an angry shout. "What the—he can't operate without his hand," said the agent.

When Joe opened his eyes, the criminal was scrambling up from the other side of the skiff where he was shoved, and the agent was towering over his colleague and the captive doctor. "I will not do your surgery," Joe gasped out, somehow raising himself on his elbows.

"You won't be doing *any* surgery," snarled the criminal. "We'll chop *you* into pieces and sell you around the world."

"Primum non nocere," Joe said, voice weak and thready. "Above all, do no harm." His elbows slipped out from under him, and he fell, hitting an already injured spot on the back of his skull. "I will not do your surgery no matter what."

Tone curiously satisfied, the agent mused, "You won't break." He bent down, his hand going to his ankle. A click... when the agent straightened, there was a gun in his hand.

Joe swallowed hard. This was the end. They'd find him dead in a boat, covered in his own shit and vomit. *Sundari, I was so bloody stupid. Please, please, please know I didn't actually do anything wrong. Fr Franco, you're all they have now.*

"Hey," shouted the criminal. "You said we need to keep him alive until we explain to the bosses what happened."

"We do," agreed the agent. There was a muffled report.

Joe waited to feel something... there was no added pain, no fresh warmth of gushing blood, no visions of the dearly departed. Slowly, he became aware of the relative silence in the boat. Except for the rumbling of the motor and the gentle lapping of the waves, there were no sounds.

The agent once again bent down, tucking his weapon back into the ankle holster. Joe turned his head to the side. The criminal was in the same position he was before. There was a hole in the middle of his forehead, blood trickling out from the edges. The bullet missed the major blood vessels on its way through the skull, Joe noted, feeling somewhat dazed.

Without saying a word to Joe, the agent walked to his dead colleague. A grunt... a splash... the corpse sank into the water.

"There's no time to explain," said the agent, sauntering back to Joe and squatting next to him. "We'll be at the ship soon. Play along if you want to stay alive."

Terror kept Joe quiet through the rest of the boat ride. He didn't dare take his eyes off the agent but was aware of each painful breath. A rib or two had to be cracked for sure. Counting his own heartbeats, he wondered if it would be the last one.

When they got to the ship, someone came down to check on him, a man the agent addressed as "boss." The muted conversation between this boss and the agent left Joe even more confused at the elaborate lies being peddled. The agent claimed the cops stopped the car used by them. Apparently, the donor—poor Mustafa—was wanted by the police on a prior charge of petty thievery. The stupid criminal colleague decided to outrun the cops instead of simply surrendering the donor and postponing the planned transplant. They managed to lose the police vehicle, but there was an accident. Mustafa escaped. Joe and the agent were in the backseat of the car and weren't seen by the cops, but Joe was badly injured. The agent managed to get Joe and the criminal into the boat under the pretext of getting medical help at the ship and killed the criminal to avoid being tracked through him. Except for an annoyed grunt or two, there was no regret expressed by the boss at the loss of a team member. "I'm going to take him back to the city," the agent finished, tossing a casual glance in Joe's direction. "We'll have to throw a couple of thousand at the hospital staff to make sure they don't report him as an accident case, but it's a necessary expenditure. Dr D'Acosta has long-term potential."

"I agree," said the boss, nodding.

After the boss returned to the ship, the agent powered the motor back on. Tone barely more than a whisper, Joe asked, "Who are y—"

"No talking," snapped the agent.

It couldn't have taken more than an hour to reach the jetty, but to Joe, each second seemed an eternity. Shivering in his wet clothes, he glued his gaze to the back of the agent's head. Once they got to dry land... Joe was in no shape to make a run for it, but there were surely a few people still out on the street. If he could shout loud enough... how was he even going to get out of the boat?

When they arrived at the jetty, a form detached itself from the shadows. "Sir?"

The agent powered down the motor and threw a thick rope around the post at the end of the ramp. "We have a problem."

The shadowed form moved into the small circle of light thrown by the bulb on the ramp—the driver who'd picked Joe up at the airport. "So I see," said the man, somehow not appearing as skinny as he did in the car.

Between them, the driver and the agent hefted Joe from the boat. "Dammit," grunted the agent. "There isn't enough space." The ramp wasn't wide enough for three grown men to walk abreast, let alone with the middle one being supported by the other two. "Lemme try it this way..." The agent shifted to move sideways down the ramp.

Joe's hand slipped off the agent's shoulder, and he stumbled, falling to his knees. Cursing mildly, the driver hauled Joe upright. "Hold on to both of us, Doc. We don't want any more injuries."

Sweat beaded Joe's upper lip. Taking short, shallow breaths, he reached for the railing. His eyes chanced on the docked boat and the name painted on the hull: *Sea Queen*. Not *Sundari*? "Is this the same boat I got into?" he asked.

"Heh?" asked the driver. "What do you mean is it the same—" He nodded at the agent. "Did the doc get hit in the head?"

"Yes," said the agent, peering at Joe's face. "Any trouble seeing?"

"I'm all right," said Joe. "*Is* it the same boat? I need to know."

With an annoyed mutter, the driver said, "Of course, it's the same boat. If you're all right, stop effing around and walk."

"But—" Joe glanced between the boat and the men with him. Why would they lie about it?

"We don't have all night," said the driver.

Yanking Joe's arm, the agent draped it around his shoulders and hauled the captive sideways down the ramp. "By the way," the agent said. "Don't get any bright ideas about escape. I'm your best way—the *only* way—out. If the people in the ship find out what you did, it won't be only you paying. They know where your family is. They know about the girl."

An Ambassador car waited at the entrance of the jetty. Joe hesitated only a second or two before stumbling into the backseat. If he tried to run, he wasn't gonna get far, and what the agent said about the criminals going after Joe's loved ones... he watched the streets fly past, not really seeing any of it. The name of the boat... he could've sworn it said... didn't matter now. His priority was escape. Mind working feverishly, he estimated the odds. Anjali, the kids, Fr Franco... if Joe could call one of them and warn... *shit*. Even if his phone were still in his back pocket, there was no way to use it without being overheard. The agent had said something to his boss about taking Joe to a hospital. Surely, there was someone who'd help Joe.

Tyres screeching, the car came to a stop by a tall gate, and the driver talked to a couple of uniformed guards. From there, it was only a few minutes before they drove under a large arch proclaiming the name of the place: INHS Sanjeevani. Ignoring the throbbing pain in his ribs, Joe scrambled up. Indian navy hospital ship? They were at a naval base?

Quickly and quietly, Joe was moved from the car to a stretcher and from the stretcher to a bed in what appeared to be an austere private room. A sharp sting went up his arm. Joe yelped.

The agent—lounging in the chair by the window—chuckled. "After the beating you took tonight, a needle is what gets you crying?"

"I wasn't expecting—" Joe held up a hand, stopping the nurse coming at him with a syringe. "What's that?"

"Sedative," she said. "We have some work to do on you."

Joe struggled to sit up. "I don't want any—"

With gentle hands, she urged him back to the bed. "We're not giving you a choice, Doctor."

"Stop," he demanded, trying to swat her away. "I need to know..." He craned his head towards the window where the agent was sitting. "Who are... are..." Joe shook his head. His vision was getting fuzzy. "You put something in the IV," he accused the nurse.

His form blurring around the edges, the agent sauntered to the side of the bed. A moment before Joe went completely under, the agent said, "DSP Naidu—deputy superintendent of police. CBI officer, working with INTERPOL."

***

Propped up by pillows on the bed, Joe didn't take his gaze off the loose thread on the sheet as the agent, Naidu, talked to the third man in the hospital room—the dean of the All India Institute of Medical Science. "I don't care for your tactics, Mr Naidu," said the dean, fidgeting in the narrow chair. "You deliberately targeted one of my students."

"No one put a gun to his head," said Naidu, slouching against the wall.

Joe heard it all right before the dean's arrival. Naidu, an agent with the CBI—the Central Bureau of Investigation of India—was assigned to the INTERPOL desk. He was sent undercover to the organ-trafficking ring and was tasked by the criminals with recruiting donors from among the migrant workers in Delhi. The crime ring employed at least one such recruiter in major metros. Naidu hoped to worm his way into the top rungs of the criminal organisation, but his lack of medical credentials meant the corrupt surgeons saw no reason to welcome his company. He never managed to ID them, and he didn't know who in the various governments and law enforcement agencies were in the pay of the criminals. There was no way the organisation was able to do what they did without help from official quarters.

Naidu needed a doctor working with him, preferably someone already employed by the crime ring and therefore wouldn't be suspected of being a mole. When the wife of the Arab sheikh blamed the surgeon doing the kidney extraction for her body's rejection of the transplanted organ, the crime ring started scouring the campuses of the elite medical colleges in India for a new medic. Their contact in AIIMS pointed them towards Joe, surgeon-in-training and the grandson of a criminal. Ambitious, arrogant Joseph D'Acosta was believed to be for sale.

The undercover cop saw his chance and volunteered to be the one luring Joe. The bosses of the trafficking ring, impressed by Naidu's apparent eagerness to get ahead in his criminal career, agreed. Plus, the contact in AIIMS didn't want to risk his job in case Joe reported the offer to the police.

Naidu rented the flat next to Joe's and quickly sized up the target as not the sort to postpone his career success to assist law enforcement. The plan was to trick Joe into one surgery and then, he'd be trapped by INTERPOL. Unfortunately, Joe wasn't biting no matter how high the offer of cash went. Naidu was on the verge of giving up when Ruksana passed, leaving Joe desperate for a way to keep his family together.

"He eventually made the right decision," argued the dean. "You said so yourself. Surely, he deserves leniency."

Naidu huffed. "Look, sir... doctor... leniency, justice, and the rest of the mercy crap is for the courts to decide. My job is to get the bastards behind this operation. I need Dr D'Acosta's help. Right now, he needs mine as well. He may not go to jail because he did change his mind, but do you imagine things will get as far as a trial? Dr D'Acosta witnessed part of the operations of the ring. They'll make sure he doesn't testify. If he somehow does, they won't merely chop off the Kochi limb to keep the master organisation intact; they'll make sure no one else gets the same idea. Every member of his family will be spread across the world in little pieces... the priest, the boys, even the child. Not to mention the girlfriend."

Joe struggled to shove the images away... gruesome visuals of his baby sister with her guts spilling out... Anjali... bleeding, her eyes pleadingly fixed on her boyfriend. Fingers gripping the bedsheet tightly, he took one panicked breath. Sharp currents of pain zigzagged all across his ribcage.

Beep... beep... beep. The piercing sound rang through the room. The two men stopped talking.

"What's going on?" asked a female voice. The nurse marched firmly to the IV pole next to the bedside and clucked. "Doctor, you should know better. Your IV won't work if the muscles are all clenched like that."

As soon as she fixed the problem and left, Naidu said, "You need to see this through, Dr D'Acosta, or no one connected with you will be able to live without fearing for their lives. The CBI is getting your family out of Goa even as we speak. They'll be placed in a safehouse for the duration of your mission. As for the girlfriend—" Meeting Joe's glance, the cop paused. "I never identified her to the gang... she's a civilian... didn't think it was appropriate. So she should be all right. There will be someone keeping an eye on her—on your circle of friends—regardless."

The dean didn't ask for the identity of the girlfriend, and Joe didn't volunteer. "How long do you expect this mission to last?" the dean asked the cop. "I don't want one of my most promising students wasting his potential, playing secret agent."

"It will last as long as it needs to," said Naidu. "The agency promised to help him return to his course no matter how much time has passed. This is the only reason the CBI director notified you. Neither you nor Dr D'Acosta may talk about this with a third party." Nodding firmly at Joe, Naidu added, "There was no option but to explain to your Fr Franco what was going on. Which leaves the girlfriend. Under no circumstances are you to say anything to her."

What *could* Joe say to Anjali? How could he tell her he'd ruined the dreams they'd woven together? How could he even look her in the eye? When she heard he wasn't returning... Joe jerked up in bed, setting the alarm off, again. "Sir," he called the dean. "I need another favour." Anjali would hate Joe to the core for what he was about to ask, but there was no other way. She needed to believe without even a trace of doubt he was a callous bastard who discarded her without a second thought, or she'd never stop searching for him. She'd put her life at risk. Heart heavy, Joe asked the dean to let his friends know he was quitting, that he was cutting off all contact with them. "Delay it until after Nikhil's wedding if you can."

"I'll take care of it," said the dean, briskly. With a rueful sigh, he muttered, "You idiot. Of all the things you could've done... why didn't you call *me* for help? I would've arranged something. Now... your career, your future... God knows what's going to happen."

"I'm gonna be removing kidneys," Joe mumbled in response. He'd be harvesting organs from desperate men and women like Mustafa who'd agreed to be chopped up only to feed their families. If Joe wanted *his* family to stay alive, he'd have to break the oath he'd taken as a doctor: primum non nocere. From surgeon, he'd be reduced to a butcher. Everything he wanted in life... the girl, the career, the security for his family... he'd destroyed it all himself in a matter of days. A sob broke from him. His shoulders shook with the force of unshed tears.

Awkwardly patting the top of his head, the dean said, "There won't be any legal repercussions, and I'll make sure you don't get into trouble with the medical board. As for the procedure part of it... I have full faith in your surgical skills. Better you than some quack with a scalpel."

After the dean's departure, Naidu sauntered to the chair and plonked himself in it. "Your flatmate will be happy."

Joe wanted the man to go away. He didn't want to talk. He didn't even want to think. Then, he frowned. "My flatmate? What's he got to do with this?"

Briefly, Naidu talked about Rishi's trip to the gay club, the night he spent at some actor's apartment.

"Son of a bitch," growled Joe. "You blackmailed him? Don't you have any ethics?" Joe *walked* into the trap, but his jackass flatmate did absolutely nothing wrong.

Eyes narrowing, Naidu said, "I can't afford to worry about ethics when there are hundreds of lives at stake, Doctor. Your friend is only one man. He was my next best option since *you* weren't biting."

"Call him," demanded Joe. "Let him know you don't require his services any longer." No one else needed to ruin his life the way Joe did.

Naidu held up a hand and explained two weeks was when the Arab lady said she'd be ready. When Joe agreed to do the job, the cop wanted to make sure he didn't get time to change his mind. With some crazy excuse offered to the bosses of the crime ring, Naidu moved the plans up. "I'll call your flatmate in two weeks as I said I would. Also, I have to ease out of the deal. If I cancel right now, he might connect it with your disappearance. After all, you actually are a transplant trainee." Plus, Rishi knew about the moonlighting offers Joe kept getting.

Two weeks. Joe wasn't allowed to see a soul other than the one doctor and the two nurses treating him. The only visitor was the cop, grilling Joe on the details he needed to know about the mission. He also brought the news Fr Franco and the kids were no longer in Goa. The cheque from Joe was retrieved by the CBI, and Dev left a note for the landlord about mailing the rent money owed when they got their father's pension sorted out. The D'Acostas were now safe in their new home in Bangalore, but there were no phone calls to Joe. "If the kids could at least hear my voice... they've got to be going out of their minds," mumbled Joe, staring out the window one afternoon. Anjali, too, but she didn't know he was in the clutches of INTERPOL. First, she'd refuse to believe he'd walked out on her. When he didn't return for days... weeks... months... she'd start hating him, wanting to erase his existence from her life. But she wouldn't be putting herself in danger, looking for him.

"No calls to anyone," said Naidu, firmly. "We can't risk any leaks." Which was the same reason Joe gave Naidu when asking him not to talk to Fr Franco about Anjali. Truth was she was the granddaughter of the priest's best buddy, and Joe didn't want his family knowing how badly he'd treated her.

The evening Joe was discharged, Naidu waited until it was dark to spirit him to a one-room apartment somewhere within the naval base. There wouldn't be much time left for Joe to worry over what he'd soon be doing. The first surgery was set for the day after. Naidu lounged in the only chair in the apartment and stretched his legs out, apparently settling in.

"You don't have to stand guard," said Joe. He desperately needed reprieve from the cop's presence for one night at least. "I'll still be here in the morning."

Shooting him a sardonic glance, Naidu seemed about to say something when there was a thundering at the door. The cop went out to talk to whomever and was an inordinately long time in returning.

Joe collapsed onto the cot and closed his eyes, hoping to be asleep before the damned fellow was back, but his brain refused to cooperate. There was a cheap digital clock on the wall, the electronically induced tick-tick-tick seemingly getting louder and louder. Through slitted eyes, Joe watched as the time approached 12 AM. The date below changed to November 27, 2008.

I AM... 1:30... silently, Joe listened to the door squeak open, the click of shoes approaching the cot. After a minute or so of knowing the cop was staring down at him, Joe snapped his eyes wide open. "What—" Naidu's brown face was almost paper white under the tan. Swinging his feet to the floor, Joe sat up. "Problem?" he asked, heart pounding.

The cop opened his mouth and put an unlit cigarette to his lips. With a huff, he took out the thing and tossed it to the floor. "Nothing major. The usual crap we deal with from politicians. You get some rest. I... ahh... will be in the next apartment, taking care of some stuff."

With the single window in Joe's room barred, all Naidu would have to do was lock the door from the outside. Shaking his head in annoyance, Joe flopped back onto the mattress.

The next day he met Mustafa, again. They weren't left alone together to create mischief this time around, but the Bengali labourer held up all ten fingers. Joe hid a satisfied smile behind his knuckles. Ten thousand euros would go a long way towards treating Mustafa's child. It wouldn't have mattered what kind of lies the cop offered to the crime ring to explain the sudden jacking of price; the surgeons doing the actual transplant would've told the wealthy patient near-perfect matches like this were hard to get. Per Joe's demand, both he and Mustafa were permitted to stay a week on board the hospital ship to ensure the donor's safe recovery.

When Joe jumped off the boat at the jetty, he expected to be allowed to visit his family in Bangalore. Naidu had promised to smuggle Joe to the city on India's other side in one of the military vehicles. Instead, the cop led him back to the office near the church by the jetty and into the small room where he'd been introduced to Mustafa.

"Is someone going to pick me up here?" Joe asked, squirming in the hard plastic chair. Or perhaps they'd go to the naval base, and he'd travel to Bangalore from there.

Without answering, Naidu went to the desk and tugged impatiently at a drawer. He took out a pack of cigarettes and glared at it for a moment or two before tossing the whole thing back in. "We're going to walk." Picking up one of the folded newspapers on the desk, he stared hard at the front page.

"Back to the naval base?" Joe didn't fancy the ten-kilometre trek right at the time. "It's been a bloody long day. Can't we at least take the bus?"

"Heh?" With a short laugh completely lacking in mirth, Naidu pointed to something outside the door. "No, we're walking over there. The naval officers' quarters." The Southern Naval Command owned multiple properties in the city, including the apartment building on Marine Drive, which they used to house their employees.

Dammit, how long was Joe expected to wait? The kids... Fr Franco... gritting his teeth in impatience, Joe asked, "When do you think you'll be done with your errands so I can go to Bangalore and see my family?" Plus, Joe needed to somehow know how Anjali was doing. The CBI made sure she was safe, which meant squat as far as her emotional state was concerned. Perhaps Naidu's pals could do Joe a favour and ask around.

Naidu took two strides to the door and snapped it shut. "Your family's not in Bangalore. They're in one of the flats in the navy quarters here."

"What—" Joe bounded out of the chair. "More of your secrecy crap, I guess. Tell me which apartment. I'm going over there right now."

"Sit," Naidu said. "There's something we have to discuss."

Seething, Joe said, "Look, man. I did what you asked me to do, and I'll continue doing so until you get all the criminals in the ring. But there's no way I—"

"*Sit down,*" ordered the cop. When Joe remained standing, the officer shoved Joe into his seat.

"You—" Before Joe could leap back up, a folded newspaper landed on his lap.

Eyes steady and fixed on Joe, Naidu said, "Read."

"IT'S WAR ON MUMBAI," screamed the headlines in *The Times of India.*

Joe looked up, confused. He glanced back down at the paper to check the date: November 27, 2008. The week before. The article talked about an attack by Islamic terrorists on India's number one city, of the nightmare unleashed on the Taj and Oberoi hotels, hospitals, on the neighbourhoods of Colaba and Santa Cruz. There was a buzz in Joe's brain. "Is this real?" he asked, his lips stiff.

The cop didn't respond. Tossing the *Times* aside, Joe clambered up and grabbed the other newspapers on the desk. "BLOOD BATH IN MUMBAI," said the *DNA.* "NIGHT OF TERROR," read the *Mumbai Mirror.*

"Oh, my God," Joe whispered. Picture of buildings in flames, bleeding bodies, crying children, soldiers on the streets... the noise in his brain got louder, morphing into loud screams and pleas for help... the smell of burnt flesh, the stench of death. Gasping for air, he dropped the papers and shoved his fingers into his hair. "Anju..." No, Anjali would've been in Delhi. She wouldn't get to Mumbai until the middle of December for the wedding in the group. Nor would Rishi and Siddharth. Nikhil was supposed to have flown in that morning. Or had it been the next? Joe couldn't think. *Please, please, please,* he begged. It had to have been the next day. Flights would've been grounded, and the wedding would be delayed, but Nikhil would be safe. "Oh, God... Gauri and Meenu... were they there?"

"They're fine," said Naidu. "I checked."

With trembling fingers, Joe wiped the sweat off his upper lip. "Good," he breathed. "They're fine; they're safe—Anju's parents? They live in South Mumbai. Did something happen?"

"No." The cop held up a hand. "They're okay, too." Grabbing one of the newspapers, he flipped it open and handed it to Joe.

Nikhil's familiar face grinned up, inviting the world to join whatever adventure was being planned. "Obituary?" Joe whispered. Twenty-four-year-old doctor, travelling to India for his wedding, dead from a bullet to the head. One of the many, many casualties of the terrorist attack on Mumbai. "No... no... *no way in hell.*" Hurling the paper across the room, Joe turned to Naidu. "Nikhil wasn't there. He couldn't have been. He was supposed to get to Mumbai the next day." Wasn't he? Frantically, Joe tried to remember when Nikhil was expected in India.

The cop didn't say anything, only throwing a wary glance at the barred window beyond which was the church.

"It's got to be a mistake," Joe insisted, his head throbbing in pain. "How could it... they IDed someone else. You know these things happen." It would've been complete chaos in Mumbai. A random dead body, a guest list from the hotel, mistaken identification. "Call his house," Joe demanded. "You'll see. I bet he's already back there, trying to get the wedding done before he returns to New York. Gauri must be going crazy."

"I'm sorry," said the cop, quietly.

"Sorry?" Joe asked. "I don't want to hear your 'sorry.' I want you to pick up the phone and call his house." When the cop stayed silent, Joe said, "I'll call myself." He shoved aside the papers on the desk, sending them sliding to the floor. "Where the landline?" Joe's mobile phone was missing in action since the first night in Kochi. "*Where's the damned landline?*" He went around the desk and tugged each drawer open, tossing out anything and everything he found—paperclips, pens, random bits of paper. No phone. Roaring in anger, he sent the chair flying to the wall.

"Stop," snapped the officer. "You'll draw attention."

"I don't give a damn," shouted Joe. "I need to know... I need to talk to Nikhil."

"You can't," said Naidu, tone steady. "Nikhil's dead. There's no mistake. His American friend was with him and watched him die. His body was cremated in Delhi. Your flatmate was there. So was Anjali. Nikhil's family took his ashes to Haridwar." Haridwar, where Hindu believers immersed the ashes of their loved ones in the holy river to free their souls from bondage.

"No," said Joe, shaking his head. The room blurred. Hot tears ran down his cheeks. "It's not possible."

"Yes," said Naidu. Sighing, he repeated, "I'm sorry."

"No," Joe whimpered.

He wasn't sure how long he stayed in the room, sobbing, remembering, regretting. The man who'd thrown his arm around Joe's shoulders the first day they met, claiming him as friend, was dead. The grin, the excitement, the joy in life... reduced to memories.

On their first day as freshers in AIIMS, Nikhil fidgeted in his seat in the sheer pleasure of being in the anatomy dissection hall, prompting a rebuke from the professor. The same evening, Joe encountered Nikhil arguing with a group of senior students, his friend—the pretty-faced jackass called Rishi—standing next to him. One of their classmates seemed to be caught between the two groups. Her plump cheeks were painfully red, and her chubby shoulders were so hunched she was practically collapsing into herself. It wasn't difficult to guess what was going on. Bullies, picking on an easy target. Nikhil, the saviour, riding to the rescue. Problem was the same seniors would make the rescuer pay for it in the privacy of the men's hostel. Casually, Joe sauntered by and took his place next to Nikhil and his friend. Strength in numbers, etcetera. Also, people rarely messed with Joe.

The simple act was enough to seal the deal in Nikhil's mind. Joe D'Acosta was one of Nikhil's best friends. The day after, Joe, Nikhil, and Rishi found themselves the heroes of the first-year batch.

It went on the same way all through their years together in AIIMS. With the jackass in tow, Nikhil would rush into something exciting/risky/heroic. Joe, exasperated to his teeth, would join only to keep the idiots from trouble. Joe used to joke Nikhil would either win some kind of bravery award or get himself—

"Was he trying to help someone?" Joe asked, hoarsely. He was back in the chair, not quite sure how he got there.

The cop was at the window, staring out into the night. "No," he said. "Dr Arora was on his way to the Leopold Café with his American friend, but they weren't inside yet. One of the terrorists shot into the crowd." With a sigh, Naidu turned around to face Joe. "Wrong place, wrong time."

That was it? There was no more meaning to Nikhil's death? Nothing more to his life than the pain of what could've been? Joe screwed his eyes shut and rocked back and forth in fresh grief.

"Bright young man by all accounts," Naidu muttered. "Everyone seems to have liked him."

The officer had done his research in the one week since the attack. "When did you find out Nikhil died?" Joe asked.

After a tense moment, Naidu admitted, "The night it happened." The night Joe was discharged, the night before he left to perform his first surgery for the crime ring. Naidu kept silent because he didn't want his reluctant partner going to pieces. He'd made sure Joe wasn't alone with anyone else for even a moment, risking the news reaching him before he completed his mission.

"Effing bastard," Joe snarled.

The cop didn't deny it.

One week passed in a world with no Nikhil, and Joe never knew. He wasn't there for his best friend's last journey, his... "Gauri... oh, my God..." The sparkly brat fluttered into AIIMS two years after Joe, Nikhil, and Rishi. She took one look at Nikhil's grin and tumbled into love. "I need to talk to her. And Rishi..." The jackass and Nikhil had been friends since before they were potty-trained. For Rishi, it would be like having part of his soul ripped away.

"You can't," said Naidu.

"I need to talk to them," Joe begged. "Please. Just once. I swear I won't say a word about what's happening here."

"Then what?" asked Naidu. "Did I mention your girlfriend and your flatmate went to Goa and filed a missing persons report? The cops from the station they approached called your dean to check. I've taken care of things with the police, and the dean already informed your friends you're not

388

returning. If you communicate with them now... what if they go again, looking for you? They're civilians; don't put their lives at risk."

***

"They're lying," Joe stated, zipping his gym bag closed. "Anju knows Rishi is gay." No matter how heartbroken she was, no matter how much she hated Joe at the moment, rebounding with Rishi wasn't possible. And to go straight to being the jackass's fiancée?

Leaning against the wall in Joe's room at the navy flat, Naidu quirked an eyebrow. "You don't think I realise it? Those two believe they're very clever, threatening me with the minister. All you doctors are full of yourselves."

There was a doggy whine from Joe's bed. Patting Scher's head, Joe shrugged. "Might've worked for real if you'd actually been a blackmailer." Anjali's family was wealthy, and money meant power. Add a minister to the mix, the Joshis were almost untouchable even by the law. Once she claimed Rishi as her betrothed and issued a counterthreat, a blackmailer would not have found much benefit in carrying on. He could always locate another surgeon, but if he insisted on Rishi, the minister would have the crime ring running for their lives. Nor would they bother going after Rishi for the refusal like they would've with Joe. After all, Rishi possessed no details on them except a few phone calls which could not be traced. If he actually showed up where he was asked as Joe foolishly did, the criminals might've risked the minister's wrath to avoid discovery.

"Quite amusing," muttered the cop. "The naïve bluster."

Without bothering to respond to the comment, Joe asked, "Did you arrange someone to get my stuff from Delhi like you said?" A few of his certificates were there. Plus, the oil sketch Anjali did of him. He wanted it... a memory to cling to until the day he could return to her.

389

"The CBI retrieved everything a long time ago," said Naidu. "It's a matter of making sure the shipment gets here without anyone from the crime ring finding out your actual address." As far as the criminals knew, their new surgeon lived in a seedier part of the town, and his family was in Bangalore.

Nodding, Joe hefted the bag and strode to the living room where Fr Franco and Dev were waiting. Scher leapt off the bed and followed.

It had been a month since Joe showed up at the flat in the middle of the night, shaking and pale from the news of Nikhil's death. Fr Franco—the forgiving soul—didn't say a single harsh word. Joe needed his xapai—his grandfather—and the priest let the boy sob on his shoulder all night. With a paw on Joe's knee, Scher offered doggy sympathy. Towards dawn, Joe apologised for his stupidity which landed the entire family in this mess. All Fr Franco said was he was in the business of faith, hope, and love.

When the younger D'Acostas woke, they were told Joe took a medical job with the military and would return to his training once they were on surer financial ground. His work involved treating high-ranking officers in hush-hush places, and his family was expected to cooperate by keeping to themselves.

Oh, yeah... as soon as Joe received his first paycheck as "technical adviser" to the CBI, he got Naidu to send the son of a bitch landlord in Goa the rent money owed. The three-bedroom flat on Marine Drive, facing the sea, was quite an upgrade from their digs in Goa, but it was a quasi-prison. Joe got a few weeks off before his next assignment with the crime ring and was ordered to stay indoors for both Christmas and New Year. Fr Franco never ventured anywhere except to walk Scher and buy groceries, but he played the part of the naïve elder to keep the kids entertained over the holidays.

It wasn't completely role-playing. The priest steadfastly held on to his faith in God and the universe He created, milking joy out of the silliest, most childish things. Joe harboured no doubts Fr Franco was simultaneously aware of the reality of what his adopted grandson was up to and imagining him as some sort of superhero/spy, fulfilling the destiny chosen by the heavens. But sending Joe off on this second trip to the ship couldn't be easy on the old man now that he was cognisant of the danger involved.

Standing at the door to the living room, Joe nodded towards the boy stretched out on the sofa. "Already asleep?"

"It's past midnight." With a worried smile, the priest stood from the upholstered chair next to the sofa. "How long will it be this time?"

"Not sure," said Joe. This wouldn't be merely another surgery for him. Naidu had explained to the bosses of the crime ring how money was only part of Joe's remuneration. Dr D'Acosta expected to be helped along in his career by the better-known members of the team. He expected introductions to the actual transplant surgeons, their contacts in various governments and law enforcement agencies without whose help the setup wouldn't have been possible. Glancing at his sleeping brother, Joe said, "You know what to tell them."

When schools reopened after the short break, Naidu's driver/subordinate would chauffeur the kids to and from the facility in the well-guarded naval base. Once home, they wouldn't be allowed out except to equally well-guarded events within the base.

Joe earned the same salary given to other technical advisers to the CBI, and the government took care of the rent and school and security, but yeah, they were prisoners. How long their sentence would last depended on how quickly he completed his task.

Over the next few months, he went wherever the crime ring sent him on his fake passport—the one provided by the CBI. Joe walked down the slums in the Philippines, talked to the prostitutes in Bangkok, trudged through the snow-covered marketplaces in Kosovo. Apparently, the criminals recently expanded the donor recruitment part of their business to include the poor in other countries. Joe sliced open patients of all colours, carefully extracting their kidneys. The fee he was paid went straight to the CBI, but each drop of blood splattering onto his gloves stained his conscience.

Joe was assisting men and women desperate for survival in selling off parts of themselves. Once they agreed to the deal, once they showed up at the designated spot, there was no backing out. Joe never had the misfortune to encounter such a circumstance, but he'd heard enough to understand what happened to the donors who did try to back away—pretty much what Naidu promised would happen to Joe and his family if he refused to cooperate. To make sure they stayed mum, they'd be killed and every possible organ harvested. Mustafa's life was spared only because he wasn't exactly unwilling to donate... he only wanted more money. The Arab sheikh didn't baulk at paying ten thousand euros to save his beloved wife. With each procedure Joe performed, he found himself battling the urge to tell the donor to run and hide, all the while praying fervently they wouldn't.

In the evenings, Joe met the transplant surgeons, dined with them on caviar and fine wines, hoping like hell the wire he wore under his shirt wouldn't be detected. Unfortunately, their contacts in the government weren't as trusting as the doctors to divulge anything incriminating before the newcomer.

"You'll need to gain their acceptance," Naidu stated. With Joe's ascendance in the ranks of the criminal organisation, the cop's stature also rose, and he went along on their trips as the doctor's personal assistant. "It will take time."

Time. Six months had flown by, and he wasn't anywhere close to getting out. Every moment that passed, the farther Anjali got from Joe.

Back in the flat in Kochi, Joe eyed the article in the life and style section of *The Times of India* and wondered for the millionth time what the hell was going on. The picture was beautiful, showing Anjali dressed in Indian clothes. She was officially engaged to the jackass? How far was she going to take this fake relationship? The smirk on the jackass's face... did he even remember

Anjali was the girlfriend of a man he once trusted with his deeply buried secret, the same truth he was now using her to hide? With an angry growl, Joe ripped the page in two and tossed the pieces onto the coffee table before collapsing into the sofa.

"Something wrong?" asked Fr Franco, plodding in from the room he shared with Joe. The younger two D'Acosta boys split a second bedroom, and little Laila got her own. The kids were already asleep. The elderly priest was also supposed to be resting, not wandering around the flat. His eyes went to the torn paper. "Isn't that your friend's engagement announcement to Ram's grandchild? Why did you tear it up? Naidu left it here because he thought you'd be interested."

When this was over, Joe was going to beat the cop to a pulp. Naidu was an expert in many martial art forms and could probably break Joe's neck in under a minute, but he'd be damned if he let this go. What was the need to thrust the picture into Joe's face except to remind him of what he was fast losing? "Yeah," Joe said to the priest. "I'm getting frustrated with this INTERPOL business. I need to get back to my own life."

Eyes sympathetic, Fr Franco lowered himself into the plush chair. "Was there a girl back in AIIMS, Joe?"

"Huh? No." Clearing his throat, Joe sat up. "Why do you ask?"

The priest shrugged. "I've been wondering... is that why you refused Lazar Noronha's offer?"

Noronha... the department store owner who'd attempted to buy Joe as son-in-law. Poor Fr Franco believed it was simply a matter of wanting a doctor in the family. The priest didn't have a clue what Noronha was actually looking for—a smart, ambitious fellow he could control. Much like Naidu was doing right now. Except, Joe's current situation was his own fault. "Girl or no girl, I wasn't going to sell myself to Noronha. Why are we talking about him,

393

anyway?" The damned vulture wasn't someone Joe wanted to remember in the time he was allowed with his family.

"He passed last week," said the priest.

Joe stared for a moment before muttering, "I hope he rots in hell."

"Joe," snapped Fr Franco.

"What?" Flinging his hands into the air, Joe asked, "Is he supposed to be a saint now he's dead?"

"No, I was thinking of his poor daughter. Your intended bride."

Joe rolled his eyes. "I never even met the woman."

"She went to the diocese and asked for you."

Jerking back in surprise, Joe asked, "What?"

The priest nodded. "She asked if the bishop knew any way to contact me... and you." The bishop was told the same tale weaved for the D'Acosta kids— that Joe was working as a medic for military officers on hush-hush operations, and Fr Franco would be helping with the family until it was done. Any messages from the diocese would be conveyed via Naidu.

"What for—" Joe shook his head. "I don't really care. I wasn't going to marry her then, and I'm not going to marry her now."

"I hear you," said Fr Franco. "Just trying to understand why. I know Lazar was... er... difficult, but the girl's rather sweet."

Incredulously, Joe asked, "You're matchmaking? *Now*, old man? Haven't you noticed what's been going on in our lives the last few months?"

Not only the damned CBI/INTERPOL mess. Dev had failed to clear his higher secondary exams, without which he couldn't go to university. He was stubbornly insisting college was not in his plans. He'd retake the exams the next year, but no, he wasn't gonna apply to any stupid university. Someday, he'd make a restaurant out of the shed back in Vagator.

Joe found himself without words to reprimand his little brother. How could he? If Dev could've stayed in the school in Goa, he might've at least scraped through, gotten some kind of college degree.

Fr Franco wanted Joe to consider bringing another person—a woman—into this chaos?

"No, no." The priest smoothed back his hair. "Before poor Ruksana passed, I was going to ask you to meet the Noronha girl... once at least. Then, I was waiting for the threat of money hanging over your head to go away. Not a good way to start a marriage. When this..." He waved a hand around. "...happened, I forgot all about her. After Naidu brought me the message from the bishop, I wondered why you thought marrying her would be worse."

"She came as a package deal with her father."

"Is it the only reason?" persisted Fr Franco, glancing at the torn pieces of paper on the coffee table. Flushing, he mumbled, "I've heard the stories from your college. The D'Acosta men were always a hit with the ladies. The last couple of years, though... the gossip was you were off women. Some of the parishioners actually thought you were making sure Lazar Noronha didn't withdraw his offer. If it wasn't the reason..."

"I decided I wanted to be a priest," said Joe, promptly. When Fr Franco guffawed, Joe grinned. If Anjali could hear him... smile fading, he muttered, "I never talked to you or the kids about the women I dated, did I? Somehow, the rumours from Delhi got to Goa. After a while, I decided to stay low key. Less drama if things don't work out."

"So there *was* something which didn't work out?"

Joe groaned. "Let it go, xapai. I'm not in the right frame of mind to think about women." If Fr Franco found out about Anjali... when the whole mess started, Joe specifically asked Naidu not to mention Anjali to the D'Acostas, claiming the last thing anyone needed was for the sentimental priest to do something stupid like keeping tabs on his old friend's granddaughter, thus risking the criminals finding out about her importance to Joe. Truth was Joe didn't want to admit to Fr Franco how badly he'd behaved with her.

Anjali was now engaged to another man... to her former boyfriend's flatmate. As soon as Joe was out of the picture, the jackass moved in on her. And for *what?* Only to save his own skin? She surely knew it but was still going along.

There was nothing—absolutely nothing—Joe could do about it. If he tried to contact her, ask why she was promising herself to a gay man... no, he wouldn't risk her life for anything. What he needed was to get himself and his family out of this damned trap and return all of them to some semblance of normalcy. He needed to get to Anjali without danger following him and beg her forgiveness. He was going to explain everything he did. Naidu and INTERPOL could simply shove the secrecy fetish up their—Joe was going to be one hundred per cent honest with Anjali about what happened. It was the only way she'd ever consider taking him back.

He wouldn't know for another year and a half how far out of his reach Anjali had gone. Shoving from his mind the wedding picture in the newspaper, Joe strode to the brothel in Bangkok masquerading as a massage parlour featuring former supermodels. The owner was a particular friend of one of the transplant surgeons.

In the luxury suite, he stared in silence at the leggy woman who could've easily graced the cover of *Maxim.* Her tone low and sexy, she asked for his preferences. All he could think of was a petite brunette with a tiny birthmark near her mouth. All he wanted to hear was a sweet, strong voice, arguing with him, teasing him, whispering words of love. All he needed was... was... Joe blanked his mind of further thought and held out a hand as though inviting an actual lover into his embrace.

The supermodel's kisses were definitely more expert than Anjali's, her touch surer. The model figured out quickly where to put her mouth, how to drive him to a frenzy. She was worth every penny of the two-hundred and fifty American dollars.

When Joe returned to his hotel room, Naidu looked up from the papers he was perusing and muttered, "Idiot."

Lying awake late into the night, Joe taunted the memory of Anjali with the story of his visit to the prostitute. While his former fiancée was on her honeymoon with a gay man, Joe was being pleasured by a stunning woman whose job was to cater to his whims.

In the morning, he asked himself what was the point. Who was he punishing? Anjali for moving on two years after her boyfriend walked out on her? Or himself for being fool enough to let it happen?

Evening after evening, Joe found himself at the brothel, each time picking a girl as different from Anjali as possible. Night after night, he jeered at the image of her in his heart, telling her how much better his life was without her in it. When the sun rose, he'd remember it was all his fault.

The most mundane of things stopped his visits to the whorehouse: money. Naidu firmly refused to sign off on Joe's expense account. If he were determined to be a self-destructive fool, he'd do it on his own dime, not the government's.

There were no more women to torment his past self with every night. When his soul bled from its self-inflicted wound, he doubled over in pain and cursed the very existence of his faithless lover. With every cell in his body, he prayed Anjali was hurting at least as much. If she were to suddenly appear in front of him, he'd... he'd kneel at her feet and beg her to take him back. There was nothing he wouldn't do, no bargain he wouldn't make, to have her again in his arms. But he couldn't. For her sake, he needed to stay away. He was trapped in a prison of his own making, no escape in sight.

Ironically, the visits to the brothel opened the gates of acceptance to Joe. Suddenly, every damned criminal in the organisation wanted to be his friend. Within another year, Naidu got enough names.

Papers across the globe reported in breathless horror on the organ-smuggling ring which preyed on the poor and the helpless. The criminals with medical degrees were hauled away from hospitals, from pricey neighbourhoods, and from their country clubs. The government officials who protected the butchers were brought before courts. The small fry involved were apprehended by local police departments. What was never mentioned were the names of the investigators. Their identities would forever remain secret precisely as they wanted.

Chapter 33

Present day

A half-moon lit the deserted cove as Joe and Anjali exited the taxi, the baby sleeping comfortably against his chest. It seemed a lifetime had passed since he walked into the temple near Mapusa with Fr Franco, encountering Anjali. Still, the two hours Joe got in the office with her wasn't anywhere near enough to say all he needed to.

"Over there," he said, pointing down the cove where a dozen or so fishing boats were shored. The waves frothed against the sandy beach as they walked, crickets keeping rhythm with each step. He took her close to the red and white skiff on the far side. Painted on the hull in royal blue letters was the name: *Sea Queen.* "I bought this from the CBI. They thought I was nuts, but I wanted it." Smiling slightly, he patted the baby's back. "I have no idea why I saw *Sundari* instead of the actual name. If I hadn't..."

"You were looking for a reason to stop," Anjali murmured. "You saw what you wanted to see."

Joe's heart latched on to the first encouraging words she'd spoken since they started this conversation. Throughout their two hours in the temple office, her shoulders had heaved in silent sobs. Every now and then, she'd whisper "Why?" or "How could you?" or "Oh, God, Joe," with tears pouring down her cheeks. Her fingers wrapped so tightly around his that her nails left crescent-shaped bruises on his skin. Her gaze never wavered from his face, not even when the temple priest mentioned it was time to close shop. When Joe asked if she'd go with him to see the boat, she simply nodded. Collecting her sleeping baby from the temple priest and Fr Franco, Joe and Anjali left in a taxi. Not a word crossed her lips the entire ride... until now.

"I stopped," Joe acknowledged. "But very late in the game."

Her hands stole around his elbow. Tone tremulous, she said, "Still, you did stop, and you were prepared to pay the ultimate price for it—your life. I can't imagine the courage it took." With a shaky sigh, Anjali rested her cheek against his arm. "Why didn't you return to AIIMS to finish your residency?"

"I didn't want to see you," Joe said, his chest throbbing from a curious mix of pleasure at her approval and the remembered pain from years ago. He'd been careful to stay away from any news of her, but he couldn't very well forget it was around that time she'd finish her internship. Even if she chose to do postgraduate training somewhere other than AIIMS, she wouldn't have gone far from Delhi where the jackass was. His former flatmate would've been playing doting husband to the woman Joe once loved. "I couldn't handle it." With his free arm, Joe gathered her against his side, holding the woman and the baby close in his embrace. "The dean wasn't happy. He even offered to call Goa Medical College so I could continue here."

"And?" she asked, craning her neck to look into his face.

"I wasn't thinking clearly at the time." Joe shrugged, making the baby mutter in irritation. "I thought maybe I didn't deserve it. After everything I did..."

He then talked about a surprise visitor who accompanied the cop to the Kochi flat: Bobby Noronha, the twenty-four-year-old daughter of Lazar Noronha. Around the time of Ruksana's death, young Bobby had been making plans which didn't include marriage. She was steeling her nerves to reject Joe when he did her a favour by vanishing. Daddy Noronha flew into a rage, spewing his venom at anyone within hearing distance. Bobby was horrified to learn the D'Acostas might've left Goa because of her, but she couldn't do anything about it until her father passed.

Then, Bobby hounded the diocese for the whereabouts of Fr Franco. Once the mission was over, the cops agreed to bring her to the D'Acostas. The young woman apologised profusely to Fr Franco for what she saw as her part in his quitting his calling. She was mollified only when assured there was no one who could understand the pain of escaping his family's past like Joe. Much to *his* relief, she announced she could do what she wanted with a guilt-free mind: join the Carmelite Sisters of St Teresa as a novitiate nun. The look on Fr Franco when he realised he'd been matchmaking between Joe and a woman promised to God was priceless. Even now, Joe snickered, remembering the sheer horror on the priest's face.

"I asked if she would mind putting in a word for me at the bank," Joe said to Anjali. "I needed a loan to open my practice." Bobby Noronha did one better. She took out the loan under her own name with her father's business as collateral. The amount was large enough to cover not only Joe's practice but also the home and the restaurant. Dev was ecstatic. He'd managed to scrape through high school but firmly rejected Joe's suggestion of at least a bachelor's degree. Dev was working in the canteen at the naval base for the second year when their ordeal came to an end. He claimed there were tears in the eyes of the naval officers when they learned the young assistant chef was quitting. Within months of the return of the D'Acostas to Goa, Café Ishq opened. "We're almost done paying it off."

"So that's why your name's not on any outstanding mortgages," Anjali stated, moving a little away.

"Yeah." Being back in Goa and knowing his family was all right brought a measure of peace to Joe's mind. If he didn't get to be a surgeon, he'd bloody well be the best general practitioner around. His patients would be well cared for. He'd lost Anjali, but she was safe. Perhaps she and Rishi decided they could be happy together. Sex, after all, was only one part of any romantic relationship. The jackass did have a lot in common with Anjali. "Some nights, it would get too much to handle. Then, I'd look at the sketch you did of me and pretend none of the bad stuff ever happened. I'd imagine what it would've been like if I looked for another way to take care of my family, if I returned to Delhi. In a couple of years, we'd have announced our engagement. We'd be married... living in your dream house... kids." He never imagined children until encountering the infant right now in his arms, but yeah...

"Joe," whimpered Anjali. Her hand came up, her fingertips caressing his jawline. The look in her eyes... the love, the longing... the quivering lips.

He bent down, intending to graze her mouth with his. Kicking his chubby legs, the baby whimpered. Both Joe and Anjali started. Laughing mildly, she stroked her son's back, soothing him. Joe gathered her back into his embrace. The three of them—Joe, Anjali, and the baby—swayed together to the song of the waves.

"Six-bedroom house," Joe whispered. "You can see and hear the ocean from the master bedroom. French windows with a rose garden right outside." He'd built the home she once said she wanted.

"Seriously?" Anjali asked.

"Seriously. My family thought I was crazy. I mean, we'd already borrowed a cartload of cash from Bobby. The house was... let's just say it was expensive, but the practice is doing well, and it should all be paid off in a couple of years."

"Poor girl," Anjali mused. "She must've felt really guilty."

"I was very clear I wasn't asking for any sort of blood money. Naidu had already told me *he'd* talk to the bank, but banks like to hear from rich people you're creditworthy. That's all I asked, I swear."

"Naidu?" Shaking her head, Anjali shrugged loose from Joe's hold. "*SP Naidu?*"

Noting with confusion she knew the cop's rank, Joe said, "He was a DSP at the time, but yeah, Naidu. He's now in charge of the INTERPOL wing at the CBI." The director of the bureau was the ex officio head of the wing, but it was run by an SP. "If you want to be accurate, you can call him the Pomeranian's owner/moonlighting agent/CBI officer-turned-INTERPOL agent. I'll introduce you sometime." By accident or by design on the part of the cop, he'd never met any of the circle of friends other than Joe and Rishi. When their partnership started, Joe made it very clear to Naidu that someday, Anjali would hear every detail of it. It was the only way to get her to consider taking Joe back. He laughed. "Maybe you won't want to be introduced. Dude heard us every time we..." Joe waggled his eyebrows.

Anjali didn't laugh or even cringe in embarrassment. "You never said his name," she said, her tone unnaturally high.

"I didn't?" Joe asked. He frowned at the pallor on her face. "Does it matter?"

Almost hyperventilating, she clapped a hand to her mouth. "I told you when you got to the temple office that the charity clinic is being investigated. The man who came to my office said he was from INTERPOL. He said both you and Rishi are suspected of being involved."

"So? They probably got the names from the old records. I'll call Naidu and ask him to talk to the investigating officer. We'll tell him there's no way in hell the Joshi Clinic is involved in any organ smuggling."

"You don't understand," cried Anjali. "The man who came to my office said he was SP Naidu. Why would he say he suspects you and Rishi when he already knows you're both innocent?"

"Son of a bitch," growled Joe. If it were really Naidu who went to the clinic, there was only one reason Joe could think of why the bastard would lie. There was only one reason the cop would avoid his partner of three years and go straight to Anjali. *She* was the suspect, not Rishi, not Joe.

Part XII

Chapter 34

Anjali kept her hands on the conference table, hoping the quaking inside her chest wouldn't show in her fingers. The last thing she needed this Monday was a surprise attack from the staff, but that's what she faced, and she was gonna deal with it all on her lonesome. There were no other Joshis, no friend/lawyer, no Joe.

After their conversation at the cove, Joe tried calling Naidu. Over the next twenty-four hours, it became clear the police officer was avoiding his former partner. Joe cancelled all his appointments for a week and hotfooted it to the airport to confront the cop in person at the INTERPOL office in Delhi. As Anjali's lawyer, Siddharth went with him. The two men were on their way back from the city, but last she heard, they didn't have any luck locating the cop. Siddharth swore he'd corner the deceptive fellow through his connections in law enforcement.

Anjali was yet to apprise her family of the new developments. There was so much background info they were going to find unbelievable that she needed time to collect her thoughts before talking to them.

Kokila arrived at the Fontainhas mansion over the weekend, and so did Meenu and Gauri. With Kokila's old home in Goa still undergoing renovations, all three ladies were staying with Anjali. Her friends would've been here to speak in support if they knew about the ambush.

In fact, Kokila was in the process of inviting the nurses she used to work with to dinner, hoping to build backing for the new CEO of the Joshi Charity Clinic. None of them had heard Joe's story or Rishi's. Anjali wasn't sure how much she could divulge. The two men needed to do it themselves, but by God, she was tired of keeping secrets for them. She couldn't even confess to her friends the full story of the breakdown she suffered the year before without bringing Rishi and Joe into it. The ladies had surely heard the rumours by now as had the employees at the clinic.

"I'm sorry, Anjali," finished the thirty-ish doctor at the far end of the conference table, his tone insultingly sympathetic. From whatever Anjali heard, he was liked by both staff and patients and was excellent at his job. "Times like these demand a stronger hand at the helm."

Anjali eyed the rest of the officeholders of the employee association—five in all—and her secretary, Chandekar. Glancing away from the moustachioed man, she asked the doctor, "May I ask where you heard the tale about the police investigation?" The staff members were reportedly worried about the official enquiry into the acquisition of generic medicines. *Thank God,* Anjali muttered in her mind. The fake story about violation of intellectual property law was bad enough, but if it came out the clinic was under scrutiny for something like organ harvesting... she couldn't even imagine the panic. Still, the cover was also meant to be kept secret.

"These things have a way of getting out," said the doctor. "I'm not going to get anyone into trouble for speaking up about what they see as a problem."

"Of course not," Anjali said, automatically. The Joshi Trust, the board of the charity clinic, Anjali, her secretary, the cops... apart from them, the only people who knew were Siddharth and Joe. Anjali hadn't mentioned any of it to her other friends. Not even Rishi knew what was going on—not the real problem *or* the cover story. The Joshis would've stayed mum about it. So would Siddharth and Joe. The police could've leaked the info, but Anjali couldn't see the purpose. The only possible sources left were Chandekar, the secretary, or one of the board members. Chandekar's actions were suspicious, but Mrs Braganza's brother was a board member, wasn't he? The nosy woman thought it her mission to mess with Anjali's life and sanity since the day she showed up at the mansion in Fontainhas.

"So you agree?" asked the doctor leading the ambush. Rumours were he was angling for a management position at one of the bigger hospitals, something he wouldn't get until he acquired more experience. The only reason he wouldn't have applied for the chief executive position at the charity clinic was the lack of a paycheck. He was reputed to be an excellent doctor. Plus, he was quite popular with the nursing staff and the patients, which was probably the reason he was chosen to confront the new CEO. None of it made the condescending smirk on his face any prettier.

"Agree with what?" Anjali asked, making a mental note to talk to the other doctors in the clinic about the self-important nincompoop. "Your suggestion that I step down to make way for someone sounder in their mind?" Leaning back in her chair, she casually crossed her legs. "I wonder," she mused, "if you realise how obnoxious you're coming across."

Uneasy mutters rose around the table. Flushing an angry red, the doctor said, "My behaviour is not the issue here. We're talking about your inability to handle the management of the clinic. Don't tell me you're not aware of the potential for trouble. I mean, you must've quit your job in Delhi for a reason. You couldn't cope with the pressure."

"I quit because..." Anjali took a deep breath. How in the world was she going to explain what happened without divulging Rishi's secrets? He'd said to her before he was hoping she would, but she couldn't take the decision out of his hands. Someday, her son would ask why she exposed his father to ridicule only to protect her own reputation, and she wouldn't have an answer to give. "I see no reason to give my explanations to you. Come to think of it, why are you here, talking to *me?* I would've thought you'd take it to the board." The members would then contact the Joshi Trust with their concerns. At the sudden silence, Anjali remarked, "The board would need actual evidence of my incompetence, wouldn't they? You couldn't find any, so you decided to try and pressure me."

"We thought we could get you to see reason," said the doctor, tone angry and stiff.

Forcing a grim laugh, Anjali said, "You're betting on humiliating me enough that I'll slink away in silence." The legs of her chair scraped the floor with a high-pitched sound as she stood. "No way. I'm not going anywhere. Feel free to present your case to the board."

Pulse pounding viciously at her temples, Anjali strode back to her office. Chandekar followed practically at her heels.

As soon as she plonked herself in the chair, he asked from the open door, "Can I get you something to drink? You need something to soothe your nerves."

What? Heading jerking up, Anjali glanced at the hallway behind him. A few employees were walking around, keeping their eyes carefully averted from the CEO's office. One of the X-Ray technicians was making a production of inspecting the gears on a wheelchair. Three women in white lab coats were gathered at the door of the phlebotomy lab. "I hope what you said doesn't mean you're used to seeing doctors drink in the clinic, Chandekarji," Anjali said, taking care to keep her tone pleasant but loud enough to be overheard. "Perhaps that explains the behaviour of the pompous idiot at the meeting."

There was a subdued gasp from outside, followed by a couple of titters. Noting the lack of surprise at the mention of a meeting, Anjali sat back. So the morning's ambush wasn't exactly a secret. How did Chandekar fail to hear of it? How did he neglect to give his boss warning of what was about to happen? Even if he didn't leak the info about the investigation into the violation of intellectual property law, he knew the news reached the staff and did not notify her.

"I meant chai or coffee," Chandekar responded, shoulders hunched in deference.

Anjali huffed. Maybe he *didn't* know what the employees were up to. He kept reminding her he'd been working there for years, but it meant nothing if the staff worried he'd rat them out to the CEO. Holding up both hands, she said, "Sorry. I was... I *will* take the chai. Also, Chandekarji? I need you to call a townhall."

"Huh?"

"Townhall," she repeated. "You know, where all the employees are invited to hear me speak and ask questions."

"Do you think that's a good idea?" the secretary asked, patting his moustache. "Madam, you should take my advice and allow someone who's been here for a while to sit in on the dealings with the cops. This morning's meeting, for instance. If they heard from *me* we were taking care of things, it wouldn't have gone so badly. I've been here a long time, and they trust me."

If they trusted him, they'd have told him about the meeting. Which again brought Anjali back to why he never breathed a word about the planned attack. "Great point, Chandekarji," she said. Now that the news went public, she would've taken the recommendation, hoping to build the same level of trust with the employees as time went by. Unfortunately, they weren't dealing with pharmaceutical crimes. Plus, if Joe's hunch were accurate, Anjali was the one under suspicion. Nope, no one else from the clinic was going to hear of it, let alone Chandekar who acted as though Anjali were a cross between an incompetent loon and a mad dictator. "I'll give it some thought. Meanwhile, please make arrangements for the townhall."

As soon as he left, Anjali strode to the door and closed it, leaning her forehead against the wood panels. She'd purposely thrown the taunt about the doctor from the meeting drinking at work, but God, she was tempted to do exactly that. The idea that the cops might be investigating her for organ smuggling was laughable. Joe was wrong. He had to be. Still, she couldn't find any other reason for the INTERPOL fellow to have lied to her.

A shrill ring interrupted her thoughts. Her phone... it was in the purse she'd stuffed into the drawer before the meeting. "Hello," she said into the device, walking to the window with it.

"Anju," came Kiki's excited voice. "Are you all right? One of the nurses I called this morning said something about an emergency meeting."

Anjali snorted. "More like a sneak attack. Umm... did your friend say why they wanted the meeting?"

"Yeah," Meenakshi said from the background. The women were clearly gathered around the speakerphone. "The cops need to stop harassing you. They have no idea what a struggle it is to get medicines to patients. Plus, your crazy neighbour lady's starting trouble, right?" Anjali had updated the women in her group on La Braganza's firm belief the Joshi ladies were keeping some kind of a male harem in the Fontainhas mansion.

Anjali wished those were her only problems! "The staff doesn't believe I can handle the job," she said, morosely. She'd called the townhall, hoping Kokila would be able to sway enough employees to her side, but how were

Anjali's friends going to help when they didn't know exactly why no one at the clinic believed she was up to the job? They'd surely heard rumours about her breakdown, and Kokila firmly designated it as gossip against a divorcée. Anjali needed to tell them—tell everyone—the truth, but how did she even begin to explain the last few months of her life without giving away Rishi's secrets? "Let's talk about it tonight. I'm going to invite Rishi to dinner." She needed to convince him to open up to at least their friends about his sexuality, if not the rest of the world. Yeah, coming out was a deeply personal choice, but his refusal kept the world thinking she went off her rocker for no reason, darn it. Anjali could spend the rest of her friggin' life claiming it was a one-time thing brought on by extreme stress, but no one would believe her without Rishi's support, not even those closest to her.

"Are you calling him for dinner at Joe's?" asked Kokila.

"Heh? What do you mean?"

Kokila clucked. "Girl, check your messages. Sid phoned and told all of us to go to Joe's house in the evening. I'm sure Rishi's already invited. *You* weren't picking up."

Anjali always left her phone in her purse, and the purse was usually stowed in the drawer. Slightly dazed, she nodded. Dinner at Joe's place?

The story he'd told in the temple office... he was lucky to be still alive. If she hadn't been so shocked, she'd have beat him to death with her bare fists for the sheer stupidity. *Argh.* The strength of will it must've taken to admit his folly and face down the criminals, thinking he'd pay for it with his life... the courage he must've needed to work with the crooks day after day, wearing a wire... Anjali's insides quaked in utter terror, imagining all the ways his mission could've gone wrong. She'd have never known it if he were killed.

Her heart bled in pain for the time they lost. One mistake, and he couldn't return. While she'd been hating the fact he ever breathed, he was fighting to stay alive, battling the criminals who would've slaughtered her and his family in a heartbeat. She curled up on her side of the bed every night of the last eleven years, willing herself to forget, not knowing the memory of her haunted his sleep.

She clung to his arm, wanting to never let him out of her sight. In his eyes, she saw the pent up longing of an entire decade, waiting to erupt. Every bit of her own longing for the man came surging to the surface. She needed to touch him... kiss him... then, he mentioned the INTERPOL agent's name.

If he hadn't, what would they have done that night? Instead of conferencing with Siddharth at the Fontainhas mansion, would she and Joe have gone to the home he built for her? Would they have kissed away each other's tears? Unwilling to waste even a moment, would they have loved madly until the sun came up?

The shock from the idea that she might be under investigation yanked away the cobwebby fog of love and desire clouding her senses. Joe never lied to her, and his story held the ring of truth, but Anjali didn't trust herself where he was concerned. Ignoring the acute yearning to rush into his arms, she asked Siddharth, lawyer/police psychiatrist, to independently verify the information from Joe. The men spent the last few days together in their futile search for the INTERPOL officer. Joe's former partner might be hiding, but Siddharth possessed extensive connections in law enforcement and could easily ferret out lies.

Still, when Anjali was exiting her car outside Joe's secluded clifftop home, she couldn't stop her heart from racing in almost panicky excitement. Tucking her yellow-framed sunglasses into the matching purse, she relished the feel of the grass-scented breeze against her face. Joe wasn't kidding when he said he'd built her dream house. There were mossy rocks in the yard interspersed between wild clusters of flowering plants and a wood pallet trail leading from the driveway to the back of the residence. The house was structured like a two-storeyed chalet with stone walls and slate tiles on the roof. The setting sun glinted off the glass windows, and the gentle roar of the ocean accompanied the flight of the squawking seagulls.

Meenakshi and Gauri climbed out of Siddharth's rental car, with him complaining about Meenakshi's choice of music. Apparently, there was an unwritten law which said the one at the wheel got to pick the songs. Shaking her head, Kokila slammed the passenger door of Anjali's yellow Beetle and marched to the house. Before she could ring the bell, the door was flung open, and she was enveloped in a bear hug.

After a few seconds, Kokila shrugged loose from Joe's hug and punched him on the shoulder. "I want to hear why——" she shouted. Brushing away tears with her knuckles, she hugged him back before stepping away. "I still want to hear why," she said. "But it's good to see you, you... you..."

With a teary laugh of his own, Joe kissed her on the forehead. "I swear I'll tell you everything."

When he moved past Kokila to greet Siddharth, Anjali nearly swallowed her tongue. God, she was in bad shape if one glimpse of Joe was enough to reduce her to a hormonal mess. He did look good in the faded denim combo. With sleeves rolled up and his black-rimmed glasses, he was every inch the sexy professor.

Self-consciously, she smoothed down her black cotton frock. Bit more formal than the rest of the group, especially with the matching gauzy scarf, but she was going to wear what she wanted, not what someone else believed was appropriate.

Joe and Siddharth performed a weird and elaborate handshake that had Meenakshi muttering, "Dorks." Shoving Siddharth aside, Joe went to Meenakshi and pulled her into a hug. When he let go, she moved her big, butterfly glasses to wipe the tears from her eyes. "You'd better have a good reason," she warned, shaking a finger in his face.

Anjali hung back, waiting for Joe to welcome Gauri, the woman who'd been engaged to his best friend. Gauri's curls were tamed into a braid, and her face hadn't changed much in the last eleven years, but the sparkle never returned to her eyes since Nikhil's death. For the longest time, she wouldn't even speak, barely eating enough to keep herself alive. When she resumed talking, it was only the minimum required. She declined all offers by AIIMS to let her complete the six weeks of internship remaining to complete her degree. Eventually, she went to work in a call centre.

Visibly swallowing, Joe pushed the square-rimmed glasses up his nose. "Hey, girl," he said, shoving his hands into his pockets.

Gauri stared unblinkingly for a moment or two before pivoting on her heel. "I wanna go home," she said, both face and voice stony.

"Hear him out—" started Siddharth.

Eyes fixed on the hood of Siddharth's car, Gauri enunciated, "I want to go home."

"Gauri, please," Anjali begged.

Flinging up a hand, Gauri called, "Meenu? You said we'd leave if I felt uncomfortable. I want to leave now." In the first couple of years after Nikhil's passing, Gauri's parents had fallen apart, coping with their silent older daughter. Meenakshi moved back home after her degree from AIIMS, not bothering to apply for the nuclear medicine subspecialisation she so badly wanted. Instead, she did her training in radiology in a medical college closer to home. She'd since turned into the sole caretaker for the entire family.

Jogging around to face Gauri, Joe said, his tone urgent, "I know what I did was unforgivable, but it wasn't on purpose. You have no idea how many times I wanted to... how many times I picked the phone... but I couldn't. Please, Gauri? Gimme a chance to explain."

"Yeah, let him explain," jeered a familiar voice. Opening one of the back doors of Siddharth's car, Rishi got out, the beard Anjali saw on him a couple of days ago still on his face. He was also dressed casually in jeans and a black tee.

No Farhan. Siddharth had said he'd pick up Rishi from the Marriott on the way to dinner, and Anjali was hoping he'd bring his boyfriend. She closed her eyes in disappointment. Rishi wasn't prepared for even his friends to know his secrets, let alone the rest of the world.

Mouth twisting in a sneer, Rishi continued, "I want to hear what kind of lies he's fed Anju this time."

Joe swung towards his former flatmate. "You——"

"Stop," ordered Siddharth. "Rishi, man. Joe's told *me* what happened, and what's more, he knows I can verify everything. You two have things to thrash out, but..." Siddharth glanced in Anjali's direction. "Right now, I suggest you get along for *her* sake." Softening his voice, he turned to Gauri. "I'm not kidding. This is important for Anju."

He led Gauri inside. Her face was still stiff, but she didn't object.

As the rest followed Gauri and Siddharth into the house, Anjali dawdled, staring at the doorstep. A hand appeared in her field of vision. When she glanced up, the gang was milling around the living room a few feet behind Joe, not even making a pretence of not watching.

Devilment writ all across his face, Joe's hot gaze sauntered over her eyes and nose and mouth, down her neck to the top of her breasts. Inside her stilettos, her toes curled.

Anjali drew her brows together. *Doing this on purpose, are we?* Quite casually, she touched the tip of her tongue to the corner of her mouth—right where the birthmark was. At his sudden, sharp intake of air, she bit back a smirk.

414

"*Touché.*" Voice loud enough for only her to hear, Joe murmured, "I'd say welcome home, but—"

"But what?" she asked.

"You left the little man behind," Joe said, still holding out his hand. "So you're not planning to stay."

Was this the same guy who took forever to confess his attraction? "Moving fast, aren't you?" she mumbled, tucking a lock of her hair behind her ear and feigning unawareness of the interested expressions on their friends' faces.

"Got to, sundari. I have eleven years to make up for." Looking thoughtful, Joe added, "Maybe you *should* wait a couple of weeks. We need to child-proof the house."

With the back of her hand, Anjali smothered an unexpected giggle. "Are you trying to bribe me, by chance?"

"Yes," he admitted, instantly. "Also, I want the baby to grow up knowing this is his home... that I'm his..." Swallowing hard, Joe finished, "...whatever you want him to call me."

Struggling to control the sudden gush of gooey warmth in her heart, she said, "I need time. The last few days... there's a lot to process." The story she heard from Joe was not the only thing occupying her mind. For eleven years, Anjali blamed his insecurities for their breakup, but *her* immaturity and impulsiveness were also part of what drove them apart. She'd simply refused to see his point of view. If she did, he might've called her when things went south. Yeah, he was responsible for his own choices, but her me-me attitude certainly didn't help. The same immaturity caused her to jump into marriage with her gay friend. She never thought through the lifetime implications of the relationship, didn't consider its impact on all involved. Trying to compensate—maintaining the façade of perfection—brought her to the lowest point in her life. Anjali would not repeat the mistakes of her past. She was no longer that naïve and thoughtless girl to leap without looking hard. "I'm not... *we're* not the same people anymore. We both need to think about this."

The twenty-four-year-old who left his girlfriend behind was a boy... arrogant, hot-headed, ambitious... loving, loyal, kind... sexily weird... but a boy. The Joe who stood in front of her today was a man. Still loyal, still loving, still kind. Still a little weird and still über sexy. But his arrogance morphed into the strength he needed to defeat the crime ring. His hot-headedness changed into a fierce need to protect those he loved—his family, his lover, his friends. His ambition was now purpose—he did everything he could to keep his patients safe during the INTERPOL mission. Joe never completed his surgical training, but he was determined his patients would get the best possible care they could ever ask for.

The girl Anjali used to be tumbled headlong into love with the boy, and the woman— *Careful,* she admonished herself. *Don't rush things.*

"So let's get to know each other once more," Joe urged, oblivious to her tumultuous thoughts. "Take all the time you need. I can wait... one week, one month, one year, forever, whatever. Just don't ask me to go away."

Anjali bit her lip hard, but she couldn't stop her hand from reaching for his. With their fingers intertwined, she took her first step into the house.

The nearest neighbour was at the foot of the hill and nowhere close enough to overhear the conversation in the D'Acosta home. Scher, Joe's canine companion, was staying with Fr Franco for the night—something about the kids at the church orphanage enjoying their doggie visitor. The rest of the D'Acostas were also not expected back until the next day. No one was around to see Joe's friends from Delhi sit stiffly in the large and airy dining hall, drinking cold beer and munching on roasted clam and crab masala from Café Ishq. Still, there wasn't much talk for the first few minutes.

"This is too big for us," Kokila announced, finally. "We're too used to the flat in Delhi."

With a great deal of clattering and laughter, the dishes were moved to the large desk in Joe's home office. Anjali stayed at one end of the blue suede sofa, Rishi next to her. She wished she'd brought the baby with her. Not because of what Joe said; poor Rishi hadn't seen his son in weeks. Meenakshi and Kokila sandwiched Gauri on the second sofa. Joe was kept busy, topping drinks and refilling plates.

Siddharth wandered around, peering through the glass windows lining one wall and inspecting the books arranged neatly on the wooden shelves. He stopped at a cubby with half a dozen hardbacks and smiled. "You have good taste."

"I want your autograph on all of them," Joe said.

"Is that my—" Kokila got up to scrutinise the photographs hanging on the wall. Poking a finger at one, she said, "My wedding picture from the newspaper announcement." She went to the next. "Look, Meenu. It's your graduation picture."

All of them went to check. There were newspaper clippings detailing Siddharth's achievements, Meenakshi's article from some radiology journal, Gauri and Nikhil's engagement photographs, and the announcement of Kokila's appointment as the youngest ever chief nursing officer at her hospital. The pride of place was occupied by a photograph of Joe and Nikhil in football tees, their arms thrown over each other's shoulders. Joe was muddy and dishevelled, and there was blood caked above his lip. One side of Nikhil was cut off as though—

"Damned bastard," Rishi swore, tone angry and hurt. "You cut me out."

"What did you think I was going to do?" Joe snapped. "Build a temple in your name?"

There were mutters from among the group in the room. "Stop, please," Anjali begged.

Running a quick glance over all the pictures, Rishi taunted her, "Not a single reminder of you, either."

"I don't need photographs to remind me of Anju," said Joe. "She understands I don't blame her for wanting a life. But you..." He bared his teeth at his former flatmate. "There wasn't much you didn't know about me. Hell, I knew you better than your family. We shared a flat for almost three effing years. *And how long did it take you to make a move on her? A week? Two weeks?*"

"How long did it take you to call after Nikhil's death?" snapped back Rishi. "Should I tell you how long I... we... waited, hoping you'd call? Poor Anju... if you hadn't run into her at the restaurant, she'd have never known what happened to you."

"Enough," said Siddharth, but the combatants weren't listening. Kokila muttered in annoyance, and Meenakshi clapped a hand to her forehead, but Gauri was simply staring at the scene, her eyes wide.

"How the bloody hell could I call?" Joe shouted. Face alarmingly red, he glanced around the room. "I needed to stay away from all of them... because of *you,* jackass. Because I didn't want to hear anything about you playing house with *my* girlfriend."

"Oh, God," moaned Anjali.

Meenakshi groaned. "Stop it, you two. My sister's having a rough enough time as it is."

Instantly, the two warring men turned to Gauri, incredible guilt on their faces. Face dark with annoyance, Meenakshi prodded her sister to the sofa, and Anjali followed.

Not giving the two former flatmates time to do more than mumble apologies, Siddharth said, "Let's sit. There's something we need to discuss. Kiki, you're planning to be at Anju's townhall meeting. Before it takes place, we need to put together info from Joe and Rishi and figure out what the hell is going on."

When Siddharth returned to the Joshi mansion from Delhi, he'd informed Anjali they needed to pool information if they hoped to get to the bottom of things. Since Naidu was plainly disinclined to explain why he was investigating Anjali, Joe stated he was under no obligation to keep secrets and risk her life and freedom. He was going to put his story together with whatever Rishi had. Kokila and the rest of the ladies were helping Anjali with the clinic, so they needed to know, as well.

"Townhall?" Rishi asked, not budging from his position near the photographs. "What do you mean?"

"Trouble at the clinic," Anjali muttered.

Kokila snorted and plonked back onto the sofa with a plate piled high with roasted clam. "I'd say there's trouble, but the clinic staff refuses to change the way they've been doing things. Instead, they're trying to blame Anju for the problems."

"How can they blame *you?*" Rishi asked. "You got there only a few weeks ago!"

Rolling her eyes, Kokila said, "Doesn't matter when she got there. She's getting divorced which proves she ain't perfect; that's enough for some people to dismiss her. Joe has nothing to do with it except in Mrs Braganza's dirty mind."

Anjali smiled in gratitude. Loyal, loyal Kokila. She simply assumed the stupid gossip about her friend's mental condition was untrue.

"I don't get it," Joe said, frowning. "I thought the townhall was only about getting the staff to trust Anju. The divorce is her personal problem. What does the clinic have to do with it?"

"I don't get it, either," said Rishi. "And who's Mrs Braganza?"

419

The ladies in the group were aware of the malicious talk about Anjali's mental state but not Joe or Rishi. Joe knew nothing of the rough time Anjali faced over the last year. How could he when he deliberately stayed away from any news of her? She hadn't even remembered to bring it up at their previous encounter. Rishi... she doubted he'd paid any attention to the whispers about his soon-to-be-ex-wife, but he was the only one who could shut down all gossip... if he so chose.

"Dudes," snapped Meenakshi. "People are saying Anju went off her rocker, and that's why she filed for divorce. One of Kiki's old acquaintances said there's talk *Rishi* wanted the divorce because of Anju's mental health. Mrs Braganza is Anju's neighbour in Fontainhas... a nosy bitch who thinks Anju's getting it on with every man she meets, including Joe. The Braganza woman's brother's a board member at the clinic, so she's got to be the one who spread the rumour. The clinic staff told Anju to her face they don't think she can handle the job."

Cheeks suddenly pale, Rishi glanced between Anjali and the rest.

Walking around the desk to his swivel chair, Joe swore. "They need to be put in their places. Or did they find out about—" With a wary look, he stopped and eyed the people in the room.

No, the employees were blissfully ignorant of the organ-smuggling case, but the combination of the pharma crime rumour and gossip about Anjali was bad enough to make them demand a new CEO. Meenakshi, Kokila, and Gauri didn't know anything about the INTERPOL case yet. Even Rishi knew only that he was being blackmailed, not the rest of the story.

Slouching against the wall, Siddharth groaned. "Too many secrets."

Silently, Anjali agreed. She needed to come clean—not only about the breakdown which was the cause of all rumours but also about the legal problems. Joe and Siddharth had already decided to risk INTERPOL's wrath and divulge the details they possessed, but the rest... Anjali glanced at her ex-husband. Without Rishi's cooperation, how was she ever going to set the record straight about their personal problems?

"Is this true, Anju?" Rishi asked, still white-faced. "Do people think *I'm* divorcing *you* because..." When she didn't say anything in response, he cursed hard. "Why don't you simply tell everyone what's been going on? You don't have to do me any bloody favours by keeping quiet."

"I'm also not going to do you the favour of making your decision for you," Anjali said, her voice tight. "What if my child asks me someday why I did it? Nuh-huh." She shook her head. "The story's not mine alone to tell."

"What story?" asked Meenakshi, glancing between Rishi and Anjali.

For a couple of moments, Anjali thought Rishi wouldn't say anything. She gritted her teeth in frustration. The law was no longer an impediment. The blackmailer issue—which was really an INTERPOL matter even if he didn't know it yet—shouldn't have stopped him from acknowledging his sexuality. His family, of course. Anjali had assured her ex-husband over and over she'd go to the extent of refusing to let the Rastogi elders meet their grandson if they didn't treat Rishi with respect, but he couldn't somehow get beyond the fear of losing them. Forget what he was doing to her, he couldn't seem to see he'd eventually lose Farhan. How long would a lover be content to stay in the shadows?

She looked towards the swivel chair behind the desk where Joe was. Anjali once promised to give him a total of three years until the end of his junior residency, but she'd reached the limits of her tolerance by the time he disappeared fifteen months into their romance. Farhan was already at two years and more.

"There's no story," Rishi finally muttered, his eyes darting to his former flatmate. "Only the truth of how I nearly killed Anju."

Chapter 35

2011

Rishi recited the last line of the Urdu *shayari*—poetry—before grabbing Anjali's hand from the top of the dining table and kissing her knuckles. Oohs and aahs went up from the gathered Joshis. It was her mother's birthday, and the one Joshi brother who was currently travelling in India—Anjali's Skinwalla Uncle who lived in L.A. with his partner and their children—was present to help the family celebrate it. Anjali and Rishi flew in from Delhi. Twenty-year-old Vikram Joshi, engineering student, was also there, but he was staring at his phone. No one at the table was objecting to his behaviour.

"*Saale saab*," called Rishi, addressing Vikram as Mr Brother-in-law. "Pay some attention to your family."

The kid looked up, anger in his glare. "I already wished Mom a happy birthday," Vikram mumbled. "She was talking to *you* at the time. Dunno if she heard me."

His parents were smiling happily at their daughter and her husband. At Vikram's remark, they turned as one to him. "Of course, I heard," exclaimed Rattan Joshi, Anjali's mother. "Thank you."

Shrugging dismissively, Vikram returned to his phone.

Bloody idiot, Rishi muttered in his mind. "People are going to think you're a sociopath."

The sudden tension in Vikram's shoulders indicated he'd heard the comment, but he didn't glance up. Instead, he shoved his chair back and muttered he was returning to the men's hostel in IIT. Apparently, Vikram's best friend—the finance minister's son—would soon be returning from visiting his father, and they were going to a cricket match. The smile on Rattan Joshi's face dimmed ever so slightly, but she didn't reprimand Rishi or her son.

Nor did Pratap Joshi, Anjali and Vikram's father. Both the Joshi parents stared worriedly after Vikram as he strode towards the front door, but the boy seemed utterly oblivious to their concern.

Later, in the privacy of their room, Rishi asked Anjali, "What is *up* with Vikram? The privileged ass doesn't seem to get how good he has it. I mean, look at your parents... your uncle..."

There was the same weird mix of incredible contentment and extreme restlessness within Rishi's ribcage he always felt when in the Joshi household. He badly wanted to ask Anjali's uncle about his life. It might have been the sappiest idea Rishi ever had, but he wanted to hear how the dermatologist met his partner of many decades, how they managed their family of five adopted children. If Rishi ever dared vocalise his thoughts, the Joshis would recognise his marriage to Anjali for the sham it was.

No. Rishi shook his head. Their marriage of six months was no sham. Sex wasn't everything. He and Anjali were a perfect match in every other way. There was a comfort in returning to their flat in the postgraduate hostel in the evenings. Visiting art galleries on weekends, arguing over music, making coffee for each other during exams... there was a bond between him and Anjali Rishi didn't know how to describe... not romantic, but something more than friendship.

"I've stopped trying to figure out Vikram," Anjali muttered, bringing Rishi back to the here and now. She was staring out the window. "You know, Skinwalla Uncle said he'd help Vikram get a job in Silicon Valley. He said no. He wants to start his own business someday."

"So?" Rishi asked, settling into the pillows piled on the bed. "Is it a problem?"

Turning from the ocean view outside the window, Anjali said, "No, not a problem. I was simply... Vikram wants to do it all himself. It won't be easy, but he made it clear he doesn't want anyone's help. He might fail, but he'll do exactly what he wants in life. I'm beginning to feel he doesn't care what anyone thinks of him."

Her tone was admiring... almost awed. Rishi snorted. "Easy to fail when he has parents like yours to pick him back up." Watching her mild smile fade, he sat up. "Problem?"

"No," she muttered. "Remembered something."

Yeah, and he could guess what. Joe's name hadn't crossed Anjali's lips since the day she tied the knot with Rishi, but every now and then, there would be melancholy washing over her face. Searching his mind for a way to divert her attention, Rishi asked, "Are you worried about going straight to anaesthesiology? You don't have to, you know."

From the day Anjali started her clinical rotations, she complained constantly about the ridiculous way some people thought hospitals should be run. She was considering working as a general practitioner after her internship, perhaps doing a hospital management course once she got a little experience under her belt. Then, at one of their dinners with the Rastogi parents, Rishi's father brought up the offer from the CEO of a pricey hospital chain. They'd sign Rishi and Anjali on as a couple, provided she completed anaesthesiology within a reasonable timeframe.

Rishi's ma firmly declared management was not appropriate for women who intended to be mothers someday. As an anaesthesiologist, Anjali would work shifts, and not a minute more than the set time.

Anjali shrugged. "Your parents are correct. We're going to want children at some point. It's easier if the mother works regular hours."

"But—"

"It's all right, Rishi. I don't dislike anaesthesiology, and hospital administration is not something I'm especially sure of. What would be the point of antagonising your parents by refusing to accept their advice?"

Rishi huffed. "You bend over backwards to please them. You don't need to; they already adore you."

"They adore who they think I am," Anjali corrected. "The girl who loves their son. I don't want to disappoint them. You know... when we decided to get married for real, I never thought about how it would affect our families. I was too busy wallowing in self-pity."

"You feel guilty now," Rishi stated.

"Don't you?" With a mischievous grin, she asked, "How many hours did you spend looking for the right poem to recite at dinner?"

Rishi laughed. "Your mom and dad love you. It makes them happy to know you're loved." He settled back into the pillows. "I didn't spend two hours on the poem because I felt guilty. I'm happy being married to you... being your parents' son-in-law. I hope you're happy, too. Life's good... perfect."

Anjali seemed about to say something, but her grin suddenly faded. Her hand went to her forehead, and with a mewl, she pinched the top of her nose.

"Headache, again?" Rishi asked. "You need sleep." He patted her side of the bed.

One step forward, and she stumbled, catching herself on the back of an armchair before she fell. When Rishi swung his feet out of bed, she raised a hand. "I'm all right. I should've looked where I was going."

Days blended together; months flew by. In December 2013, Rishi read the news that the supreme court of India set aside the 2009 Delhi High Court judgement decriminalising gay sex. Anjali didn't say a word about it, but she couldn't have missed the headlines, the threats from local politicians to arrest the same-sex partners of foreign diplomats. Rishi was safe with Anjali as his wife. She was his shield from everything and everybody—the law, his family, society.

For the first few years of their marriage, they used the excuse of their training to stay in the postgraduate hostel on the AIIMS campus. Then came a summer when there were no excuses left. Training was done, and they were expected to move to the family home to live with the Rastogi parents as was the custom in India.

The first time Rishi noticed the change in Anjali was when she came out from the bathroom one day, twisting her dark brown locks into some sort of fancy knot at the nape of her neck. "When did you stop cutting your hair?" he asked, buttoning his blazer. All through her years in AIIMS, she'd sported a shoulder-length do. Come to think of it, her bangs were no longer obvious.

"Few months ago," she muttered. "Rishi, can you zip me up?"

Obliging instantly, he asked, "Are you going for a new look or something?" The mid-calf, chiffon dress in dusty red was pretty but not really her style. She tended to go for happy colours and clean lines. The casually fashionable outfits she preferred were damned expensive, especially the shoes. Anjali was the proud possessor of a huge collection of shoes, all of them with painfully high heels.

"I'm almost twenty-seven. I need to dress my age."

Rishi chuckled. "You sound like—" Laughter turning into a frown, he asked, "Did my mother ask you to wear this?"

"Uhh... no." Grabbing the matching purse from the side table, Anjali said, "Let's go. We don't want to be the last ones to walk into the banquet hall."

"You don't need to lie to me," Rishi said.

She didn't pretend not to understand. "It's such a small thing. Not worth arguing over."

"But—"

"Plus, gossip gets around. Someone says something about my clothes to your mother. She tells me what's going on. I refuse to change. People start

426

saying there's trouble in paradise. You *know* how it goes." Smiling slightly, Anjali walked to the door. "You and I have a reputation to maintain: the ideal couple. Let's not mess it up over something silly like clothes."

Raking his hair with his fingers, Rishi followed her to the car, but the itch of annoyance within his skull persisted through the night.

The banquet hall, the hospital, the family home... the right kind of clothes, the right social circle, the right way to speak to elders. The smile on Anjali's face never dimmed, not even in the comfortable company of her old friends. It was never "anything worth starting a fight about."

"I can't take this, anymore," he exclaimed one day, flying back from visiting Gauri and Meenakshi. "This is not you. We were with Gauri and Meenu, for God's sake! You didn't need to put on an act." She could've forgotten her in-laws' dictates for one bloody weekend and worn what she wanted or gone with Meenakshi to the Sunburn Music Festival in Pune. The old Anjali wouldn't have pretended she'd grown beyond dancing at electronic music shows.

Anjali kept her eyes on the clouds outside the plane window. "What do you suggest I do?" she asked, tone more curious than anything else. "Tell your parents to back off? It will hurt them so badly, and we've already made fools out of them. Or should I switch on and off depending on who we're with?"

"I don't mean for you to start a fight with Papa and Ma, but you could... when you're around your own family..."

"I'll have to be the exact same person with the rest of our social circle as I am with your parents, or people will know we're frauds... that we were never the ideal couple... we'll be mocked behind our backs. Our families will be mocked. I won't have it, Rishi. Plus, gossip will eventually get to your father and mother. End result, we'll be adding insult to the injury we already inflicted." Anjali turned to face him. "If you're suggesting I behave differently only in Mumbai... what will happen when my parents see me with someone else? Your relatives, our colleagues, the people we know in Delhi? Don't you think my mom and dad will pick up something's off? Right now, they believe I'm happy the way I am. They believe we have a perfect marriage." She winced as though in pain. "If they see I'm different around other people, they're going to start worrying. The truth will somehow come out... about you, about me. My family will know we lied to them for years... they'll be terribly hurt... I can't let it happen."

"But—" Scowling in frustration, Rishi punched the armrest of his seat a time or two.

"No buts." She patted his hand. "Honestly... it doesn't bother me much."

"How can it possibly not?"

Glancing back at the clouds, Anjali murmured, "I know me, and so do you. Isn't it the same in your case?" When he didn't respond, she added, "In this world of six billion people, only you and I know the truth about each other. Kinda romantic if you think about it."

Despite himself, he laughed a little at the comment. "What do you know? We *are* the ideal couple."

Everyone who knew them would've agreed.

Anjali was off with Rishi's ma at some gossip columnist's book release party one day when Rishi accompanied his father to the weekly golf game with the old man's cronies.

"I'm going to nominate your son for a seat on the hospital board," the CEO said to Rishi's papa, thwacking the golf ball hard enough to pulverise it. The hospital executive squinted across the putting green of the ultra-restrictive club much as the Mughal emperors whose monuments were scattered across the course might have glared at an unfortunate animal slated to be game.

"Is that so?" asked Papa. "No doubt he'll do well."

428

"No doubt," agreed the CEO. He nodded at Rishi. "The organisation needs fresh blood in leadership positions. Young people like you and your wife will be the faces of new India—educated, globalised couple with traditional values." The executive tipped his cap at Rishi's father. "You raised a son to be proud of, Rastogiji."

Driving back home in his new Lexus, Rishi stayed mostly quiet as Papa listed the VIPs he'd need to impress if he wanted to win the spot on the board. "Anjali will need to go with you," Papa stated.

"Her parents," Rishi muttered.

Papa shook his head. "It's not merely about the Joshis and their connections. Anjali knows how to project the right image. I'll tell you something I didn't want to before. When I met the family, I harboured some doubts. Not about the pedigree but their outlook on life. I wasn't sure... yet Anjali has fit so beautifully into the role of your wife. She's adjusted very well with *our* family. You made the right choice, betay."

Later in the evening, Anjali nodded dutifully to Papa's instructions before excusing herself to go to bed.

Watching her leave, Rishi's ma happily remarked, "Thank God for Anju. One of the ladies at the book release was saying her nephew came out as gay. It was such a mess. The boy's sister's wedding got cancelled. People were sending threatening letters to the parents. I mean, these kids don't realise how much such things affect the entire family."

Papa held up a hand. "There's no need to rehash old stuff now."

"But—" started Ma, leaning forwards with her elbows on the dining table.

"I understand what you're saying," said Papa, tone firm. "*We* need to realise young people make mistakes. The important thing is our son recognised it in time and fixed it." With a hint of moisture in his eyes, the old gent continued, "Still, it *is* good to know we didn't go wrong in our children's

429

upbringing. Not every parent gets to say it. Betay, you won't understand how happy you've made us until you have a child of your own."

Two weeks later when Anjali chose a champagne-coloured cocktail dress and matching flats for their dinner with a board member, Rishi didn't object.

His seat on the board meant he travelled frequently to the other hospitals in the network, including the one in Mumbai. Plus, the VIP patients in India's largest metro sometimes requested him as surgeon. Visiting the Joshi residence in Cuffe Parade when he was in the city was no hardship for Rishi. Anjali's parents adored him. The young punk, Vikram, had completely moved out as soon as he finished college and got a job. He rarely visited the same time as Rishi, but even if Vikram were there, he could always be driven off by a cutting remark or two. He'd take his morose glares and return to his own flat in one of the shabbier neighbourhoods of Mumbai or to his friend's digs in upscale Colaba.

And Anjali... she appeared content when in Mumbai even if she maintained her persona with her family. There were the occasions when Rishi would spot puzzlement in her mother's eyes at Anjali's demeanour, but as soon as Rattan Joshi saw how lovingly her son-in-law treated her daughter, she'd nod in approval.

When they returned to Delhi, Anjali would go from being dutiful daughter to docile daughter-in-law. It wasn't until the summer after her twenty-ninth birthday that Rishi saw her flustered by his parents' demands.

They were all enjoying dinner at Delhi's priciest Italian restaurant before Papa and Ma flew to Dubai to stay with sister number three for a while. One of Papa's very good friends from his investment banking days was an Emirati who was suffering from Parkinson's disorder, and the gent wanted the company of his old buddies before the inevitable dementia set in. Rishi cannily suggested to his parents they take the chance to do some travelling, visiting the three daughters scattered around the world. The senior Rastogis would spend a year or two in the U.A.E.

Terrible thing to do, to feel relieved at the absence of his parents, but Rishi craved one bloody evening where he didn't have to watch Anjali play the role of devoted wife and obedient daughter-in-law. Except, Mr and Mrs Investment Banker were determined to remote control their son. "High time you two started thinking about children," Ma said, decisively.

"Can we please not do this here?" Rishi asked, dabbing his mouth with a napkin and glancing at the other diners. With a sideways peek at Anjali's red face, he added, "You're embarrassing her."

Papa laughed. "What's so embarrassing about it? Arrey, we're your parents. We want to see grandchildren. I'm sure everyone in this restaurant will understand our feelings."

Sitting next to Anjali on the bed at night, Rishi insisted, "It's not as if we never did it before. We simply have to make sure the timing's right."

She tilted her head, throwing an anxious glance at him. "Are you sure, Rishi? I mean, I know I want kids. But you need to be ready, too. We can't let ourselves be pressured into this."

Laughing mildly, Rishi asked, "What about the 'ideal couple' shit?"

Anjali stuck her tongue out, giving him a glimpse of the girl he'd met so long ago in the physiology lab. "Having a child is not a small decision. You can't change your mind. Once a daddy, always a daddy."

Guffawing outright, he teased, "I wasn't aware of it." He swatted off her punches and continued, "I *am* ready. I like the idea of a little girl calling me papa."

"Could be a boy."

431

"Doesn't matter." Whichever the gender, Rishi was sure of one thing: he'd love the little scrap, protect him or her from every hurt the universe might hurl. "I want this, Anju. I want a child."

✳✳✳

December 24, 2017

"Hold on, Anju," Rishi said into his phone. "Someone's at the door." He closed the web browser before calling, "Come in." He didn't need the staff at the Mumbai hospital to see what he was looking at online. Most knew his wife's family, and the gossip would reach the Joshis before his return flight landed in Delhi. Anjali's parents would know their son-in-law was checking out fertility clinics.

The door opened, letting in one of the junior doctors. "The patient's wife wants a moment with you before the surgery." The junior grimaced. "She'd like you to talk to a cousin of hers who's a physician in the U.S."

Normally, Rishi didn't mind speaking to the second wives of third cousins of an in-law if it gave the patient some comfort. The politician he was operating on today wanted absolute secrecy regarding his brain tumour, though. Hence this surgery on a Sunday—Christmas Eve, to boot. The gentleman was currently snoozing under the influence of the anticonvulsants pumped into him and would have no idea his wife planned to share the news—if she hadn't already done so.

Still holding the cell phone to his ear, Rishi mumbled a curse, prompting a snicker from Anjali. As soon as the junior doctor left, Rishi said into his phone, "You know what this means, doncha? When the patient wakes up and finds out what wifey did, all hell is going to break loose. The missus is going to look for someone to blame. The first victims will be the hospital staff." Especially so if the information leaked to the press.

"I'm sure you can smooth things over," Anjali soothed. "The hospital will want you to. That's why you get paid the big bucks as a board member."

Rishi clucked. "I'll have to wait until the patient is fully coherent to explain what happened. Our flight to Amsterdam... we'll be cutting it close."

He and Anjali wanted absolute secrecy for *their* plans, too. They'd tried the old-fashioned way of getting pregnant. Ovulation detectors... check. Viagra... check. Making sure the phone and the laptop were kept away from his babymakers... check. Then, he was required to actually perform. In the darkness, he could close his eyes and dream of Hrithik Roshan, the Bollywood God, but Anjali's stiffness was unmissable. Rishi didn't think there was a time in his life he felt as horribly guilty as when she whispered "sorry" at the end of their first attempt. A worse blow came two weeks later... the pregnancy test strip stayed stubbornly negative.

In the third month of their mission to reproduce, Rishi muttered, "This ain't working," and Anjali showed him the webpage of the fertility clinic which advertised services geared towards gay couples. Not Rishi's situation, exactly, but close enough.

They took time off on the pretext of a romantic holiday in Europe for their initial consultation. The success rate of intrauterine insemination was sixty to seventy per cent over six cycles. Thank God, Papa and Ma were already in Dubai, or Rishi would've had to invent a reason to send them there so he and Anjali could continue the treatment. After this surgery Rishi agreed to perform in Mumbai, they were supposed to travel to Amsterdam for the first cycle of intrauterine insemination.

Striding down the brightly lit corridor leading to the patient suites, Rishi continued talking to Anjali. "Just imagine... by the time we return, you might be pregnant."

"I hope so," she said, dreamily. Tone turning brisk, she added, "The chances of that happening in the first cycle are at best twenty per cent, so don't get too disappointed if I'm not."

"It'll happen," Rishi insisted. "If not now, then soon." Stride faltering, he paused by an artificial pine stuffed with every possible Christmas ornament. There was a vague reflection of him on one of the glass bells. Somehow, he was reminded of his old flatmate, Joe. He'd never been much into religious holidays, but they'd always put up a small plastic tree, even singing carols while deep under the influence of cheap wine. Rishi shook his head. He didn't need any memories of the S.O.B., but he knew why his mind was bringing up old stuff. Once he and Anjali had this child, no one could come between them. "We'll be Papa, Mama, and baby... a family. Anju?"

"Yeah?"

"You already are, you know... family, I mean."

Sounding slightly confused, she said, "We've been married seven years. Of course, we're family."

"No." He struggled to find the words to tell her without actually mentioning her old boyfriend. "You're family like Nikhil was."

After a second, she murmured, "Home."

"Yes," Rishi hissed. The bond between them wasn't remotely romantic, but it was there, nevertheless. For the last seven years, he hadn't known how to express it. Acceptance, comfort, safety... how else to define her except as his home? Now, no one could wrench it from him. "It's great," he said, laughing in sheer joy. "Simply great."

There was a surprised snicker from the other end of the line. "You want to seal the deal with a baby."

"Something like it," he admitted, continuing his stride towards the VIP section of the hospital. "Nothing... no one... will be able to take you away from me."

Chuckling at Anjali's gentle teasing, he reached the nurses' station and nodded at the ladies. One of them was gesturing towards the politician's room. After raising a hand in acknowledgement, Rishi put his knuckles to the door to knock. It was already open and silently swung a few inches in. When he stepped inside, the missus of the politician was on the couch in the living area of the suite, her eyes red-rimmed but mouth stretched into a smile.

Next to her was a man in green scrubs, turned sideways so that only his back was visible from the door. Rishi eyed the thick, black hair tied in a loose tail. A grey stethoscope hung around the fellow's neck. Another of the junior doctors, perhaps. He'd be one of the employees being groomed for higher positions, or he wouldn't have been allowed to participate in the VIP's care. Dr Ponytail was about to learn Rishi didn't allow long hair on the men in his team. Patients would not be impressed.

"Got to go now, darling," Rishi muttered into the phone before hanging up. "Excuse me?" he called.

The long-haired fellow turned in place, revealing a tiny gold hoop in his right ear. The electric grin slammed into Rishi's chest. The smouldering eyes crinkled in welcome. With muscled grace, the man stood and extended a hand. "Dr Rastogi, I presume. I'm Dr Zaidi... Farhan Zaidi, consultant anaesthesiologist."

***

Anjali paced the hardwood floor of the waiting room at the fertility clinic, her kitten heels going clickety-clack with each step. Where *was* Rishi? Okay, so he needed to stay back after the surgery to talk to the VIP patient and missed the flight to Delhi, but he'd said he'd buy a Mumbai-Amsterdam ticket. If he didn't get here on time... her hormone levels were already nicely up, and the procedure—artificial insemination—needed to happen within a day or two.

When a soft knock sounded on the door, her heart jumped. *Finally.*

It was only the silver-haired obstetrician, her hands stuffed into the pockets of her pristine white lab coat. "I'm sorry, Dr Joshi. We can't wait any longer. Not today. I have surgeries scheduled. If your husband gets here later tonight, we can try to squeeze you in tomorrow."

Back in her hotel room, Anjali refreshed the webpage listing the flights between Mumbai and Amsterdam for the thousandth time. Flopping back into the armchair, she wiped the wetness from her cheeks. *God, Rishi. Where are you?* There was nothing on her cell phone after his last text saying he was booking a ticket online. No other messages with the details of his flight. All *her* calls went to voicemail.

Telling herself again and again there was one more day before they missed this cycle, Anjali went to the window as though she'd be able to see Rishi approaching the entrance to the hotel. It should've been a perfect day, but dark grey clouds had rolled over the sky, masking the sun. Tourists were gathered in the square where the hotel was located, dancing to the frenzied beat of drum music from somewhere. Inside her mind, it seemed there was an entire orchestra of instruments, setting her skull vibrating with stormy songs.

She didn't realise how hard she was gripping the thin fabric of the curtain until it ripped. Her fingers... they were shaky as though she'd just downed a gallon of coffee when she hadn't consumed anything with caffeine for weeks to make sure her systems were in ideal condition for maternity. Yanking the curtains closed, she went to the shower.

The needles of lukewarm water striking her scalp, streaming down her body, brought no peace. Rishi *had* to get there on time. If he didn't... Anjali clapped a hand to her mouth, trying to silence the sobs.

She so, so badly wanted this. A child of her own. A baby to love. There would be no conditions, no expectations, only love. He wouldn't have to be perfect in everything to be perfect for her.

Holding both hands to her temples, Anjali shook her head. The pain... it was worse than ever. Her brain would explode any moment. It wouldn't matter to the universe. Even if her family grieved, the cosmos would know it lost nothing. Anjali was a fraud—a flawed woman masquerading as the perfect daughter, the perfect wife, the perfect daughter-in-law. The headaches were merely her mind taunting her with what she'd always known. She, a rich, pampered woman who got everything handed to her on a platter, was lauded as perfection when all she possessed was pretence.

The pain intensified, painting the air with a reddish hue. The water in the shower turned the colour of blood. Or was she haemorrhaging? Had her body decided it was the way to vent the pressure within her skull?

Somehow, she stumbled out of the shower. Anjali crouched, blindly scrounging for the pants and sweater she'd left on the floor. Clothes half on and half off, she staggered to the king-sized bed and pulled the covers over her.

Rishi would get there. In the morning, they'd go to the fertility clinic, profusely apologising for messing up the doctor's schedule. They'd go through the procedure. If they were lucky, one cycle was all it would take for her to conceive. In less than a year, they'd have a baby.

Anjali hadn't realised how badly she wanted one until the dinner with Rishi's parents. The image of an infant popped into her mind. Sweet-smelling, soft child, cuddling against her heart. He wouldn't care his mother was imperfect. All he'd want was for her to love him. She would, with every single atom of her soul. She'd teach him never to pretend to be something he wasn't. Like his Vikram Uncle, her baby would do exactly what he wanted in life, the world be damned.

The morning came, bringing with it a phone call from the fertility clinic, asking if Anjali and Rishi planned to come in.

"No," she mumbled. "I'm sorry about this. Can we make another appointment?"

The sun shining in the clear winter sky brought some much-needed clarity to her thoughts. The fertility treatments could be rescheduled, but she had no idea what happened to Rishi. She took her cell phone and contemplated calling the hospital in Mumbai. He wouldn't have returned to her parents' flat after the surgery, risking them somehow finding out about the trip to Amsterdam. He'd have stayed in the hospital until it was time to go to the airport. But if she contacted the staff, word would get around Rishabh Rastogi's wife had no clue of his whereabouts.

But what if he were injured or—her mind flashed back to a day so long ago. She was in Goa, searching for her missing boyfriend.

Anjali shook her head. No, Rishi was nothing like Joe, nothing like the boyfriend who'd ripped her heart apart and stomped on the pieces. There was a darned good reason her husband wasn't here. She could only pray it wasn't because he was hurt.

The nurse who managed the operating theatre in the Mumbai hospital giggled when she came on the line. "Dr Rastogi said you might call," she said in a sing-song voice. "*He* tried to call you lots of times, but your phone was turned off. You were in flight, right? He was going to tell you he didn't get tickets which would get him to your conference on time, so he was heading home to Delhi. Since you didn't pick up, he booked the late ticket anyway and said he'd meet you there."

"Thank you," Anjali said, hanging up. Rishi tried to contact her? He always teased her about being a stickler for rules and turning her phone off during flights, but she hadn't this time. She'd been so anxious about him possibly missing the appointment at the fertility clinic, she left it on. Some kind of service error? It had to be. Why would Rishi lie about it?

***

"It's all right, Rishi," she said, zipping her luggage. No sooner than he got to Amsterdam, it was time to leave. They, after all, hadn't planned to spend more than two days in the city. "These things happen. I hope your VIP patient wasn't terribly angry."

Clearing his throat, Rishi said, "We took care of it." He didn't turn from the scene outside the window—the tourists crowding the square, the holiday decorations, the restaurants.

Anjali frowned. Something in his tone... "Sorry about phoning the hospital. There were all kinds of stupid thoughts running through my mind."

"I thought you might call after not hearing from me for a couple of days. So I told the theatre manager you were presenting a paper at one of the hospitals, and I was supposed to join you."

"Did you sleep in the hospital, or did you go to a hotel?" Anjali asked, checking her face in the mirror above the desk for traces of the tears from last night.

"Ahh... no." Finally turning from the window, Rishi hefted her luggage from the bed. "How much did you pack, Anju?" he complained, grunting. "You were here only for two days!"

"I thought we could go to one of the restaurants after the procedure," she said. "I needed a nice outfit... matching shoes... jewellery. Plus, your stuff." Since he couldn't return to Delhi and fly with her as planned, she'd packed for him.

Rishi flushed. "Sorry," he muttered. "We'll do dinner next time, perhaps."

She inclined her head, thanking God he hadn't witnessed her tragedy queen act from the night before. The fertility drug she was prescribed was known to cause anxiety and even full-blown panic attacks. Plus, there was her usual headache. Except, the headache hurt much, much worse this time around, and it took hours to subside. Still, her emotional reaction was so silly. The baby would happen in the next few months, and she'd forget all about the drama of one missed appointment.

When they were in the cab *en route* to the airport, Anjali asked, "So what *did* you do while you were waiting for the flight?"

Gaze fixed on the glittering streets, he said, "One of the nurses in the team is engaged to a dude who owns a pub. She invited everyone to spend Christmas Eve there. Normally, I wouldn't have gone, but..." Rishi's social circle was in Delhi. In Mumbai, he spent his free time with Anjali's family. On this particular trip, he wouldn't have risked returning to the Joshi flat.

"Hope you got to know some of the people," Anjali commented. "At least the other surgeons. It's important. We all work for the same system. Plus, you're a board member."

Rishi shifted to face her. "Do you know any of the other anaesthesiologists working for the system?"

Laughing, she admitted, "I don't. But then, I'm not travelling between hospitals all the time. Who *are* the anaesthesiologists in Mumbai?"

With a nervous shrug, he said, "There are a few. I haven't met all of them."

"You must've met *one* at a minimum," she pointed out. "How many surgeries have you done there so far?"

"Five or six." After a second, Rishi blurted, "Farhan. Farhan Zaidi. He was the anaesthesiologist at the last surgery."

"Is he from Mumbai?" The city was home to immigrants from all over India and some from outside the country.

440

"Punjabi ethnicity," Rishi said. "His great-grandfather moved there from Lahore during partition."

"*Really?*" The Rastogis were from Punjab, but from Amritsar, which was on the Indian side of the province. Lahore was in Pakistan. When the Brits left, they divided the subcontinent into secular India and Islamic Pakistan, starting a mass migration in both directions—Hindu Pakistanis to India and Muslim Indians to Pakistan. Frowning, Anjali said, "That doesn't make any sense. His name sounds Muslim. Why did his great-grandfather migrate the wrong way?"

"My question, exactly," said Rishi, his tone as tickled as a child's. "Farhan claims he comes from a long line of rebels."

Anjali raised an eyebrow. "You did get to know at least one person at the Mumbai hospital."

Rishi stilled. Turning his head to cough into his shoulder, he said, "Yeah, well... he was at the pub on Christmas Eve. We talked for a while is all."

***

Chatting, laughing, sitting side-by-side in pleasant silence... Rishi wasn't a rural creature by any stretch of the imagination, but he could stay in this village tea shop forever, talking to Farhan. The medical camp organised to bring preventive services to remote areas would end in a couple of days, though. Before it did, there was a question Rishi needed to ask.

His eyes went to the tiny gold hoop on Farhan's right ear. "You know the earring code?"

Swigging water straight from the bottle, Farhan laughed, spilling some of the liquid on his face. "Right ear means gay? Yeah, I know. Silly story which started in the 'nineties."

"Are you?" Rishi asked.

Eyeing the other occupants of the tea shop, Farhan said, "Let's talk outside." When they exited the establishment, he bent and patted his right ankle. "My Beretta's right here, but I'd much rather not have to use it."

Beretta? Rishi blinked. "You carry a gun?"

Farhan threw a speaking look. "I'm openly gay. What do you think?"

Heart pounding in anticipation, Rishi followed Farhan down the mud path through the village to the riverside. When Farhan plonked himself down at the foot of a coconut tree, Rishi crouched and started brushing away the reddish clay coating a log. At Farhan's amused grin, Rishi snapped, "Dust gives me asthma attacks."

"Sure, your asthma," Farhan said, chuckling. "Sit, please. A little dust is not going to hurt your pretty butt."

With a reproving glare, Rishi asked, "You realise I'm sort of your boss?"

Devilment sparked in Farhan's eyes. "Yeah. The bigshot board member related to all the right people." The mischief faded, and his gaze went to Rishi's left hand. "It ain't tough to figure out when someone's interested, but I need to hear the significance of the ring *you're* wearing. Does she know?"

Rishi glanced down at his wedding ring. For the last seven years, it served as his shield. From the moment she acknowledged him as her betrothed, Anjali guarded him from everyone who sought to harm him.

The day he met Farhan... when the theatre nurse invited everyone to her fiancé's pub for Christmas Eve, Rishi first declined. Drinking... food... live band... nuh-huh. He was expected elsewhere. Rather, his tadpoles were. There were no excuses for him to remain in Mumbai. Farhan got to the VIP patient's room before Rishi and talked Mrs VIP out of contacting her cousin. Anjali didn't know it yet, but there was no reason for Rishi to stay in Mumbai any longer than it took to make sure the patient was stable after surgery.

In the men's room attached to the staff lounge, Rishi splashed water on his face. The ring glinted under the yellow light from the bulb over the sink, reminding him again of the woman waiting for him in Amsterdam. He took out his phone, intending to text her he was on his way to the airport. Outside the closed door of the men's room, there was loud talking and laughter. Someone was singing... Farhan? Without giving himself a chance to think twice, Rishi sent a message to his wife he'd need to stay in Mumbai at least one more night, perhaps longer.

The blue dress shirt and dark grey pants he wore would pass muster. Farhan wasn't much more formal in his all-black attire. They talked all through the party, going through the rituals of getting to know each other. When Farhan stumbled over basic Punjabi, Rishi laughed out loud, but when it was time to dance the *bhangra*, he couldn't compete with the wildly attractive anaesthesiologist. On the team's urging, Farhan took his place with the band, beating out an intense rhythm on the drums.

After a while, someone suggested the idea of a pub crawl. Rishi and Farhan sauntered behind the rest, making sure one of them paid for the drinks as the two well-salaried consultants in the group. Neither imbibed much, but Rishi's heart was flying as though he were intoxicated. Each word passing between them changed to music notes, setting up a soaring song. Hell, even the inanimate objects seemed to sway in drunken pleasure—the clouds, the air, the power lines in the crowded nighttime streets.

Somehow, the group found itself once again at the pub owned by the nurse's fiancé. The gentleman was good enough to offer the backroom of his establishment so his betrothed's sozzled colleagues could sleep it off. Cigarette smoke from the bar outside swirled into the dark room, adding to the alcohol fumes given off by the snoring bodies on the tiled floor. Armed with pillows, Rishi and Farhan manoeuvred their way to the wide windowsill. They'd have to sleep sitting up, but it was better than risking being vomited on by a drunk doctor or nurse or technician.

"*Eid aa gaya*," Farhan muttered sleepily, glancing at the sky outside.

Eid was here? *Eid-ul-Fitr* was the Islamic festival where the faithful eagerly waited for the first sliver of the moon to show up before celebrations could begin. Rishi laughed. "Isn't it in the summer? This is Christmas Eve."

Dreamy expression on his face, Farhan settled against the pillows and closed his eyes. "I wasn't talking about the actual moon. *Tu bada chikna hai, yaar.*" You're damned attractive.

Rishi slept only in fits. Sometimes, there was Farhan in his dreams, beckoning him with a mischievous grin. Then, there was Anjali holding a screaming baby... no, a phone. God, the thing was so loud. Rishi woke with a start. Massaging the stiff muscles in the back of his neck, he shifted to tug the phone out of his pocket.

Shit. Anjali. She would be at the Delhi airport, waiting for her flight to Amsterdam. He could still make it on time if he flew from Mumbai, but... Rishi glanced at Farhan's sleeping form. Pulling up a list of available flights to the Netherlands, Rishi found one guaranteed to get him there after the window the fertility specialist specified.

Brunch with the team, returning to the hospital to shower in the special suite provided to visiting board members, popping into the patient's room for a short chat, making up a story for the nurse who managed the operating theatre to tell Anjali... she'd wait until she started worrying for his safety, then she'd call. She needed to hear a plausible excuse. Rishi stayed in the staff lounge until the time Farhan said he'd show up, shaved and showered and dressed in fresh clothes.

"Sorry you have to work on Christmas," Rishi said, awkwardly. There was no one else in the staff lounge at the moment, but it wasn't as though he could announce his interest.

Farhan shrugged. "I'm not. I wasn't sure we'd meet again after today, so thought I'd... umm..."

By way of answer, Rishi said, "I do surgeries in Mumbai now and then." If there was one thing he was sure of, it was this wouldn't be his last meeting with Farhan. With a brief handshake, they parted.

When Anjali opened the door to the hotel room, she was as gracious as always, casually claiming the missed appointment wasn't a big deal. The tear stains on her cheeks told a different story. Rishi couldn't bear to look at her. Neither could he stop himself from blurting out details about Farhan. Rishi hoped perhaps saying the name in Anjali's hearing would put an end to his impossible fantasies. No such luck.

All through the next week, he found himself drifting off into dreams. He'd catch himself wondering what Farhan was up to. There was a waiting list of patients who'd requested Rishi as their surgeon but incredibly, none from Mumbai. Well... if the mountain wouldn't go to Mohammad, etcetera, etcetera. In another week, Rishi arranged a medical camp for the needy in the village at the Maharashtra-Goa border, sending a special invitation to consultants who might wish to join. When Farhan's name popped up in the list of attendees, Rishi made plans.

Unfortunately, five days went by, and this was the first chance he got with Farhan to ask the question about his sexual orientation. Now, Rishi needed to answer Farhan's question. What was the significance of the wedding ring on Rishi's finger? Did Anjali know about him?

Rishi glanced around their surroundings, taking in the tranquil river, the grassy bank, and the bright, blue sky. Birds chirped in trees, and there were a couple of boys splashing about in the water, but Farhan was silently seated at the foot of a coconut palm, waiting for an explanation. Tugging at his collar for some relief from the sweltering heat, Rishi gestured with his eyes towards the landmass across the river. "Over there is Goa." When Farhan frowned,

Rishi shook his head. How did he explain Anjali's decision to marry him? How could he give away her secret pain? "I was just... I'm not sure why I said that. Yes, Anju knows about me."

Farhan raised his eyebrows. "Either she's terribly in love with you, or you have an open marriage." Huffing, he looked away. "Sorry, Rishi. You're a good-looking man... intelligent... soft-spoken... just the sort I find appealing. But your situation... nah, not for me."

"It's not an open marriage," Rishi said, gingerly settling onto the clay-coated log he'd been cleaning. Whatever their motives, he and Anjali fully meant the vows they'd taken. But then, he hadn't met Farhan. "I shouldn't need to explain *my* reasons to you. The law... society... family." Yeah, the blackmailer was the original reason for the pretend engagement, but the problem didn't need them actually tying the knot. He could've escaped to Canada, instead. "None of Anju's reasons involved being in love with me. Don't get me wrong. We're friends—very good friends—and we meant every word of the vows we made." Rubbing his temple with his fingertips, Rishi muttered, "She wants a baby."

"Ahh. And you don't?"

"Yes and no," Rishi said. "Being a father... a family... I'm damned sure of it. I just don't know if... Farhan, I wasn't expecting to run into someone like you. I need to think about this." After the fiasco of the missed treatment cycle, Anjali asked the fertility centre for a month's reprieve prior to the next appointment, citing some unexpected side effects from the meds she needed to take. At some point before the appointment, Rishi would need to tell her about the doubts which suddenly popped up in his mind. She would want to know the reason. "I should be talking this over with *Anju*. I owe it to her. She's the only one who knows the truth about—" Glancing at Farhan, Rishi asked, "How come *you're* so open with it? Aren't you worried... you know, repercussions and such?"

With a small shrug, Farhan said, "My family has an allergy to conformism. They aren't particularly religious, either. I told you about my great-grandfather. My granny eloped with a neighbour and went to live in London. All my aunts and uncles fancy themselves more Brit than the queen, but my dad returned to India to teach Shakespeare to Mumbaikars. He and my mom are divorced. *She's* a veterinarian—and an animal rights activist." Farhan paused to toss a small twig into the water. Laughing, he continued, "You have no idea how hard it was to rebel in our household. Whatever I did, someone else would claim they'd already done it."

Rishi guffawed. "So you decided to be gay? Not how it works, buddy."

Eyes crinkling in mischief, Farhan said, "I simply got turned on by the sight of—" He waggled his brows at Rishi. The laughter which followed was tinged by simmering attraction... anticipation... something. "Yeah... my family never had a problem with it. As far as the law is concerned... they'd have to *prove* I engaged in sex with another man to arrest me. I've been careful about it. Plus, my dad made me take British citizenship when I first told him I was gay. I was around fourteen. Since the government allows non-Indian doctors to work here because of the shortage, I didn't have to leave, but I could if it gets to that point. So I've never needed to worry about the legal implications of my sexual orientation. I'm guessing it wasn't quite the same for you."

"No." Rishi gave Farhan a sketch of the Rastogi household, just enough for him to understand the reasons behind Rishi's marriage. "Anju's the only one who's stood by me." Nikhil was long gone, and Joe... the S.O.B. skipped out on every one of his friends.

"You love her," remarked Farhan. When Rishi threw a startled look, Farhan amended, "I don't mean romantically, but your tone changes when you speak her name." With a sigh, he stood and walked to the edge of the water. "Look, Rishi. When I saw you... it was like... it's hard to explain, but my first thought was 'there you are.'"

A warmth spreading through his chest, Rishi chuckled. "Love at first sight?"

"Attraction," Farhan corrected. "Pheromones, hormones, etcetera. I've been around enough to pick up on return attraction, but I knew you were married. I was gonna make sure I wasn't scheduled to work on any of your surgeries. Then, I got the email about the medical camp. Bloody fool I was, I wanted to see you, and I was trying to avoid you, all at the same time. I wouldn't have said anything if you hadn't asked... maybe I should've simply denied being gay. I don't approve of cheating on a spouse, no matter what the circumstances. Wedding vows have meaning, ya know?"

Smiling a little, Rishi teased, "I thought you were a rebel."

"Only as far as it doesn't hurt another person." Turning from the water to face Rishi, Farhan said, "You're exactly my type, but I won't help you make a mockery of your marriage. If your wife didn't know, I would've told you to suck it up and stay with her. I mean... poor woman took your word for it. Since you're certain there's no romantic love on either side, and you both knew what you were getting into, your situation's actually less problematic. Instead of complicating things with extramarital affairs, you should consider... dunno... explaining to your Anju you made a mistake and walking away with your integrity intact, perhaps?"

"Easy to say," Rishi said, shaking his head. "The reasons we got married haven't changed. Don't you pay attention to things happening around us? The courts are still playing games with gay people." Delhi High Court decriminalised homosexuality in 2009, a few weeks after Rishi and Anjali's engagement ceremony. He'd told her at the time to wait for the other shoe to drop. Sure enough, in 2013, the supreme court reversed the judgement. "It's not only about the law. My family... they'll be crushed. Yeah, Anju and I knew what we were getting into, but like I said, we meant to stay together. If I walk out, she'll be humiliated. I can't do it to her."

Farhan inclined his head. "We have nothing to discuss then."

They returned in silence to the resort housing the medical team. There were no private goodbyes when the camp came to an end.

In the next couple of months, anyone requesting Rishi as surgeon was asked to schedule their procedure in Delhi. Thankfully for him, he didn't have to tell his wife he was having second thoughts about the baby. The fertility expert deferred further treatment for Anjali until she saw a psychiatrist about some side effects she mentioned.

***

"I can handle it," Anjali insisted, trying hard not to let tears sprout in her eyes. It was exhausting to discuss what was going on without giving away Rishi's secrets or hers, but any crying would be taken as a sign of instability.

The psychiatrist—a matronly Indian woman in a cotton sari—pushed her chair back and walked around the desk. Pulling out the second chair meant for the patient's family, she sat. "Anjali, you're a doctor. If you were in my place talking to a patient, what would you say? You need to give yourself time to understand why you reacted so badly to Rishi missing the appointment. It could be a side effect from the meds—which will clearly be a short-lived problem—but what if there's underlying pathology, exacerbated by the drugs?"

"Did the anxiety score say I have a problem?"

The shrink sighed. "No." The good doctor didn't come out and state Anjali could've easily lied on the questionnaire, but the expression in her eyes made the belief evident. "How about a compromise?" she asked. "Take six months off from attempting to conceive. I want to be reasonably certain the treatments won't put your health at risk."

Anjali could handle six months. She'd handled her years in the Rastogi household when Rishi's parents were in residence. Now, it was only Rishi and her. There would be no need to pretend in the privacy of the house.

449

Except, Rishi was rarely around the next few weeks. He took on more and more work, barely coming home to sleep. They hardly ever got the chance to talk. It was never a convenient time to discuss baby plans.

In her solitude, Anjali jotted down all the times she could remember when the headache attacked. Three months later, she sat back into the sofa in the Rastogi living room, certain she'd identified the trigger. Perfection—anytime the idea was brought up, her head felt ready to explode in flames. All she needed to do was be mindful of the problem, and it would cease to have power over her.

Oh, really? Her psyche mocked her only a night later. And two nights later. And on the third night. Eyes darting around the silent living room of the Rastogi residence, Anjali puffed short, rapid breaths into cupped hands. No one had said the trigger word. She never even imagined it. Not only that, the pain now lasted hours instead of mere moments like it used to before she began the fertility treatment.

The pressure in her head was so intense that the furniture blurred, then glowed red. The phone... where was it? She needed to call Rishi. It was impossible for pain this extreme to be only in her mind. If she ruptured a blood vessel or something... the neurosurgeon's wife would be found on the floor, dead from an intracranial bleed. Joe's stepmom died from a bleed, didn't she?

Anjali shook her head. Why was her mind bringing up old memories? If she died, she wanted to go remembering the people who loved her, not the boyfriend who discarded her without a second thought. Her mom... Dad... Rishi... Vikram... Anjali never got the chance to tell her little brother how much she adored him. She was in awe of his strength, his will to take on life on his own terms.

Would she get a chance to see her family one more time? Hindus believed in the *chakra*—the wheel—of life and death. A soul went through birth after birth after birth until deemed worthy of *moksha*—deliverance. Anjali had done nothing worthy of redemption. All her life, everything was handed to her, and she still managed to make a mess of things. Her entire existence was based on pretence, on mute compliance with whatever was demanded of her. *Please, God,* she begged, not knowing what she was asking for.

She needed to get her purse from the cupboard. Her phone was in it. Anjali staggered to the bedroom and managed to retrieve the device. With trembling fingers, she tried to enter the passcode. The numbers blurred in front of her eyes. After five attempts, the phone refused to let her in. Sobbing in fear, she hurled it to the floor.

Anjali didn't remember getting into the bed. She didn't remember falling asleep. The next she knew, someone was calling her name, tone urgent. "Anju, wake up," bellowed Rishi.

She bolted upright, the top of her head nearly hitting his chin. "Rishi? What—" Rubbing the sleepiness from her eyes, she asked, "Why are you yelling? Everything all right?"

"I was about to ask you the same question," Rishi said, his gaze going to the floor where her phone lay in pieces. Her purse was also on the marble tiles, its contents strewn everywhere in the room.

Did she do all that? She was trying to call Rishi... "I must've dropped the purse," Anjali lied. "Sorry."

Rishi frowned as though he weren't quite sure what to make of her excuse. "Ahh... okay."

Sitting in her office the next day, Anjali tugged off her theatre cap and considered calling the shrink. Unfortunately, it would lead to further postponement of the fertility treatments. Too much time on her hands... too many chances to be alone with her thoughts... it was the only reason her mind was reacting so badly. She hadn't been truly alone for years. After Joe left, she was constantly with Rishi. Then, they moved in with his parents. Never a moment by herself to delve too deeply into her thoughts. Now, the senior Rastogis were gone, and Rishi was hardly around. There was nothing wrong with her a trip to Mumbai to visit her parents wouldn't cure.

Rishi was strangely reluctant to accompany her. "They're *your* parents, Anju," he said, not taking his gaze from the newspaper by his breakfast plate. "Get some quality time with them without me around."

"But—" Anjali frowned. "The six months the shrink wanted will be up soon. *We* need some time together to discuss the baby. You've been working so many hours lately."

"Comes with the territory."

"You have to do your rounds of the other hospitals, don't you? Spend a week at the Mumbai facility." Anjali spooned cold yoghurt into her mouth, relishing the sourness. She needed to prep her body for maternity with all the vitamins and minerals, but glasses and glasses of milk a day? *Yuck.* Yoghurt was a blessing to womankind. "Tell you what: you can introduce me to the anaesthesiologists there."

Rishi's head snapped up so fast, she wouldn't have been surprised if he fractured a vertebra. "Why?" he asked, voice weirdly tense.

"No particular reason. We *were* talking about the need to network, remember?"

"Were we?"

"Yeah, in Amsterdam. You told me you'd gone out with some of the Mumbai staff on Christmas Eve. What was the anaesthesiologist's name? The Muslim man whose grandfather migrated from Lahore to India?"

"Farhan," Rishi said, coughing. "Farhan Zaidi." With a loud screech of the chair legs against the floor, Rishi stood. "I have early surgery today. You'll need to take your own car to work. As far as going to Mumbai is concerned... we will if you want. Give me some time to rearrange my schedule."

Silently, Anjali nodded. She kept her eyes on Rishi's back as he strode out. *Farhan Zaidi.* Somehow, the name set her stomach churning.

Two months later, in September 2018, a month before she'd get the clearance to return to the fertility treatments, Anjali recognised the feeling in her belly as dread. Absolute fear that the veneer of perfection she concealed her pathetic self behind was about to be ripped away.

She was in her parents' duplex in Mumbai, half-asleep on the living room sofa with the television running in the background while Rishi was at the Mumbai hospital for his meeting with the nurses' union. The Joshi parents wouldn't return from their own work until evening. Anjali's brother, Vikram, had moved out long ago. Even the household employees were off on errands.

"Hold on for breaking news," said the news anchor. With a beaming smile, she announced that portions of Section 377 of the Indian Penal Code were ruled unconstitutional by the supreme court. The government declared it would not contest the judgement. "Social morality cannot violate the rights of even one single individual," said Chief Justice Misra. Just like that, aeons of legalised discrimination was over. Homosexuality was no longer criminal in India.

***

Rainbow flags decorated the streets of Mumbai. Drums rolled as men and women danced to celebrate the court's verdict. Hugging, kissing, singing as loudly as they could, India's gay community announced to the world they were finally free.

His palms on the glass windows in his third-floor office, Rishi watched the city whoop it up. Traffic in Colaba, where the hospital stood, was bad enough on a normal day, but the Mercedes he rented wasn't going to get through at all this evening. He was within walking distance from the Joshi residence in Cuffe Parade. Anjali and her parents... they'd be waiting. He didn't *want* to return.

Not just yet. Surely, the universe owed him a moment on his own to relish this... this *lightness* within his soul.

There was a knock on the door, but he didn't bother to respond. The union meeting was done. He had no surgeries scheduled. Anyone else who needed to talk to him could bloody well send an email.

A second knock set the door vibrating—a thud, rather, as though the person outside were kicking the wood panels.

Curbing his impatience, Rishi wheeled around and wiped the wetness from his eyes. "Come in," he called.

There was a strange grunt. The door opened, and Farhan shouldered his way in, his hands occupied with a wine bottle and two flute glasses. Clenched between his teeth was a folded newspaper.

Rishi's heart did a Bollywood hook step in his chest. "What are you—"

Farhan went practically cross-eyed, gesturing at the newspaper in his mouth and mumbling something totally indecipherable.

"Oh, for God's sake." Rishi strode to Farhan and tugged out the newspaper. "What *is* this?"

Spitting out a piece, Farhan said, "Celebration."

Rishi glanced at the bottle and goggled. "You have Dom Perignon stashed at work?"

"Only at work?" Laughing hard, Farhan said, "I've been storing a bottle each at home, at work, even in my bike... ready to go on the day of the verdict."

Narrowing his eyes, Rishi asked, "And how did you know it would be positive?"

"I didn't *know*." Farhan set the glasses on the desk and uncorked the champagne. "I hoped, trusted, and expected our fellow human beings would come through."

"You carry a *gun* because you're openly gay."

"I'm an optimist, my friend. Not a fool." Holding out a glass of the bubbly, Farhan added, "I heard you were here. Didn't think you'd be able to celebrate this with the wife, so I decided to share my bottle with you. Before you ask, I'm not scheduled in the theatre, and I didn't see your name anywhere on the surgery list for today."

"We're still at work," Rishi pointed out. "Oh, to hell with it. Gimme the glass." Tossing the newspaper in his hand to the desk, he grabbed the flute from Farhan.

"Wait," said Farhan. "There are a few steps before we can drink. First—" He snatched up the newspaper. "We tear this into pieces." At Rishi's puzzled look, Farhan explained, "It's the 2013 *Times* with the verdict which upheld Section 377."

Rishi growled. "Let's put the thing in the shredder."

"Nope," said Farhan. "We have to do this by hand."

They did. The paper was torn into the smallest pieces possible and tossed into the air. Like confetti, the bits floated down, settling on the furniture, on the floor, on the heads of the laughing men.

Rishi didn't bother to sip the first glass. Down the gullet went the sparkling wine, barely lingering long enough on his tongue to hint at the citrusy taste.

"Look," Farhan exclaimed, beckoning Rishi to the window. "By the electronics store."

A movie star—surrounded by her security detail—danced in time with the drums. "Shit," Rishi muttered, eyeing the two young men gawking at the celeb from a few feet away, rainbow bandanas around their heads. "My brother-in-law, Vikram."

"Is he gay?" asked Farhan, tone tinged with curiosity.

"No. He has a gay uncle, so I imagine he's here in support. I can't stand the little punk. He doesn't get how... I would've killed for a family like his, and *he* has no respect for them, whatsoever. Someone needs to knock some sense into his thick head."

Farhan snorted. "Tell me how you really feel."

Chuckling reluctantly, Rishi asked, "See the kid next to the punk? His name's Adhith... Adhith Verma. He's Minister Verma's son. Adhi's actually decent." Yet Rishi had a feeling Adhith shared Vikram's dislike of his brother-in-law. It started when Rishi once blurted something he heard at the golf club about the finance ministry. He didn't usually make such mistakes, but he'd been distracted, watching his father talking to Anjali's gay uncle. Papa knew how to handle himself in most social situations, but still... the annoyance on Adhith's face snapped Rishi back. Unfortunately, the damage was already done.

"The union minister?" With a low whistle, Farhan added, "You move in some high circles."

"Not me. The Joshis. Adhi and Vikram work for the same tech company. Adhi lives around here from what I heard. Somewhere close to the Gateway of India."

"Expensive, but I guess cost wouldn't be an issue for a minister's son."

"Yeah," Rishi turned a half circle and gestured with his glass towards the bottle on the desk. "Let's get some more of the good stuff."

After the second glass, he and Farhan sprawled on the chintz-covered sofa on one side of the room and went through the Twitter feed of celebrities, making wild guesses on which of them were closeted. Farhan harboured a passionate interest in gay badasses from history, especially T. E. Lawrence, a.k.a. Lawrence of Arabia. After twenty minutes of listening to the details of the Arab revolt against the British, Rishi begged Farhan to stop.

Sulking at having his lecture cut short, Farhan poured them each a third glass of champagne. His arm was slung around Rishi's shoulders as they watched the celebrations around the nation on the flat-screen TV.

When the sun dimmed, and the automatic lights flickered on in the room, Rishi asked, "You drunk?"

"Not in the least," said Farhan, tone easy.

"Me, neither." Turning to face the other man, Rishi asked, "Mind if I kiss you?"

A sweet, soft meeting of lips, the taste of champagne, the scent of cologne... when Rishi withdrew, his eyes were moist.

Farhan's lashes were strangely sparkly. "Damn," he swore. "It was a bit..." He coughed. "...more intense than I expected." Standing clumsily, he muttered, "I'd better go. Promised my parents I'll join them for dinner. Some kind of vegan shit my mom wants to test out on her ex-husband and only child. And *you* have to return to your wife."

***

"Why do you want to wait?" Anjali asked, the painful lump in her throat barely letting her speak. Rishi was sitting cross-legged in the middle of the bed, dressed for the night in shorts and a Polo tee, his gaze fixed on the iPad in his lap. "We already lost half a year because of the psychiatrist. She finally gave us the go-ahead, and you claimed you needed time to clear your schedule. Two more months wasted. Now, you're telling me you have second thoughts?"

"You're still going to need to take the fertility meds," he muttered. "After your reaction the first time, I'm concerned about your health."

Tossing the hairbrush in her hand to the dressing table, Anjali dragged on a thin sweater over her flannel pyjamas. "You are?" With laughter which sounded crazed even to her own ears, she asked, "When were you around to develop concerns? You're out the door before we finish breakfast, and you don't get home until after midnight. It's either more work on weekends or golfing. If I were the suspicious sort, I'd think you're having an affair."

Looking up sharply, Rishi snapped, "Don't be ridiculous."

"I'm ridiculous?" A sudden pain exploded behind her eyeballs. Anjali staggered, clutching the edge of the dressing table to avoid falling. One deep breath. She struggled to beat back the headache. If she fell apart in Rishi's presence, it would give him a genuine excuse to avoid going through the fertility treatments. "*We* decided to have a baby, Rishi. It wasn't me alone. What am I supposed to think when... everything was okay until you went to Mumbai last Christmas. What happened there? I want to know."

Cheeks flushed an angry red, Rishi said, "What an insulting question. We work in the same hospital. You know everyone on my team. Don't you think you'd have heard if—"

"I wasn't around in *Mumbai,* was I?"

"Stop imagining things." Tossing his iPad onto a pillow, Rishi stood. "The trip to Mumbai you're talking about was almost a *year* ago. I never even returned there until *you* asked me to."

"Why?" Anjali asked, her body trembling in her effort to keep from screaming in pain. The baby. She needed to remember the baby she wanted.

Rishi frowned. "Huh? 'Why' what?"

"Why didn't you return to Mumbai? Did something happen that you couldn't?" Anjali tottered towards Rishi and nearly fell against his chest, clutching the lapels of his tee. "*Answer me.*"

Rishi's hands circled her wrists, trying to tug her grip loose. "Stop, Anju. What are you—" Stumbling, he shoved her away. "Please, calm down. Nothing happened."

"Then, why can't we get the treatment?" she screeched, hot tears running down her cheeks.

"What's going on?" he asked, his brows drawn together. "Why are you acting so strangely? I simply asked for a little reprieve before bringing a child into the world. More for your sake than mine. Like I said, I'm worried about your health."

Strange... strange... she couldn't be strange. They wouldn't let her have a baby if they thought there was something wrong. Gathering every ounce of focus within her, Anjali counted her breaths, keeping them slow and even. "Any woman would get upset. We've been married for almost eight years now. I turned thirty last August. We agreed it was time for a baby. Now, you're changing your mind? Right after the court changed the law? I want to know... are you cheating on me?"

"Cheating?" His eyes widened. "My God, Anju. You're behaving as if... we're not..." Glancing towards the door as though checking his parents hadn't somehow materialised in Delhi, Rishi muttered, "I hope you haven't forgotten the reasons behind our marriage."

"What reasons?" she asked. "That you're gay? That I agreed because of—" Anjali stopped. *No,* she said to the image in her mind—that of a man with a cleft in his chin. *I don't want to remember you.* "Whatever our reasons, we made our vows. I've kept mine, and I expect you to keep yours whatever the law is now. I won't let you make me a laughingstock in front of the rest of the world."

"I swear I've kept every vow. I simply don't think it's the right time to have a child."

459

The flush on his face... the way his eyes were skittering... "Let me see your phone," Anjali said, abruptly.

"*What?*"

"Where is it?" Whirling, Anjali tugged open the drawer of the side table. The table lamp teetered, crashing to the floor, but she didn't bother to place it back. There. The phone was inside the drawer, on the charger. Before she could unplug it, a hand landed on her hers, fingers tightening painfully around her wrist.

"Don't touch my stuff," shouted Rishi, yanking her back. "What is *wrong* with you?"

She wrenched her arm free and dropped to her knees in front of the side table. "I want to see."

"Stop, Anju." He snatched the device from her. "This is crazy."

Clambering up, she pounced to get it back from him. "I'm crazy?" she panted, struggling to tug the phone from him. He wouldn't let go. They stumbled together in the room. "For trying to assure myself my marriage is not breaking apart?" The last eight years... the baby she wanted... her entire life would be destroyed. She'd have to explain to her family she was a failure. Anjali Joshi was nothing but a fraud who'd somehow fooled the world into thinking she was the perfect daughter, perfect wife, perfect *every*thing. "Give me the phone," she snarled, barely able to see through the red haze of pain clouding her visual field. Her nails scratched the back of his hand, leaving thin, crimson lines of blood.

Back against the wall, Rishi turned, trying to secure the device between his torso and the concrete structure. "*Stop,*" he bellowed, flinging his other arm out to shove her away.

The back of his hand struck her cheek. Shock. The steely taste of terror surged into her mouth. The room tilted... whirled. She was on the floor, staring at the ceiling. A splitting pain shot from one side of her face to the other. The fog of her headache darkened from red to murky grey.

Rishi faded in and out. Eyes wide in panic, he was shouting, screaming her name. He crouched next to her, asking frantically if her head struck the edge of the side table when she fell. "I didn't mean to," he babbled, his voice trembling as he tried to gather her into an embrace. "I'm sorry. I'm so sorry. I didn't mean to."

"*Don't touch me.*" Anjali scooted away on the floor.

"Anju, please," Rishi begged, sobbing. Still on his haunches, he crawled a foot closer. "I swear I didn't mean—"

"*No,*" she screamed. "Don't come near me." A hand on the bed, she heaved herself up. "I have to go." Wildly, she looked around. She didn't want to pass Rishi to get to the clothes cupboard, but her purse and car keys were already in the living room.

When she stumbled to the front of the house, Rishi followed. "Where are you—Anju, you can't go out like this. It's not safe." He leapt around her to barricade the door. "Please, darling. I swear I didn't mean to... please, don't leave." Raising both arms in surrender, he said, "Stay in the bedroom, and I'll sleep in one of the other rooms. Wherever you decide to go in the morning, I promise I won't stop you. Just don't... you *know* it's not safe at night."

Wherever she decided to go? Where *was* she going? To her parents, admitting she'd played them all for fools for so many years? Admitting to the world she was an abject failure, marrying a man who didn't love her, doing a job she never wanted, living a life made wholly of lies? "Perfect life; perfect lies," she mumbled, hot tears spilling down her cheeks.

There was only a foggy awareness in Anjali's mind of Rishi guiding her back to the bedroom, tucking her in. Vaguely, she heard the door open and close multiple times as he returned to check on her. She barely responded to the brief neuro exams he did—awareness, pupil size, and muscle tone— making sure there were no invisible injuries from his inadvertent blow to her head.

When she woke, the sun was shining in the cloudless sky outside the window. There was complete silence in the house. Rishi... did he already leave for the hospital? *She* was expected at work. Anjali tossed aside the covers and stood.

The door opened with the slightest whoosh of air. Still clad in the shorts and tee from the night before, Rishi walked in. Tone subdued, he said, "I called the hospital and told them there was a family emergency."

Jerkily, she nodded. "Thanks." The shadows under his eyes... the guilt on his face... "About yesterday—"

Almost at the same time, he blurted, "I'm sorry. I didn't mean to."

Anjali raised both hands in acknowledgement. "I know. I'm not sure what got into me."

Miserably, Rishi said, "Don't absolve me of guilt, Anju. You got upset because of what I said. And you're right... having a child is a decision we made together. I should've discussed it..." Taking a deep breath, he looked her right in the eye. "There's something I need to tell you."

Sitting next to her on the living room sofa, he showed his phone. Call after call after call between Rishi and a number in Mumbai over the last couple of months. "Who is it?" she asked, numbly. Somehow, she knew the answer before he said the name.

"Farhan." A slow flush spread across Rishi's cheeks. "Farhan Zaidi." An unexpected meeting on Christmas Eve, unintended attraction, a connection of souls Rishi never dreamed he'd find. Things never went beyond one small kiss and long phone conversations. Farhan vehemently refused to consider anything physical as long as Rishi were otherwise attached. "I couldn't, either," Rishi murmured. "Felt too damned guilty. But I wanted to tell you so badly. You're the only one who'd understand."

Anjali bit her lower lip, trying to muffle her sobs, but the tears wouldn't stop. "Are you going to leave me?" she asked, her blurry gaze fixed on a piece of paper fluttering about in the cold draught sneaking in through the gap at the bottom of the front door. "After all this time?"

"Anju—"

"The law changed; you don't need me any longer, right?" she accused, wiping the wetness off her face before turning sideways to look at the man she once trusted. "It won't matter to you what happens to me."

"No." Urgently, Rishi shook his head. "Not true."

"I spent eight years as your wife," she whispered. "I did everything I could to keep your family happy." The tears started anew. "Even my career... whatever they asked, I did. They wanted the perfect wife for their son, and I made sure they got one. Now... now..." Weeping loud, ugly sobs, she raised her eyes heavenwards. "My baby... I've been dreaming for so long." The precious, precious child she'd been waiting for... she could almost see his innocent face, feel his tiny form cuddling in her arms.

"Anju, stop," Rishi pleaded, grabbing her hand to drop a kiss on her knuckles.

"Don't do this to me," she begged, her words interspersed with harsh blubbering. "My parents, the people at work..." The whole world would know her as an impostor. She'd be mocked wherever she went.

"I'm not going anywhere," Rishi insisted. "Why would you even think... it's not only your family. *My* parents will be crushed if I... Papa and Ma are old. I could never do it to them. Then, *you*. My God, I can't lose you, Anju."

Still sobbing, Anjali asked, "And Farhan?"

An acute pain flashed across Rishi's face. "Farhan was a dream. *This...*" Rishi glanced around the room. "...is reality. I'm not willing to give it up for anything in the world."

Soon, their reality would include a child. Anjali was determined not to give the dark thoughts another chance to attack. She wasn't quite certain how she'd avoid it, but Rishi did a one-eighty from never being home to never leaving her side after work, especially when she needed to take the fertility drugs. Movies, concerts, day trips... they even went golfing together a couple of times.

Four months later, the specialist at the clinic in Amsterdam confirmed the news: Anjali was pregnant.

✳✳✳

"Ready?" Anjali asked, eyeing the doorbell at the Joshi front door. She was done with the first trimester and all set to announce her impending maternity to her parents.

"Why do we have to do it now?" Rishi grumbled. "If we'd waited an hour more at the airport, we could've avoided the little punk."

"C'mon, Rishi," Anjali reproved. "I want to tell my brother in person." Vikram was temporarily back in the family home until he found a new flat, but he'd be on his way to work in a few minutes, and she wanted to catch him before he left.

Intense irritation passing across his face, Rishi said, "You keep excusing his bad behaviour. The punk doesn't get how good he has it. Your parents will support him no matter what he does, whereas I—" Abruptly, Rishi stopped. "Sorry," he muttered.

"It's all right," Anjali said, automatically. Unwelcome thoughts intruded. Since coming clean about his attraction to the man he met in Mumbai, Rishi carefully avoided reminding her of the fact he was gay. The years of honesty between them... the comfort of acceptance... the friendship... "It'll be back," she murmured to herself.

"What?" asked Rishi, frowning.

Yikes. She never meant to say it out loud. "A TV show I want to watch," she lied. Ignoring Rishi's confused look, she pressed her finger to the doorbell.

While Anjali was greeting her old nanny-turned-housekeeper with a hug, Rishi strode on ahead to the living room where the Joshi family was breakfasting. "Hey, Mom," he called, playfully.

"We have news," squealed Anjali, unable to help the wide smile erupting on her face.

Her parents greeted the announcement with exclamations of surprise and tears of joy. Shoving his chair back, Vikram stood. "Congratula—"

"We need your help," Rishi said, talking to Anjali's mom. "The obstetrician we like has a waitlist of three months." The fertility specialist had been in charge the entire first trimester, but Anjali most certainly needed someone in Delhi.

"I'll make a call." As the chief of obstetrics in one of the nation's best medical colleges, Rattan Joshi possessed the clout to make sure her daughter was allowed to cut the line.

"Anju," called Vikram. One of his rare grins lit up his face. "This is great news—"

Their father hugged Anjali from the side and dropped a kiss on top of her head. "You two are going to be great parents. This baby's going to be one lucky fella."

"Could be a daughter," said Mom. "Doesn't matter. But you must prepare well for its arrival. Every detail is important."

"Of course," said Rishi. "We have all the prenatal vitamins, but Anju hasn't been able to keep much down."

"You *are* a little pale, Anju," Mom said, clucking in concern.

Tossing Rishi a glare, Vikram asked, "Are you feeling all right—"

Rishi interrupted, "I have chewable vitamins on special order from the U.S."

Smiling at her brother, Anjali started, "I feel f—"

"Wait a second," said Rishi, bringing his phone out. "I want to show you something."

Nanny agencies? Puzzled, Anjali glanced at her husband's face. It couldn't have waited until they returned to Delhi?

He even pulled out a list of exclusive kindergartens from his pocket. "The right school is important. The right company, the right attitudes... or..." He side-eyed Vikram.

Anjali's jaw dropped open. What the heck was Rishi doing, ridiculing her brother so viciously?

"I've got to get going," said Vikram, his face red and tight. "Don't want to be late."

"Vikram," exclaimed Anjali, her insides suddenly jittery. Her parents were also looking startled. "Rishi was kidding." That's all it was—a bad joke.

"Of course, *saale saab*," said Rishi.

"We all know how good you're at..." Mom glanced at Dad. "...at... ahh..."

"Computers," finished Dad, tone triumphant.

Forgetting her annoyance with her husband for a moment, Anjali bit back a chuckle. Vikram's degree from IIT and his job as the manager of the Mumbai division of a multinational cybersecurity firm didn't really register in their parents' consciousness. They bought a desktop more than a decade ago which was basically used to play games. In the last few years, both discovered social media, chatting with their college friends on WhatsApp.

Vikram held both hands up. "We're all good. There's a presentation coming up this afternoon. I have to get going." Laptop bag slung over his shoulder, he strode to the front door.

"Wait." Leaving Rishi and her parents talking, Anjali scurried after Vikram. "You're not going to congratulate me?"

Tone stiff, Vikram parroted, "Congratulations."

"Thanks," she said, catching one of his hands in both of hers. "You're going to have responsibilities, you know."

"Like what?"

She tossed a glance over her shoulder towards the dining room. "Like stopping the rest of us from completely messing up the child."

On a short spurt of surprised laughter, Vikram repeated, "Congratulations, Anju."

"And," she went on, "I want you to teach her to play the guitar." Or him. Anjali somehow kept thinking in terms of a boy.

Smile turning into a mildly puzzled frown, Vikram said, "I didn't think you liked my playing."

"Are you kidding me? I always wished I—"

"Hey, Anjuuu," Rishi called.

Startled, Anjali turned to check on her husband. His tone was so coo-ey. What was going on with him? "Coming," she said. With a quick pat on Vikram's hand, she returned to the living room. Before she reached, she twirled and shot Vikram a wink, surprising another grin from him.

467

For one moment, he was the brother she'd longed for, the friend she'd always wanted.

On their way back to Delhi, Anjali asked Rishi what was the idea of mocking Vikram. In front of Mom and Dad, too! She'd heard Rishi pass snide comments on Vikram before, but today... it was simply too much.

"Your brother deserved it and more," Rishi said, stubbornly. "Look what he's doing. He refused to return to the family home after his degree was done. When he lost his flat, he moved back in, no please, no thank you. If I were in your parents' place—"

"Not every family needs to be like yours," Anjali argued, getting angrier by the moment. The Rastogis insisted on their son and his wife moving into the family residence as soon as their training period was done. "My parents don't have a problem with Vikram living his own life. They'd love him no matter what he—" As soon as the words were out of her mouth, she bit her tongue.

"Exactly what I've been saying," Rishi muttered, turning to his phone.

Resting against his shoulder later in the month, Anjali wondered if the sense of openness would ever return to their conversations. Oh, they were always chatting about this and that, joking, and making plans for the baby. But since the visit to Mumbai, there was an edginess to Rishi. When he thought she wasn't looking, he'd stare at his silent phone or glance restlessly through the window or simply zone out as though he were mentally with someone else. Some nights, she feigned sleep while he left the bed to pace the living room.

Anjali would place a protective hand on her still flat belly and imagine her child. The baby was safe. Neither of his parents would let the world pile expectations on him he couldn't fulfil. Neither his father nor mother would make their love conditional on his acquiescence to their demands.

"Are you going with me to my parents' anniversary party?" Anjali asked, popping into his office after her shift in the theatre. "I know there's the neurosurgery conference in Tokyo."

Rishi looked up from his computer with a half-grimace, half-smile. "There will be other conferences."

Shutting the door behind her, Anjali said, gently, "I won't go to pieces simply because you're not with me a couple of days."

"It's not—" Rishi huffed. "Are you sure?"

"Yes, I am. You need to see a few faces other than mine."

"I don't want to miss your parents' anniversary." He brooded for a couple of moments. "But the punk will be there, won't he?" When Anjali rolled her eyes, Rishi grinned. "What if I go to Tokyo and fly straight to Mumbai on the day of the party?"

"That'll work." Smirking, she said, "Come to think of it, you *shouldn't* miss it. Mom was saying Adhi's bringing his new girlfriend." The minister's son was a fixture at Joshi events, but he'd never brought a friend of the female persuasion along before. When Rishi's brows drew together in question, Anjali elaborated, "The girl works in the same tech company as Adhi and Vikram. Adhi wants to marry her, but she's completely unsuitable according to Minister Verma. Apparently, she grew up in the slums. The minister wants Mom and Dad's take on her."

Rishi laughed. "Should be entertaining."

The Friday night she dropped him off at the airport and returned to the empty house, she lay awake, staring into the darkness. There was no headache. The agonising ache in her soul refused to indulge her. All she could think of was Rishi—the pain in his eyes, the strain in his smile, the unusual jerkiness of his movements.

This was going to be his life for the next fifty, sixty years. His parents reduced his personal identity to son. The woman he married was reducing it to father. No wonder Rishi was bitter towards Vikram who always did whatever the heck he wanted, never having to worry about losing the people dear to him.

Anjali smiled. Her little brother didn't give two hoots about being perfect. Those who didn't like it were royally ignored by Vikram. Heck, he ignored some people just because.

***

Tucking a strand of hair back into her bun, Anjali stood at the back of the elevator as it took her to the twenty-first floor of the building on Mumbai's Marine Drive. In there was Vikram, doing whatever IT managers did. She wasn't quite certain why she arrived in the city earlier than expected or why she invited her brother for lunch.

In the five minutes she made small talk with Adhith, Anjali managed a furtive glance around the cubicle maze. No, she couldn't spot handsome, fashionable Adhith Verma's fiancée. There didn't seem to be anyone resembling an urchin from the slums of Mumbai as the prospective bride was purported to be. The girl surely possessed enormous strength of character to escape the terrible circumstances of her childhood. She was now working in one of the world's largest technology firms. Anjali really, really wanted to meet this woman.

Before she could ask to be introduced, Vikram hustled her out, his arm around her shoulders.

"Pick a restaurant," he said, dodging a couple of salwar-clad ladies speed-walking their way down Marine Drive's promenade.

Tide was high, with only black tetrapod rocks thwarting the waves from lashing the coastline. Ignoring the cars and buses careening past and the skyscrapers on the other side of the road, Anjali focused on the roar of the ocean and the wind whistling in from the sea, whipping strands of hair about her face. It was sweltering, though. There wasn't a single cloud in the bright blue sky.

She wished she'd opted for something lighter than her pink tee, blue jeans, and sneakers. Poor Vikram was probably baking in his dress pants and shirt and red power tie.

Still, she gulped in a deep breath, relishing the hint of salt in the warm air. God, she'd missed this. After her marriage to Rishi, she never really got the chance to enjoy the seaside. When they visited Mumbai, it was usually for family events.

"I don't feel like lunch yet," she said, casually kicking aside a stone. What *did* she want to talk to Vikram about? The mess she'd made of her life? The worry she was killing Rishi, inch by inch?

"*I'm* hungry," Vikram complained.

Sighing, Anjali gestured at one of the vendors ubiquitous to the promenade. "I'll get you some *chana*. Okay, Vicky?"

Holding paper cones warm from the spiced chickpeas, they wandered further down the walkway. Chewing on chana, Vikram said, "I haven't heard that name since I was five or six."

She laughed. "You wouldn't let us call you Vicky after you started kindergarten." Meditatively, she added, "You were so excited to go to school with me." Then, she made one mistake of ignoring him when he was being taunted, and he cut her out of his life.

"Life's taken us both a long way from there," said Vikram.

Please, Vicky, she mumbled in her mind. *I need my brother.* Anjali pointed to the parapet separating the promenade from the tetrapod rocks. "Let's sit for a few minutes." Dropping down next to her, Vikram fidgeted on the scalding hot concrete seating. "The dust will show on the black fabric," she noted, apologetically.

Ignoring the comment, Vikram asked, "So what's up?"

I badly need to talk to someone, and the only person I could think of was you. Anjali needed to tell him about the day in the physiology lab when she met Rishi and Joe... how she gave her love and trust to a man who never deserved it... how he left her heartbroken and bleeding into her soul. She longed to admit to her brother how she ended up marrying Rishi... how she meekly took up a career she never wanted... how she turned into someone her eighteen-year-old self wouldn't recognise. Rishi's affair with Farhan... her pregnancy. If anyone could understand, it was Vikram. *He* wasn't perfect, and he didn't care who knew it.

"What are you doing back in Mumbai? Vikram continued, still squirming on the concrete parapet.

"The anniversary party."

"It's on Friday." This was Tuesday. "Don't you have to work until then?"

"I thought Mom might appreciate some help with the arrangements, so I took a couple of days off." Idiotic explanation. The party was at The Oberoi. The event manager was taking care of everything. All they had to do was show up, dressed in their finery.

"What about the—" Vikram coughed. "—your husband? Is he here, too?"

"He left for Tokyo last week. There's a conference going on. He's taking the flight to Mumbai on Friday morning." Biting back a smile at the chagrin on her brother's face, Anjali continued, "Anyway, I didn't want to stay in Delhi all by myself, so I thought I'd spend some time with my own family. You, especially."

"Why did you want to go for lunch if you didn't feel like food? You could've told me to show up on time for the family dinner."

"At home, we won't get a chance to talk one-on-one."

"What do you want to talk about?"

Where did she start? "Life in general. As you said, we've both come a long way. Vicky, do you ever... have you ever... I mean, are you where you thought you'd be at this age?"

"Sure," he mumbled. "I already knew things weren't gonna be easy. If I keep going at this pace, I'll get where I want in another five or six years. Ten, at the most."

It took Anjali a moment to understand what he was saying. The business he wanted to start, of course. "Have you ever... you know... looked back at some point and felt you made the wrong decision?"

Frowning, he said, "No, I haven't. What's this about, anyway? You have everything you wanted. Perfect career, perfect husband, perfect life."

Pain. Exquisite pain flashed down her nerve endings, clouding her vision in a red fog. Every sound from the street was magnified until there were a million honks in Anjali's brain, thousands of men and women chattering, and a monstrous ocean roaring in displeasure. Her fingers curled around the edge of the parapet. Focus... focus... she needed to take deep breaths. She needed to stay calm until she got to the privacy of her room at the Cuffe Parade flat, or they'd all know what was going on. "I was only making conversation." Anjali stood, praying her knees wouldn't buckle. "Not complaining. See you at home, Vikram."

Her next memory was of waking up in the guest room at her parents' duplex.

***

Chatting with a relative at the poolside party in The Oberoi, Anjali threw a sideways glance at Rishi. On their previous trips to Mumbai, they'd managed to avoid the sites hit by the terrorist attack of 2008. The hotel was long since rebuilt, and this wasn't the location of Nikhil's death, but she was still worried about Rishi's reaction. It was a relief to see him looking fabulous as he always did in business suits—navy blue this time, with matching striped shirt. The healthy light was back in his eyes after a long while. His absence might've given her too much time to think, but the break clearly did him good. Once the baby arrived, this jitteriness within her would also subside. They would all be in a good place.

"Perfect career, perfect husband, perfect life," Vikram's words echoed in her mind.

No. Shaking her head, she ordered the pain to stay away. It was her parents' anniversary party, and she was going to enjoy herself.

The sky was a gorgeous azure with tufts of cottony clouds, and the ocean view on the right was unobstructed. The geometrically shaped pool was empty of swimmers, and except for the palm trees and potted shrubs, the deck had been cleared for the party. Concealed lighting covered the space in a golden haze. The tuxedoed band on the far left played jazz music, and the bar on the near left was serving Vikram and Adhith. She hadn't spotted them before; did they just arrive?

Pasting on a bright smile, Anjali excused herself and hurried towards the two men, followed closely by Rishi.

"What the hell's the matter with your brother?" Rishi muttered. Vikram was glaring at Adhith, looking ready to throttle him.

Adhith didn't seem to notice his best friend's anger, though. "Looking good, Anju," he called.

Preening, she said, "Thanks, Adhi. You always say the right things." The claret-coloured cocktail dress did bring out the sheen in her dark brown hair, and the red suede shoes were a perfect match.

"So Adhi," said Rishi. "Where's your girlfriend?"

"Her name's Seema," Adhith supplied. "She'll be here soon."

Which was apparently a problem for Vikram because he was opening and closing his mouth like a fish caught in a net.

"Vikram," shouted someone. The Joshis gathered around, greeting Adhith and demanding information on this girl none of them had met yet.

Once the group wandered off, the furious glare returned to Vikram's eyes. "Let's get beer." Holding a hand up, he gestured at the bartender.

"*I* will take a menu," said Anjali, sighing. "Let me see what kind of non-alcoholic drinks you have."

Standing hunched over the counter, Vikram muttered something indecipherable in a ferocious tone. Adhith muttered back, sounding equally furious and just as unintelligible. Anjali and Rishi exchanged glances over the menu, the thought in her mind reflected on his face: what the heck was going on? After the passing of their mother's father, Adhith was the only person in the whole, wide world Vikram ever bothered with. Was there trouble between the two friends? Was that why Vikram acted so short with her before? He'd always been a bit grumpy, but—

"Excuse me," Vikram called to the bartender in a loud voice. "I changed my mind. Make mine a lemon drop shot, please."

"Mine, too," Adhith said, promptly.

"Oooh." Anjali looked up from the menu. "Shots."

"Coming right up," said the bartender, turning to the bottle rack.

Raising the tiny glass holding chilled Grey Goose vodka, Adhith said, "May this evening be all we hoped for."

"What's going on with these two?" Rishi said in a tone loud enough for only Anjali to hear. She shrugged, signalling ignorance.

Vikram downed his drink and grabbed a sugar-coated lemon wedge, sucking on it. "May we all survive to see the morning."

Nodding with all the gravity of a medieval commander leading his troops to battle, Adhith tossed the vodka straight down his throat and snatched a lemon wedge from the dish.

Rishi laughed. "I didn't know you were planning to go to war. Or I'd have stayed in Japan."

Eyeing his brother-in-law, Vikram said to the bartender, "Keep 'em coming."

As he followed his second drink with another sugary piece of lemon, Adhith said to Rishi, "Speaking of your conference in Japan... I thought I saw you here a few days back. Did you fly out of Mumbai or something?"

For a moment, the words didn't register with Anjali. She was about to say Rishi only got to Mumbai in the morning, but when she glanced at his face, the mirth was no longer present. Instead, there was dismay. Terrible dismay.

"I..." he stuttered. "...from Mumbai?"

"What?" asked Anjali, shock and fear ricocheting around in her brain. Why would Rishi have been in Mumbai without telling her? Farhan... Farhan lived in Mumbai. Rishi had sworn... he wouldn't do it to her... they had their baby to consider. "That's silly. You were not in Mumbai, right?"

"No, no," soothed Rishi, a hand on her arm. "I was in Tokyo. I wasn't anywhere near Mumbai."

"Maybe you have a lookalike," Adhith continued, looking somewhat discomfited. "Somewhere by the Gateway of India." He lived in the neighbourhood.

"The Gateway?" echoed Anjali, suddenly feeling cold. The Mumbai facility of their hospital network was near the monument. Farhan worked there. Her insides shuddered.

Eyebrows drawn together, Vikram asked, "Anju? Are you okay?"

"She's pregnant," snapped Rishi.

"Gateway?" Anjali parroted. "Are you sure?"

Rishi's warm hand cupped her elbow. "No, he's not sure. How can he be? I wasn't in Mumbai... Anju, why don't you sit for a while?"

Somehow, she found herself seated at the table farthest to the bar, Rishi in the next chair, whispering urgently. The sky was still blue, the music was still playing, and the guests were still milling around, chatting and laughing. If she reached out and touched one of them, would they respond? Would they even feel her presence? Would they see the dark red fog of pain battering her defences?

"I swear to God..." Rishi continued talking.

He spent a long time trying to convince her, but eventually, she held up a trembling hand. Through stiff lips, she asked, " *Were* you in Mumbai? Yes or no, Rishi."

"No," he insisted. "I don't know who Adhi saw, but it wasn't me. You could check with the hospital."

"If I called one of the surgeons who was in Tokyo, what would he say?"

"Tok... Tokyo? I... Anju..." Silence. Complete silence.

Screaming in murderous victory, the pain smashed through the barricades and into her brain, into every cell in Anjali's body. Everything... everything was so red... her parents, Vikram, Adhith, the uncles, cousins, everyone. Was she bleeding into her skull? Would she simply collapse and die here?

There was a warmth at her elbow, a hand urging her to stand. Rishi was saying something about Adhith's guests. Walking in were two women. Vaguely, Anjali wondered if the woman dressed in the silvery-white sari were an *apsara*—a celestial nymph. She was gorgeous enough to be one. But she couldn't be Adhith's fiancée. He and Vikram seemed to be playing tug-of-war with the second woman, the curly-haired one in the black halter top dress, sporting a ridiculous number of coppery bangles on both arms. The matching skyscraper heels in black patent leather were something eighteen-year-old Anjali would've drooled over.

Anjali was almost at the group surrounding the women when she stumbled. Rishi caught her around the shoulders and held her in an easy embrace. "Please, darling," he whispered into her ear. "I didn't *do* anything. I just needed to talk... nothing happened, I swear. We were only—"

Shaking her head jerkily, she tried to move away. She didn't want to hear him say it. If he announced the news, her life as she knew it would end in the presence of her entire family. They'd all know what a fraud she was, how she tricked all of them. *"Perfect career, perfect husband, perfect life,"* mocked Vikram.

The monster in her brain guffawed in glee. The red haze intensified, turning almost to black. She needed it to stop. *God, please make it stop,* she begged.

There was chattering all around. Rishi stayed next to her, his hands holding her upright whenever she stumbled. "I'll tell you everything that happened," he vowed. "I mean, *nothing* happened, but I'll tell you exactly... only, not here. When we get home. I don't want anyone to know... please, Anju. Will you smile? People are watching."

Anjali glanced around at the happy faces of her family. No, she couldn't break... not here. Blood was surely oozing from every crevice of her brain, but she obliged Rishi with a pleasant look.

Everyone smiled back at them, their thoughts clear in their eyes: the ideal couple.

When they turned to Vikram and Adhith and the supposed fiancée, there was only confusion at the seeming battle between the best friends over the young woman. Adhith was introducing her to the other guests, with Vikram practically stalking her around the gathering. He simply wouldn't stop staring at the girl. Anjali's mom hissed at him a couple of times, but Vikram seemed not to hear any of her admonishments. Even the apsara in silver sari—the fiancée's auntie—was clearly annoyed. The girl herself looked confused at times and at other times, thoroughly tickled by Vikram's attention. Adhith's charm didn't slip as much an inch, though.

When the anniversary cake was rolled in, Rishi strode to the front and took charge. "Everyone, please sit at your tables," he called out, clapping hands. "Saale saab. You're up here with the rest of the family." The table closest to the band. "You, too, Adhi. And your guests."

The weird vibe between Vikram and Adhith continued on their way to the table, with a bottle of champagne somehow ending up in the pool in their rush to sit next to the girl they were fighting over. The hotel staff scurried around, straightening chairs and picking cutlery off the floor. A young man appeared with what looked like a butterfly net and fished the bottle from the water.

The Oberoi hostess glided to the main table. "Are we ready?" she asked, tone strained.

"Ready or not," said Rishi, "let's start. Or saale saab might act out more than he already has."

With a frown, Seema—the fiancée—turned to peer at Rishi.

"My friend—" started Adhith, glaring at Rishi. The arrival of a waiter interrupted whatever Vikram's best friend was about to say.

The hostess led the guests of honour to the cake. The band played "The Anniversary Song" as Rattan and Pratap Joshi cut the cake. Like Anjali, her mother was short, with her years adding inches to her waistline. Dad was also short, balding to boot. No matter what physical changes time wrought, the couple remained deeply in love. When they fed each other the cake, Anjali smiled through the agony ripping her body apart. Watching her dad twirling his wife into a dip and soundly kissing her, Anjali applauded, each clap thundering along her raw nerves.

Turning to Vikram, Adhith's girlfriend said, "Oy, Vikram. Your parents are cool."

"They're wonderful," gushed Rishi. "I'm lucky they consider me their son."

Only Anjali saw the trepidation in his eyes. He didn't want their families discovering the truth any more than she did. *Why, Rishi? Why did you do it?* Didn't he know his treachery morphed into the sharpest of all knives, giving the monster inside her brain a weapon to torment her with? Didn't he understand she was bleeding as they spoke? Couldn't he see the blood filling her skull?

Somehow, she managed to make conversation with the guest next to her. Perhaps the silver-clad apsara—the fiancée's auntie—was too busy flinching at her niece's antics to notice any abnormalities in Anjali's behaviour. Perhaps the continuing tussle between Adhith and Vikram over the girl kept everyone distracted.

"I'll take more wine, please," Vikram said to the waiter.

"Another drink?" asked Rishi, a nasty smirk evident in his voice. "How many now?"

Rattan Joshi was seated next to Vikram and took his hand in hers. "Are you all right, betay?"

"He's not going to be all right for long," Rishi opined. "Saale saab, if you do this every day, you're going to pickle your brain."

The occupants of the table stilled. Avoiding everyone's gaze, Vikram tugged his fingers loose from his mother's. The girl—Adhith's supposed fiancée—widened her eyes, fixing Rishi with a furious glare.

"No need to lay it on so thick," Adhith said, wiping his mouth with a napkin. "Vikram's hardly a drunk." The battle over the girl clearly hadn't trickled into other aspects of the men's friendship.

"He is *not* a drunk," snapped the girl, her words whipping across the table.

"With all due respect," said Rishi, tone stubborn, "you two are hardly qualified to diagnose alcoholism."

Baring her teeth in a hiss, the girl said, "With all due respect, you're a little prick."

For a couple of seconds, no one responded.

"Excuse me?" Rishi finally asked.

"You heard what I said," responded the girl, stabbing at her cake with a spoon.

Both Adhith and Vikram were smothering laughter. The apsara in silver sari—the girl's auntie—moaned, both hands covering her face.

"You seem very fond of our Vikram," said Rishi, his words dripping honey. He continued talking, but Anjali didn't pay attention. She couldn't take her eyes off the girl.

"You need to get your mind out of the toilet," the girl said to Rishi.

This was the woman Adhith wanted to marry? Wasn't she supposed to impress the Joshis so they'd give a good report to the minister? She didn't seem to care two bits what anyone thought of her.

Seema was not at all like Anjali. The girl wasn't living in constant fear of being discovered. She wasn't cowering from the monster in her own mind. *"Perfect career, perfect husband, perfect life,"* Vikram taunted.

Please, please, please, Anjali begged God. She needed the night to end. She needed this pain in her head to go away.

But the party didn't end. People laughed, danced, and gossiped about the newcomer in their midst. Adhith's girlfriend apparently harboured no qualms about jumping him in the middle of the crowd or dirty-dancing with Vikram—all before sunset.

No, she was nothing like Anjali, terrified of being exposed for the fraud she was. The hot knife in Anjali's brain continued to twist and stab. Tears sprouted in her eyes. With jittery hands, she picked up the napkin as though to wipe her mouth. How could there be no bloodstains on the fabric? *I can't take it anymore,* she whispered in her mind. *Mom, Dad, I'm so sorry. Vikram, my little brother...*

*** *

One slice. Anjali was an anaesthesiologist. Even if she never cut patients, she knew how it was done. One slice was all it sometimes took to relieve pressure. Funny how detached she felt about it.

Vaguely, she wondered if the steak knife she'd stolen off the table were clean. A giggle erupted. How did it matter? Eyes fixed on the blue markings at her wrist, she swiftly drew the blade across. A line of fiery pain burned its way down her wrist. *Drip, drip, drip...* Anjali counted the drops of blood spurting from the cut ends of the left radial artery.

Standing at the sink, she eyed her reflection in the mirror. *Soon,* she said to the image. The pain would stop. Soon, she'd be at peace.

Clickety-clack, clickety-clack. Was there someone coming into the ladies' room? Transferring the steak knife to her left hand—the one with the bleeding wrist—Anjali opened the tap and let the water wash away the blood in the sink. The door whooshed open. She kept her eyes on the drain, waiting for whomever it was to go into one of the stalls.

"Are you okay?" a clear voice asked.

Anjali's head jerked up. It was the girl—Seema. Adhith's fiancée. Or Vikram's girlfriend. Or whatever. The three of them didn't seem to know.

"Anjali?" Seema called again, frowning in concern.

Pulling her left hand behind her, Anjali turned off the water with her right hand. "Yeah. Just needed a break."

"I understand," Seema said.

Go away, Anjali pleaded. What was Seema waiting for?

The frown on her face deepening, Seema glanced at the floor. Her eyes widened.

When Anjali looked down, she saw the red dots. One more. Then, one more. She gasped and raised the hand which held the knife. Blood spurted rhythmically from her wrist, coating the entire hand. Her fingers were so slippery. She switched the blade to her right hand. "Don't come near me," she said, hoarsely. "I won't hurt you. Go into the bathroom, and I'll lock you in. Someone will find you—and me—sooner or later."

Seema opened her mouth, and a gurgling sound came out.

"Go," Anjali said, swaying.

Seema took one step forward.

"I said, 'Go into the bathroom,'" Anjali ordered, her voice trembling.

"You'll bleed to death," Seema mumbled.

Anjali laughed. "Are you really this dumb? Of course, I'll die. That's the idea."

Hand to her mouth, Seema gagged.

"What are you doing?" asked Anjali.

"I'm gonna throw up," Seema said, lurching to the washbasin. One step. Two steps. With a loud scream, she whirled around and lunged.

Before Anjali even realised what was happening, before she could even make a murmur of surprise, Seema's fingers closed around the arm with the knife. In a split second, Seema was behind Anjali, yanking her right arm behind her back. The knife fell from Anjali's fingers.

Again and again, Seema screamed, "*Help.*"

"Let go of me," Anjali shrieked, kicking backwards.

"Oww," squealed Seema. "Stay still, you little *princess*. I'm trying to save your life."

Anjali struggled even more, holding her bleeding left wrist as far away from Seema as possible. "I didn't ask you to save me," Anjali said. "Go away. I won't tell anyone you ignored me while I was dying."

"How could you? You'll be dead." Somehow, both of Anjali's arms were now in Seema's hold. "*Help,*" she screamed. "*Somebody, help!*"

Anjali kicked furiously. The wastebasket toppled over, its contents strewing across the room. She and Seema teetered together on the marble floor, their feet slipping on the puddles of blood. The thick, red liquid smeared both women.

Without warning, something struck the back of Anjali's knees, and she collapsed, face down. Seema came tumbling after. Anjali floundered, but she couldn't seem to get back up. There was a weight holding her down. A pressure around her bleeding wrist. Seema was sitting on Anjali's back, frantically trying to staunch the blood loss.

A tide of darkness washed over Anjali, tugging at her feet, dragging her into a lightless ocean. Terror. Stark terror. "I can't see," she sobbed. This was not the same darkness of the headaches. This was the thick, black sea of death.

"What—are you fainting?" Seema screeched from somewhere outside the darkness. "Don't you faint on me. You hear me, princess? *Don't faint.*"

Weeping hard, Anjali thrashed around amidst the shadowy waves in her mind. "I'm scared, Seema." The waves seemed to be yanking her deeper and deeper to a place from which there would be no return. There would be no Mom and Dad, no family, no friends, no Rishi. No baby. "I think I'm gonna die."

"No way," said Seema, her voice now distant. "I *will not* let you die. *Help.* Someone. *Please.*"

"Stay with me," Anjali begged. As long as she could hear the girl's voice, she'd be able to find her way back.

"I will," vowed Seema.

Vaguely, Anjali heard the ring of a phone, Seema begging whomever to pick up. Anjali tried to keep talking, but her mouth couldn't seem to produce sounds. It was too much effort even to cry. The darkness now seemed less threatening... more peaceful.

"Hey, wake up," a voice shouted in Anjali's ear. "We need to talk."

"Acute volume loss," Anjali said in the way of response.

"Say what?"

"I lost a lot of blood," she explained. "My blood pressure is probably too low. Therefore, I cannot wake up."

"How does that work?" asked the voice, the feminine quality now clear. "You can talk, but you can't open your eyes?"

Anjali frowned. The question carried merit. Slowly, she tried fluttering open her lids. The marble floor of the bathroom gleamed beneath her cheek. Hands on the cold tiles, she heaved herself up.

And almost tumbled back in surprise. There were two people in the ladies' room—a girl, smeared all over with blood from the dying woman on her lap. The girl was screaming for help. There was stuff strewn all around—a loose shoe, the steak knife, tissue wads from the wastebasket... even what looked like a used tampon.

"Is that me?" Anjali whispered, eyeing the bleeding woman.

"And you called *me* dumb," taunted the voice from before. "Yeah, princess. It's you." Seema, her black halter neck dress somehow spotless, was sitting on the countertop, her long, tanned legs crossed.

"But..." Anjali glanced at the floor where the two women were. "I can understand I'm dead, but why are *you?*"

"I'm not dead," said Ghost Seema, sounding offended at the very idea. Jerking her head towards the duo on the floor, she added, "I don't know if *you* are, either. Your chest is moving."

Tilting her head, Anjali studied the woman on real Seema's lap. "You might be right. If I'm not dead, I need some explanation on what's happening."

Ghost Seema shrugged. "I don't know. I was waiting for you to tell me."

"Heh?"

"Clearly, you wanted to talk to me."

Anjali pointed out, "I could've talked to you when I was alive... before I fainted... or whatever."

"Oh, for God's—" Ghost Seema rolled her eyes. "I'm not really *her*. I'm you. Or rather the person you wish you could be."

Anjali laughed. "What I want to be is a foul-mouthed former urchin who's got my brother fighting with his best friend? No, thank you."

Ghost Seema glared. "Don't be rude." Tone hardening, she added, "And don't act coy. The time for pretence is over. Death does not accept anything but the truth. Death *is* truth. 'Fess up, Anjali Joshi. Why am I here in your mind?"

"Truth?" Anjali asked, bitterly. "There has never been any truth in my life. I lied to everyone, even to my own family."

"Why?" asked Ghost Seema. "Were you afraid they'd stop loving you?"

Startled, Anjali said, "Of course not. My parents aren't like that." Her dad and mom certainly expected personal and professional success from her, but they'd never disown her if she stumbled. They weren't like the Rastogis, making their affection conditional on their son's mute compliance to every demand.

"Then?"

"I don't know." Thinking back, she muttered, "Everyone always said I was perfect, so..."

"You decided you needed to be?" Ghost Seema laughed. "You met society's expectations all right, but your quest for perfection so thoroughly messed up your life to the point you decided to end it. How less perfect could you possibly get?"

"Tell me something I don't know," snapped Anjali.

"I can't," said Ghost Seema. "All I know is what you know. But I want you to tell *me* something. Am I perfect?" Glancing at the real Seema on the floor, shouting threats at the Almighty to keep Anjali alive, the ghost clarified, "I mean, is *she* perfect?"

"Not even close," Anjali muttered. The minister considered the girl from the slums of Mumbai completely unsuitable for the position of Mrs Adhith Verma no matter how steely the will she must've possessed to escape the circumstances of her birth. There was no question every guest at the party believed Seema was a potty-mouthed, man-crazy fool. But the same woman was now on the bathroom floor, crying over someone she barely knew. She was hanging on to Anjali, telling her not to give up. Eyes tearing, Anjali said, "Seema's certainly no goddess, and she'd probably laugh her head off at the idea."

"What is she then?" asked Ghost Seema.

"A human being who's more than her background, more than her flaws, more than her mistakes," whispered Anjali.

"She worked hard to make something of herself," agreed Ghost Seema. Tone turning derisive, the ghost added, "Unlike you. Take away your rich family, what's left? A fool who married a gay man and destroyed both your lives. Worthless."

"*No.*" Anjali bared her teeth. "The fool you're talking about *saved* that man from being blackmailed. My family might've been rich, but I worked darned hard to be a doctor. Anaesthesiology was not my first choice, but I give it everything I have. I... I think I'm a good friend. I *am* a good daughter." If she were the bragging sort, she'd have even told the stupid ghost to open her eyes and see if Rishi would've been where he was without his wife. Placing a protective hand on her belly, Anjali murmured, "I'll do my best to be a good mom." She didn't remember the baby when she put the steak knife to her wrist. Her only thought had been to end the pain. If the universe gave her another chance...

With a mocking grin, Ghost Seema said, "I notice you're no longer claiming to be perfect. Society doesn't like it when women are less than perfect. If you're not a goddess, you're a demon."

"Says who?" Anjali asked, chest heaving with anger. "Go and tell your precious society what I've done for the people around me." Anjali Joshi was neither goddess nor demon. Only a human being who was more than her background, more than her flaws, more than the mistakes she made. "I'm worthwhile as I am—as a daughter, as a sister, as a friend, as a doctor, as *me*. My baby will have a mom who loves him." WEE-WOO... WEE-WOO... WEE-WOO... a high-pitched shriek set her eardrums vibrating. Anjali jumped. "What's that?"

"This will only hurt a bit," said Ghost Seema, reaching out to pinch Anjali's forearm.

"*Oww,*" said Anjali. "What did you do that for?"

"We need to give you blood, sweetie," said her mother's voice.

When Anjali opened her eyes, she was inside an ambulance, a medical technician inserting an IV line into her vein.

***

The baby was all right. Anjali closed her eyes and muttered a prayer of thankfulness. She glanced towards the chair by the hospital bed. Each time she woke during the ambulance ride, Rishi was by her side. All night, he stayed in the plastic chair by the bed, never moving even to go to the restroom. He didn't say a word, but his red-rimmed eyes already begged for forgiveness a million times.

All of Anjali's family was around. Mom and Dad were clinging to each other on the sofa. Vikram... where did he go? Last she saw, he was sitting on the windowsill. And...

"Seema?" Anjali croaked, trying to raise herself on her elbows.

"Here," called a voice. Both Seema and Vikram heaved themselves up from the floor by the foot of the bed. The way he was holding on to her... Anjali bit back a smile. Vikram was in love.

489

When Anjali next woke, it was to the psychiatrist waiting by her bedside. The woman flew in from Delhi? This time, Anjali didn't conceal anything. From her first encounter with Joe to her decision to marry Rishi, she talked like she never talked before. Hesitantly, she asked for the shrink's assurance that anything she'd learn about Rishi would be kept confidential. Doctors were supposed to keep their lips zipped about patients, but Anjali needed to hear the promise. The psychiatrist didn't as much as blink at Rishi's affair or the emotional blackmail Anjali exerted to get him to cooperate with the fertility treatments.

Rishi was present during the second session. Voice low, Anjali said, "I'm filing for divorce."

"Please, Anju," he begged, clinging to her hand. "Don't do this. I swear I won't ever return to Mumbai. I'll never call Farhan. I'll... I'll quit my job. If I'm not a board member, I won't *have* to return to Mumbai."

"This is not about you and Farhan," Anjali said, sitting propped up in the hospital bed. "It's about me."

"What about the baby?" Rishi's eyes went to her still flat tummy. "It can never be about only you or me."

Anjali nodded. "I might've agreed for the baby's sake. But if we continue the way we've been doing, I won't get over the panic attacks. I won't be a functional human being, Rishi. And what about you? Either you'll stray again, or you'll die inch by inch. Neither scenario will be good for the baby."

Explaining to her family wasn't nearly as difficult as she imagined. They caught the tail end of her conversation with Rishi—enough to get the gist.

"I love you, Anju," he wept, refusing to leave the side of her bed.

"I know," she said, a protective hand on her belly. "I love you, too. Just not the kind of love which should've ended in marriage. I should've... *we* should've known better."

"Our baby," Rishi begged. "Please, don't do this. I swear I'll do whatever you want."

Anjali smiled. "You're always going to be the baby's father, and you'll always be my best friend, but if I use my stupidity to force you to change, you'll be in this bed in my place a year or two down the line."

"My family," Rishi whispered. "My God, my father's going to—"

"*We're* your family," Anjali said, tone firm. "This baby and I. If your parents can't accept you for who you are, it's their loss, not yours. Rishi, if you'll take one last piece of advice from an old friend... move from Delhi. Take your..." She swallowed hard. There was no way around letting her family in on the secret. "...partner with you and move someplace where you can be yourself." No amount of pleading from Rishi would change her mind. She'd gone into the marriage with full knowledge of his sexual orientation and still somehow ended up resenting it. Like his parents, Anjali also guilt-tripped him into pretending one part of his identity didn't exist, that Farhan didn't exist. No more. "Go to him," she urged. "All three of us need to be at peace."

Through it all, her family didn't say a word. The expressions on Mom and Dad were comically confused, and Vikram's jaw was nearly on the floor. Seema was also in the room as per Anjali's request.

After shooing her husband out, Anjali turned to the sofa where her shocked parents were seated. "You heard enough to put it all together. When Rishi and I decided to get married, I already knew he was gay. His parents were vehemently opposed to what they saw as his perversion, and I... I thought Rishi was the perfect man. I thought I could make it work. Why wouldn't it, right? The perfect Anjali Joshi would have the perfect husband, perfect career, perfect life."

"Anju," Vikram muttered, his awkward tone telling her he hadn't forgotten their conversation by the sea.

"You don't have to feel guilty about what you said," Anjali assured him. That's what *everyone* believed, and I desperately wanted it to be true." She tried to explain more, but one tiny hiccup, and the sobs started. Her shoulders shook. With an indistinct murmur, her mother rushed to sit next to her on the bed. "I saw you and Dad... you were always so proud of me. You didn't know how badly I'd messed up my life. So I did something even more stupid. If Seema hadn't come along..." Through her tears, Anjali continued talking. "I'm a failure..." Only in some of her choices, but she needed to look her mistakes in the eye before moving on. "...but I still want to live," she finished, firmly.

Anjali refused to let her parents blame themselves for what happened as they seemed to be doing, but she insisted they confront their relationship with Vikram. The four of them talked almost the entire day, cried, laughed through their pain, and told each other everything would be all right. Dad wouldn't let Vikram out of the room until it was drilled into his thick skull he was surrounded by a family which adored him no matter what, and he'd better act like he was a part of it. There was a long way to go before the wounds—real and imagined—healed, but they at least made a start that afternoon.

Anjali did consider returning to her job in Delhi, but there she'd be alone and pregnant except for the husband she was divorcing. Plus, the Rastogis. Rishi refused to deliver the news, and Anjali never wanted to repeat the highly uncomfortable phone call with her soon-to-be-former mother-in-law. Rishi's ma and papa hotfooted it back to India. Rishi moved out before their flight touched ground, but it didn't stop them from harassing him with daily calls and emails. Nope, Anjali didn't want to go through any of it. She definitely didn't wanna risk having them show up at her doorstep.

In Mumbai, she'd have an entire support system. Even if the father of her child weren't in the picture, she was pampered by her parents through her pregnancy. In late November 2019, her baby boy was born.

Four months later, Dr Pratapchandra Joshi called Anjali into his tiny home office and asked if she wanted a job. Apparently, the Joshi Charity Clinic in Goa was in legal trouble.

Chapter 36

Present Day

"No, Joe," snapped Anjali, leaping from the sofa to shield Rishi. "You're not going to do a single thing."

Struggling against Siddharth's hold, Joe asked, "How can you possibly defend... he *hit* you!" Kokila and Meenakshi were hanging on to one of his elbows, trying to drag him back to the chair behind the desk. Gauri was staring wide-eyed at Rishi as though she couldn't believe what she heard.

"It was an *accident*." Turning to Rishi, Anjali said, "Return to the hotel. *Please*."

Rishi heaved himself up from the sofa. "No. I'm done hiding behind you." Angry eyes fixed on his former flatmate, he said, "You wanna punch me? You can try. I'll beat the shit out of you at this just like in everything else."

With an enraged roar, Joe rushed.

"*Stop*," screamed Anjali, throwing herself at him.

All of them—Anjali, Joe, Siddharth, Meenakshi, and Kokila—stumbled, going down in a heap. Kokila and Anjali ended by sitting on Joe. Only Siddharth's head and upper torso showed from the bottom of the pile.

"*Rishi*," screeched Meenakshi. "Are you crazy? You can't get into a fistfight. You're a surgeon. You, too, Joe."

"He's not," snapped Rishi. "Why can't anyone remember the fact?"

493

"Get off me," Siddharth bellowed, trying to shove Joe from the lower half of his body. Unfortunately, Kokila and Anjali were trying to hold the furious man in place.

"Not until Joe comes to his senses," grunted Kokila, still grappling with his arm. Anjali clung to his neck, each hot, angry breath from him blowing against her cheek.

"*What?*" came Siddharth's voice. "You're crushing my *kidneys*." Reaching sideways, his hand scrambled over Joe's face.

"What are you—" bellowed Joe. "Take your bloody finger out of my nose!"

"Got it," Siddharth announced, triumphantly. "Joe, my friend, come quietly, or your glasses will buy it."

"My—give them back, you—"

"Give them back," Rishi taunted from behind. "He ain't gonna be able to do a single thing with or without his glasses."

Joe struggled against the hands holding him down. "I'll show you what I can—"

"Stop it, both of you." Anjali let go of Joe's neck and scrambled to a sitting position on his belly. "Listen, Joe," she said, urgently. "If I can take your word for what happened eleven years ago, the least you can do is trust me when I say it was an accident."

Below her, Joe stilled. Wild pain in his eyes, he started, "But... Anju, because of him, you tried to... oh, God..."

"No buts," said Anjali, firmly. "What I did wasn't because of him, and I'm already over it. I need you to get past it as well, or none of us will ever be able to move on. And Rishi, don't think I don't know what you're doing." Breathing heavily, she twisted around and shook a finger at him. "If you're feeling guilty, you can darned well live with it. Don't provoke Joe into a fight."

Rishi stared unblinkingly at her. A deep flush spread upwards from his neck. "Please, Anju," he begged, voice hoarse. "I can't take any more of this. I need... I just need..." Shoving fingers into his hair, he stumbled back into the sofa. "Do you understand what I did?" he asked Joe, remorse and misery etched into every line on his face. "If Seema hadn't gone to the bathroom, Anjali would've died that night. *You hear me?*"

"He hears you," said Siddharth. "We all do. But this is not the way to fix things, my friend."

With a small sob, Gauri patted Rishi's shoulder, but she didn't speak.

Crawling off Joe, Anjali said, "Both you men are going to sit down and pay attention to what I have to say, okay? No one's going to start a fight."

"Are we clear on the subject?" Siddharth asked. "Good. Now, *get the hell off me.*"

When they eventually limped back to their seats, Meenakshi mused, "So I *wasn't* wrong about Rishi."

"What do you mean?" Anjali asked, keeping an eye on the man in question. He was staring dully at the photograph on the wall—the one of Joe and Nikhil, the picture from which Rishi was cut out.

One by one, the group admitted to having harboured suspicions about his sexual orientation. Only, nobody ever tried to poke their nose into his private business except for Anjali. Gauri already knew, but she didn't emerge from her funk until Rishi and Anjali were a couple of years into their marriage. By then, no one wanted to voice worries.

Rishi didn't respond to any of the comments and continued to stare at the old photograph.

Joe said nothing, either. He'd returned to his chair, but his face was still pale, and his turbulent gaze remained fixed on Anjali. "I should've been there. Promise me you'll say something if you ever feel like——"

"I don't think it will happen again," Anjali assured him. She'd always been prone to panic attacks—the headaches which went misdiagnosed since childhood—but the psychiatrist believed the specific circumstances in Anjali's life were what caused the problem to escalate so badly. As long as she didn't return to said circumstances, she'd be all right. "But I swear I'll ask for help at the first sign of trouble."

Heaving a collective sigh of relief they weren't going to witness Joe murder Rishi for his part in Anjali's breakdown, the gang quieted. "So... aren't you gonna call him?" Kokila asked Rishi. "Your Farhan?"

Finally looking away from the picture on the wall, Rishi threw a startled glance at her.

Meenakshi ptchaaed. "C'mon. We wanna meet this Dr Zaidi." Following Rishi's eyes to the dark sky outside the window, she added, "Nuh-huh. Not tomorrow. Now. I'm sure he's not asleep. I mean, would *you* simply take a nap if you knew he'd be talking to his family about you?"

Tone bitter, Rishi said, "My family's never gonna want to meet Farhan. They'd prefer to pretend he didn't exist. Hell, I'm sure they prefer *I* didn't exist."

For a moment or two, no one reacted. Then, Joe stood, muttering under his breath. "This ain't your father's house, and we're not your damned parents. Call the poor sap. We need to talk about your blackmailer shit, and he deserves to be part of the discussion. Plus, he deserves a medal for putting up with a jackass like you."

"As if you're some prize," Rishi snarled.

"Oh, for——" Siddharth spat out a foul curse.

"*I* want to meet Dr Zaidi," said Gauri. She nodded at Joe. "Ask him here, please."

Tugging out his phone, Siddharth asked Rishi, "What's the number?"

When the doorbell chimed through the house, Anjali went with Joe to welcome Farhan. He looked as badass as always with his shoulder-length hair loose and his muscles defined under the light cream tee, but there was clear trepidation in the dark eyes.

As soon as he entered the office, everyone in the room turned to the door. Gaze darting around, Farhan said, "Hello."

Nobody responded, simply staring at the newcomer in their midst. Meenakshi elbowed Kokila and blinked meaningfully in the direction of Farhan's biceps.

Siddharth groaned. "Don't mind them," he said, resting a hip against the edge of the desk. "They're all dorks. I'm not."

"Oh, yeah?" snapped Kokila. With her index finger, she poked the lawyer/doctor in the belly, making him double over with a high-pitched giggle.

Laughter ensued. Rishi's face was somewhat blotchy, but he managed a grin at his friends. "Thank you," he said to Joe. The trembling in his fingers clearly visible, Rishi took Farhan's hand in his. "Everyone, this is Farhan. Farhan Zaidi."

Quick introductions and a round of beer later, Farhan asked Siddharth, "You said you have information on the blackmailer?"

"Not me." Siddharth glanced at Joe.

It took more than an hour for Joe to narrate his tale. No one spoke. Over every face flowed the same succession of expressions—shock at the events, terror of what could've happened, pain at the thought of all the lost time.

Then, Gauri growled. "Idiot," she raged. In silence, the rest watched as she stumbled towards Joe. A fist raised, she punched him in the chest. Sobbing harshly, she rained blows, and he took it all without protest until she collapsed against him in tears.

"I'm sorry, girl," he murmured, stroking her hair. "I couldn't call. But believe me... I never stopped thinking of Nikhil. Or of you." Joe's eyes went around the room, jerking when he reached Rishi. "*Any* of you."

One by one, the group tore into Joe for his stupidity before hugging him. Except Rishi. Chest heaving with raspy breaths, he glared at his former flatmate. When his fist went up, the rest shouted his name, but Rishi didn't throw the punch, simply continuing to glower in silence.

"Yeah, it was my own damned fault," Joe acknowledged, gaze firmly fixed on Rishi. "My arrogance and stupidity. But if I returned... if I even sent an email... it would've put Anju's life at risk. I couldn't do it, man."

"Sit, please," begged Siddharth, shoving Rishi back to the sofa. "We have things to discuss." Turning to Farhan, Siddharth asked, "Did you bring the notes Rishi got?"

Nodding, Farhan tossed the two notes onto the desk. "You think this was your INTERPOL fellow?" he asked Joe.

"Hard to say," Joe muttered, perusing the sheets of paper. "I didn't really pay attention to his handwriting. Who else could it be? It's either him or one of his officers."

"I'm not sure, man," Siddharth said. "Your theory simply doesn't fit." Grabbing a pillow from the sofa, he dropped to the floor and stretched out. The rest waited a few seconds for him to elaborate. Finally, Farhan hurled the pillow from *his* chair straight onto Siddharth's face. Swatting it aside, he groused, "What? I'm thinking."

"Think louder," snapped Rishi.

With a sigh, Siddharth sat up. "Okay, let's assume for a moment it was Naidu. What was he hoping to achieve?"

"The same as before," said Joe. "He wants a surgeon working with him."

Siddharth shook his head. "Against *Anjali?* By using her absence in Rishi's life? How would Naidu stop Rishi from going to Anjali and telling all?"

"Divorcing couples are not known for their cooperation," Farhan said.

"True," said Siddharth. "But in our case, both parties would've had strong motive to cooperate. Anjali wouldn't want Rishi working with the cops to put her in jail, and he wouldn't have wanted to do the surgeries. Plus, their child."

"Children make things crazier." Huffing, Farhan added, "When my parents were divorcing, I learned more than I ever wanted about both of them. Since we all now get along, they pretend they never said anything." Amidst the murmurs and chortles in the room, he insisted, "Divorce makes everyone go nuts."

"All right, let me put it this way." Siddharth turned to Joe. "Rishi could've been angry enough with Anjali to cooperate with INTERPOL. Or he might've thought the better of it and tipped her off. Fifty-fifty probability. You, Joe, worked with Naidu for three years. Take a wild guess. Would Naidu go for it?"

Frowning, Joe mused, "Maybe... if his back were against the wall. Mostly, he has plans A, B, and C ready to go."

"So either his back is against the wall for some reason, or..." Siddharth toppled back onto his pillow. "...it's not him."

"Shit," muttered Rishi, rubbing his temple hard. "I'm still in trouble."

"Join the club," said Anjali.

"Actually," said Siddharth. "I've been trying to figure out what possible cause INTERPOL would have to suspect Anjali. She was eighteen when she met Rishi and Joe. Unless Naidu believes she was some sort of prodigy villain, that theory doesn't make sense, either."

"She *is* the CEO of the clinic," Kokila pointed out. Grimacing, she added, "Which started only a few weeks ago."

Shaking her head, Anjali said, "I found it hard to believe, too, but SP Naidu lied to me. Sid, you were around when I talked to him the second time. You heard what he said. There was no other reason for him to do it."

"He said he was hoping to pick your brains about Joe and Rishi. He could've been trying to get you to reveal other information. About your family, for example. They're as good as you as suspects in the case."

"The Joshis?" Kokila asked, incredulously. "Why didn't this Naidu person go straight to Anju's father?"

"Unethical bastard," Joe snarled. "I know why." Turning to Anjali, he explained, "The cops won't dare go against your family until they have solid evidence. If they approached your father directly, he'd immediately contact higher authorities. Naidu's going after you because he thinks you're the weakest link. He's trying to get evidence against your family through you."

"Weakest link?" Baring her teeth, Anjali hissed.

"He's trying to play you like he did me," Joe said, eyes glinting. "Damned cop thinks you're the same girl you were in Delhi. He somehow forgot *you* put a stop to his blackmail scheme. He's assuming you snapped because your marriage broke. But like you said, your breakdown wasn't because of Rishi. The only person who's ever been able to bring you down is you. Naidu doesn't realise you were willing to take on the whole bloody society as a single mom rather than continue in a failing marriage." Indian community could be unkind to divorcées, especially those with children. "He doesn't know you *let* people call you crazy only to protect the jackass you married. The sonuvabitch cop has to return to Goa at some point. He's gonna find you're not easily played."

"None of which tells us who in the clinic is actually responsible for the organ trafficking," muttered Siddharth. "Or who's blackmailing Rishi now."

Part XIII

Chapter 37

"This ain't a good idea," Rishi muttered, swatting away a mosquito buzzing by his head as he followed his former flatmate to the one-storey building behind the whitewashed church.

"God, it's bloody hot," Joe said, tugging at the collar of his faded green tee.

All three men—Rishi, Joe, and Farhan—were dressed in shorts, tees, and sandals, but the ocean and the blazing sun teamed up to drench every living thing in Goa in sweat. A giant dark patch decorated the front of Rishi's blue Polo shirt as though he'd spilt a glassful of salty water on himself.

With not even the slightest hint of a breeze to provide relief, the green palms surrounding the churchyard were perfectly still. There were a couple of workmen scrubbing clean the statue of the deity on one side of the yard, but otherwise, the place seemed deserted.

"It's the only idea I have until Naidu returns my calls," Joe said. "My brother first told me they hired an investigator to find if I'd been dating someone in Delhi. Now, he's claiming it was Fr Franco who did the hiring. I want to meet this investigator. I thought no one in Delhi knew about Anju and me except you and the rest of the gang. Naidu, too, but he wouldn't have blabbed. There *must* be someone else who knew and talked to the investigator. Maybe this person knew about *you,* too."

Anjali had said she'd ask her cousin Mohini who did the Tinder setup from the other end. By the time the group left Joe's house, it was already well into the morning, and the CEO of the Joshi Charity Clinic couldn't afford not to show up to work. Not when the organisation was under investigation, and its staff was mutinying against the leadership. Plus, she needed to update her father on the latest developments while somehow concealing the information about Rishi's blackmailer and whatever she heard from Joe. Siddharth and Kokila went with Anjali to help arrange the townhall meeting. As her lawyer, Siddharth would also be coordinating with the Joshi family legal team on defensive measures.

Any discussion with Mohini would need to wait for the evening, but Joe could corner Fr Franco right away. "Yeah, but..." Rishi stopped at the plain wooden door to the priest's residence and glanced at the church building. "You're gonna barge in and announce to your grandfather... I have a hard time buying he'll help a gay man."

"We're not going to know until we ask," said Farhan. Keeping his tone low, he added, "If you'd rather not tell the priest you're gay, I can go with Joe."

Rishi's vocabulary wasn't good enough to describe the swell of feelings within his heart in a single word—a mixture of gratitude, love, and guilt. "Thanks, Farhan. I can do this. Got to start somewhere."

"I'm with you," assured Farhan.

Rolling his eyes, Joe raised his knuckles, but before he could knock, there came a volley of barks. When the door opened, the half-eared mutt called Scher hobbled to his master as quickly as his old joints could carry him. "Good boy," murmured Joe, dropping to his haunches to scratch the dog's back. "Did you enjoy your trip?" Scher had gone along with Fr Franco to visit the kids in the church orphanage. Joe needed to pick the dog up and planned to talk to the priest at the time.

"Joe, my boy—oh, hello." The priest stepped out from behind the door, wearing a plain cotton shirt and pants. "You brought guests." Except for the leanness of the old man's frame and his paler skin, this would be what Joe D'Acosta looked like in fifty years. The Portuguese phenotype ran strong in the entire family—Joe, his brothers and sister, and the old priest who was their biological grandfather's cousin.

"Xapai," Joe called. "These are my friends from Delhi—Rishi and Farhan." Not exactly but close enough.

An hour later, they were seated around the living room, drinking tiny glass tumblers of sweet, cool coconut water brought in by the priest's helper. Fr Franco was red-faced, looking anywhere but at his grandson/godson's companions. Finally, the old man huffed. "Some of the younger priests keep reminding us God created everyone, and there's no cleric big enough to question His wisdom." The priest threw a sideways glance at Rishi. "One of Ram's sons is gay, you know." Anjali's Skinwalla Uncle. "Ram wasn't terribly happy, but what could he do? Either take the boy as he was or lose him altogether."

Farhan seemed unaffected by the revelation, but Rishi shifted in discomfort. Somehow, he'd imagined the Joshis as this perfectly accepting clan from the origin of the universe.

"Dr Ram was a man of his times, xapai," said Joe. "But he loved his family. About this investigator..."

The ruddy colour on the priest's wrinkled face deepened. "Er... there wasn't one."

"What do you mean?" asked Joe.

"Well..." The priest looked both ways before leaning forwards. "All I said to Dev was I'd arrange for someone to investigate. He assumed it was a professional."

Joe goggled. "You *lied?*"

"No," said the priest. "I simply didn't correct his wrong assumption. I didn't want him knowing the girl's name if it turned out to be nothing."

"You lied," insisted Joe, glee on his face. "What do you mean 'girl's name'? I thought you merely suspected there had been someone in Delhi. Did you already know it was Anjali?"

The red on the priest's cheeks got even darker. He mumbled something Rishi couldn't hear.

"What painting?" Joe asked.

"The one where you're..." Once again glancing up and down the room, Fr Franco hissed, "The one with the frog. She *signed* it."

"Frog—" Suddenly, Joe's face was as bright red as the priest's. Closing his eyes, he muttered, "Damn."

"Language," reproved the priest.

A frog painting? What in the— Rishi blinked, then chortled. "You don't want to know," he said to a puzzled Farhan. Turning to Joe, Rishi asked, "You took it from the old flat?"

Apparently, Naidu arranged someone to ship all of Joe's stuff to the navy quarters in Kochi where his family was in protective custody. Joe did all the unpacking himself, but he wasn't in the flat the entire time to prevent the priest from opening his cupboard in search of something or the other and getting an eyeful.

"Then, I saw in the paper she was marrying *you*," Fr Franco explained to Rishi. "I didn't know what to think." The priest kept tabs on his old friend's family, and when he heard about the divorce, he contacted Dr Pratap Joshi, Anjali's father.

"How much did you tell them?" Joe asked.

"Only the same story we told the kids and everyone else," assured Fr Franco. "You left your course to work for the military."

Phew. The same relief was on Joe's face. Anjali was going to tell her father she heard via Siddharth's connections in law enforcement about INTERPOL's suspicions regarding the Joshis. If they already knew about Joe's past with the transplant ring, she'd be caught in a lie.

"I didn't even have to mention Anjali to Pratap," Fr Franco continued. "*He* brought up the topic."

When Anjali contacted the Joshi lawyer to locate her missing boyfriend, she didn't realise the man would feel duty-bound to inform her parents. Pratap and Rattan Joshi were puzzled their daughter didn't involve them in the search but bought the story of how she was merely helping Rishi look for his flatmate. Still, the episode was strange enough and Joe's bio close enough to Rishi's that they harboured doubts on the identity of the man in their daughter's life. The Joshi parents put it out of their minds when Anjali informed them she wanted to marry Rishi.

The doubts resurfaced when she announced the reason for the divorce. They actually asked Vikram, the cybersecurity engineer in the family, to track down Joe. A day later, Fr Franco called. Within an hour, Dr Pratap Joshi got a second phone call—SP Naidu from INTERPOL wanted answers about the illegal purchase of pharmaceuticals.

Desperate for Joe and Anjali to find happiness but not knowing how they would react to each other after so many years, the elders involved took a chance and arranged for Anjali to go to Goa under the pretext of the crisis at the clinic. Well, the crisis was real... but yeah, Cousin Mohini made a fake profile on Tinder while Fr Franco did his part through Romeo, the second of Joe's two brothers.

"The Joshis aren't involved in the organ-transplant mess," said the priest, tone obstinate as though his guests were insisting otherwise. "If they were, they wouldn't have sent their child to deal with it all on her own."

"They wouldn't," agreed Rishi. "They wouldn't blackmail me, either." First, the family would have to know about the night he spent with a former patient. If they did, they wouldn't have happily agreed to marry their daughter to a gay man. Now they knew it as the reason for the divorce, what could Anjali's parents gain from threatening Rishi? "Thank you for taking the time to talk to us," he said to the priest.

When Fr Franco grinned at his visitors, Joe said, "I'll call you later, xapai. We need to get back and figure out what next."

"Er... Joe?" the priest called. "If you're going to see Anjali any time soon, please ask her to make nice with Mrs Braganza."

Frowning, Joe asked, "Why? The woman's a pain in the backside."

"Be that as it may..." started the priest. "She went to the bishop and complained about Anju... also, about you. Something about an orgy. The old coot..." Crossing himself, the priest continued, "...wants to talk to me about it."

"You can ask the bishop to talk to me, directly," snapped Joe. "His Excellency has an appointment with me in a couple of weeks."

"It's not the bishop," the priest explained, tone earnest. "The poor man doesn't have a choice. Mrs Braganza and her brother are big contributors to the diocese."

Rishi managed to bite back the expletive springing to his tongue, but Joe didn't bother.

When they left the priest's residence, Joe said, "I'm going home to see if there's anything in my old papers which might give us a clue. Not likely because INTERPOL took everything. Still... doesn't hurt to look. I'll meet you at your hotel for dinner."

Both Joe and Siddharth showed up at the Marriott in the evening. After their preliminary discussions with the clinic staff about a townhall, Siddharth and Kokila left Anjali working late as usual. Kokila returned to the Fontainhas mansion to sleep off jet lag, and Siddharth collected Joe from his home and drove to the hotel. Anjali would join them later. The remaining three women in the group couldn't make it for various reasons.

Siddharth looked sharp in the same dress pants and shirt he'd worn on his visit to the clinic—every inch the high-profile police psychiatrist he was. Like Rishi and Farhan, Joe didn't bother to change out of the shorts and tee from the morning. And no, he didn't have any luck finding clues in his papers.

Crouching in front of the small fridge, Farhan grabbed a bottle of water. "The fact *we* think it's not the Joshis running the crime ring is immaterial. INTERPOL clearly does. Why? Let's start there."

Siddharth slouched further into the armchair. "I'm mulling another theory at the moment, but since you asked... Rishi and Joe were connected to Anjali back then, and now, the clinic is connected to the Joshis. But the Joshis didn't contact Joe and Rishi in Delhi; *INTERPOL* did. Anjali simply happened to be around. The crime ring found Joe through their point man on the AIIMS campus. Then, Naidu took over. He found Rishi in the process of recruiting Joe. The Joshis had no part in the Delhi case. Yeah, the charity clinic is definitely a Joshi problem, but I don't really understand why Naidu's linking the Delhi episode to the clinic case through the family."

"Not through the Joshis, but the two episodes cannot be unrelated," Rishi insisted, yawning. He'd collapsed into bed because he was too tired to do anything except lie down, but sleep was a luxury he couldn't afford yet. "It's impossible."

"The blackmail note you got proves they're linked," agreed Joe, staring out the window. Turning to face the group in the room, he added, "The sonuvabitch cop will show up someday. He's going to answer a few questions."

"*Naidu* contacted you in Delhi, not the Joshis," repeated Siddharth. "He found you through the crime ring's point man on AIIMS. The Joshis didn't have anything to do with it. Plus, Naidu sent the old blackmail notes, but we haven't been able to talk to him about the new ones. There is no reason for *him* to link the two cases except Anjali."

Joe blinked. "What if INTERPOL thinks the point man was someone hired by the Joshis?" He groaned. "What am I saying? Dr Ram's family wouldn't... it's got to be one of the doctors at the clinic."

The conclusion they reached the night before in Joe's house was the culprit *had* to be one of the doctors or nurses at the clinic. The AIIMS recruitment did not involve donors, so the crime ring didn't need a trained medic, but the clinic episode required the suspect to have enough medical knowledge to pick appropriate organ donors. Since the two instances were connected, the assumption was this doctor or nurse previously functioned as the recruiter of surgeons in Delhi. Problem was no such person employed by AIIMS back in 2008 was at the clinic now. No one brought up the idea the cops might be right about the Joshis until tonight, but it was simply impossible.

"No way," said Rishi. "I know Anjali's parents. Even in the one in a million chance they're involved, they'd never, ever let Anjali get into trouble for it. Believe me, they love their kids." Even Vikram, the undeserving punk.

"Actually..." brooded Siddharth. "We do need to check for connections between the Joshis and the point man in Delhi."

"Thank God Anju's not here yet," Joe mumbled. "She doesn't need to hear this dumb shit."

"It ain't dumb to consider all possibilities," Siddharth responded. "But yeah, Anju's not gonna like hearing it." He glanced at the clock on the side table. It was a little after seven in the evening. "She'll be here in an hour or so. The baby's with her at the clinic, so she won't even have to go back home to pick him up before coming here."

My son, Rishi whispered in his mind. He hadn't seen his own child in weeks. Swinging his feet out of bed, Rishi said to Farhan, "We need to take pictures—you, me, and the baby."

Farhan stayed slouching against the wall, but his eyes widened in mild panic. "Maybe when he's older. I mean, what if I drop him or something?"

"You'd better hope he doesn't fart," Siddharth said, tone dark. "Kid's a chemical weapons expert. He can take down the entire hotel in under five seconds."

Joe laughed. "That's muh boy," he said, smugly.

Inside Rishi's chest, his heart thumped painfully hard. "*My* boy," he corrected.

"Not again," Siddharth muttered. Farhan clapped a hand to his forehead.

"I wish I could forget you're the kid's father," Joe said, tone nasty. "But Anju won't agree." With a derisive huff, he muttered, " *Your* boy. You haven't even named him. The child's almost six months old."

"It'll happen," Rishi said, stiffly. He remembered the naming ceremonies of his sisters' children. The flowers decorating the house, the priests chanting hymns, the music, the laughter... the baby's oldest aunt would whisper the chosen name into his ear. Then, one of the uncles would announce it to the gathered family.

Rishi's son would have no aunts to whisper the name in his ear. One set of grandparents would refuse to show up, decline to acknowledge him. The baby's father would be an outcast, unwelcome in his own family without his wife by his side.

Rishi knew Anjali was never returning, and she was right not to. Hell, *he* no longer wanted her to. He yearned to claim the man he loved as his mate in front of the whole universe. Except the moment he did so, he'd lose his family forever. Even if they somehow managed to send the blackmailer packing, Rishi would end up alone in the world.

"My parents," he murmured. "How the hell am I supposed to do a naming ceremony without any of my family around?" He'd explained this to Anjali, but she refused to understand. Fixing Joe with a glare, Rishi added, "But *my* child's naming is none of your business."

"Listen, jackass," Joe snarled. "Lemme make something clear. If Anju lets me, I plan to be part of her child's life. Part of the family. The *whole* family."

"Oh, yeah?" Rishi started. "Lemme see how you—"

"Thank you," said Farhan, nodding at Joe. Turning to Rishi, Farhan added, "Sometimes, my love, you don't seem to see what's right under your nose."

"What do you mean?" Rishi asked.

"*Enough*," said Siddharth. "You, too, Joe. Unless you want Anju to stalk out of here, both of you'd better behave. She's not gonna be in the mood to put up with your shit."

Farhan sent a steely glance Rishi's way before turning to Siddharth. "More problems with the clinic staff?"

Siddharth nodded. "Anju thinks Mrs Braganza is the one who leaked the info about the pharmaceutical crime cover story. Plus, the secretary, Chandekar... he's problematic."

"He's used to running the show," said Joe. Apparently, Chandekar started as secretary to the chief executive in the last few months of Dr Ram Joshi's life. The succession of CEOs who followed mostly couldn't remember where the latrine was, let alone manage the clinic.

"Chandekar definitely doesn't like the idea of a hands-on boss," agreed Siddharth. "He was not happy when Kiki and I showed up. The dude actually had the audacity to ask Anju why she hired an outside lawyer without first clearing it with the board. Then, he made noises about Kiki being allowed to talk to the staff without a stamp of approval from whatever department. For a minute or two, I thought he was going to shout at Anju. Finally, he fell over himself, trying to claim he was merely trying to help. Effing toad."

Rishi raised an eyebrow and exchanged glances with Joe. Chandekar had managed the feat of riling easy-going Siddharth to the point of name-calling.

"Sounds like Chandekar *paaji* thinks he's the boss," said Farhan, using the Punjabi word for bro.

"Yeah," said Siddharth. "He's supposed to be helping Anju set up the townhall, but every five minutes, he stops to say it's not gonna work. According to him, the staff doesn't trust her, so her best option would be to put someone they do trust in charge as the INTERPOL liaison. Namely, him. Anju says half the problem is his attitude towards her which is trickling down to the other employees. She wants to fire him, but she can't. The fellow knows everything happening in the clinic, *and* he makes it look like he's doing his best to help her. He's with her right now, going over the points to discuss at the townhall. Anju said she'd work from home because she couldn't keep the nanny at the clinic this late, and Chandekar got his wife to come and babysit. So bloody supportive, right? If she fires him now, the staff will riot."

"She *shouldn't* fire him," said Rishi. "He really could help her. *My* secretary claims personal assistants always know what's going on." Laughing mildly, he added, "Apparently, there's an underground network where P.A.s trade information about the bosses." Rishi nodded in Joe's direction. "She was actually going to locate you for me, but I saw you at the clinic."

"So Chandekar could possibly give us information on the organ-smuggling issue?" Farhan asked. Raising a hand, he added, "I know, I know. Anju can't involve him." If it came out that INTERPOL was investigating the clinic for organ smuggling and not violation of pharmaceutical laws, chaos would erupt. The clinic could end up being shut down. "Still, if he's been running the place for so long, he would've noticed something, right?"

Joe shoved away from the window he'd been leaning against and paced the room. "Like what? Unless the cops told him patients who came there were disappearing, how could Chandekar possibly notice anything? The disappearances didn't happen from the clinic; they happened after."

"Know what, Rishi?" Instead of completing the thought, Siddharth drummed the armrest of his chair with his fingers and turned to Joe. "Does Chandekar have some sort of medical training?" At Joe's puzzled look, Siddharth clarified, "It just occurred to me... what Rishi's secretary said about P.A.s... if someone's going through clinic records to pick patients for organ harvesting, how did they do it without Chandekar knowing? I mean, they'd need sonogram reports, blood and urine tests, doctors' notes, etcetera, etcetera. Nothing in that place is computerised. This person would have to go department by department, collecting information. Chandekar *would* get to know. Two, our suspect would need enough medical knowledge to understand what he's looking at. If Chandekar has medical training, we have our man."

"Run it by me again," Rishi said.

Siddharth huffed. "I wish I could give you a visual demo with a bulletin board. Okay... point one: there's no way the incidents in Delhi and Goa are not connected. Rishi getting blackmail notes both times proves the fact. Point two: we've been thinking the culprit must be someone who was in AIIMS in 2008 and is at the clinic now. Point three: this person has to be medically trained to know which donors to pick, making a doctor or nurse the most likely suspect. Point four: Anjali is the only such person on our list at the moment. INTERPOL doesn't know about the second set of blackmail notes, but they know about Anjali, so Naidu's going after the Joshis. Correct?"

"It's not them," Joe said.

Holding up a hand, Siddharth said, "There is another person who was connected to AIIMS back then and the clinic now. *You*, Joe."

"*What?*" Joe snapped.

"Hear me out," said Siddharth. "Point five: I'm assuming it's not Anjali's family for right now. I'm also assuming Joe told us the truth, the whole truth, and nothing but the truth. Point six: If so, we're left with no one at all who knew Rishi and Joe in AIIMS back then and set up shop in Goa now. Point seven: I told you I'm mulling another theory. Let's backtrack and look at things from another angle. What if our culprit were not someone from AIIMS? What if he knew Joe from the clinic back in the day and got word to the point man in Delhi?"

"You're saying it might not have started in Delhi," Joe mused. "It could've started in Goa with someone who knew me, someone currently employed at the clinic, who then passed the information to the contact in Delhi."

"Wouldn't Naidu realise it?" asked Rishi.

"Naidu might not have known there was another person in the picture," said Siddharth. "He might've assumed the point man found Joe on campus. Until the Goa case, of course. Now, he thinks the Joshis did it."

"He's wrong," Rishi insisted. "It's someone else from the clinic."

"Which brings me to point eight," Siddharth said. "Like I said, I've been wondering about the possibility the culprit might be from Goa and not Delhi, so I looked through the employee directory of the clinic this morning. Anjali assures me there's no doctor common to both time frames at the clinic. The pay is simply not high enough to keep them for more than a few years. The nurses and other support staff... there are a few who've been around that long and would know about Joe. I made a list. Point nine: what we heard from Rishi. Executive secretaries do usually know quite a bit of what goes on in an organisation. In Chandekar's case, he was secretary *and* executive. There's no one amongst the support staff on my list who was in a high enough position to do this without being spotted by Chandekar. Actually, there is no one in any sort of position at the clinic who could bypass Chandekar to gather all the information required to recruit donors. Hell, even Anjali needed to go through him to get the documents for her meeting with INTERPOL. So he's either working with the culprit in Goa, or he *is* the culprit. Given the blackmail note Rishi got, he and/or his partner needed to be involved in the Delhi case as well. They gave the information on Joe to the point man in Delhi."

Rishi snickered. "You're pissed at the fellow."

"I'm serious," said Siddharth. "Chandekar started before Anjali's grandfather passed, so he most likely knew about Joe in 2008. Question is if he has some sort of medical training, or is he working with someone?"

Pacing the room, Joe said, "I remember meeting Chandekar a couple of times. But I don't believe he has any medical background. I could check with his mother-in-law if you like. She used to be a patient of mine."

"I don't know, Sid," said Rishi, shaking his head. "Let's say Chandekar has medical training and if not, he's working with someone who does. Naidu figured out my sexual orientation without help from anyone and started his blackmail scheme. How did Chandekar know about it to blackmail me?"

Siddharth ptchaaed. "Naidu couldn't possibly hide the blackmail scheme from this point man... the crime ring would know when the wrong surgeon showed up. If the Delhi point man mentioned Rishi to Chandekar... it's easier for the smaller players to hide from the law. Chandekar could be one member of the crime ring INTERPOL missed."

Stopping short in his pacing, Joe said, "His wife... I think she's a lab technician. *She'd* have at least a vague idea how to read the test reports."

"There you go." Siddharth eyed the rest. "Husband and wife, working as a team. Plus, whoever this point person was in Delhi. The more I think about it, the more I'm convinced it's Chandekar. Given his clout at the clinic, there's no way the Goa episode happened without his help. Since the two episodes are linked, stands to reason Chandekar was involved in Delhi, as well."

Staring unblinkingly at Siddharth, Joe said, "If it's the Chandekars, they know who Naidu is. They know about me. Today, you, a criminal lawyer, showed up and went through the employee directory. Plus, there was Kiki who could possibly get the staff talking."

"They must be shitting bricks," agreed Siddharth, tone sombre. "Trying to figure out how not to get caught."

"Which would be how?" asked Rishi.

Eyes darting here and there in furious thought, Siddharth muttered, "By framing someone else. Someone present in both Delhi and Goa. Someone who wouldn't be able to protest her innocence."

"Not possible," said Rishi. "Anju was the only one who was present in both places, and she'd definitely—" Heart pounding, he stopped. The only way Anjali wouldn't protest was if she were dead.

Glancing at the dark sky outside the window, Joe whispered, "Oh, my God... Anju... the baby..."

They were in the empty clinic building with Mr and Mrs Chandekar.

Chapter 38

"Weakest link," Anjali muttered under her breath, not taking her eyes off the bottles in the refrigerator in the far right corner of the operating room. The noisy ceiling fan whirred, sending warm air circulating through the empty ambulatory surgery suite of the clinic. "Stupid cop."

He believed poor, unstable Anjali could be easily manipulated. Joe's fury on her behalf was balm to her injured pride, but she had to admit most people didn't seem to think much of her capabilities. The clinic staff clearly didn't, including the man who was in the room with her, supposedly helping her prep for the townhall.

Out loud, she said, "Please add to the list... we need to ask at the townhall which other antibiotics the surgeons would like to have on hand."

There was penicillin as well as some clindamycin but nothing else. The red-capped glass vials containing the paralytic agent succinylcholine were still in the fridge as was insulin. One of the tasks she'd assigned to Chandekar was to see what would happen to patients who collapsed during outpatient surgery. The succinylcholine—a.k.a. sux—would paralyse patients and aid in rapid sequence intubation, and the clinic possessed two ageing mechanical ventilators, but there were no arrangements in place for emergent transfers to tertiary care centres. The secretary never got back to her on the question.

Anjali dusted her black, wide-leg pants and turned to face Chandekar... where was he? "Chandekarji?"

"Right here." The secretary said, suddenly materialising from behind the open door of the steel cupboard next to the refrigerator. The bright white light above glinted off whatever he was holding in his hand. "I was checking to see if we need more surgical instruments."

Anjali glanced at the scalpel. "Why did you take it out of the packaging?" she asked in irritation. "It's not sterile any longer."

The moment she said it, Anjali wished she hadn't. Not that there was any particular fondness left in her for the annoying fellow. Before Siddharth left with Kokila, he'd made it clear he considered the secretary a big problem, and Anjali heartily agreed, but she couldn't afford to alienate him. Plus, she did need accurate numbers on their inventory. At some point, she'd be able to step back and delegate but not right away. The clinic limped along with poor administration for so many years that micromanaging was now unavoidable. Also, she was trying to impress the staff with all the info she possessed at her fingertips.

"The package was already open," Chandekar said, patting his thick moustache with his other hand.

Anjali frowned. While management was deplorably lax, the charge nurse of the ambulatory surgery suite had thus far shown herself capable of doing her job, which would've included not leaving used instruments lying around. "Throw it in the sharps disposal container, please," Anjali instructed, walking past Chandekar towards the door of the surgical suite.

"Here." His hand shot out, the blade missing the left side of Anjali's neck by less than an inch.

With a short squeak, she leapt to the side. "Careful! You could've cut me." Gesturing with her head, she added, "The sharps container is right behind you."

"Sorry," Chandekar muttered. Something in the man's eyes... he knew she'd slit her wrist, of course. Patients could recover from flu, from heart attacks, even from cancer. Society simply wouldn't acknowledge recovery from psychological trauma. Even if Anjali accidentally cut herself, the rest of the world would think she'd done it to end her life. "I'm a little clumsy," the secretary said. "It's been a long day."

"We'll be done here in a few," Anjali soothed. "Your wife must be tired." Poor woman. As soon as her shift in the lab was over, Chandekar corralled her into babysitting so Anjali could continue working. The baby was sleeping, but now that Anjali was closer to the door of the surgical suite, she could hear the only noise in the empty building—the faint echo of her phone going off in the office downstairs. As usual, she'd left it in her purse. If it woke the baby, he'd be mega annoyed at seeing a strange face. Before he shattered Mrs Chandekar's eardrums with his angry shrieks, Anjali needed to return to the office. "My son..."

"Take your time," Chandekar said from behind. "The baby will be safe with my wife."

Anjali didn't want to take her time. She was supposed to meet the guys at the Marriott. Kokila was jet-lagged, and Gauri wanted a day to herself to digest everything she heard from Joe, so Meenakshi also stayed back. Anjali would be the only female at dinner, but she needed to see what the men in the group came up with thus far. In fact, the phone call had to be from them, asking when she'd get to the hotel.

Plus, Joe was there. The hots were still mutual. She'd seen it in his eyes each time they met, but she wanted him to get to know her as she was now, not simply cling to the memory of the girl she used to be. Although the way he bristled in annoyance at the cops' belief she could be manipulated... Anjali mentally patted her own back at Joe's vote of confidence. If it weren't for the INTERPOL mess, they'd probably be at dinner, talking, laughing, madly flirting. As things stood, romance would need to wait its turn until the cops were out of their lives, which wouldn't happen unless Anjali got her act together and joined the brainstorming session at the Marriott.

Chandekar didn't know any of this, so the fellow was volunteering to stay even later. Annoying he might be, but he did try to help in his own way. Sighing inwardly, Anjali wondered if there was some way she could give him a handsome retirement package and simply get him to leave instead of firing him. If only he didn't act like Anjali was a crazy woman in need of humouring, she could've somehow worked with him. "Let's go to the pharmacy," she said, striding out of the ambulatory surgery suite towards the staircase leading to the lower floor. "There are a couple of things I need to check before heading home."

Attitude like Chandekar's was something Anjali would encounter the rest of her life. The stupid INTERPOL people certainly agreed with the secretary. SP Naidu was really stupid if he believed the Joshis were in league with the organ-smuggling criminals. The next time she ran into him, she was going to make it very clear he was wasting time and money chasing after the wrong folks. He should've been looking at... Anjali grimaced.

Who would INTERPOL look at except the Joshis? The gang discussed it *ad nauseam* last night in Joe's house and came to the conclusion it must be one of the doctors or nurses at the clinic. Still, Anjali couldn't deny she was the only known factor common to the old crime ring Naidu infiltrated from Delhi and the latest problem in Goa. *No friggin' way.* Forget her emotional attachment to her own family, Anjali couldn't fathom any reason the Joshis might have to involve themselves in such criminal activities. The family trust was doing very well and supported almost every member.

While working in her office this morning, Siddharth came up with the theory someone already employed by the clinic back in 2008 recommended Joe to the crime ring. Given the fact the same person possessed enough knowhow to pick prospective donors in the present day, the culprit still had to be another doctor or nurse currently in the charity clinic. There were a few names in the list Siddharth made. Maybe tonight, they could review... it would be easier to narrow it down if she got info from someone who knew those people then and now. Siddharth needed to interview someone like Anjali's secretary who knew every detail about the clinic going back to the year before Daadaji's passing.

"Chandekarji." A hand on the post at the top of the staircase leading to the lobby, Anjali turned and came practically nose-to-nose with the man. "*Ack*," she shrieked, jumping to the side. "What are you *doing?* You could've accidentally tripped me down the stairs."

The secretary opened his mouth to say something, but there was a loud voice at the glass-doored front entrance. "We're closed now, madamji," argued the elderly watchman.

From her position, Anjali saw the door pushed open. "My brother's a board member," came the strident tones of Mrs Braganza. "I have special permission."

Biting back a yelp, Anjali slipped behind the wall at the side and peeked down the stairs. Chandekar was also peering at the woman walking in. As usual, Mrs Braganza was clad in a silk sari—green and electric blue tonight. A fat, black leather purse hung on her shoulder. There was a tall man behind her, someone dressed like a Christian priest, except there was a pinkish skullcap on his salt-and-pepper hair.

"We're going to her office right now," continued Mrs Braganza, her loud voice echoing across the lobby and up the stairs. "Let me see what answer she's going to give the bishop."

The bishop? Fr Franco's superior? Mrs Braganza would stop at nothing to drive her neighbour out of town. Anjali nearly howled in frustration. Gesturing Chandekar to her side, she hissed, "I'm waiting here until she leaves. Could you go down and make some excuse?"

A strange relief flickering across his face, Chandekar said, "My wife will send them away. We can both stay here until she leaves."

"No," Anjali whispered, keeping an eye on her neighbour arguing with the watchman. The bishop looked like he was praying for quick deliverance from the situation. "If Mrs Braganza gets to my office, she'll see my baby, and she'll know I'm still here. You need to head her off."

As Chandekar descended the stairs, the phone continued to ring nonstop in Anjali's office. She *wished* she hadn't set the volume so loud. If she could hear it from the top of the stairs in the quietness of the empty clinic, so could Mrs Braganza. What if the woman decided it was enough evidence her quarry was still in-house?

Slipping off her slingback stilettos, Anjali crept to the ambulatory surgery suite. No sense in risking Mrs Braganza looking up and spotting the target of her ire at the top of the stairs. If the woman didn't puff up like a self-righteous peacock any time she laid eyes on her neighbours, she could've given Anjali more information than even Chandekar. La Braganza's brother served as a board member since the clinic's inception, while Chandekar started only... Anjali frowned, not really listening to the echoes of the argument downstairs.

Mrs Braganza wasn't involved in the day to day running of the clinic like Chandekar was since before Daadaji's passing. Anjali never asked the secretary if he ever met Joe during Daadaji's time, but there was no way Chandekar hadn't at least *heard* about the man who found his boss dead in his home. The person who'd helped in trapping Joe was assuredly known to Chandekar since he or she must've been around at the time.

No. Anjali shook her head. Siddharth's near-instantaneous dislike of the secretary combined with his new theory of the culprit being from the charity clinic all along was making her imagine things.

Plus, the guilty party was unquestionably a medic which Chandekar was not. Yet the secretary controlled every aspect of the clinic's management. Heck, Anjali was the CEO, but she still needed him to get papers together for INTERPOL when they believed it was only a pharma crime problem. How could the culprit have gotten information about the migrant workers without Chandekar hearing about it?

The secretary was annoying, but he wasn't stupid. How could he fail to notice something was amiss? Even if he didn't know exactly what was going on, he was such a stickler for rules that he couldn't possibly fail to notify someone in authority of unauthorised access of patient info. Unless it *was* authorised by the *de facto* CEO, Chandekar. A two-person team.

Standing at the door of the operating room with her stilettoes dangling from her fingers, Anjali contemplated the partly open refrigerator door. She'd walked out in a hurry, assuming Chandekar would close it. Instead, he'd followed at her heels, nearly pushing her—Anjali once again shook her head. This was stupid. Or was it?

Her eyes fell on the scalpel on the floor, right below the sharps container. Chandekar almost nicked her carotid artery with it. Then, he tossed it aside in his hurry to follow her out. If she hadn't turned at the last moment... if Mrs Braganza hadn't pushed her way in... would Anjali now be lying at the bottom of the stairs, her neck broken? She was the only person other than Chandekar who could be connected to the two organ-harvesting cases, one in Delhi, one in Goa. Young as she was back in 2008, would she have been pegged as a tool for the Joshi clan? Would her death be written off as suicide triggered by guilt?

The weakest link, Anjali muttered in her mind.

She pivoted on her bare foot and ran out of the surgical suite, her heart thudding hard against her ribs. She needed to think about this more, but her baby was right now with the man's missus. No way was Anjali going to take a chance—

Anjali came to a sharp stop at the top step. Mrs Chandekar was a lab technician. Would she know enough to... the baby. *Oh, God, my baby.* Terror surged, leaving her quaking.

The glass doors at the front entrance swung open, and Chandekar walked in, the look on his face at once relieved and purposeful. Mrs Braganza was nowhere to be seen.

There was a loud voice in Anjali's brain. *Call out to the watchman,* it urged. *Scream for help.* Curling her shaking fingers into a fist, Anjali stayed silent. If she as much as breathed the wrong way, Chandekar would know she suspected him. The watchman was outside and would investigate the noises, but he was elderly and armed with only a baton. Somehow, he'd also end up dead, and Anjali would be blamed. Her baby... Chandekar's wife had the baby. Acidic terror churned all the way from Anjali's stomach to her mouth.

Every cell in her body demanded she run to her child's side, but she couldn't... Chandekar would follow. She needed to keep the criminal away from her son.

Without saying a word, she returned to the surgical suite. *Options... options...* Anjali closed her eyes in despair. Her phone was in her office. The landline in the operating theatre couldn't be used to send S.O.S. texts to anyone she knew. If she called on it, Chandekar would hear, and she'd be in immediate danger as would her baby. She carried no weapons, not even pepper spray. She'd never taken any self-defence classes. The only things she knew besides medicine were oil painting and classical music.

No. She wasn't going to admit defeat—not with her baby's life in danger. Wildly, she looked around. Anjali had spent nearly a decade in operating theatres. She could surely find something here to use in self-defence.

Thump... thump... Chandekar's heavy tread was getting louder and louder.

Scalpels, forceps, needles... no, the secretary would easily disarm Anjali. If Rishi or Joe were with her, they could turn surgical instruments into weapons. *She* was an anaesthesiologist, used to putting patients to sleep.

Her eyes went to the refrigerator the secretary left partly open. Some of *her* weapons were in there.

Slipping her stilettoes back on, Anjali strode to the fridge and picked up the vial of succinylcholine. She was ripping open the disposable syringe when Chandekar appeared at the door.

"What are you doing?" he asked, frowning. His voice held none of the smarmy deference Anjali was used to hearing. The man was certain he no longer needed to bow to her.

"Hmm?" Tamping down the wave of nausea, she turned to face the secretary. Average height, slightly bulky form. *One hundred kilogrammes, give or take a few.* At twenty milligrammes per millilitre, she'd need five millilitres. That is if she managed to get it straight into his circulation. Not giving herself time to think further, she used a sixteen-gauge needle to draw fifteen ccs into the syringe. "I thought I'd check one of the vials," she said, keeping her tone casual. "If it's not stored properly, it can go bad. We'll throw out the entire batch if this one looks cloudy or grainy."

The frown on Chandekar's face deepened, but he didn't say anything.

"Help me out, please," she implored, tossing the vial into the wastebasket by the fridge and squinting at the syringe with the thick needle fixed to the top.

Silently, she counted his steps. One... two... three... four... a half step. As though looking for better light, she held up the syringe and turned a semicircle until she got to Chandekar's right side.

Raising her right leg, she stomped hard on his foot.

His eyes widened in shock. With a sharp scream, he bent double.

His neck was now within Anjali's reach, but she didn't have the luxury of time to check the precise location of the blood vessels. Swinging her right arm, she stabbed the triangular area above the sternocleidomastoid muscle with the needle. One second, two. The plunger on the syringe went all the way down, the entire fifteen ccs of the paralytic agent injected into Chandekar's body.

"What—" He staggered upright. Tearing the needle and syringe from his neck, he tossed them aside and stumbled towards her.

Blood trickled from the tiny hole. It wasn't spurting as it should have if she got the carotid artery. If the medicine went into his muscle instead, it would take three to five minutes to work—plenty of time for him to warn his wife who was right now minding Anjali's child. She didn't know what the woman could do at that point, but Anjali wasn't about to stop and examine all angles.

She needed to keep Chandekar inside the surgical suite. Anjali ran to the door. She didn't have the time or the physical strength to block it from the outside to prevent him from going to his wife. All she could do was delay him until the medicine worked and mask any warning he might shout before then.

A hand landed on her shoulder, whirling her around. Stumbling, she reached sideways for the doorjamb. "You—" Chandekar snarled, voice hoarse with vicious rage. His large face blocked the rest of the room from Anjali's visual field. Droplets of spit landed on her cheeks. Thick fingers closed around her windpipe.

Air. She needed air. Anjali scratched at the sweat-slick skin of his wrist, but Chandekar wouldn't let go. Her vision darkened.

No, she wasn't going to die like this. Not when her baby depended on her. Arms flailing, she brought her hand up to Chandekar's face and jabbed his left eye with her fingers.

His angry scream reverberated through her skull. The chokehold loosened. Shoving the criminal away, Anjali ran to the top of the stairs.

"*Help*," she shouted between hoarse coughs. Mrs Chandekar would be caught by surprise and wouldn't know how to respond, but the watchman would hobble in to check. By that time, the succinylcholine would work. It had to. With Chandekar out of commission, Anjali and the watchman could rescue the baby from the criminal's wife. "*Help. Somebody, help!*"

A loud crash. The front door flung open, bouncing off the wall on the side. "What is going on here?" screeched Mrs Braganza.

Behind her were the two men in Anjali's life. "Anju," bellowed Joe, shoving Mrs Braganza aside. Rishi followed him, then Siddharth and Farhan.

"*Go the office,*" screamed Anjali, watching Chandekar stumble out of the surgery suite. He wobbled before dropping to the floor in a heap. "*The baby...* he's with Chandekar's wife."

***

Rishi couldn't see anything besides the tiny human screaming his head off in the arms of the murderous woman. Chandekar's wife was shouting, warning all the people who crowded the office to back off, but no sound was louder to Rishi's ears than the baby's panicked howling.

"Please," Rishi begged, not taking his eyes off diaper-clad infant with tears rolling down his small face. The boy held out a little arm, reaching towards the crowd.

"Please," Anjali implored, her voice hoarse. "Don't hurt him. We'll let you go, I swear."

"Stay away," screamed Chandekar's wife, retreating further into the side room of the CEO suite. "I have a knife." Extending her hand to the small table behind her, she grabbed what seemed like a utility blade.

"*No,*" shouted Rishi, his arms and legs trembling in fear. Everyone around was yelling—Farhan, Joe, the bishop, the watchman—pleading with the woman not to hurt the child.

"*Please,*" Anjali said, sobbing. "Oh, God, please. I'll give you whatever you want. Just don't hurt my baby."

The infant was waggling his small fingers as though begging the onlookers to save him. On his face was confusion why no one was rescuing him from the scary woman. If Rishi could take three steps to the front, he could touch the baby's hand. His son. His precious child.

There was nothing more important than him in Rishi's universe. No one existed in the world beyond the little boy. Rishi would give anything— *anything*—to keep the baby safe.

"Look, woman," came the Braganza dame's screechy voice. "You're not going to gain anything by this. Let the child go. One of the other doctors is taking care of your husband. You'll both go to prison, but you'll be alive."

"Go away," screamed Chandekar's wife, her eyes wide in panic and mouth spewing spittle. "You old bitch."

There was a loud hiss by Rishi's side. "What did you call me?" demanded Mrs Braganza. Her thick elbow landed on his ribs. Shoving through, she stomped heavily towards Chandekar's wife. "*What did you call me?*"

"*No.*" Waving the utility knife, Chandekar's wife shouted, "Don't come any closer."

"Mrs Braganza, stop," Joe and Anjali screamed at the same time.

"*What did you call me?*" the Braganza woman asked a third time, her voice even louder. Raising her arm, she swung her leather purse at the criminal's wife.

Rishi leapt. The baby was in his arms. He veered around, intending to run to safety with the boy. He saw Anjali's crying face, her hands reaching for her child. Joe was shouting something, his pupils wide with alarm.

A sudden, sharp pain pierced through Rishi's lower back. A feeling of warmth and wetness. "What—" he asked. The room blurred, darkened.

When his vision cleared, he was looking up at the bright LED bulbs on a surgical lighthead. There was shouting all around, the familiar clatter of instruments. He was in the operating theatre. "My son," he whispered.

"Mrs Braganza has him until the nanny gets here," said Joe. Nose and mouth shielded by a surgical mask, he came into Rishi's field of vision. "I think the Chandekar woman got one of the major arteries. We don't have time to transfer you to another facility. I haven't done major surgery in the last eight years, but..."

"Go ahead," Rishi said. "There's no one I'd trust more to cut me open."

A feminine snort came from somewhere nearby. Joe moved away, and Kokila's grinning face came into view. "Took a knife to make you admit it," she said.

Before Rishi could ask when she got there, Farhan appeared next to her, his dark eyes anxious above the green mask. "You'll be all right," he mumbled, the statement more plea than reassurance.

"I will be," Rishi swore. "You should wait outside." It was never a good idea to play doctor within the family.

"Sorry, Rishi," said Kokila. "I need his help here. But Anju will be your gas man, not Farhan. Still, he's familiar with what goes on in the theatre, so he can assist me. Meenu will, too." Briefly, Kokila explained she, Meenakshi, and Gauri—as well as Cousin Mohini—left the Fontainhas mansion the minute they got Siddharth's phone call about the situation. The terrible traffic delayed them a bit, but they arrived at the clinic right behind the men and heard Anjali scream something about the succinylcholine she'd injected into the criminal. Gauri was helping Siddharth keep Chandekar alive until the cops got there while the bishop and the watchman guarded the missus. Oh, yeah... Cousin Mohini was on the phone with Anjali's father.

"Primum non nocere," said Anjali, popping up next to Kokila and Farhan. Even a murderous bastard like Chandekar couldn't be left to die.

"You did what you needed to do," soothed Rishi, his voice weak.

Anjali shook her head. "I'm not beating myself up."

Anitha Perinchery

Joe returned to Rishi's side. "Put him under, Anju."

An oxygen mask was placed over Rishi's mouth and nostrils. "Close your eyes and take a deep breath," instructed Anjali, her tone steady.

Complying with her order, Rishi focused on his heartbeats. *Lub dub, lub dub, lub dub... thump, thu-thump, thump, thump, thu-thump.*

He frowned. The rhythm wasn't regular. Was he going into some kind of arrhythmia? He opened his eyes, intending to ask Joe to check.

Bright sunlight hit his face, making him stagger. "What the hell?" he muttered, looking around the football ground. He seemed to be back in AIIMS. The thuds he heard were the sounds of a young man kicking a ball around. Rishi couldn't see the boy's face, but his jersey was familiar—the same red and black uniform from back when Joe, Nikhil, and Rishi were big men on campus. Actually, Rishi also seemed to be wearing the same uniform right now for whatever reason.

There was no match going on at the moment. The boy was alone except for Rishi, but he was still playing as intensely as though there were two full teams on the ground, battling to score goals.

"Hey," Rishi called, raising a hand. Clearly, the surgery was over, and he'd lived. Some kind of postoperative amnesia... was he wandering around the city in his old sports uniform? He needed to return home, but where *was* home? Perhaps the boy could call for help.

The lad didn't turn around. "What?" he snapped, tone full of youthful hostility.

Rishi blinked at the unexpected antagonism. "I was only..." Suddenly irritated, he asked, "Could you look at me when we speak? It's the polite thing to do."

With one last kick to the ball, the boy turned. "What?" he repeated.

530

Rishi took half a step back and gaped. The same face he saw in the mirror every morning, the same eyes, the same bone structure. Except for the adolescent belligerence in the gaze, everything was the same. "Who are you?" Rishi asked, heart thudding.

The boy jerked back as though in puzzlement. "Something wrong with you? I'm your son, of course."

"My... my *son?*" Rishi stared. "It's impossible. He's... you're... how old are you?"

The young man shrugged. "I don't know. How old do I look? Sixteen? Seventeen?"

"What do you mean you 'don't know'?" Rishi glanced around. "You're in medical college, so you must be at least seventeen." Which meant the gap in Rishi's memory was of the same length of time, putting him in his early fifties. Funny. Rishi didn't *feel* fiftyish.

"Am I in medical college?" asked the boy, laughter replacing his previous petulance. "Why? Just 'cause you'd like me to be a doctor?"

Nothing the kid said made any sense. "Teenagers," Rishi muttered. "What's your name?"

"Heh?" The boy's laughter turned into loud howls of mirth. "C'mon, old man. How can you not know?"

"Humour me," snapped Rishi.

Mirth sputtering to a stop, the boy said, "I don't have one. You never named me, remember?"

Rishi frowned. "Don't be ridiculous. Everyone has a name. Even if I didn't, your ma would've given you one."

"Not me," said the boy, tone mocking. "All I am is Rishabh Rastogi's son."

531

"Enough," bit out Rishi. "I asked you a simple question: what is your name? All you need to do is give me a straightforward answer."

"I *am* giving you a straightforward answer," the boy insisted. "I don't have a name because you didn't give me one. My only identity is that of Dr Rastogi's son. I have your face, I live in your home, and I do whatever you ask me to. If you want me to be a doctor, I will do it. I will marry whomever you point out to me, pop out children when you're ready to be a grandfather."

Getting angrier with each word from the boy's mouth, Rishi held up a hand. "Stop. You're my son, and I understand you're at an age when you want to test limits, but I won't tolerate disrespect."

"What are you going to do?" asked the boy, curiosity on his face. "Throw me out of the house?"

"What the hell are you talking about?" Rishi growled.

"I want to know if you're going to cut me out of the family. Why will you refuse to acknowledge my existence when I've done everything expected of me?"

"Why would I deny you even if you didn't?" Rishi huffed in annoyance. "Listen, you little punk. Don't try to pretend I asked for blind obedience. I want you to be a decent human being, which includes not mouthing off to your father. Even with your blatant disrespect, you're always going to be my son."

"Will I?" asked the boy. "Were you?"

"Huh?"

"You did whatever your parents asked, but none of it was enough. The one thing you refused to do... the one thing which shouldn't have mattered to anyone but you... didn't they say you're no longer their child?"

"They... I... ah..." Rishi stuttered, not taking his eyes off the young man.

The boy nodded. "Why should I believe you're gonna be any different? You don't see anything wrong in their behaviour towards you even when you fulfilled every bloody expectation the world could have from a man. Except for the one thing so intensely personal, nobody else should've had a say in it. Fulfilling expectations wasn't enough, was it? They couldn't let you have your own identity; it needed to be submerged into theirs."

There was a loud buzz in Rishi's head. "Who are you?" he asked, his entire form suddenly trembling.

"Your future," said the boy. "Actually, the future you sketched out for me."

"No," Rishi said, shaking his head. "It's not supposed to be like this. I promised to love you and keep you safe, not decide who you are and what you will be."

"I don't believe you." The boy turned as though to walk away. "If you meant it, you wouldn't have tried to use me to get my mother to return even after you saw life with you was literally killing her. If you meant what you said just now, you would've named me a long time ago. Instead, you're all right with me being merely the Rastogi baby—an extension of you, not someone with my own thoughts and feelings. If you meant it about not deciding my life for me, you would've asked your parents to do the same. You would've told them they're wrong. You would never have so selfishly used my mother."

"I do mean it," Rishi said, urgently. "My parents *are* wrong. *I* was wrong in what I did to Anju, and I will not repeat the mistake with you. Like I said, all I want is for you to be a decent human being, a productive member of society. Beyond those basics, your life is yours to live."

The boy chuckled, the sound almost babyish. "Prove it," he said. "Live *your* life."

"I will," Rishi swore, reaching out. "Give me another chance, please."

"Guh," said the baby, his tiny hand patting Rishi awake.

Part XIV

Chapter 39

The best way to make sure the hospital staff showed up at meetings was to provide food. Piping hot samosas, spicy chicken croquettes, tomato rice with pickled green mangoes, all followed by *bebinca,* the traditional Goan dessert prepared with coconut milk. Chatter hummed around the buffet tables in the auditorium.

Eyeing Anjali seated on the dais in her greenish-blue business suit, Rishi nodded his encouragement. He wished like hell he could do more than offer moral support from the audience, wearing an old grey tee and black drawstring pants over the thick bandages covering his lower back. Without her, he wouldn't have gotten where he did in his career in less than a decade, but he didn't have a place on the stage today. This would be a one-man show.

Farhan was in the seat next to Rishi's wheelchair, the protective angling of his body towards his partner causing a few curious stares to be tossed their way. The clinic employees knew Rishi was Anjali's former husband, of course.

Even if he couldn't go up there and announce the reason for their divorce wasn't mental fragility on her part, he could let the world draw its own conclusions.

Mrs Braganza and her brother were in the front row of the packed auditorium. In the one week since the Chandekar incident, the woman developed a strong fondness for Rishi and Farhan, arriving at Rishi's bedside once a day with food he wasn't supposed to eat until cleared by the surgeon. At least she'd stopped hassling Anjali. Admitting an error and apologising? Nope, not so much. Anjali said the best she could hope for was the uneasy truce currently in place. Plus, the older woman did save the day—kind of.

The cops ordered Mrs Braganza in no uncertain terms to keep her mouth shut about the new organ-trafficking ring she accidentally helped capture. Rishi told Anjali to harbour no faith the matter would remain under wraps. If not Mrs Braganza, someone else would blab. The watchman, Chandekar's extended family, the board members... many people now knew about it. Well... they knew about the part which involved the clinic but nothing of the episode in Delhi with Joe, Rishi, and INTERPOL. Apart from the cops, only Joe, Anjali, Rishi, and their friends were privy to the entire story. Plus, Fr Franco.

Anjali gave the same carefully edited tale the board heard to her parents. Edited or not, she wouldn't want the information going public. If it came out that patients were targeted for organ harvesting, the low-income community served by the clinic would panic. The staff was told Chandekar got caught selling medicines from the clinic on the black market and attempted to attack Anjali when she discovered his crime. Also, that INTERPOL dropped the pharma investigation. The same lies would be repeated today at the townhall.

The entire gang from Delhi was in attendance, seated at a safe distance from Mrs Braganza. It was damned weird seeing Joe dressed in something other than the worn clothes he donned in Delhi. His sister apparently picked out the designer charcoal pants and steel blue Oxford shirt. This was an important day for the D'Acosta household, after all. Joe was finally going to meet Anjali's parents.

He was fidgeting in his chair, trying his best not to turn to the back door and check if they'd arrived. It didn't matter the Joshis knew nothing of his part in the organ-smuggling saga; Joe was still sweating bullets at the idea of meeting them. Spotting Anjali glancing meaningfully between Joe and the back of the auditorium, Rishi smiled. Pratap and Rattan Joshi must've walked in.

As the crowd settled into the seats with plates of food, Anjali started, "Friends and colleagues..." The financial situation of the clinic, the desperately required structural improvements, lack of adequate supplies, need for digitisation... she spoke for fifteen minutes. Then, she elaborated on her plans, promising to create teams to debate ideas and execute them. The loudest applause came when she brought up the possibility of a daycare centre attached to the clinic for the children of the employees. Finally, she mentioned Chandekar. "I'm sure you've heard what happened in the clinic last week..."

When the cops arrived, Chandekar's wife blabbed quite a few details in her panic, leaving no doubts about the veracity of Anjali's claim of self-defence. Plus, Goan police contacted SP Naidu to verify info, and he finally ferreted out the connection between Chandekar and the crime ring's point man in Delhi—the gent was a cousin of Mrs Chandekar.

None of it was mentioned at today's meeting. Anjali repeated the story put out in public. She informed the stunned audience if they harboured the slightest concern about the legitimacy of her claims, they could check with Mrs Braganza who'd witnessed the entire incident.

The employees didn't exactly give her a standing ovation, but nor did they seem to outright reject her assertions. Anjali's huff of relief was visible from Rishi's position. She already had plans in place to slowly win her staff's trust, but it was always better if every inch were not a battle.

***

The throbbing pain along the incision in his lower back intensifying with each word from the phone, Rishi sat on the edge of his bed in the guestroom at Joe's house. Farhan and Joe were leaning against the windowsill, waiting for Rishi to finish the conversation with his parents. Gauri was at the door. She'd arrived there five minutes ago to go over her role in the naming ceremony coming up in two weeks, but the phone call from Delhi interrupted their discussion.

On Rishi's request, the Goan cops had informed the Rastogis about their son's injury. He was hoping... he didn't know exactly what, but the tremor in his mother's voice wasn't from fear for her son's life.

"Oh, God, I'm so thankful," said Ma. "When we heard you quit your job... we should've known you went to Goa to get Anju back. You've made me so, so happy. Your papa, too. He's right next to me. Anju did agree to come back, didn't she?"

"No," Rishi tried saying, but she went on babbling. "Ma, stop. It's not why I came to—" It had been, but the life he lived before this trip was never something he wanted with his heart. His parents knew it; they merely didn't care. Rishi selfishly used Anjali to keep them happy. He arrived in Goa to persuade her to return only because he believed there were no other options. Rishi apologised to her a thousand times since waking from anaesthesia, but all she said in response was the baby made the eleven years worthwhile.

Over the phone, Ma continued, "Women get emotional when they become pregnant. It's the hormones. Plus, Anju must've been lonely. Her hours at the hospital were regular, but you were working day and night, and there was no one else at home. It's not surprising she got a little unstable. We'll get her to see Dr Bharti. You remember her, don't you?"

The conversion therapist? Rishi hissed. "That woman's never going to get anywhere near—Ma, don't you want to know how I'm doing?"

There was a chiding cluck from the other end. "Of course, betay. Your father and I nearly went out of our minds when we heard. But there's a silver lining in every cloud, right? It made Anju appreciate what you did. No matter what she found out about your past, she can't deny you're a good husband. I hope she's there now, taking care of you."

"Anju has always known about me," Rishi bit out. "And no, she's not here." Taking a deep breath, he said, "Farhan is."

"Heh? Who?"

"Farhan Zaidi," Rishi said, the smile on the face of the man by the window setting his heart aglow. "I'd like to introduce him to you."

"Introd—*what?*" screeched Ma.

In the background, Papa instructed, "Cut the call, Jaya."

Voice tremulous, she started, "But—"

"*Cut the call,*" snapped Rishi's father. "From this moment on, he's no one to this family."

Heart splintering into a thousand sharp-edged pieces, Rishi said, "I'm still your—" The high-pitched tone from the phone told him Ma was no longer on the line. Tossing the device onto the mattress, he muttered, "I should've known better than to expect anything else."

Gauri mumbled, "Sorry, yaar." The others in the room might've heard only half the conversation, but it was enough to tell them what happened.

Maybe it was just as well his parents cut the call. What Rishi wanted to say was not what they wanted to hear. Rishabh Rastogi would forever remain their son, but it was only one part of his identity. There were many other things Rishi was—a brother, a friend, a doctor, a father. According to society, he more than fulfilled expectations in all his roles. He was also a living, breathing human with his own thoughts and ideas and feelings which included being gay.

539

His homosexuality shouldn't have mattered any more than his friends' heterosexuality, but it did. Unless he agreed to fit into the mould his family built, nothing he achieved would *ever* be enough. No, his son couldn't grow up thinking the same. It was time to draw the line. *Take me as I am*, Rishi declared to his parents—to the world.

***

The bright, white rays of the sun peeked through the bluish-grey monsoon clouds, glinting off the glass windows of the old jewel-toned mansions in Fontainhas. The garlands of red roses wrapped around the wrought-iron balcony and porch railings of the Joshi home infused Rishi's every breath with the scent of new beginnings.

Funny, Rishi thought, dreamily. While his airways did squeeze slightly, reminding him of his allergies, he wasn't battling near-unconsciousness from lack of oxygen. The pollen count was probably down because of the rain from dawn. Droplets of moisture still clung to the air, shrouding the cobblestone street with its antique lampposts in fairy tale mist.

If it weren't for the sounds of distant traffic and the muffled chatter and laughter from the people gathered in the Joshi mansion for the celebration, he could've believed he and the man next to him were alone in some kind of magical realm. But no. Reality awaited them inside the house. Beautiful, beautiful reality.

"Farhan," Rishi called.

Manoeuvring his bike to a safe spot between the Joshi and Braganza residences, Farhan paused. "Incision hurting you? I told you we could call a cab if you didn't feel up to riding pillion."

Rishi waved a dismissive hand. "I'm okay." One month had passed since the emergency surgery. "Listen. I want to tell you something before we go in."

He halted. How did he say this without feeling like a bloody idiot? "It's been two-and-a-half years."

"Since we met? Yeah. We should celebrate on Christmas Eve... our third anniversary."

Rubbing his temple, Rishi said, "Sure. I was trying to say... thank you for hanging on when most sane men would've given up." Between Anjali's decision to file for divorce and the beginning of the recent blackmailer shit, months went by with Rishi insisting he wanted to get back with his wife.

A grin lit up Farhan's smouldering eyes. "Who told you I'm sane?" When their laughter petered out, he added, "Unlike you, I used to have a... umm... busy love life. When we met, it was..." Farhan snapped his fingers. "All my smart-arsery, my self-centred attitudes, ended the same day. I knew you were interested, but I'm not sure it would've mattered if you weren't. Everything I dreamed of... all I was never aware I wanted was you. There was nothing beyond you. There will be nothing after you."

Each sweet word stormed into Rishi's heart, swirling, whirling, filling his every sense. "Damn," he muttered, thickly. At Farhan's confused look, Rishi clarified, "*I* wanted to say those things." Watching Farhan snicker at the idea of Rishi coming up with romantic nonsense, Rishi drew a deep breath for courage. "I love you," he blurted.

Farhan straightened. "I lo—"

"Wait, please." Rishi held up a hand. "I was bloody afraid of saying it before. I mean, it's a commitment. Not like I could've taken it back when my family objected. You would've kicked my ass out the door, and I'd have deserved it. But..." He squinted in the direction of the house before smiling at Farhan. "I can't spend my life being my parents' extension. If they come around, great. If not, the man I love will still be the man I love. Is the offer still open?"

"Heh? What offer?"

"You know..." Gesturing vaguely with his hand, Rishi continued, "Move to Bombay or Delhi or London or join Doctors Without Borders? As a couple, I mean." Yeah, they'd be making frequent trips to Goa to see the baby, and Anjali wouldn't object to letting the boy stay with his father now and then. "The divorce came through yesterday. I'm a free man but hoping not to be one for long."

Farhan's eyes snapped wide open. Glancing up and down the street, he said, "Rishi, my love... you do pick your spots to make these announcements... ah, hell, I don't care." In two quick strides, Farhan was next to Rishi. Fingers digging into each other's hair, they kissed.

A shrill whistle broke their embrace. "Get in here," snapped Kokila. "You barely have time to change into Indian clothes." Apparently, the priest from the temple near Mapusa just announced the auspicious time was on them for the ceremony. Plus, Kokila needed to get to the airport soon. She'd already extended her holiday by three more weeks than intended, declaring she'd leave right after the naming ceremony,

***

There were roses in every nook and cranny of the Joshi living room. All of Anjali's family was there, including Vikram, his buddy Adhith, Seema, and Seema's auntie. The D'Acostas, Mrs Braganza, and a couple of other neighbours were present. Every single one was dressed in Indian finery—kurta/dhoti for the men and colourful silk sarees for the ladies. Even Joe's dog wore a crimson silk bow on his collar.

Glance falling on the gent talking to Vikram, Rishi straightened in surprise. Sister number one's hubby? The Yank? When did he fly in from Boston?

The man greeted Rishi with a bear hug. "Your sister's scared shitless of your father, dude," said the Yank. "She'll come around. I'm working on her. The other two will come around, too."

Rishi had asked Farhan to invite the Zaidi parents, but neither was currently in the country. Until a moment ago, Rishi was resigned to the idea the baby would have only Farhan and the Delhi gang from his father's side for today's ceremony. *Resigned* was the wrong word. They *were* family to Rishi. Still... "Thanks," he said to the Yank, barely able to speak through the welling gratitude.

Across the room, Anjali plucked the screaming infant from the decorated swing. He absolutely refused to stay in the contraption, his angry bellows practically drowning out the Marathi *barsa* music playing in the background—songs meant for naming ceremonies.

In fifteen minutes, Rishi took his son into his lap and sat cross-legged on the makeshift stage across from the priest. Farhan took his place on the stage on Rishi's left. Anjali and Joe were on the right. She apparently saw no incongruity in her wish to have him next to her at this event despite insisting they needed time to get to know each other as the people they were now.

After the priest from the temple near Mapusa completed his prayers, poor Gauri—as the baby's paternal aunt—knelt on the floor to reach the infant instead of simply bending towards the swing as originally intended. In a hushed whisper right into the child's ear, she told him his name. It was the duty of the baby's maternal uncle to draw the navy-coloured curtain covering the wall where foam letters in glittering blue spelt out the boy's name. Hot tears rolling down his cheeks, Rishi listened to Vikram make the announcement. "Nikhil Ram Rastogi."

Chapter 40

Watching the women in the group crowd around Kokila's bedroom as she did some last-minute packing for her return to New York, Joe told himself to simply blurt it out as Anjali advised. They'd spent hours on the phone the last couple of nights, discussing his plans at length.

"Gauri," he called. When she turned towards the door, he continued, "I talked to the dean at AIIMS. You know... to see if they'd let me complete my training."

All chatter in the room came to an abrupt stop. The men behind Joe—Siddharth, Rishi, Farhan—stilled. "And?" asked Gauri.

"The governing body of the college will need to approve it, but he's positive they will." After all, Naidu once again swore to bring pressure from the CBI on the college authorities. It was the least the sonuvabitch could do after declining to apologise to Anjali. According to Naidu, friends and lovers of former CBI consultants were not beyond suspicion. The bloody cop would demand proof of innocence from his own mother.

He did offer an apology of sorts to Rishi for the attempted blackmail. Finding out Joe's former flatmate's sexual orientation was a stroke of luck for Naidu. He happened to be on the street with his dog—the loud Pomeranian—when Rishi stumbled past the entrance to the apartment building. Naidu heard the young doctor wheezing and originally intended to offer help when he saw Rishi walking into the gay bar. The cop went in as well and ordered a couple of drinks, watching Rishi chat with the actor. Naidu followed the duo until they disappeared into the actor's flat and decided Rishabh Rastogi would do fine as his partner on the case.

And yes, Siddharth turned out to be correct. Naidu needed to give Rishi's information to the crime ring to get their approval. The INTERPOL fellow never realised the contact in AIIMS who pointed the crime ring to Joe was related to a lab technician at the Joshi Charity Clinic in Goa. The corrupt cousin and her husband—Chandekar—planned to use the low-income patient population of the clinic as a source of additional revenue, and when the chance came to recommend a surgeon, they pushed for Joe, hoping to get a referral bonus.

When Joe returned after the collapse of the criminal network, the Chandekar couple realised the surgeon they recommended was a plant. For a few years, they stayed out of trouble. Then, some of the minor players in the sector started a new setup, and the Chandekars were back in business. There was one problem: they still wanted a surgeon from a brand-name college for the higher-profile patients, but Joe was not an option.

The news of Anjali's divorce reached the clinic before she did. Chandekar knew Rishabh Rastogi had been the alternate choice. While the criminals were busy sending notes to Rishi, unknown to them, INTERPOL was brought in on the case, and Fr Franco was plotting to get Joe and Anjali together. A perfect storm of events, ending in Chandekar's arrest.

Joe almost lost his shit when he realised Anjali and the baby were alone with the criminal. Now, he was so damned proud of her. Twenty-something Joe was madly attracted to the prim and proper girl with the streak of wildness no one else seemed to see. The woman Anjali became was a ferocious warrior in her own way, a lioness protecting her cub. The way she took down Chandekar... Joe's insides still quaked at the memory, but with her life no longer in danger... by God, Anjali Joshi was hot stuff. Murderous criminals? As she said later, *"Pfft."* Recalcitrant employees? Pfft, again. Social scorn? Double pfft! Everyone who heard about the incident at the clinic would know not to mess with her, including the police.

Naidu deigned to return Joe's calls only when news of the arrest reached the INTERPOL office in Delhi. The cop flew to Goa and visited Rishi in Joe's home, mumbling he wouldn't have gone through with the blackmail even if Rishi refused the moonlighting offer. Small comfort after the trauma of the past eleven years, but Naidu also promised Rishi's transgression would forever be wiped off official records. And yeah, the CBI would help with Joe's readmission to AIIMS.

But certain conditions needed to be met before Joe returned to his training. Glancing away from Anjali's encouraging face at the back of the room, he said to Gauri, "If everything works out, I'll start in January."

Squealing, Gauri clapped her hands. "It will work out. It has to."

"Depends on you," Joe said.

"On me?" She drew back in surprise. "What do you mean?"

"It means I'm not going unless you go with me," said Joe, keeping his tone easy. "You have a few weeks of internship left. The dean says it won't be possible to do only a few weeks after all these years, but he'll consider it if you're willing to do the entire year over."

"I... umm... Joe..." Her eyes filled with tears. "I don't know."

Stepping into the room, Joe took her hand in his. "I won't tell you Nikhil would've wanted you to move on. You already know it. All I can say is if I can do it, you can, too. Please, Gauri? The whole group lost something in that one week. Let's go get it back. A new beginning for everyone. What do you say?" He did mean *everyone*. If Gauri agreed to return to AIIMS, Anjali would get the rest of the gang to nag Meenakshi into applying for the nuclear medicine residency she sacrificed for her sister.

With a small sob, Gauri fell against Joe's chest. The rest crowded around, patting her head and shoulders.

Except Anjali. Smiling through her tears, she stayed in the back of the room and blew Joe a kiss. He let his gaze wander over her face to the small birthmark by her mouth. Watching her sputter in mirth, Joe shot her a wink. They'd work it out.

Anjali hadn't solidly committed herself to being in his life, stating her naïveté and impulsiveness surely contributed to their breakup. Not intending to repeat the mistake, she was determined to take her time before making any life-altering decisions. Plus, she was insistent on them getting to know each other as adults.

Joe would wait as long as she demanded, but the thirty-five-year-old doctor was as crazily attracted to the tough, shrewd CEO of the charity clinic as the young tutor had been to the first-year medical student. He didn't need another second to figure out he wanted to spend the next fifty or sixty years as mate to this gorgeous woman—this warrior mom—after which he'd die with his head on her lap. She was the other half of him, dammit.

Chapter 41

Apart from her family and circle of friends—Fr Franco and the cops, too, obviously—the one person Anjali was certain wouldn't breathe a word about the actual reason behind Chandekar's arrest was the doctor seated across the desk. The pompous man once tried to squeeze her out of the CEO position, but he was well-liked by the employees of the clinic. Plus, his reputation as an excellent doctor meant patients trusted him. Anjali took Joe's advice and asked her nemesis to a one-on-one meeting, spending the morning going over the details of what really happened, *sans* the part about the men in her life.

Dr Dileep Kumar sat in stupefied silence. When he finally made a sound, it was a gurgle.

With an inner snicker, Anjali offered him a deal. Assist her in running the clinic for a few years, and she'd make sure he got the administrative position he was angling for at one of the big hospital networks. Dileep Kumar would be her second-in-command in every aspect of the clinic's management. How long the pharma crime cover would last was anyone's guess, but Dileep would need to do his best to keep the organ-harvesting story from leaking. If and when it did leak, Mrs Braganza's politician brother would help the clinic frame it to the media and the public.

Anjali would soon have one more ally. Kokila and her Russian-American hubby were moving to Goa within the year. Mr Kokila made enough money on his IT start-up that Kokila could afford the pay cut which came with being the chief operating officer at the charity clinic.

Anjali would take all the help she could get juggling her career and love life. She and Joe had already lost more than a decade, and no way would she postpone her plans for five more years until he completed his training and joined the faculty at the Goa Medical College. Nuh-huh. Wasn't gonna happen. Anjali was still determined to take her time before making a firm decision, but getting to know each other wouldn't come about when they lived almost two thousand kilometres apart.

Her heart jeered at her every night for dithering, telling Anjali what she already knew. His protectiveness... the fierce determination to make things right... his passion for transplant medicine which never dissipated even when he believed it was forever beyond his reach... Joe D'Acosta in his fully grown form was as attractive to Anjali as he'd been all those years ago. There was a sense of completeness in her soul when he was by her side. Plus, her toes curled at the very thought of his sexy professor look.

No, she couldn't *stand* the idea of them being apart. They were going to finalise certain plans over dinner at Café Ishq tonight. Joe would fly to Goa as much as he could, and he and Anjali would rent a flat near the AIIMS campus—preferably one with sound-proofed walls. On the weekends when Anjali flew to Delhi, she'd take the baby to Rishi and Farhan's place. The private hospital network requested Rishi to withdraw his resignation. They weren't gonna lose one of the best neurosurgeons in the nation over his sexual orientation. Plus, having Rishi as a board member let them check the "woke" box as Farhan stated, rolling his eyes.

Leaving her baby with his father, Anjali could return to the flat and proceed to jump Joe. They'd be living in glorious sin until they knew for sure where they were headed. Anjali was quite certain both their families would be mortified, and Joe would try to hide any time he ran into her parents, but neither was willing to waste one more day from the rest of their lives.

***

"*No,*" Anjali whimpered, kicking the door of her yellow Volkswagen Beetle. "Oww, oww, oww." She hobbled around, screwing her eyes shut against the pain in her stubbed toe.

No amount of kicking was going to open the door or make the keys magically appear in her hand. She'd gotten out of the car for a mere moment when the dashboard said the tyre pressure was seriously low. She did seem to have a flat, but how she managed to lock herself out when the darned software was supposed to make it impossible was anybody's guess. Eyeing the purse lying on the passenger seat, Anjali bit back a sob-laugh. As usual, her stupid phone was in there.

There was no helping it now. She'd have to walk across the beach to Café Ishq. With a quick glance at the grey clouds in the dull blue evening sky, she started her trek. Monsoon was on them, and it had been raining all afternoon. She needed to get to the restaurant before the small break in the stormy weather was over.

At least there weren't any drunk tourists to avoid this time around, and no sharp odour of feni. Except for a few white people meditating on the sand with a guru in saffron robes in front, the place was empty. The world smelled like wet earth and crushed leaves, with the air practically shimmering from moisture. Even the coconut palms gyrating in the brisk breeze darkened in hue until they took on an ethereal quality.

Red suede stilettos sinking into the wet sand, she trudged as fast as she could. A white-hot streak of lightning broke through the clouds, followed by crashing thunder.

"Not again," exclaimed Anjali, plodding towards the electric torches marking the entrance to the café. "This is *not* happening." Rain fell in sheets, soaking through her sleek new haircut, sluicing down her torso, plastering the red floral maxi to her skin. "Argh," she shouted, shaking a fist at the universe.

The meditation group, including the guru, was also running towards the restaurant. Getting wet in monsoon storms was not conducive to the contemplation of the meaning of existence.

The electric torches on top of the gateposts flickered as she walked through. "Anju," shouted the man in the dark blue suit and yellow shirt waiting at the glass double doors, the single bulb casting a golden glow over him. Pushing the black-rimmed glasses further up the bridge of his nose, Joe sprinted towards her.

"You're gonna get drenched," Anjali hollered over the downpour.

"I already am," Joe bellowed back, mud now splattered all over his brown dress shoes and the hem of his pants. The slightly overlong dark brown hair was plastered to his scalp. He leered at her wet form. "But the view's worth it." When she didn't respond, his grin faded. "Anju?"

She blinked away the drops clinging to her eyelashes and looked around at the dark skies, the wild squall, the restaurant, the ocean. She heard the roar of the storm and felt its power in every one of her hair follicles. When monsoon season was over, the beaches of Goa would be cleansed of the waste of the year before. The mistakes of the past would be washed away. Everything would be the same, but everything would be new.

Anjali laughed in sheer joy and twirled once, her arms raised above her head. The heavens pelted her upturned face with needles of water.

Grinning at her antics, Joe asked, "Rain dance?"

"Maybe. This is kind of romantic, don't you think?"

"Ishq?" asked Joe, gesturing with his head towards the restaurant. The Urdu word for fiery amour... wild, unrestrained love mingled with tempestuous, no-holds-barred passion. His light brown eyes remained fixed on her, heat rising between them with each passing moment.

"Ishq," Anjali acknowledged. Raising trembling fingers to his wet cheek, she asked, "Hypothetically speaking, shouldn't we kiss or something?"

All at once, nothing existed except Joe's hot gaze, his shaking hands wandering all over her back and hips, and the fresh green scent of his cologne filling her lungs. "Hell, yeah," he rasped.

Her body quaked in remembered pleasure suddenly made real. Or was it his form shuddering in response to her touch? When his soft lips parted hers, she moaned a plea into his mouth never to stop. He swore not to until the end of time. Anjali told him it wouldn't be enough. There was no way she would ever get enough of the cinnamony taste of him.

Again and again, they claimed each other with kisses, unmindful of the rain soaking them through, uncaring of the whistles and catcalls of those watching from the restaurant. They didn't pause until the sun came up the next morning outside the master bedroom in her dream home.

***

Much to the relief of the Joshi parents and Fr Franco, Joe and Anjali never got to live in sin as she planned. Six months later, two weeks before the new batch of surgical residents were supposed to start in AIIMS, the gang from Delhi descended on Vagator for another Goan holiday and a beach wedding.

THE END

Note from the author

Dear Reader,

If you liked the story, do tell others about it. You can use the links below. Also, writers thrive on reviews. They help us figure out what worked and what fell flat. They help other readers make up their mind. Please do leave a comment on Amazon and/or Goodreads.

https://www.amazon.com/dp/B081V1GWFB

https://www.amazon.in/dp/B081V1GWFB

https://www.goodreads.com/book/show/48390355-a-goan-holiday

Sincerely,

Anitha

P.S. Do visit www.AnithaPerinchery.com for a bunch of other fun stuff.

P.P.S. For those who're wondering:

Yes, I did publish this in 2019. Also yes, I edited to include a sentence here and there about certain events from 2020, but the story remains unchanged.

Coming in 2021...

Siddharth's story.

Made in the USA
Coppell, TX
31 January 2021